Arab

Tales of the City
2

# Arabella

A Romance
of the City

Twenty Years On

## Michael Summerleigh

Dancing
Wolf
Press

Copyright 2024 - Michael Summerleigh
Corrected and reviSded – October 2024
Book design by Michael Summerleigh
Floral Borders by David Oxley (UK)
Dancing Wolf logo by L.S. Madden, SeeShell Graphics,
With inspiration from a design by DansuDragon (UK)
Dancing Wolf Press
P.O. Box 194
Tamworth, Ontario
Canada K0K 3G0

with thanks
for a lifetime of adventure...
William Morris
Austin Tappan Wright
Leslie Barringer
H. Rider Haggard
Sterling E. Lanier
Talbot Mundy
Henry Bedford-Jones
Edgar Rice Burroughs
Robert Louis Stevenson
Arthur Conan Doyle
Fritz Leiber
John Buchan
Alexandre Dumas
Rafael Sabatini
J.R.R. Tolkien
Jan
for the rocket fuel
and Amy B
for making everyone real again

# Arabella

# Chapter One – AT THE SIGN OF THE MOONSTRUCK MERMAID

Arabella Wyndham raised her head and realised she'd fallen asleep on her blanket; that there was a distinct warmth attendant upon her bare backside that would not have been there at all if someone else had been looking after her as promised.

"'Rissa?" she called drowsily.

She roused herself up onto her knees, wriggled back into the light cotton shift she'd worn to the seaside, wincing at the twinge of more sunburn than she'd bargained for in places that didn't normally see daylight. She shaded her eyes against the westering sun, scanning the deserted beach for Stella and Jamie, but they were nowhere to be seen. Kerissa waved from the surf and began wading her way back up onto the beach, then long-leggedy leaping across the sand, racing the shadow of a gull flying overhead.

"You let me fall asleep," said Arabella. "Now look...my bum's all burnt."

She pouted and lifted the hem of her shift to show the full impact of unmitigated sunlight upon her *derriere*.

"It's still a beautiful bum," Kerissa Davies said in a most complimentary tone.

Arabella frowned with mock petulance.

"Yes well it's lovely you think so, but it's not going t'help me get comfortable in bed tonight."

Kerissa's appreciative regard of the afflicted portion of Arabella's anatomy became more pronounced.

"Then I think you should let me look after that," she said. "It's the very least I can do, given that I've been so derelict in my duties."

She grinned impudently and embraced her, their bodies and lips meeting within moments of each other. Arabella abandoned concern over her sunburn in favour of the simple pleasure of Kerissa's silken skin beneath her fingertips.

Together they were of a near equal but modest height, both young women somehow having managed to combine the best features of their respective parents. A week in the sun had turned Arabella's generous curves into a perfect complement to the slender Kerissa's dark coppery skin, derived from the pale ginger complexion of her father and the deep chocolate of her exotic mother, her hair a halo of tight molten bronze curls to her friend's near waist-length tumble of honey-blonde. Arabella's eyes, now closed as she nosed about Kerissa's left ear, were emerald-green to the other's strange and hypnotic amber. They made contented noises, until Arabella remembered that the twins in their care still were unaccounted for.

"They were tired of being in the sun all day so I sent them back towards the village," said Kerissa, who was three years older than Arabella's seventeen and officially in charge of making sure their holiday went smoothly before the two of them were off to university. "I told them we'd not be much longer, to wait for us up on the headland where they'd have some shade under the trees."

"We can't leave them for too long," cautioned the blonde girl. "Who knows what they'll get into if we're not around to curb their *enthusiasm*."

Kerissa laughed softly and nodded a kiss into Arabella's right ear. "I'm sorry your bum got burned," she said, gently resting one hand there. "I promise I'll make it feel better..."

She knelt beside their blanket and shimmied her way into her own cotton shift, and after collecting their gear, both shouldered a canvas pack and began to slog their way up the beach, to the path that led to the top of the cliffs above them, and the track leading back to the seaside village of Bedford. They climbed easily, both young women so day-by-day active that the effort was no effort at all. At length they reached the top of the rocky headland and Kerissa pointed to a pair of smudges in the shadow of a stand of windblown cypress a quarter mile away.

"Doesn't look like there are any imminent disasters."

"One can hope," said Arabella.

They trudged on at a good pace that brought them up to the children in less than ten minutes, found them both oblivious to the world as each peered through a brand new pair of field glasses they'd received as birthday presents the week before, so they could "look at stuff far away".

"Whatcha lookin' at?" asked Arabella, perching beside them where they stood on an outcropping of rock beside the path. Kerissa scrambled up next to her, and they followed a line of sight out into the shimmer of the sunset sea.

"Sea monsters," replied Stella, without lowering her glasses. "Jamie saw them first."

The twins were only just beginning to grow out of their childhood, two sturdy mirrors of each other—snub-nosed round faces framed by dark mops of unruly curls, dreamy blue eyes that managed to spark almost constantly with curiosity, and dispositions they seemed to have inherited from their adoptive parents, Stella having Alain Devreaux's unshakeably sunny optimism, Jamie taking after Andrew MacKinnon's more cautious version.

"Sea monsters," echoed Kerissa, careful not to sound overly skeptical.

"Out there," said Jamie, pointing to a horizon growing more and more nebulous as the sunset drenched itself over sea and sky. "I think they've gone now, but we saw them, didn't we, Stel?"

Stella nodded emphatically, lowering her glasses and bestowing one of her glowing smiles upon her "cousins".

"We did!" she gushed. "Jamie said and then I looked and sure enough there it was."

"I thought you saw more than one," said Kerissa, in her role as an advocate of Truth and reality-grounded perception.

"Oh," said Stella. "There was only one, but two is better so I put an extra S on..."

"Were you scared?" asked Arabella.

Jamie said, "A little bit..." but Stella said "Nope!" and did one last look through her glasses.

"Gone now," she said. "We can go home."

So they did, their guardians bringing up the rear and shaking their heads as their charges charged all over the place along the way, investigating anything that struck them as worthy of investigation. As they came to the steep descent to where Bedford lay nestled beside its own snug harbour, they lost the sun, moved along in a twilight that became full with the scent of salt wind off the ocean, the eventide whir of swallows overhead, the shrill cries of gulls seeking shelter in the hollows of the cliffs they had left behind.

Brand new electrical streetlamps began to wink into the dusk as they came down the high street, at length stopping beneath the sign-board of their lodgings—a rock-bound mermaid staring up with longing into a silvery full moon riding through a gap in the cloud-ridden night sky. The twins of a sudden grew quiet, huddling closer to 'Rissa and 'Bella, sunshine and the day's excitement finally catching them up in a drowsy contentment.

Once through the door of the inn, however, some new furore raged among the patrons of the taproom. These were almost entirely fisherman still in their slickers and waders, all milling about the bar and standing rather than sitting at any of the tables. The level of their voices raised in conversation was almost impenetrable. Arabella squirmed her way through the press.

"Hello Jacob!" she called to the proprietor, who stood at his taps ready for the almost constant call for refills.

"Hello, Miss Arabella. You might want t'wait on yer supper for yourselves and the children tonight," he said apologetically. "Our boys are all standin' about waitin' for the boats t'come back down the firth so they can go out again."

She knew from earlier visits that the fishermen's cooperative always ended their day by taking the day's catch up the estuary from the bay, to the processing plant where a railhead had been established to connect them to the new criss-cross of train lines being laid down across the country. She must have looked a question without saying a word because Jacob leaned towards her and lowered his voice.

"Maire Dowd's boat didn't come in wi' the fleet," he said, frowning. "Today around noontime somebody saw her out at the edge of things, but nobody can remember seein' her boat after that...D'you mind supper bein' a bit late?"

Arabella shook her head, said they'd be down once things had quieted down some, then worked her way back through the press at the bar to where Kerissa and the twins waited.

"Today, let's see if we can get the two of you bathed *before* supper," she said, herding everyone off to the stair leading up to their room on the second floor.

"What's all the business about?" asked Kerissa.

"One of the fishing boats went missing," explained Arabella. "They're all waiting t'go back out to look for her."

The twins stopped climbing stairs.

"Told you," said Stella, and Jamie nodded. "Sea monsters..." they said in unison.

Bath-time became an hour-long struggle to get the twins free of sand and salt crustiness, whilst at the same time keep them safe from the jaws of the sea monsters they swore were lurking at the bottom of the big copper tub. Eventually Kerissa was forced to leap to their rescue, thereby ensuring no one truly got clean of the aforementioned sand and salt, but providing for a very soggy floor upon which Arabella laughed herself into a state of near exhaustion.

Next came the towelling stage of the evening's festivities, wherein Stella quietly but with great specificity remarked to Jamie that "one of these days I'm gonna find out why you have one of *those* and *we* don't", which only served to renew 'Bella's fits of laughter to the point where she had to lie down again.

"C'mon guys," said Kerissa. "Did you *really* see a sea monster?"

Once again Stella nodded, leaving no room for doubt that she and her brother had seen *something*.

"...Truly, 'Rissa," replied Jamie, with the earnest face both she and Arabella knew well from prior experience could mean everything and nothing at all as far as reality was concerned. "It had a big long snaky neck and one big horrible eye."

"And both of you saw this creature," said Arabella from where she hung over one side of their bed. The twins nodded. She and Kerissa exchanged glances, the kind you gave the other grown-up in the room tasked with keeping things *in order* for the children.

"Well then, I suppose if we all get dressed again we can go downstairs and have dinner."

The common room was empty of the local fishermen when they arrived, a few of the older residents quietly bent over their mugs of ale, discussing the unlikelihood and utter improbability of one of their own suffering some sort of misadventure with the entire fleet within hailing distance; and then there was the seasonal contingent of visitors, those at the seaside for business or pleasure, who sat around curious or uninterested, but more intent upon what lay on their plates or in their own glasses.

Arabella, Kerissa and the twins found a cosy table in a far corner, somewhat removed from the rest of the goings-on, happy for some quiet in the soft glow of candle-light.

"The electric lights are magical," observed Jamie. "How come there's only candles here?"

"I like candles better," said Stella. "Just 'cause we can do stuff like that doesn't mean we have to. Some old things are good too."

Jamie put in a few more votes in favour of progress and a debate ensued regarding the relative merits of flickering electrical light as opposed to flickering candle-light. In the midst of this discussion, Jacob's wife Nancy arrived with a wax-sealed cream-coloured envelope addressed to Arabella Wyndham c/o the Moonstruck Mermaid.

"Jake says this come for you this aft, Miss 'Bella," she apologised, "but it were so busy what with Maire gone missing that he forgot t'give it you. I'll have your suppers out for you in a jiff."

She bustled off and Arabella did a tour of the envelope.

"It's from my da," she said, inspecting the wax seal on the back flap.

She broke the seal and extracted a single sheet of matching paper covered in a flowing script.

"Well my mum wrote this for sure," she laughed. "The only thing da can make legible are notes on staff paper."

"What's it say, 'Bella?" chorused the twins.

She read in silence for a minute or so, a small frown making a crease between her eyebrows as she read down the sheet of paper. After a another quick look inside the envelope she folded the letter into it and set it down beside her silverware.

"We've got t'go back tomorrow," she said quietly. "Mum and Da say it's not dire or anything like that, but somethin's come up and it would be best if we were home again."

Jamie and Stella protested, but only until she informed them that the envelope from Uncle Windy and Annie Branny also contained train tickets to whisk them back to the City in record time. They had come to Bedford in dusty carriages; this would be the first time any of them had been on the train.

"New stuff is better," said Jamie.

"Sometimes," said Stella.

"We're goin' on the train!" he said.

"It will be nice," replied Stella.

Dinner arrived, both Jacob and Nancy apologising profusely (again) for late suppers and late delivery of letters. The twins tucked into their food with no encouragement.

"What's it all about?" asked Kerissa.

Arabella shrugged. "I don't know, 'Rissa. They didn't say any more than I just said, but I guess we have t'go, right?"

Kerissa nodded and soon all four of them were slashing away at fat spicy fish fillets pan-fried with onions and mushrooms and shallots, fresh-baked buttered bread, all washed down with big mugs of ale for the girls and lemon-water for the children.

Kerissa observed it wasn't at all bad for an unexpected last meal on holiday; Jamie was too busy with another slice of bread to say anything at all, but Stella had stopped in mid-swallow and now appeared to be a bit put out by something. She seemed reluctant to enlighten either of her cousins as to why, but relented after directing a frighteningly adult glare across the common room.

"They're staring at us," she said.

"Who's staring at us?" asked Arabella.

"Those men...four of them...over there in the other corner..."

"They're allowed t'do that," offered Jamie with a mouthful of bread. "Alain says you can always look as long as you're polite about it. I don't quite know what that means, but I suppose as long as we don't have t'stop eating it's okay."

"Well..." huffed Stella. "One of them is very rude...he's staring so big his eyes are drooling..."

Arabella raised an eyebrow in Kerissa's direction, as she could see the rest of the patrons from where she sat against the wall.

"He certainly seems interested in you, 'Bella," she said. "Tall dark and probably quite dangerous from the look of him....but he's quite handsome. Shall I be jealous?"

Arabella's curiosity got the better of her. Stella whispered urgently *No no don't look!* but she did, if only for a moment.

"He *is* very handsome... " she said, and ducked her head to where she could look up at Kerissa from beneath lowered eyelids.

"Oh you fickle beast!" cried Kerissa softly.

"Don't be silly, 'Rissa...he couldn't ever be handsome enough that I would ever even *think* of dreaming of anyone but you."

She leaned sideways and they kissed for what seemed an extraordinarily long time. The twins giggled. Stella poked her tongue at tall dark and dangerous on the other side of the taproom.

At length they finished their supper and decided the day had been long enough. Arabella glanced back at the far corner of the taproom, but the table her admirer had occupied was empty. They went back upstairs after asking Jacob to get them a carriage first thing in the morning, to take them to the train station at the head of the firth.

# Chapter Two – STRANGERNESS ON THE TRAIN

"...Did they find the boat went missing yesterday?" Kerissa asked as they plunked themselves down on the padded seats of their travelling compartment.

The twins were oblivious to everything but the gleaming locomotive, smoke swirling up into a cloudless sky and steam hissing out over the tracks. The morning had been a frenzy of activity, packing the last of their things, getting them fed and dressed and out on the high street in time to meet their carriage. The trip to the railhead had been a headlong clatter, with Jamie and Stella shouting at each other in anticipation and excitement whilst Kerissa and Arabella just kept things in order, forgoing conversation until they were finally on their way back to the City. Arabella shook her head.

"Jacob said the fleet was out most of the night but they didn't find anything, not even a splinter of that poor woman's boat."

"How many were with her?"

"Two sons and her husband's father."

"Makes you wonder if maybe these scamps really did see something," replied Kerissa. "If something dreadful happened, you'd think there'd at least be some indication...you know...wreckage...nets...whatever..."

"Gone without a trace," said Arabella.

The train lurched forward, steel wheels screaming at steel rails, slowly picking up speed for the slow climb up past the seaside cliffs that enclosed the firth. Jamie and Stella had their field glasses aimed at a dozen things all at once, making exclamations of delight and wonder as they looked down on the western ocean and then turned their attention to the upland countryside as it began to seemingly race past them.

"Just look at one thing at a time, kids," cautioned 'Rissa, "else you'll get dizzy and next thing y'know we'll all be saying hello to your breakfasts again."

The twins giggled and pretty much ignored the advice, which was no more and no less than either of the girls expected, but it wasn't long before they too fell under the intoxicating spell of speed and the world rushing by like kaleidoscopes with legs.

Amid *oohs* and *aahs* and *Look, Jamie!* and *Stella, look at that!* they enjoyed the luxury of being amazed and overwhelmed by sharing a totally new experience, exchanging very grown-up glances of adoration while at the same time feeling much like children themselves.

Eventually the twins decided that there was more to their first train ride than watching the world go whizzing by. Respectfully requesting permission to run riot on the rest of the train, they disappeared in a flash and the girls availed themselves of the peace and quietude to engage in more conversation, and speculate on the nature of the "emergency" that had cut short their holidays.

"I guess it could be anything, 'Bella," observed Kerissa, "but you said your folks said it was nothing dire."

"That's what's so puzzling about it," she replied. "If it wasn't horrible or earth-shaking then how come it was enough of something t'make a next-day train-ride home so necessary?"

Kerissa shrugged and made an *I dunno* face that never failed to draw Arabella into her arms. In the process of getting there, she rustled across a newspaper thrust down between the seat cushions, pulled it out and did an about-face where Kerissa could wrap her arms around her while they both read the paper.

"That would explain it, then," she said, as both read the full page headline. "Someone on the morning run from the City must have left this here."

In massive boldface type that spanned the entire eight columns of the front page, they learned of the passing of Queen Caroline de Montigny.

"This is terrible," said Arabella. "Mom...Dad...they said it was nothing dire!"

"Well it don't get direr than this," said Kerissa incredulously. "What's gonna happen now? Who gets t'run the country now she's gone?"

It was common knowledge that Caroline had not given birth to an heir in all her years on the Amaranth Throne; that once upon a time long ago and early on in her reign there *had* been a child, but it had not survived.

"There's somethin' funny going on, 'Rissa."

"Funny peculiar not funny haha," they said in unison.

"You'd think Mom would know something," said Arabella. "After all, she's the second assistant t'someone-or-other in the palace."

"You'd think," agreed Kerissa.
"Definitely funny peculiar," said Arabella.

"...Your mom doesn't do much painting or drawing anymore, does she?"

"Sometimes she does," said Arabella. "I know she used t'be really keen about it. Your da and Tom and Andrew and Alain, they all talk about some of the beautiful things she did on paper and canvas. They're all hung all over the place in our houses, but you're right, she doesn't seem to give it much thought anymore.

"I asked her once and she said one of her dearest friends got her the position at the palace, and after a while she realised that in order for her to be truly appreciative of something like that she ought t'give it most of her attention."

"It's kind of too bad," said Kerissa. "She's *really* good. I've said so a couple of times and she's gotten all embarrassed and tried to make me think she's just pottering around, not capable of anything exceptional."

"That sounds like my mom," said 'Bella. "More when I was small, but she's always run herself down in favour of just about anyone else she felt needed running up."

Their compartment had gotten stuffy and hot as the day wore on; oftentimes when they opened the windows wide to get some cooler air what they got instead was a great sooty cloud of whatever from the locomotive. In consequence they got drowsy, and were grateful the twins were amusing themselves elsewhere but with the consideration of checking in every now and again, just to let them know they'd not managed to do themselves in or set the train on fire.

An hour later, now descending from the coastal highlands onto the Findhorn delta that enclosed the City, Arabella declined to open her eyes, burrowed under what she assumed was Kerissa's sundress, licked at coppery brown skin and smiled.

"I like trains," she said.

"Oh...?' inquired Kerissa. "And why is that?"

"Don't be mean 'Rissa you know why."

She tucked her cousin back into her clothing and snuggled down again.

"Where's the kids?" she asked.

"We're right here," said Jamie and Stella together. "We didn't wanna wake you but..."

It was the *but* that brought both Arabella and Kerissa out of their cuddle.

"But *what*?" demanded Kerissa, making sure she was entirely tucked.

"Stella maybe did something bad," said Jamie.

"Oh...?" inquired Kerissa...again.

"He's here," said Stella.

"Who's here?" said Arabella, sitting upright.

Jamie stared. Stella did too.

"Do I get those when I grow up?" she asked.

Arabella was not tucked into anything that resembled clothing.

"Only if you like aching muscles and occasional back pain," she snapped cryptically. "Who's here?"

"Him," said Jamie.

# ARABELLA

"The one from the inn," added Stella.

"We were trying t'get something to eat and we bumped into him," said Jamie.

"Are we talking *bumping into* as in a casual encounter or actual physical contact?" said Kerissa, who was of an eternally inquiring mind.

"I don't know what that means," said Stella. "We ran into him. He was real polite this time, but he asked who you were."

"And...?" the girls asked together. Raised eyebrows were involved.

"Stella said you were our cousins and we were on holidays together, and then I said no that was wrong we were orphans and had been kidnapped."

Jamie appeared to be waiting for some sort of commendation for quick thinking.

"Where is he now?" said Kerissa.

The twins shrugged. Kerissa looked at Arabella and suggested a bit of clothing would probably be a good idea just then.

"...This guy definitely has something in his trousers for you and we may need t'make a run for it once we get into the station."

As things transpired, both Andrew and Nicholas were waiting on the platform when the train chuffed its way into the shiny near-new cavern of the steel and glass station. The twins wraped themselves around Andrew; 'Bella ran into her father's arms with no small amount of concern on her face. Windy kissed her hair reassuringly.

"We know, Da," she said.

"Not quite everything, honey," he replied. "It'll be okay I promise. Let's get your things and head home."

The newly-arrived passengers from all points west to the seaside quickly cleared the platform as the train whistled its departure for the Eastern townships and began to leave the station. Stella frowned and pointed to a window in one of the departing carriages.

"There he is again," she said distastefully.

# Chapter Three – THE PAST BECOMES THE PRESENT

It was a sober gathering of friends who sat about in the great room of the Wyndham house in St John's Mews in late afternoon the next day. It had been years since anyone could remember even laying eyes on Queen Caroline, yet history had given them all good reason to believe that someday, one of the de Montigny line might actually live forever. That she had surpassed almost eighty years, more than sixty of them upon the Amaranth Throne, came as no surprise; but Death, never anything but unwelcome to all save those for whom Life had become too great a trial in one way or another, never came in any way but unexpectedly. There were only two people in the great room who had the most cause to grieve painfully, but they had done so twenty years earlier, in secret, and this day was meant for secrets to come into the light.

"I'm going to leave this to Brandy," said Nicholas quietly. "It's her story to tell more than mine. I'm going upstairs with the scamps to make some music..."

There were a few streaks of grey in the pale blond hair, but in all wise else to everyone there, Nicholas still was Windy—the one who had seen them through the most difficult times in their lives, provided a sense of family and refuge to a band of orphans and strays. The twins looked pouty.

"We should be able to hear Annie Branny's story too," said Stella. Jamie stood steadfast in agreement beside her, glaring about as if to challenge anyone who might disagree. Aunt Brandywine had been too much for them when they had arrived almost four years earlier. Annie Branny was easier, and had become her name for all the children, grown or otherwise.

"Not today, Stella," said Nicholas. "I promise I'll explain a little bit when we get upstairs, but today's for the grown-ups..."

The twins remained unconvinced, but followed Windy upstairs nevertheless; moments later horrific sounds fled from the music room...the clavichord in distress... until a door was closed and the twins' torture of taut steel strings became muted. Eight pairs of eyes turned to Brandywine.

"I hope you won't be angry with me," she said beseechingly, looking at each of them in turn. "Windy and I never meant to keep things from you, but I made a promise for so much of it, and the rest...well...it seemed possible that knowing might be dangerous so we never said."

A score of years had changed her, but almost not at all. Brandywine had become more than the uncomplicated girl who had nothing in her heart but concern for all living things. Her hair yet shone with a golden light of its own, her sun-browned shoulders radiated more strength than before...but her eyes, startling green, though now more knowing than when first she had wandered through the City, remained those of a child, windows into the soul of

# ARABELLA

someone always ready to be struck speechless with delight and wonderment at the simplest of things.

She looked at the open windows of the great room, that overlooked the courtyard of the Mews. Zoraya, who had in no way changed or seemed to have grown older than a day for every year gone by, whispered:

"We are safe. Hasan and Grim keep watch. No one but the eight of us shall hear what you say."

Diana asked, "Branny, should Edmund and Sebastian be here? The university has closed down for a month of mourning, and they're on their way home, but the train from the university is still half a day behind everything else."

She leaned forward, away from Thomas' arm around her shoulders. Brandywine shook her head.

"They've done their part and never questioned, Di," she said. "You can tell them about all of this when they get home."

"So it's pretty serious stuff," said Thomas. He had remained bearlike, lumbering and contentious, but only grown deeper into the service and devotion of Diana, who had married him, and provided a great measure of Peace in what had been his angry soul.

"It is, Tom, oh I feel so badly...all this time...never being able to tell..."

Alain the ever cheerful said, "Well now you can and no one of us will ever hold it against you, Bran, you know that."

Brandywine ducked her head down where her hair covered her face and all but the sound of a half-suppressed sob. "I do. I do I know it's true...all of you...you're all I have I love you so much..."

Arabella felt a gentle hand belonging to Kerissa, that urged her up from the floor where they sat together, up onto her knees before her mother. Andrew stood there beside her, a score of years having done nothing to lessen his adoration of the sun-child who had befriended him first before all others.

"Mum it's okay," said 'Bella. "I think we've all known there was *something*...we just wanted to know so we could help...whatever it was..."

She took her up into her arms and held on. Brandy flung her hair back:

"Andy...Alain...that wonderful day when Ambrosius...when he announced...before all of us...d'you remember...? And d'you remember the beautiful woman who came...?"

They both nodded. Gareth, who had gone a bit more grey and a trifle more stout than Windy, said, "Marie... your friend Marie..."

Brandy started crying.

"That was Caroline," she said. "That was Caroline...*the queen*..."

She told them of the afternoon she and Windy had spent, twenty years before, on the day the rest of them had gone to the gala at the palace. How Marie who in truth had been Caroline de Montigny, had found them at the Silver Rose, and then cautiously followed them all over the City.

"...And we ended up here that evening. Windy played for her, and I made a drawing..."

"The one framed in your studio," said Andrew. "Marie in Magic..."

Brandy nodded.

"It was a gift to her, but she returned it to me just before she died."

"But you've had that sketch in your studio for years," said Diana.

Brandy nodded again. "That's part of the secret, Di. Marie didn't die a few days ago. She died less than a month after the day when you all saw her here..."

"She didn't look a day older than any of us," said Tom incredulously.

"That's the secret too," said Brandy. "It's why we're here now."

There was a rustle of the long caftan worn by Zoraya, her usual white linen embroidered in arabesques along its edges with threads of red and gold, blue and silver and green. She sat quietly in a corner a bit removed from everyone else, but the whisper of her voice was clear and unwavering.

"You have the flower, don't you, Brandy," she said. "You've had it all along...ever since that day..."

Brandy looked startled, and though she was sitting, reached a hand to her daughter's shoulder as if to steady herself from falling.

"Zori, how did you know?"

"Perhaps now it is time for all our secrets to be shared," was her reply. "My Gareth knows some of this...and perhaps Nicholas does as well, because soon after you welcomed me into your family I know he spent many hours in the libraries, and likely found the one reference to me that, in all of your history, would be the only clue..."

ZORAYA'S STORY

"...I was born over three thousand years ago in a place that no longer exists. My parents were of two royal families, and in many ways their union was a marriage of political convenience...but with one unlooked-for consequence more than the joining of two houses aligned against a third. They did not know what I would become as I grew older; they did not know that by the length of their family histories, their roots were older than ancient and had flourished in 'soil' that allowed some of their ancestors to see and be capable of things no longer thought possible. I dreamed of these things, and became able to dream in such wise that I could also make others see my dreams..."

She smiled at Gareth, and here it was that together they related the circumstances of his visions, and how creating her in stone had provided the doorway that released her from thousands of years of imprisonment at the hands of a rival sorcerer.

"...He walked the empty corridors of the palace I grew up in...the same place all of you visited briefly on the day of the mirage that hung over the ocean just beyond the harbour. He found an image of me, as I had intended him to do, and in *finding* me found also someone who would love him for his spirit and for the strength of the talent that would free me...and give me the beautiful daughter who is the beloved of our own Arabella."

She raised her hand to Gareth's face in a caress so intimate that a flood of warmth filled the room, sent a rush of emotion through all of them.

"I am what you call a witch...or that is what I became. As a child I saw things no one else could see, heard songs no one else could sing, tasted of miracles that no one could even imagine. My parents had their own concerns; I looked only to the stars and the infinite possibilities we as humans had abandoned to earthbound desires and enterprise. I began to grow in knowledge, and became irresistible to all things I desired and to those whom I chose to desire me...

"On the day of my first bleeding, when I was thirteen years old, everything that had come to me before seemed to increase a hundred times. At first I was overwhelmed, sometimes so full of pride and superiority that I became arrogant and selfish...but then I made a small transgression, and so learned the way of the Threefold Law that was an immutable premise to my kind..."

In response to a handful of mystified expressions, Kerissa explained a law of Magick:

"It's a rule," she said. "It means that whatever good or evil you do with what the Goddess has given to you, it comes back to you three times over."

"So you learn to behave yourself if you can do magick," added Gareth, "or you learn in the worst ways possible that there's a price to be paid for everything."

Arabella turned from Brandywine and levelled a look of astonishment at them both.

Kerissa smiled a cryptic smile she had learned from her own mother, and blew her a kiss. Zoraya smiled a smile of her own and continued:

"Three years later, I had grown to be much of what I am now. Being the only child of a noble house, I had many suitors clamouring for my attentions, for far too many reasons that were, of course, of no consequence to me. If I desired physical love I had only to snap my fingers to know ecstasy; if I desired more wealth and jewels than that already belonging to my family, a careless word or a favour bestowed would have it come to me without question or request. But one day a young man of a lesser house came to me with an ancient scroll of papyrus as a gift; it was in this scroll that I learned of a flower... *amaranthus veneficus*...a treasure of legend long lost if it had ever even existed at all...and I became obsessed with the thought of it, this singular flower, that grew from the single stem of a single tree that grew upon the shore of a tideless inner sea in a land no one could remember."

She paused, and in one fluid motion rose from her chair, went to a sideboard where she poured wine for herself from a crystal decanter, and then, in an almost ritualistic manner, first served a glass to each of those who sat spellbound, of a sudden lost in her tale.

"It was said in this papyrus," she began again, having resumed her chair, "that this amaranth was a thing of great power, able to bestow upon its owner an endless life so long as it was worn by day and lay nearby at night; that the measure of its power was bounded only by the knowledge and imagination of he or she who wore it, and was *so* great that it transcended even the Threefold Law, so whosoever could find and wear it would be capable of almost anything, without consequence of any kind."

The afternoon light had gone from the great room. In the courtyard dozens if not hundreds of cats'-eyes winked in the gathering gloom. A fox yipped a brief message that Zoraya alone seemed to understand. Kerissa and Arabella rose together, and went about lighting the gas lamps sconced upon the walls.

"The purple flower that Marie wore," said Brandy in a whisper. "The purple flower that's belonged to the de Montignys for as long as they've ruled our country. Caroline...my friend Marie...told me no one could say when or where it had come from, but she thought it had come back with the pilgrim-warriors of her family when they returned from the Indus wars."

"She gave it to you the day of Andrew and Alain's joining," said Zoraya. "I did not see it, but thereafter, whenever we would come here, I sensed something hidden away."

Brandywine nodded slowly and sipped wine from her glass, both hands about the stem, like a child tasting at a rare treat.

"That's the rest of the secret, Zori," she said, "but you should finish your story and then I'll finish mine."

Zoraya bowed her head in acknowledgment of what no one else there knew.

"I wanted the flower," she went on. "My every waking moment became filled with the determination to find it, to live forever and remake the earth into a paradise for all who lived upon it. At night as I slept, I went further afield, dreaming impossible journeys to places far beyond the borders of my country or any other...and on one of these journeys I realised someone else knew of the flower and was searching for it with even greater desire than my own. Someone who was *not* good, who wanted it to serve him rather than allow him to serve others..."

"His name was *Chakidze*, someone I knew of by name only, from far far away to the south of my home. That I knew of him at all, his reputation for evil, was enough to convince me that stopping him was more important than finding the flower. We met in a place not of the earth, lightning-blasted through the endless dark of a place between the worlds, where black stars cast no light at all and swallowed down the lightning bolts as you or I would swallow our breakfast tea...

"I survived only because of his contempt for a sixteen-year old girl who dared to challenge him. The spell he cast would have blasted me apart had I not been his near equal, but even as I felt it tearing at me I cast my own net upon him, and it was only his stunned surprise that saved me from complete dissolution. Before the great silence of Time enclosed me I heard him scream in disbelief and anger. And then I waited...three thousand years...for my beloved to free me..."

# Chapter Four – THE PRESENT BECOMES THE FUTURE

Again Zoraya reached a hand to Gareth's face, smiling the enigmatic smile that spoke of an Eternity in the endless reaches of her imagination. Everyone in the room who once had journeyed with her to a mirage floating over the ocean, felt themselves returned from that place all over again.

"Marie had no idea," said Brandywine at length, "only that the flower cast a spell of its own over her ancestors, enough that they kept it close and learned they could live a lot longer when they did. But she was tired...so very tired...

"She wanted to know why I was the only one who didn't come to her gala that day. No one outside the palace would have recognised her. She found me and Windy and she came home with us and then a few days later she asked to see me. I was so scared, and then I was so scared even more because she wanted *me*...she wanted me to take the flower from her and become the queen. It was so silly. Me, *the Queen*? But I couldn't do it...I told her...it would be more than I could bear to watch Windy...and all of you... grow old...while I would have t'go on without you..."

She began to cry again, lifted up the hem of her dress to dry her eyes.

"We saw each other a lot after that...we became such good friends. It was a secret, of course, but I started to realise how horrible it must be for her, and then I couldn't bear the thought of her alone like that, so tired and no one to help her, so me and Windy talked and decided it would be a good thing if I sort-of took over...let her go on without having to worry. I promised I would take care of the City and everyone until I could find someone who could do it better than me...

"So I'm not really the Second Assistant to the Royal Stationer. That was something we made up so I could be at the palace whenever I needed to talk with all the people who really belonged there. Marie arranged it...I was sort of the queen....I got to be the one t'tell the people who knew how to run things properly what they should run things properly for... what t'do with money from taxes and trading with other countries, like looking after hungry people or homeless people, like Ambrosius did after he left the Church...or when the Findhorn flooded so many farms up north...and the trains she wanted for the country to make things easier for everybody."

Diana shifted uncomfortably in her chair, a dark frown creasing her forehead.

"So what you're saying is—?"

"No Diana I know what you're gonna say. It wasn't like that at all. You've all made your way to where you are now because you're all so good at the things you do. Gareth's statues and stuff are all over because they're wonderful; Thomas writes magical books that everyone loves; Andy writes beautiful poetry; Zoraya weaves wondrous tapestries, and Windy's music makes me want t'dance and cry at the same time...but when it came time for someone to become the director of the dance school, it wasn't me said it had t'be you. Your name was on the list because the ones who were supposed t'choose knew what a good dancer you were...same as Alain's market...he didn't get t'be the one who stocked the palace kitchens because of me, it was because his food and services were better than anyone else.

"Marie said I could make all of you Royal Everythings if I wanted to...that it would be okay...but she knew I would never do something like that...how could I play favourites and still be what she wanted me to be?"

She looked at her daughter, her eyes begging for understanding.

"I couldn't tell, 'Bella, not even you. I'm so sorry."

There was a long silence as everyone in the room absorbed the immensity of all they had just heard. Finally, Kerissa broke the silence.

"'Bella, your mom's been in charge of everything!" she cried. "That is *so* great!"

Arabella looked dazed. Everyone else looked a bit dazed as well.

"What's it all mean, Mum?" she asked after a while.

Brandy got down on the floor next to her and they disappeared into each others' arms.

"I'm not sure, sweetheart," she said. "I think there's been some bad things goin' on for a while, and now that everyone thinks Marie just died something's gonna happen..."

Thomas piped up, "Branny you've really been running the show for almost twenty years? I'm not saying it's unbelievable, but..."

Brandywine laughed.

"Tom you are such a poophead. But you're right. Maybe Marie thought me being in charge would be something no one would believe, and that would make it easier, but she knew I'd always have all of you in case things got t'be too much for me..."

"So what's really happening now?" asked Alain.

"You and Da said it would be better if we were here," said Arabella.

Brandywine.hugged her daughter, stroked her hair and could be seen to be searching for the right words to tell what was going on.

"There's plenty of people in the palace who've known all along that Marie died twenty years ago," she said thoughtfully. "But what happened this week wasn't an *official* announcement. I think someone's been waiting for a long time...the *right* time...t'let everybody else in on the secret..."

"Which means there's a good chance they've been planning something—" offered Andrew.

"And now they're ready," finished Brandy, "and that's not good, because we don't know who they are or what they've been up to."

"But Mom, surely we've got our own people...unofficial y'know...keeping an eye out in other places?" asked Arabella

"Spies you mean?" said Brandy. "I guess we do, honey, so what I get to hear are all the things they find out...but so far there's nothing, and suddenly it's all so strange I don't know what t'do..."

Diana stood and crossed the great room.

"That's why we're here," she said, and leaned down to kiss the top of her head.

Brandywine looked up. "What *can* we do t'help?"

"I'm not sure," said Brandy, frowning. "I think I've finally found two or three people who might be the right person to take Marie's place, but now would be the worst time ever to tell if there're people have their own ideas about it and will make trouble."

"Can we afford t'sit around waiting for them t'make their trouble?"

Brandy shrugged helplessly. "I don't know, Gareth, I just don't know...not yet, anyway."

---

Windy and the twins reappeared. It was suppertime and they were hungry and all over again huffy about not being able to sit in on the "secret squirreling" of the adults. Eventually, they all migrated into the Wyndham kitchen and there was a mass conjuration of evening meal for everyone in attendance. Whilst Alain, Windy and Tom looked after the food preparation, Gareth and Diana set a table for ten. The twins curled up with Arabella and Kerissa. Zoraya sat alone in a corner, seemingly in some sort of deep communion with a rusty red dog-fox that somehow had managed to find his way into the kitchen without anyone noticing. Brandywine started towards them; the fox slipped behind Zoraya's skirts as she came to sit beside her.

"Wasn't that Hasan, Zori? Are you all right?"

Zoraya's uncanny eyes were clouded and her lips had gone pale, almost bloodless. She shook her head at the sound of Brandy's voice and became herself again.

"Something is not right, Brandywine," she said softly. "Perhaps we shall not stay for supper tonight."

As had always been the case in the last score of years, when Zoraya became *mysterious* the others had learned to wait until she was ready to provide explanations.

"Are you sure? Shall I tell Gareth and 'Rissa?"

"Please if you would. I'm so sorry..."

Brandy shook her head. "It doesn't matter, Zori...but now that you know about the flower...I should talk t'you soon?"

Zoraya nodded and they rose together. "Very soon, Brandy," she said quietly, "but from now on you must be very careful in all things. Take nothing for granted and look beyond what you may see with your eyes."

For a moment, there was a flash of fear in Brandywine's green eyes, but it was gone almost at once, replaced by a strong determination not to succumb to it. Twenty years of necessity and deep responsibility had given Brandy Lloyd some time to learn of her own strengths.

"Well okay then," she said brightly. "'Bella wanted to spend the night with 'Rissa, though. If that's all right I'll send them along right after we've had dinner."

Zoraya tilted her head to one side, her hair a soft rustle of dark glistening curls.

"Tell them to be careful," she said.

She moved towards the arched doorway that led to the front of the house. Hasan was nowhere to be seen.

There was only a glimmer of daylight in the sky when Arabella and Kerissa said goodnight to Nicholas and Brandy and started across the cobblestone courtyard of the Mews. When it narrowed down to the laneway leading out past the Church of St John towards the Boulevard, stars magically appeared overhead and shadows crawled upwards to wind about the branches of the apple trees and shroud the dozens of snoozing felines awaiting full darkness to go in search of adventure. Kerissa put a protective arm around Arabella's shoulders and remarked:

"Your mom's worried."

"Yours too, 'Rissa."

"I know. I haven't seen her this serious about anything in a long time...actually... never..."

"Gareth and my da are funny."

"Funny haha or funny peculiar?"

"Haha, silly. They're both so...ferocious?...about being in love with our moms that they don't let anything get in the way of it."

"Like me and you."

'Rissa heard 'Bella smile.

"Yeah," she said.

They stopped just short of the church and got wrapped up in each other for a while. When they were both breathless with that they giggled, put their hands on each other's faces and their foreheads together.

"I love you so much, 'Rissa," said Arabella.

"Oh…you'll find some charming young stranger like the one in Bedford and throw me over in a second."

"I will not never!" cried 'Bella. "And you're so cruel t'me sometimes maybe I will!"

"See…what did I tell you!" laughed Kerissa, but suddenly her lover was staring past her shoulder, back the way they had come along the laneway.

"Look 'Rissa…there…I can see lights around the curtains of that house."

"It's almost night-time, 'Bella, not everyone wanders around in the dark like the two of us."

"No 'Rissa, that house was where Teodor…Father Ambrosius…that's where he lived and looked after anyone needed a place t'stay or food or—"

She pulled herself from Kerissa's arms and started back down the laneway.

"'Bella…?"

"Kerissa, nobody is supposed t'be there! Father Ambrosius died last year and the house has been empty ever since. My da knows the woman who owns it…"

The older girl stood still for an instant, then had to run to catch up the younger, all the while fighting off a wave of cold and inexplicable terror. She grabbed Arabella by one arm and wouldn't let go.

"Don't, 'Bella!" she cried. "Come away…please…come away now…"

Kerissa was in tears, for no apparent reason frightened out of her wits and begging.

"Please…'Bella…"

# ARABELLA

Gareth's stable/studio on Old Princes Street had undergone some changes over the years.

Once Zoraya had taken up residence, some of the chaos had been taken in hand and turned to a more practical and efficient use of the space involved. Above the open expanse of what once had been an empty ground floor filled with the obstacle course

of his many ongoing projects, stairways had been constructed that led up to a broad walk, and rooms overlooking the carnage below. One had become Zoraya's workroom,

still another the bedroom she shared with Gareth. A third, on the farthest end from these, to afford a measure of privacy, was Kerissa's room. The girls huddled there, together in her bed.

"I'm so sorry, 'Bella" she said. "I have no idea what came over me. Suddenly I was so scared...I couldn't let you go..."

It was not often that the younger played older to the elder, but on this night Arabella was the one who enfolded her love, cradling her in her arms and crooning softly to allay the terror that had overtaken Kerissa in the laneway of the Mews.

" 'Rissa what happened?"

"I don't know," she shivered. "I just knew it would be horrible if I let you go back there, knocked on the door..."

"We're safe now, baby," said Arabella. "I won't let anything bad happen t'you."

" 'Bella I wasn't afraid for me!" cried Kerissa. "I don't know what I was afraid for..."

"Well we're safe now," said Arabella again. "Go t'sleep 'Rissa I'll take care of you..."

In time Kerissa stopped shaking in Arabella's arms, drifted off into a sleep of complete exhaustion. 'Bella stared up into the dark for hours, with the image of light behind curtained windows in a house that should have had no one there to make that light.

Eventually she too drifted off...

...Woke with the sensation that something was crawling over her...hundreds of tiny pinprick feet, a strange physical manifestation of an ill-intentioned gaze...hungry... devoid of anything but that hunger...chittering with anticipation.

She struggled against it in her sleep, aware that her survival, and that of Kerissa in the bargain, just might depend upon her *not* allowing this creature of dream and nightmare more liberty than it had already taken.

As dream and nightmare somehow converged with reality, she opened her eyes and found Kerissa curled into a little ball against her, face buried between her breasts as she wept, whimpered and squirmed in the flood of leprous moonlight that streamed past curtains now thrown wide, through the broad windows of her bedroom. Arabella roused herself up to shield the girl from the near-physical torrent of malice pouring over them, seemingly sourced by the moon itself, its normally placid glow in the night sky now tinged with a sickening aura of diseased colour that had yet to be identified by name.

She burrowed herself and Kerissa beneath the bedclothes, but felt the light scouring away at the fabric, shredding it apart as it strove to reach through to them. The pinpricking on her skin, lessened for a moment, renewed itself tenfold as the linens covering them seemed to fall away in tatters. She tried to scream for help but could make no sound...

...And then there was the crash of the bedroom door flung back, muttered curses in a familiar voice raised in fury. She dared to open her eyes again and saw Zoraya naked in the obscene flood, tearing the curtains back across the windows, drowning the insect voices as she chanted meaningless sounds guised as thunder.

In blessed darkness, she felt Kerissa come awake in her arms, found Zoraya at their bedside, outlined by the light of an oil lamp held by Gareth, who stood in the doorway.

"Zori...?"

Gareth came to stand beside her. Zoraya knelt beside the bed and gathered her daughter up into her arms.

"I think you have done something miraculous, Arabella. I don't know how, but I am certain my daughter lives because of you."

"What was it? Zori, I've never been so frightened in my life..."

Lit from behind only by flickering lamplight, Zoraya's face remained for the most part in shadow, but her amber eyes shone through the dark, and then to glisten...

"I don't know, Arabella," she said hoarsely. "I begin to suspect, but it is something I would have thought to be impossible. Nevertheless...for now it is over, and we are in your debt forever for the strength of your love."

# Chapter Five – THE GIRLS GO NORTH

"...I believe it would be best if Kerissa and Arabella went away for a short while," said Zoraya.

"Mum, y'know we're both standing here and for the most part adult enough to have *some* say..."

Kerissa put on a frown of intense dissatisfaction on her face that made Arabella look away to hide her smile. Four of them sat at the broad trestle table that took up most of the Davies' kitchen space—Brandywine and Windy on one side, Gareth and Zoraya on the other. Their daughters stood together at one end, arms about each other as they'd been for most of the day. Zoraya replied with a look of caution.

"Last night was serious, my love," she said.

"Oh you don't have t'tell me believe me I know!" said Kerissa. "'Bella told me everything that *she* felt was going on, but for me it was like being locked inside of someplace that had no doors or windows with something I couldn't see tearing the skin off me every time it got close enough to take a swipe at me."

There were a few uneasy moments of silence as her words sank in. Brandy shifted uneasily, reached for Windy's hand beneath the table.

"'Rissa, we don't mean t'be treating either of you like children," she said. "This is somethin' new...and scary...

"I know there's been piles of things I've had t'keep from all of you, but your mom knows more about what happened last night than any of us, you and 'Bella included. If she thinks the two of you should be away from here for a while then likely it's the right thing t'do?"

Kerissa became sheepish, put her head down where her hair put sneezes in Arabella's nose. They laughed together.

"I'm just being huffy," she said apologetically. "It's more than scary, like you said. Where will we go?"

"The Carillon," said Nicholas. "I'll send a wire to my folks and you can stay with them a fortnight or whatever...make up some for the holiday we cut short."

The girls consulted each other with raised eyebrows and unspoken questions that ended in unspoken affirmatives between them.

"All right we'll go," said Arabella.

"But with no pretensions of being put out," said Gareth with a grin and one upraised forefinger. "Nobody here will believe you anyway."

Everyone smiled, an easing of tension in the aftermath of terror.

'Rissa said, "Once the twins find out we're haring off again they're gonna be just as huffy as me a little while ago."

Again everyone smiled.

"They're seven years old," said Nicholas. "I'm sure the trauma and bitter disappointment, not to mention the utter injustice of it all, will fade from their memories by next week."

Arabella shook her head.

"Don't be betting on that, da. They're like little wild creatures that can't write anything down, so they have to remember *everything*."

"When do we go?" asked Kerissa.

"The train north tomorrow morning?" said Windy, looking at Zoraya. "We'll stop t'send a wire t'my folks and by the time you arrive they'll have the red carpet out and the whole crew there as a welcoming committee."

All of *les enfants des Boulevardiers* had spent many a summer in the Carillon with Windy's parents. The twins too had been there once or twice, but all of the others had spent their growing up years riding horses (and a large variety of farm animals) all over the vale, at the same time becoming crack pistol shots as well as vastly proficient with the older traditions of duelling swords, short blades and double-curved hunting bows that were perfect for use on horseback. In the midst of all that bloodthirsty work, they'd also become hugely appreciative of the world they lived in, and the good fortune that allowed them to enjoy it so freely.

"So it's settled?" asked Gareth.

"I'll start packing again," said Kerissa. She kissed Arabella and headed for her bedroom.

"Are you okay with that, honey?" asked Brandy.

Arabella nodded, but a frown followed quickly.

"There's something else, mum," she said, and looked at her father as well. "Before everything that happened here..."

Everyone's sense of cautious relief began to evapourate.

"When me and 'Rissa was walking here last night I saw lights in the windows of Robertson's house."

"The place has been empty since Ambrosius passed," said Windy. "No one's been living there since then…"

"I know that, da," said Arabella. "I said so to 'Rissa and was goin' back t'see what was what, but suddenly she got so scared. She begged me not t'go…"

The four adults exchanged glances and what little sense of relief that remained from the decision for the girls to go north for a while disappeared entirely. Zoraya was heard to sigh deeply, and when all eyes fell upon her in response it was obvious that some deep emotion was at work in her heart.

"Perhaps you saw Hasan come to me last night," she whispered. "He could not tell me exactly what it was that made him nervous while we all were talking; but I have had suspicions for some time, and his news only added to my dismay, yet still I have nothing substantial to show me if this is something truly to be of concern."

"Zo, you're being mysterious again," said Gareth.

"I know, my prince…and I am so sorry…please…let me deal with this until I am certain one way or another?"

"Zori, are we gonna be okay? Me and 'Rissa will stay here if you think we…she…is in any real danger…"

"No 'Bella, but for now it would be best if you did go, and it will give me time…but don't let her know…?"

"And I'll look into the thing with Robertson's house, honey," said her father.

She swallowed once and nodded to both.

---

Leave-taking at the central station the next morning was an event of mixed emotions, to the accompaniment of gleaming locomotives hissing clouds of steam onto the spotless platforms, the high whistling of their departures and the distant call of imminent arrivals.

The girls hoisted themselves into their carriage car; one shared case between them had been stowed aboard earlier, so they flung their shoulder packs down once having found their compartment and then hung out the windows, waving apologetically to the twins and trying to maintain an air of carelessness that no one of them felt. Andrew called out to wish them a safe journey; Alain did the same with the added request to "bring us back something nice".

"I don't see why we don't get t'go," said Jamie.

"They said it wasn't really a holiday," said Stella. "'Rissa said they were going because they needed t'do stuff could only be done the two of them."

"Like what?" he persisted.

"Like I don't know, Jamie, but 'Bella promised we could go with for Yuletide, and that's a lot more fun than getting all cooked along the way now."

Stella's maiden voyage back from Bedford, in a train car not quite yet ventilated properly, had been exciting but somewhat overly warm. In consequence, she felt justified in viewing herself as a veteran of rail travel, and entitled to be critical where necessary.

The last passengers boarded the train. With a blast from its steam whistles, the engine lurched forward and then slowly began to move more smoothly out of the station. The girls continued to wave until the tracks carried them out onto the approach to the bridge over the Findhorn, fell back onto their seats once the station had fallen behind them.

"Well...we're off again," said Arabella. "It'll be wondrous fine t'see Grampa Fred and Grammy Alex again...we can ride all over the place and go fishing and thwack the daylights out of all the boys who think girls don't know what t'do with quarterstaffs or practice swords."

Kerissa was pensive, the goodbye smiles now gone. Arabella knew she still was haunted by the horror that had come upon them two nights before.

"I was really frightened too," she said, and launched herself across the compartment to where she could snuggle into Kerissa's arms. "But y'know, we did okay...the two of us...and here we are again the two of us, so we don't have to worry so much. We'll make some adventures of our own..."

She came around to straddle Kerissa's hips, bent down to kiss her face. The older girl began to smile again.

"You're so amazing, 'Bella," she said. "Sometimes I feel like you're so much older than me...days when I just wanna be small again and have somebody take care of me...and you always know what t'do and what t'say t'make me feel better..."

"It's my job," replied the blonde girl. She put her face into 'Rissa's crown of curls and wriggled it around making growling noises all the while, until they fell apart, laughing.

"Maybe we'll meet mysterious strangers," suggested Kerissa, "like the one in Bedford, and on the train home."

Arabella shivered. "I hope not," she said. "He was nice t'look at but he gave me the wiggins."

"The wiggins? That's a new one. What is it?"

"It's what we had two nights ago, but not as nasty. It's when whatever it is isn't what you're comfortable with."

"The wiggins?"

"Yep," grinned Arabella.

"That's the technical term, right?"

"Yep."

"I love you, 'Bella," said Kerissa.

"You better," she replied.

---

They settled in, cozied up together as the train crossed the river and then turned in a slow arc to the north, leaving the City behind them in the late morning sun. Every now and again a great gust of smoke and dreadfulness from the engine would roar in through their open windows, but mostly they revelled in the sweet smell of late summer over the countryside—open fields redolent with one last harvest of hay or new corn, the smell of pasturage and the fleeting sounds of milk cows, goats and sheep, the hum of cicadas and the rush of birds winging past them, racing the train northward. They watched a frenzy of sparrows chasing an impertinent bluejay across the sky, a red-tailed hawk rocket to the ground only to have the rabbit it had chosen for dinner swerve at the last moment and disappear into its den belowground. They drowsed in the heat, pulled down the blinds, locked the door of their compartment, and made love to each other until they fell asleep...

---

...Woke hours later as the train again rattled over the Findhorn, but now the fields and trees that bordered the rail line had taken on the colours of an early fall season, and the air coming through their re-opened windows seemed a bit sharp with the smell of leaves turning to red and gold. Arabella turned in silhouette against the westering sun of the late afternoon, stretched languorously with teasing of forethought and leaned close to whisper in Kerissa's ear.

"We must be almost there, but I'm starving, 'Rissa. D'you think maybe we can get something small t'nibble on until...?"

"If you mean will I get dressed and find us something to eat, then yes," grinned Kerissa. She reached past Arabella for her knickers, blouse and skirt. "I'll expect something in return for the effort, though..."

Arabella wiggled once and blew a kiss. Kerissa slipped on her sandals and ducked out of the compartment door. Within minutes she was back again, but her grin was gone and there were no nibbles.

"'Bella I think we have to get off the train," she said.

"Now this instant?"

Kerissa nodded. "I just figured out what you meant by *the wiggins*," she said. "He's here on the train...tall dark and dangerous from the Moonstruck Mermaid in Bedford. He saw me and I think he recognised me because all of a sudden his eyes got this narrow look and I could feel him watching me as I came back here."

"Maybe we should just go on, 'Rissa," said Arabella. "Once we're with Grams and Grampa we should be okay."

"Baby, I don't think we want him *t'know* we're with Grams and Grampa."

"But why?"

Kerissa scowled, shaking her head.

"I dunno...I just feel like we need to be gone right now." She looked out the windows, at the first low hills of the Carillon vale rushing by. "I think we have t'cross the river at least one more time before we get to Élysée. That means there's gonna be a big curve where we should have t'slow down for at least a quarter mile... "

"And we're gonna jump off the train?"

Kerissa nodded. "Grams and Grampa will know something's up when all they see is our travelling case."

It was Arabella's turn to be concerned.

"'Rissa are you sure it's what she should do?"

"Nope...but it sure feels like I should be sure."

"It was definitely that guy from Bedford?"

"It was, 'Bella," she replied. "And if he gave you *the wiggins* then and gave me *the wiggins* just now, I'm thinking we'd best put some distance between us."

It was a measure of the trust each of them held for the thoughts and opinions of the other. Arabella was dressed in moments, collecting their things and stuffing them into their backpacks.

"I guess maybe it's a good thing we kept our pointy things with," she said, and unsheathed her own duelling sword.

***

The light was beginning to fail on the eastern side of the line when Kerissa's speculation proved to be prescient. The train roared across one last trestle; the Findhorn foamed and rushed beneath them...and then the train began to slow its progress through the sharp curve taking them eastward once again. Arabella and Kerissa shouldered their packs, crept cautiously into the companionway and moved to the rear of their carriage, looking back only once, but long enough to see *tall dark and dangerous* at the other end of their car, with unfamiliar faces directly behind him.

They raced for the end of the car, slammed the doot shut. 'Rissa spiked a long dagger through the handle and turned to Arabella.

"Time to go, my love," she said, and launched her backpack into the closely-trimmed brush beside the line before leaping from the narrow platform between the carriages. Arabella followed suit. Behind them they heard inarticulate cries of what could well be rage and frustration, swiftly carried away as the engine began to gain speed for its final run to the station in Élysée.

# Chapter Six – THE BEVERLEY BOYS GET THEIR MARCHING ORDERS

In mid-morning Edmund and Sebastian sat patiently in the great room of the house in St John's Mews. Uncle Nick served them steaming mugs of coffee and apologised.

"Brandy was called away," Windy said. "She shouldn't be much longer."

"The Palace then," said Edmund, with a disconcerting certainty.

They might have been twins themselves for all the difference could be found between them. Scruffy and eternally dishevelled, they had their height from both parents, but it was Thomas' girth that made them appear almost mountainous to those meeting them for the first time. At twenty Edmund was the elder of the two brothers, Kerissa's immediate contemporary; Sebastian shared seventeen years with Arabella. Both were thoroughly enamoured of their *cousins*, in despite of full knowing the girls were thoroughly enamoured of each other. Nevertheless, they remained good-natured and blindly devoted to them, in the way that brothers might become ferocious in defense of their sisters.

"Big doings, Uncle Nick," observed Edmund.

"And Annie Branny running the show," said Sebastian, with no small amount of wonder.

"That's exactly what your father said," said Windy, laughing.

"We figured there was *something* going on," said Edmund drily. He took a big swallow of his coffee, looked at the bottom of his mug with a woeful expression.

Nicholas was just coming back from the kitchen with a full pot for refills when Brandy came through the front door.

"I'm so sorry," she said. "I wanted t'be here when you arrived."

The brothers stood to receive welcoming hugs and Windy went back into the kitchen for a mug for Brandy. When they all were settled, she cradled hers in both hands and smiled when Edmund got back up on his feet and saluted her with his mug.

"Beverleys reporting for duty, ma'am," he said with a grin.

"We're not so formal as all that," said Brandywine. "You know what's going on?"

Both young men nodded. "We got most of it from Mom and Dad, including all the question marks *and* the nasty bits," said Sebastian. "'Riss and 'Bell are okay?"

Brandy nodded and sipped at her mug.

"They're fine, Sebastian, but whatever it was, Zoraya thought it would be best if they took another *holiday*, away from here. They took the morning train up to the Carillon yesterday t'stay with Grams and Grampa. Why don't we go into the kitchen, you guys must be hungry..."

The Beverley boys laughed in unison, sloshing coffee down their shirt-fronts.

"Why is it everyone tries t'feed us?" asked Edmund. "Do we look like we're starving?"

"No of course not," said Brandy, "but every time I see you two it seems you've grown some more and I just worry a bit you're not getting anough meals t'keep up."

That drew more laughter from everyone.

"You needn't worry on that score, Auntie," said Edmund. "We ate a horse for breakfast, with all the trimmings..."

No one was interested in what *all the trimmings* could possibly be, but they wandered into the kitchen anyway, and Brandywine quickly filled a platter with cheese and biscuits and slices of honey-flavoured apples. The boys got hungry again in a hurry. Through a mouthful of crunchy bits, Sebastian asked:

"So do we finally get t'find out why you wanted us t'keep an eye on Evrard de Montenay? It was a bit of work to t'get close to him."

"Sebastian was the one finally managed it," offered Edmund. "They ended up in the same political science class, and then the three of us started prowling together...you know...pubbing, sports, lectures...the usual college stuff...

"He was pretty quiet at first, kept to himself most of the time, and really serious about being there...but he came round when Sebastian went out of his way to give him some extra tutoring for the first semester exams. After that he was a lot more comfortable with us."

Sebastian went on from there. "He never talked about his family or when he was growing up, but he seemed grateful for some friendship, like he'd always had t'be cautious around other people.

"He was planning on staying in the residence once the university announced it was closing down for a month of mourning for the Queen, but as soon as the news came out he got a message calling him home. We got the impression he didn't get any kind of choice about it, either. And he seemed really unhappy about having t'go..."

Brandywine drank coffee and paid close attention, every now and again interjecting a comment or question regarding the younger de Montenay's outside interests, his temperament, the things he did in his free time. Inside of an hour it became evident that her two "nephews" had taken their task quite seriously, and, at the same time, found in Evrard a comrade they themselves would have chosen entirely on their own.

"...So what's next, Auntie B?" asked Edmund.

"Have you made any plans while you're waitin' t'go back to school?"

Both shook their heads, and Sebastian said, "Not really. We'd thought we'd just kick around the City some, hang out with the girls, that sort of thing.... Have you got something else in mind?"

"I do, but I don't want t'ruin your extra time off," said Brandywine.

"We had plenty of time off through the summer, didn't we, Ed? The offered courses were pretty thin this year so our professors really didn't keep us all that busy."

Brandy looked thoughtful, deferred to Windy for a confirmation of something they had discussed earlier.

"Will you go north as well?" he asked. "We thought you could join the girls briefly, and then go on to the Dales, t'keep an eye on your friend. My folks would see to getting you rigged up properly, and when you got to Glen Carrick, a woman there named Camille Ardrey can see to your lodging and if necessary provide you with a bit of made-up history and a reason for being there. I'll write you a letter of introduction."

"All in aid of just *keeping an eye* on Evrard?"

"Without letting him know that's what you're about, if you can manage it."

"We'd just be rambling around, taking the tour up from the Carillon," said Edmund.

"Sure," agreed Sebastian. "We could manage that no problem at all."

"In a couple of days?"

Both boys nodded, and there was a faint knock at the front door that Nicholas rose to investigate. He returned a minute later with an envelope in hand.

"It's from my folks," he said, breaking the seal and extracting the wired message within. He read the contents quickly, his face growing dark with dismay.

"The girls weren't on the train," he said hoarsely. "Their travelling case was delivered up onto the platform, and Mum and Da waited until the train left...but the girls either didn't get off, or they simply weren't on the train to begin with when it arrived."

Brandywine put her coffee mug down on the table carefully, exchanged a look of terror with Windy. Sebastian said:

"We'll go this afternoon..."

# Chapter Seven – ON THE CARILLON MOORS

They rolled and tumbled through the sharp grass and brambles beside the rails, crawled into each other's arms and spent a long while just hanging on to each other whilst catching their breath and re-discovering their sense of balance in relation to the rest of the world.

"You heard him," said Kerissa.

Arabella nodded. "You were so right," she whispered. "It sounded like if he could've killed us with words we'd've been dead ten minutes ago."

It was a sobering thought.

"Thank goodness the twins knew what a jerk he was just by looking at him," said Kerissa.

"Whoever he is," added Arabella.

"It would be a good thing t'know," agreed Kerissa. "Meanwhile, I guess we've got at least a night out here before we can get t'Grams and Grampa's place."

"It might get cold tonight," said 'Bella. "We're a lot further north..."

"No worries there, my love," said Kerissa. "We've got each other and a bit of help from my mum as well."

"But I'm still kind of starving," said the blonde girl apologetically.

"We'll do what we can," said Kerissa. "You and me we're tough as rusty nails and bloodthirsty in the bargain."

"Oh, that we are..."

"So no worries then?"

Arabella growled in her throat and licked playfully at an ear.

"None at all..." she said.

---

They doffed sandals in favour of heavy-soled hiking boots from the bottom of their packs, and after a brief lookabout decided their path led up onto the Carillon moors a quarter mile away.

"It'll be at least an hour before the train reaches Élysée," said Kerissa.

"And hours more in the dark if he truly intends us harm," said Arabella.

"Then it's holiday time again," said Kerissa gaily. "Tramping about in the gorse and the heather and—"

"Well we'll see about that," said Arabella. "I've never been on the moors, the only heather I've ever known was a thoroughly objectionable girl from the Eastern townships, and I've no idea what a gorse is."

"Me either."

"Oh we're gonna do just swell then," laughed the blonde girl, "as long as we find someplace where the moon can't find us."

Kerissa became serious. "It's not full anymore, 'Bella, so I think we'll be okay. I think it has t'be a full moon for any kind of damage t'be done."

The climb became much steeper, so Arabella didn't bother to ask how Kerissa would know something like that. They huffed and puffed their way upwards, angling across the face of the steep slope until they came to its crest and stood in the last rays of the sun going blood red on the horizon behind them. The Carillon moors stretched away from them in every direction, details becoming lost in the burgeoning shadows, though the heather was undeniably purple, and gorse turned out to be spiky with yellow flowers gone a bit burnt orange in the sunset. They sighed together.

"No hot baths or clean sheets tonight," said Arabella wistfully.

"I was hoping for some of your Grams' pratie soup," said Kerissa in equally woeful tones.

"That guy has got a lot to answer for..."

"I can do without the answers, 'Bella. Let's get into this and see if we can find some shelter sooner than later?"

Three hours later they were well into *this,* and, with the benefit of their afternoon snooze, only just beginning to feel the strain of weaving their way through the aforementioned gorse and heather, and the ups and downs of the undulating moorland. They came to a small stream that seemed to have lost its way along its way from the mountains far to the north, but gratefully stripped off their boots and stockings to bathe their feet in water as cool and clean on their toes as it felt down their somewhat dry throats.

With bright stars and an unthreatening waning moon high overhead in the black vault of the night sky, they carried on, alternately striding and stumbling along as the terrain dictated their pace. Sometime both surmised to be near midnight, Arabella took a tumble down a declivity that seemed to open up under her feet, losing her pack along the way until she lay spread-eagled and flattened in a small cleared space at the very bottom of a ravine that ran off to the northeast to their left and curved southeast to their right. Kerissa followed in seconds.

"Are you hurt, baby?" she said, but suddenly her concern turned to something else. "Oh look! 'Bella look you found our place for the night thank goodness I didn't have the heart t'tell you my blisters were getting' blisters..."

Arabella turned her head and found a small rather splintery little door set into the hillside made by the declivity. Beside it was a small pane of heavy glass, with bubbles inside that caught the starlight and made it seem like a welcome of warm light from within.

"I think I've got a burr in my bum," she said.

"Stay where you are," commanded Kerissa. "I'll scout the inside and then we'll see about what's what in your knickers..."

---

The offending bit of spiky vegetation lodged in Arabella's knickers was but the work of a moment to remove; thereafter the luxury of an abandoned shepherd's cottage as shelter for the rest of the night gave the girls a needed sense of security.

"I'll get some of that gorse-y stuff for a fire," she said, nodding towards the small hearth that somehow had been put together in such a way that it seemed likely to vent on the top of the hillside. "It's gettin' a bit chilly..."

Kerissa dug into her pack and extracted a small bundle of cloth with a flourish.

"We don't need a fire, honey," she said, shaking it out in half-light that became less so.

"My mum made this. She called it *Equatoria*, and while it won't keep our tummies from rumbling, it *will* keep us both warmer than toast."

The sunburst woven into the centre of the cloth seemed to radiate warmth, and a soft but reassuring light. The girls threw their clothing down on the leathern lattice-work of the wooden bed frame that stood in a corner of their refuge, and somehow managed to keep the shivers at bay...

---

Arabella woke to the sound of something scratching at the door of the cottage...

*Oh gods not again!* she thought.

The scratching stopped, began again. Then it moved to sharp scrapes at the little window, and outlined by the faint aura of light from their blanket, Arabella saw a sharp-muzzled face with bottomless black eyes appear and disappear as whatever it was on the outside leapt up into the air, over and over, to see what was inside.

" 'Rissa wake up!" she whispered urgently. "I think we're in the soup again!"

Kerissa came awake at once, with 'Bella's fingers gently across her lips.

"There's somethin' outside tryin' t'get in."

Kerissa bobbed her head once to let her know it was understood; together they keeked out from under their blanket until she had caught her own glimpse of the thing outside. Arabella reached for the scabbard of her duelling sword where it lay beside the bed, but Kerissa stayed her hand and then slipped from her embrace, moving cautiously across the earthen floor.

"Be careful, 'Rissa."

The dark girl nodded in acknowledgment, but put her hand on the latch of the door, and then swung it wide. A small vixen darted into the cottage, yipping frantically as it leapt up and down and nipped at Kerissa's hand, trying to move her out into the night.

"'Bella we're not in any danger..."

Arabella was out of bed in an instant, dragging her blade free as she moved past Kerissa and into the doorway.

"Oh yes we are," she said, and pointed.

Perhaps half a mile from the door, in the deep shadows of the ravine, a trice of flickering lights moved along slowly, accompanied by the faint murmur of voices.

"We gotta get our stuff together and get out of here," Arabella said. The vixen yipped once more, made circles around them as if to goad them off to anywhere else but where they were, then stood motionless in the doorway, waiting.

The girls went into a frenzy of activity, stuffing Zoraya's blanket, their boots and clothing into their packs, while the vixen made *hurry-up!* sounds.

They followed her outside, keeping low to the ground, letting themselves be led along as they headed south down the ravine in the opposite direction until it curved away to their left and then began to climb back up into the moonlight. Making sure they couldn't be seen from below and tucked down out of sight of anything above or around them, they went through their packs and managed to get back into most of their clothing before the shivers took too much of a hold on their bare skin.

"They can't be looking for us, can they, 'Rissa? I mean...Tall Dark and Dangerous...he couldn't have sent those people out after us so fast..."

Kerissa shrugged in the moonlight. "All of a sudden it feels like *everybody's* out looking for us, 'Bel...oh damn! Damn damn damn!"

"What?"

"I'm missin' my knickers, 'Bella!"

"You don't need them, honey—" replied Arabella, then stopped with a look of dismayed comprehension and said *Damn!* herself.

Kerissa finished lacing up her boots and leapt to her feet. "If I left 'em behind in or anywhere near the cottage they're gonna know somebody was there..."

"...And maybe be out after us in no time," finished Arabella with a short laugh. "I never dreamt I'd ever be sorry 'bout you losin' your knickers."

Kerissa grinned in response, but now the vixen was getting anxious again, trying to move them away as quickly as possible. They'd not gone more than a dozen yards when Arabella stopped.

" 'Rissa wait! Listen...even if they're not after us, there's an awful lot of them t'be out wandering around the moors in the middle of the night. That's somethin' funny peculiar. We need t'find out who they are."

"I knew you were gonna say that," whispered Kerissa.

They crept back toward the edge of the ravine, hunkered down again and waited. The vixen made a small despairing sound behind them, but fell silent and followed reluctantly. Minutes later they heard what sounded like the tramp of a score of heavily-shod feet, and the clank of steel on steel.

"They're soldiers," said Kerissa. "I bet they're soldiers..."

She risked a cautious look from their hiding place and almost immediately threw herself back down beside Arabella, wide-eyed and definitely spooked. In the ravine below they were now close enough that snatches of conversation could be heard as well.

"I'm right, 'Bella, and there's a whole bunch of 'em but they don't look like any of our soldiers."

Arabella closed her eyes and listened intently.

"They're Scandians," she hissed angrily. "Armed Scandians over a hundred miles south of our border. We gotta tell somebody!"

She motioned that now it *was* time to go. They crawled back to where they had left their packs, shouldered them, and followed the vixen deeper into the heart of the moors at a dead run.

# Chapter Eight - CONSPIRACY

"...And you say she jumped from a moving train once she caught sight of you?"

Sevrain de Montenay stood in his father's study, becoming more and more uncomfortable with each passing moment. He nodded wordlessly in reply to the question, already knew where the rest of the conversation would take them, and silently cursed the yellow-haired bitch on the train.

"Could you go over the entirety of this, your latest disaster, for me one more time?"

Renard de Montenay rose from behind his desk, poured himself a brandy from a decanter on the sideboard and resumed his seat, once again placing himself in a flood of western light through the broad diamond-paned windows at his back. He sat in silhouette; his elder son stood blinded by the light, in what he knew quite well to be the merciless glare of his father's regard. That he tried to emulate his father in all manner of appearance and attitude seemed suddenly to make no difference when it came to his failures. And Sevrain was very certain he had in some way, again, failed.

"I first saw her in Bedford, in the common room of the inn. She was with an *afrique*, no doubt a servant, and two small children. They were having dinner. I was with *our friends*, those you had instructed me to meet with, across the room..."

"Go on."

"Someone...likely one of the children, noticed I had taken an interest in her and made some sort of remark. She turned briefly. We left before they had finished their meal."

"Why did you take an interest in this girl, Sevrain? I know the reason very well, but please, I wish to hear it from your lips."

Sevrain trembled, prayed it was nothing his father could see. To the world he presented himself as *tall, dark and dangerous*, black-eyed and elegantly handsome, a neatly trimmed Van Dyke and moustache giving him an air of mystery and the promise of unbridled passion; before his father he presented himself in the only way he had ever been able to face him—as some inferior creature unworthy of respect or consideration. He bowed his head and had to repeat himself twice before his father was satisfied.

"She was...handsome," he said.

"You mean she was a large-breasted cow," said his father, sipping brandy.

Sevrain, again, nodded.

"And because you stared at her from across the taproom of an inn, she found it necessary to leap from a moving train in order to escape from you."

"Father I told—-"

"I said I wanted to hear it again!" shouted Renard de Montenay. The cut crystal of his balloon glass shattered across the surface of his desk as he slammed it down, spattering his waistcoat with brandy. "We've waited a thousand years for this moment. Do you have any idea what your stupid infatuations may have cost us? Tell me the rest of it, you brainless twit!"

Sevrain closed his eyes, fighting back against fear, shame, and a withering hatred.

"On the train back to the City I encountered the little girl in one of the companionways. I made some sort of compliment to her, and then asked after the name of her guardian."

Renard de Montenay could be heard to be grinding his teeth.

"You were told to make yourself as inconspicuous as possible, and yet you did the exact opposite in the hopes you could fuck some nameless trollop. What did you learn from this little girl?"

"She said her guardian was her cousin Arabella and they were returning from holiday. When I pressed her for more she became wary and ran off."

"No doubt to inform *cousin Arabella* that the halfwit stranger from Bedford now was asking questions about her. Was that the end of it?"

"No, sir. They all left the train when we reached the City, but the little girl pointed me out at my carriage window as we departed for the Eastern townships."

"And you saw her again on the northbound train as you returned here..."

"I saw the *afrique*, and assumed she would be travelling with the girl."

"So you went looking for her."

"I did."

The featureless shadow behind the desk fell silent. Sevrain could see his father's head bent forward to his chest, but nothing of his expression. When they came, his words seemed to come from between clenched teeth, barely audible even in the silence.

"And all of this in such wise as to give her cause to *take notice of you*...suspect you of something...and flee from you."

"Father she's likely dead on the moors by now. The night was unseasonably cold. They had nothing with them but small backpacks."

"And if she is not?"

"If she is not?"

"If she is not dead, you fool! What then if she has survived, with a story of being harassed by someone of your appearance? Though not well, we are known in Élysée, perhaps enough that the authorities will know full well who it is they are looking for."

Again Renard went silent, lost in thought long enough that Sevrain grew doubly uncomfortable waiting for his next outburst.

"And while in Bedford you thought that a fishing boat lost from the local fleet was not worth mentioning?"

"Boats go missing all the time—"

"Not like this time, you idiot! The weather was clear, the ocean was calm."

"Father—"

"Shut up! For god's sake shut up and let me think."

There were vague mutterings as Sevrain was left standing in the haze of light come from behind his father; he grew warm in the heat, hot with rage and frustration when his father's inner voice became externalised with a fervent wish that the intelligence of his younger son might have been bestowed upon the elder instead. Yet all he could do...all he had ever done...was await his father's pleasure.

"Describe her to me, this girl," said Renard de Montenay.

Sevrain did so, in the most minute detail and in such a way that only increased the measure of his father's contempt for him. De Montenay again rose from his desk and, this time, disappeared into an adjoining room, left his son sweltering in the heat for the better portion of half an hour before he returned and and threw a photograph onto his desk.

"Is this the girl?"

Sevrain leaned forward and examined the photograph.

"Yes," he said quietly.

"No," said his father viciously. "*That* is the girl's mother, some minor functionary in the palace staff, married to a musician named Nicholas Wyndham. The girl is their daughter, Arabella Wyndham, and by following your cock wherever it leads you, there is the distinct possibility that your behaviour may lead the authorities to me."

"I'm sorry—"

"Your contrition means nothing, Sevrain. I cannot wire this to our friends. You will go back to Bedford immediately, and inform them we may need to act much more quickly."

Sevrain nodded.

"I'll go first thing in the morning—"

"You will go tonight," said his father quietly, "and you will cut your hair, take off your beard and moustache, and travel in clothing borrowed from one of the stable boys. Am I clear?"

"Yes, sir".

"Good. Go pack your bags. You can find your supper on the evening train. Now have someone come in here to clean up this glass and tell your mother I wish to speak with her."

---

Margaret de Montenay slipped quietly through the door of the study She was rather more fair than her husband or first-born, but also tall and statuesque and of great physical beauty—a prize that had been won more than a score of years earlier in a place far away from the country in which she had come to be with her betrothed, his reward for services to be rendered.

She moved a chair into the place where her elder son had stood, but away from the blinding sunset that now came through the windows at his back.

"You scorn him for being just like you," she said tonelessly. "You treat him worse than you treat our kitchen maids, when you are not fucking them..."

De Montenay looked up from some papers before him and smiled without the faintest trace of amusement.

"He is not just like me, my dear wife," he said. "He is a thick-witted clod pretending to royalty."

"And what then are you, Renard?" she asked.

"I am this country's rightful sovereign, now the old bitch has finally died without issue."

She clasped her hands and looked away.

"What did you want of me?"

"Where is Evrard? Why has has he not come to me?"

"You know as well as I."

De Montenay scowled. "Gods but I am tired of this. Could you not have given me more than one son who is a moron, and another so selfless he has no clue what is good for himself or his family?"

Margaret de Montenay caught her breath and in it, a sound that may have resembled a sob of despair.

"You have three daughters besides."

"I have no use for daughters," snapped her husband. "Not until I have the throne and can marry them off where they will do us the most good."

"You mean where they will do *you* the most good."

De Montenay bore this rebuke with another mirthless smile.

"Perhaps you should look after our evening meal..."

Margaret knew when she had been dismissed, said nothing as she passed a servitor entering the study to clean up after her husband's fit of temper.

"Get Rochambeau in here," he said, when the glass and brandy had been swept and mopped up.

The faceless creature bowed once, said "Yes, m'lord" and backed his way out of the study. Rochambeau, the master-at-arms, appeared minutes later, in that moment equally as faceless in the eyes of his master.

"We're riding into the Carillon," said de Montenay, without looking up from a map spread across his desk. "Get our people together and be ready in an hour...and make certain Evrard rides with us..."

# Chapter Nine - THE FURTHERANCE OF ALL THINGS

The afternoon train caught up with the night as Edmund and Sebastian went north in search of their cousins. The locomotive belched smoke and sparks into the burgeoning darkness, and their compartment filled with shadows until Sebastian remembered that there were filament bulbs powered by the revolution of the train's wheels to provide them with illumination. He flicked a switch by the door, turned a small dial to lower the glare of light to a soft glow, and turned to his brother, suddenly overwhelmed by the thought of losing either of the girls, stricken with speechless eloquence...

"I know," said Edmund, no less terrified by the prospect. "But I've been thinking, Sebastian. They'd not abandon ship without a reason, and if they jumped anywhere along the way it would only have been when the train was moving slowly enough that it wasn't suicide t'do it..."

"Then it would have t'have been near to one of the northbound village stops along the rail line."

"Right. And if that were so, then they would have wired Nick and Brandy right away t'say what they'd done, and why..."

Sebastian nodded. "So that means—"

"They were already further up the line than any of the villages..."

"...And the only place they could've safely jumped ship was when the train turned east to Élysée after crossing the Dunsmuir Bridge."

"Exactly."

"So they're on the moors."

This time Edmund nodded. "And will be spending the night there, whilst trying t'make their way east to Élysée, or Gram's and Grampa's place.

By instinct, Sebastian looked to his older brother to make a plan of action for the two of them. Edmund grew silent, staring sightlessly out through the windows of the carriage into the spark-strewn darkness.

"Will you trust me?" he said.

Sebastian nodded.

"I'm going t'get off the train at Élysée. You're going on to Glen Carrick in the Dales, to contact the Ardrey woman, and see if you can find Evrard."

Sebastian made to protest, but thought better of it immediately. Edmund continued:

"I can be at Gram's and Grampa's by sunrise, and an hour later on the moors heading westward for 'Bella and 'Rissa with all of their people."

Sebastian nodded again.

"When you get into the Dales...Glen Carrick...find Camille Ardrey and then go about what we were coming up here for in the first place. Find Evrard. Tell him whatever you think is best. I don't know what else is going on here, but Annie Branny wants him so you just say something he'll believe and then if something happens, get him the devil out."

Sebastian nodded a third time. They looked deeply into each other's eyes.

"I'll find them, Sebastian," promised Edmund.

"Swear it t'me!"

"I love them as much as you do. I'll find them and get them out of whatever they're into no matter what kind of Hell stands in the way..."

---

Though concealed by darkness, the vixen moved them cautiously across the highlands, instinctively keeping them out of sight of anyone or anything they might encounter by leading them down through streambeds and washes that would remain dry until the spring thaws brought snow-melt from the mountains. With sunrise they were tramping due east directly towards Élysée, though likely still not far enough north to come off the moors comfortably near to the Wyndham estate. Arabella was struggling.

"'Rissa I'm really tired," she said, almost in tears. "I don't know why. I don't mean t'be such a baby..."

Kerissa was concerned. Arabella had become steadily more unsteady as the damp and chill crept through their light clothing, until the younger girl was stumbling constantly, and remained on her feet only through the warmth of Zoraya's blanket wrapped around her and the supporting arm of her companion. The she-fox had left them for half an hour at a time through the night, roving back and forth along the path they had taken, returning with a lessening sense of urgency, but showing concern for Arabella's sudden weakness.

Kerissa was not unfamiliar with it. There had been times when they were growing up that Arabella had become frantic with hunger, and then slowly lapsed into a state similar to the one she was in now. Briefly, she contemplated finding some hidey-hole and going on alone, leaving the vixen to watch over Arabella while she sought help at a faster pace, but couldn't bring herself to leave her.

"We can rest soon, honey," she said. "They stopped following us a long way back, and we must be getting close to somewhere by now. We just need t'find some food for you and then you'll be fine..."

---

De Montenay rode in a fury, lashing his black gelding every time the horse slackened its pace. Rochambeau rode well behind them, still dazed from the riding crop that had whipped across his face and knocked him from his saddle.

"...I'm quite certain I told you Evrard would ride with us," de Montenay had spat in the garth-yard, whilst two dozen of his servitors armed themselves and massed round him.

"I couldn't find him, m'lord," the hapless Rochambeau had said. "He was nowhere to be found. M'lady said he'd gone into the village for some reason or another. She'd not say more..."

Now they thundered *en masse* a mile out from the western edge of Glen Carrick, crossing one of the many small streams that fed the Findhorn, and then onto old tree-shrouded cart tracks seldom used and well away from unwelcome eyes. De Montenay led them toward what the locals called the Moorgate—a path through the hills enclosing the Dales that led directly up onto the highlands.

Renard was not happy. His younger son had managed to thwart him without actually being aware he had done so, and so could not be held to account; the evening past he had watched his elder son slouch away into the village to board a southbound train like a whipped peasant dog, and while it had given him pleasure to see Sevrain stripped of his empty pretensions, it was infuriating as well. Not for the first time, he wished there had only been one son, of subservience *and* a modest amount of creative intelligence so *he* was not forever forced to think for the both of them. He had already decided that Arabella Wyndham and her *afrique* would die if there were no circumstances to prevent it; the what and whyfore of her flight from his eldest son's attentions were of absolutely no consequence to him. He simply did not want unwanted attention, for any reason.

The Moorgate was nothing more than some crumbling stone ruins beside the path. A league further and they began to climb up onto the moors.

Daylight was still hours away when the train carrying Edmund and Sebastian arrived in Élysée. They had spent the entirety of their journey in a quiet frenzy of impatience and speculation fuelled by the revelations and inexplicable occurrences of the last few days. To add to the mysteries, before they had left, Nicholas informed them them that someone...some *thing* perhaps...had indeed taken up a brief residence in the old Robertson house, and left a small patch of burnt flooring in testimony.

"... I've no doubt it had something to do with the girls' nightmares," he said. "Zoraya insisted on coming with me, and seemed to agree, but only became more close-mouthed when I pressed her for what she thought it might mean..."

All things taken into consideration, the boys realised they were working on blind faith alone, trusting that whatever they did in some way would serve to mitigate the strangeness of it all until explanations could be found. During the short layover, before Sebastian continued on to the Dales, they had one last deliberation.

"...I'll send word t'you as soon as the girls're safe," said Edmund. "You just be wary of running afoul of any of Evrard's family."

"His father, you mean," said Sebastian.

Edmund nodded. "I suspect he might be the real reason Branny wants us looking out for Evrard, but like everything else, who knows for what reason. One thing that *is* certain is that Renard de Montenay is no more a friend of our family than was his father Dorion..."

"I'll be careful," Sebastian promised. "You go...now...."

Edmund shouldered his own pack and went in search of a horse or motor car to take him the last twenty miles to the Wyndham estate.

※

The vixen bounded into the small hollow where Kerissa sat cradling Arabella in her arms, tugged at her sleeve until she gently laid the barely-conscious girl down and followed at a scamper to where she could look to see whatever the fox had found demanding of her attention. She breathed a sigh of relief; less than a mile away, heading in their direction, was a small wagon being drawn slowly across the moors by a pair of dray horses. She returned to her companion, began coaxing her back onto her feet.

"C'mon, 'Bella, we gotta move, honey. This time I'm pretty sure it's a good thing..."

※

De Montenay halted the progress of his party as they crested the last rise, scanned the empty expanse of open country before them. He directed half his men to scatter across the moor to the southwest, while he and the rest went directly south.

"One way or the other I want these two found and brought to me," he said. His tone suggested he was careless of their condition upon delivery. "We should be able to intercept them whether they travelled the night or not."

He cast one last meaningful glance to each of his men.

"If you find them and bringing them to me becomes troublesome, kill them both..."

---

With the eastern horizon aglow with the first dayight to spill out over the Carillon—at just about the same time that Arabella and Kerissa gratefully were climbing into the wagon of a farmer on his way to the market in Élysée—Edmund Beverley and Frederick Wyndham stood in the paddock before the latter's stables. The last of his crofters arrived, and as they mounted their own horses, Alexandra Wyndham strode towards them in riding skirts, silenced any protest with a single gesture, and ordered her own mare to be brought out and saddled. With the rising sun at their backs, they rode westward to the moors.

---

Sebastian found himself skulking. When he gave it some thought he realised there was no *reason* for him to be skulking, yet he was no more than a few dozen strides from the railway platform with the mid-morning sun at his back when he realised he was trying his best to be inconspicuous, even stealthy.

*This is silly* he told himself. *You're wandering down the high street in a village where everybody knows everyone else...with a pistol, a longbow and a longsword strapped to your pack... and you're trying* not *to be noticed?*

Thereafter he stopped skulking, straightened himself up to his full height and strode along as if he owned the world.

He stopped at the hostelry and inquired after Camille Ardrey, received directions and went on his way. Twenty minutes later he found the old smithy at the edge of the village and let himself through the front garden gate. The door of the old timbered house opened as he climbed up onto the porch, and a grey-haired woman looked at him curiously.

"Can I help you?" she asked.

"Are you Camille Ardrey?" he asked. "My name is Sebastian Beverley."

When she nodded, he said nothing, but handed her the envelope containing his uncle's introduction. She foraged about in the pocket of her apron, brough out a pair of spectacles and read silently for a minute or so. Her smile was immediate.

"And your brother...?"

"...Decided t'stay on a while with Uncle Nicky's parents in Élysée," he replied.

"Well come in then, Sebastian, and welcome to Glen Carrick," she said. "Please call me Cami, everyone else does. I imagine you must be starving after your train up from the City..."

Sebastian grinned. He was, in fact, pretty hungry...

---

Sevrain de Montenay took a room over the stables at the Moonstruck Mermaid, spent the day drowsing in the heat, alternately raging against his father and wishing for some respite from his contempt. At sunset he trudged through Bedford without stopping and out onto the road that ran the clifftops to the west. Then he climbed down to stand on a deserted beach, staring out across the western ocean to where it met the sky. He lit an oil-soaked rag on the end of a piece of driftwood, lifted it above his head and moved it back and forth for the better part of five minutes before burying it in the sand and looking about for some place to spend the hours he knew were likely ahead of him before his signal might be answered.

---

The farmer had bread and cheese and a flagon of ale still cool from its bed of hay beneath his wagon bench. While Kerissa tore off morsels and slowly fed them to Arabella, he sneaked glances over his shoulder and found himself marvelling that a boring trundle across the moors to sell potatoes and garden vegetables had become some sort of mysterious adventure, complete with two pretty young women.

He never saw, and only just barely heard the whistle of the arrow that struck through his left eye as he turned his head forward again. Soundlessly he toppled from his seat, and hung for a moment before bouncing off the floor of the wagon and into the brush beside the track. Another hail of arrows took down one of the horses. Kerissa looked up as the survivor snuffled once and then stopped, nosing at the corpse of his fallen comrade. When she keeked up out of the wagon bed, what she saw approaching from the north was a smaller contingent of what they had left behind at the abandoned cottage.

"Oh 'Bella hurry up and feel better," she said. "This time it's the soup again. I don't think they know we're here, but I'm kinda thinkin' it's not gonna be fun once they find out..."

She lay down flat in the wagon-bed and managed to have both their bows strung by the time Arabella stirred beside her, reached out a hand to her face.

"I'll be okay in a minute or two," she said weakly.

"One minute would be more helpful..." suggested 'Rissa with an urgent smile.

---

Sebastian and Cami Ardrey spent the rest of the morning getting acquainted, during which time it was determined that should the need arise, he was a distant nephew and she was an aunt twice or thrice removed from the central trunk of their family tree; that he was in the Dales for a holiday of hiking...

"...In truth I'm supposed t'be playing nursemaid-at-a-distance to someone," he explained, "though he's not supposed t'know that's what I'm doing. We became friends of sorts at the university. His name's Evrard...Evrard de Montenay."

"The de Montenays are the oldest family in the Dales," she said with a frown. "They own the manor house overlooking the village and most of the land surrounding Glen Carrick, but they aren't very well loved here, Sebastian. I imagine Nicholas told you that...?"

Sebastian nodded. "Well...Evrard's all right, I guess. We've gotten along fairly well once we got to'know each other a little. He's pretty quiet though, keeps to himself more than not."

"Just remember that if you end up anywhere near his father you need to be very cautious."

"I'll remember," said Sebastian, "and thank you so much for putting me up on such... well...no notice at all, really."

Cami Ardrey smiled. "Your uncle and I have a great deal of common history, and I've known him and his family almost from the time he was born. You're most welcome here, Sebastian, for as long as you need to stay. If you'd like to wander about the village, I'll look after your things and get a room ready for you. Supper's usually around six this time of year..."

---

"...How many of them are there, 'Rissa?"

"I quick-counted about a dozen or so."

"How many arrows do we have?"

"Maybe a half dozen more than that."

Arabella sat up cautiously, the dazed look that had been in her eyes now turning to a sharp green awareness. She did her own fast reconaissance and slipped back down beside Kerissa.

"They're still just a bit too far away t'make a surprise from us anything more than a waste of them."

"We could cut the other horse loose and run for it," suggested 'Rissa.

Arabella thought that over for a moment and then shook her head.

"It would just be an invitation t'end up like that poor farmer and his horse...and besides, I want t'know why armed bands of Scandians are running around our countryside."

"We're gonna t'try to take one of them?"

Arabella face became a mask of determination.

"Maybe...but first I want t'pay them back for the farmer and the horse," she said coldly, reaching for her bow and drawing a handful of arrows from the quiver on 'Rissa's pack.

"Good job we've got target arrows, though. I saw ring-mail. If we're lucky, the target points will sneak their way through."

They lay beside each other for a while, breathing heavily as fear wound its way into their hearts.

"They must be close enough by now," said Kerissa finally, nocking one arrow to her own bow. "I can hear them. On three, then?"

Arabella nodded. 'Rissa counted them down and they stood in the wagon-bed. At thirty yards her first arrow slipped through chain-mail chest-high and dropped the foremost of the Scandians in his tracks. 'Bella's first took the one beside him in the throat.

"So far so good," she growled. As they crouched down behind the wagon bench to put another pair of shafts to their bows, they heard shouts of surprise and outrage from the Scandians. "Again," she said. "We can't let them get too close."

'Rissa nodded and they counted together. This time only one arrow did its work, the other glancing off the ring-mail of a flaxen-haired giant, who broke ranks and charged at them, bellowing incoherent threats as he drew a longsword from the scabbard on his belt. Arabella stayed on her feet, faced him down and put her third arrow through his open mouth, refusing to stand down as he continued towards them, finally dropping to his knees a dozen strides away before pitching facefirst into the heather. She ducked an arrow, unconsciously counted seven more still on their feet, shouting for Kerissa to loose another of her own even as it whistled past her ear. Then there were only six Scandians... then only four as they loosed again in unison...but now they could quite clearly see the anger and lust in the eyes of their attackers.

"Close quarters now, my love," she called to 'Rissa, and casting aside her bow, she drew her duelling sword from its sheath and leapt fom the wagon-bed. As she charged the Scandians she could feel Kerissa at her side, and smiled, but it was only with her lips. The first Scandian to come at her could only wonder that someone who appeared to be so harmlessly female could be possessed of eyes so frighteningly intent. Arabella parried his first wild stroke at her head, then a second riposte before opening his throat with the point of her sword. Kerissa kept the remaining three at bay, long enough that when one drew an arrow to his longbow to shoot at point-blank range, Arabella's throwing knife made short work of him, and paid him back for the farmer's death.

One of the two remaining Scandians said something conciliatory...*Put down your weapons we won't hurt you*...and smiled wolfishly. The girls smiled back...

"You can die here," hissed Arabella. "Or not..." she said carelessly.

The inference to be drawn was clear. The Scandians began to show a growing disconcert, suddenly faced with two young women standing their ground, with swords and poniards drawn, who showed them no fear and only a confidence that was, in spite of their own ingrained feelings of superiority and strength, daunting. One of them cursed, made disparaging remarks, and intentions that now promised nothing *but* hurt. Arabella shrugged and spat.

"Come and take us then," she said quietly...

---

Sebastian strolled. Occasionally he sauntered. Glen Carrick's tree-lined high street was wide enough for both, bathed in a cool late summer breeze that allowed for all manner of commerce afoot and on horseback, all in a sleepy haze of light that encouraged anyone on the street to stop and engage in conversation with neighbours and strangers alike.

As he strolled and sauntered and, now and again, nodded in a friendly (and most hopeful) fashion at a pretty girl, his thoughts were yet filled with the mulling over of plans that might bring him into contact with his university friend without arousing suspicions over his true intent. As things transpired, such thoughts proved entirely unnecessary. Sebastian heard someone call out his name, turned, and found Evrard de Montenay approaching him from the opposite side of the street.

"Sebastian, is it really you? What on earth are you doing here?"

Evrard was more the mirror of his mother's heritage, of medium height and build, much lighter in colouring than his older brother. His face was an appealing mixture from both parents, yet lacked the hard sharp planes of his father's features. There was room for kindness in his grey eyes. Sebastian feigned surprise as they embraced.

"I could ask the same of you," he said, "but then too, I know you're from the Dales. I just didn't think I would run into you here in Glen Carrick. Are you thirsty? Take me somewhere the ale is good and poured by the pitcher..."

Minutes later they were tucked in a corner of the local tavern, toasting each other's health and good fortune in having encountered one another.

"I'm staying with a distant relative...Cami Ardrey..." said Sebastian, finding himself quite comfortable as he slipped on what Andrew and Alain's twins would have called his *secret squirrel face*.

"Me and Edmund've never been this far north and thought we'd try some hiking about until it's time t'go back to school."

"Edmund's here with you?"

"He'll be along in a few days," said Sebastian with a comradely grin. "Just stopped in Élysée to say hello t'somebody or another..."

"It's good t'see you," said Evrard quiety. "I've actually been thinking about you and Edmund a lot lately..."

The initial pleasure of having so serendipitously encountered a friend slowly fell away from his face, leaving it drawn and creased with something that might have been total exhaustion.

"We were both hoping we could threesome our way until classes began again, " said Sebastian. Evrard began to look hopeful.

"Can I trust you, Beverley?" he asked earnestly. "Can I please trust you?"

"With anything," he replied. "We're mates...we are...truly..."

Sebastian felt a mild twinge a of guilt at this bit of subterfuge, but cast it out from his thoughts immediately when he admitted to himself that it had been become a Truth not long after Annie Branny had ever asked him and Edmund *to keep an eye* on him and report on his behaviour.

"I didn't want t'come back here," said Evrard, staring down into his tankard of ale. "I don't know what you know of my family...my father, actually...but you don't get much of a choice in anything once he's made up his mind on what *he* wants."

"That's kind of the impression you've given all along, Evrard."

"Well... I was ordered to come home until classes start up again, but now I can't stay..."

Sebastian said nothing, examined the contents of his own tankard...and waited...

"My father is ambitous and he is not a kind man," said Evrard. "Even those of us he professes to love have learned there is a vicious knife edge to his *affections*. And now I think he's involved in some activity that I cannot, in any conscience, excuse him. I can't denounce him, but neither can I...will I...countenance what I think he intends..."

Sebastian again said nothing, but only met his friend's searching gaze with what he hoped was a look to inspire trust *and* confidences.

"If I tell you, will you swear that it will stay between the two of us?"

There was a look and sound of desperation in every word, every gesture made by de Montenay. Sebastian sought middle ground.

"I won't betray *you*, Evrard," he said simply. "*You* are a friend. For the rest, I can't be making any promises until I know…"

The young de Montenay swallowed once at his desperation, and again at his ale, seeming to come to a decision in the process.

"For as long as I have lived, from before I was even born, my father's thoughts have often turned to taking a throne he believes was wrongfully stolen from our side of the family. Once upon a time a thousand years ago we too were de Montignys."

Sebastian nodded. "I know that history," he said. "Michael the First held more support than his brother once the Scandian wars were won and the country safe from invasion. The nobility of the time proclaimed him king, and your branch of the family was, for all intent, banished to the Dales, and forced to change your family name."

"With Caroline's death…with no heir to the throne…my father has started talking about it more than ever, and my brother seems to listen, seems to have become convinced that the Amaranth Throne rightfully belongs to our family.

I think he...they...contemplate treason; I think they conspire with foreigners to help them take it..."

Sebastian came to a decision immediately.

"You're leaving, aren't you?"

Evrard nodded.

"Where are your things?"

"Mostly I left anything of value to me at school. I have a travel bag waiting beside a horse in the stables here. I must be gone soon, before my father knows I'm gone..."

"Then will you trust *me* now?" demanded Sebastian.

"What of your promise?"

"For now you have it, Evrard. I may change my mind, but not without your knowledge of it first. Is that enough?"

The young man gave it thought, inclined his head once...slowly...

"Good," said Sebastian. "Then it's time I introduced you to Cami Ardrey, and *we* make plans to have us both gone from here..."

---

Arabella sat in the scrub beside the track and wept, dragged herself into Kerissa's embrace and sobbed as if her heart were breaking.

"...Damn them, 'Rissa! Damn them! Why are they here? Why couldn't they just leave us alone...?"

Kerissa had no answers, only knew that when the last two Scandians had died on their swordpoints, Arabella had crumpled to the ground, flung her sword away and no amount of consolation or rationalisation could stem the flow of her tears. She said nothing, just held on and rocked the younger girl in her arms. Exhausted, they seemed to take no notice whatsoever as a group of horsemen from the east converged upon them in almost the same breath as another from the north.

Alexandra Wyndham threw herself from her saddle in a swirl of riding skirts, and heedless of the corpses surrounding them, went to her knees beside the girls, took them both in her arms. Frederick, Edmund and the others on horseback quickly encircled them as they turned to face the riders approaching from the north.

Renard de Montenay drew his people up a few yards from those facing him, deigned to acknowledge Wyndham with only the barest inclination of his head. At the same time, he took in the carnage surrounding them almost casually.

"I see you've found them," he said. "Hopefully none the worse for wear. Are these not Scandians lying about?" he added distastefully,

"I believe they are," replied Frederick Wyndham. "It would appear they made the mistake of thinking my girls were easy prey...but what d'you know of them, Renard? Surely they must have come through the Dales..."

"What are you implying?"

Wyndham smiled. "Nothing at all, my friend. I imagine there are ways through the mountains that could have brought them here without your knowledge."

"They have no business in our country. If I had known, they would not have gotten this far."

"We can agree on that most certainly, but the government must have word as quickly as possible, especially in these times."

"I'm sure you will see to that, Wyndham...meanwhile...the women are safe..."

He spurred his horse round as if to leave, signaling to his men to do the same.

"What of the crofter, Renard?" called Wyndham. "He's a dalesman by the look of him."

De Montenay looked over his shoulder at the body of the farmer.

"His name is David Herrin. He owes me the better part of a year's rent..."

So saying he spurred his horse again and went off the way he had come, with his men trailing behind. Edmund dismounted and ran to his cousins. Alexandra came to stand beside her husband, watching the dust rise up in de Montenay's wake.

"How did he know the girls were out here, Frederick?" she asked pointedly.

"And why were none of his people in livery, and armed as if expecting trouble?"

"Yet he seemed to have no knowledge of the Scandians."

Wyndham grimaced. "Renard de Montenay can seem many things without being any of them, Alexandra....meanwhile, as he said...the girls are safe. We should get them home at once, and send word to Nicky and Brandywine. They can deliver a letter to the palace as well."

Alexandra turned to direct her attentions once more to her grandchild and her friend.

"This is not a good sign, Frederick," she said. "Not with Caroline scarcely in the grave."

Wyndham nodded. "I know. I think I'll have the boys back here to secure our holdings, and start on a quiet muster of anyone can hold a weapon."

He turned to his estate manager of more than thirty years.

"Can you see that Herrin's people have word of this, Aaron? We can bury him here, return his horse and wagon and the proceeds once his goods have been sold in the market...and draw enough from our accounts to see that his rent is paid to de Montenay in full, for this year *and* the next."

---

"...Cami, this is Evrard...de Montenay."

She nodded cautiously, said, "You've grown up."

"Mostly," said Evrard. "I remember you now. When I was small my father brought my brother and I into the village and I wandered off...got lost...ended up crying in front of your house. You gave me a glass of milk and a biscuit and stayed with me until we found my father again."

Now she smiled. "You were a very sweet child then. I couldn't believe—"

"That Renard de Montenay was my father."

"Yes."

A silence grew uncomfortable, until Sebastian rejoined the conversation.

"Cami...Evrard needs...wants...to leave Glen Carrick...quietly if he can, with *no one* being any the wiser of it. I'll be going with him."

"Serious business, then?" she asked quietly.

"For me it is...yes..." said Evrard.

She looked at Sebastian and inquired when it would be best for them to be gone.

"Tomorrow? The first train south...?"

"That would be mid-morning," she said. "You can both stay here the night, and I'll walk you to our station so there won't be any surprises. Now, let me go down to the market to see about our supper..."

When she had gone the boys helped themselves to a pitcher of ale and went to sit on the back porch of the old smithy, where they would not be seen or overheard.

"She's seems quite remarkable," said Evrard. "It must be wonderful to know someone like that...asking no questions...trusting as a matter of course...How long have you known her?"

Sebastian grinned. "We met this morning," he said. "But she's got long history with my parents and their friends. We've all become family to each other."

Evrard shook his head in wonderment and, as it had happened in the tavern earlier, searched his mug of ale for something in the way of illumination.

" I can't imagine something like that," he whispered, without looking up. Sebastian saw the glisten of a tear find its way into Evrard's mug.

"From now on you don't have t'try," he said. "You'll stay with me and Edmund. My folks have plenty of room for you. It was the same for them when they were our age, all of them from families that were broken or gone...except maybe for Annie Branny and Uncle Nicky, who brought them all together."

Evrard put his mug down and made a poor show of being able to deal with a heart's desolation that had become more and more unbearable with each passing year. Sebastian laid aside his own glass, took his hands and then drew him closer.

"You're going t' be fine," he whispered. "You're going t'go stupid with being safe and happy and among people who don't demand anything of you that isn't who you already are."

De Montenay made to draw away from him, then made a small, heartbreaking sound and wept silently on his shoulder.

"...When I was ten years old my father sent me away...to the City...to the palace. For two years I was a page there. For two years whenever I would come home there would be photographs of all the people I had met, photographs I was made to identify for him, until he knew almost everyone I knew and dealt with on a daily basis...

"I never even saw Queen Caroline, not once in all the time I was there, but not once was I ever treated poorly, not once was I ever cursed for being a de Montenay. There was one woman who was the kindest most beautful woman I'd ever seen, who never failed to be friendly, ask if I was being treated well, if there was anything at all...

"She was an assistant to someone or other in the palace, but everyone showed her a special kind of deference I never saw given to anyone else...she was like sunshine... they called her Miss Lloyd..."

Sebastian took him by the shoulders, drew him away to arm's-length and laughed out loud with delight.

"She's my aunt, Evrard. *She* is Annie Branny. She's the reason I'm here, and you're not gonna believe the things she's gonna tell you..."

Just after supper there was a knock on Cami Ardrey's front door. Evrard ducked into the kitchen, while one of the locals delivered a wire addressed to her, but containing a message for Sebastian from Edmund. He read it quickly, breathed a sigh of relief and sent a reply off with the delivery lad:

*dM in harness. Heading back south in the morning.*

Then he read Edmund's message one more time.

*The girls are safe...but there's a ton of peculiar going on that's not funny at all.*

"You don't know the half of it, Edmund," he said aloud to no one...

---

It was nearing midnight when, in response to his last signal fifteen minutes earlier, Sevrain saw a faint bob of light on the horizon, that slowly drew closer and closer to where he stood at the water's edge.

A longboat grated on the sand. Three oarsmen leapt from the gunwales and dragged it further up onto the strand. Three more stayed with the boat whilst another three came slowly towards him.

Sevrain shook in his boots. He never quite knew what was truly expected of him, and now his companions from a few nights earlier stood before him once again, no less daunting to his frail sense of self.

"What is it now?" said the foremost, nothing but a shadow making sounds in the night.

"I come from my father," said Sevrain nervously. "He says there are new developments. We may have to move more quickly than we had planned."

The shadow laughed. "We have been ready for years, and we will move when it pleases us. What is your news?"

Sevrain outlined everything that had enraged his father, leaving out the parts where his behaviour had precipitated most of it, and adding that the "disappearance" of a local fishing boat had been ill-advised. The shadowy leader of them sneered at his concern.

"Well then...what can I say to him from you?" Sevrain asked.

"Nothing at all," said the shadow. "Turning to the two others beside him he said, "Cut his throat. It will be one less of them to deal with later..."

# Chapter Ten – BRANDYWINE THINKS THE UNTHINKABLE

Everyone slept in after arriving on the last train from Élysée. Just after noon, the entirety of *les Boulevardiers* and their families once again converged on the Wyndham house in St John's Mews, now with additions to their ranks in the persons of Evrard de Montenay and Alexandra Wyndham, who had insisted on accompanying her grand-daughter and Kerissa on the trip south.

Once they all were comfortably crammed into the upstairs music room, Gareth and Zoraya were soberly reunited with their daughter, before she went off with Arabella, Edmund and Sebastian, for an hour-long with Brandywine and Nicholas, who were waiting downstairs in the kitchen. It was apparent to all, including the twins, that something untoward and utterly unwelcome was in the wind, but Alexandra took them in tow like a mother hen—to the amusement of Andrew and Alain—and it didn't stop either of them from providing an informal welcome to the somewhat stunned northerner.

"Don't mess with 'Bella or 'Rissa," advised Stella. "They've got the big smoochies for each other. Sometimes when they kiss each other I can see their tongues doing stuff."

# ARABELLA

Edvard continued to be a bit stunned, but nodded and swore he had no designs on either of the two girls he'd only just met. Jamie, in his own way, felt it necessary to make certain.

"They can do all sorts of guy things too, way better even than Edmund *or* Sebastian," he informed the newcomer. "Also they take their clothes off a lot...mostly when they think nobody else is paying attention."

"Really," said Evrard. "That must be interesting..."

Jamie shrugged. "They're girls..."

Alexandra laughed uncontrollably while Evrard turned red.

---

Downstairs, Brandywine and Nicholas held council with *the girls* and the Beverley boys, considerably more serious than any of them had ever seen them before.

"So now you *all* know," she said, looking at Edmund and Sebastian ruefully. "Your uncle Windy has always been here to help me, along with all the official people at the palace, but today I have t'find out as much as I can from all of you so I can tell them. I think we're in trouble..."

Arabella served tea for everyone, then sat beside her mother.

"When Grampa and Edmund found us, Renard de Montenay showed up moments later. He looked just like the person who scared us off the train. We had no idea who he might be except he'd been paying us too much attention ever since he saw us at the inn in Bedford."

"It had to have been de Montenay's elder son, Sevrain," said Windy. "He looks just like Renard and he's fairly well known for that sort of thing when it comes to pretty women... but I wonder what he was doing in Bedford...and you say he stayed on the eastbound run leaving the City, but then you encountered him again when you headed north..."

"He was sitting with three men in Bedford," added Kerissa. "I didn't pay them much attention at all because Stella was making a big deal over de Montenay, but thinking back they didn't look like they belonged there any more than he did. They could have been Scandians..."

Edmund spoke up, quietly, but with an edge in his voice that spoke of outrage on behalf of his cousins.

"So it's safe to assume Sevrain told his father what happened on the train...but it explains nothing as to why de Montenay felt it his reponsibility to ride out on a rescue mission for the grand-daughter of someone everyone knows he despises..."

"And according to Evrard there's a good chance he knew who 'Bella was, so why did he bother?" added Sebastian.

Kerissa said, "He certainly didn't breathe any friendly sighs of relief once he realised Grampa and Edmund had found us."

Brandywine sat quietly listening, frowning with concentration as everyone at table added pieces to a puzzle no one had seen as a complete picture.

"De Montenay was surprised to see the Scandians?" she asked.

"Grams said he seemed to be," said Arabella, "but Grampa said he could pretend that sort of thing any day of the week."

"Yet it still doesn't change the fact that you and 'Rissa saw *two* armed bands of northerners well within our borders. That much we can assume is a bad thing and needs to be dealt with, especially since it's come directly after the announcement that Caroline had died."

"They're planning another invasion," said Edmund angrily, "and de Montenay is helping them." He turned to his brother. "Sebastian, did Evrard give you any indication that might be true?"

The younger Beverley looked uncomfortable.

"I've made some promises to him, Edmund," he said apologetically. "We need t'tell him what we think we know and let him decide what he wants t'tell us in return. One thing I *can* say is that when he met you as a page in the palace, Branny, you made a real big impression on him for going out of your way to be kind to him...and he felt badly that whenever he would go home, his father had photographs of just about everyone and made Evrard tell him who they were and everything he knew about them."

Windy looked at his wife. "What d'you think, Branny?"

"I think we need to make sure everyone in the Dales and the Carillon are safe as soon as we possibly can," she said, and looking at Kerissa and her daughter, "Evrard's brother might simply have been following after the two of you because that's what he does when he sees pretty girls...but from all appearances their father is plotting to betray his country in order to take the Amaranth Throne and thinks this is the best time t'make it happen."

There was dead silence, long enough that everyone could hear their own heartbeats for far longer than it was comfortable.

Edmund looked at Nicholas. "I think Gramps came t'the same conclusion. He said he was going t'have your brothers start a quiet muster of everyone in the north who could carry a weapon."

"Then I guess it's time we talked to Evrard?" said Sebastian.

Brandy nodded unhappily, asked them to give her and Uncle Nicky a moment before they joined them upstairs. When they had gone, she turned to him with tears streaming down her face.

"Windy what am I gonna do?" she sobbed. "I promised Caroline...Marie...and I knew there were going t'be times when I would be sorry for it, but I loved her so much, and she needed someone...so she could finally rest...but I never thought it would come to this."

He took her in his arms and they said nothing, of a sudden cast back in time twenty years before, when they had finally *found* each other, joined themselves to each other and to a woman who had, by her birth, become a victim of circumstance.

"...That last night, when I went to the palace...Windy she was so sad...and so grateful. We undressed each other...and we...we did stuff...but later when she put her arms around me and we were falling asleep together...for the first time in my life I felt like my mum had finally come home to me..."

He had no words for that, his own mother never having failed to be near when he needed her. For the rest, he could only try to lessen the horror of what he knew was the one choice given to her.

He bent his head down to her, brushing his face against hers.

"Branny, she knew," he whispered. "She warned you, and she loved you enough to try and spare you this by warning you—"

"Windy, people are gonna die because of me!"

"Let's hope then that the ones who don't die will be the ones she wanted you to save."

"Windy—" she wailed.

"Branny sometimes we don't get the luxury of making a choice and having everything about it be everything we want it to be."

She looked up at him, and he down at her, and his heart broke for her, who had nothing but goodness in her own.

"I love you," he said. "I love you more than I know how t'tell you, Annie Branny...and if it would spare you this hurt I would make all these choices myself, so they would never touch you...

"Some people say that Love isn't supposed t'be where you get so happily lost in the person you love that eventually you lose yourself in the whatever it is the two of you have become together...but I don't believe that, Branny. I don't believe that at all. Being lost in you has been the path to finding me; if I'd not gotten lost in you I would have been lost in Nowhere...so what *you* have t'do now is what *we* are going t'do... because you promised. It won't change how horrible the choice is, but it's not going t'be just you. Caroline...Marie...chose you because she knew that you would know how t'make the best choice that could be made."

He kissed her forehead, the place where the spun gold of her hair swept away into the years of his life to make him rich with the wealth of her giving.

"Let's be about it then?" he said....

---

Jamie and Stella were still "entertaining" Evrard when Brandywine and Windy came upstairs, Evrard himself sneaking curious glances at Arabella and Kerissa simply because he'd been warned off of them; while everyone else were stifling amused smiles, there was an underlying current of unease once the girls and the Beverley boys reappeared.

Brandy interrupted the proceedings by shoo-ing the twins off Evrard, who stood nervously to receive her greeting.

"Hello again," she said softly. "It's been a few years and now you're all grown."

He offered his hand to her, but Brandy leaned forward instead, placed a brief kiss on his cheek.

"I never thanked you..." he said, blushing. "Most everyone was so kind, but no one more so than you."

Brandywine only smiled and said, "I was as much out of place as you were," and turned to the rest of her friends.

"Evrard was ten years old when his father sent him to us at the palace, and for over two years he was always a favourite, and always there ready to help whenever you needed him.

"It's so good t'see you again, Evrard, though I wish it were not under such worrisome circumstances. I'm afraid you've been spirited away into the middle of things even we don't really understand. We're hoping you can help us..."

Evrard seemed nervous, now casting doubtful looks at Sebastian.

"No one has betrayed any of your confidences, Evrard," Brandy reassured him. "Please believe me...and please don't be afraid. The first thing you should know is..."

And she proceeded to tell him a bit of the story of how she came to be a regent in the shadow-government that had perpetuated the reign of Caroline de Montigny for twenty years after her actual death.

"...And so now, it looks like there are people who think she's only just died, and feel it's time that things should change. From our own experiences in the last week, it looks a lot like your father is one of those people...

"Somehow he came to believe that my daughter Arabella and her friend, Kerissa, posed a threat to him, and when they were forced off a train onto the Carillon moors by your brother, he came looking for them. He arrived just after they had managed to fight off a dozen Scandians who had no business on the moors, and according to my daughter and Kerissa, were at least one of two bands of them who had no right to be within the borders of this country. Sebastian's brother and my husband's parents arrived just before him..."

Her intimation was clear. Evrard began to look uncomfortable. Brandywine tried to reassure him.

"We're not here t'make you say or do anything you don't want to, Evrard...but I have t'think about what I promised Caroline I would do, and if there's anything you can tell me that will help..."

EVRARD'S STORY

He sat down again, looked around at a sea of strange but not unkind faces, all waiting for him. Stella took the opportunity to escape from the confines of Alain's lap and come back to stand beside him.

"It's okay," she said, putting one hand on his knee."Annie Branny's the best. She's not gonna hurt you."

Evrard smiled somewhat painfully, obviously in need of more reassurance. Diana was next to speak up.

"Stella is right, Evrard, and my son Sebastian knows better than to betray confidences. All of us here belong to the same family, and you're more than welcome to join us."

"At what price then?" asked Evrard hoarsely.

"No price at all," said Andrew. "Edmund and Sebastian have spoken for you. That's more than enough. If you can help Branny, though...it's her promise we've promised to help her keep."

Evrard weighed Andrew's words, spent the better part of five minutes searching the faces around him, always returning to Brandywine, who had knelt in the centre of their broad circle, and now faced him with as much kindness as she could impart through the gaze of her green eyes. He swallowed once.

"I don't know anything about the Scandians," he whispered. "If my father had had anything like that t'do with them, though they've never once in my knowledge ever been t'the house...or met with him, though I suppose I can't say any of it for certain. I do know that every now and again we'd see small groups of them trading in the village."

"D'you know why two bands of them were tramping around our northern moors a hundred miles from their own border?" asked Thomas quietly.

Evrard shook his head. "I told you, I don't know anything about them...but there *is* one thing...I just don't know if it's important..."

Brandy said, "Evrard, you don't have t'say anything else...we're talking about *your* family, asking you to speak against your father and your brother. No one here will hold it against you for being loyal t'them."

Evrard bowed his head, took several breaths before he looked up for a moment, and found something in Brandywine's earnest gaze to compel him to do what *he* felt was right.

"You already know the worst part of anything I could tell you." he said with downcast eyes, "so there's no point in me trying to pretend that my father and brother are doing something I'm comfortable with.

"When I was small...maybe four or five years old...I remember three men I'd never seen before come to our house. They stayed for a few days and I've not seen them since. All my father ever said was that they were *my mother's people*. It wasn't until I was older that she herself told me what that meant.

"Long before any of us were born, my grandfather Dorion sent my father abroad, ostensibly to develop relations independently of our own country's treaties and trade agreements. He travelled extensively, often taking ship far across the western ocean. In Antillia it seems he found what my grandfather intended him to find—an ally and an agreement with the ruling house, with my mother as Renard's incentive to seal their bargains."

"De Montenay allied with Antillia, against the Amaranth Throne here?" asked Zoraya. There was no outward physical emotion in her question, but so much contained anger in her voice that it was all the more disquieting to Evrard. He shook his head, sought the shelter of Brandywine's regard.

"I don't know," he whispered. "Truly...I don't know...but my mother and my sisters... and I...we've all felt like we were of no consequence at all to my father; that our thoughts and dispositions were so far removed from whatever he contemplated over the years that we lived under his roof on sufferance...just an unwelcome aspect of whatever he had agreed to in Antillia."

"You aren't your father," said Brandywine. "You don't have to be ashamed on his account."

"Then what's going to happen now?" he asked, looking to her as he had done so often when he had served in the palace. "What else can I do?"

She got up, went to kneel beside him; taking his hands in her own she said, "Nothing else, Evrard. You've done more than we could have asked of you. As for what happens next... there are the people in the palace who've looked after the details...helped me t'find the right course t'take once I'd come to some sort of decision on something."

"Then there's going t'be violence," he said.

"Probably," she replied unhappily.

"I'll fight...I'll do whatever—"

"No you won't, Evrard! I won't allow it!"

There was a stunned silence in the wake of Brandywine's pronouncement, no one in the room able to remember her ever imposing her will on anyone else, for any kind of reason. Evrard blinked as if she had struck him. Arabella rushed to her side...

"Mom? What's goin' on?"

Brandy looked mortified, yet behind the apologetic words she offered to everyone,

those who knew here recognised something never seen before—that Annie Branny had made up her mind about something, and would brook no opposition to her wishes.

"I'm sorry," she said, embarrassed, and seeming to beg for forgiveness. "I didn't mean to t'snap at you, Evrard, or be so huffy with you all of a sudden. I have t'go t'the palace *now*, t'tell everything we've been talking about..."

---

When *les Boulevardiers* were all gone home, Evrard with the Beverleys, Brandywine went upstairs to dress more formally, declined to have Nicholas or Arabella accompany her. At the door she was still apologetic, and suddenly miserable with weight of responsibility that was totally beyond her ken.

"I might be late so don't wait supper on me," she said, and rushed away across the courtyard.

Nicholas and Arabella put together a meal of leftovers and sat down beside each other at the long kitchen table, not saying much of anything, each of them preoccupied with their own thoughts, their own ways of dealing with a shared reality neither of them had ever dreamt would become real at all.

Dishes and pans got washed. Arabella sat quietly on a couch in the music room, looking over her shoulder, out into the twilight deepening over the Mews. Windy played for her, quiet piano sonatas that were so seemingly born of sadness they were a comfort of sorts to both of them. Night crept inwards, coiled itself around them. Arabella yawned and then got up to kiss her father goodnight. He played on for a few more minutes...found himself lost in the middle of music he had made himself...listened to a few notes fade away into the dark...missing Brandywine...missing...*something*...that had fled away in what he knew quite well had been an unofficlal council of war.

He got up and went down the hallway, knocked on his daughter's door and found her curled up in a corner of her bed, buried under her blankets. He sat down beside her, reached to stroke the honey-coloured hair that shone even in the absence of light.

"...Are you okay, 'Bella? Your mum's gonna need you a lot the next little while."

"I know, Daddy," she said, disembodied in the dark. "She's so unhappy with what she's got t'do...at least now I've got some of the right experience to help her."

"Sweetheart it's easy for me t'say it wasn't your fault—"

"They were gonna hurt us, Daddy...they were gonna hurt 'Rissa!"

"I know that, but it doesn't make what happened any less dreadful. It doesn't wipe any slates clean in your heart or the things you remember. It was something horrible that needed doing, and you did it. Try...try not t'let it ruin anything else..."

"I was so angry...and scared...and then I was just angry and I just wanted t'kill them! I wanted them all t'be dead so we could be safe...so 'Rissa would be safe."

She started crying, crept out from under her blankets and crept into his arms. Windy couldn't think of anything else to say, so he rocked her gently until she was quiet again, wiped her eyes and her cheeks with his sleeve and realised all over again what a miracle Brandywine had bestowed upon him.

"We'll get through this, honey, and Time will make a faded memory of the things that are hurting you now. Until then you've got me and your mum and you've got 'Rissa. She's so good, and the two of you are so good together. That's going t'go on for as long as you live..."

---

Brandy came home hours later. Windy was sitting in candlelight in the great room downstairs. She came to sit beside him and they put their arms around each other.

"It's gonna be horrible," she said.

"I know."

"Is 'Bella all right? It's so hard t'think of her as anything but happy and smiling and wishing only good things for everyone."

Windy shrugged.

"I don't know, Branny. She's sleeping now. That's what we should be doing. The rest of it can wait until tomorrow."

They left clothing on the stairs.

# Chapter Eleven – A BRIEF MUSICAL INTERLUDE

Brandywine was away again in the morning, and for the better portion of the day. When Nicholas received a brief note requesting his assistance with a project before the City's orchestral committee, Arabella was left to her own devices, wandered off on her own for a stroll round the City.

Though the day was bright with sunshine, the weather had taken a turn towards cool, northern winds bringing on a bit of the night she'd spent on the moors. She dressed in corduroy trousers and a jersey, with knee-high boots and a hooded woollen poncho, went searching for some company, but could find no one to fit the bill.

On Old Princes Street she found Gareth banging away at a tangled flurry of sea otters in stone, but 'Rissa and her mother had neglected to mention to him where they might have gone. Likewise, Thomas was clacking away at a new novel, but Diana was away to the dance school overseeing classes whilst Edmund and Sebastian had spirited Evrard away for a day of riding in the country. She found Andrew at home, and spent a hour having tea with him, but both were inclined to avoid any conversation having to do with the day before.

Then she made her way down to the Water Street market where Jamie and Stella, happy to have another month of holiday from school, were "helping" Alain by stocking bottom shelves with a wide variety of mis-placed canned goods. They were all glad to see her, but it was a busy day so she only stayed long enough to undo the most glaring errors before moving on.

Once on the Boulevard, she window-shopped and stopped at the Silver Rose for another cup of tea and a buttered scone, but she let them grow cold, became restless and unhappy before she wandered on in the direction of the animal park and the Emerald Gardens. There she found Grim the Grey, regal and ancient, sunning himself on one of the benches that lined the walkways. The tall trees surrounding them rustled in a light breeze, already beginning to shed their summer green for the red, golds, yellows and browns of autumn.

"Hallo Your Majesty," she said, bowing once before sitting down beside him. He lifted his head in her direction, obviously demanding his due as King of the City's cats. She curled her fingers and gently scritched the uplifted chin.

"I guess things are gonna get *interesting* in a hurry," she observed a bit sadly. "Not that *you* have t'worry so much. Any new kittens around? Maybe some lovely little girl kitty to lick your ears?"

Grim responded to her ministrations with some impressive rumblings, but declined to enlighten her on the questions of squeaky little weans or new romances. Arabella sighed.

"Sometimes it's just no fun being on your own," she said wistfully. "It's fine for you. No matter where you go there's always gonna be someone or something t'keep you busy... but I'm stuck today, Grim...somehow everybody forgot about Arabella..."

He licked her fingers by way of offering sympathy, got himself up a bit creakily on all four paws, to arch his back, curl his tail, and flex his toes in a luxurious upward stretch. Arabella smiled, realised it was her first smile of the day, and properly thanked the cat before moving on, buying a small sleeve of critter treats at the entrance to the animal park, and making her way to a corner of the park where a skulk of five grown foxes amused themselves by watching four kits leaping over each other and chasing round after each other's tails. Arabella smiled her second smile of the day.

"Anyone seen Hasan today?" she asked, trying for some brightness in her tone. The adults looked away from the children for a moment, seeming to grin at her in recognition. She recognized the proud parents and the kits, but there were three newcomers. She shook her head in mock bewilderment.

"It's a wonder nobody ever notices there's only supposed t'be two grown-ups here," she laughed. "How d'you guys manage to get fed? I suppose it's possible if somebody turned the card upside down and a six turned out t'be a nine...but don't worry, I'm not telling anyone..."

She pitched the crunchy bits in her sleeve of critter treats through the bars of the enclosure and waved goodbye...

There was a part of the City, on past the east bank of the Findhorn to a small branch of it that moved sluggishly on to the delta further to the east; once there, if you happened to cross one of a handful of small bridges, and then followed your feet down towards the water, one could easily get a bit lost in the mostly-deserted-by-day mazy winding of older streets and alleys.

Arabella rarely visited that part of the City, had never done so on her own, but as the afternoon wore on she found herself there, and though not uncomfortable with the thought, realised it would be a wiser choice to regain the west bank and get back to places with which she was more familiar. She turned to retrace her steps and after a few meanders in as many directions, came to the conclusion that she had led herself seriously astray without being any the wiser of it.

*Best t'look for the sun, then* she told herself, and made her way to a cross-street where the sun was clearly visible and she could with some assurance point her nose back in the direction she wanted to go. Once having determined (at last) that west was west and east was now definitely behind her, she strode on with a bit more confidence than before, taking short-cuts through alleys and small shadow-filled lanes. At the entrance to one laneway she encountered a small hand-painted sign tacked to the brick of a rundown warehouse on the corner, stopping to read the curiously-formed letters:

THIS WEEK ONLY
direct from the farthest reaches
of the Dark Continent

## AZIM SHARAD
### and his orchestra

Arabella was intrigued. Throughout the day she had gone in search of diversion, anything to take her thoughts away from the unpleasant events and revelations of the last week. She followed a series of smaller signs, each with a stylised finger pointing farther along the laneway, until she came to a door with a duplicate of the one that had caught her attention in the first place. This one noted a small admission fee as well, but going through the doorway and finding no one to collect it, she shrugged and made her way down a short corridor to a small darkened theatre.

The room was dimly-lit and, judging by the hum of muted conversations surounding her, seemed to be full of others as curious as she. Arabella found a empty seat at the rear of the theatre and settled herself down, huddling a bit in her poncho against a chill dampness that filled the room. Soon after, the dimmed lights around her disappeared and a small stage emerged from the gloom on the far side of the audience as a series of electric lamps grew brighter. Those in attendance hushed; dead silence prevailed as three robed figures moved onto the stage, bowed once to the audience and commenced to tune an array of drums and stringed instruments, all of which were totally alien to Arabella. She shivered in the dank air, briefly considered leaving before her natural curiosity got the better of her.

*I can always leave* she murmured to herself, and inched a bit further to one side in her seat when someone occupying the seat beside her coughed horribly. Then the stage-lights dimmed but for one in the centre, and Azim Sharad came to sit on a low stool.

Arabella had never seen anyone quite like him. He was very tall and seemed misshapen even through the sweep and swirl of his voluminous garments—embroidered layers of dark cloth that revealed no other details of his person—yet his long-fingered hands deftly took a stringed instrument...a lute of some sort...and proceeded to strum and fidget with its tuning pegs until chords shimmered away into the dark to his satisfaction. Arabella shivered again, but this time with anticipation. The random sounds that Sharad coaxed from his instrument were delicious...intoxicating...so much so that she barely took notice of the fact that every now and again his face, hitherto of an exotic and startling beauty, seemed to turn itself inside out, become a dreadful caricature of itself—hairless, with mottled white skin ritually-scarred and broken by an hideous ingratiating smile, words of welcome softly murmured through bloodless lips, teeth broken and filed to points.

Azim Sharad nodded once to his fellow musicians and the music carried her away...

---

He played endlessly, each new piece introduced with a few words, but never interrupting the flow of notes from the four on the stage. Sharad's fingers were mesmerising, delicate and precise though they flew over the strings, arousing and insistent when he played them over his drums. Arabella became thoroughly involved in the music, swaying from side to side, eyes closed, every inch of her body tingling with it.

She forgot that she had ever considered leaving before the performance had begun; forgot even how she had come to be there at all...only that it was wonderful beyond words and she wished it would go on forever...

Until she became aware it had stopped; that the stage was empty and most of the others who had been witness to the concert had already gone. Arabella rose unsteadily, made her way to the corridor in half-light, and thence out through the door to the laneway. She stopped there for moment, puzzled though she could not say why, but as she walked back to the corner where she first had encountered the sign announcing the concert, she realised two things in almost the same breath—that all the signs were now gone, and though she had been listening to Azim Sharad for hours, the sun seemed to have hardly moved in the sky.

---

Arabella couldn't find her way home. The sun had disappeared behind the towers and spires of the City to the west, leaving her on the east bank of the Findhorn, wandering about in the gathering gloom, trying desperately to find one of the bridges that would take her back to somewhere she could recognise...but somehow, no matter which way she turned, or retraced her steps along a street or lane she thought to have been on before, no one of them took her where she wanted to go.

She found herself close to tears with frustration, yet at the same time wondered that there were brief instants when she seemed to move outside herself, and become a bystander to her confusion, her inability to find her way out of a maze that she could swear shifted every time she felt she was on the right path. Exhausted, she leaned against a wall and fought back the tears, closed her eyes and renewed her determination to *go home*. When she opened them again, Hasan was waiting patiently at her feet, tugged once at the knee of her trousers and made it clear she should follow him...

Once again on the west bank, he disappeared, but in his place came the large grey tom-cat with whom she'd briefly shared a bench in the Emerald Gardens earlier in the afternoon. In a like manner to the dog-fox, Grim made it known she should follow him, and soon thereafter heard a familiar voice calling out to her...sighed and gave way to her tears as Kerissa raced towards her.

"'Bella are you all right?"

"I am now, 'Rissa...but I had such a strange afternoon..."

"We'll stop at my house for a little bit, and then we'll get you home, okay?"

Arabella nodded, let herself be cuddled and coddled along by Kerissa until she brought them both back to Old Princes Street, where her parents stood in the door of the stables beside Gareth and Zoraya, all of them showing signs of distress.

"I'm so sorry," she said. "I wandered all over the place all day, and when I ended up on the other side of the river I got lost and I never meant to be so late I'm *so* sorry..."

Kerissa hustled them all indoors and when Arabella was comfortably warming in front of a small stove fire, set about putting dinner together for all of them.

"I should 've left a note," she said apologetically.

"It doesn't matter now you're safe," said her father. Brandywine scooted her chair over to where she could put her arms around her daughter as twilight turned to dusk and dusk in turn became evening.

"I shouldn't've left you alone so long," she said.

"Oh Mum you're always trying t'make everything your fault when it's not. I'm not a baby anymore, but *I* should've known better than t'go somewhere I'd never been before."

"So where *did* you go, 'Bella?" asked Gareth . "Adventures a-plenty? Portents and wonders?"

"Mostly I was just lost," she said, venturing a smile. "Thank goodness Hasan and Grim came t'rescue me...but I did have an adventure of sorts..."

"Oh...?" said Zoraya. Tilting her head to one side she regarded Arabella with a puzzled expression, and then seemed to sniff the air in a manner the girl found more than a little disconcerting.

"Well...I saw this sign for a music recital in a strange little place and that's where I was for a long time, but when it was over it was like no time had gone by at all."

"Really," said Zoraya.

"Well it seemed that way," said Arabella, "but I guess I've been pretty dopey all day, t'have gotten lost like that."

"But you sat through a music recital?" asked her father.

Arabella nodded. "I did! It was wonderful! I saw this little sign and followed pointy- finger signs to a tiny place I don't think I could ever find again...and then I listened to Azim Sharad and his orchestra—really only three other musicians—from the farthest reaches of the Dark Continent. It was magical, Daddy...I got so dozy and dreamy that when they stopped I must've been asleep or…well…whatever…because I never even saw them finish…"

Kerissa interrupted their conversation with a giant platter of cheesy scrambled eggs with toasted bread, thick slices of bacon and sizzling sausages on the side. Midway through their meal, Hasan appeared out of nowhere, nosed at Arabella's knees if to assure himself she was thoroughly rescued, and then curled himself in a corner next to the stove. Zoraya looked at him curiously, and he at her until he put his nose down and went to sleep.

Eventually the day caught up with Arabella and, as she began to yawn continously, Zoraya bundled their guest up for the walk home to the Mews, and brought a coat for her daughter as well.

"I think 'Bella would like company tonight," was all she would say. Neither of the girls could think of any reason it should not be so.

---

Kerissa made happy noises under the blankets, playing with her girl, soothing and kissing and laughing out loud with pleasure whenever Arabella would squeak or sigh.

"…You're the yummiest girl a girl could ever have," came her muffled voice.

Arabella reached down and drew her up where they could kiss.

"I'm afraid t'go t'sleep. 'Rissa," she said later, when both were damp and drowsy with making love to each other. "I don't know why…"

Kerissa licked her nose and said, "This time I'll protect *you* from the nasty wiggins..."

Arabella laughed softly and said "Then I won't be afraid," and they fell asleep.

# Chapter Twelve – ZORAYA TAKES A HAND

He read the message hidden in the innocent-seeming wire, his hands balling into fists as he crumpled the flimsy paper and flung it away into the fire that flickered in the small hearth of his study.

"Dead," he snarled. "The idiot couldn't wait for one of the wenches here. At least they will have little or nothing to connect him to this house...just one more fool to have been murdered in an alley behind the local whorehouse."

Though it was yet early in the day, he poured himself brandy, downed it in one gulp and poured another. As he paced back and forth across the floor, his mind raced over a half dozen plans he had formed as contingencies to crisis, pondering how each of them might best be turned to his advantage. None of them took into account the death of his oldest child.

He fought back the impulse to throw things, shatter glass and splinter furniture. That Evrard had literally disappeared from the house only enraged him further. Briefly, he thought to summon his wife and inform her of Sevrain's pathetic end, but decided she could be left to learn of it whenever the news arrived on its own. There were more pressing matters to concern him. Sevrain had barely even been useful, but now he would have to find someone else with whom he could share the details and intent of the plot his own father had put together decades earlier.

---

Had there been anyone abroad on the high street in Glen Carrick soon after dawn the following morning, they might have encountered a shadow that moved from the shadows of the lane beside the local tavern, and then moved about where shadows had no right to be. As the sun rose higher it appeared to take on a shape, a form, and some measure of substance, yet still it was no more than a smudge in the air, perhaps only a trick of the light. Had there been anyone abroad on the high street in Glen Carrick that morning to witness this inexplicability, they no doubt would have attributed its existence—real or otherwise—to an overly long night spent in the tavern.

Zoraya walked out of the shadow and became herself.

---

Camille Ardrey had not become so familiar with unexpected knocks on her door as to be unsurprised by them, instead simply viewing them, in one sense with a large measure of prescience, as something to be unexpectedly expected. When she opened her door and saw a slender woman with skin the colour of dark chocolate and a halo of dark curls sparking in the morning sun 'round a face of almost ethereal beauty, she made a mental shrug and simply invited the woman in for morning coffee.

Once in her kitchen she said, "You can only be from the City," and poured a large steaming mug from a pot newly-made on her stove. "And coming from the City, you must know Nicholas...somehow...and have come here for something that concerns him?"

Zoraya slipped from her coat, and sat at Camille's kitchen table.

"*You* must be a creature of magic to know that," she said with slow smile. "My name is Zoraya. My daughter Kerissa is his daughter's beloved."

"I've never met Arabella," replied Camille, "but I know her father well, and, it would seem, I know a nephew...Sebastian...?:"

"He is the younger son of Thomas and Diana, who are two in Nicholas' family of the heart. In this way, my daughter is his niece and I am an aunt to his daughter."

"Well it's lovely t'meet you. Is this your first time in the Dales?"

Zoraya nodded. "I have business with Renard de Montenay," she said coldly.

Camille looked troubled. "Some of Frederick Wyndham's people were here yesterday, up from the Carillon, asking if I knew anyone in the village who could be trusted to help *organise*...that was the word they used...*organise*...in the event of an uprising. It was intimated that I should know what they were talking about."

"De Montenay is very likely engaged in activities less than beneficial to our country. As well, he requires a measure of chastisement for something he intended against my daughter and Arabella."

"Renard de Montenay is not a nice person..."

"I know that very well."

"You should be very careful with him."

Zoraya's smile was frighteningly cold.

"Not so careful as he needs to be with me," she said.

"So you intend going up to the manor house...alone?"

Zoraya nodded and smiled again, this time warmly, and reached for the older woman's hands.

"He cannot do me any harm," she said reassuringly.

Camille took them out onto the back porch where they sipped their coffee in silence, watching the house sparrows flutter and squeak at each other as she scattered bread crumbs out over the garden path below. She also watched her guest, marvelling at the intensity of emotion she sensed in her, and how it was in no way mirrored by her outward calm.

"What do you intend?" she asked at length.

Zoraya shrugged. "I have yet to decide upon what course I must take with him....but I will be very careful..."

---

Somewhere along the the way from Camille Ardrey's front door and the de Montenay manor house on the hill, a rust-red dog-fox joined Zoraya, listening intently to whispered instructions before dashing on ahead of her. She went leisurely, letting the mid-afternon slide by. Hasan returned with advanced reconnaissance; then she bade him seek the comforts of his home in the south, knowing there was a new vixen in his life and the imminence of yet more kits to swell the ranks of those who might shimmer in and out of reality in the City.

She was unconcerned. Everything she had heard of de Montenay gave her neither pause nor regret for what she intended. A brief conversation with Brandywine had been enough. When she reached the manor house, a tall elegant woman was waiting for her as she came to the door.

"He is in the coach house," said Margaret de Montenay. "He likes the idea of having his own little army. You will find all of them there. This morning he received some word that has made him foul with anger."

Zoraya nodded, laid a reassuring hand on her arm and informed her that she and her household were of no interest in the matter at hand.

"My business is with your husband," she said. "Ready your daughters. Go wherever you feel you will be safe. Camille Ardrey in the village has said she will be more than pleased to help you."

Margaret de Montenay inclined her head.

"Years ago I had no idea I was nothing more than a reward...something to be bartered, like a horse or some trinket..."

Zoraya sighed. "Someday it may change," she said kindly. "For now we must do the best we can, and hope for the best."

"What will you do to them?"

"Whatever seems appropriate."

"Will you hurt him?"

Zoraya shook her head. "Not today. Today I must simply stop him in his tracks, and trust whatever he has been involved in can be turned aside by his absence."

Margaret said, "Thank goodness it's finally over. Do whatever you must do."

She turned to go back into her house.

"Evrard is safe," said Zoraya. "If you would go to the City, you will find him there, and good hearts awaiting you if, at the palace, you ask for Brandywine Lloyd..."

---

The carriage house was a thing of ancient brick and mortar, somewhat removed from the main house, fronted by paving stones, covered in ivy and grapevine. Zoraya trod barefoot across the cobbles, leaving her coat behind, and in an embroidered robe opened the double doors only so much as necessary to allow her entry.

Inside she heard the murmur of voices overhead, swept her hand in a slow arc to gentle the horses in their stalls on the ground floor. She climbed a wooden staircase, turned at its head and found a great open space before her, filled with two score men-at-arms and one man who railed at all of them. That one saw her immediately; the others turned as they realised there was an unannounced stranger in their midst.

"Good day to you, Renard," said Zoraya, conjuring an impudent smile. Much as she had assured Brandywine of her reasonably peaceful intentions, there was in her heart a spark of anger and outrage that she fully intended he should be made to account for. She strode slowly into the centre of the open space, surrounded by his people. De Montenay scowled.

"Who are—-wait! I know. You are the Wyndham trollop's *afrique*..."

"I am the *afrique's* mother," she said coldly. "You have committed a deadly affront to me."

"I tremble."

"You *should* tremble, Renard," she assured him. "I know the truth of you. I know your treason, and I know your pathetic trust that the Antillians will actually let you rule in this place."

"In time I will not need their leave," said de Montenay scornfully. "I have other resources for tomorrow...but today, I think I shall amuse myself with you."

Zoraya shook her head as she would to a misbehaving child. "I am older than Antillia, Renard, and your *resources* mean nothing to me, but you may take comfort in your mistaken belief if it pleases you."

He signed to those surrounding her that they should take her, but she muttered a few words in a language that had been dead for three thousand years, made a careless gesture, and two score men-at-arms found themselves rooted to the floor when they tried to move towards her. Then they simply collapsed where they stood. She smiled at de Montenay.

"So now you will learn you are not inviolate," she said quietly. "That there are indeed consequences to ambitions that are wholly selfish, and feed upon the lives of innocent people who have done you neither harm nor insult."

She reached to the embroidered collar of her robe and undid a clasp, letting it fall to her feet so she stood naked before him.

"*You* come and take me, Renard" she taunted him. "If you can..."

# Chapter Thirteen – IN THE AMARANTH PALACE

Brandywine resigned herself to the seemingly endless day-after-day at the palace. Each morning she would dress appropriately for her official position as Second Assistant to the Royal Stationer; but once within the the vast echoing corridors hung with tapestries and framed portraits of a millenium of de Montigny royalty, she would always find her way to the royal apartments behind the throne room, where a score of ministers and advisors, even after twenty years, yet found it strange to be answerable to someone named Brandy Lloyd, whose almost apologetic nature could suddenly turn to an unyielding stubbornness when policy clashed with what she felt was best for Caroline's people.

With the unwelcome news that roving bands of Scandians had managed to cross their northern borders with no one being any the wiser save perhaps Renard de Montenay, those who knew best how to deal with such incursions laid out their plans to combat the invaders, and then awaited a final judgment from *the girl*. Midway through these proceedings, a page interrupted them with a brief message that a woman of colour named Zoraya wished to speak with Miss Lloyd on a matter of some urgency.

Brandywine excused herself and met her friend in one of the small reception rooms beside the royal apartments.

"He will not trouble you further," said Zoraya with a grim smile. "All of them are peacefully nowhere on the second floor of the de Montenay carriage house. You may have them collected whenever it is convenient. His wife and daughters likely will seek sanctuary with you some time in the next few days."

Brandywine's eyes became very large.

"Zori, what did you do?"

She laughed. "I teased them and then put them to sleep for you."

Brandy felt shaky, sat herself down in a thoroughy uncomfortable but elegant-seeming chair.

"Renard too? What did you say to him?"

Zoraya nodded, looking quite pleased with herself.

"I told him we knew everything, and whether that may have been true or not, I made him believe it. But he is a fool, Brandywine...so very heavily armoured in his own sense of self-worth that he chose to ignore my warnings to him, and instead chose to try to *seduce* me with physical strength. He was astounded to find that he could not rise to the occasion, or that I could turn him into jelly without saying a word."

"So he's...?"

"Sleeping, Brandy, along with his merry band of traitors. They await your pleasure..."

"Really?"

"Really."

"Did he admit to anything?"

"I didn't ask, Brandywine. Do we truly need confessions from him?"

"I suppose not. Even if we don't know the half of what he's been up to, it's enough we know that he's been up to a lot of *something*."

"Exactly," nodded Zoraya. "And I should go home now. I'm sure there's one thing or another I should look after. You are all right here?"

Brandywine nodded. "Much better now, Zori...thank you..."

---

She went back to her meetings and consultations, received word from Nicholas that his father and brothers were out scouring the moors for Scandians, and that nearly the entire adult population of the Carillon *and* the Dales had been roused to alert and watchfulness.

"...We should send some of our people north look after things?" she asked a stolid old gent who had been militarily disposed for a lifetime without ever having been called to arms. He was, as well, one of a handful of Caroline's inner circle who had eventually been won over by Brandywine...the passionate insistence that in spite of her absence, they continue all of the programs and policies that had hallmarked Caroline's reign.

"Indeed," he replied. "We'll help keep things in order and coordinate if the Scandians decide skulking about our empty spaces is not enough to win them our country."

Brandy then broached them the subject of Renard de Montenay, who was known to every adviser and minister as a constant source of unrest, but in no wise thought of as an insurrectionist. There were skeptics. Brandy just wanted to go home.

"He's been plotting," she said with finality. "If not with the Scandians, then most definitely with Antillia."

"Impossible," said one lesser official. "Antillia? He would not dare...besides, they are an ocean away..."

"But he *has* dared," replied Brandywine. "We became aware of it totally by chance... misadventure and, for de Montenay, just plain bad luck...but there is no doubt, only very little detail right now. Nevertheless, when we send our people north, he and *his* people should be collected at once, and held to account."

"And if they resist?"

Brandy made a small face that could have been a smile of indulgent self-satisfaction. Mostly she had spent a score of years being accorded a level of respect she would never have dreamt as her due...yet every now and again it became evident to her that she knew more than all the people who were supposed to know everything, and this was one of those moments.

"I don't think they're going to put up any kind of fight," she said, and told them where de Montenay and his people would be found. "And maybe we should let the Scandians know we know what they're up to, and we're not so happy about it?"

"That's letting them off quite mildly," said the old military gentleman.

"I know," said Brandy, " but if there's a possibility we're going t'have t'go t'war with Antillia, we can do without another one with the Scandians if there's any way we can avoid it."

There was a murmur of agreement went round the room as Brandy stood up to leave.

"I want t'say thank you to all of you, for all the times you've put up with me not knowing stuff...all the times when I know some of you felt I had no right or reason t'be here at all except for me being Caroline's friend.

"I think maybe we're in a lot of trouble right now, and more than ever I'm grateful for your help and your patience...but Caroline asked me to look after things in the best way I could and I've tried t'do that. She also asked if I would find someone t'take the throne... someone who would carry on with all the things that were important to her..."

There was a another murmur run through the assemblage, this time of astonishment.

"I've tried t'do all the things I felt Caroline herself would have wanted me t'do in her place... but being the one t'choose someone to take her place has been...well... it's been scary, and I've been afraid of making a mistake..."

"You mean *you* are the final arbiter of who next will sit on the Amaranth Throne?"

Brandywine nodded.

"Why did you not simply do so yourself, if Caroline was so much the dedicated friend you claim her to be?"

"She asked if I would do it."

There was disbelef in the murmur went round a third time.

"And...?"

"I told her I wasn't someone who *could* do it...that I wasn't royal anything t'be able t'be a queen instead of her. I told her...promised...I would find someone else."

She put her chair quietly back beneath the long table.

"Some of you here know I'm telling the truth...have notes written to you by Caroline so I could do the things she wanted me t'do. When this business with Antillia is over, if we've still got our country to ourselves...I know who will be Caroline's successor. I think I've finally found the right person..."

---

The conference room was empty—the shocked silence that had given way to demands for more enlightenment... the quiet acceptance of those who had been Brandy's "inner circle" for years...all of it had gone away, leaving her alone, still standing beside her chair. A door behind opened and closed quietly, no doubt one of the staff come to clear away glasses and discarded scraps of paper. A voice she recognised called her by name.

"M'lady," said Antonia Ballard, who had been Caroline's last personal attendant.

"No *m'ladies* for me, Antonia," said Brandy. "You know that. You've got more right t'be where I am than I do."

Antonia Ballard was in her seventies, having "served" a shadow queen for twenty of them, and most of the prior half century in total devotion to the real one. She was unbent by her years, still very much everything one would expect a lady-in-waiting to royalty should be, and her loyalty to Brandywine had been unshakable from the very start.

"That's as may be," said Antonia quietly. "I know you were hoping to be on your way home by now, but could I have just a moment...?"

"Of course...always..." said Brandy. She pulled her chair back out from the table, and another for Antonia, so that they faced each other, knees-to-knees, as they sat down together.

"I don't know if I'm being presumptuous or not," said the lady-in-waiting.

"I don't think you've ever been presumptuoous, Antonia. You don't even know what it means so you can't be," said Brandy, laughing.

"It's from a long time ago, Miss—"

"Brandy..."

"Brandy. Word gets a round quickly here. There's a rumour you've found someone to take her place."

"To follow her, not replace her. I think so, but there's stuff needs t'be taken care of first."

"Then now may be the right time...one last thing Caroline asked me to tell you when it seemed appropriate."

Brandywine felt a small shiver run up her spine, memory instantly taking her back to the night she had spent with Marie Santinelli...no longer Queen Caroline...only her friend, who had asked the world of her by giving it into her care.

Now the palace staff arrived to clear away the debris of the official meeting, light gas lamps to chase off the gathering gloom. Antonia sat quietly, hands clasped in her lap as she weighed the words she was to pass on to Brandywine, and how to frame them properly...

### ANTONIA BALLARD'S STORY

"After that last night...the one the two of you spent here together...she was so happy, as if all her cares had been lifted away and she could finally be at peace. She had already put away the flower, so her life was already catching up with her, but she was radiant that next morning; she just shook her head at the grey streaks in her hair, the wrinkles that suddenly crept round her eyes and her lips...but her eyes danced and she laughed and smiled and felt like she had finally been given all and everything of her heart's desire—a lover, a child, someone who she knew, without any doubt, would be true to her word and *her* own hopes for the future of our City and our country.

"You cannot imagine how much she loved you after that night, Brandywine, how utterly grateful she was to have found you."

Antonia drew a handkerchief from her sleeve and dabbed at her eyes, unable to look at Brandy, who, in turn. found herself unable to say anything in response.

"...We went away the next day, to the place where she had been born, up in the hills that run round the southern edge of the Carillon, where the royal family had always kept a summer palace. It was only the two of us, and someone to cook and look after things in the house, another to keep up the grounds while we were there...so we were truly quite alone and I wondered why she had chosen to simply go off and fade away...and why she had chosen me to be the one to stay with her."

Now she could not go on, only wept silently and wrung the handkerchief in her hands as though to make room for her tears. Brandywine used a sleeve to wipe her nose and eyes, something not lost on her companion.

"You're so much like her," said Antonia. "Sometimes, and only when it was my place to look after your needs while you were here, I would forget that *she* was gone; that in some strange way she'd come back to us again, this time as a delightful young girl as fair as she had been dark, who lacked nothing of her kindness and concern for everyone around her.

"She grew more and more fragile with every passing day, yet it never seemed to bother her when the reflection in her glass slowly became that of a stranger. You and I...we have years and years to watch ourselves slowly grow old; for Caroline it was a matter of weeks. When finally she grew too weak to even get out of bed in the morning, she would tell me stories of her childhood, or ask me to read to her. My heart was breaking and she begged me to forgive her for being the cause of it...but she was never less than joyous to my heartbreak, always the one to offer comfort, something positive for tomorrow, when it was my place to be there to ease her last days.

"Less than week before she died, it seemed she woke up and realised there were dozens...hundreds of people whom she had known almost exclusively as servants... people to whom she owed a lifetime of gratitude for always being there, loyal and dedicated. She said:

"In my heart I knew all of them would have died for me if ever it had become needful. I don't want one of them, not one, Nia, to think I *didn't* know. Please promise you will go to all of them and tell them...'

"We spent frantic hours making arrangements so all of them would be looked after. It was exhausting for her. I could see her energy...her *life*...drifting away from her, but she wouldn't rest until she was certain no one would be forgotten...and then we came to you, who were first in her thoughts all along...

"She could barely speak. I don't think she could even see me, knew that her windows were wide to the sunshine only by the scent of leaves turning to dust in the growing autumn. Our last day together, as I tucked her in for the night, she drew me close to her and whispered:

"'Tell her, Nia, tell the blonde-haired girl she gave me all I had ever hoped for...and someday...you will know when...there will come a time when you *must* say these words to her, so she will know I knew how much her sacrifice to me had cost her, and there was never a moment of doubt that I had made the right choice.'

"She made me repeat the words several times, and after all these years I can still hear her voice in my ear. She told me to tell you *Things as they have been in the past do not necessarily need to be part of the future.*

"The next morning when I came with her breakfast, she had gone peacefully in her sleep..."

⊙≈≈⊙

Brandywine sat alone with a borrowed handkerchief, long past the hour when she knew she should be home with Windy and 'Bella, but she would not move, only asked for a small candle when the staff came again to douse the gas lamps.

She watched it flicker away in the dark, in a sense actually living through the passing of her friend, as it had been told her by someone who had loved her mistress no less than she herself had loved her unlooked-for friend.

She whispered goodbye one last time and went home.

# Chapter Fourteen – WINDS OF CHANGE

The manor house standing on the hill above Glen Carrick was empty, its occupants hastily-packed and away to the south. The livestock in the surrounding outbuildings and paddocks had all been loosed to become themselves without benefit of the attention of human beings, though most, having known nothing of existence save what had been fashioned for them, seemed content to stay on, going aimlessly about their usual routines until hunger drove them back out into the world...

The carriage house was another issue, utterly silent save for the soft pasage of a strange misshapen thing, cowled and cloaked in rough cloth, that climbed the staircase to the second floor and surveyed the slumbering "army" of Renard de Montenay sprawled about the floor as if in drunken obeisance to their slumbering master. A long-fingered hand reached out from beneath the cloak and made swift patterns in the stillness, that left trails of sickening green light that hung in the air until they fell apart and drifted like dust to the wooden floor. Renard de Montenay stirred where he lay in the midst of his servitors, blearily raised his head.

"Get up," said the intruder impatiently. "You are almost as useless as your dead son." His voice was a growl and hiss of contempt. "Your *friends* move with or without you."

De Montenay struggled to his feet and surveyed the fallen men around him.

"What am I supposed to do by myself?" he demanded.

Again the concealed hand thrust itself into the light and made deathly patterns in the air; two score men-at-arms scraped their way back into consciousness.

"Now you are not alone anymore," sneered the faceless voice, "though the witch was right to think you pathetic. I call you a fool, to have never seen the Truth in twenty years."

"And what *Truth* would that be?"

"You have been gulled, my stupid friend, by a street wench..."

Renard's truculent gaze faltered.

"What are you talking about?"

"I am talking about a cow...a Brandywine Lloyd...who runs about the palace as if she has not a brain in her head...and has ruled this realm since the death of your precious Queen...twenty years ago!"

De Montenay was stunned, disbelieving.

"It is impossible."

"You may believe what you wish. You could have forced her to her knees when her daughter was within your grasp, yet you let a witless girl slip through your fingers. I have done all I can for you, Renard de Montenay. You have ambition enough for all of these fools lying before you, but only the soul of a bully to guide you to its fulfillment. You will never sit on the Amaranth Throne."

The was a faint echo of those last words, and a whisper of derisive laughter.

"What of the witch?" he demanded, but the cowled figure was gone. De Montenay found himself shaking as if with a virulent fever; then he cursed, and went about kicking his men up onto their feet.

He found his manor house standing on the hill above Glen Carrick empty of family or staff, and heard the whisper of derisive laughter all over again.

---

"...Windy I should go back," said Brandywine. "I have t'start doing things to protect the City, and get people all over to start watching out for—"

Nicholas put his lips gently on hers, hands in her hair trailing down her back as he kissed her into silence.

"That's what all the people in the palace who are in charge of that stuff are doing now, Branny," he said. "You've been there all day almost every day this week; they can manage t'do the job without you for a little bit."

She seemed skeptical.

"Windy I promised—" she began, but he kissed her again, until their eyes went a bit dreamy and they both stopped thinking about anything except how peaceful it could be when the world left them to their own devices.

"And I promise they'll manage without you for the rest of the day," he said, kissing her a third time, longer than the first two..

Eventually she relented, and he could feel the tension in her drain away into invisible puddles around their feet. He smiled at down at her, and she up at him. Arabella wandered into the kitchen whilst they were still getting over their last kiss.

"I hope I'm not interrupting anything," she said with an impudent grin, "but if I am, please don't stop on account of me. I can go away...really fast..."

That said, she managed to insinuate herself between them and became an Arabella sandwich that went on for as long as the last kiss before she provided one to each of them.

"Is it okay if 'Rissa comes for supper and spends the night?"

"Do we really get t'decide?" asked her father.

"No of course not," she said. "I'm a brat and you're the best parents anyone could have so it's only right I should take advantage every chance I get...I wanna maximise my bratness-without-consequences while I still have a chance."

"Well then, me and your mom are going out," said Nicholas. "I'm her social director for the rest of the afternoon and evening; as long as you and Kerissa promise t'stay out of trouble, you can do as you please and we'll see if we can bring something nice home for both of you."

Arabella said *thank you* with hugs, and went off to collect 'Rissa. Brandy cozied up to Nicholas again.

"So what am I doing this afternoon?" she inquired archly, slipping one hand inside his shirt. "I know something we can do until 'Bella' comes home, and then we can do whatever *you* thought we should do."

Nicholas found her very persuasive, enough so that when their daughter and Kerissa arrived an hour later, they somewhat hurriedly got dressed while the girls waited patiently outside the kitchen.

"Have a good time, whatever you're doing," called Arabella from the door of the house.

Arms round each other they strolled across the courtyard, down the laneway and out onto the Boulevard.

"So what *are* we doing?" she asked.

Nicholas shrugged and smiled.

"I thought we could just wander. There were days when that was all we needed."

"You stink-bomb," she said. "No plans at all…?"

"None," he replied, with smuggitude. "How about the Silver Rose…and *then* whatever…?"

---

When her parents had gone, Arabella looked at Kerissa and Kerissa looked at Arabella. They seemed to be thinking the same thoughts, spoke at almost the same time:

"We should get the boys…see what they think…Maybe we can even get them t'take us out for supper…"

They shared a smile only those who are utterly devoted to one another can share, and in doing so realised the shared thought itself was not one to be taken lightly.

"Our folks are gonna be unhappy," said 'Rissa.

"Yeah…I know," replied 'Bella. "But we can't just sit here, can we?"

'Rissa shook her head. "Nope…and I know the boys are gonna feel the same way."

"Then we better get moving…"

De Montenay struggled with himself. His first instinct was to whip his men back onto their horses and wreak havoc upon whoever first had the bad luck to encounter them. Yet every time the anger came roaring back into his brain, when he wanted nothing more than to rend and tear and be the source of someone else's misery as payback for his own rage and frustration, he heard the faint laughter of his cowled "ally" and felt twinges of doubt...and in his heart what he knew was Fear. Then he would become calm for a time, and quietly look for a course of action that would feed the savage hunger of his hatred.

---

The Silver Rose might have been deserted for all the sense of bustle and business those on its terrace and indoors in the dining room failed to engender in the usually warm atmosphere of the place. Nicholas and Brandy chose a table in a corner of the terrace, somewhat removed from the lack of hustle and bustle, and wondered how anywhere could be so busy and so quiet at the same time.

"Windy what's goin' on?" she asked.

"It's pretty strange, whatever it is," he said, by way of agreeing that *something* was going on, but having no clue as to what it might be.

"It's like everyone is kinda dopey. Like they're all here to have a good time but suddenly they don't know how?"

"That sounds right," he said. "At least we've not gone that far...May wine for you?"

"And strawberries?" she asked hopefully.

Windy drank cognac with his strawberries, and made quite sure Brandy didn't wear any of the whipped cream from hers in any of the embarrassing places it had visited in the past. Nevertheless, there was an overpowering *hush* in everything going on around them, including even the wait staff, who always came by to say hello or advise them of the best things on the menu that day, but now seemed to be sleepwalking through even that...

"This is very funny peculiar," said Brandywine. "And look at all the people wandering by, Windy...it's like they're only-half awake..."

Late afternoon on the Boulevard was usually a non-stop parade of revellers, and people on their way home from work with a constant lookout for some gang of friends to hail them from a started-earlier-in-the-afternoon party. The conversation on the sidewalks and terraces was an unstoppable hum, but now it was mostly a disquieting quiet.

There seemed to be a flow to all of it. Everyone seemed to be moving in one direction, intent upon some mysterious destination. Windy reached over the terrace railing and tugged at the sleeve of a passerby, apologising for doing so, but also asking what it was that had everyone on their way to wherever. The man shrank away from him with a look of what might have been wide-eyed terror, saying nothing before hurrying on. Windy looked at Brandy and she looked at him.

"Are we curious?" he asked.

"I think so..." she replied.

Within minutes they were immersed in the slow-moving tide of humanity, edging away from the Boulevard to some of the smaller cross streets and eventually coming to the front of what had been, until recently, an abandoned warehouse, but now sported a freshly-painted façade and a professionally printed sign beside the door:

THIS WEEK ONLY
direct from the farthest reaches
of the Dark Continent
AZIM SHARAD
and his orchestra

They queued up with the rest of those who had lined the Boulevard and any number of the side- and cross-streets along their way, still feeling somewhat removed from the strange lack of...*something*...in everyone around them. As it came near to the time for them to pay for their admission, Brandy spoke to the couple directly behind them in the queue, asking if they had ever attended one of the concerts before.

"Oh at least a dozen of them," said the woman enthusiastically.

"He's quite remarkable," added her partner. "Listening to his music is like being lost in things that we've only ever dreamt of..."

Nicholas and Brandy exchanged glances that were equal parts incredulity and unease.

"Windy, isn't this the musician 'Bella saw last week?"

He nodded.

"*This Week Only* seems to be pretty flexible."

"I had the same thought myself."

They paid for their tickets and let themselves be carried along by the curiously silent crowd, through a broad open space and then along a darker corridor into a large dimly-lit room of seats scattered haphazardly across the floor. They found a pair of them on the far side of the hall, settled down with Windy's arm around Brandy's shoulders as she snuggled up to him.

Soon after, the dimmed lights around them disappeared and a small stage emerged from the gloom before them as a series of footlights grew brighter. A breathless sigh ran through those in attendance; then dead silence again prevailed as three robed figures moved onto the stage, bowed once to the audience and commenced to tune an array of drums and stringed instruments, all of which were totally alien to both Nicholas and Brandywine. The stage lights dimmed but for one in the centre, and Azim Sharad came to sit on a low stool.

They had never seen anyone quite like him. He was very tall and seemed misshapen even through the sweep and swirl of his voluminous garments—embroidered layers of dark cloth that revealed no other details of his person—yet his long-fingered hands deftly took a stringed instrument...a lute of some sort...and proceeded to strum and fidget with its tuning pegs until chords shimmered away into the dark to his satisfaction. Brandy shivered, half in delicious anticipation, and half with a burgeoning sense of terror.

The random sounds that Sharad coaxed from his instrument were delicious with promise...intoxicating ... so much so that they barely took notice of the fact that his face, hitherto a visage of exotic beauty, would sometimes appear to turn itself inside out, become a dreadful caricature of itself—hairless, with mottled white skin ritually-scarred and broken by an hideous ingratiating smile, words of welcome softly murmured through bloodless lips, teeth broken and filed to points.

Azim Sharad nodded once to his fellow musicians and the music became inexorable...

"Windy something's wrong...we need t'go right away..."

The urgency in her voice was something he had learned never to discount for any reason of his own. If Brandwyine had reservations, doubts or fears about anything he had always been willing to deal with them after the fact. They got up from their seats, moved to the back of the hall and began to edge their way to the door in which they had come in...and found themselves doing so in silence...in the glare of the musician on the stage who had stopped in mid-performance and now followed them with eyes that blazed with hate...

---

He determined that at first light the residents of Glen Carrick would learn the measure of respect they had always denied him; that now, with his world crumbling around him, he would make them all pay, and then find a way to revenge himself upon those whom he held responsible for its destruction. He found another bottle of brandy and this time, felt no need for a glass.

Nicholas and Brandywine walked home quickly in darkness, under a sky of cloud-ridden stars, the moon turned the colour of something foul and nauseating.

"Windy we didn't stay long enough," she said. "Why is it the middle of the night when we went inside before dinner time?"

He shook his head wordlessly, now infected with the same unease that had moved her in the theatre. For a brief instant he felt as if he had stirred out of himself, as if their sudden, irrational, yet shared sense of impending danger belonged to someone else. He tightened his grasp around her shoulders, trying not to alarm her further by increasing the speed of what he incredulously recognised as *flight*...the thing one engaged in when confronted with an insurmountable threat to one's life or well-being. Nevertheless, he knew this was what they were doing...

Running.

---

De Montenay awoke from an alcoholic stupor, in a waning of daylight that served only to make him more foul-tempered than he had been before emptying the bottle of brandy. He was alone in his study, but now could hear others moving about *his house*, without his leave, and it only enraged him further. He called out for Rochambeau, but it was a dull-faced brute who went by the name of Embry who answered his summons.

"Rochambeau's gone, m'lord," he said, trying to convey a semblance of the newfound authority he'd won with a couple of well-placed fists. "He took off as soon as he realised..."

"Realised what, pray?"

"Well, sir...he said you was shit-faced in here so now was as good a time as ever t'be on his way..."

"Truly," said de Montenay in a whisper.

"Yes sir," replied Embry, too dense to hear the note of violence couched by the soft reply. "There was a couple o' the others thought t'go with him, but I set them right, yes I did."

Renard grinned. "Well you're a fucking paragon, Embry, and I'll not forget it."

Embry of a sudden looked uncomfortable. He wasn't at all familiar with the word itself, nor had he any idea what *a paragon* might be, or what kind of influence *being* a paragon would have on his life.

"Thank you, m'lord," he said, ducking his head to acknowledge what even he realised sounded more like a harbinger of something dreadful in store for him as much as it sounded like a promise of reward for his loyalty.

"Fetch me another one of these from the cellar, would you?" said de Montenay. "And please inform *the others* that we are riding again in the morning and I'll not tolerate laggards."

"Can I tell them when, m'lord, and wheres we're goin'?"

"You may not," snapped de Montenay. "Now bugger off and get me that fucking bottle..."

***

Arabella edged Kerissa off the sidewalk into a doorway as a tide of dishevelled humanity slowly surged past them in dead silence, looking neither to right nor left as they shambled along, oblivious to anyone or anything that lay in their path.

"'Bella these people don't look—"

"Like they're even awake," she said. "They look like somebody just roused them out of bed, dressed them badly and then sent them on their way."

"I'm getting tired of funny peculiar."

"Me too, 'Rissa. Ever since word got out that Caroline had died—even if it *was* twenty years late—everything's gone a bit wonky all over."

"Wonky?" said Kerissa with a raised eyebrow. "Is that related to when you get the wiggins?"

"Don't make fun, 'Rissa. Wonky is things getting that way by themselves, when the stuff you expect t'happen doesn't. Getting the wiggins comes after...maybe."

"So what you're saying is that things can be wonky, but not necessarily enough t'give you the wiggins?"

Arabella closed her eyes and sighed.

"You know I love you, 'Rissa," she said wearily, "and I know you love me, but just because you're older doesn't mean you get t'treat me like one of the twins."

Kerissa pretended to be contrite, and apologised profusely whilst swearing she would never again comment critically on Arabella's unique way of viewing the world, or the way she described its vagaries and unlooked-for occurrences. Then they burst out laughing, waiting for a break in the plodding foot traffic to cross the Boulevard arm-in-arm, on their way to Thomas and Diana's loft to collect Edmund, Sebastian and Evrard... who just happened to be on their way to see them.

## ARABELLA

Kerissa shouted to them half a block away, received an answering cry of welcome and then turned to Arabella with a devilish glint in her eyes.

"Isn't it amazing, 'Bella? Here we are on our way to see the boys when I bet they were on their way t'see us at the same time. That's gotta be wonky enough t'give anyone the wiggins...don'tcha think?"

Arabella's eyes got big as tea saucers. "You big poophead! I'm gonna get you now!"

Kerissa took off in the direction of the boys crying "Sanctuary! Sanctuary! 'Bella's gone bonkers!"

"Bonkers nothing!" Arabella cried out after her. "It's gonna be torture time when I get my hands on you, Kerissa Davies. Run away all you want now, but I'll catch you up don't you worry...!"

They both arrived at about the same time, entirely breathless but still full of mischief. Kerissa threw herself upon the mercy of Edmund and Sebastian, ducking round to hide in their mountainous shadows; Arabella took one look at Evrard's eyes bugging out at the sight of them approaching and decided it would more fun to tease him than tickle Kerissa to the pavement. She had no idea that Jamie and Stella had warned him off; she wrapped herself around him and appealed to his sense of justice.

"She's bein' mean t'me, Evrard. You have t'tickle her to death!"

He looked to Edmund and Sebastian for guidance. Saw Kerissa keeking out from behind them. Looked back at the Beverleys and realised he was on his own.

"I'm not sure I'm allowed t'do that," said Evrard.

"Of course you are," said Arabella. "I said it was okay."

"But—"

"Who's in charge?" she demanded.

Again, Evrard looked for outside guidance and found none, only two large young men purportedly his friends, and a pair of extremely attractive young women, all grinning at his discomfiture. He shrugged in resignation.

"I guess I have t'tickle you t'death some time in the near future," he said to Kerissa, trying to be diplomatically apologetic.

"Traitor" she cried. "You swore undying devotion!"

"I did?"

Kerissa nodded and turned to Edmund and Sebastian for confirmation.

"You must have," said Edmund. "We don't even get t'look at them unless we swear stuff like that every other week."

"And don't forget how you promised t'feed us whenever we decided we were hungry," added Arabella.

"That too," said Sebastian.

"So where are we going for supper?" asked Evrard in total capitulation. "I'm the new guy in town..."

Over dinner they agreed the only thing they could do, in all conscience, was travel north yet again, to join Arabella's grandfather in clearing the Carillon moors and the Dales of unwanted Scandians.

---

Though it was late, Nicholas and Brandywine opted for a detour to the converted stable on Old Princes Street, seeking out Zoraya in search of some explanation for what had occurred. Cautious rapping on the stable doors brought a response almost at once. Gareth swung one of them open, ushered them onto his studio floor, and thence up to a sitting room in the loft. Zoraya looked tired, sitting before a small fire, but not at all surprised to see them.

"You saw him, didn't you?" she said quietly. Firelight shadows sought shelter in the frown that creased her forehead.

"We saw *somebody*," replied Windy. "Or some*thing*..."

"And Time decided to play games with you."

Nicholas and Brandy nodded together, explaining how they had inadvertently wandered into what was supposed to have a been a concert performance that had begun with the sun well up in the afternoon sky, but after only minutes inside had left, and found themselves outdoors again, but in full nighttime darkness.

"Sort of the same thing upset Arabella so badly," said Brandy, "except now there are hundreds of people listening to him, instead of the small audience she was part of...and they all seem to be wandering around in some kind of silly mindless haze, talking like they've known his music forever.

"Zori, the worst part was when we left. He just stopped playing and looked straight at us and it was like he wanted t'tear us apart..."

Zoraya nodded. "I thought I was through with him," she said. "I hoped it might be someone else...but I think it *is* Chakidze, the one who imprisoned me. I think I have known all along.

"To be on the safe side I set ward-spells around all of us after Arabella's fright, so now there is little or nothing he can do to any of you, but as I have never forgotten him, so it seems he has never forgiven me. I'm the one he wants, but he will do as much damage as he can to those I love. That he has taken total strangers from the population of the City and spellbound them is not good."

"What do *we* do?" asked Windy.

"Nothing, Nicholas, but only avoid him in any way that you can. It is my place to deal with him."

Brandy raised an objection.

"We're all of us family, Zori. We can't let you be all alone against him."

Zoraya smiled sadly.

"Time will prove your magic is much stronger than mine, Brandywine, but if he cannot harm you because of it, you can be sure he will find other ways to make you suffer, *because* I am part of your family.

"Please...just be careful and go home. I have work to do tonight, but I will come to the palace in the morning to see you..."

---

The piles of arms and clothing scattered about in the great room told Brandywine and Nicholas all they needed to know upon their arrival. They heard their daughter and Kerissa stomping round upstairs making further preparations, but had no chance to exchange anything but a look of profound concern coupled with exhausted resignation.

A few minutes later the girls came crashing down the stairs and stopped short in the doorway.

"I know I should've asked first," said Arabella.

"You weren't gonna just go without saying anything, were you, 'Bella?"

"No of course not, Mum. I would *never* do something like that, but you know that we should go. We can help. And Evrard needs to prove that he's had no part of anything his father's involved in...."

Windy said, "So when are you planning on leaving, sweetheart?"

"The boys will be here at first light," 'Bella said apologetically. "We're on the morning train north."

Brandywine looked heartbroken. Nicholas briefly considered not allowing either of them to go...and decided it was not truly his decision to make.

"Promise you'll all be extra careful," he said.

"Swear you'll come back safe," said Brandy.

Both girls nodded solemnly, and no one slept soundly that night.

When the Beverley boys and Evrard arrived half an hour after sunrise, Nicholas was there in a dressing gown to extract the same promise from them. And five minutes after that they were gone.

---

Brandywine's meetings began early the next day, she herself rousing all of her advisers and ministers to the conference room before they'd had the chance to even consider breakfast. That itself was an haphazard affair, food and drink taken as they conversed.

As always, her presence drew a lot of polite condescension from those who even after twenty years still felt she had no business meddling in affairs of state; the news of two messengers, one from the western coast and another from the Dales, did nothing to help her in their eyes. She relayed the first message—that Sevrain de Montenay had been found murdered in an alleyway in Bedford—then fought back a shiver of equal parts frustration and fear as she read the printed communiqué from the leader of the party that had been despatched to arrest his father. After the briefings, she was in the corridor outside the conference room when a page brought Zoraya to her.

For a moment neither said a word, but embraced each other as two parents whose only children had gone off to war. That much was one terror and heartache shared by both of them, and they felt no shame at shedding tears together, not even when palace staff encountered them in a shadowed alcove beside the conference room.

At length, Brandy shared her news from the northlands.

"...Zori, they said the entire manor house was empty...and the coach house as well. His wife said things were very *quiet* when they left..."

"Where is she now?"

"She and his daughters, most of the household...they're all in a wing of the palace being treated as guests, but all the ministers of this that and whatever think I managed t'bring them here as hostages."

"But there was no sign of de Montenay or his men-at-arms."

Brandy nodded. "Northing, Zori. The stables were empty too."

Zoraya frowned. "Brandywine, I did not see this. "

Brandy knew better than to seek for illumination. Zoraya kept her own counsel in such things; instead, she simply asked:

"It's trouble?"

"It can mean only one thing, my love—that I was right. The one I thought I had defeated so long ago has somehow returned and I have been careless. I cannot allow anyone else to be involved."

"Zori, we can help."

"No, Brandywine, no one can help. This Akim Sharad...who cannot be anyone but *Chakidze* though I do not know how it can be...he knows how to play upon the wants and desires of mankind, bend them all to his lust to rule the world. In his time he held entire countries in thrall, and no one but he could have loosed the bonds I placed upon de Montenay and his men; that he did so means it is likely he is the one behind everything that threatens us now. You can deal with Scandians and Antillians who have had their dreams of conquest fuelled by his lies and deceit, but as I told you before—dealing with him is for me alone..."

# Chapter Fifteen – WORD FROM THE WESTLANDS

"...He was right, you know," said Edmund. "Never mind that he shouldn't be out here himself, bein' as old as he is, but with you close by he could so busy making sure you and 'Rissa don't get hurt that it becomes dangerous for him. And then there's Grams... and *nobody* wants t'get on *her* wrong side when she's so damn ferocious about keepin' the two of you safe."

Arabella pouted. She knew Edmund was right to take her grandparents' side, but it still rankled that she and 'Rissa had been relegated to support staff and rearguard duty.

"So how come you guys don't get into the soup for it?" she demanded. Kerissa already knew the answer to that, but also knew better than to be the one to inform 'Bella.

"We're guys," shrugged Sebastian. "It's our job t'do stupid stuff and kill things. Girls are the ones get t'clean up after we're finished being stupid."

"That is so *wrong*!" cried Arabella. "Me and 'Rissa can go twice as long as any of you on horseback...and we're just as good if not better with swords and bows and pistols!"

"We know that," said Edmund, "but Frederick and Alexandra are still *your* official grandparents, so what're we supposed t'do?"

# ARABELLA

Arabella rounded on Evrard, looking for some support from somewhere she hoped that unassailable logic had not yet had time to find a solid foundation.

"What d'*you* think?" she demanded.

Somewhere on the trip north, Evrard had learned the ins and outs of dealing with *the girls*. He knew quite well from observing Arabella and Kerissa together that his fantasies were likely never going to be anything more than just fantasies; nevertheless, he felt compelled by adoration and admiration to take their part anyway.

"I think it's horribly unjust," he said, in his most earnest and diplomatic tones.

Arabella looked like she was ready to murder him. Kerissa began to laugh hysterically, and went out of her way to wrap herself around him in a hug that had nothing to do with thanking him for his support and everything to do with making him crazy.

"You are so sweet!" she said, and kissed him to prove it. Evrard turned red and decided it was time to just stop talking. Arabella ranted on.

"Well...me and 'Rissa aren't gonna just sit around and crochet doilies!"

Edmund grinned. "I know. So does your grandfather. That's why all of us have our own special little band of brigands to follow us around while we ferret out bad guys. Your Grams is still a bit huffy over it, but Evrard got really charming and explained to her how we felt that we all needed t'do our part."

"Oh you lovely boy!" exclaimed Kerissa, who had yet to let go of Evrard. "I knew you were wonderful!" She kissed him a second time and he blushed on cue. "'Bella when all of this is over we need to take him home with us, don'tcha think..."

Arabella just shook her head and headed towards her horse.

"Where's our guys, then?" she demanded. "It's all well and good for us t'be havin' a swell time t'gether out here in the middle of maybe a war, but we really should get into the business if we're gonna bother..."

***

Farther north in the Dales, Camille Ardrey was drinking her first cup of morning tea on the back porch when she noticed something in the air that had nothing to do with leaf-turning, or the usual things that accompanied the end of summer and the beginning of autumn. She looked up and through the patchwork of seasonal desolation to her maple trees and saw great clouds of black billowing smoke, caught the unmistakable signature scent of it on the wind. She heard raised voices coming from the village and raced back into the house, threw aside her apron and found a pair of stout-soled shoes. Once outside in her front garden, it was plain that somewhere along the dirt track that wound from Glen Carrick up to the de Montenay manor house, a croft was on fire. At her garden gate she joined the first rush of her neighbours and friends...

"...It's the Rawdon farm!" cried Tatty McArdle. "My boy was there for some eggs when *His Highness* come down from the manor with his bully-boys and set the barn on fire."

All around her the people of Glen Carrick surged up the track toward the Rawdon farm with buckets and pots and anything that might hold water. Cami gathered up her skirts and strode forward to the head of the procession, full of foreboding and anger. Both found their object a quarter mile up the track, where Renard de Montenay and his men emerged from a cloud of dust kicked up by their horses' hooves.

"Stand aside, we have business in the village!" shouted de Montenay.

"Burning a few more houses then, bastard!" came a voice from behind her.

De Montenay seemed to take a perverse pleasure in receiving the insult. He slowed the headlong pace of his men, signed for them to stop, and then cantered slowly forward to within a length of the crowd barring his way. Cami was there to meet him.

"Go away, Renard," she said quietly. "We've had enough of you."

Behind her there was a murmur of assent. Someone threw a clod of earth that struck at the armoured chest of his horse. Another called out derisively:

"Where's the Lady de Montenay and your girls this morning, my *lord*? Gone away with the stable-boy?"

A tide of laughter swept through the crowd as de Montenay's self-satisfied smirk of superiority slowly darkened into something dangerous.

"I heard he went all night with all of them, my *lord*. Is that true? Did he let you watch until you'd had too much to drink?"

De Montenay's face went bloodless. He spurred his horse forward, but Cami Ardrey would not move and his riding crop slashed once across her face, drawing blood. Cami Ardrey still would not move.

"I saw them off myself, Renard," she whispered, "*and* your son Evrard, who knows you for the pathetic traitor that you are."

She turned to those behind her.

"He deals with foreigners, to betray our country to them."

"I've had enough of you and your fucking family!"

"You and *your* father still owe me for the death of my brother and your own Rochelle de Montenay."

He would have trampled her down then, but the people of Glen Carrick surged around her and went for him and those who followed.

"Run away, Renard," she called again. "Run away as long and as far as you like. Justice will find you...for everything..."

De Montenay snarled and wheeled his horse, even as a handful of his men were pulled from their saddles and the rest turned tail in flight. He followed them in a hail of rocks and clotted earth.

---

Frederick Wyndham had sent his eldest sons to range the high deserts to the north of the Dales—thousands of square miles of near-unspoiled wilderness, populated only by those who had sought as little to do with *civilisation* as possible—that stretched from the northernmost hills of the Dales, rising steadily to meet the mountains that formed the natural border with Scandia and, for a thousand years, had proven to be the greatest deterrent to any further incursions after their rout by the first King Michael de Montigny.

What they had found were hundreds of Scandians roaming the plateaus, heading south and destroying anything that lay in their path. That the onset of winter in the northlands was scarce more than a month away served only to move them to greater haste and increase their appetite for laying waste to all they encountered. The Wyndhams paid one life for every five they took, but still found themselves in desperate conflict almost daily. Even with no knowledge of the Antillian threat from the west, they knew with absolute certainty that the realm had come to a massive crisis, and its very existence hinged upon their continued efforts to stand against the invaders.

To those out on the moors and to the west, it was only a matter of time, waiting upon Disaster to find its way to them...

---

Arabella peered through the pair of field glasses that Stella had insisted upon sending north with her. In amongst a small band of crofters who owed allegiance to the Wyndhams, she sat her horse beside Kerissa, Evrard and the Beverleys, and looked down off the edge of the moors to the empty tracks of the railway line below.

"This is where we jumped the train," she said aloud. "I wonder what happened to the Scandians we saw that night."

She scanned south and east, to the bridge and the roil of the Findhorn rushing down from the north. As if in answer to her question, she caught a glimpse of movement off to the west—a small body of men perhaps four or five miles away, but moving quickly on foot towards the river. Then she caught further movement, a lone figure no more than a half a league in front of them, by all appearances running for his life.

She passed the glasses off to Edmund, pointing in the direction of what she had seen; he in turn passed them to Kerissa, and she to Evrard. Sebastian took the last look.

"Whoever he is, he's not got more than a half an hour before they catch him up."

"And the people chasing him don't look at all like they belong to us," said Kerissa.

Arabella looked to each of them for a consensus of opinion.

"Can we get to him in time?"

"Edmund said, "You or Kerissa on your mares. The rest of us are all too heavy."

Arabella nodded, pointing the way for all of them, and spurred her mount down the slope, racing towards the bridge where the railroad spanned the curve of the river.

They careened down the hillside and upwards again to the raised bed of the tracks, their horses' hooves striking sparks in the gravel between the ties as they thundered across the bridge. Kerissa and Arabella set the pace now, outrunning the rest of them by twenty yards, looking back to make sure they would be close enough to engage those pursuing the lone runner if a confrontation became necessary.

"'Bella, you have t'go you're way faster!" cried Kerissa. "But be careful it's gonna be really close."

Arabella clapped her heels to her mare's flanks, spoke softly into one ear, and leaned forward across her neck, as together they seemed to leap forward yards at a time, the ground rising and falling beneath them as she spurred across the rolling hills. She heard the cries of her companions urging her on, and then only the pounding of her horse's hooves as she left them in her wake...

Only once did she turn to look back, on the crest of a hill, in time to see 'Rissa and the boys and the half score of her grandfather's liege-men, cresting a rise a quarter mile behind her. She turned herself forward again, reaching for the clasp of the leather sheath that held her double-curved bow, stringing it at a full gallop and making sure her arrows were within easy reach. The mare ran effortlessly, revelling in the clench and release of muscles that for two days had known only the slow pace of a canter, the only evidence of her exertion now the faint sheen of perspiration that began to glow across her flanks. Arabella whispered more encouragement, let go the reins and gave the mare her head, now laughing out loud in the rush of wind past them. She could sense herself nearing the runner, could almost feel his desperation as his pursuers closed in on him.

One last hill rose up before her, and then below her in the trough formed by it and the one beyond, she saw him stumbling with exhaustion...and the first of his pursuers reaching the top of the farther hill...drawing an arrow of his own...nocking it and coming to a wide-legged halt. She nocked one of hers, calling out to the man below as she bent the bow into a diamond-shaped instrument of death. The double-curve sent it forward like a gunshot, arcing across the space between the hilltops and burying itself to the fletching in the Scandian's chest.

Arabella plunged downward, calling out again, this time able to clearly see the look of relief in the fugitive's eyes. She tucked her bow down under one thigh as she nodded to him, leaned forward and reached for his outstretched hand, the mare never breaking stride as she swung him up behind her and swerved down the trough to put some distance between those following the archer she had downed.

She reined her horse a dozen yards out of bowshot, wheeling round to come at the invaders from one flank, as she knew Kerissa and the boys would do the same from their side, to encircle them and leave them with no place to run. The man she had rescued spoke urgently into her ear:

"My name is Robin Adair, come from Snowdon on the north coast, running with news for the City until these dogs took my horse out from under me and came at my heels. There are ships…dozens of them moving south to Bedford. Is't true the Queen is dead?"

Arabella nodded. Robin cursed under his breath.

"You cannot be alone," he said.

"No," she said over her shoulder. "Friends come right behind me. We're going t'take at least one of them."

She felt his breath on her face. "Good. Then give me your sword and let me pay them in steel for hounding me like an animal, while you make them think twice over it with that bow of yourn. Twere a fine shot you made a moment ago, m'lady. I've not seen better…"

Arabella grinned into the wind, inclining her head.

"You're too kind, Sir Robin," she said. "I think these may be some who would have treated me even less kindly had they been able to catch me. Let's collect our due..."

---

There were three dozen and more of them, but it was not long before they realised their prey had come upon unlooked-for relief from their attentions as Kerissa, the Beverleys, Evrard, and the Wyndham crofters ringed them round and demanded their surrender. Receiving only defiance from the northerners, they danced their horses on the edge of their bow range, charging forward to drop one or another of them with one of their own arrows. There were a dozen left standing when Adair slipped from behind Arabella's saddle and went for them on foot. The Beverleys fell upon them like thunderbolts, their longswords like the blades of avenging angels, slashing down through chain mail and flimsy helms as though through butter. Kerissa feathered a handful like porcupines, until only two remained and, after surveying the carnage around them, dropped their weapons and put up their hands.

---

"...I've never seen ships like them. Steel-sided—and at least one that seemed to sail *under* the water!—with great guns bigger than anything we've got, I'm sure. Dozens of them. They just pounded the daylights out of us from better than half a mile out t'sea, and then waded in to clean things up.

Luckily, most of the Snowdon fleet saw them coming and managed to get word to us before heading south. Everyone in the village fled inland, me included."

Adair's face was a rueful mass of light and shadow in the flicker of the cookfire, framed by a shaggy mop of shoulder-length brown hair. At close inspection he was thirty or so years old, not so tall as Edmund or Sebastian, but well-muscled from hauling nets and felling trees.

"No..." he said in response to a question from Kerissa. "I'm from Bedford, but we took four boats north for some cold-water catch before winter. Three days ago we drew straws t'see who'd get to take a dinghy in *for supplies,* so that's how I cam' t'be in the village at all. I hope my people got out with word t'the south. My wife and kids are in Bedford."

"Where were you heading?" asked Sebastian..

Adair shrugged. "Anywhere I could find a place t'send word t'the City," he said. "I lit out east and south and was doin' just fine until those norland bastards got wind of me."

"Trowbridge can't be more than a day's ride south from here," said Arabella. "That's the northernmost town before the rail line doglegs toward Élysée and then up t'the Dales. We can send a wire from there down t'the City. My mum probably knows what's in the wind, but it can't hurt t'be sure."

Adair shot her a curious glance.

"It's a really long story," she said, "but the short one that most nobody knows is that Caroline died a long long time ago; that my mum was her friend and promised her t'look after things until ...well...whenever..."

"I didn't know I was bein' so familiar with royalty."

Everyone laughed.

"Well you're not," said Arabella, with a small smile. "Maybe someday you'll meet my mum and you'll see...but the truth is that we're all just plain folk ourselves, tryin' t'be helpful."

Edmund daggered a chunk of something out of the pot on the fire, looked around as he chewed.

"Where's Evrard?"

"You mean that cute friend of yours who gets all flustered when girls kiss him?" asked Kerissa with mischief in her eyes.

"'Rissa can you leave off with that *please*? The two of you have got him t'where there're times he can't even speak properly."

Kerissa and Arabella exchanged glances of immense satisfaction.

"Okay...so where is he?" asked the blonde girl.

"Havin' a chat with our *guests*," replied Sebastian matter-of-factly.

"Evrard knows Scandian?"

"It would appear so. When he first wandered over t'pay call on them he said something that got them really quiet."

Evrard appeared a few minutes later, sat himself down and accepted a bowl with his supper from Kerissa, who made a point of being quite formal with him whilst sticking her tongue out at Edmund and Sebastian.

"Your grandfather's people are good," he said. "We've got a decent perimeter and back-up on four-hour shifts....*and*...we can see a ways in every direction from here and things look pretty quiet."

"And our guests...?" inquired Sebastian.

"Were pretty close-mouthed at first. Actually quite rude......made some interesting suggestions about what I could do with any number of body parts, but I convinced 'em that loosening their tongues would be a good thing."

Five pairs of eyes glittered in the firelight, demanding more illumination. For once, in the presence of Arabella and Kerrissa, Evrard seemed to be thoroughly comfortable.

"I explained t'them that the only reason they'd not been ventilated like the rest of their people was that we expected information from them...a helpfulness that might be rewarded with the possibility of them actually going home, rather than just being left out here for the badgers; that if they didn't feel much like conversation, then there really wasn't any reason why that shouldn't happen."

"Really? You actually said that to them, Evrard?" asked Kerissa, visibly impressed.

"They were tied up. I thought I could get away with it," said Evrard between mouthfuls.

Kerissa made google-eyes at everyone else around the fire, as if to say *See...I told you he was special...* Arabella just shook her head.

"Someday you'll be a grown-up too, 'Rissa."

"Not right away, I hope."

"No...definitely *not* right away."

"Oh for god sakes can you two just stop!" laughed Edmund, trying not to choke on his own supper. "Evrard, just tell us what you got from them...quickly...before either of these hellions can conjure up any more devilry."

Evrard was no longer giving up any ground. Knowing full well he had, in the past, voluntarily entered into an almost pathetic thralldom to the two young women, he was not about to give up the opportunity to come into his own, a place of some solid if not quite equal footing within the camaraderie of *les enfants des Boulevardiers*. He made a great show of one more mouthful, carefully chewing and swallowing. The girls, who knew exactly what he was about, smirked in a kindly fashion. Evrard came clean.

"These two are just foot soldiers," he said. "Their orders were to check things out, disrupt things as much as possible wherever it wasn't too obvious, and then just sit around until the *real* Scandian army got here. The curious part was that it was common knowledge it all started when someone...*someone*...approached the government there and convinced them now would be a good time to take back what was rightfully theirs; that the death of the Queen had been a fabric of lies for two decades."

"Someone?" said Arabella.

Evrard nodded. "A foreigner. Somebody who fired up old grievances and scared the daylights out of most of them at the same time, more than enough to set things in motion. They said there was talk of him not even being human, that he seemed more than half some horrific sort of animal..."

*Les enfants* exchanged ominous glances, noticed at once by Robin Adair.

"You know about this fellow?"

Kerissa said, "I think we've encountered him. My mum certainly thinks so, and 'Bella's mom thinks he's responsible for everything going on now..."

"Sounds like whoever he is, he needs some serious attention," observed Adair, in tones that were unmistakably less than peaceful.

Everyone nodded in agreement, and talk became desultory while the meagre fare doing dinner duty was consumed. Afterwards, Arabella did a turn about their camp, making conversation with many of the Wyndham crofters she knew from her childhood visits. At the edge of the camp she made a point of turning away from their battleground of the afternoon, where it was obvious that nocturnal foragers had wasted no time in availing themselves of their own unlooked-for dinner meal. Robin Adair came up quietly beside her.

"I wanted to thank you for my life," he said. "I didn't have much time left."

Arabella's face shimmered in the light and shadows cast by the cookfires scattered across their camp. She smiled and shook her head.

"We can't have good honest folk being hunted down by outsiders in their own country," she said. "My mom would be furious over something like that, and she's the most peaceful person I've ever known, except maybe for my Da...and Andrew and Alain... and 'Rissa's parents...and...well...Edmund and Sebastian's folks as well, though they both show a bit of temper every now and again."

She laughed and won him for life.

"You're all so easy with each other," he said. "It's a good thing t'see...warms you up inside..."

"Our folks were the best of friends from when they were just about my age, and we've all grown up together so we've been brothers and sisters since forever...and lovers too...me and 'Rissa. She looks after me..."

Adair nodded. "I thought there was somethin' between the two of you, but it's good, all of you one great family."

"I guess that's what we are," said 'Bella. "What about you, Robin, you said your people are in Bedford?"

"My folks, my wife and three kids`...Darya, the girls Devon and Daryl, and my son Daniel. He's the youngest...five years old..."

"I thought you looked a bit familiar. All of us have taken holidays in Bedford over the years. We gotta get you back t'your family as soon as possible."

Adair's face in half-light showed gratitude all over again.

"I was goin' t'beg you another favour," he said. "A horse if you can spare one...and me as well, as far as the wire t'your people in the City is concerned."

Arabella considered that for a moment.

"First light then" she said. "Sometimes my mare doesn't even touch the ground, so you can have her and I'll ride with 'Rissa. The two of us can run down to Trowbridge together and be back in a couple of days to find the boys wherever they've wandered off to."

"Bless you, m'lady," said Robin Adair.

"But you have t'promise to return her someday, is all," said Arabella, " and t'stop with that *m'lady* stuff..."

# Chapter Sixteen - THE STANDING STONES

As promised, Robin was off at first light, freshly armed from the vast store of weaponry that now belonged to no one but corpses. Arabella and *les enfants* had conferred longer into the night, determining that her plan, while leaving them on their own in spite of their promise to Arabella's grandparents, was likely the fastest way to get news to her mother.

"You just have t'swear you're not gonna get into anything dire while we're not around," said Edmund, "else no one of us will be able to go home when all of this is over."

The girls only laughed, and chaffed the boys for having no faith in their abilities to give as much in return as anyone might be inclined to give them in the way of trouble.

"...We'll come back t'this spot," said Kerissa distastefully, looking over her shoulder to where dead Scandians mouldered—and became food—in the darkness. "What about our guests?"

Evrard offered a solution.

"We can let them pile up their own people and the weaponry...give them a fiery send-off. That's what they do...and after that we can just let them go home?"

"With instructions t'tell whoever runs things there that they'd best not try running anything here," added Sebastian.

And so it was settled. The Scandians were put to their grisly work as Robin rode west; the girls had a quick breakfast of hard cheese, bread and tea, and then went gaily on their way, waving at the boys with 'Bella comfortably snugged up against Kerissa's bum-side as they ambled over the first low hill.

"Well...here we are again," she said.

"That Evrard sure is a cutie," said Arabella.

"Oh don't you start!" warned Kerissa. "Look what happened the last time."

Arabella reached round to make any further recrimination pointless. At mid-morning they stopped alongside a stream and lazed on the ground whilst the mare drank her fill and cropped at the still-summer-green grass beside it. Kerissa stretched her willowy length across her riding cloak; Arabella curled up in her arms.

"I hope Robin gets home safe," she said. "He's really sweet, but I made him promise to return my horse. It seemed like if I did that...made him promise...then it would be like for certain we'd all get through this....but did you hear? Boats that can go under the water! And we thought the twins were just having us on with all their talk of sea monsters."

"It's not really much fun anymore," murmured Kerissa glumly.

"I don't think it was ever fun, 'Rissa...it was just us bein' dopey...*the girls* goin' off on adventures...'xcept it turns out the adventures are more serious than the ones we read about in books."

Kerissa nodded drowsily. "So we gotta get goin,'" she said. "Chances are we don't have much your mom doesn't already know, but like you said, it would be a lot better if we made sure. And Trowbridge is a ways off yet..."

They were up and on their way again within minutes, this time 'Rissa behind Arabella. The west bank of the Findhorn lent itself more to rolling hills and pastureland than farms. They rode at an easy canter, not wanting to overwork the mare, making steady progress southward across broad meadows starting to go wheat-coloured with the end of summer, where sheep or cattle in the distance grazed on grass not quite gone to autumn. The morning sun sparked colour out of the stands of leaf-turning maple and oak that skirted the meadows; occasionally a small rill or brook crossed their path so they were never thirsty, but an hour past noon found them staggery and a bit woozy with sunshine and heat. Kerissa rode front again for an hour or so, then Arabella, alternating through the afternoon, as the sun sank down towards the hills and forests to the west. Arabella had dozed off, her arms around Kerissa's waist; suddenly she came fully awake with an ominous foreboding, her eyes darting nervously around them.

"'Rissa we should be getting close now," she said.

"I've been tryin' to edge us closer to the river," she replied.

"Me too," said Arabella, "so how come the last little while every time I look up I've got the sun in my eyes?"

Kerissa wobbled her head back and forth a few times.

"You're right. I never even noticed until you said just now."

"Head east, 'Rissa...over there towards that outcropping of rock sticking out of the hillside...and close your eyes for a minute..."

Arabella did the same, and when both girls opened their eyes again, the sun was filtering through the trees to the west, directly in front of them. They both said *Funny peculiar!* at the exact same moment.

'Rissa immediately added, "And not in a way that makes me feel warm and fuzzy inside. All of a sudden I got a big case o' the wiggins."

They tried the experiment three more times with the same result, each time ending up closer to the western edge of the meadow they had been crossing—trying to cross—for the last hour...until the ground dipped away through a stand of spruce to the left of them, down into a hollow with a round, almost flat bit of tableland rising up in the centre, crowned with a ring of huge menhirs of jagged black basalt that seemed to absorb the gathering shadows. Under a different set of circumstances it would have been a cause for wonderment, for neither of them had ever been aware of the existence of stone circles in their corner of the world, but it was the strange procession below them that gave them cause for further concern, and banished any sense of *Wow!* from their consciousness.

In single file and absolute silence, they watched dozens of men, women and children wind their way through a break in the hills to the east, all of them milling forward as they began the ascent to the stone circle. Arabella materialisd Stella's field glasses and began to tremble.

"'Rissa it looks like they're all asleep. They're walking with their eyes closed...it's like when me, and then my mom and dad went to see—"

"Azim Sharad." said Kerissa. She took the glasses from Arabella and trained them on the illusory figure that stood in the centre of the circle, atop what might, in an earlier time, have been an altar stone. "I can feel him, 'Bella...calling...drawing them in...and us along with..."

"Why aren't we down there with them?"

"My mom...remember...after the night I was so scared...she said she did ward-spells for all of us."

"But not our poor pony."

Kerissa nodded thoughtfully. "My mum said we'd be safe."

"And my mum and your mum both think he's the cause of all our troubles."

"We could end it right here."

"We could," whispered Arabella. "We could go charging down the hill with our bows and—"

"Get ourselves into something way deeper than we can manage."

"I know I know...but...what if we could do it, 'Rissa? What if...?"

Kerissa shrugged in resignation. "Why is it always the soup for us, 'Bella? It sure would be nice if we could avoid stuff like this."

Arabella smiled cautiously and slipped from the mare's back. Kerissa followed suit, following the blonde girl down the hillside after looping the reins of the horse over a low-hanging spruce bough. Halfway down the slope they stopped, strung their bows, and after one last look of encouragement to each other, nocked arrows and let them fly.

They flew unerringly, straight to their target...and then completely through it as though through empty space, the only visible result being that the nebulous shape that had moved and gestured in parody of a human being suddenly took on the form and substance of the misshapen musician that Arabella and her parents had seen in the City. The once impossibly beautiful face that turned in their direction was vile, its gaze as unerring as their arrows, and found them crouched on the hillside, baring its teeth, pointing towards them and shrilling strange meaningless sounds that seemed to enrage the sleepwalkers surrounding him. Even from a distance, the girls could see their closed eyes flutter open, and hear a collective sigh of outrage as they all turned from the circle and its perimeters to slowly toil their way up the hillside towards them.

"Always the soup, " murmured Kerissa bitterly..

"They don't even have any weapons!" wailed Arabella. "We can't just shoot them down."

"We don't even know if we *can* shoot them down, 'Bella. Who knows what that thing has done t'them."

They put aside their bows and drew their swords and daggers, standing back to back in the gathering gloom as the mindless horde crawled towards them, their eyes empty of anything but a nauseous light that seemed to ooze down their slack faces, at the same time focusing its sickening regard upon the two of them. The creature in the centre of the circle began to shriek at his minions, a ululation from the depths of despair and ruin.

Arabella began to cry. "'Rissa I'm sorry next time I have a dumb idea just tell me t'be quiet...please..."

At first they were able to beat off the foremost of their attackers with the flat of their blades, but as they were crowded round and round by more and more of them, both instinctively began to use the points, thrusting into arms and legs and trying desperately to fend them off without having to kill anyone. Kerissa fought quietly, muttering curses to herself; Arabella became savage and wept uncontrollably each time her sword drew blood.

Below them they could hear Azim Sharad chanting...making sounds that made them sick to their stomachs, railing and raging words that drove those in his thrall to actually throw themselves upon the sword-points of the two young women. Moments from being overwhelmed, Arabella heard Kerissa cry out in her own anger and defiance, turned in time to see her make one last, small defensive gesture with an upraised hand. In that instant two things happened.

The first was a rumble of dismay that ran through the ranks of the sleepwalkers that surrounded them, followed by what could have been an invisible wave of...*something*... that flung them violently backwards, away from the girls.

The second occurrence came in the form of a massive shadowy tide of small rusty-furred creatures that appeared on the rise behind them and then flowed downwards into the stumbling retreat of the sleepwalkers, leaping upward to nip and tear at unprotected flesh and clothing.

Drenched in perspiration, the girls fell to their knees and thence into each other's arms, exhausted, watching as the foxes flowed down the hillside. When they looked up, the thing in the centre of the circle was gone...and the ring of stones with it....

# Chapter Seventeen – THE DESOLATION OF TROWBRIDGE

" 'Bella are you okay?"

"I think so. How about you?"

"I think I'm okay too."

"'Rissa, what happened?"

"What happened is that we probably just got rescued by most of the foxes that live within a hundred miles of this place."

"No...I mean right *before* we got rescued. What'd you do?"

They were still on their knees on the hillside. Evening mercifully descended upon them, cloaking the corpses of those who had ended their lives on the point of their swords; twilight that turned the girls into disembodied voices, and most of the foxes that lived within a hundred miles of them a mass of furry little shadows that chirped and rustled around them, nosing curiously at their hands and faces.

"I didn't do anything 'Bella."

"Oh yes you did, honey! Right before...you put your hand up and all of *them* just seemed to bounce off of us."

"Well I don't know. I closed my my eyes. I didn't wanna see them once they got to us."

"You must've done something, 'Rissa Davies, because I could feel them breathing on me and then they were gone...falling down the hill...running away..."

"Did I say anything?"

"You didn't make a sound."

"I thought I heard myself say *Go away leave us alone!*"

"Nope. You just waved an invisible magic wand and made them run away. If I'd not been so scared I would've been really impressed. Did you learn that from your mom?"

"'Bella, my mom has never once really tried t'teach me anything like that."

"Well she did a good job of not tryin' 'cause it worked really well."

Kerissa hiccuped, a bit of the adrenalin-fueled confusion giving way to a sob of laughter. They found each other in the dark again, exchanging caresses in between reaching for the dozens of foxes—young and old—that came to nuzzle at them in celebration of their "victory".

"Are you up to going on, baby? We can't be far from the river now...and there should be enough light once the moon comes up..."

Kerissa moved her face up and down against Arabella's, felt one of the foxes tugging at her sleeve and saw two gleaming black button eyes winking at her through the gloom.

"She says we shouldn't go, 'Bella," she said. "She says it's a bad place now, that nobody's there anymore."

"Who says?"

"This one," said Kerissa, reaching down to pick up the vixen. "I don't know how it could be, but I think she's the one saved us on the moors."

"I don't know how *you* know she's saying anything at all, 'Rissa..."

That stopped the both of them, gave them pause to consider again what the cocoa-skinned girl had *not* learned from her mother. They struggled up onto their feet and retraced their steps up the hillside, followed by dozens of the vixen's *relatives*. She stayed tucked in Kerissa's arms, chuckling and squeaking contentedly, but with an underlying note of the warning she had passed on to her.

"Tell her we have t'go," said Arabella.

"'Bella how?"

"I dunno. You're the one doin' all the witchy stuff all of a sudden."

Kerissa *told* her, not making a sound, heard what passed for a foxy sigh of resignation and then a warble of what could have been acquiescence.

"She says she'll take us there," said Kerissa.

---

*There* became a problem. Once they were on horseback, the vixen and a small entourage of her friends and relatives took them eastward, but half a mile on and one last towering rise before them made it plain she had not been exaggerating. The top of the hillside was outlined against the sky, silhouetted by the lick of flames somewhere on the other side, that rose up into the night to twice its height, and turned the silence into a hiss and crackle of a town being eaten by the fires of Hell. At the top of the rise they stopped in disbelief and horror.

Below them lay a broad sweep of greensward angling down to the river, but the Findhorn itself was a mirror of disaster, waters that should have been dark and shot with silver starlight, the surge of foam over rocks below its surface, now beginning to actually steam with the intense heat of the conflagration consuming Trowbridge and the wooden trestle that spanned the river. The vixen made unhappy noises in Kerissa's arms; her family darted behind them, peering fearfully over the top of the hill. Arabella slipped to the ground and stood speechless, one hand reaching up to Kerissa's thigh as she tried to keep herself upright. When she spoke she had to shout in order to be heard above the roar of the flames on the other side of the river.

"'Rissa someday I'm gonna make him pay for this," she said quietly. "There's still people alive in the middle of that...and there's nothing we can do..."

Kerissa dropped one hand to her shoulder, wordlessly trying to console her. The vixen crept cautiously down from her embrace until Arabella felt her forepaws round her neck, reached upwards to cradle her as Kerissa had done. They watched in silence as the flames devoured the bridge supports and sent it crashing down into the flood. In the town, they could see dark figures lit up and darting like holiday rockets until they collapsed into the inferno. They thought to hear the screams of people being burned alive...charred to cinders...but knew it was only what they made of it all in their imaginations. The flames swallowed everything—sight and sound—and the stench of burning flesh rose up into the night...

※

They camped on the far side of the hill, surrounded by the foxes, though there was no rest to be found even in the brief moments when exhaustion rendered them the mercy of sleep.

For a moment, when they awoke in the desperate clutch of each other's arms, there was still vivid memory of what they had seen the night before. Together they scrambled back over the top of the hill, hoping it all had been some nightmare spawned by the nightmare they had encountered at the standing stones, but fingers of flame still licked among the ruins of the town, and in the dawnlight they could see more clearly the utter destruction that had been wrought there.

Once again, Stella's field glasses brought them closer inspection, but it was clear to Kerissa that however the holocaust had come to pass, it had destroyed everything, down even to the rail lines at the river's edge that seemed to have convulsed themselves into a tangle of smouldering ties and twisted steel. She found herself overwhelmed by it, sucked into the heart of it, unable to tear herself away from the horror.

"Let me look, 'Rissa." said Arabella.

Kerissa shook head, wrenched the glasses from her eyes and tucked them away in her pack before she turned to Arabella.

"Baby you don't wanna do that...please don't look..."

"We need t'find a way across the river...send word...."

"We can't, 'Bella, there's nothing left. Nothing. Some of them are lying on the riverbank. They tried to escape to the water and *they killed each other* along the way."

"*Let me see.*"

"No..."

"'Rissa let me see!"

The vixen, of all the foxes, had stayed the night with them, but now drew away from the agonised note in Arabella's voice. The girl flew at Kerissa, reaching for the field glasses in her pack, tears streaming down her face.

"Let me see..." she said one last time...pleading...barely able to stay on her feet.

Kerissa shook her head again, threw her arms around Arabella so she would not fall, and then fell to sobbing with her, the pair of them like children abandoned on the edge of Purgatory.

"'Bella you can't fix everything..."

The blonde girl looked wild-eyed, unseeing, suddenly mad with grief and rage. Kerissa clung to her, struggled with her, pleading:

"'Bella stop...please 'Bella...stop..."

Arabella stopped. She looked at Kerissa as if awakening from a dream that had come apart at the seams, and then just wept.

"I don't know why you love me," she whispered. "I don't know how I get to deserve you...or anyone..."

Kerissa fed her...old cheese and bread that would have been a bit more edible a day earlier...but after a while the wild look in Arabella's eyes went away and Kerissa just rocked her until she was come back from whatever horrible place she had been.

"The little girl-fox is taking word to your mum and mine," she said. "Everything Robin told us...and this.... I told her she should look for Hasan and all the news would go where it needed t'go..."

Arabella nodded, quiet now, but still with a dazed look in her eyes that frightened Kerissa more than anything they'd been through in the last twenty-four hours.

"Whenever you're ready, 'Bella," she said. "We should get back t'the boys as soon as we can to let them know, too."

Again Arabella nodded.

"We have t'go soon," she said. "The wires are down...and now there's no trains can come and go. It's like we got cut in half..."

There was a querulous note in her words, as if she, who always had been ready to face any kind of emergency or unlooked-for happenstance, now trusted...needed...Kerissa to be the one to make decisions for them.

"You just say when you're ready, baby, and we'll be on our way..."

# Chapter Eighteen – EN PASSANT

De Montenay fled the Dales in a frenzy, knowing full well that having fled, with his men and the entire village to witness his flight before Camille Ardrey's unwavering defiance, and his family's desertion, had cost him dearly in their eyes; that somehow all his plans, that once he had held to be careful and prudent and a foolproof path to the fulfillment of his ambition, had come apart in a matter of days; that his years of overlordship in the Dales had come to an end. In his mind he no longer had anything left to lose; when his retribution upon the folk of Glen Carrick took so untoward a turn, it only left him further enraged, and determined to bring ruin upon anything and anyone he encountered in the days before him.

Once again he led his men to the Moorgate, determined now to make his way to the western ocean, there to join with his Antillian allies to wreak what havoc could be wrought with the full weight of a true force of arms behind him. He lashed his small body of followers across the moors in two days, ignoring their whispers and sniggers around the campfire that one night, and then led them across the Findhorn into the Westvales, with the better part of a week of travel to reach Bedford. He looked forward to encountering crofters and settlements that could be ravaged at his pleasure.

---

Frederick Wyndham winced as his horse leapt a streamlet flowing down from the wall of mountains before him. One rear hoof failed to fully clear the rill, and he heard a faint crackle as the skim of ice on its surface splintered. He wrapped his cloak more tightly around him, dropped one hand to his right thigh were a Scandian arrow had caused him more discomfort than actual harm, and swore if the Wyndhams survived this conflict, he would give serious thought to moving himself and Alexandra south to the city, where he could depend upon Nicholas and Brandywine to provide some peace and quiet.

Before him lay a broad expanse of upland meadow, now grown dull and brown with the onset of much colder weather than had been expected so early in the season. Above him rose the northern mountains, their crowns already capped with snow, with pennons of ice in the chill winds that whipped round their summits, and whistled down from the heights to presage the onset of an early winter that could not have been more welcome. He shivered once in the cold, shook crystals of ice from his head of greying hair, and looked for a large tent in the middle of the encampment staged a mile from the outlet of one of the mountain passes from the north. Both Aaron and Finn came to help him dismount, taking care not to jostle his wounded leg.

"What news, sir?" asked Aaron. All that could be seen of him was a bearded face gone pale with cold, and two blue eyes the colour of winter sky above a tightly-wrapped scarf.

Wyndham found his footing, welcomed Finn's shoulder to lean on as they traversed the small expanse of ground leading up to the tent.

"I think we're good," he said, watching his breath coil and smoke in the air around him. "I've seen Chaunce and Raymond and it looks like we've driven them all back into the lower reaches of the mountains. Now it's simply a matter of which way they'll move before snowfall—back from where they came from, or to us, and a welcome of steel and shaft from our ten thousand. They can't come at us with any advantage now..."

"Or...they could simply stay where they are and freeze t'death making up their minds," offered Aaron with bitter smile.

Wyndham answered it and nodded. "*That* would not be unwelcome, my friend," he said. "But if it ends up we're needed in the southlands, still we cannot leave until we're certain of the outcome here."

"Then for now we've just t'keep our fires burning," said Finn.

"And the wine warmed up a bit," added Wyndham. "Speaking of..."

---

"...I hate it," said Brandy. "I hate not having her close by...not hearing her voice...not knowing what she's doing or if she's okay."

She was curled up on a settee beside his harpsichord, having wandered into the music room while Nicholas played with a riff and trill of notes he felt would make a lovely central theme for a concerto. She'd waited until he left off playing, smiling when he looked up at her, but waiting nevertheless. Windy saw the care and unrest beneath her smile, and came to sit beside her.

"She's got 'Rissa and the boys t'look after her, Branny," he said. "They'd die before letting anything bad happen to her."

Brandywine folded herself up in his arms, staring down at her hands clasped between her knees.

"I know...and there's some things happen whether you want them to or not," she said miserably. "I miss her, Windy...I miss her so much...she's still my little girl and there're times when all the years seem t'have gone by so fast and now she's almost all grown up and it's almost like losing her. I can't bear that. I never dreamed I could ever have someone like you t'love me...or we could make someone so special...

"I'm tired, Windy...so tired... Why couldn't they all just have left us alone...?"

---

Zoraya stared sightlessly into the palms of her hands, seeing only things that were not really there, feeling her heart and mind reaching out to her daughter and her daughter's beloved, Diana and Tom's boys, the young man Evrard. She felt the same misery as a blonde-haired girl living in St John's Mews, but, like her, could only wait upon Time to show her the outcome of her efforts and small magicks to keep them all safe. She clenched her hands into fists, dispelling the visions, looked up and found Gareth standing silently in the door of their bedroom, knowing well enough not to interrupt here when she gave herself up to the Sight.

"They're all safe for now," she said softly, "but something is not right with 'Bella. I can feel it...she is so terrified of what she thinks she has become. 'Rissa is scared too. They have seen things too terrible to be borne lightly, and done things that haunt them, though they know they had no choice..."

Gareth sat beside her on their bed, reached for her hands.

"When I first dreamt of you," he said, "I couldn't imagine where the dreams had come from, or why they would have come to me at all. And then came your sending...this thing of living stone that held you and Hasan waiting for me t'find you. Zori it never once occurred t'me to wonder *why*... it was just the way it was, and I felt myself led around in the dream until one morning I woke up and saw you for the first time in the image I had found in the stone, and then found you for real standing outside my door while the statue I had made of you turned to dust."

He put his hands in the crown of curls that wreathed her head, leant forward to kiss her closed eyes.

"The world turns," he said. "We can only turn with it."

Zoraya looked up at him, now with tears flooding down from the wonder of her golden eyes.

"My world is different from yours, my prince," she said. "I am just a visitor here, someone who should have died long ago..."

"...You can go faster, 'Rissa."

"This is good."

"At the rate we're going it will take us a week, and then we have t'find the boys again."

"It's still good, baby. You just keep on hanging on t'me and we'll get things sorted out when we do."

The truth was that Kerissa was every bit as exhausted from worrying about Arabella as Arabella was herself, from dealing with whatever it was that had made her so miserable. The first flush of their return journey to the edge of the Carillon moors had languished in a malaise neither of them could explain or even recognise. Kerissa simply let the mare wend its way in her own time, paying just enough attention to keep her nose pointed in the right direction. From her place behind her, Arabella clung to her, arms clutched round her waist as if hanging on for dear life. Kerissa didn't need to see her face to know that her beloved was suffering.

In mid-afternoon they stopped beside a stream to let the mare drink her fill while they tucked into the dwindling supply of food and drink they had taken with for their mission south. Arabella seemed locked in a prison of her own device, staring into nothingness and sometimes needing to be spoken to two or three times before she responded. Kerissa was half-crazed with concern, and frustration that her every attempt to draw 'Bella from her shell of misery met only with silence or tired wags of her beautiful head. They went on...slowly...the sun throwing evening crimson across their path, darkening as it sank lower in the sky.

"We'll stop soon, honey," said Kerissa.

"Okay," said Arabella listlessly.

"Honey what's wrong?"

For Kerissa the silence went on interminably, and she thought to stop them where they stood, though it were out in the middle of a broad open field. Finally she felt Arabella stir.

"I don't know, 'Rissa," she said, in a voice that Kerissa remembered from when they were children together. "I'm really tired and I feel like I'm not who I'm supposed t'be... that I made a wrong turn and now I'm so lost I don't know where t'go..."

"Baby it's been dreadful for you...I know it—"

"But why 'Rissa? Why do I get so crazy angry? And then when I do it's almost like I *want* t'be this bloodthirsty creature...and kill everything that can hurt you...or all the people I love..."

Her arms tightened around Kerissa's waist, and she could feel the blonde girl shuddering against her, head down between her shoulder blades, sobbing uncontrollably.

"I feel different, 'Rissa, like I'm not me anymore."

She turned and took Arabella from the waist, set her side-saddle before her and let her curl up in front of her.

"We'll find the boys and give them our news, baby...and then I'm gonna take you home..."

# Chapter Nineteen – TIMELY MET & SADLY PARTED

They sat their horses well off from the towering flames of the funeral pyre, moving constantly around an invisible perimeter whenever the heat of the blaze brought a shift in the wind and the stench of Scandians burning their way to back to the heavenly halls of fallen heroes, full-breasted women and their childishly vengeful deities.

After waiting just long enough to ensure their efforts brought about the desired results for their departed comrades, the two who had surrendered now could be seen trudging their way northward, well-provisioned but without weapons, and now perhaps a month from any chance of encountering any more of their countrymen. What the boys had been about had seen to that, scouring the moors before Chance, two headstrong young women, and a lone fugitive had led them down into the Westvales.

"What now?" asked Evrard. "Those two won't be causing us any more trouble."

Edmund and Sebastian looked to each other for inspiration, but an obvious course seemed not to thrill either of them. More of the same seemed to be the order of the day—more riding and tramping and nights growing longer and longer under a chill sky deepening into winter as they made their way back to the Wyndham steadings in Élysée. Edmund was the first to give voice to what the other two were thinking.

"Once the girls are back we should go west," he said. "If what Adair had to say was at all accurate, the towns and villages on the west coast will be be hard-pressed soon enough. If Grandfather's people aren't inclined to follow us then we three should go on anyway"

Both Sebastian and Evrard considered this briefly, and found themselves of like mind. It was agreed then that they would go due south and try to collect Kerissa and Arabella as quickly as possible, thereafter to turn westward and do what they might in delivering the coastal towns and villages from the invaders. When this plan was presented to the Wyndham crofters, to a man they agreed to go wherever the situation would take them. In twilight they turned away from the pyre, the boys determining they would ride through the night until they came upon their cousins.

---

Arabella seemed to grow stronger as they travelled, some of her despair slipping away so that she and Kerissa talked quietly of the days to come. As they retraced their path inland along the west bank of the Findhorn, suddenly the season caught them up in the flutter of leaves across their way, gusts of wind that stripped them from the trees as if autumn had arrived overnight and now must needs rush its way towards winter. Beeches gone a dull green fluttered and became troves of silver. Overhead they saw arrows of geese winging southward; whenever the meadow tracks came near to stands of trees or the margins of forest-growth, they heard the rustling of small creatures, busy with their preparations for the coming snow. The sky grew pale, in the span of just hours fading from deep blue to a colour that seemed to presage the onset of cold weather. Arabella shivered against 'Rissa's back, grew silent again, her head turned to it's own burrowing into her warmth.

"When we get home we'll do just like the critters, 'Bella. We'll get all naked and climb into bed with food for a week...and blankets all over and a big fire and—"

"And the world will still come knocking, 'Rissa. Someday maybe it will be like that, but not soon...not right away. You know it and I know it too."

"Well then maybe for as long as it takes the world t'find us again?" offered Kerissa, once again hearing the note of despair in her voice.

"That would be nice. I wish things could be the way they were, but I guess that's just something Jamie and Stella would believe in because they're kids and don't know any better."

Kerissa couldn't find anything else to say, only dreaded that there would be so many miles to be travelled before she could bring even a temporary respite to her girl.

"We'll find the boys and then I'll take you home, baby," she said again, and then continued to say it to herself, over and over, like a conjuration she could forge into existence from the raw materials of her desperate concern.

---

They spread themselves out in groups of three across the hills, never more than a half mile from any other trice of them, each holding aloft a burning torch to serve as a beacon to themselves and the girls who were, hopefully, already riding north to meet them. Edmund and Sebastian rode with Evrard, ever mindful of the task Annie Branny had set to them, and finding in him some things they had not consciously noted before.

"This is all so strange," he said, struggling to stay awake in the saddle.

They had been moving slowly southward for hours; midnight had found them following an *halloo* from one of the Élysée crofters, who appeared to be able to track anything at any hour, day or night. An hour earlier he had discovered pony tracks that, by their depth, could only have belonged to a larger member of their troop, or perhaps two young women astride one horse.

"How's that?" asked Edmund, responding to sound of confusion in Evrard's voice.

"It's just that I've never felt like I belonged anywhere," said the younger son of Renard de Montenay. "Certainly not in the manor house at Glen Carrick...but now here I am with the two of you, having betrayed my family, and I've never felt so much at peace with anything I've ever done...that I've finally found out where I *do* belong."

His face in torchlight was a study in conflict—the child of a bitter ancient tradition at odds with the lure and promise of better days to come.

"Evrard, you've not betrayed your family," said Sebastian. "Not the ones that matter, anyhow. By now, *they're* all likely safe as houses, in the City with Annie Branny and *our* family, which is where *you* should have been all along."

"Somehow I have t'find a way to make up for all the damage done. My father alone—"

"It's not your problem," said Edmund. "You're not responsible for what he's done in the past, Evrard, or for what he's doing now. That's on *his* head, not yours."

"I know that in *my* head, but it doesn't really change anything in my heart. When Sevrain and I were children together we used t'play at being kings and princes because it was all we ever heard about from our father—the Amaranth Throne belonged to us as much as it ever belonged to the de Montignys. But we were happy at it. There wasn't the anger or the sense of having been wrongfully deprived of anything...

"And now...when I think of how much hurt my family has caused...and how much hurt has yet to be measured out in the days to come..."

He shook his head ruefully. Sebastian rode closer to him, reached to take his hand. There was a shout from one of their own to the east...

---

"'Bella are you awake?"

Kerissa felt Arabella's head move up and down against her shoulder blades.

"I can't sleep, 'Rissa. Every time I close my eyes...it's horrible..."

"I think I fell asleep, baby I'm sorry. We should have stopped hours ago. I have no idea where we are..."

She felt 'Bella's arms tighten around her waist and heard her crying softly.

"Honey you should have something to eat, okay...like right now..."

She lightly reined their horse to a standstill, turned so she and Arabella could slip to the ground together, reaching into her pack for the embroidered coverlet her mother had named *Equatoria,* wrapping Arabella in its folds as she searched for the last of their bread and cheese. The mare turned her head a moment to see what betid, then fell to cropping night grass as Kerissa lowered 'Bella to the ground, broke off small morsels of the bread and cheese that she lifted to the girl's mouth. Arabella chewed each mouthful slowly, barely awake now, her face drawn and, in the shadows of starlight, showing ancient... scarcely alive.

"'Bella please don't give up. I don't know what I would do without you."

Kerissa stroked her face, continued to give her small bites of food, and water from a wineskin at their saddle-bow. At length she laid the girl down with their packs as a pillow for her head, running her fingers through the honey-gold hair, untangling knots and twists long ignored.

"We'll just stay here for the rest of the night...but I gotta pee, honey. Will you be okay for a minute or two I promise I'll be right back..."

'Bella nodded where she lay, no longer half awake so much as mostly asleep. Kerissa moved off a dozen paces or so and shimmied her riding skirts down around her knees as she bent them to go about her business. She wiggled once when she was done, shrugged it off as the best she could manage under the circumstances. When she sank down again beside Arabella she could see starlight reflected in her green cat's-eyes, wide open now, staring up into the spatter of silver stars in a black velvet night sky.

"Where did the stones come from, 'Rissa? And how did they disappear like that? And how can anyone be so cruel, to set those poor people on us like that when they have nothing t'do with any of this...or turn them against each other...burn down their entire lives...?"

Kerissa said she didn't know, only set herself to stroking Arabella's hair and face until she drifted off to sleep. Having nodded off while they were on horseback, she felt herself far from that luxury of unconsciousness, nor would she have even considered it in any case, they being out in the middle of nowhere, with nothing to shelter them from whatever might come their way. She unsaddled the mare, thrust her duelling sword into the ground as a picket-post. When she looked up, she saw flares of light spaced across the hills that rose up around the northern perimeter of the meadow where they had stopped, all now converging upon them. She had never truly felt her heart sink before, realised that even in starlight they must be plainly visible to whomever had chanced upon them, a deeper shadow in the middle of the sprawling meadow. Briefly she debated with herself whether or not to wake Arabella; she sighed, reached to string her bow and then to stand all their arrows in the turf beside her.

"I love you, 'Bella," she whispered. "No matter what happens I won't let them take you..."

She watched them draw closer, reached for an arrow and held it ready, apologising to their mare, knowing that the first arrows from those approaching would take her down. She felt herself growing numb in self-defense, the surety that she and Arabella would not survive this encounter and it fell to her only that she take as many of the riders as possible with them. She was a breath away from loosing her first arrow at one of them when she heard her name being called...and 'Bella's...

She dropped her bow and stood in tears, shouting back ...

Three by three the Élysée crofters came to her, many of them knowing her well from the visits that all *les enfants des Boulevardiers* had made to the Wyndham farms over the years. They took her hand, asked of what service she was needful, but grew quiet as she cautioned them to silence, nodding towards Arabella sleeping. They stood away, so that when her cousins and Evrard arrived she was knelt beside her, and the mare, now made nervous before armed and mounted men, stamping before them. Wordless she rose to greet them, first Sebastian and then Edmund, but for Evrard, who had hung back from them, she strode forward and kissed him as she had the others.

"We're all right now," she told them, "but 'Bella's not so good as she might be. She needs to eat little meals all the time, but it's not been like that...we've forgotten...and too many horrible things have happened..."

As the rest of their troop arrived, the boys ringed them round for the night, posting sentries and lighting cookfires long overdue. They went to see 'Bella, but she did not stir, so at length all came to sit beside their central fire, where

Kerissa gave them news and somewhat of the history of all that had befallen the two of them

"...I don't know if my mom ever said anything of *Chakidze* to any of you, but you know the story of how she came to be with us in the City. This creature, whether or not he is the same one, or some hellish reincarnate of the one who imprisoned her, now is known to us as Azim Sharad, and..."

She told them of their encounter at the standing stones...of those who threw themselves mindlessly upon their swords, how the vixen had brought them to the desolation of Trowbridge, and how Arabella had seemed in the aftermath of all to lose heart, and then to damning herself for having survived at the cost of so many innocent lives.

"...I have t'take her home. I'm scared for her," she said, "but we needed to let you know that Trowbridge is gone...destroyed.... The wires are down and the rail line is broken... nothing is left..."

Edmund's face grew pale even in the firelight.

"We've had no word from the north," he said. "Winter is much closer this year than any before and I think Gramps and the uncles will know how best to make that work to our advantage with Scandians, but we've decided to go west to the coast, to wait for whatever comes of the Antillians."

She told them how the she-fox had gone her way south at once to find Hasan, and bear all they knew to her mother and Annie Branny, but...

"We can't go with you," she said. "I know 'Bella would choose otherwise—"

Evrard said, "No...you're right, Kerissa. You say she needs t'go home and you know her better than any of us. The two of you have been through enough, done more than your share. We'll look after the rest of it."

They all looked to him then, and remarked silently to themselves that there was in his voice something that had not been there before. Evrard grew warmer than the glow from the fire on his face. Sebastian, who of the two brothers knew him somewhat better than Edmund, smiled to himself.

"Go in the morning then, 'Rissa," he said softly. "We're here now t'keep you both safe through the night, but this time if we let you go you have t'keep a better promise t'stay out of trouble."

He grinned and even Kerissa could be seen to join him, Edmund and Evrard as well, relief and determination writ largely upon their faces. She leaned sideways about the fire and punched Sebastian in the shoulder hard enough to rock him sideways.

"That's because I love you," she said. "All of you. And also because I'm tired again, and 'Bella needs company under her blanket."

They watched her go from the fire, three pairs of eyes that looked at her through veils of unquestioning loyalty and devotion.

Very quietly Evrard said, "I don't know how you two manage t'deal with them the way you do."

Edmund shrugged and said, "They're our sisters...and even if we wish it were more than that for either of us, still they'd only be what they would choose t'be for themselves, and we to love them for it..."

"Losing them would be like the end of the world," said Sebastian with finality. "It doesn't have much more t'do with anything but that..."

Evrard watched Kerissa become lost in the dark beyond the glow of their fire...

---

...And in early morning the next day wistfully watched her and Arabella as they crested the rolling hills to the south of their camp, newly provisioned, leaving Kerissa's mare behind in favour of a heavier draft horse to carry them both. Sebastian spurred his own mount alongside him.

"After a while you get over the part where you just want them," he said. "You begin to realise that what they've got is more than anything you could ever offer...and that they're a gift to us, the two of *them* together infinitely better than what any one of us might find if we ended up in bed with either of them.

"You should be grateful you didn't grow up with us. When we were small we always insisted on sleeping together. That went on just long enough for me and Edmund t'wish it had gone on a lot longer."

Evrard only shook his head, staring at the hilltop that had come between them.

"I'm grateful I *didn't* grow up with them," he said. "Not in the Dales, anyway. Neither of them would have escaped my father...or Sevrain, once he was older..."

"It doesn't matter now," said Sebastian. " You're one of us, Evrard. When you finally bring someone home the girls will be just as ferocious in their love for her...or him...as they are in their own for each other."

"Even so..." said Evrard.

"Even so," agreed Sebastian, with a rueful smile. "Edmund and I would lying if we pretended every now and again they didn't show up in our dreams..."

# Chapter Twenty – IN THE CITY

Brandywine and Zoraya sat in a corner of the Silver Rose, nursing mugs of mulled wine against the chilly wind that came through the doors whenever someone else wandered in with the same thought.

"... Hasan has a new friend from the north," said Zoraya. "He is happy, yet the news she brought was very good and very bad all at once."

Brandy looked frightened. Zoraya reached for her hand.

"The girls are coming home, Brandywine, on horse from just west of Trowbridge, so they should be here in a few days. The boys have decided they will go west to meet whatever the Antillians have in store for us. For now, that is the very good. The very bad is that the girls encountered Chakidze, who we know now as Azim Sharad, and managed to divert his *interest*, but at a cost that has badly unsettled Arabella. Trowbridge is gone, the rail line and wires destroyed along with the town and, it would seem, all who dwelt there. He has become more and more indiscriminate, mad for his vengeance upon me, and has learned to channel and augment his power through standing stones that he conjures for the purpose..."

"But they're all right...'Bella and 'Rissa and the boys?"

"I think so," said Zoraya. "'Rissa made certain to convey they are all unharmed, but shaken badly. 'Bella especially. That is why she's bringing her home, to give her some rest from her own nature...

"Do you remember when they were children...how sometimes Edmund and Sebastian would tease Kerissa...make fun of her for one thing or another...and how 'Bella would become furious with them, so much so that she would fly at them..."

"...And threaten t'do dreadful things t'them if they didn't stop."

Zoraya nodded.

"Your girl cannot bear to see innocent creatures being hurt. Trowbridge was the end of a nightmare for her. The she-fox was there with them and said what she saw was too terrible for even her own kind to speak of, they who have no great love for us who hunt them..."

Brandywine cupped her mug in both hands as she dipped her head to drink, hiding behind the fall of her hair about her face.

"Zori I don't know how much more I can go. 'Bella is the same as me. I promised Marie, but sometimes it's so hard t'do stuff I don't really know how t'do. Windy never ever complains, but all of a sudden sometimes I miss him so much even when we're alone together...sometimes there's just too much..."

Zoraya cwched her chair around to where they could sit beside each other, took her friend's hands in her own.

"Let me do more then," she said. "I know what all of this means. With the rail line broken, when the Antillians come for us we will have little or no help from the north. The she-fox also brought news of one who was in Snowdon to see their fleet come upon us...great steel-bound ships with guns far greater than anything we have, some that can travel beneath the surface of the water...all likely now on their way south to come at us here..."

Brandywine raised her head, startled, suddenly like some small creature faced with an unimaginable...unavoidable...threat to its life.

"I can help you," whispered Zoraya. "For all this time...twenty years...twenty years of happiness I've never known before...all of it has been a mystery to me how or why your Gareth became the one to bring me here...but now it becomes clear. Nothing comes without its price, and I have been blessed with so much love...yet it may well be that I am the one who has brought all of this horror down upon us...and even if that is not so, still, for all the love you and your loved ones have given to me, it is for me then to be the one to drive it away if I can. Listen to me, Brandywine...trust me please...I bear thee nothing but my infinite gratitude...this is what we must do..."

---

While Alain and Andrew were conferring with Brandywine in the parlour, Stella stole a sliver of glazed carrot from Jamie's dinner plate, waited for his usual explosion of *Hey stay away from my food!*, but found him wanting in any sense of outrage. She stole another slice, and received nothing for her trouble.

"Jamie?" she said. "What's goin' on with you...?"

"Nothin'," he replied, pushing his fork around his dinner plate, and being so unlike his usual self that in despite of her fleeting moment of guilt for taking advantage of such an opportunity to chaff her twin, she stole two more slivers and looked smug in the bargain. Jamie shoved the better portion of his dinner in her direction.

"You can have all of it if you want, Stella," he said. "I'm not hungry."

This was unheard of. Jamie was never not hungry. She could hear him being silently huffy, but it was so much a breach of protocol between them that she slid off her chair and found herself hugging her brother...which in the past had been yet another something that should never have been allowed. Jamie was not happy.

"They've been gone forever," was all he would say. "Everything is bad."

Stella knew exactly what he was talking about.

---

Gareth whacked stone splinters out of what should have been the beginnings of a flowered vine twined about the leg of a forest dryad and stood back with a sense of immense but cranky accomplishment. Hasan perched above him on the remains of a rendered-superfluous floor joist and looked curious.

"Sure," said Gareth. "Easy for you, all furry and mysterious, and now you've got yourself this new honey from the northlands and there's all sorts of whatever flying about and what the devil do I know? Nothing, it seems. Zori's off making magick out of the ordinary. My daughter is haring about who knows where doing who knows what with her girlfriend, and all the while there's this bunch of barbarians invading our country and here I am knocking bits of stone around like it was important."

Hasan tried to look sympathetic, but foxy faces being what they were, mostly it just seemed like he was looking down upon the sculptor with what seemed to be a genial but decidedly condescending smile. Gareth pitched his mallet and chisel on a workbench.

"Fine," he said. "Be that way. See if it makes any difference. I can't help it if my magick was a one-time-only deal...see if I care."

He stamped off to find something to drink, preferably with overwhelming alcoholic properties. Hasan ceased sprawling on the floor-joist end, gathered up his hindquarters beneath him and leapt down to the workbench. Gareth's head came round as if he'd been slapped.

"What'd you say?" he asked.

Hasan's foxy smile became a grin. Gareth sat down on the floor...

<hr />

Thomas flung his pen across the length of the studio, spattering ink along the way until it smacked into the far wall, never to spatter ink anywhere ever again. Diana looked up from her own writing table, setting aside notes for a choreography and lesson plans for the day when the world wandered back to normal again and she could start up her dance classes with some hope of properly finishing them up in a semester.

"What?!?!?" she said.

"I'm sick of this," he replied. "I'm sick of making up stories when our world is collapsing around us."

"It's not gone *quite* that far..."

"Well it feels that way. I'm sitting here getting fat writing fairy tales while the kids are dodging arrows and who knows what else."

"Tommy I love you dearly but you're being an idiot."

"Oh...and how is that?"

Diana uncoiled herself from her chair and slunk her way down to Thomas' end of the studio, every now and again sneaking a glance at the bank of mirrors that lined the long wall behind a barre and a pile of mats she kept for teaching her preferred students the best way to take a tumble without breaking bones. It was an old habit born out of vanity and insecurity, to make certain she was still everything she demanded of the young men and women who came to the school.

"Edmund and Sebastian and the girls have actually taken some training in how t'deal with whatever they're dealing with now. You, on the other hand, can perfectly recount a tale of cataclysmic conflict and murderous this that and the other, but we both know you only *write* a good game; that you don't have a murderous or cataclysmic bone in your body...and if maybe once upon a time that was nor the case, it's different now."

"And the children are murderous and cataclysmic?"

"No...that's not what I said."

"Then what?"

"They mostly understand their limitations. You would go rushing into the shit and then they'd have t'rescue you."

She sat down in his lap and put her arms around his neck, pushing her face at his face until her grin met his lips and became something else. He resisted only just long enough to realise that resisting was counter-productive and definitely not as much fun as surrendering. Eventually they came up for air.

"Well it's just lovely you think so well of me," he said.

"You're being an idiot again."

"I'm gonna talk to Windy today. Maybe we can put our heads together and find a way to get useful."

"Go see Windy," she said, doing her best to sound supportive. "I love you, Tommy, forever and ever, but sometimes any one of Grim's millions of kittens has more sense than you."

---

"...Does she ever look tired," said Alain as he and Andrew watched Brandy wander off. They'd walked her out into the street, trying to be outwardly cheerful for her sake, not wishing to add to her troubled thoughts by worrying her with their concern for her. Andrew slung his arm across Alain's shoulders as they stood in the doorway.

"Sometimes I wonder how she's gone on this long," he said. "We've all done as much as we could to lighten the load, but I guess we've never been that much help in actually *doing* things for her. Moral support and mostly uninformed advice only go so far..."

Alain burrowed into his embrace. "What're we gonna do with the twins, Andy? Jamie's really upset that the girls are gone, and the best thing we might have done was send them up to Élysée until all of this was over—"

"Except that things might get to be just as bad up there as they seem to be going here. And with the rail line only good to barely past halfway, it wouldn't be easy..."

Alain c ould only agree. "It's better if they stay with us...and since she's here anyway, I know Alexandra won't mind looking after them while we're looking after the stuff Brandy wants done."

"Well...tomorrow we can get started," said Andrew.

"Andy, I can manage on my own."

"Don't be silly. We'll drop the kids off with Grams in the morning and then I am most definitely coming to work with you. I can write the epic poem of our deliverance from the Antillians once we've been delivered. Meanwhile, we need to figure out where we can replace your stock that comes from north of Trowbridge, and cut back on all the fancy stuff that normally goes t'the palace, start sending them a stockpile of basic food and supplies instead..."

"And spend the rest of this day and night with the twins," said Alain quietly. "Jamie's the one who's showing it, but Stella's no less unhappy about not having the girls around... and they know a lot more than what they let on. I think they're really scared, even if they don't know exactly why."

They stood a few minutes more in the gathering twilight, kissed each other long and hard for luck, and went inside.

"...Good morning, Nicky," said Alexandra Wyndham. "Can I make you something for breakfast?"

A small fire crackled peacefully on the kitchen hearth. She stood at the rear door that opened into the small enclosed garden behind the carriage house, watching the rain come down on a grey dismal day. A brief visit to return her grand-daughters to their rightful homes had become an extended stay; she wore one of Brandy's fleecy housecoats, her hair loosely flung about her shoulders and down her back, showing firelight colours in the pale platinum and grey.

"I'll just have some coffee, Mum," he said, and poured himself a mug before he came to stand beside her. She leaned into him, shivered herself up against him even though it was more than warm enough in the kitchen.

"Brandy's still in bed?"

Nicholas nodded. "It was a long one for her yesterday, and today's not like t'be any better. Are you okay?"

"Mostly," she said. "I'm worried about your brothers and Freddie, and I hate not having him close by at night. It's worse knowing there's not going to be much news at all for a while."

"Dad's tough, and he doesn't ever tell you tales so that arrow was just painful is all, just like he said. And as for my brothers...well... Raymond, Chaunce and William are pretty much impervious to anything but red ink in their ledgers, so you can stop worrying."

"Oh you're dreadful! That's not the only thing they think about. They've got families now too..."

"I was just teasin', Mum," he said. "They're all right...I mean, they're out there freezin' their butts off to defend the realm. I don't fault them for anything, and I shouldn't be talking about them in any case. I'm not doing much of anything useful these days."

"Nicky you're keeping Brandy from being crushed under the weight of her promise to Caroline de Montigny."

They sipped coffee for a few minutes, watching the rain strip the trees of their leaves, listening to it rattle against the windows panes.

"'Rissa's bringing 'Bella home," he said at length.

"I overheard Brandy tell you last night."

He nodded. "From the sound of it she's been through a bit more than she can deal with comfortably. I keep getting this feeling that I never should have let her and 'Rissa go with the boys; that *I* should've been the one gone off with them."

Alexandra laughed softly. "And done what, Nicky? Fought off the Scandians or whomever with a sparkling arpeggio...or a blistering crescendo? Smack them over the head with a violin? Baby you grew up well out of the way of such things. Your father and I wouldn't have wanted it any other way."

Nicholas shook his head and sighed.

"Stop, Nicky. Until this is over we've all got t'do the best we can with whatever talents we have...but your part is *not* running off to play with sharp deadly toys you've never played with before."

"It's a small comfort, Mum," he said. "Branny sat down with Zoraya yesterday and they've hatched *something* that needs most everyone living round the harbour to be moved inland, and the levees built up along the river from Linden down into the bay. Once she's up and about, I'll see where she wants of me, but I need t'do something...at least until 'Rissa and 'Bella get home..."

---

She opened her eyes and closed them again quickly, reached for Windy and realised he'd already gotten up for the day. She could hear him down the hall in the music room, softly at the piano, an old sonata he'd written the day after Arabella was born. In between the notes there were whispered voices—Windy and his mum—and to either side of her the spatter of rain on the windows, leaves slapping once before sogginess overwhelmed them.

She drew a deep breath and let it out slowly, reluctant to be awake enough to consciously recognise all the things needed to be done, even on a grey day in late Windfall. She huddled down under her blankets and wished for the times when her daughter and Kerissa would come bounding into the room at daybreak, bouncing all over the bed, up and down over body parts desperately in need of a visit to the bathroom before anything else...belling with laughter...two beautiful little faces belonging to two beautiful little girls...

*"G'morning g'morning are you guys awake...?!?!?"*
*"Well we are now..."*

The echo of the laughter faded away, back again into her *today*...unavoidable...the rain slashing, rattling the windows when the wind would drive it against the glass. There was a soft knock on the door, and Alexandra bumped her way into the bedroom with a tray of tea and toast and orange marmalade she could smell and taste at twenty paces.

"Hi g'morning, sweetheart, are you awake...?" she asked with a smile.

Brandy burst into tears...

# Chapter Twenty-One – FATHER & SON

One day into the Westvales they sacked a small village and burned it to the ground. Whether or not anyone escaped from the conflagration concerned Renard de Montenay not at all. He watched the flames from a hilltop a quarter mile to the west, already thinking…day-dreaming…of the next village…conquest…what he would do with his first day on the Amaranth Throne…

He celebrated with a bottle of brandy one of his people had "rescued" from a burning cottage. Seventeen Dalesmen of his two score and then some suddenly found it difficult to keep up with him as he rode into the night, quietly falling behind until they could no longer hear those in front of them before turning back to the north.

"I won't be doin' this shite no more," said a carle known to his mates as Mad Jack Parham. "It may be I'm fuckin' crazy when I've 'ad too much t'drink, but I'm no up t'the sacrilege of what that bastard intends. I've done enough murder and cracked enough heads for him. I'm goin' home afore the first snow and he can do his own devil's work…"

"...I grew up in this part of the Vales," said one of the Wyndham crofters, pointing to a glow further on in the western sky. "Swinton is off that way..."

"In flames, from the look of it," said Edmund darkly.

"They can't have come that far so quickly," observed Evrard.

"Scandians *or* Antillians," added Sebastian.

They had only just dismounted, ready to make camp for the night among the ruins of an old monastery tumbled into the shelter of what the locals called the Three Sisters, a trice of limestone outcroppings through which ran the Murvale Race, on its way east to join the Findhorn at Colbourne town.

The crofter said *We should go on*, quietly, and the rest raised their voices in agreement. No one of the boys was inclined to disagree. They were on horseback again within minutes, spurring over the starlit grasslands at a pace that brought them to Swinton- on-the-Race within the hour. They reined their horses above the village, narrowly avoiding a tide of refugees turned to survey the fiery end of their homes. Evrard was on his feet in an instant, striding amongst the villagers, seeking for an answer as to what had happened.

"...Thirty forty men...just come out the hills like yourselfs and fell upon us..."

"Foreigners," said Evrard. His face was mask of barely-controlled anger, something neither of the Beverleys had ever seen before.

"Nay, sir," said the one questioned. "They was no foreigners. They spoke our ruin in plain enough words, put fire to ever'thin' and then just rode away, the evil bastard leadin' 'em laughin' the while."

"Rode away where?" demanded Evrard.

"There," said the villager, pointing west again. "Taunton lies maybe twenty miles ride that way..."

"Can we be of any help t'you?" asked Sebastian, leaning down from his horse..

"You can catch them all and pays 'em for us."

Evrard took to his own horse again. "That I will," he said. "You have my word," and without waiting for any of the others spurred west.

---

Embry came up beside de Montenay, glanced quickly at half a bottle of a burned-out villager's brandy in his master's gloved hand and thought better of saying anything.

"What d'you want, Embry?"

"Nothin', m'lord."

"Please don't make me ask you a second time."

Embry trembled, desperately in search of something to say that would be stupid enough to be dismissed outright as unworthy of reply.

"Are you having a crisis of conscience, Embry? Were we perhaps overly enthusiastic in our dealings with that village?"

"I just didn't see the reason for it, is all."

"The reason for what?"

"For burning the place down, m'lord."

De Montenay turned to him, face masked in shadows and half-light, but with an unmistakable smile of amusement on his lips.

"It pleased me to deal with them in that fashion."

"But you didn't know a soul there! No one of them has ever laid eyes on you, nor you on any of them. What served t'do what we done?"

De Montenay lightly reined his horse to a walk and thence near to a standstill; behind them the rest of his people took to a similar pace and milled about the track uncertainly.

"I believe I just answered that question, Embry. If it's not quite enough to satisfy your curiosity, or assuage whatever feelings of guilt have suddenly found their way into your shitpile of a brain, from now on I suggest you keep your questions to yourself. Have I made myself clear? Do you understand *exactly* what I mean?"

Embry trembled further, and nodded rather than risking more words.

"Good," said de Montenay, now fully amused. "I hope you've derived a bit of wisdom from this exchange, so when we encounter another village, you will understand why it is I expect you and every one of the halfwits following us, to do whatever I ask of you..."

Embry bowed his head and murmured "Aye, m'lord", praying his own horse would slacken its pace further so he might fall from his master's regard without scathe. De Montenay smiled into the night, drank deeply from his bottle of brandy, and felt himself well on his way to a well-deserved lordship of the world in general.

"...We're not far behind them, Edmund," said their tracker. "Half a mile at most. They don't seem t'be in any kind of a hurry."

Evrard had become like one possessed, racing ahead of them, reining his horse back impatiently whilst they all came up with him again. Edmund nodded, content to go at a pace that would leave them untired, yet bring them up to those whom they followed well before they encountered Taunton village. Sebastian sought to keep pace with their friend, reaching for his bridle to slow him that they might talk.

"Leave off, Sebastian," snapped Evrard.

"What's gotten into you?"

"It's him. It can't be anyone but him, to lay waste to innocent souls and go on his way *la-de-da* as if it all belonged to him to be served at his pleasure."

"Evrard, who?"

"My father, Sebastian! The great fucking Renard de Montenay, who's made life a hell for my mother and my sisters and my poor brother with not enough brains to fight for his soul...anyone unlucky enough to ever cross his path."

"Evrard you can't know that for—"

"For certain? *Pfft*...I know...I can smell him, Sebastian. Suddenly my world reeks of him..."

"Evrard go back t'Swinton. Do what can be done for those people. Let us go on t'deal with this and we'll come back for you."

Evrard only shook his head and put his face forward. Sebastian could see tears glinting in the starlight as they streamed down his cheeks.

"I'm done making excuses for him, Sebastian. Overlooking his cruelty. Telling myself I need not deal with him at all because I was in no wise like him...but if I'm truly his son it will be t'my shame for as long as I live..."

---

In one way it all ended within the next half hour. They came upon Renard and his men in the middle of a broad field studded with the shorn stalks of newly-harvested corn, small patches of shadow covering the ground as it closed between them, hooves crunching down over stubble and the breath of their mounts steaming in the air as the night turned to deepening dark and early winter coolth. Now Evrard charged forward again, screaming challenge to the one who was furthest from them, daring him to turn and make account for his transgressions.

Edmund and Sebastian turned to each other in consternation, the same thought running through their minds as they raced after him, turning only long enough to beg the crofters of Élysée to keep up with them, that they would not come alone into the ranks of those who rode before them. Swords rang out from their sheaths, pikes lowered themselves to run parallel with the ground beneath as the score of village-burners ahead of them turned to face the onslaught.

What ensued was only Chaos. In the dark, it was almost impossible to tell friend from foe, yet the clash of steel and the cries of mortally wounded men rang out into the night, and if there were any creatures of wood and field nearby to bear witness, they could only do so in wonderment at the folly of those who would hunt *themselves* unto death. In the midst of it, a young man from the Dales came upon a madman from the Dales, and stood wordlessly, glaring across the corpses of men no longer innocent.

"Your brother is dead," said de Montenay. "They killed him."

"It is your doing, father, not mine *or* theirs," said Evrard.

"The throne should have been ours long ago," said his father.

"A throne is no use to anyone without the courage or kindness to sit on it," replied his son, striding towards him. "Sevrain's death and every last ounce of wretchedness that has ever come upon our house are on your head, all returned to take form and substance in the pettiness and cruelty of your life. Someone has to make an end of our pathetic history."

Renard de Montenay reeled backwards as if the spoken words had been a physical blow. For a moment, the errant light of a misguided star struck something in his obsidian eyes that might have been dismay, but it was quickly replaced with rage.

"Then let this be my legacy to you!" he hissed

From ten paces, Evrard de Montenay's father flung a long-bladed dagger at his only remaining son's breast, and Sebastian Beverley took one step forward to stand between them...turned...looked down once...shaking his head at where the blade had buried itself in his chest. From his knees he looked up at Evrard and shrugged helplessly.

"I couldn't go home without you," he said apologetically. "I promised Annie Branny I'd look after you..."

# Chapter Twenty-Two - THE CHILDREN HEAD HOMEWARD

The world went away as Sebastian swayed on his knees, one hand stretched out to keep himself from pitching forward. Evrard knelt beside him immediately, lowering him gently to the ground, calling out for his brother. Edmund was there in moments, his eyes widening in the closest he'd ever come to horror in his life.

"He took the blade for me," said Evrard.

"Well I had to," said Sebastian, looking up at Edmund. "I promised...and besides, there was no way I was gonna let his own father kill him. Something like that is just plain wrong."

"Just shut up and let me see what you've done," exclaimed his brother. "Mom is gonna have my head..."

"It's not your fault," groaned Sebastian. "And *I* didn't do anything, I told you, it was Evrard's father..."

"Gods you're an idiot!" said Edmund. "Be quiet and don't move."

"I don't think it's as bad as all that, Edmund. Really. It doesn't hurt at all."

"That's not a good thing, Sebastian. It means you're going into shock. We've gotta keep you warm and—"

"Let me, Edmund," said Evrard. He reached to pull back Sebastian's coat, then with his own dagger expertly sliced a path through the shirt underneath so they could see what kind of damage had been done.

One of their people brought a lit torch to hold over them, reporting the while that they had accounted for all of de Montenay's raiders, saving de Montenay himself. He was nowhere to be found.

"Of course not," sneered Evrard, lightly running his fingers around the haft of the blade in his friend's chest. "He's run away. No surprise that. He needs other people around him to do his dirty work, people he's terrorised into believing him more than a coward and a bully. Sebastian are you having any trouble breathing?"

"It hurts a bit now, Ev, but no...I told you...I don't feel all that badly..."

"Can we see if anyone's got some brandy or something I can run over this? It's bloody miraculous but I don't think the steel has gone near anything t'cause any real damage."

Sebastian went a bit cross-eyed.

"Well thank goodness for that then," he said, and passed out.

Evrard undid his own coat and laid it down over him.

"We need t'get him somewhere someone who knows what they're doing can have a look at him," he said to Edmund.

"I think we're as near to Taunton as we are to Swinton."

Evrard thought for a moment.

"Then let's go back, Edmund. There's got to be someone amongst them can see t'this, and while Sebastian's resting we can do what we can t'help them, now they've got nowhere t'go." He looked around at the bodies surrounding them distastefully. "How many of our people did we lose?"

The crofter with the torch spoke up.

"Three, young sir, with another handful banged up some or stuck nothin' serious."

Evrard nodded. "Edmund, look after him while we bury our three, and then we can head back to Swinton. I think he'll be all right as long as we don't bounce him around too much on the way."

He rose and put one hand on Edmund's shoulder for a moment, before going off to see to their dead. Edmund followed him with his eyes until the shadows swallowed him up. To no one in particular he murmured:

"I think I'm beginning t'see just why Annie Branny set us t'look after you..."

⁂

"...'Rissa I'm feeling a lot better. We should go back t'help the boys."

Kerissa had found them a little hollow on a south-facing braeside, where the moon wouldn't smack them in the eyes as it rose into the sky. The air was chill, but with both of them snuggled beneath the blaze of *Equatoria*, they were warm and comfortable; drowsing in each other's arms, stars shimmered and winked above them, while the great midnight-coloured dray horse named Diomede cropped at nearby patches of withered meadow grass, bluebonnet and cranesbill.

"'Bella, by now your folks and mine are expecting us. Tomorrow we'll find the river again and then we'll have an easy time of traveling. Home in two-three days…"

Arabella began to protest but was silenced with a kiss, and then allowed herself to do what she would never admit to doing—letting someone else take care of business—by wriggling deeper into the warmth of Kerissa's embrace.

"Colbourne's the next town, right?" asked Kerissa, under no illusions that Arabella might not realise she was changing the subject on purpose. Arabella nodded against her chest.

"Then Bancroft and then Linden and then home," she said sleepily." We can see Grams and the twins and—"

"And take a rest from adventures?" suggested 'Rissa.

"I suppose so," said Arabella. "I just worry about the boys…and Mum worrying about everything even when she knows she's done as much as she can…"

"Is that like worrying about everything the way you do?"

"Don't be mean."

"I'm not being mean, 'Bella. You and your mom are so much alike it's spooky."

Arabella was drifting off.

"Uncle Thomas is gonna want t'hear every detail so he can write a story."

"Then we'll be famous," laughed Kerissa.

"And Diana's gonna get all huffy with him and insist he take her home."

"So she can give him more things t'write about."

"'Rissa you're awful…"

"I know."

"I love you anyway…forever…"

"Me too you, 'Bella. Now go t'sleep."

For a while they listened to crickets and furry little four-foots scurrying around in the night. Kerissa was halfway to Snoozeland when Arabella's voice came to her through the dark.

"How come all of a sudden you can talk to critters and understand what they're sayin' t'you?"

"I have no idea, 'Bella. Go t'sleep..."

---

It was easy to retrace their way back to Swinton. The lick of towering flames in the night sky had subsided to an unhappy glow on the eastern horizon, but even had their been jet-black ink for the air around them, the smell of the village burning would have led them unerringly back along their way. An hour before midnight they found the folk of Swinton camped on the heights above the furnace below; in exchange for the news that those reponsible had been "paid back", a stead-wife who served her neighbours in leech-craft was summoned to look after Sebastian.

Half the survivors of the village along with Evrard, Edmund, and the Wyndham crofters looked on as she examined him, made cryptic pronouncements, and then, after numerous applications of a poultice both horrifically smelly and of an equally unsettling aspect, slowly withdrew Renard de Montenay's dagger from his chest. Sebastian occasionally regained consciousness during the process, drank from a decoction equally as vile as the ingredients of the poultice, and appeared to be unfazed throughout the process. He was awake when the blade was finally taken from the wound, and was visibly impressed with himself at having survived.

"That wasn't so bad," he said somewhat drunkenly, as she bound up the wound. "Big knife though, eh?"

"Gods you're an idiot, Sebastian," said his brother again. He turned to the wise-woman and asked,"Will he be all right then...his body if not his brain?", who nodded briefly and walked away without a another word.

"Don't mind her," said one of the villagers. "Nor think us ungrateful at least for the payback on them as have ruined us."

Evrard spoke up immediately. "We'll stay on a bit t'help clean things up, get all of you into some kind of shelter before winterfall."

"That would be a kindness," replied the villager. "But mayhap we'll just leave off rebuilding anything until the spring, get ourselves off to Colbourne or Taunton before the snows."

He left them to look after his own family, as the Wyndham people went about making sure everyone was warm enough and had something to eat. Evrard stood to one side, staring sightlessly off into the dark before he turned to the Beverleys, knelt again beside Sebastian.

"Thank you," he said softly. To Edmund he said, "You two go home. I'll stay on with your grandfather's people, moving west, and go wherever they have need of us."

"That's not gonna happen, Evrard," said Sebastian. "If that's what you think you have t'do, then me and Edmund will be right there t'make sure you don't do anymore stupid stuff like going after your father. Besides, he's alone now, he can't do any more damage."

Edmund said, "My idiot brother is finished with swashing and buckling for now. As soon as he can sit his bloody horse someone has t'take him back t'the City...and like it or not, Ev, you're the one gonna do that. I'm sure Robin Adair is rousing up the westlands as he heads home to Bedford; I'm going t'follow him t'make sure."

Sebastian looked at his brother and, from experience, thought better of protesting; however, by firelight it could be seen that for all his contempt for the one who had sired him, in Evrard was a spark of temper he had inherited in despite.

"What is it with you two?" he demanded. "I'm not your child. You don't have t'wipe my nose every time I sneeze."

Sebastian began to laugh where he lay on the ground, and then to swear a bit with discomfort.

"Shows what you know, Evrard," he said, when he'd stopped laughing and coughing. "That's exactly what me and Edmund are supposed t'do."

"Your Annie Branny must be something else when she gets pissy," he replied.

"Not at all," countered Edmund. "She never *gets* pissy. It's not in her nature...and she's the gentlest soul we know, her *and* her daughter...but once she's made up her mind on something she's pretty fierce about it. You belong to us, my friend, until such time as Aunt Brandywine says otherwise. Get used to it..."

Evrard looked incredulous. Edmund raised a hand in warning.

"We'll truss you like a chicken if we have to."

Evrard grew even more wide-eyed with disbelief... and then shook his head.

"I suppose Sebastian and I are leaving first light in the morning."

"Second or third maybe," offered Sebastian from under his blankets, "but yeah... tomorrow for sure." In response to his brother's look he said, "I can ride. We just have t'go slow..."

---

The girls weren't hurrying anymore. When a mid-morning sun finally keeked through an overcast sky promising rain, they stayed where they were, Zoraya's blanket steaming over top of them, hissing occasionally, whenever a drop of moisture fell upon it. Kerissa coaxed a small fire from early winter deadfall and they breakfasted on tea, dried fruit and a chunk of hard cheese. Diomede nosed at their pack of provisions until Arabella ponied up a pair of apples.

"'Rissa d'you remember Amadeus?" she said.

"Of course...when we were small and used t'visit up north...you grandfather would take us out riding on his back and we could hardly stay there because our legs weren't long enough."

"I'm pretty sure this guy is one of his colts."

"He's about as big as Amadeus for sure," said Kerissa. "And it seems like he knows us...or at least likes us enough not to pitch us into a ditch first chance he gets..."

"So what's goin' on with you and the critters, 'Riss?"

"'Bella I already said. I don't know...except that if I pay attention I can... *hear*...it isn't really the right word...but I can hear them. And then if I talk back in my head it seems they can *hear* me too. I'm gonna check in with Mom on that soon as we get home."

"I read somewhere that if you're gonna be a witch, stuff happens once you have your first period..."

"Then I guess I'm just a really late bloomer,." laughed Kerissa, "'cause it's been a while."

"I suppose we should get going?"

"Sure. Anytime you like, honey. We should get t'the Findhorn around lunchtime. After that it's a clear run home t'the City."

"I still think we should've gone back."

Kerissa leaned over and took Arabella's face in both hands, shaking her head.

"Nope. From now on we'll find other ways t'be helpful. I'm not taking us anywhere there's a chance you can get hurt..."

---

At half past noon under a lowering sky, they rode leisurely through one last succession of hills and found themselves overlooking the town of Colbourne, grateful that the scene below in no way resembled the inferno they had witnessed at Trowbridge. Whatever had been the cause of the madness and disaster there had not reached Colbourne. The river was a slate-grey ribbon running peacefully through the centre of the town; on the east bank they could see carts laden with goods and produce approaching from the countryside, and the occasional motor-car on the paved road that ran beside the rail line. Diomede snorted something in the way of what might have been equine anticipation, and in a flurry of mane, tail, and feathered hooves took them down the long sloping approach from the west.

Once on the outskirts of the town, they found a small inn where the stallion's anticipation found fulfillment in the form of a brief banquet of hay, carrots and grain; the girls drank mulled wine and filled up on fresh-baked bread, steaming bowls of beef and barley soup.

A quick trip across the river on foot brought them to the railway, and a line still in working order, where Kerissa sent a message to her parents, with updates on what was going on, and a more detailed version of their encounter at the standing stones. Back again at the inn, they both thought longingly of a room and bed for the night, but Arabella demurred.

"It would be nice," she said, "but last night was nice too...and even if it decides t'rain on us, we can at least get halfway t'Bancroft and you can find us another cosy spot to camp out for the night."

Diomede was reluctantly drawn away from his feasting and by mid-afternoon, they had put a handful of miles behind them, following the river with brief forays back up onto higher ground. By sunset three hours later, they were well on their way in the gathering twilight, Arabella riding front with Kerissa behind her amid the welter of their packs and weaponry.

"'Bella I think somebody's following us," she whispered.

Arabella nodded. "Me too. I've had the wiggins runnin' up and down my back the last hour."

"Maybe we should stop here, or go back t'Colbourne?"

"No let's keep goin', 'Rissa...but just long enough t'conjure up a plan for when we do stop..."

"I was hoping we could take a break but...looks like we're in for more adventures."

Arabella nodded again. "Oh well...right?"

Kerissa dipped her head once against Arabella's back. At that point they were moving slowly not far from the river, the sunset well beyond the heights above.them. Kerissa grew silent, only the sound of her breathing in Arabella's ear grown slow and measured. After a while, she spoke again.

"Up on our right, 'Bella...you don't have t'look it's one of our foxy friends. He says there's a man on horseback moving behind us a few hundred yards back, keeping just below the ridgetops."

"What's he look like?"

"Our little guy doesn't really distinguish that way. He knows t'recognise friends more by touch and smell, but he's not anxious t'have anything t'do with our shadow so I'm thinkin' he's not after bein' a guardian angel."

Arabella thought awhiles.

"'Rissa, can you get the packs up close t'me so it looks like you're still there?"

"What've you got in mind, 'Bella?"

"I don't want him on the higher ground above us, so I'm gonna climb up there ahead of him. Get your bow and quiver ready, and just before we crest the hill slip off and wait for him t'go by. Me and Diomede'll go slow, and I'll head down the far slope pretending t'look for a place t'camp for the night..."

"And when he decides t'get friendly I'll have your back."

"Just don't let one of your arrows mistake me for him if it comes down t'that, okay?"

"Not a chance, my girl."

"Good luck to us then," said Arabella, and turned Diomede up the slope, as 'Rissa secured the straps of one pack across her shoulders, bundled another below it.

Just before they came to the top of the hill, she slipped to the ground and waited—an eternity of Time that in reality was no more than two or three minutes—until she heard the quiet passage of their stalker as he rode by. She strung her bow and crept along, keeping him a dozen yards ahead of her, at the same time keeping her eyes on Arabella's shadow as she angled down the far slope, outwardly appearing to be looking for a place to shelter for the night.

---

Evrard and Sebastian arrived in Colbourne that same evening, after a longer day of travel. Once they had seen Edmund off westward with the Wyndham folk, the two of them had plodded along in much the same direction as the girls, but at a considerably slower pace.

Evrard left off being huffy about being chaperoned without his consent, but found his good humour returning once "on the road" with Sebastian; he, on the other hand, though well aware of the miracle of his survival, found that miracle or not it still hurt like the dickens to have survived it. They found lodging for the night on the outskirts of the town, the innkeeper who served them their supper just happening to overhear their conversation.

"Yer no talkin' about two girls wanderin' about on a great black mountain of a horse, are ye?" he inquired.

"One fair and the other dark...both lovely as a dream in Paradise?"

"Aye, that's them for sure. Friends of yours?"

"Cousins," replied Sebastian eagerly. "When did you see them?"

"This aft," said the proprietor. "They took some time for a meal and t'send a wire down t'their people in the City, then left three or four hours ago. Ye don't want t'be goin' north just now. Word is, there was some kind of great fire near burned Trowbridge t'the ground two nights gone...but if ye're on yer way south, I don't imagine they'll have reached Bancroft t'night, so like as not you can catch them up tomorrow..."

When they were halfway through their meal, Sebastian looked over at Evrard and grinned knowingly.

"I'll do my best if you want t'try," he said. "I know the feeling, but I've had a bit more time t'find my place with them in the world. I was about a year old when 'Bella was born; 'Rissa was maybe three years old then, and after that we all just grew up together."

"Were they always so—?"

"Keen on each other, y'mean?" Sebastian said, nodding carefully. "From the moment they laid eyes on each other Kerissa was in love, and 'Bella seemed to simply take it as a matter of course that they should be together. Once we were in school and all of us grown enough t'be takin' notice of such things, we used t'laugh ourselves sick at all the boys trying t'get into their knickers. Then we'd pretend like we were the chosen ones. Bein' family we just naturally did stuff together, so outwardly it looked like we were the wee boys. Me and Ed caught *so* much envy and jealousy, but we weren't about t'let anyone in on the secret."

Evrard appeared to join the ranks of the madly envious, shaking his head over the dregs of a mug of early October ale.

"Sevrain was the oldest...and then there was my three sisters before me...but once we started getting older my father semed to enjoy pitting us against each other, and he had no use for the girls. All in all, it was pretty hellish."

"You don't get t'choose your people, Evrard."

"I know that. Still, it hurts...but I'll wager not so much as that hole in your chest."

Evrard smiled ruefully. Sebastian shrugged.

"I think your father has gone a bit round the bend, Ev. I can't say since I never had anything t'do with him until I met up with you, but he seems t'be running around in some kind of reality that doesn't really match up with ours."

"That's not an excuse, Sebastian. It wouldn't matter one way or the other if he was only torturing himself with all those damned dreams of empire and whatever...but he's spent my entire life making everyone around him pay for his delusions. He *chose* t'be a bastard, even to all the people he was supposed t'love..."

Sebastian reached for his face, cupped his chin and stared into pale eyes a breath away from agony.

"All of that's over now, Evrard. I told you, and you met Annie Branny and just about everyone in our *family*. I remember her telling me about the day she met Alexandra, Nicholas' mom, for the first time—on the day that Andrew and Alain stood for each other. Alexandra whisked on past everyone that day and said *Now you belong to us* and hugged her. I have no idea why she decided t'make us your nursemaids, but I swear you'll never regret the day she decided t'do it."

He winced once as he leaned over to kiss him. Smiled.

"I'm tired," he said. "If we want half a chance at catching the girls tomorrow I'd better get some sleep…"

# Chapter Twenty-Three – DE MONTENAY AT LAST

Kerissa kept low to the ground, blessing and cursing the overcast skies in the same breath.

In the almost Stygian gloom there was very little chance their unknown stalker would discover her, become aware that he himself was now being followed; at the same time, she found her eyes playing tricks with the darkness, creating shadows where they didn't exist, making it difficult to determine where her prey ended and the night began. She realised with a start that Arabella and Diomede, the blot of darkness further down the slope beyond him, had disappeared. She forced herself to drown a surge of panic, the frantic temptation to call out...picked up the pace of her own descent, praying that wherever Arabella had gone was her part of the plan to entrap the man following them.

As she moved closer to him his silhouette became more distinct, and she heard him muttering profanities under his breath, suddenly spurring his mount forward. Kerissa heard the smallest whisper of a sword being drawn, saw the smallest glint of steel where there had been no glint at all. She drew the fletching of her arrow to where it tickled her right ear and prayed that wherever 'Bella had gone was not in its path if she overshot or missed her mark. She took a deep breath and let fly. The shaft become invisible for a heartbeat; then she heard it *thunk* into something, and another flurry of profanity as a cloud drifted apart long enough for her to recognise it buried in the thigh of her prey. Her second arrow was already in flight, this time taking the rider from his horse as it plowed through his left shoulder.

"'Bella he's down!" she shouted, drawing a dagger as she raced down the slope.

The clouds scattered at her cry, and she saw Arabella atop Diomede thunder out from from the shelter of the hillock that had hidden her from view, her own sword drawn and assuredly glinting in moonlight as she bore down upon the fallen man. He struggled to rise, brought his own weapon up too late. Diomede's left shoulder sent him screaming and sprawling back to the ground, with Arabella coming off the horse's right flank to land *en garde* beside the stranger. Again he struggled to rise, though now the point of her sword pricked at his throat.

"Whoever you are I think you'd best serve yourself by not moving at all," she warned, and as 'Rissa came up with them, he raised his head to where there was more than enough light to hazard his identity.

"It's him," she said. "The one from the train..."

"From the moors, 'Rissa," amended Arabella. "The one who somehow knew enough to come hunting for us there. The one on the train was his son...Evrard's older brother. This is Renard their father...Renard the traitor ..."

She reversed her grip on the haft of her sword, leaned forward and struck him in the forehead with its carved pommel.

Moment later Kerissa saw the blonde girl sway on her feet, realised they'd not eaten for hours, and the occurrences of the last quarter hour had again sent Arabella reeling. Ignoring the prone figure of Renard de Montenay, she found Diomede presciently beside her, dragging one of their packs down from his back, and furiously searching for something to stave off her dizziness. Arabella fell to her knees, her eyes unmistakably dazed and unfocused even in half-light.

"'Bella stay with me, baby, don't go away please 'Bella talk to me..." she wailed.

She found an apple, bit into it and half laughing half crying flung it off for Diomede, chewing savagely before she pressed her lips to Arabella's mouth and in that way fed her the sweet pulpy mess; then there was cheese and another apple, only half eaten and again shared with horse and girl. Kerissa started counting Terror by the number of her own heartbeats, desperately waiting for Arabella to come back into the world....

"Hi..." she said sleepily. "It happened again..."

Kerissa nodded, tearfully, leaned over her and kissed her face.

"Y'gotta remember sometimes, 'Bella," she said. "I know it's hard and I try t'be the one but I forget too."

"I'm sorry."

"Baby it's not something y'have to apologise for, but we need t'be more careful, okay?"

Arabella nodded slowly; then the sleepiness sparked away from her eyes and she tried to sit up. Kerissa held her gently down under the blankets.

"It's okay, honey, I took care of him."

They were camped in the shelter of the hillock, another one rising up to the west crowned with a stand of alder and maple bathed in moonlight under a rapidly clearing sky. A cold wind chasing the clouds southward whistled above them. Arabella turned her head where she lay and saw the baleful glare of two dark eyes belonging to the trussed figure who lay belly down not far from the fire Kerissa had struck with flint and steel.

"No worries now, baby," soothed Kerissa. "I won't let him hurt you."

"I'm hungry, 'Rissa. Can I have something t'eat? Is Dio okay?"

"We're all okay, honey. The big moose is wandering around looking for his own supper. I made us some soup. It's really just some broth with vegetables and a potato and stuff, but it's warm."

"That would be nice..."

"Can you sit up a little, honey? "

She gently raised Arabella up against one of their packs and spooned broth to her lips. Diomede reappeared and tried to nose his way into the small pot hung over their fire, snorted once and stamped backwards when it encountered too much heat for comfort.

Kerissa laughed. Arabella smiled wanly.

"Aren't you the cutest little couple," came a voice from the edge of the firelight, dripping with contempt.

"Nobody asked for your opinion," snapped Kerissa. "Why were you following us?"

"I know who you are," said de Montenay. "The darkie's precious little mongrel bitch, and the street-whore's whelp...the pair of you deserve each other. You're both gutter scum."

"Shut up!" said Kerissa.

"Or what?" sneered Renard.

"Or I can manage it for you."

"Why don't you untie me? I'm sure I can do things to both of you that you'll never be able to do for each other."

Kerissa made as if to stand up, her free hand reaching for the dagger on her belt until she felt Arabella's fingers about her wrist.

"They're just words, 'Rissa. It's all he's got now. We'll take him back t'the City and let my mom's people in the palace do what needs be done."

She sat up carefully, taking the bowl from her friend and turning to face de Montenay.

"The gutter scum have you on your belly like a worm in the grass," she said slowly. "You let a mongrel bitch and a street-whore's whelp do that. You let two *girls* do that, my dear *Monsieur* High-and-Mighty."

De Montenay ground his teeth and said nothing. From where they sat the girls could feel the waves of malice and hatred coming off of him.

"I'll see to you both very soon," he said. "I'll make you forget why you ever wanted to have anything to do with each other."

"Of course you will," said Arabella. "But until then you should be quiet. 'Rissa has much more patience than I do, especially when it comes to vicious children playing at being high-born."

"I'm bleeding."

"Good. Bleed all you like...but if you won't be quiet I'll make sure you bleed in silence....and help the process along a bit in the bargain."

✦

"...'Bella you didn't mean what you said."

"I did, Rissa. He called you names. He called your mom and my mom names, too...and then he threatened t'hurt you..."

"They' re just words, 'Bella. You said."

"I know, 'Rissa, but they're not just words for him. They're the only thing he's got between him and knowing what a mean-spirited creature he really is. He doesn't have the courage to stand up on his own. He lashes at people t'make them do his dirty work and then pretends afterwards he's had nothing t'do with any of it. It makes him feel like he's important..."

✦

It was the shrill roar of anger and the stamping of Diomede's hooves on the ground that woke them, saved them from de Montenay. It was the towering ferocity of his presence that stood between them in the faint glow of their dying fire when de Montenay managed to free himself from his bonds, and kept him from their weapons and his intent to use them on his sleeping captors. In frail moonlight shrouded by tatters of cloud, they disentangled themselves from their blankets in time to see him limping away up the far hillside... watched him turn...heard the mockery in his voice:

"I met up with some of your friends, you know. Two great hulking louts wandering around with my pathetic excuse for a son. I killed one of them...the young one, I think. He got in the way of a dagger I'd intended for my own dear little shit Evrard."

Kerissa stood in stunned silence, her hands clutched in Diomede's mane as she watched him turn again, fleeing upwards to the stand of trees at the crown of the hill. She didn't hear Arabella's wail of anguish, or see her scrambling for her bow, stringing it in seconds and waiting...waiting...waiting until de Montenay thought he was safe as he went for the shelter of the trees.

Her first arrow took him between the shoulder blades and pinned him to the trunk of the tree in front of him. The next four made certain he would never fall to the ground before the crows came to feed on his corpse.

# Chapter Twenty-Four - AMARANTHUS VENEFICUS

Once again, *les Boulevardiers* were gathered in St John's Mews, only waiting upon Brandy to return from yet another day at the palace conferring with ministers and advisers. In her almost day-long absences, Alexandra had taken it upon herself to act as the mistress of her son's house, preparing meals and, once Nicholas himself had gone off to add his efforts to the defense of the City, making certain all things were where they should be when needed.

On this day, Nicholas had returned home early, well before nightfall, and the two of them had conjured up a fire on the kitchen hearth and a small feast to serve as everyone's supper. Andrew and Alain had brought the twins, who had in their own fashion sensed something important in the wind, and sat quietly together, reading in front of the fire.

At the broad clerestory table that occupied one end of the kitchen, everyone else sat back from their plates, a bit groggy with a surfeit of food and warmth. Conversation flurried for a few minutes at a time, then flagged under the weight of endless speculation. There had been news from the north and west from reliable sources, but an equal amount of rumours had come through their daily associations with other denizens of the City, all trying to maintain a sense of normalcy whilst preparing for the worst. Once they had stripped every morsel of flesh from the bones of hearsay and gossip, they lapsed into a mostly satisfied after-dinner languor. Only Zoraya, who had asked for them all to come together, seemed less than subdued, moving about the kitchen restlessly as they waited for Brandywine. No one seemed to notice the rust-red dog-fox that had materialised on top of one of the kitchen cupboards during dinner.

"You're not gonna let us in on anything beforehand, are you, Zori?" said Thomas. Diana, who was no less curious than anyone else in the room but never the one to let such things show, took his hand and smiled indulgently. Zoraya almost did so, but shook her head.

"Better to wait for Brandywine," was all she would say.

Alexandra was pouring tea and Nicholas was cracking open a bottle of sherry when she arrived, looking harried and a bit blue with chill from the wind gaining strength outdoors. She declined dinner in favour of a glass of claret and a welcoming hug from him, and everyone else on down to the twins, who looked expectantly to her and Zoraya.

"Well some of it's not so good," Brandy said once settled beside the fire. There were dark smudges beneath her eyes, and the brilliant emerald green colour she shared with her daughter had a haunted look in their depths. "We all know what came in the girls' wire when *they* came to Colbourne, but not much more than that.

"In the west it's different," she continued. "The Antillians were *discovered* off our northwestern coast by the fishing fleet out of Snowdon, and they all but levelled the village in what looked like them trying to keep them from raising an alarm. Since we're still receiving wires from Bedford, the people at the palace seem t'think they know we know they're here, so they're not gonna waste anymore time. Zoraya says they'll be coming straight for us here within the week..."

She turned to Alexandra.

"Mum, we actually got word from Frederick, north of the Dales," she said. "He and all of Windy's brothers are fine but getting frozen...sent a rider south just as a huge snowstorm came over the mountains, thinking to send the message from Élysée. When his man heard the wires had been destroyed along with the rail line in Trowbridge, he ended up taking three horses from your stables so he could go on to Colbourne without stopping. In his message, he said Gramps couldn't say for certain, but the Scandians had nowhere to go once the storm came down on them, so he's pretty sure afterwards there won't be enough of them left alive t'cause us much trouble...and as soon he can confirm that he'll be coming south again hoping to get here before the Antillians."

Alexandra left off pouring tea, relief written all over her face as she embraced her son.

"What we've heard from the girls and recent news from the west has everyone in the palace really worried because we don't have much of anything that can stand up to what they've got in store for us. One of the ministers says the only chance we've got is if we somehow get them to come at us on land, rather than what they did to Snowdon. At the same time, it's not likely they're going t'fall into something like that when all they have t'do is bombard us from the

# ARABELLA

harbour, which is why we're trying t'get everyone safely away and fortify it as much as we can."

"We're basically looking at the end of the City," whispered Alain, "if not worse."

Brandywine nodded solemnly. "Right now it looks that way, Alain. I don't know why, but we never gave any thought t'what's happening now, or how t'deal with it if it did happen. We just never got round to making weapons like the ones they have..."

"So we're just sitting around waiting for the worst t'catch up with us?" growled Thomas.

Brandywine looked stricken, until Alexandra sat down beside her.

"He's not blaming you, Brandywine. Caroline didn't intend for you to look after every last detail of everything all on your own. We've just never had to deal with something like this. We've never even considered trying to impose our way of life on anyone else; the thought itself is...it's just not something that would occur to us..."

"She's right, Branny," said Gareth. "We got lazy...believed everyone felt the same way we did. Now we have t'pay a price for it."

Zoraya spoke up, suddenly seeming far more than just the most exotic member of their family. Her eyes darkened from amber to swirls of bronze sparked with gold.

"We have a plan for something, Brandywine and Nicholas and I," she said. "It's why I asked all of you here...but before that, I have news of the children."

She looked first to Diana and Thomas..

"For the most part, they are all well," she said slowly. "The boys encountered Renard de Montenay in the Westvales with a small contingent of his people, laying waste to anything in their path. It seems he went mad, and even flung a dagger at his own son before he fled. It was Sebastian who stepped into its path and took a grievous wound, yet he survived and is on his way home with Evrard to look after him. Edmund chose to continue westward, which would give us good reason to believe Sebastian was not in any danger."

"Zori how do you know all this?" asked Diana quietly, who had gone pale where she sat beside Thomas.

Zoraya smiled wanly, looked over her shoulder to the top of the cupboard where Hasan watched them all with unwinking eyes.

"What about 'Bella and 'Rissa?" cried Jamie. The twins stood up from their place beside the fire, excitement and anticipation now turned to an unreasoning terror. Alexandra raced to their side, thought to take them from the kitchen, but Andrew stayed her with a hand lightly on her shoulder.

"Grams, they need to know as much as we do…perhaps even more so…"

"Are they all right?" demanded Stella, squirming from Alexandra's arms. "Are they all right, Zori, are they all right? Tell me…!"

Zoraya knelt in front of them, smoothing the folds of her caftan over her knees and taking them both into her arms.

"Kerissa is fine," she said softly, so as not to alarm them further, but loud enough so they all could hear. Gareth too had gone pale, sensing unwelcome news, and in turn Nicholas had sought to reassure Brandy by moving closer to where she sat, scarcely daring to breathe. Zoraya hugged the children, hushed them with her hands gently on their lips.

"Arabella is not hurt at all," she said, "but she and 'Rissa also encountered Renard de Montenay, who must have fled south and chanced upon them as they came down from Colbourne. As things transpired, Arabella killed him, and that, along with...along with all the *other things* she and Kerissa experienced, has taken its toll upon her. Hasan has told me they are now close to home; that his folk saw them coming down from the Vales onto the plains near Linden. Evrard and Sebastian are not far behind them.

"They will be here soon..." she promised the twins, but neither Jamie nor Stella was entirely convinced, clinging to her until Diana and Andrew came to look after them.

Zoraya looked at Brandywine.

"It is time?" she asked. "You are certain of doing this?"

Brandywine nodded slowly. "It's really all we've got, isn't it. Zori?"

"I believe so. For the immediate future, yes..."

"I hope so," said Brandywine, and turned to her husband. "Windy...would you... please...I don't think I can even stand up right now."

Nicholas nodded to her and went to a door in the corner of the kitchen that opened onto a flight of stairs to the basement of the house. Brandywine swallowed the last of her claret, one after the next looked at everyone in the kitchen. Moments later, Nicholas returned, with a small carved wooden casket in his hands that he gave to Brandywine.

"Nicky and me are the only ones in this room who have ever seen this," she whispered, "though not long ago we told you about it. This is the last gift Caroline gave to me."

"She wasn't wearing it on our day," said Alain.

Brandywine shook her head. "No. She'd already decided...*we* had already decided that I would hide it away until...now, I guess."

She took a small brass key from a pocket in her dress, inserted it into the lock on the casket given her by Nicholas. There was small *snick*, barely heard over the crackle of the fire on the hearth. Everyone in the room rose to surround her where she sat, and as she lifted the lid there came into the air around them a breath of... *something*...ancient and indefinable...sweet with promise. Where a moment before there had been Despair, now there seemed to be Hope. Brandywine lifted a purple flower from the casket that glowed with a soft inner light.

"*Amaranthus veneficus*," breathed Zoraya, her eyes gleaming. "I've only dreamt of it...for thousands of years...the unfading flower..."

Brandywine offered it up to her, and Zoraya was seen to be overcome with a vast trembling as she took it in her hands, her eyes closing for a moment before she stood back from all of them. She took a deep breath, as one who might stand on the edge of a precipice of decision with only one choice, yet saw the abyss of Infinity beyond.

"I asked all of you here to be witness to this," she said hoarsely, still struggling in her vision. "Among my kind, an oath made...a simple promise even...is strengthened a hundred times over by the number present of those to whom the oath or promise is made."

She too surveyed every face before her, slowly, nodding to each in turn so they would know they were of that number, even to Jamie and Stella.

"I swear to Brandywine, and all of you, that I take this thing of Power only in trust, in the time of our greatest need; that once it is served, it shall be restored to the one who is its rightful keeper. I swear it, and if I fail in this promise it shall be of my own doing and I will pay for it with my life..."

She pinned it to the front of her robe, and one by one went to kiss each of them—forehead, eyes and mouth—to seal her promise, even as she seemed to grow in stature until everyone there felt her to have become a towering presence of something completely remote and alien to the person they had known. She turned to Brandy and Nicholas and said:

"Now we must make our plans in earnest..."

# Chapter Twenty-Five -
# WATCHING & WAITING

Edmund and Robin Adair sat their horses on the same Bedford headland where, seemingly a lifetime ago, Jamie and Stella had discovered "sea monsters" out where water met the sky in a distant haze. Halfway to the coast, Edmund had sent the Wyndham crofters back to their homes in the Carillon, as it became obvious that Adair had been there before them, and roused up every man, woman or child able to bear weapons of any kind. As a result, the Westvales had become an armed camp of sorts, ready and willing to move west or south to the ocean on a moment's notice. Below them and well out to sea, the twins' imaginings filled half the horizon as they steamed southward, trailing plumes of smoke like the breath of black dragons.

"They're passing us by," said Robin incredulously.

"A small mercy, but one gratefully received," said Edmund soberly. "They're running for the City now. Whatever plans for secrecy they had don't apply anymore...but it strikes me that they're going to land somewhere between here and there."

"A land force to move east and clean up what's left of the City when they're finished with it from a distance," said Adair.

"And that's where we have t'get in their way," replied Edmund. "I hope my aunt has got some tricks in her sleeves t'deal with those long guns they've got, but either way, we can't just let them overrun us without any kind of a fight."

"And we've still got the railway here. We can move with them, as many of us as we can cram on the trains, and meet them anywhere they try t'land."

Edmund grinned. "We've turned into pretty desperate characters, eh?"

Robin grinned back, but without any humour. "True enough. I've never met a one of these Antillians, but I know for a fact that when I do, I'm gonna dislike the hell out of them."

"Bad luck t'them then," said Edmund. "Time t'wire the latest off to Annie Branny..."

They reined their horses round and headed back to the village.

---

*Les Boulevardiers* sought each other's company almost constantly as the City more and more took on the character of a city under siege. Communal meals became an almost daily occurrence, as once upon a time they had been when they all were newly-forged family to each other. As in that earlier time, the carriage house in St John's Mews became the place where they came together, out of habit, and now, because of all their homes, it lay the greatest distance from the harbour, in the heart of the Old City. Diana made an unsettling observation the next evening.

"There's an awful lot of people just milling around like they're asleep," she said. "It's been going on for a while, and then I'll bump into someone I recognised from a few days before but now they're okay again."

"I've noticed the same thing," said Andrew. "Once me and Alain got the warehouse cleared out and all the dry goods and perishables off t'where they need t'be, I started in trying t'help with getting people away from the harbour and on their way t'the camps set up on the south side of Linden. They stumble around for a while and then, all of a sudden they wake up again."

"It's very funny," said Alain, trying to lighten the mood. "Funny peculiar, not funny haha."

"What's *peculiar*?" asked Jamie.

"You are," offered Stella.

"Play nice," said Thomas, poking her in the ribs. She giggled and Jamie said:

"Yeah...play nice, poophead."

Alexandra said, "Brandy, you mentioned something funny peculiar like that a few days ago, and Nicky said he was in the shop where he always buys his wine and the proprietor acted like he'd never seen him before."

Everyone looked to Brandywine, who put down her knife and fork and looked apologetic.

"The palace people didn't want me pointing it out... but you all remember that night when Windy and I went t'that strange concert? When it seemed like we'd only been there for a few minutes right around suppertime, but when we got outside it was hours along into the night?

"Zori knows more, but it's happening a lot all over the City..so we're going t'put out an alert warning everyone away from anything t'do with the *musician* Azim Sharad, and we've got our people watching for him."

A curious silence descended upon them. Zoraya would not respond to the glances that came her way, only said to the children, "Go see who is in the courtyard", which sent them dashing from the kitchen to the front of the house, returning in seconds...

"They're home! They're home! It's 'Rissa and 'Bella and a giant black horse...!"

Sebastian and Evrard arrived two hours later, led to the Mews by an escort of cats. Arabella took one step toward them, relief and disbelief on her features, and then would have fallen if Kerissa had not caught her as she sank to the floor.

---

Gareth heard the click of four paws on the stone floor of the studio, then soft footfalls ending with two arms about his shoulders and a nuzzle of one nose into one ear.

"Good morning, my prince," she whispered.

Gareth closed his eyes, praying there would be no tears, at least none to which Zoraya might be witness. Somewhere, she had tucked away the carved casket with the flower it held, but from the moment she had pinned it to her breast in the kitchen in St John's Mews, her touch had become a source half of sorrow and half of unmitigated terror. The princess he had freed from a prison of stone a score of years before had become someone...something...else...outwardly the same…yet now, her proximity brought to him visions of places and things he had never dreamt of, nor wished to ever see in any lifetime. She was the beloved of his life, become a stranger.

"I'm meeting Nicholas and Brandywine today," she said softly, yet the tenor of her voice had become infused with thunder and lightning and the upheaval of things that in untold millennia of existence had never once moved.

"When are you going?"

"I will see them this afternoon, but I have things I must look into before then."

She kissed his cheek and murmured something in a language known only in antiquity…

"I love you too, Zori," he said, and was grateful when she was gone.

Hasan had remained. Looked up at him, head tilted to one side, gleaming eyes holding his own. Gareth forced himself to speak.

"You've had her forever," he said. "What am I gonna do without her?"

---

Andrew and Alain finished packing essentials into a small travel case, moved it and the extra things for the twins into the foyer beside the front door of the house. Then they went from room to room, aimlessly, moving furniture away from the outer walls that faced the harbour, fastening shutters over the windows, making work for themselves to put off yet another moment of unwelcome Reality intruding upon their lives. When one of Alain's delivery carts had been loaded, and had rumbled off to the Old City, they stood in the foyer again and looked at each other, neither one of them willing to concede to the inevitable.

"I guess there's nothing else for it," said Andrew. "We can go anytime. Windy and Brandy said this is an invasion they don't mind so much at all."

Alain shook his head. "I'll be along later," he said. "We've pretty much emptied everything—the shop, the stalls and the warehouses—so I want t'be sure they're locked up *and* all of my people have food and shelter, someplace safe until this is over..."

"I could go with..." offered Andrew.

"I'll be all right on my own, Andy. Besides, the weather's just plain wretched today. You go on t'the Mews and I'll be along as soon as I'm done."

They stood there awkwardly, until Andrew got a stubborn look on his face.

"We'll look after it together," he said.

Alain smiled gratefully. "That would be nice..."

---

"...Tommy, have we got everything we need?"

Diana stood in the middle of her studio, in candlelight, shaking her head at a mirror reflection of someone in ragged workclothes, who resembled her in too many ways for that someone not to be her, but looking harried and dog-tired. Up until the decision for all of *les Boulevardiers* to move into the Wyndham digs in St John's Mews, she had been working side by side with them, filling sandbags beside the river, herding her neighbours off to the country when they were awake enough to know where they should be going, watching a tide of four-footed creatures heading northward in the wake of a great grey tom-cat. The broad-plate glass windows overlooking the street below had been boarded from the inside; Thomas' books, her notebooks, the boys' things...all had been tucked in with their clothing, bare minimums to last for as long as they needed to last. Thomas' bellow came from the bedroom.

"It's all downstairs just waiting on Alain's cart t'get it all over to Nick and Brandy's."

"Sebastian? Evrard? Shake it up, guys. Who knows what we're in for this afternoon. The sooner we're gone from here the better..."

Those two appeared in the door of the bedroom they had shared since their return, where Evrard had taken it upon himself to attend to Sebastian's recovery in such wise that Diana had found herself a bystander, offering help for things already looked after.

"We're almost ready," called Evrard. "This one decided t'take his time about getting out of bed this morning."

"I'm an invalid," protested Sebastian.

"You're lazy," said Evrard. "And nowhere so close to death as you'd have us believe."

That last was for show, evidenced as they came into the great room and she watched her younger son move ever so slowly to Thomas' writing table, where his friend lowered him gently into a chair.

"You'll want a head start on the stairs," said Evrard.

"You know where you can put that idea," snapped Sebastian.

Evrard turned away and grinned at Diana.

"Y'see, he's feelin' much better today."

Diana looked at herself in the mirrors one last time, shaking her head.

"What a wreck," she murmuered. "Tommy! the brat from the Dales is gonna need some help getting Sebastian downstairs..."

---

Nicholas buttoned up his coat, wrapped a scarf a bit more tightly round his neck and made his way out to the windswept Boulevard. Outside the warmth of his home, it was far more intrusive, whipping round him, crawling into places where his clothing didn't fit quite snugly enough. He knew a great portion of the chill had nothing to do with the wind, and that knowledge only served to deepen his sense of unease.

For the first time in all the time he and Brandywine had known each other, they had come close to actually *having words* with each other, and he had *lectured* her on her place. That morning she had been crushed with remorse at how her promises dragged her from their house at all hours of the day and night; that their daughter lay upstairs in her bed suffering, and she was off...wasn't there beside her.

*"...Branny you and I made those promises together, and now you need t'do what you said you would do...what you promised t'do...and it's important, more important than anything right now, because no matter how you feel about your part in looking after this country for the last twenty years, you've been its guide and light for all that time. Caroline's*

*ministers and advisers...who knows what they would have done in your place...*

*"Maybe they would have followed the same paths that you set for them, but think, honey...think how much you've put up with from them, all the while just trying t'do what you knew in your heart Caroline would've wanted.*

*"Bella will never call you to account for that. She'd have done exactly what you're doing now....and I swear t'you...Branny...my mother loves her every bit as much as we do...and the twins are here...and 'Rissa, every day.... She's being taken care of, we're all looking after her for you..."*

He slipped gloves over his frozen fingers and put his head down against the wind, startled to find small ragged tatters of snow swirling around his boots and scurrying along the foundations of the buildings he passed. The walk to the Silver Rose had never seemed so long and endless before. When he arrived, he found Brandywine and Zoraya squirreled away at a shadowed corner table beside the kitchen. The remnants of a mostly-neglected lunch lay before them; the same could not be said of the carafe of red wine. Windy ordered whisky.

"...We've gotten word from Edmund that the Antillian fleet is moving south along the coast from Bedford," said Brandy. "He and a man from the village named Robin Adair have gathered up a ragtag army to get in the way of a land force they're pretty sure will get left along the way."

"And up north, any word from my father?"

"The Scandians won't be bothering us anymore. He's trying to outrun the storm, t'be here as quick as he can."

"So how long have we got before the Antillian ships reach the City?"

"A few days at most," said Zoraya.

"Zori thinks we can get through this," said Brandy. "With the flower...and you..."

He listened quietly as Zoraya explained the part she would have him play in defense of the City, and how it would serve her own efforts. As she outlined her plan he became aware of the cause for the uneasiness he had felt on his way to the café; that Zoraya had changed, in ways only those who had known her for any length of time could see. The disconcerting beauty, the mesmerising flash of her amber eyes, her entire presence had become *unsettling*. She seemed to vibrate with something overwhelming, an almost palpable force that was wild and threatening, in no way resembling the placid composure of the young woman who had stepped through Time to become a part of their lives.

He thought *This is what Brandy might have become if she had chosen to wear the flower,* and he shuddered inwardly, suddenly grateful they had decided to hide it away from the world, because Zoraya no longer *felt* quite like Zoraya.

"Do you undertsand how this will be of help to me?"

It was like she was speaking to a child, condescendingly, as one supremely confident and utterly sure of her dominance over another living thing. He nodded without speaking, more saddened than incensed, and for a moment the aura surrounding her came apart and he again recognised her as the mother of the girl his daughter loved. He saw an instant of confusion light in her eyes, a look almost of supplication, before she was become again the alien presence. He looked at Brandywine, and realised that she too was less than entirely comfortable in the company of their old friend.

"What about Sharad, Zori?" she said in a whisper, as if she too were a child, cowed by the authority of a parent in daring to even ask a question.

"I will deal with him later," she said. "He cannot trouble us now."

Windy forced himself to speak, knowing Brandy had had to summon up a reserve of courage to speak at all.

"Can you be certain of that? He's managed to sow fear and confusion at every turn, Zoraya. He destroyed an entire town..."

She smiled, and he could feel Brandy's hand clutching at his own under the table.

"I am the one he wants, Nicholas. All his efforts against the City and our people have been a challenge and a pathetic desire to seek my ruin through the ruin of innocents; to work the destruction of the life around me to wear down my defenses in order to breach them.

"He knows I have the flower and he will not dare to challenge me now."

# Chapter Twenty-Six – FATHER & DAUGHTER, MOTHER & SON

Nicholas realised that the hand he raised to knock on Arabella's bedroom door was trembling; that his heart was pounding away in his chest like a hammer on an anvil, and some strange emotion he had never truly felt before when it came to his daughter was making it difficult for him to breathe. He realised he was afraid...deathly so...not *of* her, but *for* her...for the memory and image he carried in his heart—of a little girl who was fearless and unfailingly joyous in everything she said or did, and so in love with the adventure of being alive that anyone who had ever come in contact with her could not fail to fall under her spell. Watching her grow into young adulthood had been as great a gift to him as a long ago declaration of love from a young woman named Brandywine...a day that he looked back upon as the very first day of his *own* life, a living and breathing that belonged only to him.

It had been three days since Kerissa had brought Arabella home. Though she had tried to appear cheerful and unaffected by the horrors they had witnessed together, there had been a haunted look in her green eyes that belonged only to herself, at once so painfully obvious that both he and Brandywine had been reluctant to even begin to draw her out of it, for fear of only making it worse. Within a day she had fallen into an abyss of misery, padding silently about the house for a few moments at a time, saying almost nothing, her face drawn and her hair gone to a tangle of tarnished gold. Kerissa had come to visit daily, staying with her almost every night, in the morning coming to sit with them at breakfast before bringing a tray back upstairs to remain almost untouched by evening. At the end of the week she had left in tears, without saying a word.

He forced the trembling in his hand to go away, and tapped softly at the door.

---

Arabella was only half-awake. Though already mid-morning, the curtains shrouding her bedroom windows kept away most of the light, and she tossed restlessly, lost among the spectral visions of her nightmares, trying to escape the ghosts that lurched and staggered through them. She shrank from a weight at the edge of her bed, not daring to open her eyes.

"'Bella...?" whispered her father. "Wake up, honey, it's just me you're safe now."

She shook her head violently, refusing to open her eyes for fear of what might really be there, calling her by name, but only to draw her deeper and deeper into the darkness. She felt a hand touch her gently on the cheek and whimpered, tried to escape, but she knew there was nowhere she could go, no pace great enough to outrun the creatures howling and snapping at her heels.

"'Bella listen to me...please...come back...*kitten-face please...*"

This time in the voice there was something she thought she recognised through the mindless shrieking in her head...a name she remembered from when she was small... that always made her laugh and drew her into waiting arms that belonged to someone gentle and loving and strong...who never raised his voice to her in anger or hatred... always turned away from whatever else there was in the world to be with her.

"Daddy...?" she said, pleading for it to be so.

The hand came away from her face and another joined it on her shoulders, came to gather her up from under the empty frozen waste beneath her blankets.

"You're safe now, kitten-face," said Arabella's father.

She dared to open her eyes. Praying for absolution through her tears she sobbed:

"Daddy I've done such bad things..."

---

He sat beside her on the bed and combed the tangles from her hair, grateful for the sunlight that flooded over them once the curtains were drawn. finally come to bring a measure of warmth back to her, chase away the chill hands that had taken hold of her in his absence.

"You had no choice, 'Bella," he said softly. "Kerissa told us everything. We never should have let the two of you go. We didn't know then what was really happening."

He put away her comb and stroked her hair, her face, brushed away tears. She curled herself into a little ball, crawled into his arms and shivered.

"I had *one* choice, Daddy," she said miserably.

"I know, 'Bella...but you didn't know he was lying, or that he thought he was telling the truth. You can be forgiven for that."

"Have you ever killed anyone?"

"No, honey, not ever. But I've been lucky enough to have never been in a situation where I was afraid for my own life enough t'kill for it."

"But he was running away...and all I could remember was the nasty things he'd said about Mom and Zori and 'Rissa, and how he'd promised t'do terrible things to all of us. He was running away, but I thought if I let him go then he would always be out there trying t'make his horrid promises come true."

Nicholas reached round to take her shoulders again, gently moved her to where she sat back, on her knees facing him. There were tears streaming down her face, and he realised there were tears running down his own face as well.

"I don't know what t'tell you, 'Bella, not for something like that. I can't say if what you did was right or if it was wrong. I wasn't there. And it may be in a time and place like that, rightness or wrongness don't even exist—"

"Daddy I—"

"No, let me finish, baby. I'm hoping it somehow makes some kind of sense so you'll stop hurting so much. I've never been in a place like that, or been faced with that kind of a decision to make, so I just don't know....but I *do* know who my little girl was before the world outside decided to come crashing into her world, and I *do* know that my little girl would never have dreamt of harming anyone or anything unless it was to keep the people and living things she loved from harm.

"I'm not saying there's any kind of excuse for some of the things we find ourselves doing, but what I *am* saying is that sometimes, because we're not perfect beings, some things should be *excusable*...so we can learn from them, try to forgive ourselves, and try like hell never t'let them happen again.

"It may very well be that what you've gone through will be nothing compared to what Antillia may bring to us in the next little while. I used t'think there was no excuse for any kind of violence, but there's a lot of people in the world don't feel that way at all. Renard de Montenay was one of them, and the people coming to make war on us are like that too. They have no regard for anyone but their own interests, their need to have power and dominance over anyone who can't stand up t'them. So we have t'fight them; we have t'bloody our hands in order t'stop them from bloodying our lives."

He stopped, choked by his own emotion, and they brushed away each other's tears and wept again.

"How do we know?" whispered Arabella. "How do we know when it's okay...?"

He put his arms around her again, his face in her hair.

"I don't think there's any way to answer that with any kind of certainty, sweetheart. Some things are just right and other things are just wrong. They're obvious, there aren't any questions. We can only hope all our choices are that easy, and then just do the best we can when they're not."

Arabella let herself drift with the thought, struggling to find a place where she could live with the times when there was no certainty of ever being certain. And then she let it go, finally solaced by the one certainty who was her father, and the sound of his heartbeat keeping time with her own. She whispered:

"I love you, Daddy."

And he said that he loved her too, held her closer, given a small gift of Memory—when she had been the child in his arms and added a certainty to his own life.

"Daddy, I have t'go see 'Rissa. Yesterday I made her cry."

"You didn't make her cry, baby. Kerissa was crying for *you*, because she didn't know how t'stop you from hating yourself. Besides, she'll be here later today, and since we won't leave your Mum or Zori here on their own, we've decided this is the best place for all of us. Jamie and Stella have been here since the day after you got home; everyone else will be here for the duration by this time tomorrow. We've all been worried about you."

"I'm sorry. I didn't mean to..."

"You don't have to apologise, Arabella. We're all we have—the people we choose to love, the ones who choose to love us back, who know our failings and can forgive them in the light of their own shortcomings."

"Is Mom home today?"

Nicholas sighed. "She's off again at the palace. We're expecting the Antillians any day now."

"She promised the Queen t'care of things."

"She did...and she's still trying t'keep her promise. You're just like her, y'know. You would've loved Caroline...the woman we knew first as Marie. You would've loved her every bit as much as we did.

"Honey, d'you think you might try some dinner tonight? Grams would be so happy t'see you up and around some..."

---

Alexandra was in the kitchen looking after supper and the twins, while Andrew and Alain snugged into their corner of the coach house. She looked up at Nicholas, hopefully.

"There'll be one more for dinner tonight, Mum" he said, smiling cautiously. "I think she's going t'be all right..."

He turned to Jamie and Stella.

"You guys just have t'give her a little bit of time, try t'keep her from getting too worked up over anything. You've been really good so far."

They both nodded solemnly

"We won't ask any questions about the bad stuff, either," offered Stella.

"That's my girl," said Nicholas with a grin...

---

Arabella came downstairs a few minutes later, sat quietly through their meal, barely touching the bowl of soup in front of her—chicken and rice with mushrooms and onions and celery, her favourite from the moment that Alexandra brought it to table in Élysée, fifteen years before—and fresh-baked oat bread straight from the oven, slathered with butter. Alain and Andrew sat at table with them, but uncomfortably, being newcomers to having to deal with her since her return. She said almost nothing unless spoken to directly, and then responded with only a few words, before the haunted look came back into her eyes and she tried to hide behind a spoonful of the soup.

"'Bella, if Uncle Nicky will make a fire for us in the music room, will you read to us?" asked Stella cautiously. "Everybody's been real busy while you were away and..."

Her voice trailed off into an awkward silence, and her face showed a momentary panic until *Uncle Nicky* nodded, to reassure her the request had been a good one under the circumstances. Arabella looked at everyone at the table, especially the twins.

"I'm gonna be all right," she said hesitantly. "Really. I will I promise...and I'd love t'read t'you guys after supper..."

She wanted to help clean up, but Nicholas led them up to the music room and laid a fire for them, insisting that *he and Grams* could look after that. He left them with the twins clamouring for yet another read through Uncle Thomas' very first book, *The Snow-King's Daughter*...descending to the kitchen again, where his mother had yet to look after anything in the way of cleaning up after dinner. She looked up at her son from the table, obviously as much in need of reassurance for any number of reasons as they all had been in the previous weeks.

"Alain and Andrew are making themselves small somewhere," she said. "Nicky, I'm so afraid for her."

He made to start clearing dishes from the table but she reached for his hand and drew him down into the chair beside her.

"Come sit with me," she said, almost pleading with him. "Sometimes it feels like we're all wandering off in different directions, alone in our own private little nightmares. I keep thinking what if something bad happens to your father or your brothers...or what if something truly horrible had happened to 'Bella or 'Rissa...or to any one of us...just the thought of Sebastian coming so close to dying...I can't imagine what it's been like for any of the children...even the twins...so terrified of all these things going on that they can't even begin to understand...

"Nicky I know how foolish it sounds...like I'm some querulous old woman afraid of everything—"

"Then we're all becoming querulous old women, Mum," he said. "Believe me you're not alone in feeling this way. Ask any one of us and we'll know exactly what you're talking about."

Alexandra drew him closer, touched his face, stroked his hair, all the while her pale grey eyes seeking some kind of solace in the mirrored gaze of her youngest son. He put his head down on her shoulder—something he could not remember doing in all the years since he had come to the City—and as her arms encircled him felt his own terrors tearing loose inside of him, roaring at him from the place where he had tucked them neatly aside, where they would not intrude upon the daily round of things needing to be done. And then for an instant he knew an inviolate sense of *safeness*, the feeling he had known as a child whenever his mother had come to him in the wake of his small childhood disasters and disappointments.

"We'll get by, Mum" he whispered. "I can't imagine a tomorrow where we've all failed t'get through the days ahead...to where things *can't* be normal again...whatever *that* might be..."

"Normal seems like such a long long time ago," she said.

He laughed softly and took his turn at reassuring her, taking her up into his arms and, with a shock of dismay, realising she had become so much smaller...seemingly more frail than could he ever remember, where once she had been the unshakable foundation of his life.

"I don't like getting older, Nicky," she murmured. "I don't like it at all. It makes you afraid...afraid of losing all the people and things you love to...to some nameless faceless cold empty darkness. Poor 'Bella...and 'Rissa...they went away dreaming of grand adventures and excitement because we helped them grow into being more than just *girls*...and now they've come home with their hearts bruised and their souls shaken...

"I want your father to come home soon....so badly..."

"Mum, we'll survive this," he said again. "You once told me not t'be so careful with my heart, and then Branny came along. After that I stopped being afraid, because I knew I had you and her and all of these people I'd met who had become another family for me...and I began to realise that when we open ourselves up to what the people we love have t'offer us...when they do the same thing, accepting what we have t'offer them...we leave ourselves open to the possibility of incredible loss and heartache, and yet we do it anyway, because in that weakening of our defenses, we find out how t'be strong for ourselves and for those who've become important to us."

They heard seven-year-old shrieks of terror and delight, and the soft answering laughter of the seventeen-year old girl reading to them. Alexandra lifted her head from Nicholas' shoulder and smiled, took a cloth napkin from the table and wiped at a single tear that had escaped her notice. A current of cold air snaked its way through the house into the kitchen and they heard the front door slam.

"Hey I'm here!" called Kerissa. "Anybody home...? I'm starving..."

Alexandra stood up, smoothing the front of her apron.

"We'll get by," she said. By noon the next day, *les Boulevardiers* and their families would all have come to stay in St John's Mews. Alexandra became all business.

---

Nicholas sat before a dying fire in his music room, nursing a glass of whisky and listening to the wind whistle down the chimney, reminding him of a similar night two decades earlier, when an artist neighbour had come to him *in extremis* and told him a tale of lost love and heartbreak. Robertson the painter—who in truth had been a man from the Dales named Alain Ardrey—was gone nearly all of those twenty years, but on this night Nicholas considered the possibilities of loss and heartbreak for every one of the friends and family now sheltering under his roof. Once before he himself had acknowledged having lived a life entirely free of such things, but tonight the prospect of disaster weighed upon him personally, and he poured another whisky in deference to, and in defiance of his fears.

Lost in his thoughts, the house but for the wind utterly quiet with everyone gone to bed, he didn't hear slipper-shod feet scuffing at the floor, or even noticed when Evrard sat down to face him in front of the fire.

"Mister Wyndham...sir...?"

Windy looked up from his glass, found Evrard de Montenay staring at him.

"Nicholas would be fine," he said, smiling.

"All right then...Nicholas...I need t'talk with you, please. It's about your daughter..."

"Arabella?"

"Yes, sir. I know she's not been well and I don't want to add to the things that have made her ill...but at the same time I feel like I owe a debt to gratitude to all of you and...I'm afraid just seeing me might—"

"You know about your father?"

Evrard said, "I know it was 'Bella who killed him. I heard it from Diana and Thomas... and then Kerissa...but I want 'Bella t'know that it's not something I'll ever blame her for...ever... I just don't know how t'tell her that, or if trying will only make it worse for her. I'm leaving tomorrow morning and—"

Windy offered a glass that Evrard declined. He went on:

"I'm going west again, to meet Edmund and Robin Adair along the rail line to Bedford. They seemed quite certain the Antillians would try t'land a ground force to come at the City from that direction, once their fleet had taken a turn at us."

"You've seen your family here?'

Evrard nodded. "I have. Annie Br...your wife...was kind enough t'get me into the palace t'see them the day after I got back with Sebastian. They know my father's dead. Brandy told them, but also said it wasn't important for them t'know how it happened...and honestly, he never gave them any reason to love him overly much so I guess it doesn't matter whether they know or not...but 'Bella..."

"She's sleeping now."

"She is."

"And you'll be leaving early?'

"First light if I can."

Windy sipped at his whisky, stared into the sparks and glowing embers of the fire, heard the wind shrilling at the sorrow and travail of people at the mercy of their desires and failings.

"She's still keeping to her bed for most of the day, Evrard, but why don't you let me speak to her tomorrow. By the time you get back I'm sure she won't be so...well... whatever it is had you worried about seeing her again."

Evrard looked relieved.

"Thank you, sir. It's not my place, but she...and Kerissa...all of you..."

Windy smiled. "I know. I've had them all in my life since before you were even born and I still feel the same way. They're gifts, who care about me in spite of the fact I've done precious little t'deserve their concern."

"I've heard too many stories told otherwise t'believe that."

"That's as it may be," replied Windy. "Just be damn sure you come home to us."

"I'll do my best."

"Do a bit better than that, for all of us."

"I will, sir."

He rose and offered his hand.

"G'night, sir." he said.

"You've got a comfortable place t'sleep?"

"I do."

"Then I'll see you the next time I do, Evrard. Travel safely...and be careful..."

Evrard went downstairs and Nicholas drank the last of his whisky, was about to go off to bed when Brandywine came in from the hallway, head-to-toe in a flannel nightgown.

"I missed you," she said, "and then I didn't want to interrupt while you and Evrard were talking so I went t'sit with 'Bella for a little while."

"She's all right?"

"Not so restless as before. I think having everyone here will help...but I wish Evrard wasn't going off again."

She curled up in his lap and he tucked the hem of her nightgown round her toes.

"It's something he needs t'do, Branny" he said. "I don't think he'd even consider what you have in mind for him if he didn't take the chance t'make up for his father's treachery."

"I wish we could stay like this forever," she said wistfully. He didn't say anything, just hugged her closer. "But what d'*you* think of him, Windy? This is really the first time you've had a chance t'talk with him."

Nicholas thought awhiles, finding thought somewhat of a challenge with her in his arms.

"I like him," he said. "I'm pretty sure he thinks he's in love with 'Bella and 'Rissa, enough that he's trying pretty hard not t'cause them grief or upset...but I think it's part of his nature t'be that way about anyone he sees as being in need of anything. He's managed not t'lose himself in the wasteland his father created around him and his family.

"He's a good choice, Branny. For lots of other reasons as well."

"He's a lot like you, y'know." she said softly.

Windy smiled into her hair, shook his head..

"I think you and me should go t'bed."

# Chapter Twenty-Seven – IT BEGINS

"...What the devil are *you* doing here?" demanded Edmund.

Evrard shrugged. "I got Sebastian home, and then I heard you were still out here causing trouble, so I thought I'd come along to help."

He climbed down off his horse to join him where he stood beside the railway line with Robin Adair and a handful of westerners. The slopes overlooking the line were crawling with them, hundreds of men, women and older children, utterly silent unless they spoke to each other in whispers. Hands were offered and taken all around.

"Sebastian is mending, but Arabella came home badly shaken," he said. "She took no physical hurt, but I guess my father was moving southward as well. He stalked them, and the girls set a trap for him."

"'Bella and 'Rissa captured your father?" said Edmund incredulously.

Edvard nodded. "In the middle of the night he got free of his bonds, but before he fled he had to taunt them with having killed Sebastian with the knife he'd meant for me. He was running away and Arabella put five arrows into his back, pinned him to a tree and left him for the crows. After that she ...she just seemed t'come apart."

"So where're they now?"

"Everyone's at Annie Branny's. Being in the Old City, it's the safest of all your family's houses. They're all looking after her, 'Rissa especially, but I didn't see her. Your Uncle Nicholas thought it would be best if he spoke with her about it before I did.

"As for the rest, Annie Branny filled me in, and it seems she, your uncle and Kerissa's mom have conjured something up for the Antillians." Turning to Robin, he said, "Did you get t'your family?"

Adair nodded. "And everyone else in Bedford, as you can see," he said, looking over his shoulder. "Our fleet has been leading them south and east, luckily with a wind at their backs. Once the bastards realised we knew they were here they just took up the chase and went right on by…"

"But you're expecting them t'land?"

"Edmund thought they would, and he called it right. They've already started…"

Edmund said, "Come have a look for yourself."

He turned and led the way up the hillside, exchanging greetings and news with those camped there. Evrard wondered at the absence of fires of any sort, even as gusts of wind tore at them, and flutters of snow swirled in the air around them. Nearing the crest of the hill, Edmund stayed them with a cautioning hand and began to crawl forward, until they could look out over the ocean that lay beyond. The reason for the lack of campfires became obvious.

Standing out to sea were dozens of Antillian ships, already in the process of sending boats ashore. Soldiers milled around on the beach below, waiting for the rest of their comrades.

"They were fools t'do this so late in the season," murmured Edmund, "but they thought t'surprise us, take us unawares. They also didn't take a couple of girls into account."

"The bad news," said Robin," is that there's an awful lof of them. I think they're gonna outnumber us quite badly."

"But the good news," said Edmund with a decidedly pleased look, "is they haven't a clue that we're here...and knowing the ground better than they do, we also know that there's no way they can march directly t'the City from this shoreline, so they've got t'come inland..."

Robin finished for him. "... And because they don't know where t'get through these coastal hills easily, they've decided t'come to us here."

Evrard brushed hair from his eyes, thinking as he watched another boatland of Antillians come ashore.

"I rode past a break in the hills riding this way," he said.

"They're easily found from the landward side," said Robin. "Not so much from the water. There's another break t'the west of us." Tossing his head in the direction of the beach below, he went on: "They just looked for a large open stretch of sand..."

"So when they start climbing up towards us, you've already got people coming in from both flanks to hem them in."

Both Robin and Edmund now grinned openly.

"That we do," they said in unison, looking quite proud of themselves. "And they can't use their guns on us, either..."

Under a grey sky, the City seemed deserted, the streets empty, windows that faced the harbour shuttered and boarded up as the beginnings of the earliest winter storm on record scoured in from the north. In the parlour of the carriage house in St John's Mews, in the warmth of the fire roaring on the hearth, Annie Branny, surrounded by *les Boulevardiers* and their families, held court along with a small group of bewildered officials, summoned from the palace earlier that morning.

"Miss Lloyd, I believe you owe us an explanation," huffed her defense minister, the stately old soldier whose army career had been totally devoid of soldiering. "This is highly irregular. *Who are these people?*"

"My family, sir," said Brandywine proudly. A small part of her, where she refused to acknowledge the horrible ramifications of their situation, smiled with delight. Her prime minister scowled, though through the past twenty years he had been been one of perhaps a handful in the palace who had been willing to work with her without too much fuss and bother.

"Miss Lloyd, you led us to believe you had made contingency plans. These cannot be shared with just anyone."

Brandy nodded. "Mr Prime Minister...sir... respectfully...but most of what you palace people have called our *intelligence* over the last little while has come *from my family*. Do you recall how one or the other of you would always be asking me *How do you know this, Miss Lloyd?*

"If not for my daughter and her friend, Kerissa—"

"And us too," piped up Stella. "Me and Jamie saw the sea monsters!"

"Yes...both of you as well," said Annie Branny with a smile. "If not for them, we might've learned too late of what Renard de Montenay was up to. My daughter and her friend Kerissa were the first to encounter Scandians within our borders, and to make me...us...aware of them. My daughter and her friend also were the first to encounter the man we have known as the musician, Azim Sharad...who was known to Kerissa's mother from her own past as a danger to all of us, the one responsible for the panic and confusion of the people who live in the City, the one responsible for inciting the Scandians *and* the Antillians, though de Montenay's treason with *them* began long ago."

The palace officials appeared dumbfounded. Brandywine suggested brandy; Nicholas served it round and she continued:

"My husband's father and family, and Thomas and Diana's two sons," she said, nodding at Diana, "are responsible for clearing the Carillon moors of Scandians and driving them back into the northern mountains where the storm growing outside our windows right now buried them days ago.

"And it's been Zoraya, Kerissa's mother, who's managed t'keep Azim Sharad from doing any more damage than the disaster he caused in Trowbridge."

The Minister of the Interior spoke up then.

"There's talk that de Montenay is dead...and you've secreted his family in the palace."

Brandy nodded. "That's true," she said. "It was my daughter Arabella who killed him, in the Westvales outside of Colbourne, and his wife and daughters have been my guests at the palace for weeks. His elder son was murdered in Bedford, likely by one of the Antillians his father was conspiring with. His younger son Evrard is with Tom and Di's older son, on the rail line to Bedford a day's ride west of the City, waiting to discourage the landing of an Antillian army."

"Why was I not informed?' demanded the old general.

"We don't have a large standing army, sir. I thought we'd be best served if they stayed here, to oversee evacuating parts of the City, and the building of levees along the river."

"What about your daughter and her...*friend*...this woman's daughter?" asked the Prime Mminister, looking at Zoraya. "We should speak with them..."

Brandy shook her head. "I'm sorry but I can't allow that," she said as kindly as possible. "My daughter has been ill because of the things she had t'do in defense of our country. Kerissa is looking after her. If you have specific questions I'm pretty sure one of us can answer them."

"This is unheard of," observed another official.

"Same as me being in charge is unheard of," said Brandywine. "But you've all been good enough t'respect the wishes of our last Queen, who was my friend, so we've all had a nice long while t'get used to *unheard of*, haven't we?"

"So we're simply to trust you and the plans you've made with—"

"My family. Yes."

Brandywine stared them all down eye-to-eye, daring them, politely, to gainsay her. They all looked away from the look of unwavering determination in her eyes.

Without looking up at any of them, Zoraya said, "They will be here tomorrow."

The Prime Minister was heard to sigh into his brandy.

"Miss Lloyd, it seems you have taken your responsibilites every bit as seriously as we have taken ours," he said, with meaningful glances at his colleagues. "It's a bit late to be changing horses in midstream where our defense is concerned.What are your plans, then? What can *we* do to further them…?"

---

Edmund, Robin and Evrard crouched in the shelter of an outcropping of rock at the foot of the hillside. Night had fallen quickly, bringing light squalls of snow on a wind rapidly gaining in strength and its ability to chill them to the bone.

"We can't just sit here through the night," said Evrard. "Without fires we're either going t'freeze t'death, or be so cold that by morning we may as well walk into their camp and offer to lead them t'the City."

Robin and Edmund had been thinking the same thought.

"So it's simply of matter of when," said Edmund.

The other two nodded in agreement. Robin swore at the cold as he got to his feet.

"I'll start spreading the word, send riders to our flanks," he said. "Within the hour?"

Evrard murmured his assent. "At our signal. They're still at landing the last of their soldiers; those already ashore have set up tents and cookfires. We can use that to our advantage, come at them in their own firelight while they're at supper."

Robin disappeared into a swirl of snow. Edmund was a disembodied voice in the darkness.

"You're good at this," he said to Evrard..

"My father was good at it too, when he wasn't half-crazed with anger or pride. Sevrain just wanted the girls, never paid attention the times he tried t'teach us things he thought we should know, but I did..."

"How are you with this, Evrard, knowing he's dead and Arabella the one killed him?"

"D'you mean am I angry with her...bent on vengeance...with murder in my heart...?"

"Well...yeah..."

"No," said the young man who now was de Montenay. "Not at all. Never. I didn't choose him t'be my father, though I often wished I'd had a choice...someone...anyone else...

"'Bella thought he'd killed Sebastian and she was mad with grief. I would have done the same..."

They were quiet for a few minutes, lost in their own thoughts, Edmund's filled with images of his brother with a knife in his chest...Arabella and Kerissa...his own parents...

"I saw my mother and my sisters before I left the City," said Evrard. "They said they were totally horrified by the news, somehow convinced that with him gone they would be at the mercy of the people who hated him, those who had suffered at his hands come to take their revenge on them. And then it came to them that they finally had been given their freedom from him, and those responsible for it had not the faintest intention of doing them anything but kindness. I'd already learned that lesson, thanks t'you and Sebastian...everyone else..."

"Annie Branny...and the girls," said Edmund.

He could hear Evrard's sad smile.

"Indeed," he said. "Annie Branny and the girls..."

They heard the muffled hooves of two horses riding east and west. Robin reappeared beside them.

"Twenty minutes or so." he said. "Another thirty for them to get ready."

"We go at them in an hour, then," said Evrard. "We'll light up arrows when we reach the top of the hill, and then scream our brains out as we go down the other side. The more noise we make, the less they'll hear of orders from their captains to stand against us."

---

Nicholas and Zoraya stood in the courtyard of St John's Mews. Nicholas was shivering with the cold, in spite of boots, a heavy coat, gloves and a knit cap; Zoraya was barefoot in an embroidered caftan, and the snow tatters seemed to shrink away from her, leaving her in a small circle of windless calm. On the breast of her robe was a purple flower that gave off the scent of an hundred orchids in summer, and her eyes shone with the light of molten gold in the darkness. Behind them, their family stood at the windows of the music room and downstairs parlour.

"I don't think this is going t'work, Zoraya. The cold will make it impossible t'keep in tune."

"Nicholas," she said, in a voice he didn't recognise, "you will not need all that clothing. Bring it now. The sooner we begin the greater my chance of success."

He retraced his steps back into the warmth of the carriage house, where a chair and his cello stood waiting in the foyer. In the parlour, Stella came away from Alain and Andrew and her brother, watched him as he shrugged off his outer clothing.

"You can do it, Uncle Windy," she said supportively. Behind her, Jamie appeared as back-up, nodding in agreement.

"Do what, honey?" he asked, leaning down to kiss her cheek.

She looked at her brother and then back at him, smiled and shrugged.

"I dunno," she said cheerfully. "But you'll do good, whatever it is."

"Thank you, Stella," he said. "I hope you're right."

With chair in one hand and cello in the other he went back outside; the twins carefully closed the door behind him, and went back to the parlour windows. In spite of the cold Nicholas stopped in mid-stride, overwhelmed by a tide of warmth that came rushing to enfold him from a circle of flames that now rose from the paving stones of the courtyard, with Zoraya a looming presence in its centre. He turned, looked up to the music room windows, where Brandy, his daughter and Kerissa stood, watching him. Zoraya's voice thundered through the shrill of the wind.

"It is time, Nicholas. Have I not spoken truth to you? It is foolish to wait any longer..."

She reached for him through the flames, drew him into the circle, where there was neither wind nor snow, nor any sound but for that of his breathing and her voice.

"It's been a very long time," he said.

"It was only yesterday," she replied.

She placed his chair in the centre of the circle and led him to it, and true to her word twenty years of the past were become a yesterday and midsummer of a night when the City had first whispered to him. He sat down, and began to tune the cello under her watchful eyes, and when it was done he drew his bow, tentatively, across the strings and looked for her, but Zoraya was gone...

The darkness beyond the circle deepened, became taut and electric with an anticipation he recognised after all the passage of Time, crowding into the Mews in a kaleidoscope of jumbled perceptions. Somehow the moon had won itself free from the shroud of the onrushing storm, bathing the courtyard in a brilliant wash of silver light that joined with the auric flames surrounding him. Then, as he bowed the strings of his cello again, came the same insistent humming sound that had first come to him so many years ago...

He bent over the neck of his cello, placed a finger cautiously on its bass string...drew his bow slowly across it and felt the cobblestones beneath his feet trembling with the sound.

"Yes..." he breathed, confident now, and having found the note, he closed his eyes and sought the chord, bowing it strongly...

"Yes," he said again, feeling the cobblestones leap beneath him, resonating with joyous strength to match the resonant thrum of his cello.

He felt the flames crowding round him in a hurricane of warmth and now he cried out a third time, but inarticulately...accompanying sound with no meaning, only the outpouring of an indefinable tide of sensation...with a chord becoming a flow of sound, and the flowing of sound become a sonorous explosion that filled the Mews as once again the City found its voice and *sang*, but now in a torrential chorus that was the voice not only of the City, but of the Findhorn...and the Westvales...and the Dales to the far north and the mountains beyond them...the heartbeat and soul of every living thing in the realm...the realm itself...crying out in defiance and defense of itself...

---

Edmund stopped in his tracks, halfway to the top of the hillside, aware that he was not alone; that all around him the people of the Westvales...his army...had stopped...and the ground beneath them seemed to shift and tremble and a sound unlike anything in his experience filled the air, driving snowfall upward and strangling the wind into stillness. Evrard and Robin looked at each other and then to him; desperately he signed for the signal arrows to be loosed into the air, knowing full well that their enemies on the seaward side of the hill would be now be startled into wakefulness.

"Whatever it is, we've got t'go with it," he shouted, and then, like a tide themselves, they surged over the crest of the hill and fell upon the Antillians below.

# Chapter Twenty-Eight – ANTILLIA & THE CITY

Windy played intermittently through the night, at times almost asleep, lulled and washed over by the hum and heartbeat of the earth that lay beneath the cobblestones under his feet. The storm that had threatened the City never materialised, though the air remained blisteringly cold, but within the ring of flames surrounding him he was warm, and drowsy, intoxicated by the intensity of what he had called up from the vast slumbering silences of his homeland.

With the sunrise, he roused himself up from a dream wherein he and Brandywine lay naked together, suspended in space, joined to each other, rocking back and forth in time to the irresistible thrumming. He opened his eyes and realised the flames around him had slowly begun to sink down into the stones, leaving him unprotected against the chill.

A voice whispered in his head:
*Now your work is done...*

From the far north above Snowdon, down the coast to Bedford, and then in a curve south and eastward, the shoreline of the realm was a series of inlets and estuaries of the many smaller streams and rivers that sometimes sourced as near to the coast as the highlands and hills that stood in greater or lesser degrees less than a mile inland. As one might expect, the harbour of the City was the largest of these, a broad almost circular expanse of water fed by the Findhorn and its delta on one hand, and the ocean on the other. Between them were two arms of earth and rock, that rose up on either side of the mile-wide entrance to the harbour like a doorway lacking only a lintel overhead.

Throughout the morning, the sun had slanted sideways across the expanse of open water, providing light if not warmth, as if the early winter storm that had failed to materialise during the night had left something of itself behind in retribution. Now, in early afternoon it shone upon the advance guard of the Antillian fleet, entering the harbour with its own brand of retribution, in payment for the rout and slaughter of its land force on a beach a half-day's sail to the west. Tentatively, one by one, they entered the harbour, reporting back to the body of the fleet; when it became obvious that the City had mounted no discernible means of defending itself, that the harbour was entirely empty of any waterborn craft but their own, small gunships gave way to heavily-armed dreadnoughts, over fifty craft in all. The indiscriminate shelling of the City began as the last of them entered the harbour. When no guns answered them from the shore, they moved closer, now destroying specific targets, extending the measure of their destruction nearer and nearer to the Old City.

A lone figure in an embroidered robe watched them for a time from the rubble of one of the first warehouses to be destroyed, and then moved purposefully through the wreckage of the paved Promenade until it stood barefoot and knee-deep in the water, oblivious to the cold. Zoraya closed her eyes, inhaling the dense perfume from the purple flower on her breast, humming to herself...

---

Windy all but fell into Brandy's arms as everyone in the house rushed to his side. Thomas and Gareth took him up and carried him indoors; Alain took great care with his cello; the twins took charge of his chair. Once inside, Diana and Andrew were waiting with hot cider and blankets as they all jammed into the front parlour, and stretched him out before the fire. In the silence that followed his "rescue", each of them became aware that the vibrations that had been a background to their night-long vigil now were slowly intensifying...a deep rumbling that began to grow in volume and strength until they could feel the carriage house vibrating around them, hear dishes and glassware in the kitchen rattling in the cupboards.

The girls hung back from the rest of them, Arabella visibly disturbed, casting anxious glances at the walls and ceilings as Kerissa stroked her hair and face, trying to calm her. Only the twins seemed to be unfazed by the strangeness of it all.

Jamie poked his sister in the ribs and said, "Neat, huh...?"

---

"...They didn't give you any idea what they were up to?" asked Edmund.

He shifted a bit where he sat near the top of their hill, looked out past the blood-stained sand and the Westvalers' resurrection of the Antillian camp to where the ocean shimmered blissfully away into infinity. Closer to shore he saw the bodies of the Antillians they had backed into the sea bobbing up and down in the surf, like children's toys in a tub of water. The shallow bullet-wound in his side itched when it wasn't throbbing in time to the now everpresent thrumming of the earth beneath him. Evrard shook his head every bit as carefully as Edmund moved; the flat of a sword-blade had taken him across one cheekbone, drawing blood from the impact and leaving the side of his face swollen and dark as a thundercloud.

"Nothing at all," he said quietly. "Kerissa's mother seemed to be riding herd on them, like she was running things, and that seemed t'be okay with Nicholas and Brandy. Thing is..."

Edmund darted a questioning glance in his direction.

"I don't know her that well...not as well as pretty much everyone else... She looked the same, but she seemed like a totally different person, kind of like her eyes weren't seeing any of the things in front of the rest of us..."

He appeared ready to say more, but Robin came up from the beach, no worse for wear in spite of the mass of cuts, nicks and bruises beneath the blood-stiffened tatters of his clothing.

"How are we?" asked Evrard.

"It's gonna be a long winter for some of our folk," Adair said ruefully. "I don't know how many of the Antillians we laid t'rest, but we've paid for it—at least two hundred dead and as many wounded, at least half of them seriously."

"I'm getting tired of this," said Edmund.

Evrard nodded. "I can't imagine what they thought t'gain here. It would have been so much easier if their people and our people in the City had just sat down and thrashed something out that would serve everyone."

"It doesn't seem t'work that way," said Robin. "Have we got any plans for...now?"

"Hadn't given it any thought," replied Edmund. "Evrard...?"

"What else can we do here?"

Adair said he'd be staying on. "They're my people...and my road home runs past all of theirs. I guess you two will head back t'the City?"

"We've done what we can," said Edmund, struggling to his feet. "I'm hoping what's going on under our boots is Zoraya's doing, and it's all in aid of dealing with that mess of damned ships. Evrard and I might as well go back..."

"Not before we see t'everyone here," said de Montenay. "We need t'thank them for trusting us ..."

Evrard started down the hillside alone, two pairs of eyes following him.

***

She sensed their notice, knew that as the only thing moving on the shore they would focus on her, train a shell in her direction, if only for sport. They could not see her smile, could not begin to understand the place from whence she looked down on them. At her feet, amid the natural wash of water aganst the shoreline, ripples appeared, moving in time with the underlying vibrations awakened by Nicholas' cello.

She spoke words in silence. Her fingers stretched and curled at her side, then clenched into fists as the muscles in her arms tensed and her lungs filled with a single breath drawn from the winds of antiquity, spell-castings held in the very air...waiting...

Her eyes fluttered open, now unseeing as the Unseen filled her, arms slowly rising...an invitation offered to the ships in the harbour, drawing them closer as the waters of the harbour began to run backwards into the waiting mouths of the Findhorn delta. The world seemed to stop, somehow seemed to draw an inward breath...a moment...and then Zoraya screamed, levelled her arms at the Antillian fleet, and the rumbling of the earth in seconds grew into thunder.

"...Has anyone seen 'Bella...?"

No one had seen her leave the parlour. Now Kerissa looked for her and could not find her. The urgency in her voice startled everyone there from the hours of numbness brought on by worry and concern over Nicholas, and the unceasing assault of sound and vibration upon their senses . The twins called out her name and all of them looked round as if awakening in the midst of an ongoing nightmare.

"Find her," cried Andrew. "I'll stay with Windy..."

They scattered through the house, stumbling against walls, each other, and through open doorways. They clutched at bannisters as they tried to move up or down on the stairs, the floors creaking and rocking beneath their feet, windows rattling and shattering in their frames. Kerissa reached the second floor ahead of anyone else, with Stella trying to keep up with her, racing frantically from room to room until she reached Arabella's bedroom.

Wind had splintered the windows into shards on the floor, and swirled through the room, battering at the furniture, tearing the bedclothes into dervish dancing through the air. In one corner, behind the closed door of the closet, Kerissa found Arabella crouched on the floor, trembling, tears streaming from her closed eyes, hands pressed against her ears as she screamed in terror.

"Stella, tell everyone I've got her!" she shouted. The little girl nodded once and disappeared back into the hallway. Kerissa knelt into the shadow of the closet, closed the door behind her.

"'Bella I'm here now," she said, reaching for her in the darkness. "I'm here you're okay just hang on t'me and things will be all right..."

---

Those upstream of the Old City and those who had chosen to remain in their homes watched from the upper storeys of their houses as the waters of the Findhorn seemed to rear up like a wild animal, before plunging forward at such speed that when they rose above the height of the makeshift levees they created a vacuum that dragged them back into the flood. The roar was deafening, now so increased in volume that conversation was impossible; the ground shook with such intensity that movement of any sort became an invitation to be thrown bodily across the floor. The three bridges that served as entry to the City itself collapsed and were swept away, scything everything that stood in the path of the river as it swept over the delta. The wind created by its passage tore roofs from the buildings before the water buried them.

Zoraya stood in the eye of a storm unlike any ever seen, unmoving, untouched by the river as it seemed to part around her, to grow into a mountainous wall as it approached the Antillian fleet. A last barrage directed at the City from the dreadnought guns was swallowed in it. The sky grew dark and the air became filled with debris, all of it now directed at the invaders.

Stark and staring, Zoraya pointed, closed her eyes, and smiled as the first wave crashed over the front line of the ships, lifted them up, tossed them backwards one upon the next. In the voice of the storm her own voice rose into a shrill of challenge and then triumph as the fleet was slammed against the headlands enclosing the harbour and driven out into the open ocean.

# Chapter Twenty-Nine – IN THE WAKE OF THE FLOOD

"You're drawing again."

"I am. Your father thought now that we had some time I should take some for myself."

"I don't remember the last time you did that."

"Before you were born...maybe..." Brandy laughed. "I don't remember, either."

They were in a newly-fitted studio in the attic, one of Nicholas' priorities once basic repairs to the carriage house had been done. North-facing windows looking out over a largely-undamaged portion of the City let in a clear white light; a small hearth provided warmth. Brandy turned away from her easel to where her daughter stood in the doorway.

"Come in, sweetheart. How're you feelng today?"

Arabella inched into the small room, her head down, twisting strands of her hair between nervous fingers as she came to look over her mother's shoulder.

"That's pretty," she said, but not with much enthusiasm "The harbour... before..."

"It's from a sketch I did about the same time I met everybody for the first time. See... Uncle Alain's warehouse ended up here."

She pointed with her drawing pencil, but Arabella had already gone to one of the windows.

"I didn't see Grams downstairs, and nobody else is here, either...even Jamie and Stella."

She didn't see the look of puzzlement that crossed her mother's face, only stood at the window in a long flannel nightgown and stockinged feet, her hair a tangle down her back.

"Honey, Grams went home last week, don't you remember? She didn't want Grampa rattling around in the house on his own, said it would be a bigger disaster than the City if she left him alone for too long."

"I forgot. I thought Grampa was coming to visit *us*."

"Change of plans, baby," said Brandy. "Grams said we'd see them for Yuletide, for sure."

"So where're the kids...and everyone else."

"School for the twins. One of the first things we got up and running so all the grown-ups could start on rebuilding. That's where your Dad and everyone else has gone."

"I should go help."

"'Bella come sit with me. Nobody expects you t'help if you're not feeling well. You did your share and then some..."

Arabella turned reluctantly and it was all Brandy could do to hide her dismay. Her daughter's face seemed almost lifeless, with deep shadows beneath eyes that had become more haunted than ever. She shuffled over to Brandy and curled up on the floor beside her chair, laid her head down on her mother's knee.

"Would you sit for me, 'Bella?" asked Brandy, searching for something that would elicit more than the past week of shrugs and listlessness. "I'd like t'do a portrait of you for 'Rissa ...for Yule..."

She stroked Arabella's head, curved her hand round to her cheek and held it there, trying not to show her concern...to somehow pretend to take a casual attitude about watching her daughter waste away before her eyes.

"Maybe you could come up here with me and try drawing something. You used to, y'know, when you and 'Rissa were small. I bet you'd be good at it, better than me any day."

"I'm good at other things, Mom," she whispered. "Like killing people..."

She stood up abruptly and ran downstairs, leaving Brandywine to stare at a pencilled memory from a different lifetime.

---

In her bedroom, Arabella dragged her pack from the closet and started stuffing clothing into it, trying to keep her thoughts together long enough to do it with some kind of rhyme or reason. Her bow and a quiver of arrows fell out onto the floor in front of her and she began to cry soundlessly, tears streaking her face. When she realised she couldn't think of anywhere to go she crawled into the closet and closed the door.

---

At lunch time the kitchen became crowded with *les Boulevardiers* and their families, though Evrard and the

# ARABELLA

Beverleys had moved back into their digs, as had Gareth, Zoraya and Kerissa. Alain, Andrew and the twins were the only semi-permanent guests now, and as they all bumped hips and elbows at the kitchen table, conversation had revolved around the progress of efforts to bring the City back to a semblance of what it had been.

"...I saw Grim this morning. All the cats are coming back to the City. The harbour is the worst, though," said Alain through a mouthful of creamy chowder. "A lot of it is just going t'have to wait the spring...but with the warehouse in a pile and most of the market area as bad, it's kind of nice t'be home, or helping out elsewhere."

It became obvious that the absence of Arabella and Zoraya at table was a topic to be avoided. Tom and Diana had baked crusty bread to go with, both of them looking quite pleased with themselves.

"It's a bit on the heavy side though, Tom," chaffed Andrew. Alain sputtered into his bowl. "Did you sit on it when it was in the oven?"

"Hey be quiet," said Diana. "I mean it's not like either one of us has ever done this sort of thing before. It's a miracle it came out at all..."

"It's pretty good," said Jamie enthusiastically, reaching for another slice. "Can I have some butter?"

"I like it," said Stella. "Also the soup, Annie Branny. What's the chewy bits?"

Jamie poked her. "The're clams, Stella," he said. "That's why it's called *clam* chowder..."

"At least now we know why these guys can cook," said Gareth, nodding towards Edmund and Sebastian."

"It was self-defense," replied Edmund. "That or mooching dinner from all you guys every night."

"Mostly it was because Mom and Dad forgot about eating a lot," offered Sebastian. "Suppertime would come round and he'd be knee-deep in writing something, or Mom would have had a burst of inspiration and would be trying out a new dance routine."

"Well...at least the hardship didn't stunt your growth any," said Evrard. "Someday when I'm grown up I wanna be as big and strong as you guys."

"Watch it, brat," warned Diana. Evrard grinned and Sebastian, recovering quickly under the constant ministrations and care of his family, leaned his way enough that he came off the bench and ended up on the floor.

"How's your mother and sisters doing?" asked Brandy, helping him up. "I haven't been t'the palace for...wow...it's been a whole two days..."

---

Kerissa had not spoken at all through lunch, only sat quietly beside her father. Now she stayed behind when everyone else had gone, nursing a mug of tea at the table while Brandywine cleaned up the last few bowls and dishes before joining her. Both suddenly seemed exhausted, and 'Rissa made some inarticulate sound before she wriggled her way into Brandy's arms.

"Nothing I say or do is getting through to her anymore," she said miserably.

"It's horrible," said Brandy. "I don't know what t'do or say either. This morning she came upstairs and watched me draw for a few minutes and when I suggested she should draw stuff with me she said the only thing she was good at was killing people...and then she ran away. When I went looking for her later I found some clothing stuffed into her backpack....like she was leaving...but she was in the closet, 'Rissa. She was hiding in the closet with the door closed. I managed to get her back into bed, but..."

"I'll go see her in a minute. We have t'keep trying..."

Brandy nodded, reluctant...uncertain how to broach another subject both of them knew to be on her mind. Kerissa saved her the trouble.

"I haven't seen much of my mum, either," she said unhappily. "She's not been here?"

"Not since the night before," said Brandy. In the last week Time had become measured in the days *before* the Antillians had come to the City, and *after*...

"She's changed too, Annie Branny. She looks older now, and she gets this faraway look in her eyes...like she's turned into a total stranger...and then she sort of wakes up from wherever she's *been* and things are okay for a little while before you see it...the flower... drawing her back again."

"She has t'give it back."

"I know...she promised...but I don't think we're allowed t'force her t'do it..."

---

Arabella was a shapeless lump under her blankets when Kerissa quietly opened her bedroom door, edged into the half-light that snuck round the edges of the curtained windows. She sat on the edge of the bed and softly called her name.

"Go 'way, 'Rissa...go 'way please..."

Kerissa said "No...not anymore 'Bella. I miss you so much I can't breathe. I don't care if what you think you've done is so horrible you can't be with me anymore. Whatever it is it's nowhere near as horrible as not having you."

"I hate myself, 'Rissa. I'm afraid t'look in the mirror."

"Then I'll have t'love you enough until you change your mind."

She slipped out of her clothing and crawled into bed beside her, waited until Arabella stopped pretending to be a board under the blankets, let herself be coaxed into her arms.

---

Zoraya came to Brandywine the next day, supposedly looking for her daughter, but as Brandy walked beside her to the kitchen, she realised that beneath her cloak was the carved wooden casket that had lain hidden in her basement until a few weeks ago. Brandy made tea. When she turned with two mugs in hand, Zoraya was standing beside the table and it lay beside her.

"I'm sorry it took so long," she said, accepting her mug.

"You saved us all," said Brandy.

The curious amber eyes grew brighter in a face that suddenly seemed to have aged ten years in the few minutes they had been together. She saw the faraway look that Kerissa had spoken of.

"I did, didn't I?"

"Yes, Zori...you did..."

"I was wrong though, Brandywine...about there being no consequences to using it. I should have known; there's a price for everything. I feel so old now. I've never felt this way.

"I could have done *anything* I chose to do, but at a cost. I even considered breaking my promise, keeping it for myself, and then realised the flower itself would exact payment from me if didn't return it to you; that it doesn't make you into something apart from your own humanity; that it exists to make you see it, feel it even more keenly than before. It draws its power from those who have learned how to use it. It's like a bargain, a contract between you and it. The de Montignys knew only a small part of its capabilities, passively drew upon only it's natural ability to prolong Life."

They stood an arm's-length from each other, until Brandy put her mug on the table beside the casket, took the one from Zoraya's hands and placed it there as well.

"It's over now, Zori," she said softly, moving closer to her. "Now we just need t'get back to *before*..."

Zoraya said, "Soon..."

## Chapter Thirty - THE SORCERER

"...She's gone again," said Kerissa unhappily. "This is the third time. She never says anything, just does that disappearing thing and we don't see her for days. My father's going a bit crazy with it."

They were in Kerissa's bedroom, in the loft over Gareth's studio on Old Princes Street. When it was announced that classes at the university would resume after All Hallows, Arabella had shown no interest in beginning there; Kerissa had decided to stay with her, unwilling to jeopardise the slow but steady progress of her recovery.

*"I'll go back when you're ready, 'Bella,"* she'd said. *"It wouldn't be any fun if we weren't there together."*

Arabella had been pretending to read a book, but laid it down beside her on the bed.

"What about Hasan? " she asked. "Didn't I see him in the kitchen when we came in? She never goes anywhere without him."

"She does now," replied Kerissa. "He got huffy the first time, but it was just her being away that was really upsetting him."

"How'd you know that?"

Kerissa made a half-hearted smile. "I'm half magical too, remember. But even Dad can hear him now. The flower did all sorts of weird things..."

"He never talks t'me," said 'Bella. "I think I make him uncomfortable."

"Don't be silly. He's just being careful because...well...you know.."

"Yeah. Arabella's on the edge. Who knows what will set her off again..."

"'Bella stop it's not like that at all..."

The blonde girl shrugged irritably. "I'm just tired of everyone tippy-toeing around me, 'Rissa. Even you do it."

"I don't mean to..."

"I know that...but I don't wanna be sick anymore, and sometimes everything just crawls back into my head and I can't stop it."

"You have t'give yourself time, baby, that's all."

"What d'*you* think she's up to?"

They both knew the answer to that question, though Kerissa had been careful never to make mention of the primary cause of Arabella's "illness".

"She's looking for *him*, isn't she?" challenged Arabella harshly.

Kerissa grew panicky, searching her face for any indication of yet another *relapse*. Then she nodded cautiously.

"I think so. We're all so grateful t'be free of Antillia and Scandia and...well...we keep forgetting who started it all. Mom hasn't forgotten..."

"D'you think Hasan knows where she is now...and he's just not telling...?"

Kerissa nodded again.

"I do. I'm pretty certain he knows, but she's told him not t'tell, so there's no chance anybody else can get hurt."

"Maybe he's gone, 'Rissa. I heard my mom saying they've been watching for more of his 'concerts'...stuff like that...but there's been nothing. Maybe he's gone..."

Neither one of them believed it for an instant.

---

The day promised snow, great lowering clouds to the north darkening the sky as they drew closer to the City. In despite, Brandywine had proposed a shopping expedition for Kerissa and her daughter, something to distract 'Bella from getting too deep into her thoughts and memories. They dressed for the outdoors in the foyer of the carriage house in the Mews, bundling themselves into woolen caps and trousers and billowing cloaks.

As they stepped into the courtyard Kerissa froze, a stricken look on her face.

"She's in trouble," she said. "Bad trouble."

"Who, 'Rissa?"

"My mom."

"Where is she?"

"I don't know, 'Bella, I don't know."

Kerissa was frantic, the calm she had maintained at all costs for Arabella's benefit thoroughly deserting her. Together they stood helplessly in the doorway of the carriage house, each of them suddenly aware of Time ticking away, every second feeling like the imminence of yet another disaster come to visit itself upon them. Neither one of them noticed the dog-fox flicker into the air at their feet, dancing about their knees and yipping at them before he leapt into Kerissa's arms.

"He knows where, 'Bella!" she cried. "He says we have t'hurry...that I have t'try t'do magick—"

"Not yet, 'Rissa. Wait for me don't go..."

She raced back into the house, climbing the stairs to her bedroom three at a time. Once there she went to the closet, wrenching the door open, drawing her swordbelt and pistols from the hook to one side of the door before bounding downstairs again, out into the courtyard. Hasan was squirming in Kerissa's arms, his cries becoming shrill and desperate.

"'Bella hang on to me, hang on tight...Hurry!"

She wrapped herself around them, closing her eyes as the courtyard reeled dizzyingly around them she felt the cobblestones dissolve under her booted feet...an eternity of nothingness swallowing them up and carrying them away...left them stumbling in a foot of snowfall under a featureless grey sky broken only by what appeared to be a lightning storm high up on the cliffs to the west of...

"Bedford!" shouted Arabella. " 'Rissa we're in Bedford!"

They stood in the middle of the deserted high street.

"Where's your mom?"

Kerissa opened her eyes and pointed towards the cliffs.

"Hasan says she's there."

"Then why are we *here*?"

"'Bella I'm nowhere near strong as my mom...this is as close as me and Hasan could get us..."

Arabella cast about in desperation, belting sword, daggers and pistols around her waist. He eyes lit upon a signboard above the door of the local inn—a mermaid on a rocky shore, staring yearningly upward to a full moon.

"I'll be right back, 'Rissa."

She burst through the door of the Moonstruck Mermaid, ignoring the stares of a taproom full of villagers too lately delivered from destruction at the hands of Antillians to dare what might await them on the clifftops.

"Miss Arabella!"

"Jacob I need horses! I need them now! Please..."

He nodded wordlessly, and she was gone back into the street, to the stables beside the inn, leading two horses by their rope halters to where Kerissa stood beside Hasan in the snow, leaping and barking in a frenzy. Arabella was astride one of them in seconds, Kerissa an instant behind as she kicked it into a gallop on up the high street, snow churning in its wake, and turned onto the track running out to the ocean...

---

As the girls charged up the last incline to the top of the headland, the snowfall thickened around them and the very air seemed to come alive, take on a quality of some vile viscous translucency that held within its constant movement a folding in upon itself, over and over again, a welter of coruscating light amid a gelid spectrum of nightmare rainbows, as if the very nature of Reality was being twisted and tortured to the will of something beyond comprehension. The horses began to labour upward as it engulfed them; Kerissa and Arabella found themselves desperate for breath.

Their ascent became an exercise in futility, an hammering of despair and loss of hope that brought them to an agony of tears, even as they recognised it for sorcery and in their hearts knew it for what it was. Arabella could hear Kerissa choking back curses, ranting mindlessly to defend herself, to keep her resolve from disintegrating in the onslaught. They bent forward, kicking their booted heels at the flanks of their horses, and scrambled on. When finally they came to the plateau overlooking the western ocean, it was in time to see the stand of cypress erupt into flame, and Zoraya, no more than a score of paces from the track they rode, falling to her knees as the winds of Chaos shrieked and swirled around her, physically battering her into the ground. Kerissa broke away from her companion. Arabella followed the track, and would have wept out of sheer terror if only she had the breath to fuel it.

The thing that stood facing them on the cliff's edge was monstrous, something out of nightmare, an unholy creature formed of man and beast that stood well over seven feet tall against the lowering sky, fanged and clawed, its skin a leprous mottled white, scaled with mouldering scraps of fur, and hackles raised up along its spine that whipped in the winds it created and flung from the centre of a circle of black stones at the weakening soul that had walked as Zoraya.

It spewed hate and defiance out of snarling lips, jaws borrowed from the skulking scavengers of sun-blasted plains and steaming tropical forests. Its eyes blazed through two empty holes of desolation in a snouted face, nostrils twitching, lips drawn back in a howl of conquest. She recognised it now as the abomination that had posed as a musician, mesmerised audiences into believing they had been entertained, all the while its sole purpose bent upon this moment. Arabella spurred her horse forward towards it. She heard Kerissa scream out her mother's name, saw a rust-red blur racing across the headland beside her, now outpacing her horse.

Closer and closer they came, and for a moment she saw the nightmare's hideous grin of triumph distracted by Kerissa's wail of dismay. The rust-red blur became a dog-fox named Hasan, launching himself upon the beast. Arabella saw him fasten his jaws on its throat and then, watched heartbroken as he was swept away like a broken toy, tossed aside with one swipe of a clawed hand. She felt the horse beneath her thighs tremble, heard its hoarse moan of terror as she bore down upon the thing before her.

The impact as they collided was immeasurable. The creature was driven backwards even as Arabella leapt from her saddle full into its face. She drove her poniard upward from beneath its jaws, saw an incredulous light of disbelief in its eyes...for a moment...before the point found its way up into its brain.

And then...together...they went over the edge of the cliff.

# Epilogue – THE SORCERESS

It had been months. A desperate winter of murderous snowfall and bone-chilling cold, as if the laws of Nature had been abrogated by conflict, leaving the world at the mercy of Chaos and the frightening disorientation that followed in the wake of violence. At Yule-tide, Evrard had been crowned as a de Montigny, the first of his name, yet even that joyous celebration did little to return the country to normalcy. With spring, the City finally... slowly...came back to itself, but for those who knew all that had gone on in the shadows, who had, perhaps, paid a much higher price than any others in the process of having saved themselves from invaders, there was no sense of anything but an endless and overwhelming grief.

Diana continued to dance. Thomas continued to write. Edmund and Sebastian resumed their studies at university. Alain rebuilt his market stalls and warehouse on the harbourfront, whilst Andrew wrote heartbreaking poetry. Even Gareth spent time in his studio with clay and stone...but over all there was nothing that could fill the emptiness that had entered and filled the lives of *les Boulevardiers*. Brandy and Nicholas seemed to move in a never-ending nightmare. She spent more time than she cared to admit burying herself in the transitions necessary to legitimise Evrard's ascendence to the throne; Nicholas would just sit for hours at his piano or clavichord, or make harrowing sounds if he bent bow to a cello or a violin. Only Jamie and Stella wept; being children gave them neither the emotional strength nor knowledge to combat or rationalise the reality of Death, the loss of someone whom they had adored.

Kerissa became a dedicated but listless nursemaid to her mother, having no wish for anything more than to simply care for her needs during her convalescence. She rarely went out, even when there was a break in the inordinate cold; and though the friends she had shared with Arabella occasionally came to call, she was so unresponsive that soon even these well-intentioned visits ceased. It seemed the only thing left for her to share was the grief...when Brandywine or Nicholas came to keep her company as she watched over her mother...or the twins...all the rest of their family... No matter the attempts at conversation or distraction, they always seemed contrived, premeditated and useless... The only real constant was the dreadful absence of Arabella.

Zoraya spent weeks when she was barely conscious, crying out in pain or distress, as if wherever her combat with Chakidze had taken her was a place of hopeless and utter torment. She reached constantly for a dog-fox who now slept on a headland on the west coast. It was only after Evrard's coronation, when Brandywine finally was able to give over her secret regency and once again attend to her loved ones, that her presence seemed to draw Zoraya out of her prison. One morning she opened her eyes and found Brandy and her daughter sitting at her bedside.

"I'm so sorry," she whispered, reaching for both of them. "Brandywine I...I thought myself to be more than I was ...prideful...as arrogant as de Montenay in my sense of ...whatever...I don't know... I'm so sorry...so sorry...so...very...sorry..."

She drifted into what seemed like a normal sleep for the first time in all the time since her rescue on the Bedford headlands. Brandywine and Kerissa felt their own hearts come apart, and finally joined the twins in the outward manifestation of their desolation.

---

In all of this, Brandywine somehow managed to keep the nature of her promise to Caroline uppermost in all the things she said and did in the aftermath of her daughter's death. It spoke of her strength, that no one a score of years earlier would ever have dreamt belonged to her, that she would not rest until *she* felt that her promise had been fully kept.

The conversation she had had with Antonia Ballard—now something she thought of as having occurred in another lifetime—came back to her constantly as she endeavoured to fulfill the last of what she held to be her responsibilities. Caroline's last words to her, conveyed by the one who had been with her when she died:

*... Things as they have been in the past do not necessarily need to be part of the future...*

And their own last words together, that final night in the palace when Caroline de Montigny...the queen...her friend

Marie...on that night her mother and her lover...had tried to reassure her...

*"You will know the right thing to do, Brandy. No matter if it is unheard of, you will know what is right...you will be the one to change things...everything if need be...for the better..."*

She and Windy had many long winter nights to try and determine what was *right*...what needed to be changed...and how best to ensure that what Caroline had intended for her country came to pass. There was a course to be taken in her mind, on a morning in April when she managed to convince Kerissa it was necessary for her to take time away from her mother; that she wouldn't stir from her bedside until Kerissa returned. When Zoraya awoke, Brandy was there, shaking her head and pressing fingers to her lips to silence the apologies she knew would come.

"It's done, Zori," she said wearily. "We can't fix everything. 'Bella would have done what she did for every one of us. That was her way. We have t'figure out the best way for us t'go on...t'honour her love and her courage...and I've got just one more thing I have t'deal with now, and I think you're the only one who can really help me decide."

Zoraya struggled upright and took Brandy in her arms. They wept together, long and loudly enough that Gareth rushed into the twilit room that had sheltered his wife for months, and stood helplessly until he joined them.

"I'll get some tea," he said finally, not even bothering to wipe his nose or his eyes.

When he was gone downstairs again, Brandywine brushed away her own tears...and Zoraya's...

"Will you help me please, Zori? This is so scary. I need t'know as much as I can before I decide..."

Zoraya fell back against her pillows, her face a mask of desolate sadness.

"It's so hard to see my girl so heartbroken," she said, turning away. " 'Bella was like light...we lived and revelled in her simply being here among us...and now she's gone and we don't know what to do."

"There's only what's left for us t'do, Zori. 'Bella would have carried on no matter what. We've got t'do the same thing...so I need to ask you stuff...about the flower..."

Zoraya's expresion became one of infinite regret.

"I should never have allowed you to give it to me," she said. "I know it saved us from the the Antillians, but giving it up was not something I would have chosen if I had not sworn to everyone that I would do it...that it was only a temporary thing.

"Brandy it was wonderful and horrible all at the same time. I was the very first person to truly understand what it was...what kind of power it could bestow upon someone who *knew*..."

"That's why I want t'talk with you, Zori. One of the very last things Caroline said was that she trusted I would always do what was best for the City...everyone in our country...

"Before everything got nasty I talked with the woman who was with her when she died and she said that Caroline...Marie...had said something she didn't understand at the time...that I didn't need to let the past dictate what would be best for our future.

"You and me, Zori...the rest of our family...we're the only ones who know the truth, the secret and the power of the amaranth. No one who has ever served the de Montignys in the palace...a thousand years...no one of them has ever known, even now...

"I didn't even say a word to Evrard."

"What are you thinking, Brandywine?"

"Zori, I'm thinking that the flower in its own way has done as much harm as good; that maybe the House of de Montigny, now that it's safe again, doesn't need for each one of them to live a hundred years at a time."

"You're going to keep it hidden away?"

"I want t'destroy it, Zori. I want it t'go away forever. I want us t'live and be without the promise *or* the threat of what it can do. Renard de Montenay was willing to betray all of us just for a throne he thought belonged to him. Can you even imagine what he might have done if *he* had known...?

"Can you help me? Please. It's what I think is the best for all of us. Marie said I would always know what was best..."

Zoraya appeared to age a hundred years in an instant. One hand crept across the counterpane to take Brandywine's in her own. They stared into each other's eyes for what could have been hours but was, in truth, no more than the time it took for their broken hearts to bleed the same blood of loss and desperation.

"Will you trust me a second time in this?" she asked.

Brandywine nodded.

"Then give it back to me, Brandy" said Zoraya. "I will see that it repays all of you for your heartache, and that it never troubles the world again."

In June, a small wooden casket that had, but for one brief period, lain hidden in the basement of a house in St John's Mews for twenty years, once again came into the light for as long it took to transport it from its hiding place to the hands of a chocolate-skinned sorceress living in the loft of a stable on Old Princes Street.

Zoraya took it from Brandy's hands, trembling, her eyes wet with tears.

"Look for a tree of life," was all she said as she kissed Brandy's mouth. "You all have been so good to me. Tell my Gareth and my Kerissa I love them forever. Tell everyone."

---

On a bright sunshine morning in midsummer, Alain was making breakfast for Jamie and Stella. For some reason he could not explain, staying home that day had seemed the right thing to do. Andrew didn't complain. When dawnlight had crept between them, he had found Alain's face wet against his own. They kissed in the same moment that Thomas and Diana grew stupid with desperate loving of each other...the instant that Brandywine and Nicholas found themselves anxious to greet a new day for the first time in months.

Stella said, "We need t'go t'the ocean..."

Her pronouncement was given credence when one by one and two by two *everyone* appeared at the door to the Devreaux/MacKinnon household; when all of them spent the morning on a train moving westward to the railhead in

Bedford, and then slogged their way, arm in arm in total bemusement, to the cliffside and down to the water's edge where they had lost Arabella.

Only Zoraya was missing from their ranks. Gareth strode along beside his daughter, and if he alone truly understood why they had come the way they had come, it was evident that he had come to terms with its reality, and found the past twenty years to be enough recompense for the immensity of his own loss.

They stood on the slick wet sand, watching the tide rolling in, and on it, in the distance, a small something... floating...closer and closer until the incoming tide brought it to a clog of sand and cloth at their feet.

Brandywine sobbed out loud. Windy ran to kneel with her beside the figure that lay on a water-logged tapestry, embroidered with infinite detail. Kerissa knelt beside them, gathered up the blonde-haired girl who lay there.

"It's the Tree of Life," she said. "This was what Mum was working on for months. She finished it two nights ago...she's been gone since then..."

Arabella Wyndham raised her head and opened her green eyes, now sparked with a curious amber colour, that once had shone from the eyes of a Nubian princess.

"Hello Mum. Hello Daddy. Oh 'Rissa I've missed you all so much. I remember falling... it seemed like forever ...I was afraid, but after a while it felt like I was a bird in the sky... flying somewhere...I guess I was just dreaming..."

**Desperately Seeking Europe**

# Desperately Seeking Europe

Alfred Herrhausen Society
for International Dialogue

Editors: Susan Stern
Elisabeth Seligmann

Archetype
Publications

London

First published 2003 by Archetype Publications Ltd.

Published and distributed by:
Archetype Publications Ltd.
6 Fitzroy Square
London W1T 5HJ

www.archetype.co.uk

Tel: (+44 207) 3 80 08 00
Fax: (+44 207) 3 80 05 00

Alfred Herrhausen Society for International Dialogue

A Deutsche Bank Forum

Tel: (+49 69) 91 03 43 57
Fax: (+49 69) 91 03 60 90
www.alfred-herrhausen-society.org

Editors:
Susan Stern
Elisabeth Seligmann

Coordination: Maike Tippmann

Translation team:
Kathleen Cross, Marc Lowenthal, Bill McCann, Igor Reichlin

ISBN 1-873132-19-0
**British Library Cataloguing in Publication Data**
A catalogue record for this book is available
from the British Library

© Alfred Herrhausen Society for International Dialogue
Cover: Schaper Kommunikation, Bad Nauheim

All rights reserved. No part of this publication may be reproduced,
stored in a retrieval system, or transmitted in any form
or by any means, electronic, mechanical, photocopying, recording,
or otherwise, without the prior permission of the publishers.

Printed in Germany

# Table of Contents

Josef Ackermann
Desperately Seeking Europe . . . . . . . . . . . . . . . . . . . . . . .   9

## Them and Us

Slavenka Drakulic
Europe Tastes Better . . . . . . . . . . . . . . . . . . . . . . . . . . . .  21

## Through the Eyes of the Outsider

Michael Walzer
Europe and the 9/11 License . . . . . . . . . . . . . . . . . . . . .  29

Joseph Nye
The European Experiment . . . . . . . . . . . . . . . . . . . . . . .  37

Richard Perle
Europe: Ally or Counterweight? . . . . . . . . . . . . . . . . . . .  44

Sergej Karaganow
From Russia With Love . . . . . . . . . . . . . . . . . . . . . . . . . .  53

Tommy Koh
Learning from Europe . . . . . . . . . . . . . . . . . . . . . . . . . . .  67

Ma Canrong
The Chinese View of Europe .................... 72

Robert Weinberg
The Post-War Scientific Renaissance in Europe ....... 76

Chenjerai Hove
Mind the Gap! ................................ 83

## The Shape of the Union

Ismail Cem
Turkey in Europe ............................. 95

Michael Portillo
Plea for an Untidy Europe ..................... 101

Avi Primor
The Israeli Connection ........................ 114

Jiří Pehe
Central Europe Returns to the Fold .............. 123

Vaira Vike-Freiberga
A Dream in the Making ....................... 133

Janusz Reiter
Eurocivic Pride ............................... 141

Andrei Pleşu
Between Musk and Must:
Europe of the Eastern Europeans ................ 148

## The Developing Organism

Jacques Le Goff
The Roots of European Identity ................. 159

Ilija Trojanow
Forgotten Roots Remembered ................... 169

Friedrich Cardinal Wetter
Europe's Religious Origins and Future .............. 178

David J. Goldberg
The Diversity of Jews in Europe ................... 189

Yaşar Nuri Öztürk
Islam in Europe: Confrontation or Embrace? ........ 198

## Implementing Visions

William Wallace
Organised Europe: its Regional and Global
Responsibilities ................................. 213

Ralf Dahrendorf
Workaday Europe, Soapbox Europe:
Who Will Close the Gap? ......................... 224

Ulrich Beck
Cosmopolitan Europe: A Confederation of States,
a Federal State or Something Altogether New? ....... 235

## The Architects

Valéry Giscard d'Estaing
The Calligraphy of History ....................... 257

Romano Prodi
Reform and Proximity: The European Union
Defines its Borders .............................. 265

Pat Cox
Europe's Constitution in the Making ................ 275

Jean-Claude Trichet
European Monetary Integration .................... 282

Günter Verheugen
Construction Site Europe .......................  292

Noëlle Lenoir
France and Germany: The Odd Couple or
Future Motor of an Enlarged Europe? ...............  302

Matthias Berninger
Europe – A Continent for Consumers ...............  314

Ernst-Ludwig Winnacker
Joining Forces: Plea for a European Scientific
Research Centre ..............................  327

## The Core

Peter Ruzicka
Unfinished Europe, United in Music ...............  335

Adolf Muschg
The Splintered Plinth of Europe ...................  345

Cees Nooteboom
Kruisbestuiving ...............................  356

László F. Földényi
A Longing for Metaphysics: Europe and its Literature .  368

## Appendix

The Alfred Herrhausen Society
for International Dialogue ......................  382

Josef Ackermann

# Desperately Seeking Europe

*Console yourself, Europa! It is Zeus who has abducted you; you are the earthly wife of the undefeated god, immortal shall be your name, for the foreign land that has taken you in shall henceforth be called Europa!*

When an immortal being and a princess get together, something extraordinary is bound to happen. Europa's family is a large one – her offspring could hardly be more varied in size and appearance, they are scattered widely over land masses and islands, and they speak in different tongues.

And yet do they belong to one another? What is it that unites Europe and its people? A common cultural space, the so-called Christian humanist West, a common history, an identity even – or merely a stretch of land located between the Atlantic Ocean and the Urals, the Mediterranean and the North Cape?

What is Europe? Rarely are so many different answers proffered in response to a simple question. The quickest one might be: the European Union. Until yesterday it was an exclusive club of fifteen, a political island among the countries situated on this Eurasian spit of land. Tomorrow it will have twenty-five members and the day after tomorrow – with the accession of Bulgaria and Romania – twenty-seven. But we cannot reduce Europe to a political entity. Nor do we want to, because one thing is for sure: Europe and the EU are not synonymous. Europe has many contours and many faces; not everyone who is a European is necessarily a member of the Union club – and vice versa.

Nevertheless the EU may serve as a starting point for our observations. The European project of unification is unparalleled in the history both of Europe and of the world. Its impressive and successful history shows us a model of Europe as a dynamic community made up of very different members united by common interests. This unity offers them a basis for cooperation in promoting democracy on our continent, preserving peace, safeguarding prosperity and progress, maintaining and further developing a common cultural heritage and – so it is to be hoped – self-confidently fulfilling their tasks on the international stage in the future. After centuries of tearing one another apart, this truly is a 'European miracle'! We must not underestimate this fact, still less overlook it, no matter what difficulties arise from day to day in the course of working together economically and politically.

## Europe – theme of the year for 2003

The year 2003 provides a special occasion for casting a critical gaze at Europe. Now that the December 2002 Copenhagen Summit on enlargement has taken place, the EU is faced with a two-fold challenge: that of enlargement on a previously unknown scale and simultaneously the equally urgent need for consolidation of the integration process. The acceptance of eight Central and Eastern European states and two Mediterranean countries into the EU represents a major step towards the return of Central and Eastern Europe beneath a common European roof. However, as the boundaries of the EU progressively shift, so certain basic assumptions that were supposedly secure are now open to discussion. Does a larger club membership mean that core European ideas will be diluted?

How seriously must we take concerns about loss of identity in the wake of an enlarged EU? Are there limits to the enlargement process?

With so many accession candidates, the enlargement process might begin to conflict with the goal of consolidating unification. The EU's efforts to push forward with integration while remaining capable of political action are reflected in the establishment of the European Convention. The task of the Convention is to draw up a constitutional treaty ready for presentation this year. The aims are to guarantee that an enlarged EU is still capable of acting both at an institutional and political level, to create a democratically legitimated framework for seeking agreement and to achieve an appropriate distribution of tasks and areas of responsibility. All this poses a real test for the EU.

## Europe – between identity creation and self-discovery

Europe finds itself undergoing a tremendously dynamic process as it continuously searches for itself. This causes a permanent tension between the desire for unity and the centrifugal force of diversity. On the one hand it is necessary to have an idea of Europe, an image of the goal of unification, in order to mobilise the political, economic and cultural forces required to achieve this; it is only out of a strong sense of community that serviceable political decisions can emerge. On the other hand, however, structures and mechanisms need to be open enough to leave sufficient space for the different cultures and needs of the regions. The 'idea of Europe' must not be perceived as a centralising principle, as a strait jacket.

It is interesting to note that the view from inside contrasts with the view from outside: more and more countries see the EU as highly attractive and membership in it as desirable.

Even my fellow Swiss citizens are increasingly taken with the successful model of the EU, as indicated in recent referenda. In contrast, however, levels of acceptance and satisfaction among EU citizens regarding European integration have been diminishing for some time. The fear of a superstate that seeks to penetrate and standardise all areas of our lives is just as real for many people as is their scepticism towards the process of enlargement.

## Economic zone Europe – the power behind integration

It is not unusual these days to hear a clamour of voices questioning whether politics have taken over the reins from the economy. One thing, however, remains undisputed: from the very start the economy – one thinks back to the founding of the European Coal and Steel Community – has been the powerhouse and foundation of European integration. And ever since the common internal financial market has been nearing completion, the European internal market has acted as a pioneer of globalisation in the region. It provides companies with a springboard into international markets. This is also true for the Deutsche Bank as a global player with a strong foothold in Europe.

Furthermore, the European economic and social model is in competition with the Anglo-American one, from which it differs in a few crucial aspects. If Europe is to overcome the paralysis currently making itself felt in relation to economic growth and caused by holding onto the status quo, then it will have to adapt this framework, developed in the 1950s and 1960s, to the conditions prevailing in the information and service society of today. The revivification of the market economy, declared a goal by the European Council in Lisbon in 2000, is an urgent necessity. Mechanisms such as benchmarking and mutual recognition of standards and norms do better justice to many of the different political and economic structures existing in the EU than do standardisation and harmonisation. The accession of countries such as Poland, Estonia and the Czech Republic contributes a new economic dynamic to this, as well as a willingness to implement economic policies that are more liberal than those currently operated by some longer-standing members of the EU. The time for this fresh push could hardly be better: it represents an opportunity to carry out urgently needed internal reforms. A unique opportunity for the enlarged internal market lies before us, and we should make the most of it without hesitation.

The European Monetary Union is in a difficult test phase. A financial policy lacking in both solidity and coordination is jeopardising confidence in the common currency. However, the stability and growth pact does provide a guiding light for sound fiscal policy as well as a point of orientation for new member states. Re-establishing a consensus over the basic principles of economic and financial policy is of crucial importance if the European economy is to continue to prosper.

## Good governance for Europe

When the EU was founded, its institutions were designed to create a balance between national and Community interests, and the democratic legitimacy of European decisions was not a priority within this. However, the more core areas of national sovereignty that are covered by European cooperation – as in the case of monetary union, common legal structures, a common foreign and security policy – the more crucial direct democratic legitimation becomes.

Enlargement of the EU pushes the question of the Community's capacity to act more strongly to the fore. Thus, since February 2002, the European Convention has been seeking to establish a binding consensus with respect to the distribution of responsibilities, a more precise delineation of the EU's tasks and the balance between institutional structures and their respective decision-making procedures. It is agreed that federal and supranational elements have to be expanded. A number of promising approaches are being debated, some of which are discussed in this book. They include strengthening the Commission in its role as protector of treaties, reining in the centrifugal forces of an increasingly heterogeneous Union; a more significant role for the European Parliament in the decision-making process; and more efficient decision-making structures in the European Council.

Important political and economic issues require a European response, the democratic legitimacy of which, however, causes difficulties. It will probably not be possible to resolve this dilemma, which in all likelihood will continue to exist alongside the process of European unification. More democratic structures will not necessarily give the EU a greater capacity to act or make it more efficient. In those areas where the current institutional structures work satisfactorily – such as the internal market – their legitimacy is not explicitly called into question, simply because they are perceived as successful. What is decisive is the match between responsibility and mandate: only in this way is it possible to avoid the EU being subject to exaggerated expectations.

The EU is a project without precedence. The search for appropriate frameworks, processes and institutions is inevitably proving to be very much more arduous than proceeding along well-trodden paths. The constant process of self-examination and self-critique may at times seem laborious, painful and paralysing – but without it we would not be where we are today.

## Europe – on the way to becoming a global player?

As necessary as democratic structures and procedures are, they cannot replace the political will to tackle challenges and solve problems together. Years ago Alfred Herrhausen referred to this issue as follows: 'The more unity we develop in Europe and the more we speak with one voice, the more effectively Europe can participate in finding common solutions to global economic problems.'

Europe must come of age at the international level. In economic terms, the EU already is a global player. It is a different story in the area of foreign policy, however: even though progress has been made here over the past few years, the members of the EU still find difficulty in presenting a united position. And the telephone number that Henry Kissinger demanded in order to be able to talk to Europe is the same one being sought in vain today by the United States, Russia and China – and they are not alone. The need for a coherent approach that is shared by all the EU states is demonstrated only too clearly in the current foreign policy situation. This deficiency has internal consequences as well: inadequate agreement on current foreign and security policy leads to a lessening of solidarity among the citizens of the EU.

The EU must continue to assert itself as an exporter of stability and peace. It must take a keen interest in maintaining peace in its surrounding neighbourhood which, after enlargement, will border on many unstable regions. But one thing must also be clear: such an approach must not be limited to candidate countries. Rather, what is required is a convincing plan for achieving the European goals of democracy, stability and prosperity even without the prospect of accession.

And what role does the US play in this? The authors represented in this book are not the only ones to suggest that the EU can afford to dedicate itself to exporting peace and security only because the US is watching its back. This design flaw is perceived not just within Europe: on the contrary, there is a global need for a powerful European voice as a countervailing power to the US, the voice of a Europe that shares in decision-making and is prepared to take risks. Engaging in constructive competition with the 'other' superpower for social and economic models, as well as devising strategies for global conflict resolution, must be our long-term goal.

## Desperately seeking Europe

The current debate concerning the end point of the enlargement and integration process makes one thing crystal clear: hardly any clarity exists at all in relation to the basic assumptions about what keeps 'us Europeans' together. This is why it is so urgent that the citizens of Europe come together again to discuss their commonalities, visions and aims. In view of the shifting boundaries of the EU, Commission President Prodi is calling for an urgent debate on 'Europeanness', to which *all* Europeans are invited to contribute. This is because, as mentioned at the start, Europe and the EU are not synonymous and we should not wear blinkers. Europe has many contours and many faces, far more than those of the Union.

'Desperately seeking Europe' – it is no coincidence that this heading stands as a leitmotif over the articles written especially for this book. So let us ask once again: what gives Europe its identity? Do we Europeans share a common history, a common culture? What about religion, common values? Is there a European literature, European music? And in any case, who is 'European'? Not all of them are represented in the political club of the EU. What does Europe mean for a Norwegian or a Swiss? For a Turk? An Israeli? For a Croat? Where are the borders of Europe? The school atlas surely cannot be the sole criterion.

When Peter Ruzicka states in his chapter that 'in terms of music, Europe had already long been united when the trenches between hostile fatherlands were still being dug', it becomes clear that it is short-sighted to consider only the political or economic dimensions. What of the common European experience? Is it epitomised, as the Swiss Adolf Muschg thinks, in the Ghent altar of the Brothers van Eyck? Is it the 'Europe of ideas', that for Dutchman Cees Nooteboom stands above a continent repeatedly torn apart, or is it rather the 'untidiness' that does Europe good, as in Englishman Michael Portillo's view? Why does Hungarian László Földényi believe that Tolstoy and Dostoyevsky belong to European literature alongside Kafka and Proust? And how does Andrei Pleşu experience the opening of his home country of Romania to Europe – as a setting off or as a returning home? To what extent is Islam, in the eyes of Yaşar Öztürk, a constitutive element of the European experience? And what can Europeans learn from looking at their continent from an African perspective?

We are well advised to reflect on the commonalities and differences that exist within Europe and to make our contribution to the discussion about Europeanness. The Alfred Herrhausen Society for International Dialogue, the sociopolitical think tank of Deutsche Bank and our forum for dialogue and intellectual debate, has set itself the task of finding 'Europe' both within and beyond the EU. This search has developed into a passion: the more intensively we have grappled with the material, the more complex, the more contradictory and multi-layered appear the responses to our supposedly straightforward question: 'What is Europe?' International experts from the fields of history, politics, religion, culture, business, the arts and the sciences have joined us in our efforts to identify what it is that keeps Europe together, what role it plays and where it is going. This book is the result of the quest.

In putting the book together, we asked for several non-

European perspectives on given topics, because very often, views from different parts of the world open our eyes to aspects that hadn't occurred to us. But even the view from inside can sometimes be revealing and unexpected. At this point, I would like to thank all of the authors for their highly differentiated and enlightening appraisals.

The contributions are of great significance for Deutsche Bank. The positioning of our company within global financial structures depends among other things on the development of our home market, Europe. A stable, secure and simultaneously dynamic and energetic environment is of vital interest to our business.. Naturally we are well aware to what extent the so-called 'soft factors' enable us to operate successfully in the first place. I am convinced that a company that stands by and acts upon its social responsibility can contribute in a lasting way to its own shareholder value.

I hope that this book and all of our events and activities revolving around our theme of the year 2003 will make a significant contribution to the debate on the future of Europe. If we Europeans want European integration to continue to be a model of success, then we need to live a common vision supported by the millions of our fellow Europeans – a vision that brings about genuine identification as a consequence. Identity leads to confidence; this is the key to Europe's way ahead.

**Josef Ackermann**
Born in Mels, Switzerland, 1948. Spokesman of the Board and Chairman of the Group Executive Committee of Deutsche Bank AG, Frankfurt am Main since 2002. Board Member of Deutsche Bank AG since 1996. Member of the Crédit Suisse Executive Board from 1990, President of the same from 1993.

# Them and Us

*A European returns home. Her welcome is ambiguous. Across the ocean, she was simply European but what is she in Europe? What kind of European class society are we dealing with? Does belonging to one class or another rest on political, economic or ethnic factors, or simply on luck and the current fall of the dice? Who is a real European and who isn't? What are the criteria and who makes the decisions?*

Slavenka Drakulic

# Europe Tastes Better

After spending a year in the United States, I came back to Europe. It seemed so natural to say 'Europe' when I was asked where I was going. After all, I'd spent the year telling people that that's where I came from. Europe – just Europe.

But am I really an European? In my experience, that's either a very easy or very difficult question, and the answer depends entirely on which side of the new European Union border you happen to be from. I suspect that the European identity we wear so easily when we're far away in the US already starts to fade on the return plane trip – or even before. When you line up to board in, say, Washington Dulles airport, you begin to notice differences among 'Europeans'. You know from your experience, your senses, that the accent, looks, clothing, perhaps just a simple gesture, will soon reveal that the man next to you is Eastern European, while the one behind you is Western. You'll probably first make this East–West distinction (because you are so used to it), and then you'll go on to make more subtle distinctions. You'll take note of the shade of the man's skin, the shape of his face. A Pole? A Brit? But you don't have just geography on your mind – you will also conceptualise the man in terms of history and politics, and load him with all the prejudices you have about the particular nation you think he's from. Because in Europe people live together so closely, they can detect the smallest differences. What's more, they insist on them. At this point, you, a passenger returning to Europe, subconsciously embark on the process of division and exclusion: we/them, friends/enemies, better/worse.

Once you land in Frankfurt, the notion of Europe no longer exists. At the very least, there are two Europes, and this hits you as soon as you go through passport control and have to choose between two booths: one marked EU Citizens and the other NON-EU Citizens. Right there, at Frankfurt airport, you are confronted with the new division of Europe. Your European identity (if it has remained intact after the flight) collapses. You ask yourself: Who or what the hell am I? Does NON-EU have anything to do with being Eastern European, or what? And the answer is quite simply, yes, it does; if only because, unlike the Norwegians or Swiss, for example, you are not in the position to choose to belong or not to belong.

So immediately upon your return from the US, it's right there in front of you. The words are written in neon, yellow letters on a blue background surrounded by stars. The neighbour you spent the flight pleasantly chatting with takes a step to the left (EU), while you take a step to the right (NON-EU) and wave him goodbye. The line is long and moves slowly. You watch the EU line disappearing, people flashing their passports and policemen barely even looking at them. And while you wait, a very familiar feeling of frustration stirs in you. You know it all only too well: the official's very careful scrutiny of your face and your passport (and you are only too aware that you don't look anything like your picture, especially at that ungodly time of the morning), the checking of your name against the invisible (to you) list of criminals, drug smugglers and spies, a possible question about your ticket, what brings you here (business? pleasure?) and the intended length of your stay, that familiar dryness in your throat and the knot in your stomach...

Again? Yes, again.

You thought that the fall of the Berlin Wall had created one Europe, but how wrong you were. Or rather – maybe there is one Europe, but that's something called the EU. And if the country you are from doesn't happen to belong, well, you're not European. And it is of little consolation to you when you see Norwegians and Swiss (or Japanese and Americans) standing in the same line with you. There is a difference between you and them, and you know it. They, too, will be waived through because they don't need a visa.

Visa. Yet another word that has to do with identity, that represents an invisible barrier, an invisible border. It makes you think that at least now you *can* travel, even if you need a visa. But it also makes you think of long queues in a street in front of a foreign embassy, the humiliation of standing there waiting like a beggar. As, indeed, you are – you are begging the EU to let you visit the promised land. You may be let in, and then again, you may not. After all, you are a NON-EU citizen; you belong to a different category, another class. You belong to some unspecified *rest* of the Continent, the part that remains outside the EU.

Suddenly, as you are approaching the NON-EU booth, you feel an urge, almost a physical compulsion, to leave the line, turn back and take the first plane back to the US. There you can be European, feel European, and no one will question your identity, even if you come from a country of which no one has ever heard.

The exclusive power of language hits you hard, maybe because you understand it so clearly for the first time. NON-EU. It makes you feel like an outcast, a pariah. Does that bureaucrat examining your passport, your visa, think you've come to steal a job from a genuine, bona fide EU citizen? You feel, almost palpably, the load of historical and political prejudice emanating from the 'real' Europeans. You know you belong to 'the others', the 'non-us'. You know non-us people yourself; usually they belong to an ethnic minority, or they are gypsies or Jews, and we all know what *that* means. These non-us people are *marked* for being non-us, and every so often they are picked out to be resettled, ethnically cleansed or killed.

Non-us means 'nothing good' – that's what makes it so horrifying in our post-communist world. After the end of communism, we foolishly thought that we no longer belonged to the 'others'. And for a brief moment, we – all the Eastern European nations – were treated like heroes. But when reality settled in, we discovered that we were still the others of Europe. All of us lumped together: Poles, Czechs, Albanians (and we had thought that we had little in common...). For Eastern Europeans, Western Europeans – indeed, for most of the inhabitants of the European continent – the unqualified word 'Europe' means Western Europe. Is this for historical, economic or political reasons, or simply because our mentality does not change as quickly as does the political system? Whatever the reasons, nothing changed after 1989.

But if we are NON-EU citizens to Europe, what is Europe to us? Europe is obviously the entity to which we aspire to belong, but this has more to do with dreams, illusions and myths than with any reality. Walk down the streets of Prague, Zagreb, Budapest or Warsaw, and you'll see hotels, shops, cafés, or just holes in the walls with exotic, Western, English-language names: Europe, Paris, Hollywood, Hemingway, Four Roses, White Horse, etc ... as if the sheer magic of Western words, the use of a foreign language, could instantly transport us right there to where we really belong – to Europe. And then turn the craziness on its head: there was once a proposal in the Croatian Parliament to ban all foreign names in public life. 'Foreign names are confusing: they could lead a tourist to think he were in London rather than Zagreb', said the MP who proposed the law. If the tourist were blind drunk perhaps...

The myth of Europe – Europe the way we imagined it while we lived under communism – remains with us. A flashback in my memory: an Albanian family with two teenage daughters sitting in their living room, waiting eagerly for the

Italian TV advertisements, their only window to Europe. This was a dreamland populated by beautiful young people with white teeth and shining hair, driving fantastic cars and having fun. When I was small, I collected sweet wrappings – from foreign sweets, of course, ours didn't have any. And how precious those small squares of cellophane were; how wonderful they smelled among the pages of my textbook!

Our imagined Europe smelled, tasted and looked better than the real thing. It was better, more advanced, more developed, more civilised. If ever we become part of Europe, we thought, all our problems will disappear. And despite the disappointment we experienced after 1989, Europe remains our yardstick for quality. If you want to praise a piece of music, a movie, a book or a painting, an idea, a concept, a hotel or a dinner, you just have to say it's European; a guarantee of high standard.

And yet – we should know better. We've been through the recent Balkan wars. We've experienced ethnic cleansing in Croatia, Bosnia and Kosovo. It was quite pathetic to watch how unarmed and unprepared Bosnians naively expected Europe to rescue them from Serbian aggression. 'Europe will not let us down', they said. They sincerely believed that they were in Europe. They were fatally mistaken – Germany, France and Great Britain thought otherwise. They had other political interests. There was no such entity as Europe and anyway, the war was happening to 'others' in a foreign place, not Europe.

Now some of us are being considered for club membership; membership in Mecca. But we're learning that we have to first jump through a lot of hoops. We are expected to fulfil certain political and economic conditions – this is what our European identity is being reduced to. Some of us are closer than others to fulfilling these conditions, and this alone is causing frictions and divisions between us. Some of us are richer and better; others, badly hit by war, are poorer and less developed. We certainly don't want to be identified with 'them'. And so the pattern repeats itself, as we compete to get 'in', to obtain a visa, to get past the booth marked NON-EU Citizens, to cross the threshold to paradise and get away ... from what? Into what? Certainly not Europe.

Standing in that line in Frankfurt, I look at my fellow Eastern Europeans. How do they feel as they wait in line in Frankfurt or elsewhere to get into one of the fifteen EU countries? How many of them will have to return to the US, Africa or Asia to be 'Europeans'? As usual, the devil is hidden in the language. It occurs to me while I'm showing my passport to the suspicious official: *the name Europe has been appropriated.* It has been appropriated by the more powerful Europeans at the expense of the others. I am afraid that my European identity is being snatched from me by a bunch of small yellow stars in a closed circle. Of course, I can go on hoping that my country will be accepted into the circle, that we'll all be let in, but until then...

**Slavenka Drakulic**
Born in Croatia, 1949. Author and journalist, currently commuting between Vienna and Stockholm. Publications include: *How We Survived Communism – and Even Laughed; Café Paradise or Longing for Europe: A Novel About the Balkans.*

# Through the Eyes of the Outsider

*Perspective often belongs to the outsider. Has Europe emerged as a meaningful world power? Or is it trying to rattle metaphorical sabres – without any real sabres to rattle? Is it enjoying its Kantian paradise while relying on its Hobbesian US protector? Has the European experiment become a shining example of peace and security, mutual understanding and cooperation for the less developed continents of the world or has Europe become irrelevant? Is King Midas at work – or are the Europeans still building with the same old cobblestones of the past?*

Michael Walzer

# Europe and the 9/11 License

Here is one useful way to understand what Europe is and might be: consider the question from the perspective of an American liberal-leftist who is looking for a more balanced global order and a better division of political/military labor. I long for a more politically active, engaged and responsible Europe. I am not interested here in the physical borders of the European Union (unless its expansion makes coherent engagement less likely); I am interested in the extent of its role in the world. And the immediate source of this interest is my anxiety about the extent of the American role.

Often in political life, it is necessary to focus on things that did not happen and on expectations that were not fulfilled. After 9/11, many of us (political intellectuals and activists associated with the liberal left) thought that the ideological unilateralism of the Bush administration would have to be modified. It hadn't made much sense before, even if one thought narrowly of American interests; it made no sense at all afterwards. The 'war on terrorism', however it was conceived, would require international cooperation, and how could the United States expect other countries to cooperate with us if we were so radically unwilling to cooperate with them? Surely, we thought, the American position on issues like global warming and international criminal justice would now change, reflecting a new disposition to promote a 'united front', at least with Europe, but also more widely. And if there was to be unity of action, there would have to be compromise and mutual accommodation.

A year and a half later, there is little sign of either. The US seems to have cobbled together a second coalition against Iraq, and we managed to win a unanimous vote for coercive inspections in the Security Council, but this was accomplished by threatening to go to war all alone. And the ideology of 'all alone' is a powerful factor in Washington. Our government describes 9/11 terrorism as an attack on democracy, on the West, on the values of civilised life, but it responded as if only America had been attacked and only America could defend itself. Other countries were invited to join the defensive struggle, but only on American terms. In fact, there does seem to be extensive cooperation at the level of police work, and I assume that this involves some degree of practical give and take. But our foreign policy generally is as ideologically unilateralist as it was in the first months of the Bush administration. What explains this hard line?

First, the sense of imperial hegemony and responsibility, fortified by what I will describe later on as the '9/11 license'. Second, the self-confidence – 'hubris' might be more accurate – bred by military dominance. Third, the strength of the American economy (a little in doubt after the losses of the past year but by no means in eclipse). And there is one thing more, perhaps the most important thing: the conviction among American leaders that alternative agents are, literally, absent from the global scene. If America acts alone, it is because our leaders believe that there is no other source of effective action. So, fourth: a feeling that borders on contempt for all possible allies. I want to stress and expand on this last point because it poses in the most direct way the question of whether and how American unilateralism can be challenged.

Consider the issue of criminal justice: the American refusal to join the International Criminal Court and the insistence on exemption from ICC prosecution for American soldiers operating anywhere in the world. I make no excuse for this; I think that the Bush administration's policy is wrong. But it is not crazy or incomprehensible if understood roughly along these lines: in the past, when war has been just and necessary (as in the Gulf in 1991 or in Kosovo in 1999), it was the US that bore the brunt of the fighting. Our European allies oppose American unilateralism only this far: they want a role in deciding when war is just and necessary, but they are content, once the decision is made, to leave most of the fighting to American soldiers. Americans are supposed to accept the risks of war (and are criticised, often rightly, for fighting at long range so as to reduce those risks), and now they are also supposed to accept the legal liabilities. It is American soldiers, and hardly anyone else among our allies, who will be accused of war crimes – and Americans will be accused both when they should be, when there are legal reasons to *believe* that crimes have been committed, and when they shouldn't be, when there are political reasons to *pretend* that crimes have been committed. Why should the US government expose its soldiers to this liability when, in practice if not in principle, no other country's soldiers are similarly exposed?

In truth, of course, the Bush administration has been unwilling to accept the Court's jurisdiction even in cases, like that of Bosnian peacekeeping, where multilateral engagement and multilateral liability are already in place. But so far as actual fighting goes, the administration has a point. European states today (Britain is a partial exception) are in the morally ambiguous position of claiming a role in decision-making while remaining unready to share equally in the risks of decisions made. Bush exploits this moral ambiguity to argue against any serious multilateral decision-making. But liberals and leftists in the US and Europe, it seems to me, should be arguing the other way around: against unilateral war-making. We should have seized the occasion of the ICC debate to insist that the best way to avoid exposing American soldiers to politically motivated prosecutions is to make sure that European (and other) soldiers are similarly exposed. Given a genuinely multilateral military engagement (whenever engagement is just and necessary), and given a general willingness to accept the Court's jurisdiction, it would be very difficult for the US to claim legal immunity for its own soldiers. In the face of a serious multilateralism, the unilateral option would fade away.

But serious multilateralism requires a greater European investment in military power – not on the scale of the American investment, but sufficient for at least some of the humanitarian interventions and wars against aggression that are likely to be necessary in the next decades. If Vietnam could shut down the killing fields of Cambodia, if Tanzania could overthrow the murderous regime of Idi Amin in Uganda, surely European states, together or even separately, can play a far larger role than the one they have chosen for themselves. And every expansion of their role would mean a reduction in that of the US.

Now consider the most worrisome example of American unilateralism: the threatened war against Iraq. The argument for such a war doesn't have much to do with the September 2001 attacks, but the legitimacy claims of the Bush administration are based on what I have called the 9/11 license. The content of the license is very simple: because the US was attacked by terrorists and because our losses were so great, we are entitled to lead the war against terrorism. Iraq's weapons of mass destruction are – or will be – terrorist weapons, since they can only be used effectively against civilian targets, as they have been used in the past. Therefore we are entitled to fight against and overthrow the regime that is developing, or has already developed, these weapons.

European (and other) states mostly deny the license and argue for a political rather than a military response to whatever threat Iraq poses. They are certainly right on the first count and probably right on the second. But their argument is not really about what ought to be done; it is about what the US ought to do (or, in this case, not do) – as if they accepted the Bush administration's claim that only the US is an effective agent in international politics. In fact, Europe could have acted long before it did to deal with the threat of war. If a united front of European states (it would have had to include France and Russia, Iraq's chief trading partners and political protectors) had delivered an ultimatum to Saddam Hussein demanding that by a certain date he allow the re-establishment of a fully effective United Nations inspection regime, and threatening to use force (or even just to support its use) if he did not agree, I don't believe that he would have had any choice but to accept the inspectors. And once there were UN inspectors in Iraq, moving freely around the country on their own time schedule, an American war would be politically impossible. That seems the likely outcome now, as I am writing, but it appears that only the American threat persuaded the Europeans to support the imposition of a strong inspection system, which they were never ready to impose themselves. Why not? I don't know how to answer that question except to suggest that Europe's leaders lack what American social scientists call 'a sense of efficacy', a belief in their own capacity to change the world. Americans have rather too much of that sense, Europeans far too little. The result of their passivity is that the reckless threats of the Bush administration – which we (on the American left) opposed, but mostly ineffectively – may well appear in retrospect to have been necessary to achieve a just and safe Iraqi settlement.

One last example: the Israeli–Palestinian conflict. Here American policy is certainly colored by 9/11, which has led an administration that most people thought would tilt toward the Arab states in general – and toward the Palestinians in particular – to break in the most radical way with Yasser Arafat. Palestinian terrorism has had many counter-productive results: it has strengthened the Israeli right, virtually destroyed the left, and it has forced Bush to conclude that the concessions he once favored would, if made in the immediate aftermath of suicide bombings of civilian targets, enable the terrorists to claim a victory – and encourage them to seek further victories. So US policy is to insist upon and wait for the creation of a new Palestinian leadership, 'uncompromised' by terror, with which it would be morally possible to negotiate.

The policy of the European states, on the other hand, has been to complain about American policy. The US should deal with the leaders that exist, European diplomats say; it should deal now, without regard to terrorist attacks; and it should press Israel to deal also. All that may well be right – it is certainly right that only America has the power and credibility to press Israel – but it is not right to suggest that Europeans have nothing to do themselves except complain about Bush's failure to do that. Once again, imagine a more self-confident Europe with a more lively sense of its capacities and responsibilities. Though the Americans send more money to Palestine than Europe does, our money is given mostly for relief; European money pays the salaries of a substantial part of the Palestinian civil service. If, after the first terrorist attacks of the second intifada in late 2000 or early 2001, European states, acting together, had told Arafat that they would provide no more money (and no more invitations to visit their capitals) unless he stopped the attacks, that would have been, I believe, the end of Palestinian terrorism. It's not only that Arafat's ten or twelve security agencies and secret police forces were all intact at that point (they still are intact in Gaza), but the ideological support structures for terrorism – the mosques and schools – were largely in his control. Had his European friends insisted, he would have had little choice but to comply. And make no mistake: Israel could not have resisted a non-terrorist Palestinian resistance, nor would it have had American help in trying to do that. Though the Bush administration would no doubt look for some kind of marginal differentiation, President Clinton's peace plan of December 2000 (for two states, along roughly the 1967 lines) would turn out to be its plan too.

The belief in the 9/11 license is fairly powerful in the US today, but it's not universal by any means; there are a good many people in Washington and in the rest of the country who would welcome a more cooperative and internationalist foreign policy. But there have to be plausible partners for such a policy before these people can form a coherent opposition. Europe today is the only possible partner, and it is the right partner both because of its moral/political affinities with the US and because of its differences. But it doesn't look like a plausible or willing partner. It doesn't look engaged, responsible, ready for forceful action (and, to quote William Shakespeare's *Hamlet*, readiness is all: I don't think that force would be necessary in any of the current cases if there were a visible capacity and determination to use it). With regard to Iraq and the Palestinian National Authority, what the Bush people see – what I suppose they want to see – is a Europe still driven by the politics of appeasement. That doesn't seem right to me. I think the problem is passivity, a kind of political laziness and self-indulgence, an unspoken and unadmitted willingness to let Americans do (most of) the work so long as Europeans can complain about what we do.

But there is no hope for a genuinely internationalist politics without European engagement. And engagement requires independent action. Had European states acted independently of the US in the early days of the Yugoslav crisis – not merely to recognise this or that secessionist regime, or to provide humanitarian aid, or to send 'peacekeepers' (when there was no peace to keep), but actually to stop the killing and ethnic cleansing – the world today would look different than it does. It would look different tomorrow if Europe acted in the ways I have described vis-à-vis the Iraqis and (even now, though success is less likely than it would have been two years ago) the Palestinians. Different in what ways? In the aftermath of a successful European intervention in any major crisis (success is obviously important here), no one in Washington could claim that only the US had the capacity or the will to act. American opponents of unilateralism would be able to insist on the possibility of serious multilateral action. There would be a partner, or a set of partners, with whom the Bush administration would have to negotiate – and if there were disagreements, with whom it would have to bargain and compromise. I admit that Americans might take a while to relearn the politics of compromise and to surrender the 9/11 license, but we would manage in time to do both these things. Accusations of imperial arrogance or of cowboy machismo won't turn Americans into good internationalists. The necessity of acting in a world that includes other competent and confident national actors, who are not our enemies but who are also not our followers –that would begin, at least, to do the job.

**Michael Walzer**
Born in New York, 1937. American sociologist and professor at the Institute for Advanced Study, Princeton. Editor of the journal *Dissent*. Considered to be the key theoretician on the liberal left in the USA. Numerous publications include: *Just and Unjust Wars – A Moral Argument with Historical Illustrations; On Toleration, Thick and Thin – Moral Argument at Home and Abroad.*

Joseph Nye

# The European Experiment

An Interview

*When you talk about Europe these days, it seems you are specifically referring to the European Union.*

I tend to refer to the European Union because I think it is an extremely important part of international politics and international affairs. If you look at the Europe of fifty or sixty years ago and you look at Europe today, you cannot help but notice the enormous change that the EU has made. The idea that France, Germany, Britain, Italy will never think of doing battle with each other again, the feeling that Europeans are all in one boat together – this is new in history. It has been new since the start of European integration and it is immensely important. It demonstrates to the world that in some long-term future, it is possible to imagine better ways for nation-states to relate to each other. Although there are those who regard Europe as simply another nation-state – a nation-state in formation – I don't believe it is. Moreover, we shouldn't pretend that it is. I think the core of the EU is *sui generis*. Obviously, as polls show, old sentiments drawing on national identity still exist: the Germans feel German, the French feel French, the British feel British. However, they don't feel the way they did sixty years ago, and they have lost the fear that there is potential danger coming from each other. In other words, even if many Europeans consider themselves not so much in one supranational boat, but in national boats tightly lashed together, that is still an extraordinary change for politics. So when I think of Europe, I think of a zone of peace or security in which states no longer relate to each other as in the past – in the classical balance-of-power situation which has existed since time immemorial – but in very new and more productive ways. That's what Europe means to me.

*Left to its own devices in an ideal world, the Europe you envisage could perhaps maintain a state of peace. But Europe does not exist in isolation; it exists in a larger and more hostile context. How does that function?*

This is one of the hard problems for Europeans today because as some have argued, in many instances the Europeans have created a Kantian solution within a regional arrangement and yet they are living in a larger Hobbesian world. So it is erroneous for Europeans to say, as they sometimes do, that if it works in Europe it must work worldwide. But clearly things that have worked in Europe don't work in the Middle East or in East Asia, where traditional views of power politics are much more dogged and where respect for the rule of law or international treaties is much weaker. I think it is difficult for Europeans today to reconcile the extraordinary difference that has occurred inside Europe with the fact that much of the rest of the world has not changed to the same degree. Robert Cooper, the British diplomat, talks about the world being divided into three parts: the pre-industrial world, the industrialising world, and the post-modern world. Much of Africa is pre-industrial and many of the conflicts that exist there can be explained in that context. China, India and Brazil, on the other hand, are industrialising. Europe has reached the post-modern stage. It's past the industrial age and is looking at a different form of culture. I believe the fact that the world is not uniform means that while it is important for Europeans to be proud of what they have accomplished, and to cherish and nurture those accomplishments, they should not assume that the whole rest of the world is like they are.

*Should they be trying to change the world in their image? You talk about soft power as the art of convincing people to do what you want them to through the force of argument and persuasion. Does Europe have soft power?*

In my recent book, *The Paradox of American Power,* I argue that hard power is the ability to get others to do what you want through bribery or coercion, carrots or sticks. You get them to do what they otherwise wouldn't do or want to do. Soft power is getting the outcomes you want with others wanting the same things you want. They are attracted to you. Soft power grows out of your culture, your values, your policies. Europe has a good deal of soft power.

*But does it have a single soft power? Is Europe unified enough to have common 'wants'?*

Each culture within Europe has a certain soft power of its own. French culture, for example, is very attractive to some Germans. Traditionally, European cultures have always been attractive to others in different parts of the world. But what is new is the idea of Europe itself having soft power. A good example of this would be what happened after the end of the Cold War. When the Wall came down, nobody really knew what would happen to Central Europe. Would it become a zone of indifference which would eventually deteriorate into small authoritarian states, or would it become a zone of democracy and prosperity? The fact is that throughout Central Europe from the very start there was an orientation toward Brussels, a shared view that in the long term, Brussels was at the heart of where Central Europe wanted to be. It wasn't that the EU used coercion, although obviously there was some economic incentive albeit in a fairly distant future. Becoming part of the EU wasn't going to happen to Central Europe overnight. No, even before any formal negotiations were set in motion, it was the attractiveness of Brussels that gave the people of Central Europe their direction. And when a politician emerged who was headed in another direction – when, for example, Meciar in Slovakia tried to ignore the inclination towards Brussels and the fact that Slovakia's future was in a larger Europe – he was faced with an inhospitable domestic climate.

There are still, of course, some tendencies in different directions, but by and large, I think the attractiveness of Europe has given it a great deal of soft power. Just as the EU has been a magnet for the countries of Central Europe, it is also a magnet for Turkey. The fact that the Turks want to be part of Europe in the long run gives Europe the ability to try to persuade them to change some of their human rights laws. One of the things I fear is that European leaders will not do enough for, or be responsible enough towards, Turkey. Should this happen, a future generation of Turks may grow up feeling that the Europeans have rebuffed them, and that they should therefore no longer orient their expectations toward Europe. Fortunately, this has not yet happened. I think it is very healthy for Europe and very healthy for Turkey that within Turkey itself, there is still a consensus that joining the EU is worth striving for.

*Europe today is essentially a Judeo-Christian culture. One of the perceived problems with Turkey is that the Turks would introduce a different culture, a Muslim culture, which so far, Europeans have been able to downplay. The accession of Turkey to the EU would make a radical difference.*

There are a large number of Muslims in Turkey, but if you look at the present situation in Europe, if you look at the number of *Gastarbeiter* who never went home, if you look at the French and the proportion of Muslims already in their population, you come to the conclusion that Europe has really outgrown its image of itself as a narrowly Judeo-Christian culture.

*Nevertheless, Europe still has land or sea borders with the vast Muslim world. With the inclusion of Turkey, Europe becomes one with a world it considers strange, different – indeed hostile.*

But it's a world that you can't escape or avoid. You can't pull up the drawbridge and live in a medieval castle. Embracing an Islamic country like Turkey, which is comfortable with a secular, post-modern world, is extremely important for the future of Europe itself as well as for the future of Turkey. Turkey is in fact a good and important test for a modern Europe: can that Europe come to terms with the diversity that transnational relations are creating within it? The argument I hear from some politicians that the Turks are too different and that we can't do anything about them is a mistaken perception. The Turks are not going away. And would you rather have them looking and acting like Europeans or have them looking and acting like alien foreigners?

*We have been discussing Europe as a bloc, one that is about to be enlarged by ten or so countries, including eventually Turkey. However, since September 11th, the world has been reassessing its component blocs. How relevant are they now in a world where the lines are being drawn differently?*

Well, I think the issue of terrorism has put a new set of items on the agenda for countries throughout the world. It is something that we should have foreseen before September 11th, but September 11th made it blinding clear. It grows out of deeper trends that I described in my book *Globalization and the Information Revolution,* which are essentially about empowering transnational actors and non-state actors in a way in which they have never been empowered before. These issues that grow out of transnational relations are ones that cannot be handled by any one country alone. They are issues which require considerable cooperation among states. So it is not merely cooperation among and between the European countries which is necessary here, but cooperation among and between a much broader set of countries. For example, take an organisation like al Qaeda: this is a network which has been set up in sixty different countries. To deal with such an organisation requires intelligence-sharing, police cooperation across borders, effective customs arrangements which allow inspection in other countries before you ship, and so on. All this is going to entail much greater and deeper cooperation between countries. To some extent, the European experiment provides a basis for doing this. But Europe itself will have to participate in a global cooperation with other parts of the world well beyond its own borders.

*Europe has very little military might. Some say it can afford not to provide for its own security because the United States can be counted on to jump in militarily when necessary. Does this still work?*

Well, if we take the long-term view, if we look ahead many decades, I think Europe represents a point of optimism. The European experiment shows that countries which were once bitter enemies can in fact develop a totally new way of relating to each other – this alone is reason for the experiment to be cherished and nurtured. But it is also true that the European experiment does not solve all the problems or threats that we face. Transnational threats such as we see from terrorism are not resolved by having a social compact at home, so there is still a need for (military) cooperation with other countries. There is still a need, I would submit, for an Atlantic alliance. And one of the things I hope will not happen is a divorce between Europe and the US, because at the deepest level, Europe and the US share more political values than do any other parts of the world. It is extremely important to keep in mind that even though Europe and the US differ from time to time on particular policies, in terms of these political values we are a part of a common civilisation. If we focus too much on the friction, we may forget those larger common interests we both have at our core. So I would see a world in which Europe continues its experiment, but also realises that in dealing with the outside world – the Hobbesian world – it makes sense to maintain its strong Atlantic alliance.

*Thank you.*

*The conversation was conducted by Susan Stern*

**Joseph S. Nye, Jr.**
Born in South Orange, New Jersey, 1937. American sociologist and political scientist. Dean of the John F. Kennedy School of Government, Harvard. Former U.S. Assistant Secretary of Defense for International Security Affairs. Publications include: *The Paradox of American Power: Why the World's Only Superpower Can't Go It Alone; Understanding International Conflicts.*

Richard Perle

# Europe: Ally or Counterweight?

The Western victory in the Cold War liberated millions in Central and Eastern Europe and in the Soviet Union. It also liberated Western Europeans from nearly half a century of acquiescence, often grudging, to American culture and policy.

The attitude so commonly expressed among Europeans these days – that the United States is arrogant, overbearing, culturally and politically domineering, unsubtle and unsophisticated – always existed just beneath the surface during the Cold War, but for the most part it remained suppressed out of a sense of dependence on American military power. After all, without the US, without NATO, Europe could not defend itself against the massive military power of the Soviet Union. So Europeans swallowed hard, limited their criticism to intellectual circles, and invariably did what Washington wanted.

But now that there is no longer a menacing Soviet presence in Europe, and the US is no longer perceived as essential to Europe's very survival, long pent-up misgivings about American policies and power are now free to rise – *gush* – to the surface. The result is a flood of resentment from one end of Western Europe to the other.

The center of gravity of this European disparagement of the no-longer-essential US is the Franco-German consortium for the promotion of 'European' interests. Its spokesmen are

Gerhard Schröder, Jacques Chirac and a gaggle of lesser characters such as Chris Patten and his fellow bureaucrats in Brussels.

The charge against the US sometimes reflects real differences of policy on matters that are clearly debatable, issues about which controversy is normal and appropriate. But sometimes criticism of the US is churlish or simply silly. The idea, for example, that there is something 'imperialistic' or 'hegemonic' about the success of American fast food outlets in Europe or the evident appeal of American movies, music and fashion, would be laughable if it were not so generally accepted.

Any American participating in seminars and public forums in Europe these days will have encountered derisive remarks about American culture, invariably coupled with references to the superiority of European culture. Often an uneasy silence ensues when it is pointed out that Americans are the single most dynamic force for the preservation of that same European cultural legacy. The development of Monet's house in Giverny, the Guggenheim Museum in Bilbao, the renovation of museums and landmarks in Vienna – all have been accomplished with American leadership and resources.

It is certainly true that European art and architecture have given mankind an extraordinarily rich legacy. Europe's aesthetic legacy is a great and lasting treasure – no American cities can compare with the splendid architecture of Paris or Florence or Prague. But what of contemporary culture? Is not New York the music capital of the world? (I spend a lot of time in France. On a good day I can get one radio station playing classical music – at home in Washington, I can pick up half a dozen.) Where are the most innovative paintings and sculptures? Where should one look for breakthroughs in science and technology? Where are most of the universities doing leading-edge research? Forget the flowers. Where have the Nobel prizes gone? Contemporary American culture is alive and well: energetic, vibrant, diverse.

Many Europeans believe that culture should be managed by bureaucrats – they have ministries that do nothing else. Americans entrust far more to the private sector and embrace a market-driven approach (alongside generous philanthropy) to art, music and literature. This does not always produce what a selection committee of officials would have chosen, which may explain why the management of culture in Europe is more productive when applied to legacy art, architecture and music than to contemporary culture.

I don't believe that a fair assessment of the strength of American culture warrants the condescending tone with which it is described by many Europeans. But there can be little doubt that a smug attitude towards American culture emboldens many Europeans to take a dismissive view of other things American, especially American social, political and foreign policies. The sharpest European criticism of American policy centers on the related themes of 'unilateralism' and 'hegemony'. Within the general criticism of American foreign policy as unilateralist and hegemonic, there has been a steady stream of hostile comment on US policy toward such specific issues as Iraq and the dispute between the Israelis and the Palestinians, to take two of the most incendiary controversies. All of these issues deserve comment.

What some Europeans decry as *unilateralism*, many Americans regard as *leadership*. The concept of leadership certainly implies a willingness to act even – indeed, especially – when others are reluctant to do so. 'Let's go!' is not a phrase for followers. First Bosnia and then Kosovo should remind us of how feckless Europe has been on those occasions when the US recoiled temporarily from a leadership position, only to return to lead a coalition that produced results. For all its brave ambitions, there is not a single recent instance in which Europe has undertaken any significant action in the absence of American leadership.

When European critics of American policy condemn American unilateralism, they often have in mind the instances in which the US has refused to embrace some European supported policy. And when that happens, they resent the independence of the American position all the more because US opposition is often sufficient to block the result desired by the Europeans. The de facto American 'veto' rankles.

One case with which the US has been pilloried incessantly is the Kyoto agreement on the mitigation of greenhouse gasses. It is an agreement that affects different countries in different ways: there is no single standard applied with equal effect to all. Because the US consumes more energy per capita than other countries, the burden of diminishing greenhouse gasses for the US would, under Kyoto, be vastly greater and much more costly than for other countries. So much greater, in fact, that there was no chance the US Senate, controlled at the time by the Democrats, would vote to ratify the Kyoto Treaty – had it been presented to the Senate, it would have been overwhelmingly defeated.

During the negotiations leading to the Kyoto Treaty, it was proposed that countries should be allowed to meet their quota for the abatement of greenhouse gasses by undertaking new forestation programs. (Forests absorb and thus neutralise the pollutants that are believed to lead to global warming.) If the US had been allowed to meet its obligations in this way, it might have achieved the same result as a reduction in the production of greenhouse gasses, but at a lower cost and with less disruption to American industry and transportation. At Kyoto, however, the European Union blocked a provision that would have permitted the planting of forests outside the US as a means of meeting its quota. No serious reason was given for this position, although there is suspicion among American environmentalists that some European (especially French) officials opposed the idea that the US might 'buy its way out' of an obligation that they wished to make as painful and disruptive as possible.

So the American view of Kyoto was different from the European view. Is this what is meant by 'unilateralism'? Surely nations are free to decide which treaty commitments they will accept and ratify and which they will reject. If that is unilateralism, then we are all unilateralists.

Other agreements that the US has decided not to join are also said to prove that it is unilateralist: for example, the International Criminal Court, the treaty banning nuclear testing, or the protocols to the treaty banning biological weapons. In each case, the US has put forth its reasons for objecting to treaty arrangements that it believed would damage its interests. In every instance we have also argued that the benefits to others are illusory; these are not cases of American selfishness forcing injury on others. Surely the American arguments merit debate. But instead of serious debate about the effectiveness of these agreements – like the ability to verify the biological weapons treaty (it can't be done) or the wisdom of foreswearing the laboratory testing of nuclear weapons for safety and security (a high-risk policy with no obvious benefit) – we get only accusations of 'unilateralism' that *assume* those agreements are effective, and further assume that any country not signing up to them must be wrong.

American refusal to accept the jurisdiction of an ICC has provoked endless European whining. But the US has good reason to prefer its own courts to some international tribunal that may or may not measure up to the very high standard that the US Constitution guarantees to its citizens, even those accused of crimes. Few criminal justice systems around the world, if any, accord defendants the rights that Americans enjoy. These rights are important to us. The idea of allowing Americans sent abroad on peacekeeping missions, for example, to be hauled before a tribunal whose standards and procedures we do not and cannot know is unacceptable to most Americans. Moreover, the blatant politicisation of the bench in many countries could mean politically motivated actions against American officials. Even without an international court, one of America's great statesmen, Henry Kissinger, has been harassed around the world by magistrates looking for headlines.

Differences across the Atlantic concerning the ICC actually reflect a profound, underlying philosophical division over the role of global agreements in advancing national security, and the protection and extension of liberal democratic values. While this is not strictly speaking a controversy between Americans and Europeans, many of those who take the 'globalist' approach are European, and most who question it are Americans.

The globalist conceit is that the institution of international agreements that are global in scope – to which all the world's nations become parties – is the surest means of promoting a peaceful international order and, therefore, protecting the security of individual nations. Globalists are eager to see a broad range of international treaties covering everything from nuclear testing, biological and chemical weapons, the manufacture and use of land mines, cluster bombs, nuclear proliferation, human rights and the like. It is a primary objective of globalists to get as many states as possible to sign up to these global treaties, including the countries and regimes most likely to violate them – the more agreements we can get the worst regimes to sign, the better.

For globalists, it is good that Iraq is a signatory to the nuclear non-proliferation treaty, even though we know that Iraq used its representatives on Hans Blix's International Atomic Energy Authority to learn better how to hide Saddam's clandestine nuclear weapons program. That the United Nations Human Rights Commission is chaired by Libya, a dictatorship in which human rights are non-existent, is also viewed by globalists as being good.

Globalists believe that only the UN can confer legitimacy on the use of force across internationally recognised borders. They reject the idea that NATO, the EU or a 'coalition of the willing' can properly use force to keep the peace or restrain an outlaw or rogue state. They elevate the UN to a degree of moral and political authority that many Americans find absurd in light of the frailty of that institution – to say nothing of the corruption that afflicts it. (It is, after all, common knowledge that votes at the UN are bought and sold, that many member dictator-states are thoroughly corrupt and that the Secretariat, whose composition is politically determined, is often less competent than the governments of many member states.)

The alternative to globalism is what one might call the 'posse' approach to international security. In this approach, what matters is not that some universal agreement has been reached, but that the liberal democracies have banded together to achieve such things as keep nuclear weapons out of the hands of states that might use them aggressively, deny those states access to chemical or biological weapons, and apply pressure to broaden the community of nations according their citizens' fundamental human rights. For the posse school, action by NATO or the EU, even including the use of force, is every bit as legitimate as action sanctioned by the UN. After all, just what does an endorsement by China or Russia add to the weight of the Western democracies?

Inclusiveness matters little to the posse school – in fact, when inclusiveness requires that dictatorships and rogue states are accorded respect as state members of the international community, it actually undermines the strength and cohesion of an international order based on liberal democratic values.

Not all Europeans fall into the globalist camp and not all Americans belong to the posse school (Clinton administration officials such as Madeleine Albright and Sandy Berger were more globalist than many Europeans). But the thrust of European thinking is globalist, just as Bush administration policies tend toward the posse approach – and that was true even before September 11. Since that fateful day, there are few Americans who are ready to place their faith and confidence in international treaties, even though polls show that Americans would much prefer US policies to win wide approbation from our democratic allies.

To many Americans – certainly to the current American administration – the worst regimes in possession of the worst weapons pose an intolerable threat to us and the world. This explains the administration's UN demand that Saddam Hussein give up his weapons of mass destruction as the UN has repeatedly resolved. The US believes that UN resolutions must be enforced – ideally by the UN itself – but, failing a consensus there, by the US and those of its allies prepared to join in a coalition of the willing to remove them by force.

Many Americans are troubled by the weakness of the Europeans in facing up to the danger – and challenge – of Saddam Hussein's Iraq. Again and again the French, and often the Germans, appear to be siding with Saddam. Opinion polls in parts of Europe in which a significant fraction of those polled regard the US as a greater danger than Saddam Hussein cause understandable consternation in Washington. For many of us, the deterioration of European support for an American policy that faces the reality of the dangers of Saddam's chemical, biological and (eventually) nuclear weapons is an appalling failure of Western solidarity.

The dispute between the Israelis and Yasser Arafat's Palestinian regime is another issue that has become increasingly divisive across the Atlantic. It is clear that sentiment in Europe has become deeply hostile to Israel while in the US, Israel enjoys wide popular and political support. To many Americans, the Europeans – and especially the EU – have turned a blind eye to the most egregious acts of terror against Israeli civilians. We see a chronically feeble European reaction when Israeli children are targeted by suicide bombers. Indeed, we see EU money continue to flow freely to Arafat despite Palestinian terror and massive corruption within the Palestinian National Authority. Claims that EU funding of Arafat has been audited with no finding of corruption misses the point: despite its role as a money bag for Arafat, the EU has failed to exercise even minimal influence on the Palestinian National Authority; and, needless to say, it has done nothing to support President Bush's call for a new Palestinian leadership. Europe's refusal to recognise that Hammas is deeply involved in terrorism, its mere whisper of protest as Iran trains and finances Hizbollah – these are the sources of a deep division between us over approaches to Middle East diplomacy, the latter being largely in the hands of the US. (European ambitions for a role in the Middle East are laughable: lacking the trust of the Israelis and the respect of the Palestinians, the most the EU can do is meddle without significant effect.)

These differences will not be settled in the near future – if anything, they are likely to deepen. And those Europeans who think that everything will be all right when a few 'neoconservatives' in and around the Bush administration depart will be deeply disappointed. Divergences across the Atlantic now flow from fundamental differences in philosophy made more salient since the September 11 attack on the US. Moreover, the differences are not entirely, or even largely, among officials – they are deeply felt, on the American side, at least, by the vast majority of Americans.

In the end we will find a way to cope with these differences because there is so much more that unites than divides us. But it will take time.

**Richard Perle**
Born in New York, 1941. Chairman of the Defense Policy Board, an independent consultancy group of the U.S. defense ministry. Member of the American Enterprise Institute (Washington). U.S. Assistant Secretary of Defense for International Security Policy from 1981 to 1987.

Sergej Karaganov

# From Russia With Love

The events of September 11th didn't change the world radically: the world was already in the midst of a deep and rapid transformation. However, the tragedy that took place on that day dealt a crushing blow to our outdated and inadequate view of the world, forcing us to reconsider many concepts which until then had seemed to us axiomatic and politically correct.

The relationship between Russia and the European Union, the western and eastern parts of Europe, is one such concept. It has to be urgently re-evaluated – or at least re-examined in an unorthodox way – primarily because the environment that has helped form the relations between Europe and Russia has been going through a drastic and unstoppable change. In addition, the institutions and policies which have provided the framework for such relations to develop and function are themselves in a state of flux or even crisis. Finally, the shifts underway in Russia and the process of rapprochement between Russia and the EU have created new opportunities as well as new problems.

## Environmental hazards

Let's start with the political environment. Accelerating globalisation and the erosion of the rigid structures created by the Cold War adversaries in order to regulate international relations have destabilised such relations in a lasting and fundamental way.

Informational transparency has made the North–South conflict, long a cause of concern to the international community, even more acute. It would be almost impossible to rectify this situation even if the rich countries were to suddenly decide to follow the calls from many European nations to sharply increase their aid to poor countries. Our television screens will go on showing that the gap in the living standards between the viewers and the viewed remains great – and may become even greater.

It may be just as impossible to overcome the most dangerous aspect of the North–South conflict, namely, a growing gap between currently relatively successful Western cultures and the once-advanced but presently backward Islamic civilisation. The widening of this gap has fanned the flames of radicalism and boosted anti-Western sentiment in many Islamic societies.

A decade-long sponsorship by the international community of national liberation movements and of the right of nations to self-determination, and even full independence, has led to a steep rise in the number of failing or defunct states whose governments are unable to provide their citizens and economies with appropriate frameworks for existence. Such states have become hotbeds of instability and terrorism.

Nuclear proliferation and a nuclear arms race have started up again for real. In the process, one of the potentially most unstable southern states – Pakistan – has acquired nuclear weapons. Scores of other nations are amassing the expertise and technology that will allow them to produce their own nuclear bombs or other weapons of mass destruction (WMD). More than a hundred states possess sufficient stocks of fissionable materials that could be used to create so-called 'dirty bombs'. Such growing instability and widespread perception of social and military inferiority combine to whip up the demand for WMD.

This, then, is the background for a new wave of terrorism – even more threatening now because it is increasingly possible for terrorists to get their hands on ever-more powerful weapons, including WMD.

What we're facing now is the growing threat of a deeper and broader instability, a threat that is spreading from the Middle East, from Central and South Asia into the neighbouring regions and into the rest of the world. The climate of international security, which appeared to dominate after the end of the Cold War, has quickly disintegrated, resulting in military power re-establishing its traditional role in global politics and security issues placed firmly back at the top of the international relations agenda. Such a development has far-reaching consequences for the EU, which prefers to use 'soft tools of power' that promote the economy, finances, socially responsible state structures, human rights and so on.

It is important to stress that international security has not been universally undermined. Military and political confrontation in Europe has been all but overcome on a practical level, although it still lives on in many people's minds. The issue of European security as it existed in the past is no longer of concern. What have remained are mini-problems in the former Yugoslavia and micro-issues in some European and Europe-contiguous states of the former Soviet Union.

Thus, the threat to Europe's (and to some degree Russia's) security no longer comes from within Europe; rather, its source lies increasingly outside the Continent.

## Enfeebled institutions

This development has demonstrated painfully just how dysfunctional or inadequate the institutions entrusted with European security are. This is yet another reason why a new approach to relations between Europe and Russia is urgently necessary.

While it has achieved most of its strategic goals – and in the process become one of the most successful military alliances in history – NATO is becoming feeble and outdated. In the early 1990s, it missed a historical opportunity to reform itself thoroughly and thus create the basis for a global assurance of security against future threats. It still had this chance when it was faced with the choice of whether 'to get out of the zone of responsibility or die'. It failed to make that choice and instead adopted a new motto: 'to enlarge or die' and introduced a package of cosmetic reforms. As a result, NATO has been slowly decaying, a process that became especially noticeable when the second round of NATO expansion got underway. Now NATO leaders are setting new goals for the Alliance that should help it fight the new threats and Russia is prepared to back their efforts within the framework of the Group of 20. However, doubts about NATO's future usefulness as an effective partner have persisted: 'What if the Alliance's change of heart has come too late?'

In addition, as the defence capability gap between the United States and Europe increases, Europe's influence in the North Atlantic Alliance diminishes. While NATO is weakening and the EU's foreign and security policies are apparently stagnating, the Organisation for Security and Co-operation in Europe (OSCE) has been slowly but surely fading away. Just like NATO, this organisation fulfilled its key missions during the Cold War and the period immediately following it. The OSCE suffered from thoughtless expansion – to a greater degree than NATO – by allowing the admission of all the ex-Soviet republics as members, including those which, almost by definition, were unable to meet its basic principles such as human rights and democratic freedoms. Moreover, due to fears that the OSCE would become a competitor to NATO, neither the organisation itself nor its mandate were adjusted to match the changed political environment.

Weak as it may be, the OSCE still creates a lot of confusion by competing with the Council of Europe – a considerably more efficient and defined international body – since it operates largely within the same area. Since Russia was wrong to hope that the OSCE would take the lead in the European security system and would thus protect Russia's political interest, the fact that it failed to do so has created yet another institutional problem in Russia's interaction with other European states.

## EU's policies stumble ahead

The EU's own security and foreign policy is developing with great difficulty and is failing to meet the pressing needs of the fast-paced international environment. However, this doesn't apply to that part of foreign policy which deals with protecting and promoting the common economic interests of EU members. Here, the successes speak for themselves. But this aspect of foreign policy is losing significance in a world in which security concerns are becoming pre-eminent. One cannot help but acknowledge the EU's progress in formulating and implementing a common foreign policy – be it the opening of common diplomatic missions, creating the position of an 'EU Foreign Minister', or intensifying efforts to conduct joint policy in defence procurement and military research. Likewise, it is impossible to overlook its drawbacks, primarily its immense red tape and slowness, with its decision-making process based on the lowest common denominator. The EU's common foreign policy generates practically no new ideas; should any ever be formulated, they are invariably torpedoed by the EU member states or drowned in EU bureaucracy. Far too often such common foreign policy squashes national proposals which show considerable promise. What has become of Joschka Fischer's initiatives, or of Jacques Chirac's interesting idea to create an internal security alliance between the EU and Russia?

It would be advantageous for Russia to work side by side with an EU that acts as a more powerful and efficient partner in foreign and security policy areas. Most of our views and interests are similar. Despite our rather friendly current relations with the US, no one in Russia would support the idea of Washington becoming a sole, dominant power or the weakening of Europe's usually positive impact on US policy.

Russian leadership, especially with Vladimir Putin at its helm, has come to an agreement with the EU, primarily where foreign and security policies are concerned. Europeans have ceased to complain that Russia prefers exclusive bilateral relations, 'fails to pay attention' to the EU, or bases its foreign policy towards the West around its relationship with the US. Nevertheless, the EU remains a complicated and inefficient partner. Its regular contacts with Russia have yielded few results. Moreover, such contacts have all too often become a mere formality. Within three years of more frequent contacts, the two parties have come to understand each other better and are getting used to this new form of communication. Yet, the list of mutual achievements is still far too short if we discount the recent, piecemeal, enormously time and effort consuming – and I believe not very satisfactory – solution to the Kaliningrad issue.

## Russia policy out of focus

Finally, the EU has still failed to define its new strategy towards Russia. During the 1990s, the EU had other priorities: it needed to adjust to the changed status of its neighbours and integrate its immediate periphery – the states of Central and Eastern Europe and the Baltics. Russia was a lesser priority, although it, too, was treated in a rather friendly, if superficially, way. Now, Russia has moved up the priority ladder.

Policy towards Russia seemed to be undergoing a transformation at the turn of the millennium. The goal of integrating

Central and Eastern European countries appeared to have been reached, so the 1999 Cologne Summit announced that the EU's strategy was to refocus on achieving rapprochement with Russia. There followed a number of ambitious formulations, such as 'the Prodi Plan', aimed at integrating the energy policy of Russia and the EU, or the creation of a 'common economic space' between the two – and indeed, the dialogue between Russia and the EU has intensified. However, dialogue is where the EU has usually drawn the line. It has conducted a restrictive policy on Russia's exports and has been a key factor in blocking Russia's entry into the World Trade Organisation (WTO) – despite numerous supportive statements by the German, French, UK and Italian governments.

Furthermore, Russia has to meet requirements that are even more stringent than those imposed on China. The EU long resisted agreeing to an obvious step – granting to Russia the status of a state with an established market economy, in spite of the fact that in many respects, Russia has a more liberal and capitalist system than most EU countries. Indeed, many believe its capitalism has gone wild. The EU's agricultural policy and its almost universally regulated energy prices are good examples of state intervention in the market functioning in some EU economies. (The EU finally gave in, by the way, but only after the US accorded such status to Russia.)

Personal travel by Russian citizens is being hampered by EU enlargement and a further expansion of the Schengen Treaty, making it difficult for them to maintain their personal contacts in Europe. Conversely, there seem to be only a few known cases of representatives of Chechen separatists or major criminal figures and terrorists being refused visas to travel in the EU.

I could continue to list the institutional problems and difficulties standing in the way of efficient cooperation and good relations between the EU and Russia. But one particular issue is paramount: in what direction and how will the EU develop once twenty-five or more states join the club?

## Moscow must act

A considerable, if not major, responsibility for part of the problem in the EU-Russian relationship should be placed firmly at Russia's door; most obviously its economic backwardness. The country's level of corruption and criminality, frequently illegal interventions by the state into economic activity, and the sorry state of its court system cannot but baffle and infuriate not only Europeans but also the majority of democratic, liberal or simply rational-thinking Russian citizens. The level of political culture in this country is also quite low. Combined, all these deficiencies certainly help create considerable structural problems that hinder EU-Russian harmonious relations and integration.

In addition, while Russia has made the decision to build up its strategic relations with the EU, it has still failed to create the framework necessary to ensure that the executive and legislative branches of power follow this course. Russia still has no special agencies or institutions either in the government or in the Parliament that could monitor the progress of such rapprochement, produce necessary initiatives or make sure they are implemented. A growing paradox exists: while the EU's policy towards Russia is largely hampered by too much red tape, Russia's policy towards the EU suffers from too little administrative capacity and from the general weakness of the Russian state. And although the state is becoming stronger under Vladimir Putin, neither its outmoded administration nor its defence and foreign policy live up to the needs of the country.

Despite government claims that rapprochement with the EU is a major priority, one strongly endorsed by the general public (opinion polls show that over 50 percent of the respondents would like to see Russia as a member of the EU), as well as by many in Russia's business community, Russian elites want to go a step further. They believe – and I support their opinion – that to modernise and organise its economy and society, Russia has to set itself a long-term goal of full integration into the EU, rather than settle for just an association with it. Almost everyone would like to be 'part of Europe', but to give up many old as well as newly acquired habits, to work hard at reducing the gap between the EU and Russia in bringing Russia's laws, regulations and standards to the EU level are measures that remain less than universally popular.

Moreover, there are enough powerful interest groups, including some in the business community, who care little about achieving fast-track cooperation with the EU, or membership of the WTO – or even general partnership with the West. While fearing competition, they would also like to keep their business operations in an opaque 'grey area' for as long as possible.

## Old and new hurdles

Russia's structural problems in bridging the gap with the EU, institutional hurdles on both sides, plus the doubts among the political and business elite over the desirability and efficiency of good relations and mutual integration have created a paradoxical situation in which Russia is starting to drift towards its traditional position of 'US first' despite its declared course of 'Europe first'. It is not so much the growing – in absolute and relative terms – power of the US that is causing such a drift. Despite all the disagreements between Russia and the US; despite the greater distrust that Moscow has of Washington than of any other European capital; even despite the US tendency toward unilateralism – Washington still gives the impression of being a much more efficient and transparent partner than Brussels. In addition, the Bush administration has formulated a clear position on developing a partnership with Russia; the EU's position, beyond its rhetoric, is a lot woollier.

There is yet another considerable historical and cultural factor which affects the relationship between Russia and EU countries. Having missed out on over 70 years of development enjoyed by most European states but abruptly ended in the Russian Empire in 1917, Russia has discovered that it has fallen below the others by at least one rung on the ladder of political and cultural progress. Despite the huge leap it has made over the past decade, from the point of view of socio-political culture and elite-building, Russia is still stuck in the historical period that other, more fortunate European states experienced 40, 60 or even 100 years ago. And because the Soviet Union fell apart so recently, Russia as a nation is still undergoing its formation process.

Russia exists in a different geopolitical reality as it finds itself lodged simultaneously, as it were, on the cusp of two socio-political fractures. On the one hand, it is positioned somewhere between the rich and the poor nations, while on the other, it is caught between an Islam that is losing a current cultural-historical battle and the West that is winning it so far. This gives Russia the advantage of being in a better position than most other nations to recognise new challenges and to understand the need to cope with them decisively. Hardly surprising then that after September 11th, voices in Moscow could be heard claiming with a somewhat justifiable arrogance that it wasn't a case of Russia joining the West in its fight against terrorism, but vice versa. This should not be interpreted, however, as an excuse for the exceedingly drastic, even cruel, and often ineffective methods used to combat terrorism and separatism in Chechnya.

If Russia, by operating on a different geopolitical and historical plane, is better equipped to cope with the latest 'recurrence of history', with its instability and bloody conflicts as well as new challenges to international security, the rest of Europe is having a problem accepting such a new reality.

Western Europe has no desire to leave the belle époque which it has experienced in the past three decades. Its almost non-stop economic growth has taken place within a highly stable and increasingly more secure international environment. The likelihood of a major conflict, despite some alarmist rhetoric, has undoubtedly diminished. Challenges from non-European areas of the world were safe to contemplate from behind the back of the US. The full demise of the bloc confrontation after the events of 1989–91 made the belle époque seem even more splendid. Celebrating the end of the Cold War distracted people's attention from sobering forecasts that the world could once again become dangerous, if not more so than before. Europe was happy to forget its difficult history; it even started working on its own new political (or 'politically correct') culture which banned, among other things, the death penalty even for acts of mass terror. Europe also revised its security policy by replacing the right to use military force by such 'soft' means as political dialogue and economic aid. To some extent, the US followed the same route while backing the Europeans by its growing military might.

However, this bucolic trend was at odds with reality. One has only to recall a string of cruel wars in Africa in the 1990s with their millions of victims, the bloody collapse of Yugoslavia from which the world failed to draw a lesson, or even the start of the proliferation of nuclear weapons – escapist or well-meaning politicians and governments have managed to ignore all these telltale signs. Some European countries are doing just that: look at the United Kingdom, Spain, Greece or Italy, the states that border on instability-prone regions. This trend, at least in part, helps to explain why the West has failed to appreciate Russian activities to combat the threat of separatism, terrorism and Islamist extremism that Chechnya has generated.

This long list of problems blocking the path to rapprochement between the EU and Russia, the weaknesses and failures of their policies, should, however, not be seen as reason for despair. First, one can exaggerate problems and difficulties. I sincerely hope this is the case but insist it would be wrong to hide anything. Secondly, it is obvious that both Russian and EU policies towards the rest of Europe and the world are inadequate, albeit in a different way. It is, however, important to understand where the roots of problems lie, figure out where interests clash and then start acting decisively in a way that reflects the new realities – something that both parties have avoided in the past decade.

It is obvious to me that Russia, despite its growing interests in a dynamically developing Asia and its firm relationship with the US, has an historically important stake in the strengthening of the EU's role in global politics and the global economy, and is keen to achieve maximum possible co-operation with the EU, but naturally on mutually beneficial conditions. The challenges that have replaced confrontation have put Russia's interaction with the EU and the US in a strikingly new context. In its past of confrontation or competition with the West, Russia was often anxious to see active disagreements between the transatlantic partners. Now that the new threats have become mutual, Moscow is concerned that its de facto allies in combating instability in Asia, terrorism, and WMD proliferation should remain as united and efficient as possible. As a result, Russia's politicians and intellectuals are beginning to worry about the deepening of the cultural, ideological, and political disparities between the US and Western Europe.[1] As unthinkable as this would have been in the not-too-distant past, there are voices in Russia today calling for the country to start working on overcoming such contradictions, and to take on an 'an integrator' role in the transatlantic relationship.[2]

At the same time, Russia's interest in achieving rapprochement with the EU is also predicated on an increase in the efficiency of the EU's foreign policy, which could counterbalance that of the US and help prevent a victory by hegemonic and biased interest groups there – a victory which would be dangerous for all the parties involved. Finally, Russia's desire to have the best possible access to Europe's financial, research and educational resources in order to modernise itself is also understandable.

It is clear that the EU leadership and elite have to decide whether they will benefit from a strategic agreement and integration with Russia. It is obvious to me that the EU, by maintaining an arms-length relationship with Russia, is seriously weakening its international standing, particularly at a time when international security and geopolitics are regaining priority status. It would be hardly possible for the EU to take the lead in a global economic competition without comprehensive cooperation with Russia in at least some areas, such as aerospace or energy.

## New context

At the same time, it is quite likely that the globalisation of economic and information flows, and the global challenge presented by the new threats, have created a new context for the interaction between the EU and Russia. The number of important issues that can be resolved bilaterally is diminishing, while multilateral decisions are becoming necessary for an ever-growing number of problems. We need urgently to review and re-examine our legacy institutions and ways of dealing with conflict situations. Parallelism and competition between such institutions are becoming increasingly counterproductive. The institutions need to be restructured and perhaps reformed or even replaced by new ones – creating new organisations may be more productive since it is rather difficult to overcome bureaucratic inertia. We urgently need, for example, a new security alliance based on the G8 with the subsequent inclusion of China, India and other responsible and influential states.[3]

It is also necessary to put the dialogue between the EU and Russia into a new format, moving from general declarations to the discussion of concrete issues. One way to do this might be by creating an EU-Russian security council (within the framework of a broader security alliance) that would coordinate policies on, for example, WMD, terrorism, organised crime, drug trafficking, illegal and legal migration.

The lists are long. The key issue, however, is to understand that a qualitatively new situation makes it imperative for Europeans across the entire continent to radically review their previous policies and accelerate sharply their search for adequate ways to deal with and adjust to it. Searching together is certain to be more efficient.

Yet each side has to make its own choices and decisions. If Russia claims it needs a close alliance with the EU, it urgently has to create structures that will cope with this task. And if the EU leaders have decided to make Russia its priority partner, then it is high time their decisions were turned into reality.

Notes

1 Cf. Robert Kagan 'Power and weakness'. *Policy Review*, June/July 2002, pp. 3–28.
2 Cf. an article by a leading Russian politician, V. Lukin, 'A Russian bridge across the Atlantic', *Russia in Global Politics*, No. 1, pp. 100–107 (www.globalaffairs.ru).
3 Cf. the article by K. Kaiser, S. Karaganov and G. Allison in *International Herald Tribune*; also V. Nikonov, 'Back to the Concert', *Russia in Global Politics*, No. 1, pp. 78–99 (www.globalaffairs.ru).

**Sergej Karaganow**

Born in Moscow, 1952. Political scientist, Chairman of the Russian council for defence and foreign policy. Deputy Director of the Europe Institute of the Russian Academy of Sciences, Moscow.

Tommy Koh

# Learning from Europe

For Asians of my generation, Europe looms large in our experience and imagination. What is Europe?

First, it is geography. By Europe, we mean all the lands stretching from the Urals to the Atlantic, and from the Arctic to the Mediterranean Sea.

Second, Europe was the source of our colonial domination from the 18th to the 20th centuries. Most of the countries of South and East Asia were, at one time or another, ruled by the British, French, Dutch, Portuguese and Spanish. The colonisers were all referred to as 'Europeans'. The colonial experience is remembered as partially good but mostly bad; there is therefore a certain love-hate attitude in the psyches of many Asian rulers and intellectuals towards Europe.

Third, Europe was an exemplar of modernity. During the 19th and 20th centuries, Asian intellectuals looked to Europe for ideas on how to modernise their societies. The five big ideas which Asians learned from Europe were: secularism, science and technology, industrialisation, democracy and the ideal of progress. These European ideas continue to dominate the agenda of Asian modernisers.

Fourth, Asians think there is a European civilisation. (Gandhi was once asked what he thought of European civilisation: he replied that it was a good idea.) The highest peaks of European civilisation are occupied by writers such as Dante and Shakespeare, musicians such as Beethoven and Verdi, artists such as Leonardo da Vinci and Pablo Picasso, scientists such as Newton and Darwin, philosophers such as Socrates and Descartes, social thinkers such as Marx and Weber, economists such as Adam Smith and John Maynard Keynes, and other European icons such as the Magna Carta and Rousseau's Social Contract. Europe has a high culture and it is this culture which gives Europe its identity. I do not share the view of some commentators that Europe is destined to become a lot more like America. Although Europe and America are part of the Western civilisation, the European cultural box is and will always be different from the American cultural box.

What in fact are the major differences between Europe and America? There are several important ones. For example, capitalism in Europe is different from that in America. The American system is based upon the value of self-responsibility; the American ethos favours low taxes and a minimal social safety net. The European system has a much larger element of social equity and social cohesion. European society is relatively stable and orderly. In contrast, America is more dynamic and chaotic. The American milieu, however, seems to produce more creative and innovative people. Also, Europe seems to be more inward-looking and less welcoming of foreign, especially Asian expertise. In comparison, America has welcomed millions of talented and hard-working Asians, many of whom have distinguished themselves in all walks of American life.

When Asians think of Europe today, they tend to equate Europe with the European Union. One reason is that the fifteen member states of the EU constitute the military, political, economic and cultural heart of Europe. Another reason is that the EU story is very inspiring to Asians – we see at least two miracles in that story.

The first European miracle is the reconciliation of historic enemies. Asians often wonder how to replicate the historic reconciliation that has taken place in Europe, between France and Germany, between England and France, and between

England and Germany. No such reconciliation has taken place in Asia between China and Japan, or between Japan and Korea. Many Asians seem to be pessimistic and fatalistic. They seem to think that either no such reconciliation will ever take place or if it does, it will take a very long time.

I do not accept this view. In my attempt to refute the sceptics, I have pointed to the example of Europe. I have argued that it is not inevitable that China and Japan, and Japan and Korea must continue to distrust each other. If France and Germany, and England and Germany can be reconciled, I do not see why the Asian countries cannot be reconciled. President Kim Dae Jung of Korea and the late Prime Minister Obuchi of Japan had, in fact, begun the process of reconciliation between their two countries. The road has been bumpy but, at least, there is an agreed route leading to reconciliation and peace. Currently, there is no agreed road map between China and Japan. Chinese and Japanese of goodwill should redouble their efforts; they should not be discouraged by past disappointments. They should draw inspiration from the historic reconciliation that has taken place between France and Germany, whose 40th anniversary we will celebrate in 2003. The lesson for Asians is that history need not repeat itself and that it is possible for visionary and strong leaders to change the course of history.

The second European miracle is the integration of Europe. The story of European integration – beginning with the European Coal and Steel Community in 1952, progressing to the European Economic Community in 1957, to the single market in 1993 and to the European Economic and Monetary Union in 1999 – is very inspiring. It is a story which continues to give hope to many of us in Asia who are engaged in the processes of East Asian regionalism.

What is the relevance of European integration to East Asia? Let me mention two examples. The first concerns the future of the Association of Southeast Asian Nations, ASEAN. After thirty-five years, ASEAN has become one of the most successful regional institutions in the world. Its most important achievement is that it has kept the peace in South East Asia. In the economic field, it has several concrete achievements including the ASEAN Free Trade Area (AFTA), the ASEAN Investment Agreement (AIA), and e-ASEAN. However, ASEAN is still a family of ten separate economies and markets.

In order for ASEAN to compete more effectively with China and India, it has to emulate the experience of Europe and transform itself into a single market of 500 million consumers. At the recent ASEAN Summit held in Cambodia, its leaders embraced the vision of scaling the next peak – the peak of an ASEAN Economic Community. I am sure we will encounter many obstacles on our way to this new goal. We can, however, derive courage and encouragement from the knowledge that our European friends travelled along a similar road and have gone on to conquer an even higher summit.

The story of European integration is also highly relevant to the ongoing process of uniting North East Asia and South East Asia and building an East Asian Economic Community. This process began in 1997 when Malaysia invited the leaders of China, Japan and Korea to meet the leaders of ASEAN, following their annual summit. The 1997 meeting was billed as a one-off event. However, the same group of leaders met again in Vietnam in 1998 and in the Philippines in 1999. By the time of the meeting in 2000, in Singapore, the leaders of East Asia, modestly referred to as ASEAN + 3, had decided to institutionalise the grouping. Since then, the momentum has quickened. In 2001, ASEAN accepted China's offer of an ASEAN-China FTA, to be completed in ten years. In 2002, ASEAN and Japan agreed to conclude a closer economic partnership. I am confident that Korea will not want to be left out and will make a similar proposal to ASEAN.

Based on the above developments, I would venture to suggest that there is a realistic prospect that over the next ten years, the world's largest free-trade area – comprising North

East Asia and South East Asia – could emerge. The East Asia free-trade area will have a combined population of two billion consumers. If we succeed in bringing this about, part of the credit should go to the EU.

Asians applauded the recent decision of the EU Summit, taken at its meeting in Copenhagen, to admit ten new members in 2004. They did so for two reasons: first, it will bring peace and prosperity to the new members; and secondly, the expanded EU will have a combined population of nearly 500 million citizens. This will give the EU a greater collective weight and benefit the world by making it more multipolar. Asians were also pleased that the EU did not close the door to Turkey – it is in everyone's interests to have Turkey inside rather than outside Europe. Kemal Ataturk's dream of a modern Turkey will be fulfilled when Turkey becomes a member of the EU. A modern, democratic and prosperous Turkey will constitute an important role model for the Islamic world.

To conclude with a response to the question, 'What is Europe?': I see Europe as a concept based on geography, history, culture, economy, common political values and legal tradition, and a shared vision. With expansion almost completed, I hope that the EU will work hard to forge a common foreign and security policy. When that is accomplished over the coming decades, I wonder if the next generation of Europeans will share Churchill's vision of a United States of Europe?

**Tommy Koh**
Born in Singapore, 1937. Director of the Institute of Policy Studies, Singapore, and ambassador-at-large in the ministry for foreign affairs, Singapore. Executive Director of the Asia Europe Foundation between 1997 and 2000. Prior to this, Singapore's ambassador to the USA.

Ma Canrong

# The Chinese View of Europe

Europe has always played an important role in the history of the development of human civilisation. As the home of Western culture and modern science and technology, Europe has constantly exerted a major influence on the world at large. But Europe also gave rise to two world wars as a result of rivalry for resources and areas for expansion. The European states became the main battlefields in these wars, which, like the subsequent 'Cold War', led to incomparable human and material losses, and left bitter memories deep in the hearts of the nations involved. The lesson to be drawn from history is that mutual rivalries and wars cannot produce positive long-term development for any European country. Only unification can promote general prosperity and make Europe as a whole more competitive internationally.

Coming to terms with their history in the aftermath of the Second World War led the European nations to reject hate and distrust and start along the road to unification. In this sense, European integration should not be seen merely as the result of a decision made by politicians, but also as an inevitable historical development. Over more than half a century, European integration has achieved successes that are recognised worldwide. The creation of political and economic unity, the introduction of the euro, the development of a common security and defence policy as well as the setting up of the Rapid Response Force all indicate the determination of the European states to achieve further integration. The recently agreed expansion of the European Union is leading for the first time to the unification of Eastern and Western Europe and is a milestone in the history of European integration.

In view of the progress of economic globalisation and political multipolarisation, the furthering of European integration will increase the centripetal power of the European continent, thus strengthening it; it will also increase the status and the role of Europe on the world political and economic stage.

Of course the process of European integration is not advancing without friction – it is subject to many difficulties and gives rise to many challenges. Developments in recent years have shown that the EU still has many obstacles to overcome. There are particularly awkward problems connected with, for example, harmonising the heterogeneous interests of the member states and carrying through the institutional reforms. For the Eastern European prospective member states, it is not easy to fulfil the criteria which the EU demands of them. Europe needs not only a united but also an independent voice when speaking to the outside world in order to become a genuinely important centre of influence in the world, and to play an appropriate role in international affairs. Nevertheless, there are also concerns that the consolidation of Europe could lead to new trade blockades. A united Europe should, however, continue to be open and contribute to the development of free trade rather than introduce a new level of trade protectionism.

China is observing the development of European unity with great interest. We understand and support the efforts of the European states to achieve integration. China sincerely hopes that Europe will play a more active role in international affairs. From the Chinese point of view, the EU should fill an important position in world politics because of its economic strength and its potential political influence. A united Europe that stands up for peace and international development will benefit the multipolarisation of the world – and in the current international situation that is of particular importance. For a long time China has attached great importance to its relations with the EU from a strategic point of view and will do whatever it can to achieve long-term, stable cooperation. Currently, Chinese-European relations are in the most positive phase of their history. Since 1998, the leading personalities of both sides have already met five times. The foreign ministers meet twice yearly: at the UN General Assembly and during the Asian-European Conference of Foreign Ministers. There are also lively political consultations on a number of other levels: dialogues on human rights, symposia on questions of law and women's rights as well as consultations about the non-proliferation of weapons of mass destruction and the combating of illegal immigration take place regularly. Economic and trade relations are developing well and expanding on an ongoing basis. In recent years the annual increase in bilateral trade has been in double figures. The EU and its member states are today China's greatest importers of technology, second-largest investors in real terms and third largest trade partners. And for the EU, China is the fourth largest export market and fourth largest source of imports.

Because of their differences in matters of social order, value systems, historical and cultural traditions as well as in their level of development, it is natural that China and Europe do not always agree on every question. We live in a diversified world. There cannot be just one civilisation, one social order, one development model or one system of values. Every nation and its people has made its own individual contribution to the development of human civilisation. It is nonetheless important that dialogue and cooperation should take place on the basis of mutual respect, complementarity and benefit, and that differences should be set aside in the search for points of mutual agreement. China and Europe are central powers on the international stage, and both find themselves at an important stage in their historical development. In the face of the current complicated world situation, the views of China and Europe on important international and regional questions are increasingly in agreement. Both sides today share many common views on a whole series of basic problems such as, for example, combating terrorism, preserving the global strategic balance and promoting multipolarisation.

The further strengthening of Chinese-European relations is not only in the interest of both sides, but also a viable alternative in view of the changeable world situation. The Chinese government will view and conduct Chinese-European relations undisturbed by strategic considerations and will devote itself consistently to a strengthening of mutual cooperation.

**Ma Canrong**
Born in Jiangsu, China, 1945. Ambassador for the People's Republic of China in Germany from 2002. Assisting minister in the foreign ministry of the People's Republic of China from 1999 to 2001.

Robert Weinberg

# The Post-War Scientific Renaissance in Europe

An Interview

*How do you, as an American scientist, view the state of the art in Europe?*

I'm going to focus on the field of biology, biomedical research, although I'll go beyond pure cancer research. I think some history is useful here. After the Second World War, Europe, which had once led the world in biomedical research, was pretty much shattered in terms of research, certainly on the European continent. The Brits were actually the first to lead the pack in Europe; indeed, the double helix was discovered in Cambridge in 1953. At the same time, there was also a focus of activity at the Pasteur Institute in Paris. The Dutch too re-established their research competence soon after the war. But the great German centers of biology no longer existed. Many of their biologists had been driven into exile, either because of the racial laws or because of politics, and German science was in absolute shambles. Science in the rest of Europe was also minimal. Italy had a little bit in terms of biology; Spain had almost nothing. The Scandinavian countries had relatively little with the exception of the Swedes in Stockholm. The American juggernaut began to grow, and by 1970 American biomedical research had vastly overshadowed whatever remained in Europe. The Brits, who had made a good showing in Cambridge in the 1950s, continued to contribute to the events of the 1960s and 1970s. But relative to what was happening in the United States, they had an increasingly smaller share of the pie in terms of leading cutting-edge experiments. And then, starting around 1980/1985, the Germans started getting their act together. By about 1990, German biomedical research – at least in areas of basic molecular biology – was quite comparable in quality but not in quantity to that of the US. Today, Germany is in the European forefront. The Dutch have maintained a very high quality, although by necessity it is quantitatively much smaller than most other countries. France, I believe, has mismanaged its scientific research agenda. The Spaniards are moving ahead very quickly, and with every passing year one sees more and more really good lines of research coming out of, for example, Madrid. The Italians, who started very far behind, also have an increasing number of credible researchers. Scandinavia, which always had good quality, has not changed very much; it has been relatively static, to my mind, in terms of overall contributions. But in the rest of Europe, there is almost nothing: almost nothing in Greece, very little in Portugal, very little in Belgium, a little bit in Denmark, very little in Norway. So there is in modern Europe a great patchiness in terms of quality and obviously in terms of quantity. Increasingly, the large powerhouse is likely to be Germany in terms of regenerating a role in scientific research, two generations after the debacle of the Second World War, causing them to be one of the centers of gravity alongside the US, and to a lesser extent now, Japan.

*Who funds scientific research?*

Well, science is funded very differently in Europe than it is in the US. In the US there are many more sources of money, both public and private, and it is much more of a polycentric universe in terms of power. In most countries in Europe, power is concentrated in a very small number of institutions or granting agencies. There is almost no private money except, to my knowledge, in Britain and in a little bit of Scandinavia. The Brits have a great cancer research campaign which funds some excellent institutions and there is a little bit of that in France. But basically, the funding of science is viewed as a public obligation in Europe. This is quite different in the US, where there are significant foundations that support a lot of first-class research and where it is considered worthy to contribute to various disease charities to support research in those areas. What this has meant is that it is easier for individual scientists to acquire research funding in the US than it is in Europe.

*Is it possible to talk about Europe as a single entity or is it still a patchwork quilt?*

Well, it used to be the tradition in Europe – more so than in the US – for each research institution, never mind country, to be its own autonomous entity, and as a consequence, collaborations did not come as easily as they did here in the US. The professor sat on the top of a very hierarchical array of associate professors and dictated what should happen below. In this country, already after the Second World War, there was a much more democratic empowerment of younger people, especially younger professors, who were granted much more independence. And a scientist in Boston would never have said, 'I'm not going to collaborate with so-and-so because he's in the State of New York or the State of New Jersey'. What happened in the 1980s and 1990s – and is happening to a lesser extent now – is that many young European scientists with fresh doctorates came to the US, saw how research is done here, and went home to reform the way European science was organised. They began to make it much less hierarchical, with much less power granted to older people, and much more of a democratic and horizontal distribution of influence and funds.

And that has been one of the reasons why German science in particular has surged. At the same time, inter-European collaborations have also flourished and are now very extensive. One is increasingly seeing the knitting together of the European scientific community, at least in biomedical research, not because of any national government or European Union imposed pressures, but because in many areas, European scientists have become aware that if they want to compete qualitatively with the Americans, they simply have to establish collaborative arrangements with scientists elsewhere. Very often, those collaborative arrangements have to be, by necessity, with neighboring countries. So there is now ample precedent for international collaborations within the European Community, and they are growing with every passing year. Moreover, in many laboratories in continental Europe, people are communicating with each other in English. Not because of American cultural domination but because they have chosen English, perhaps arbitrarily, as their *lingua franca*. And only by having a common language can anyone get anything done in many of the laboratories in Europe. Clearly, by breaking down the language barrier, it has become possible to knit together the European continental countries.

*Do the young European scientists who come out to the US usually return home?*

As a rule, I'd say yes, when it comes to long-term careers; the Germans prefer to stay in Germany, the French almost insist on being in France. So people go back to where they came from even though they may have spent time abroad. In no small part this may also be due to certain academic constraints which require teaching in the language of the country and so forth.

*Is there anything significant happening in Eastern Europe as far as biomedical research is concerned?*

Nothing to speak of. Before the fall of communism, Eastern European biomedical research was pitiful. In Russia it was held back by people like Trofim Lysenko and bizarre communist ideologies. They had some very smart people there, and they still do. But for all practical purposes, scientific research does not exist east of the Oder-Neisse Line. So once you go east of continental Europe, the next respectable research you find is in Israel. Then you find a bit of high-tech development, software development, in India, and then you have to go to Japan and Australia and the little island of Singapore. It's not as if scientific research is equally distributed across the planet. There is virtually nothing that goes on in South America or Central America.

*Do you count Israel as European?*

I suppose I do. The fact is that, first of all, Israeli academic science was founded by Europeans. Israeli intelligentsia are still very Eurocentric. Israel correctly perceives that unless it has strong intellectual ties with Europe, it will die on the vine or become 'Levantinised', become another Levantine country. Almost all of its neighbors are extremely backward, obviously – even in Egypt there is almost no sign of scientific research. So the Israelis realise full well that if they don't establish some umbilicus to the European scientific community, there is no hope for Israeli science.

*Many American scientists have a European background. Does that make them European scientists?*

No, they've been in the US for too long, so the European loyalties of American scientists have been muted. This is not to say that American scientists are against Europe. It's just that Americans will interact with Europe on an opportunistic basis. When it looks as if there will be some good scientific synergy or collaboration, we'll work with Europe. And if it doesn't make much sense to work with Europe, we won't do it out of sentimentality. Which is fine. The Europeans view the Americans as a scientific juggernaut and a threat. The Americans don't have a corresponding feeling of rivalry with the Europeans, maybe because there is no reason for them to feel threatened. But in any case, over the past decades, the American scientific community has been enormously hospitable to a whole generation of young European scientists which it has trained, often at American expense. These are the young scientists who then return to Europe and get European scientific research moving. The same is now happening with Chinese scientists. Some of them go back to China. I'm not saying that all American-trained scientists go home, but many do.

*Do you see any immediate problems emerging in the EU?*

One problem as the European community becomes more and more integrated is that the decisions as to whether individual scientists are given money to do research may increasingly come from the EU. At the moment, decisions are not made by administrators as much as by what are called peer review panels, where a group of individuals gets together, looks through all the applications and decides on awarding research grants. And that is very good, because in most countries in Europe, the scientific community is so small that the people involved really don't have enough distance from one another, so that everybody ends up scratching everybody else's back. So these international peer review panels are good. The problem I foresee with the EU is that there is increasingly an implicit requirement that each country has its own representative on one of those decision-making bodies. So there is one Portuguese and one Greek and one Pole on one of the study sections. If that is pushed to its limits, it will destroy European science simply because it's not necessarily the case that in each specialised research area there is a qualified Portuguese, a qualified Greek or a qualified Pole to make the right decisions. I don't know how that problem will be resolved.

*Thank you.*

> *The conversation was conducted by Susan Stern*

**Robert A. Weinberg**
Born in Pittsburgh, Pennsylvania, 1942. Professor in the Department of Biology, MIT, Cambridge. Pioneer in cancer research, awarded the National Medal of Science in 1997. Publications include: *One Renegade Cell: How Cancer Begins.*

Chenjerai Hove

# Mind the Gap!

A little boy in an African village is playing in the sand. He is learning to write his name and the names of his friends, brothers and sisters. He is years past school-age, but in the 1950s and early 1960s, birth certificates do not exist. While he is playing, the excitement of writing makes him forget the calves and goats he is supposed to be watching. They vanish and destroy other people's crops. The father of the boy comes and whips the boy, but the boy insists that he wants to go to school like all his playmates. The father feels pity for him and decides that since he is no good at keeping cattle and goats, the best place for him is the white man's school.

At school, the boy first learns how to write his name, and then how to read the Bible. Everything is in English.

The boy recalls the day the district commissioner came to the village and none of the children were allowed to get near the white man. The children were not well dressed, had no proper trousers, not to mention underpants. The children, the boy among them, look through the kitchen hut window to see the white man, maybe to hear him talk the complicated nose language of his home country, England. The language sounds good and magic, since it seems it is the only tool that allows him to wield so much power over the rest of the people of the land – the blacks. All the time, the boy sees his parents and the neighbours nodding and saying something like 'hes hes hes hes'. His parents seem more subdued than he has ever seen them before.

Thoughts crowd the mind of the little boy. His head goes wild. One day, if he learns to speak the language of the white district commissioner, he will be as powerful as the white man.

English is the language that is first offered to the boy, with no choice of any other. Life becomes a dream for the things that come with the wind. It becomes a big dream of the power that the young man could wield if he could ever get the white man's education and language.

Even the clothes he is forced to wear are a vast departure from the loin cloth (mukofo) which he has been wearing for so long now. He does not even know how to wear the short trousers which are compulsory school uniform. He cannot sing in the school choir if he does not have the full uniform.

'If I learn the language of the white man, or even better, if I can go to the land of the white man and learn the ways of his life, I will be like him', the boy thinks.

And for those who did not want to go to school, the teachers come to the village, wielding baskets full of sweets and sugar. They give the boys the sweet things and tell them if they come to school, there is more to be had there. And there is even more in the white man's land, because that is where they are made.

So, school becomes associated with the sweet things of life! In school, the boy studies the English language really hard so that he can go to secondary school, university and all that. He does well under the circumstances. His first shoes are earned when he has to go to a Catholic boarding school. The Catholic teachers are French Canadians, the Marist brothers from Montreal, Canada. As a matter of course, they also teach him a little French. He has no choice. He now owns two strange languages: English and French.

Thus begins the journey of the African imagination into Europe, the continent which he has been told is equal to Canaan, the land of milk and honey. He dreams that if ever he gets there, all his village memories will be a thing of the past, to be set aside and forgotten. He will be playing with white children and be like them in the land of plenty, the land of freedom. And he knows that he is not the only one. All his friends who persist with the stream of this dream are with him. They want to go overseas. The films they watch under the tree, screened on a rough wall, say so too: the land of plenty is over there, out there where the whites are, where everyone is 'as white as snow'.

Years later, after the boy has been to Europe and seen the wealth and poverty of the Europeans, nobody believes him when he tells them there are poor people in Europe, people without homes, people without food or even hope. They cannot believe it. They think that since the young man is a storyteller, he is inventing all these stories to make them stay in abject poverty in the village or in the African city, where if a dog is run over by a car, it remains rotting on the tarmac for a week or even a month.

That little boy has become a young man and an oldish sort of man. His name is Chenjerai Hove, the now famous writer-poet, novelist and journalist.

## Europe: a dream

In the minds of so many African inhabitants, Europe is a big dream of plenty. The television that is supposed to be African shows them European and American wealth. The only thing to struggle for in Europe and America (they do not quite take in the difference) is the size of the money pot, plus a beautiful woman and a mansion to top up the whole story. That is what the film stories on television say. Once you are in Europe, it is ridiculous to write home and say you do not have money to send them. They laugh and call you an arrogant (selfish) fool!

Every African – from villager to academic – seriously believes that Europe is a continent of plenty, that the European sky is made of cake and honey for all to eat. No one starves in

Europe, so the myth goes, a myth based on the images to which Africans are subjected all day, all night, on television and in the newspapers. Those images become a permanent part of the relationship between Europe and Africa, at all levels, especially in harsh times of dictatorship, famine and other natural disasters.

## Mind the Gap!

'Every time I take the underground in London, a forlorn voice shouts: Mind the gap! Mind the gap!' I wrote this many years ago before I had the experience of the European Union, which was still being shaped as another quest for a European identity in all sorts of complicated ways.

Minding the gap becomes the symbol of that economic gap that has continued to widen between countries of the south and the EU.

> *Before I build a wall I'd ask to know*
> *What I was walling in or walling out*
> *And to whom I was like to give offense*

'Mind the gap!' – the ominous voice continues to echo in my mind and heart and soul.

Although Europe has adopted the adage that good fences make good neighbours, Robert Frost's lines from his poem *Mending Wall* (above) remind us of what has happened between Europe and the rest of us, especially on the African continent.

The new gospel of international relations in Europe is a gospel of exclusion. The EU, the European currency, the exchange rate mechanism, are all institutions set up to exclude anybody else from the European 'table of plenty'.

While the European tongue in Africa preaches open market policies, our countries are subjected to the brutal forces of quotas spelled out in this or that version of the Lomé Convention, designed to obtain African and other goods at give-away prices. Slavery has been dressed in new uniforms.

After all, the free-market policies are worth laughing at if we put the goods manufactured by villagers in a small country against those mass produced by an American company with the latest technology at hand.

Whether anyone likes it or not, Europe has embarked on the politics and economics of racist exclusion, a new form of exclusion; and this at the end of a century renowned for its crop of fine fighters against apartheid.

The fake integration of a one world without borders, united by a common vision of humanity is now being thrown to the dogs. Instead, the wall of apartheid has been extended beyond the borders of South Africa to the very heart of those who once wielded the flame of freedom, free speech, free movement and free thought.

I remember many years ago an EU commissioner spelling out the terms of the new engagement between African and European realities. The man was talking to his so-called Third World partners. The message I got was simple: you Africans are alone in the search for your own destiny. Economically, culturally and politically, we would rather be dealing with the countries east of us where old borders have been broken down.

The EU has now found other partners to whom it can relate more harmoniously culturally and institutionally, since it is no longer faced with the 'evil empire' called the Soviet Union. Instead of evaluating what mistakes the Europeans have made in their assistance programmes for Africa, it is easy to simply brush off everything and say: aid to Africa does not work.

Look at what happened in Rwanda! The Europeans simply looked the other way and did not bother to think that the guns used to butcher innocent victims had a European origin of some sort.

It is commonly understood in the EU that anyone from Africa or Asia wanting to visit is likely to want to stay on. But the bureaucracy of the new large state of Europe does not stop to consider why someone would go under the belly of an aircraft and freeze to death in an attempt to reach Europe. Even if the guy miraculously survives, he is likely to be sent home. No one wants to leave their mother and father, wife and child for no particular address, no identity. If it happens, the authorities in Europe will have to look at other political and historical perspectives in order to understand that personal, socio-economic and historical drama.

## Borders and boundaries

Since the beginning of the last century, the world has been trying to do away with all the limitations to human contact and movement. But borders are now being celebrated by the EU, they have become instruments to confine humans and their cultures at every level. The creators of borders and boundaries are specialists in the art of separating people and ideas, and in the art of isolating the human soul. The EU, in the long term, could become a house of isolation because as the excluded nations begin to feel the pinch, they could easily impose their own isolation on others. The fight for space is on both sides of the fence, especially in times of political and economic desperation. But for now and for the future, Europe has said that borders are viable and useful for self-preservation. That self-preservation can also be a profound form of cultural anguish on both sides of the high fence.

As far as I can see, Europe is wearing a huge mask, pretending that it can survive without others, including Africa. Africa and Asia are now open markets and a source of cheap labour for the comfort of others. Foreigners are not seen as humans who cry when they are pinched: they are simply the suppliers of raw materials which are processed and sent back to the Africans and Asians to buy and enjoy some kind of artificial comfort in the midst of naked poverty.

The EU might even give us soft loans to buy their own goods and skills originating from the forgotten continents. Our lands become tourist destinations where humans are invisible and animals are the talk of the holiday-makers. We become part of the jungles and nature. (Observe how many films are shown on European television screens about animals and how many about African human life.)

Everyone is entitled to their own foolishness, I think. So are states, big and small. But sometimes the consequence of that foolishness is a burden for generations to come.

## Shrinking the world

'But then, how do I tell her (my mother) about the new happenings of the city where high walls, barking hounds and warnings on the gates are a common presence. "Beware of the dog" say most entrances to houses in the city's good suburbs. Usually the owners of the house mean it, with huge hounds barking like lions from inside the high walls of the "fenced and gated" house,' I once wrote many years ago about my country. Then everyone was fencing themselves in, and fencing others out.

The EU has decided to fence itself in and out. As you fence others out, you also fence yourself in.

'Walls and gates remind me of prison', wrote Zimbabwean writer Dambudzo Marechera. But then he did not go further to say the prison officer who locks me inside is also locking himself outside. So, both are locked outside of the other's experiences. Thus, the walls of the EU are a way of creating silences on both sides, or many sides. The coin is not made of two sides: its has four, including the space where it is resting and might fly.

Closed doors and high walls are a sign of a certain malaise afflicting the homestead. That is why it is so easy to apportion blame to foreigners whenever a crime is committed in a European country. The silences that are created by these high walls cause frustration and lack of confidence in the system. A friend of mine, a poet, once sent me these lines:

> *the bird flies*
> *but does not finish the sky;*
> *a fish swims*
> *but does not finish the ocean.*

For the world only shrinks if the imagination of the inhabitants shrinks. In my language, we have a proverb which says: If a mouse trap falls on it, the mouse thinks the whole world has ended. Shrinking spaces are based on a consumerist perspective, a view which thinks the more we are in one place, the more we are likely to exhaust the air we breathe. If the world adheres to that belief, there will many homeless souls under this beautiful sky given us by the creators. The fact is, there is still enough space for us all on this earth; but most of it is taken up by greed and artificial boundaries.

I hate shrinking spaces, whether they are invented by Africans or Europeans. The shrinking spaces of Europe make one think that the whole idea of multiculturalism is dying. What it means is that the EU will select who to involve in the multicultural society which they want to create. The intellectuals, academics, writers and musicians who can mingle with high society; those are the ones who will be able to come to Europe, not the low culture subordinates who dream of other worlds without the palaces and chateaux of Europe.

The frightening possibility about the EU is that it is putting in place exactly the agenda which it says should not be: one constitution, similar laws, and in the near future, possibly one language. For goodness' sake, who wants a Europe which speaks one language? One language for so many people is, to me, like a prison uniform. It is like two million children wearing one uniform, speaking one language, walking to one rhythm.

A monolithic society is the worst thing that can happen to a people! It is a form of exile for the 'other' when it should be a search for that mysterious 'other', for the mysterious social, cultural and economic space, however small, which 'others' occupy.

> *red hills and the smell of exile*
> *exile breathing over our shoulder*
> *in a race that already looks desperate.*
> *red hills, and the pulse of exile*
> *telling us this is home no more.*

So I wrote in 1983 in my poetry anthology, *Red Hills of Home,* trying to show that a monolithic society is only a futile attempt to erase 'the other' from our memories.

The danger is that the EU will, in the end, bring this monolithic union into the education system to the extent that the children of Europe will know no other continent except theirs. This is what has happened to the United States' mis-dream.

In the process of competing with the American dollar and economy, there is the danger that Europe will commit the same errors that have created some of the most serious political and religious problems which are facing the whole world.

The fear of difference is the beginning of dictatorship. It is frightening to contemplate that one day, Europe may have one president, one parliament, one law for all. The American mis-dream is there for all to see. So-called globalisation is a process of further weakening the weak and strengthening the strong so that the money remains where it was before. An old villager does not know what it is all about, and no one seems to be ready to explain to her why the prices of her cotton crop are determined in far away places with no cotton fields at all.

**Chenjerai Hove**
Born in Zimbabwe, 1956, currently living in Paris. Freelance journalist and author. Founding president of the Zimbabwe Writers Union (ZIWI) from 1984 to 1992. Publications include: *Shebeen Tales; Bones; Shadows; Ancestors; Blind Moon.*

# The Shape of the Union

*Europe – the part that's Unionised. Some of those that belong don't care or would rather not anyway; others who don't belong – yet – would give their eye-teeth (and some have). A few who don't belong don't want to. And others figure that they might as well get as close to the EU door as possible, knowing that the door is likely to remain shut in the foreseeable future. And still the question remains: what are the hidden criteria for EU membership? If they were democratic values, respect for human dignity and a healthy economy alone, we'd have the US as the most favoured member (perhaps), while some of the present members would be denied application forms. How does the notion of a superstate jibe with a desire to preserve national sovereignty? So many questions and more...*

Ismail Cem

# Turkey in Europe

As the new century unfolds, Europe is finally putting the memories of two devastating wars and a long and bitter Cold War behind it. The first decade of the 21st century will continue the process of rectifying these historical errors and misfortunes which have affected the lives of millions of Europeans. Indeed, Europe is genuinely seeking internal harmony and integration, pursuing a dynamic initially set in motion in the 1950s. The Continent is gradually uniting, with a view to achieving common goals, from west to east and from north to south.

The main question that needs to be addressed is: will the future of the European Union be limited by religion and race, or will it reach out and boldly contribute to the diversity and unity of a much larger geographical area? How will Europe's identity and geography be defined? Which criteria will direct these choices? What will be the parameters and the priorities? Obviously, the definitions for a European identity and a European geography are interlinked. Together, they define the borders of Europe, a definition that has become fairly synonymous with the EU.

It seems to me that Europe has not yet firmly decided on its strategy vis-à-vis the challenges of emerging political realities: whether it is interested in embracing vast new economic, historical and cultural opportunities; whether it wants to go the extra mile in furthering harmony in a world endangered by the much-discussed clash of civilisations; whether it will assume greater responsibility in the attempt to create a better world for all. Europe has to decide on its identity, its vision and its mission.

The identity of Europe – or of the future Europe – can be defined through its geographic and cultural dimensions. The emphasis given to the various constituent factors and the synthesis of very different priorities involved are likely to determine the final definition. Geography alone is a simple way to establish the borders of Europe and define who is European, but it is insufficient; it does not take into consideration the dynamics of cultural and political change that Europe has gone through.

On the other hand, if Europe and being European are considered mainly as cultural phenomena, we may get closer to a more relevant definition. And here we come to the crux of the matter. How are we supposed to understand culture? If Europe and Europeans are defined by religious criteria, if the EU is a 'Christian club' then the setting is not appropriate for an encompassing identity and a far-reaching mission. But if European culture is defined as the Council of Europe, or as the EU officially claims by factors such as democracy, human rights, rule of law, gender equality, and secularism, then we are looking at the prospect of a far larger geographical area and a more complex and diverse European identity.

It is obvious that the definition of European borders will vary according to different sensitivities, concerns and goals. Lines drawn from a purely economic point of view will differ radically from those drawn from a viewpoint that gives top priority to defence and security. A citizen marked by history might desire a monolithic Europe and determine its borders accordingly. A forward-looking citizen would certainly map out the Continent very differently.

When borders are drawn, priority is generally given to the concerned entity's geo-strategic goals, assuming that this entity has the means to achieve its goals. Therefore, the ultimate decision as to the borders of Europe (for the purposes of this discussion defined as the EU) will depend on a consensus which will have to be reached by the member states; they will have to come to an agreement based on a multitude of shared and non-shared interests. This synthesis of interests, in turn, will be determined mainly by Europe's strategic vision; its geo-strategy. What then, one might venture to ask, is that strategic vision on which the future of Europe is to be built?

The answer is that Europe does not have a clear strategic vision at this point in history. Sooner or later, a choice will have to be made that will either provide Europe with a crucial bridge of conciliation with civilisations of other characteristics, or it will be discriminatory and either have no effect on the existing dichotomies or even worse, increase them. Europe has to decide on the demarcation. Will it reach the historical boundaries of Europe? Will it include Turkey and thus move the fault-line further to the east? Or will it divide the Aegean into two by encompassing Greece but excluding Turkey? The way this issue is decided will have important historical consequences.

A Europe that does not include Turkey will have its eastern borders in the Balkans and in the Aegean; the front-line countries will be facing Turkey on the other side of the border. Symbolically and in real terms, Turkey and Greece will be facing each other as potentially conflicting parties on opposite sides of the European divide. This is not an environment which holds out any promise for peaceful and promising relationships; not for Europe, nor for Greece, nor for Turkey. On the other hand, including Turkey in Europe would eliminate the division between Greece and Turkey and move the EU to the east. This will enhance the cooperation between the two Aegean neighbours and will provide further stability to the region. In strategic terms, the European security zone will thus be extended.

The past bears witness to the fact that integration has become imperative for Europe. If peace and prosperity are to take root, then European nations must integrate in a deeper sense: without prejudice, fear or animosity.

The place of Turkey in the future EU will constitute one of the determining factors for the future of Europe and for its identity. This for an obvious reason: Turkey is naturally a European country; it is not in need of formal recognition by other European nations. But it has a unique strategic characteristic: it is Asian as well as European. Turkey views this plurality as an asset, therefore, Turks are disturbed when their European identity is questioned. If being European is a historical or geographical definition, for over 700 years of its history, Turkey has lived in Europe as a European power. Turkish history was moulded as much in Istanbul, Edirne, Tetova and Sarajevo as it was in Bursa, Kayseri, Konya and Diyarbakir.

If being European is a purely cultural matter, things get a bit more complicated. If religion is considered to be the main component of European culture, Turkey is an outsider. But this is a very narrow view of culture. If European culture is defined by democratic and secular values, then, in spite of the need for further progress on some points, Turkey has shared and contributed to this contemporary European culture for more than eighty years.

This is not the complete picture, though. Turkey has also shared its history and culture with the Middle East, the Caucasus and Central Asia. All these regions, which form part of Turkey's historical and cultural geography, have contributed to the development of the country. Since the central stage of the next millennium, many observers agree, will be Eurasia, Turkey's historical, cultural and actual presence in this emerging reality is a new and relevant factor. Given the trends in production, communication and information technologies, Europe and Asia will be interlinked and interdependent. Both will gain substantially from this linkage. Turkey's roots in Eurasia, generally defined as the territory stretching from Western Europe to Western China, date from before the Ottoman and Seljuk period. This ongoing relationship has acquired a new dimension in the last decade.

The post-Cold War period has witnessed the reappearance or reconfirmation of several independent states. Almost all of these 'new' states in the Balkans, in the Caucasus and in Central Asia are ones with which Turkey shares a mutual history and cultural affinities; with several a common religion and a common language is also shared. The emergence of Eurasia and its independent states has provided Turkey with a new environment of enhanced historic and cultural dimensions. Furthermore, these new nation-states quickly embarked upon the task of rebuilding their economies as well as opening them to foreign investment and competition. Turkey, as a longstanding actor in these geographies, has become a vital partner in their economic restructuring.

In this vast socio-political geography, Turkey has the most dynamic economy, the most advanced armed forces and the oldest democracy. Thus, it is optimally situated to contribute to stability and to enjoy the opportunities presented by the new 'Eurasian Order.'

If the future Europe cannot consider as European a country firmly planted in Europe, carrying a contemporary European culture but with a strong Asian dimension, then all claims at being a multicultural, multi-ethnic, multi-religious new Europe would be devoid of reality. It is for the rest of Europe to decide whether it can define and identify itself with a country which, though European, has an equally significant Asian dimension. Therefore, the way other Europeans view and treat Turkey will reflect their understanding of the future Europe, of Europe's role as a secluded monolithic body or as a far-reaching, multicultural, multi-ethnic, multi-religious, secular entity.

What Turkey can contribute to an integrated Europe is the historical experience that only a country that for centuries was the centre of a huge geographical area and a genuine civilisation can provide. It actually has a unique role as a model: as the only country with a predominantly Muslim population which has the ideals and practices of a contemporary pluralist and secular democracy, Turkey is a particular paradigm of modernisation.

For a long period of history, Western Europe and Turkey considered each other as 'The Other', to use Edward Said's term. Each was the anti-thesis, the outsider. Now there is growing evidence that this is no longer the case. It is our mutual responsibility to ensure that this positive trend develops further. The future Europe should become a Europe of solidarity, which strives for the propagation of European, but at the same time deeply universal, values. The goal should be the creation of a community of European nations whose strength lies in its ethnic, cultural and religious diversity. This is indeed the very philosophical dimension which will qualify Europe to lead the struggle against the threats of intolerance and the clash of civilisations.

**Ismail Cem**
Born in Istanbul, 1940. President of the New Turkey party. Turkish foreign minister from 1997 to 2002. Member (from 1987 to 1997) and Chairman (1996) of the Turkish delegation to the Parliamentary Assembly of the Council of Europe.

Michael Portillo

# Plea for an Untidy Europe

An Interview

*Most people in Britain – you included – talk about Britain and Europe as 'us' and 'them'. Isn't Britain part of Europe?*

I don't think you should read too much into the fact that the British refer to the Continent as Europe. We are an island. There is a piece of water between us, and it has always been a special journey to cross that piece of water. I think the vocabulary of talking about the Continent as Europe was probably at least reinforced, if not invented, during the Second World War: Britain was the only country which didn't lose its democracy or be overrun by invading forces. Referring to the Continent as Europe, does, I suppose, betray a certain psychological orientation among the British, but it isn't meant in any hostile way – it is just a figure of speech.

On the other hand, it's legitimate to ask where Britain fits into Europe. I think most British people think that it is on a sort of bridge between the United States and the Continent. First of all, there's the shared language, which puts us in touch with the US in a very immediate way. The relationship between the British and the Americans has been strong since the First World War. It was reinforced by the Second World

War, and in recent times, it's been further reinforced by a common perception of liberal or Anglo-Saxon economics. That may date from Mrs Thatcher's time. But what is interesting is that the perception continues under Tony Blair, who also seems to believe that in some ways, the economic policies of the United Kingdom are halfway between fairly free market American policies and the rather more interventionist policies pursued on the continent of Europe.

*You have come out fairly strongly against Britain joining the Eurozone and as you have pointed out, your opposition has less to do with monetary policy than with politics.*

For many years I have been arguing that introducing a single currency is not so much monetary or economic – it's political, and that what really drives most of our partners towards a single currency is that it is one of the attributes, one of the qualities, of a state. Other attributes include a flag, a common foreign policy, a common border, a common security policy, and a head of state. And indeed, many of these goals are well on the way to being achieved. Our partners view a common currency as a step towards statehood. But I've gone slightly further recently in saying that in the end, having a single currency comes down to a state of mind. One of the things I think our partners find difficult to accept is that scepticism about joining in the European project is not limited to the Conservative Party, which, as you see now, is a minority in Parliament. Scepticism is far more widespread. After five years, Tony Blair has still not committed himself to entering the euro, although he personally has been quite enthusiastic about it. He knows, and opinion polls confirm, that the British do not share the dream, envision the ideal, that many of our European partners do. I cannot, of course, speak for countries that I am not part of, but I do think that the dream has caught hold on the Continent, perhaps partly because of a different political tradition in which dreams and rhetoric play a much bigger part of the political process. In its political dialogue, Britain is pretty downbeat. People don't very much talk of dreams, and rhetorical flourishes here are rather more constrained than in continental Europe. So it's partly that political tradition and it's partly historical experience. Because we weren't invaded and because in a way, the Second World War was our finest hour, the British don't feel the great imperative to make political changes to ensure that a Second World War doesn't happen again – an imperative which I think still motivates some of our continental partners.

Then again, Britain is a country with a curious mixture of self-confidence and lack thereof. In many ways we lack self-confidence; we are always running ourselves down. If you look at the press any day, it's always full of bad news stories and unfavourable comparisons with other countries. But on the other hand, I don't think that most people have, as it were, given up on Britain. It's not that they have grandiose ideas about Britain's place in the world, but they don't feel the need to become part of a bigger entity in order to have status in the world. I think the French government in particular is driven by the idea that Europe has to be a counterweight to the US or that Europe has to be a big economic entity; that it has to be politically powerful and maybe even militarily powerful; that it has to be a bloc. I would guess that that way of thinking is fairly prevalent throughout much of the Continent. But it's pretty much absent here. You don't on the whole get masses of people saying, 'Gosh, I wish we were part of a bigger bloc and then we could be a counterweight to the US'.

*Nevertheless, aren't we all in NATO together?*

Yes, but NATO is a very different kind of body, and in fact, demonstrates rather well another problem Britain has with the European Union. We often refer to these organisations that we belong to as clubs, because club is a very English term. And NATO in a way is a club, because it has very clearly defined rules and the rules don't change. I don't think there have been any rule changes since NATO was established. NATO is a bringing together of sovereign governments, because even under Article V of the NATO Treaty (the Washington Treaty), which stipulates that a violation of the territory of one is to be regarded as a violation of the territory of all, each government is invited to participate in mutual defence. But participation remains a sovereign decision by each government. The EU, on the other hand, is clearly a process. Its rules change all the time and in two ways. They change because the governments meet together about every three years and draw up another treaty: a Maastricht Treaty, a Nice Treaty etc. These treaties are part of an evolution. And the EU also evolves through decisions of the European Court of Justice. European Court decisions are taken in accordance with the Preamble, which states that the purpose of the court is to further an ever-closer EU. So there is already a bias in the way the court will resolve a case. These are the two ways in which the EU moves forward, and the moving forward causes difficulties for the British. The rules are in flux. Now, a lot of people might say: 'We are quite happy with everything that's happened so far, but we don't want to go any further. We don't want the single currency. We don't want a single government. We want to stop the evolution.' But there's a feeling among the British that they are on a conveyor belt, and that even though they may have chosen to jump off at times – when the social chapter of the Maastricht Treaty or the single currency came along – sooner or later, some other issue will pop up because the conveyor will have moved on, and the British will once again find themselves dealing with an unwanted situation.

*But how does this make Britain different from France? France too wants to protect its sovereignty and is loathe to give up any part of it. And yet the French are still going along with this whole European process. Perhaps because they see themselves as part of the core, the ones dictating the process. But Britain too is part of that core. There's a process, a historical process going on within Britain itself. Nothing remains static. The question is: who controls the process? The French obviously believe that to a great extent, they do. Surely, if the British were right in there in the mainstream, they could direct it better?*

I think the problem is that we don't have a consensus about where the process is taking us. Broadly speaking, I think most of the members of EU other than the United Kingdom do want to create a pan-European superstructure of some sort, be it what one could call a government, be it what one could call a state. I think most of the countries of Europe would like this to happen in due course, but on the whole, I think the British do not. It is very interesting that in the UK, most advocates of closer union – even advocates of the single currency – refuse to argue in favour of moving towards that sort of superstructure. They claim that all fears that this is going to happen are misplaced and that the currency is simply an economic question. There are no constitutional questions involved, they claim. The government says it has looked into the situation and sees no problems. But that is absurd. The constitutional questions are huge and ought to be discussed. Indeed, the debate in most other countries in the EU indicates there is a positive enthusiasm for major constitutional change. Denying that, as we do here, is dishonest. One of the things I find most depressing is that even today, most people in the UK will tell you that they do not understand what the arguments for and against the euro are. Labourites and other European enthusiasts refuse to admit that there is an enormous constitutional question involved; the Conservatives and other euro-sceptics, on the other hand, have been reluctant to talk about the subject at all, because they are divided over it. And I must admit that when they have spoken about it, they have been somewhat exaggerated in the arguments that they have made.

*Is Tony Blair going to hold a referendum on the euro, and what do you think the outcome will be?*

He'll have it because he's promised it – there is no constitutional imperative since we have no written constitution. However, I'm not altogether sanguine about the fairness of the referendum because it's already clear that much more money will be spent towards promoting a 'yes' vote than a 'no' vote. And since the government is in control of the question, it could be extremely tendentious. Moreover, a referendum that doesn't go the way the government wants can simply be repeated. That happened recently in Ireland, and before that, it happened in Denmark.

*You often talk about a democratic deficit in the EU. What exactly do you mean?*

Let me go all the way back to the very respectable case that is made for being in the EU, which is that you link the countries of Europe together so that there will be peace. By the way, I think that is a wonderful concept and ideal – I wish we heard it argued more in this country. But it is not argued in this country because we are always being told that a single currency is just an economic question. So you cannot argue about peace and war, and constitutional change, and linking people together, because it doesn't fit that particular way of arguing. I've always recognised that there is a very strong idealistic case to be made for the EU and the visions of the founding fathers. By linking France and Germany, the prospect of war is reduced, that's true enough. But there are other causes of strain which can eventually lead to war, and these include ethnic minority groups feeling they have no way of resolving their problems, and people feeling that in far too many cases, they have no democratic way of expressing their wishes. What gives me the most hope about Europe in general – not just the EU, but also the bits of Europe beyond it – is that we've already witnessed a major spread of democracy. And democracies as a rule don't go to war with one another, so that is our greatest guarantee of security. But here comes the supreme irony: while more and more European states are democratic, the EU itself is not democratic. This is simply not understood, or ignored. Take the Basques, the Catalans – the Scottish for that matter – all those who think that by joining the EU, they are escaping the clutches of Madrid or London. What about the clutches of Brussels? One thing is sure – wherever the EU ends up being run from, the power centre will be a great deal farther away (figuratively as well as literally) than London is from Scotland or Madrid is from the Basque Country. And I'm worried how Basques or Catalans or Scots will be able to make their democratic wishes heard in a European arrangement or a European state where the government is very, very distant.

The fact is that we are going on and on without anybody being able to answer the question of the democratic deficit. The British government has just produced an idea that there should be an elected President of Europe, elected by the Council of Ministers – the Council of Prime Ministers, I believe. This looks to me like a rather *ad hominem* suggestion; it looks as if it were designed for Mr Blair. According to the British proposal for a European constitution, this person, elected by his fellow prime ministers, would then be in position for four years. What would happen if during his presidential term, there were a change in the government of his own country? You see, even the British government is a very long way from suggesting anything that looks truly democratic. The democratic deficit problem is not one that can be just wished away. If you want people to elect something or someone they will have in common – whether it's a government or a president or whatever – those people, the electorate, have to share certain political values. This works in the US, because from one coast to the other, people over time have developed shared political values. Indeed, they probably started out with shared political values if you think of the Pilgrims, the founding fathers and so on. Liberty and choice, religious freedom and a separation of religion and state – all those things are their shared values that were established from the beginning. But across the continent of Europe, we do not share what I call specific political values. I guess we are all in favour of human rights and democracy in the broadest sense. But specific political values are another matter. I have in mind the role of religion in the state, or the relationship between the individual and the state. The British, by and large, always favour the individual over the state. We have a tradition of raucous free speech – just look at our press. Are these specific political values shared across Europe? I don't think so. It's not just a matter of a common language – you can have a democracy in a multi-language environment as India shows. But then again, language does make a difference, especially during election campaigning. When Europeans vote simultaneously for the European Parliament, the fact is that fifteen different elections are taking place at the same time. No British voter has any idea about any European issue in his or her mind: they are just voting Labour, Conservative or Liberal Democrat. And I suspect that much the same is true in every other country: by and large, voters are voting for or against the government of their country. So we are a very long way from developing a sense of political identity, and unless you have that, you cannot really have a proper democracy. I can't see how a President of Europe, however elected, could be democratically accountable.

Let me illustrate what I mean with an example – a rather unhappy one, but a very good one. Years ago, when I was a member of Mrs Thatcher's Conservative government, we introduced the Poll Tax, the so-called Community Charge.

It was so unpopular that within the same Parliament (that's a period of four or five years), the same government got rid of the legislation it had introduced because it felt the pressure of public opinion. It had no choice. As I say, as miserable as it was for the people involved, in a way it was a brilliant tribute to British democracy: a government had to repeal its own legislation because it felt the pressure of public opinion. How would you replicate that across Europe? Until you have some sort of commonality between the individual countries, how would a centralised European institution, a government or whatever, be accountable, responsive, to the will of the people?

*That European institution you've just mentioned is supposed to supplement national institutions, not replace them except in matters of common interest. As in the case of monetary policy. National sovereignty in most areas is supposed to remain sacred.*

'Pool sovereignty', as some people say. Let's take three concrete examples of where we already are now. *Trade policy*: because it participates fully in the EU, the UK has no right to strike a deal with the US, for example. And much of what happens in trade policy we find immensely disagreeable because thanks to the Common Agricultural Policy, we have to maintain external tariffs which we find pretty objectionable, which don't sit at all well with our sort of general national view under Conservative or Labour that we want to move towards global free trade as fast as possible. *Foreign policy*: it's abundantly clear that the two big players in European foreign policy are Britain and France. Now (and I don't want to exaggerate this because I have probably exaggerated it in the past), these are two countries which are used to having a global outlook and global positions. In our attitude to the US and our attitude to the Arab world, just to take those two examples, we are pretty different. And for either one of us to adjust to the other is difficult. It worries me a lot that many of the people who favour creating a strong Europe see it as an effective foreign policy bloc, a counterweight to the US. In fact, if you take the fifteen present member states, let alone the ones who are going to join in the future, what you may find is that the diversity of views is so great that the only positions we'll ever be able to agree on are inert positions. As a result, Europe may simply become a non-player. At least at the moment, whatever you may say about the two positions, Britain and France are still players. One of the reasons I don't want to exaggerate the differences is that when I was Defence Secretary, I was dealing with France over Bosnia. In theory the French were impossible, but in practice they were great.

*Can you give me an example?*

It was very difficult to deal with them in meetings. Maybe they wanted to issue a communiqué as pure grandstanding. I felt it was rhetoric divorced from reality and we used to have huge arguments about what to say. But when it came to putting troops on the ground, the French were marvellous. They were very effective, very well trained, very well organised. I think we're seeing the same kind of grandstanding now, and it does amuse me. The French have got everything in terms of prestige that they possibly could out of the negotiations on the Security Council resolution on Iraq. And I'm sure they are telling a very good story to the French people. The fact is, however, that they haven't prevented the US from getting exactly what it wanted from the resolution: an unconditional ultimatum with absolutely no need to go back to the United Nations for permission to do the next thing. Now to my third example of where we are now. Obviously, that's money, *economic control*. It isn't working. The common interest rate isn't working. The Irish at the moment have inflation and their interest rates are too low. The Germans have high unemployment and their interest rates are too high. The loss of sovereignty here is very, very material. The rules were never appropriate in the first place and now, to make this even more worrisome, the Growth and Stability Pact is coming under heavy criticism, even from people like Signor Prodi. I think it's extremely dangerous to create the impression that you just want to throw out the rules, because to create confidence in the common currency, you have to make people believe that there is a really serious system of discipline which will keep the weaker economies of Europe in check. Right now, we're in a crisis phase.

*What do you think the effect of enlargement will be? Britain has not opposed it.*

You're right, we have been so fixated by the euro in Britain that we have scarcely discussed enlargement. Personally, I think enlargement is potentially very, very important, and like most British people, I'm in favour of it because we are very keen on underpinning new democracies. That's why we've also been very supportive of those democracies joining NATO, too. Now, I have to admit that lying at the back of the British mind, we may have the idea that the larger the EU becomes, the harder it will be to deepen it. The more economically diverse the accession countries are, the more likely it is that the British model will commend itself and Europe will end up as a union of sovereign states in which each nation can elect to participate or not participate. I mentioned this earlier. Britain is not in the single currency, for a long time we weren't in the social chapter of the Maastricht Treaty, and we are not in the Schengen, so partly by design and partly by accident, the British have put this model into practice. This is an untidy sort of Europe and I'm very much in favour of an untidy Europe. I'm hoping – I think most of us in Britain are hoping – that apart from being good for the new democracies, enlargement will create an untidier Europe.

Michael Portillo

*Does Turkey come into your untidy Europe?*

Quite definitely it does. Our main fear now is not a repeat of the Second World War; we have other worries. Turkey is at the moment a country where the majority of the population is Muslim. It is a secular state. It is pluralistic, and it is pro-Western. It seems to me it must be strongly in our interest to maintain all of those conditions because Turkey is an important ally, occupies a very important square on the strategic chessboard and so on. But for a long time, some European leaders have been making it very clear that they would rather have anybody in the EU other than Turkey. This is partly because they have a huge population, partly because of their human rights problems...

*... and because they are not Christian...*

... and they are not Christian. Giscard d'Estaing has come out and said this pretty clearly in the last few weeks. For a long time, I've been arguing that opening the door to Turkey is a top priority. I'm not saying that Turkey should join the EU tomorrow, but we have to give them hope. The other night I was at a dinner at which Richard Holbrooke said that in his opinion, the greatest single mistake the Europeans were making was in not addressing the Turkish issue, solving the Cyprus question and opening the door to Turkey. I very much agree with him. Ironically enough, until recently we actually did have an untidy Europe. We had lots of different organisations and everybody belonged to one or some of them. There was the OSCE, there was the Council of Europe, there was NATO, there was the EU, there was the Western European Union. And membership of these organisations was very, very complicated. Turkey is in NATO and was, I think, in the WEU, probably in the OSCE, but not in the EU. In a way, that didn't matter too much, because Turkey was clearly part of things. Even Russia could be a member of a number of these organisations. What has changed recently – what has fundamentally changed – is that the EU has become the only organisation that matters, and none of the others really count. Now countries are either in or out. Being out, diplomatically and politically speaking, is very, very difficult. And let me make one last thing clear. Turkey does have a huge human rights problem, no doubt about that. But until recently so did Poland, the Czech Republic, and others. A lot of things change over time, but they are most likely to change if you encourage people, not if you tell them that whatever they do, they are not going to be welcome inside.

*Thank you.*

*The conversation was conducted by Susan Stern*

**Michael Portillo**
Born in London, 1953. Member of the British House of Commons. Shadow Chancellor of the Exchequer from 2000 to 2001. British defence minister from 1995 to 1997.

Avi Primor

# The Israeli Connection

In November 2002, the President of the Convention for the Future of European Union, France's former President, Valéry Giscard d'Estaing, dropped a bombshell that may have embarrassed many a European (although, at the same time, probably to the secret pleasure of most of them), when he claimed that Turkey was not a European country and that the Turks were not a European people. Thus there was no reason to accept Turkey as a member state in the European Union. Giscard naturally hastened to add that he was not a racist and had no religious prejudices – he respected Turkey just as he does any of the great non-European countries with which the EU fostered close relationships, and yet felt no need to accept it into the EU family. In this declaration Giscard d'Estaing was probably thinking more about the future and the success of the EU than about a precise definition of what constitutes a European.

The EU today, with its outdated organizational infrastructure, is already too large to function efficiently. It is now faced with the necessity for further extensive and complex expansion, inevitable for historical, political and psychological reasons. Turkey – which, because of its demographic development, will soon be even more populous than Germany, currently the largest country in the EU – could bring the development of the EU to a standstill if it became a member. The debate about the Turkish candidacy, within the framework of culture, tradition and religious difficulties, the concerns about the ethics and values of the Turks and their ability to adapt to the European way of life, stem not necessarily out of hypocrisy. We cannot deny the existence of fundamental differences between Turkish culture and that of the majority of European countries and this is the main concern of the most honest and passionate supporters of the idea of European unity. But there are also major cultural differences between European countries themselves, including some that may be very difficult to bridge. The chasm between what was previously Soviet Eastern Europe and the democratic West is admittedly very deep but will, it is thought, be bridged with the passage of time. On the other hand, the differences between, say, Prague and Vienna cannot be compared to those between Amsterdam and Tirana. Indeed, the differences between Amsterdam and Philadelphia, Frankfurt and New York, Paris and Montreal, are smaller than those found between some parts of Europe itself. Let us try to imagine the impact of the United States or Canada declaring their interest in obtaining membership of the EU: wouldn't sensible EU experts say that this could torpedo the aim of a unified Europe? They might even describe it as the Second Flood! However, no one would cite cultural differences or different value systems as a reason for refusing membership to North America.

So what is it that really binds the states together within the geographical frame we call the 'continent of Europe'? First, and most importantly, the builders of European unity emphasize the geography of Europe. But this is actually somewhat arbitrary: why is Cyprus, situated southeast of Istanbul, a geographical part of Europe while Ankara is not? Is Dublin really much further from the East Canadian shore than from Larnaka? The fact is that the Europeans have to draw a borderline somewhere; but, if it were only a matter of artificial geography, why is no Brussels politician talking of countries like the Ukraine as possible candidates for EU membership, while Russia is totally out of the question? Can we deduce from this that the yardsticks that measure EU policies are based on pragmatism, on the wisdom that says that politics is the art of the achievable?

The ideas and vision of the founding fathers of the EU were influenced by the terrible experiences of the first half of the 20th century. A peaceful Europe, they thought, could only be founded on cooperation and by unifying their institutions; in reality, the common development of the founding states of the European Community was soon to be guided by economic factors. How can the EU today integrate its new member states, and how can it absorb expansion and still remain viable? To respond to this gigantic challenge, the EU has to reconsider its major objectives with which it was preoccupied before the changes of the early 1990s: in what manner can the EU assert itself today, and in what form? The question of an economic union is no longer controversial for the majority of Europeans; but what, one should ask, was the aim of the monetary union and what should it achieve if successful? Is an economic union by definition meant only to ensure the prosperity of the citizens of Europe and increase their wealth? Whatever the aim might be, a successful economy needs protecting; a common currency must be defended. Without a common defense and foreign policy, it will not be possible to support and promote a common economy. So all the signs point to a process of gradual federalization of the EU.

Switzerland can be cited as a suitable miniature model for the Europe of the future: a federation of different people, with different languages, cultures and traditions, populations of different sizes and different economic importance, but which do not threaten or fear one another, and for whom the EU-invented term 'subsidiarity' has long been something that goes without saying. A federation will bring the Europeans, whose eyes are still directed towards the US, increasingly closer together. Today, students want to go to America, business people look towards America, researchers see ideal working conditions in America. Europeans enter into discussions with their European neighbors only as a by-product of what comes back from America. This must change if Europe does not want itself to be a byproduct of and led by the US. An assertive Europe will achieve equality with the US, indispensable for its own development. A self-confident Europe will carry a totally different weight in world politics and its neighbors will feel the benefit.

In the Middle East and North Africa, events are having a deleterious effect on the peoples of Europe; political upheaval in poorer bordering states is flooding prosperous Europe with immigrants and refugees with whom it cannot always cope. This impedes the course of public life in the European countries as well as their relations with the neighboring countries. Therefore, a Europe that asserts itself will not only make itself more attractive to the neighbor states and to immigrants, but will be able to exert greater influence on the course of events in these states for its own benefit.

After the ratification of the Treaty of Rome in 1957, whereby the European Community was established, few governments and even fewer of their citizens – even those of the core countries of the EC – were aware of the importance and the meaning of the new shape of Europe. Among the small number who were cognizant of this fact was the Israeli government of the time. It was one of the three governments that was prepared to recognize the EC and to offer to establish diplomatic relations with it. The majority of the member states of the present EU had not gone so far as to recognize the Community, and some even attempted to undermine it. Israel's early willingness to conduct relations with the Community brought the Jewish state a number of advantages. Thus, in spite of political difficulties, Israel concluded a trade agreement with the EC as early as 1964, and signed a free trade zone agreement with it in 1975. Implementing the treaties was not always without its problems and took some time, but was ultimately successful. Have these treaties given the EC, and later the EU, any real say in Israeli politics in the development of the Middle East conflict? Obviously not. For years the European Council complained that it was unable to exert sufficient influence on the Middle East conflict until it finally gave up any concrete hopes of achieving anything and aligned itself with the US in this particular sphere. The question still remains: can the EU exert any influence in the Middle East? Should this be one of its objectives?

The weakness of the EU lies mainly in the fact that it still has not achieved a common foreign affairs and security policy. But, as in the case of economic and currency union, most member states will eventually come to an agreement on this issue as well. A world power that the EU will then become cannot afford to ignore such a centrally important conflict as that of the Middle East. Moreover, the nascent European world power, being the direct neighbor of the Middle East, is influenced by, and suffers the consequences of the conflict in that region. If one thinks, too, of illegal immigration from the Islamic world – a problem that does not directly affect the US – then the difference between Europe and America in this respect becomes clear. The countries of the Middle East, and in particular the small isolated nation of Israel, understand, or will soon begin to understand, that their relationship with the EU will increasingly gain in importance; the question is why neither the Europeans nor the Israelis draw the correct consequences from these facts. The man on the street in Israel has supreme faith in the unlimited and almost unconditional support for Israel by the US – he perceives it almost as a sine qua non. Like so many Europeans and Americans, he fails to remember that the US has by no means always supported Israel; there were many times when it went as far as boycotting Israel. The US has often put Israel under serious pressure and forced the Israeli government to move in directions, which, in the eyes of many Israelis, were dangerous and shortsighted. Today, the Israeli Prime Minister is received every few weeks as a guest of honor in the White House. In contrast, David

Ben-Gurion, the founder of the Jewish state, visited the US only twice during his fifteen years in office, and then only privately. As a private citizen, Ben-Gurion was received just once by American President Harry Truman, who was regarded as a friend of Israel, and that was only to be presented with a refusal of his request for economic and military aid. It was only in the mid-1969s under Lyndon Johnson that the Americans began, very hesitantly at first, their rapprochement with Israel. This new American policy is often attributed to pressure from the powerful Jewish community in the US. If this was so, then one can only wonder why this community remained silent between the proclamation of the independence of the State of Israel in 1948 and the mid-1960s. The fact is that although American Jews have very close emotional bonds with Israel, they wish, above all, to remain good American patriots. Only after Washington defined Israel as being of strategic interest to the US in the 1960s did the Jews, as 'good Americans', attempt to intensify this support for Israel still further.

But unlike the EU, the US is not a neighbor of Israel, and if circumstances so demand, American interests could again change in the future. The EU, which is today Israel's largest trading partner (twice as large as the US), remains a permanent major political factor, or at least a political factor of growing importance for Israel. Nevertheless, as already stated, both the Europeans and the Israelis continue to look towards the US. Nothing, however, remains static. In 1991, in the aftermath of the Gulf War and in view of the apparent forthcoming Middle East Peace Conference, the European Council of Ministers invited the Israeli Foreign Minister to talks in Brussels, with the aim of persuading the Israelis to accept the Europeans as patrons of the conference, on a par with the Soviet Union and the US. After some initial hesitation, the Arab countries agreed, as did the Soviet Union and the US; only Israel resisted. The President of the European Council of Ministers, Italian Foreign Minister, Gianni de

Michelis, put forward an interesting argument in an attempt to convince the Israelis. He identified Israel's greatest demand and need as being, quite justifiably, security. Europeans were now prepared to genuinely guarantee Israel's security in a way no one else could. According to de Michelis, the definition of security did not just include fighter planes, submarines and tanks, but more importantly, the insurance that Israel was not isolated. Even if Israel made peace with all its neighbors and established close cooperation with them, it would not become part of their family. Plans for mutual supra-regional development, which were then being considered in the hope of advancing the Middle East and developing the mutual interests of the Middle Eastern countries including Israel, would not lead to a deep-rooted bond between Israel and the Arab states.

The Middle Eastern countries, apart from Israel, share a common culture, a common religion, a common language and tradition. Israel is not and cannot be part of this. So to avoid long-term isolation and ensure permanent security, Israel has no choice but to become part of the European family. Neither the Russians nor the Americans could offer the Israelis anything similar in terms of community. De Michelis was not talking about accepting Israel as a member state of the EU, but rather of a close institutionalized connection, a kind of anchoring of Israel in the EU. Indeed, in December 1994, at its summit in Essen, the European Council under German presidency did in fact unanimously declare that it was willing to offer the state of Israel privileged status in its relations with the EU, provided this was reciprocal. The reason for this generous European offer was, as always, a mixture of interests and values. Even in the state of war in which Israel has lived ever since its declaration of independence, democracy and human rights had never been threatened – at least in its core territories. The European-Israeli project was, however, never translated into action. Following long delays and theoretical discussions about the definition of this privileged status,

Netanyahu's accession to power in 1996 ushered in an atmosphere of change, and since then the offer of privileged status has been put on hold. If serious negotiations about this status after 1994 had taken place, the EU today would mean something very different to Israel – it would have become a major source of interest and hope. Differences of opinion between Jerusalem and Washington occur quite frequently, but although they are sometimes serious, they never lead to a major breach between the two nations. In contrast, the most superficial differences of opinion between Israel and the EU can lead to ill feeling. The reason for this is obvious: the Israelis consider their relations with the US to be of importance for their survival, whereas they do not yet properly understand how important Europe could be for Israel. Putting the privileged status into effective practice could have revolutionized this.

So is the EU a community of values? It is, without doubt, based on the common values of democracy and human rights. The EU cannot afford to take a country which does not respect these rights into its midst. Conversely, this does not mean that every country with a system based on these criteria can become a member of the EU. The EU is still led by national politicians. The power of the members of the Council of Europe is derived from the internal politics of the relevant member states, that is to say, national politics. The German Chancellor, the French President and the British Prime Minister are members of the Council of Europe, the main and decisive council of the EU, only because they have won elections in their own countries.

There is a French proverb that states that governments and states are cold monsters; that they have no feelings, merely interests. If this is still true of the democracies of the 21st century, then it is true only to a limited degree. Thanks to the increasing involvement of the individual citizen in politics, even in international politics, there has never in history been a war between two true democracies. Therefore, the leadership of the EU must respect principles and values. This does not, however, mean that interests should not ultimately gain the upper hand in their decisions. So we have a combination of values and interests, which probably explains Giscard d'Estaing's reservations about Turkey becoming a member of the EU. But it is precisely this combination of values and interests that should lead to the anchoring of Israel in Europe.

**Avi Primor**
Born in Israel, 1935. Vice President of the University of Tel Aviv since 1999. Israeli ambassador to Germany between 1993 and 1999. Vice President of the Hebrew University in Jerusalem from 1991 to 1993 and founder of the Helmut Kohl Institute. Publications include: *With the Exception of Germany* (in German).

Jiří Pehe

# Central Europe Returns to the Fold

A Czech's view of accession to the European Union

Following the disintegration of the Hapsburg Empire, Central Europe was for most of the 20th century one of the main sources of instability in Europe. The small states that emerged from the Hapsburg monarchy were not only too weak to serve as a buffer zone between the Soviet Union and Germany; they also suffered various ills related to their lack of democratic traditions. Nationalism ran rampant in most of these new states, reinforcing, in turn, the wave of militant nationalism that swept across Germany. For the Nazi regime, the small, powerless states of Central Europe were seen as a power void waiting to be filled.

The Czechs – who after the First World War found themselves in a common state with the Slovaks and more than three million ethnic Germans – were among those who suffered due to the weaknesses of the Central European successor states. Although Czechoslovakia turned out to be the most democratic of the newly created countries, its fate was sealed when an expansionist totalitarian regime was established in Germany. Truncated after the Munich Agreement in 1938 and occupied in 1939, Czechoslovakia proved to be a difficult construct to maintain in the fragmented space between Germany and the Soviet Union. With Germany defeated in 1945, Czechoslovakia ultimately ended up under Soviet dominance.

The reason for this brief outline is to show why the European Union means much more to the Czechs and some other Central European countries than just an area of economic cooperation and solidarity. To Central Europeans, the EU is, indeed, an essential provider of stability and security that makes it possible for the small countries of Central Europe to build a sovereign and peaceful future without fear of turmoil. Conversely, including Central Europe in the EU and NATO is the best guarantee for Western democracies that the historically volatile region will not produce new instability. Even if the planned EU enlargement in the end proves to be economically more difficult than expected, it is still the best investment for current EU members in their own security.

## Uniting a common space

The inclusion of Central European countries in the EU also has other, less tangible benefits. Before its disintegration into small nation-states, Central Europe was a unified area in which many different groups and cultures coexisted. Although this coexistence was not always entirely peaceful, overall the region produced its own specific brand of culture and gave the world leading intellectuals of the time. Central European culture can perhaps best be defined as both a creative confrontation and a specific blend of German, Slavic, Hungarian and Jewish influences in the part of Europe that served for centuries as a vulnerable buffer zone between two large European powers with universalistic aspirations. As a result, Central Europe's cultural identity was formed more by defensive attitudes than global ambitions. In a letter he wrote in the 1980s to his Czech counterpart, Ivan Klima, Philip Roth defined the basic difference between the West and communist Czechoslovakia: in the West 'everything goes and nothing matters', whereas in the communist Central Europe 'nothing goes and everything matters'.

In fact, while the Hapsburg monarchy in its final stages was a crumbling, weak giant, it was still an intellectual and cultural superpower. Sigmund Freud, Ludwig Wittgenstein, Edmund Husserl, Gustav Mahler, Egon Schiele, Gustav Klimt, Franz Kafka, Robert Musil, Franz Werfel, Hermann Broch, Jaroslav Hasek, Oskar Kokoschka, Josef Roth and Leos Janacek are just a few examples of an amazing array of talents which the region managed to produce in a relatively short period of time.

Milan Kundera and many other Central European intellectuals of the late 20th century later bemoaned the loss of this unified cultural space that continued to exist to some extent after the demise of the Hapsburg Empire until the Nazis occupied Central Europe. At the same time, many of these intellectuals rightly pointed out that Central European culture was more than just the sum of the artistic and intellectual creativity of various nations that shared a geographic region. The centuries-long interaction and blending of various cultures in the region gave rise to a common identity.

Not all the characteristics of what is considered to be the Central European identity are positive, however. The region, under the Hapsburgs, was a buffer zone not only between two great European powers but also between East and West. Its political culture was a mixture of Western traditions and Byzantine influences; its political institutions were relatively weak. The Anglo-Saxon type of open democracy based on a civil society was an alien concept in Central Europe; a centralised, bureaucratic *Rechtsstaat*, with its many absurdities described so ably by Franz Kafka, prevailed.

This is why many successor states to the Hapsburg Empire found it difficult to build functioning democracies. Czechoslovakia was a notable exception, partly because it was, to a greater degree than other parts of Central Europe, industrialised and urbanised when it emerged from the Austro-Hungarian state. Due to its particular history, Czech society was more plebeian as well as more middle class and, as such, perhaps more open to democratic procedures.

However, all Central European nations, regardless of their successes or failures in building democracies, inherited from the Hapsburg Empire a degree of provincialism, weak political institutions and bureaucratised systems of civil services. They were also saddled with weak political elites.

Central Europe is thus an interesting paradox. Its unique place in European history and geography – as well as its special blend of national cultures and religions, including a strong Jewish community – gave rise to a powerful culture and a plethora of impressive intellectual achievements. However, the region that produced hundreds, if not thousands, of widely acclaimed writers, musicians, philosophers and other academicians, gave the world, in comparison with the West, very few prominent politicians. Moreover, some Central European politicians, such as Adolf Hitler, rank among the 20th century's greatest political monsters.

All Central European countries inherited strong cultural identities, combining their own national cultures and common Central European features, but they also inherited weak democratic cultures and political institutions. As a result, even during relatively democratic periods of the last century, intellectuals and cultural figures often substituted for weak politicians in public discourse – a characteristic that persists even today.

## Central Europe as Europe

As unique as it has been, Central Europe has always been at the core of European culture and identity. Certainly, when seen from the outside – for example from the United States – European identity owes a great deal to Central Europe. Its cultural achievements are as important as, for example, Anglo-Saxon political traditions, French rationalism, Italian art, or German intellectual and industrial successes.

The core values created by the European civilisation – such as liberty, equality, solidarity and human rights, as well as the concept of rational discourse – were slow to reach Central Europe, but were eventually absorbed. The region has directly, or indirectly, participated in all major European intellectual revolutions of the last thousand years: from renaissance to enlightenment to the scientific revolution. Moreover, Central Europe coloured those ideas its own way and returned them enriched to the mainstream European thought.

The division of Europe under communism was thus a most unnatural phenomenon. Although communism itself was just one of the blind alleys of Western rationalism, the model that was practised in the Soviet Union and its satellites was a blend of the Western idea of equality and industrial modernisation taken to the extreme on the one hand, and of the Byzantine political traditions of Russia on the other.

Surprisingly, forty-something years of communism left relatively little mark on Central European identity. More than thirteen years after the collapse of communist regimes in Eastern Europe, we can observe a forceful re-emergence of old 'Central European' patterns of cultural and political behaviour.

Until now, the re-emergence of Central European identity has been limited by the fact that what also emerged from the fall of communism were the relatively small states that came into existence in 1918 – some of them, such as Czechoslovakia, did not survive in their original shape and disintegrated into even smaller units. At the same time, however, those states were fortunate to emerge into what is, from a geopolitical point of view, a totally different environment than the one that existed before the Second World War. While the years 1918–1939 were not conducive either to the existence of small states in the centre of Europe or to the survival of democracy, today the new Central European democracies are surrounded by democratic states that have encouraged the growth of a market economy and democracy in the new states, without jeopardising their independence.

This democratic encouragement and a relative international stability are totally new historical phenomena for the populations of small Central European nations. It is clear that their own internal stability – which might be threatened by the re-emergence of some of the more negative political traditions of Central Europe – depends to a large extent on their integration into common European structures.

## A new Central Europe?

The planned enlargement of the EU will recreate Central Europe as a common space without borders or administrative barriers. Most territories and cultures that constituted the Hapsburg Empire will again be under one roof – a development that is likely to strengthen the Central European cultural identity. The renewal of a common political space may indeed function as a catalyst for a cultural and intellectual interaction that contributed so much to Europe over a hundred years ago.

It is apparent that a new Central Europe will emerge, based more on modern political institutions than the Central Europe of the past. The benign influence of the EU has already contributed greatly to the modernisation of institutions and political culture, as well as to implementing a modern rule of law. From that point of view, Central Europe will never be the same. After all, some of the identity of 'old' Central Europe stemmed from its archaic political institutions and the absurdities of a bureaucratic state, which, in turn, represented a challenge for creative minds.

## Czechs in the EU

For most Czechs, integration into the EU cannot be separated from the integration of other Central European states. In fact, very early after the fall of communism, Czechoslovakia, Poland and Hungary established the Visegrad grouping, the main purpose of which was to coordinate their steps on the way 'back to Europe'.

Going 'back to Europe' has always been understood as an institutional and legal integration with the West, and not necessarily as a confirmation of the fact that the Czechs and other Central European nations belong to Europe culturally. As the westernmost nation in the post-communist world, Czechs have never had doubts about their European identity. Most Czechs have also taken it for granted that once the country is rid of communism, it will quickly reintegrate with the West. Indeed, some Czech politicians turned the fact that the post-communist Czechs were economically more advanced and geopolitically more Western than their neighbours into an ideology of Czech superiority, which almost destroyed regional cooperation in the early 1990s. However, cooperation was eventually restored as Poland, Hungary, Slovakia, and the Czech Republic realised that they share a common fate on the road back to Europe.

Central Europe also became a desired denomination for some countries that historically were never part of the region. While the Visegrad grouping remained limited to the four above-mentioned countries, the Central European Initiative, for example, has grown to include seventeen countries including Romania, Bulgaria, the Baltics and Ukraine. When speaking of Central Europe, careful distinction should be made between Central Europe as a cultural phenomenon relying on a common past and Central Europe as a new political entity after the demise of communism.

However the region is defined, it is already apparent that Central Europe will eventually become the most influential regional subgroup in the EU. Regardless of whether it includes only the countries that once, at least partly, belonged to the Hapsburg Empire, or other states that today aspire to become Central European (because they do not want to be seen as East European), the political voice of Central Europe in the EU will be very strong.

The Czechs, just like the other Central European countries (with the possible exception of Poland, which may have its own ambitions) realise that they can only achieve their goals in the EU by cooperation with all the small states in the region. They, just like Hungary, Slovakia and Slovenia, can rely to some extent on the expertise and experience of Austria, which also managed to escape the Soviet orbit and has been an EU member for several years.

## The past and the future

In order to again share a common destiny, however, the Central European nations need not only to look into the future but also to deal seriously with their pasts. Each Central European nation has numerous skeletons in its cupboard, some of which directly affect its relations with its neighbours. For the Czechs, for example, it will be necessary to address openly, and without prejudice, the issue of the Sudeten Germans – former citizens of Czechoslovakia whose property was confiscated after the Second World War. Eventually, some three million (virtually all) of them were driven out of Czechoslovakia. Most Czechs, including their political elite, are reluctant to admit that the expulsion constituted one of modern Europe's biggest acts of ethnic cleansing, based on the principle of collective guilt. They find it difficult to come to terms with the notion that the expulsion of the Sudeten Germans was a Stalinist act that greatly contributed to the victory of communism in the country.

The fact that the expulsion was sanctioned by the victorious powers at a conference in Potsdam has been used by Czech politicians as an alibi. But this 'alibi' needs to be acknowledged for what it is: Czechoslovakia was not ordered to expel its Germans; it was an act of free will.

The Austrians, Slovaks, and Hungarians, too, need to come to terms with their own historical failures in the period between the disintegration of their common empire and the end of the 20th century. If they fail to do so, their renewed coexistence under a common roof may initially be rather acrimonious. Some current, cross-border disputes between, for example, the Czech Republic and Austria, are charged with high emotions partly because they see each other as mirrored somewhat unpleasantly.

On the other hand, if the new common framework of the EU forces Central Europeans to face, among other things, their past, and discuss it openly, Central Europe may become a region of very fruitful cooperation; a region whose strong identity may once again be a major contributor to European culture.

The Czechs can only benefit from such a development. The independent Czech Republic that was created, somewhat reluctantly, after the split of Czechoslovakia in January 1993, is culturally no match for what Czechoslovakia used to be. While politically stable, the country whose territory was once a model of multiculturalism and home to numerous ethnic groups is now 99 percent ethnic Czech.

It can be argued that this has not been an advantageous development for a nation whose greatest cultural and intellectual feats were achieved mainly when the Czech people were part of a productive environment in which they had to confront other ethnic groups. It therefore seems that for the Czechs, a return to Europe through the reincarnation of Central Europe is much more than just a political step. It is a step towards rediscovering their national identity, parts of which were amputated with the departure, or disappearance, of Germans, Jews, and finally Slovaks from Czech lands.

**Jiří Pehe**
Born in Rokycany, Czechoslovakia, 1955. Director of the New York University, Prague. Director of the Political Department of Czech President Václav Havel from 1997 to 1999. Continues to act as political advisor to Havel.

Vaira Vike-Freiberga

# A Dream in the Making

For centuries, the dream of a secure, stable and prosperous European continent has been an elusive one. Now, at the beginning of the 21st century, the current and future member states of the European Union and the NATO Alliance are being presented with the historic opportunity to create a stronger and more united European continent.

When the foreign ministers of Nazi Germany and Soviet Russia secretly signed the Molotov-Ribbentrop pact in August 1939, they divided Central and Eastern Europe into German and Russian 'spheres of influence'. Latvia, Estonia and Lithuania were erased from the map of Europe for more than half a century. Hundreds of thousands of individuals from the three Baltic countries were either killed or sent to slave labour camps by the Nazis and the Soviets, while hundreds of thousands of others fled into exile.

For five long decades, the economic, social and cultural development of the three Baltic countries – which before the war had attained Western European levels – was severely curtailed. This immoral division of Europe into two opposing camps illustrates that we must be able to learn from the errors of our past in order to make wiser decisions for the future.

In November 2002 in Prague, the NATO member states made a historic decision by inviting Latvia and six other countries to join the Alliance. This represents a significant step in redressing the injustices of the 20th century and in eliminating the last vestiges of the Second World War.

Equally important was the summit of the EU Council in Copenhagen, which took place in December 2002. There, Latvia and nine other Central and Eastern European countries received official invitations to become member states of the EU. I am convinced that this next round of the EU's eastward expansion will help to reduce the economic disparities that currently exist in our continent, and that it will serve to bring Europe's diverse nations closer together.

## Stability and prosperity

I believe that the two parallel and complementary integration processes of EU and NATO expansion are vital for Europe's continued stability and prosperity. And I am certain that we all – both the current and future member states of the EU and NATO – will benefit greatly from an expanded transatlantic partnership.

Together, Europe's democratic nations, both young and old, face the challenge of creating a Europe that can deal effectively with such pressing global concerns as unemployment and poverty, illegal immigration and cross-border crime, drug addiction and disease, environmental pollution, and international terrorism. These urgent issues present such serious challenges in our globalised world that they can only hope to be addressed by uniting the efforts of all European nations.

In order for the EU to capitalise on the opportunities provided by the accession of its newest, rapidly developing countries, its institutions will have to be reformed so as to render them more effective, open and transparent, less bureaucratic, and closer to the people they have been designed to serve. The fact that only 38 percent of eligible voters participated in the most recent elections of the European Parliament indicates that many Europeans feel alienated from the institutions of the EU. The governments of both the member and candidate countries must therefore devote more effort to explain the EU's policies to their electorates.

German Foreign Minister Joschka Fischer rekindled the debate on Europe's future during an address at Humboldt University a few years ago. Now, the Convention on the Future of Europe, which began its deliberations in 2002, is providing a useful forum for the expression of a wide variety of opinions, and we are pleased that parliamentary deputies and government officials from Latvia and the other EU candidate countries are actively participating in the Convention's discussions.

The Convention is preparing the ground for the next Intergovernmental Conference (IGC), which will take place after the Convention ends its work. The member states will decide on how the EU will function after enlargement – a decision that will directly affect both existing and future member states. I am confident that the decisions of the next IGC will reflect the views of all parties concerned.

One of the EU's principal strengths lies in the vast diversity of its nations, cultures and traditions. I believe that the EU must remain a powerful union of national states, where this diversity is preserved. Jacques Santer, former president of the European Commission, has said that he does not see a viable alternative outside the EU for a country as small as his native Luxembourg, which has never had as much influence in international politics as it does now. Latvia, as another small European country, also believes that it will be better able to realise its interests as a member of the EU.

## Expanded borders

Following the enlargement of the EU, the eastern borders of Latvia and her neighbours will become the outer borders of the EU. This will place tremendous responsibility on the three Baltic countries and Poland to prevent the influx of illegal drugs, clandestine immigrants, terrorists and criminals into the territory of the EU. The reinforcement of Latvia's eastern border has already been a priority for several years, and the financial support of the EU under the Phare programme has been invaluable in this regard. Joint financial responsibility for the control of the EU's outer borders by all of the member states will allow for the most effective protection of Europe's security.

The enlargement of the EU and NATO should bring positive changes to the relations between the three Baltic countries and their eastern neighbours. The advantageous location of the Baltic States at the crossroads between East and West, along with their knowledge and understanding of Russia, Belarus, the Ukraine and Moldova, could serve to facilitate Europe's political and economic relations with these transition countries. Latvia's long-term experience in border control cooperation with Russia and Belarus, for example, could prove useful in furthering the EU's cooperation with the CIS on justice and home affairs.

The potential contribution of the Baltic States in both supplying energy resources for Europe and at the same time ensuring a clean environment in the Baltic Sea are just two other examples of how the Baltic countries can invest in Europe's future.

## Remarkable transformation

Although Latvia has not yet attained the prosperity and economic development of its Western neighbours, the transformations that the country has undergone since regaining its independence in 1991 have been remarkable. Latvia has successfully replaced a totalitarian system of governance with democratically elected political institutions. It has become a country where human rights and basic freedoms are upheld and respected to the same degree as in other liberal democracies.

After the collapse of the Soviet Union, Latvia had to assume the monumental task of overhauling a bankrupt, state-run economy and finding new markets for its exports, all of which for decades had been sent eastward to Russia and other Soviet republics. Today, Latvia's transformation to a liberal market economy can be considered a success story of rebirth and renewal. During the past few years, it has enjoyed one of the fastest economic growth rates in Central and Eastern Europe (7.7 percent in 2001), as well as one of the lowest annual rates of inflation (below 3 percent) and a stable national currency. These have consolidated the country's macro-economic stability.

Latvia has been successful in finding new markets for its products. More than 60 percent of Latvia's exports are sent to the EU: Germany was its biggest trade partner in 2001, accounting for 16 percent of its total foreign trade. Germany is also one of Latvia's most important foreign investors. Today such respectable German banks as Norddeutsche Landesbank, Dresdner Bank AG and Vereinsbank Riga are successfully operating in Latvia's financial market.

## Uniform development

While the Baltic States and Poland have achieved remarkable progress during the decade that has passed since the fall of communism, they have yet to reach the same level of development as their Western neighbours. Today, more than eleven years after the collapse of the Soviet Union, Europe is still far from homogenous in the standards of living, level of prosperity and life expectancy that its inhabitants enjoy. This remains as a daunting challenge to our common future: how to erase the economic disparities between the EU's current and future member countries, and how to do it in as few years as humanly possible.

As a model, we can look to the impressive track record of

the EU, which has raised the standard of living of one country after another as each in turn became a member state. We have the example of countries such as Ireland, Spain, Portugal and Greece, which have prospered dramatically since becoming members of the EU. The mechanisms that the EU is able to deploy for reducing regional disparities are effective. The various equalisation programmes of the EU are able to produce viable and tangible results. There is no reason why the next wave of member states should not be able to achieve exactly the same positive results. Nevertheless, we have to recognise that the equalisation within the EU itself, while impressive, is neither complete nor perfect. Within the EU, economic activity remains concentrated in a relatively small and central area known as the 'blue banana' – a triangle extending from North Yorkshire in the United Kingdom to Franche-Comté in France and Hamburg in Germany. Others have defined this region as a pentagon extending from London to Paris, Milan, Munich and Hamburg. Research and development in the EU, along with other strategic and high value-added activities tends to be concentrated in these central regions. If development in the EU's other regions is not sufficiently stimulated, then we may witness growing regional polarisation in the EU, along with the concentration of low value-added activities in its peripheral areas.

## The Baltic Sea region

This is where the Baltic Sea region could show the way for the future as it has the genuine potential for becoming a new and dynamic growth centre in Europe. The former German Minister of Foreign Affairs, Hans-Dietrich Genscher, had a clear vision of the Baltic Sea region as a prosperous and stable part of a united Europe more than a decade ago. He actively promoted the creation of new cooperation structures in the region and was instrumental in the formation of the Council of the Baltic Sea States, which has gained a respectable place on Europe's political landscape. Through the Council of the Baltic Sea States, Mr Genscher also wished to provide an opportunity for the new, post-Soviet Russia to increase its participation in processes occurring around the Baltic Sea – and Russia has indeed become an active participant in various regional activities.

Among just some of its assets, the Baltic Sea region has ten metropolitan areas with populations of one million or more. It is home to well-established companies and product brands. It is the leading IT-producing area of Europe and has the highest cellular telephone penetration in the world. Some 45 percent of Russia's total foreign trade passes through Baltic Sea harbours, which are endowed with well-developed infrastructures. The educational level in the whole region is high, particularly in the natural sciences and technology. And in the western part of the region, more is spent, on average, on research and development than in most other European countries.

Private businesses and governments must be encouraged to invest more into the eastern shores of the Baltic in order to capitalise on the technical know-how, scientific creativity and business innovation of its inhabitants. These investments should yield rich returns in expansion and profits.

I am pleased that Latvia will be hosting the next annual summit of the Baltic Development Forum in Riga in October 2003. Many innovative and practical ideas have been generated there in the past, and I hope that the Forum continues to foster a deepening sense of solidarity among the countries of the Baltic Sea region. The Baltic Sea – which only recently still divided the East from the West, the rich from the poor, and the free from the oppressed – is now serving to unify the diverse countries of the Baltic littoral. I hope that the Baltic Sea region becomes a model of successful partnership for other regions to emulate as we strive to create a Europe that is truly secure, stable and prosperous.

**Vaira Vike-Freiberga**
Born in Riga, Latvia, 1937. State President of the Republic of Latvia since 1999. Director of the newly established Latvian Institute in Riga in 1998. Professor of Psychology at the University of Montreal from 1965 to 1998.

Janusz Reiter

# Eurocivic Pride

An Interview

*How much national feeling does a people – the Polish people, for example – need?*

Because of its turbulent history, Poland has long had problems with its national self-confidence. But now there is a degree of stability, which is a necessary requirement for the healthy process of taking a step back and viewing oneself critically from a distance. To take one example, a critical debate about our own past has recently begun in Poland. Such a discussion was previously unthinkable, since the Poles had a very defensive attitude. The basic tenor of the argument was: if everything is taken away from us, we will at least not let them take away our sense of nationality, and we are proud of our history. Since then we have entered a climate which makes it possible to adopt a self-critical attitude when coming to terms with our own identity and with our own past. This process will not lead to the erosion of Polish identity, but on the contrary, to revitalising and strengthening it.

*Keyword Poland and Europe: prospects and anxieties…*

Poland is going through a transitional phase. The realisation that things cannot continue as they have so far is becoming more and more widespread. But the prospect of an open Europe, with no dividing – but also no protective – borders makes many people feel insecure. It is not a matter of whether it is pleasant or not pleasant to live in Europe but is Europe really the right place for Poland? Does this Europe really want Poland? Or will Poland become a second class member?

Fortunately there is a lack of alternatives in Europe today. Previously, the peoples of East Central Europe were torn between their longing for the West and their bonds with the East. Even if the pro-Western attitude predominated, there was always the pro-Eastern feeling to oppose it. The basis for this pro-Russian tendency was a feeling of insecurity, of anti-Western resentment. Every Pole knows how often the West has left Poland in the lurch. This means that distrust goes very deep. On the other hand, he feels attracted by the West. This ambivalence between fascination and distrust has marked Polish attitudes up to this day. Russia made use of pan-Slavism to whip up anti-Western resentment and to tie the Slavonic peoples to them. Now, it no longer has the power to do so. The present situation is really unique. The European Union is offering a lot, and the East is providing the arguments for linking ourselves with Western Europe.

*What do you understand by Europe and what ideas do you connect with the EU?*

For me the EU is a community for peace. And I believe that a European federation is the right form of organisation for Poland. I am not at all afraid of living in a state that is part of a European federation. I also have no reservations about living in a Europe which has a European government or a European executive. National parliaments and governments are not being abolished, but in some areas they will not have much say. Which is the way it is today anyway.

*Recently, there have been ever-more frequent arguments about the competence and functions of the nation-states. What decisions within the EU should be taken at a national and which at a European level?*

We'll have to create a new balance in this area. But 'checks and balances' of that kind cannot be produced by decree; they are much more the result of lively discussion between different interests and diverse traditions. For me, for example, the question of how European defence and foreign policy should be organised, whether it should be within the purview of individual governments, or whether it should be organised at a Community level is completely open. But we must prevent this security and foreign policy becoming the instrument of a few larger countries, say France, Germany or Great Britain. One could not call that truly European politics.

*For example, education. In Germany this is a matter for the individual states (Länder). What if Brussels decides to standardise education throughout Europe?*

I'm not very impressed when I hear that the national states should take care of education and culture, because the states that are now entering the EU are financially weak and will not be able to keep up with the richer EU countries in matters of education. We would need financial solidarity within the EU to prevent an education gap growing between the old and new members.

*After the attacks on September 11th, the question of internal security in the EU has become much more pressing. How could a European security policy be organised?*

The new threat of terrorism has opened our eyes to the fact that freedom always has to be won anew and defended. The EU offers the best framework that Europe has ever had for this purpose. What we need is a change of mentality – but that is a long process beset with risks. What I cannot imagine is a European security policy in which Europe is responsible for itself, while the United States is responsible for the rest of the world. That would mean the provincialisation of Europe. The Europeans must share the responsibility for global security with the Americans.

That also means, however, that we will one day have to spend money on military operations in such far places as Asia. Many people in Germany, or in Poland and Portugal, will ask themselves what Asia has to do with them, and why they should waste their money. The Americans have it easier in this respect. When the US President says 'That's where we have to fight for our values, that's where our interests are threatened', that is sufficient for the political class. And public opinion follows the political leadership. In Europe that will be far more difficult.

The US has a far more uninhibited relationship with power politics because they have never misused their power as thoroughly as the Europeans. The Europeans are conscious of this, so Europe cannot simply play the great power and send a few divisions to Asia or Africa. That will still take a lot of time and some difficult discussions, but I hope that we will go this way in any case. I also feel that a little more pride in Europe would be good for us. The solution to our problems lies not in scrapping Europe, but in opening it up.

*Insecurity and a nation's complicated sense of its own value – how can this be reconciled with the possibility of integration in the EU?*

If a country enters the EU it will at first suffer setbacks. We cannot allow ourselves any illusions about this: all countries are susceptible to self-doubt and crises of identity. It is hardest for countries whose sense of nationality is not sufficiently formed or established. With regard to ability and readiness to integrate we should not be thinking in terms of the less sense of national identity, the better, but quite the contrary: the more intact the sense of national identity, the better. And the more insecure a nation feels, the worse it is for it.

Only people who are sure of themselves, whose sense of their own value is secure, can be prepared to share their sovereignty with other peoples. A state which doesn't have this will, of necessity, be afraid of integration; of giving up its identity; afraid of excessive foreign influence; of the dominance of those who are more powerful, stronger, bigger. That is an old problem which dogged the Central European states, especially the smaller ones. But today we are experiencing a revolution. The peoples of Europe are gradually freeing themselves of their trauma and are ready to share their sovereignty with others – not to give it up, that is not the point of the matter. This process is not a revolution from above, but a mental revolution. It hasn't affected everyone, and it will not do so. But it is carried forward by the majority.

*What opportunities are there in this eastward expansion, firstly for the EU as it is now, and secondly for the accession countries?*

The new countries, especially Poland, have a profound understanding of Eastern Europe, the Ukraine, Belarus, and also of Russia – very important regions for the EU. That is where the future of the EU will be decided, and that is why the EU will be able to make good use of the abilities of the new members.

In addition, when they meet their new neighbours in the EU, I hope that Western Europeans will be reminded a little of the beginnings of the Community. At that time it wasn't a matter of distributing milk quotas but of ensuring peace, of solidarity and the future of Europe in the world. I know that this will be more difficult in an expanded EU, but it could spur people on to think about the actual nature of the institution. And also about what ballast should be thrown overboard.

And another thing: the prospective members are bringing markets into the EU, markets that are far from being satisfied and have an enormous potential for growth. These countries could develop a powerful dynamic. If they succeed in overcoming their inhibitions, their provincialism and their complexes, they could become enthusiastic Europeans, federalists, supporters of the common foreign and security policies. This will not be simple, because many Europeans today are still very provincial anyway. Individual peoples, the French and the British for example, are reputed to be open to the world – but as Frenchmen and Britons, not as Europeans. Expansion could lead either to further provincialisation of the EU or to more openness, and thereby to a greater sense of responsibility for what goes on in the world. I would like to live in an EU of that kind.

*Your vision of Europe?*

Europe is really the hope of my life. When I consider where I was twenty years ago, and where I could be in twenty years' time, I become euphoric. I do not wish for a European superstate. Nor do I believe that a federal Europe can be built on the ruins of the nation-states. If there is one idea that could unite Europeans today, one that is really worth working for, then it is the vision of a federal Europe, one that begins in Portugal and ends, let's say, at the eastern border of Poland. An area in which not only is peace secure, but also one governed by common democratic rules, where people can move around freely and choose their place of residence at will. What this Europe will look like in reality, I cannot tell. But what I want is something like a common sense of mission, similar to that in the US: the conviction that one's own model has a universal character. I would be glad if Europe could preach its values a little more aggressively, stand up for them and be willing to take risks to defend them.

In view of the speed of developments in Europe and all the

unknowns attached to them, there is no point in speculating what will exist in thirty or forty years from now. I would say quite pragmatically that the nation-state was supposed to give Europeans a sense of security and safety, because they felt Europe to be more of a risk than an opportunity. The more secure they feel as Europeans, the less they will need the nation-state. Perhaps we will wake up in twenty years and realise that not much is left of the nation-state. Not, however, because we have dismantled it, but because it has simply become superfluous. But look out if anyone tries to take it away from us. Then we feel threatened. The experiment has begun and I think we have a very good chance of success. But we should not rush our fences: too much boldness frightens people off.

*The conversation was conducted by Armin and Ethel Pongs*


**Janusz Reiter**
Born in Koscierzyna, Poland, 1952. President of the Centre for International Relations, Warsaw, since 1998. Ambassador to Germany for the Republic of Poland from 1990 to 1995.

Andrei Pleşu

# Between Musk and Must: Europe of the Eastern Europeans

The unification of Europe has progressed further on the institutional level than it has on the more discreet, but nonetheless decisive area of consciousness. There is still no such thing as a vital and spontaneous sense of belonging to Europe. To be Dutch, German or Italian – that is a fact. But to be a European is so far only a metaphor. In other words, as a French lawyer once said during a colloquium, it is unlikely that anyone would be prepared to die for the European Union. This is true and I'm glad that it is so. In the course of European history there has been more than enough dying – for lands and utopias, for principles and ideologies. People have died sublimely and hysterically for values that were often circumstantial, overrated or counterfeit. It is time to discover or establish values that can be defended reasonably and in a balanced way, without triumphant poses and without pathos. We have spent far too much time under the star of love as passion (that 'amour-passion' which Denis de Rougemont saw as the hallmark of European affectivity). We could now do with a period of 'amour de tête', cerebral love – which is, granted, less spectacular and bloodthirsty, but also clearer and more lasting. European patriotism could provide us with a new way of loving our values; it would ultimately be a peaceful, clear, sunny patriotism.

However, I do not believe that we have got that far yet. It may well be that no one would be prepared to sacrifice his or her life for the EU – after all, no one wants to die for an administration. But Europe is not the EU. I do not hesitate at all in affirming that people in the East definitely died for Europe during the decades of Communist dictatorship: they died for more freedom, for true democracy, for rights; they died as a result of totalitarian despotism and absurdity. But basically, they died to regain those rights which form the image of modern Europe. When blood flowed in the streets of Bucharest in December 1989, the demonstrators were not just overthrowing a dictator. What was at stake was the reinvention of a political, social, economic and cultural space from which the Romanians – like all other Eastern Europeans – had felt themselves excluded. What was at stake was nostalgia for Europe.

To build a united Europe, Western and Eastern Europeans must have a common image of Europe in mind. In reality, however, we are dealing with two differing ideas which will be very difficult to reconcile unless we grant each other the necessary attention. For the Europeans in the East, Europe is first and foremost an image, a symbol of the past. In Prague, in Budapest, in Belgrade or Bucharest, in Krakow and in Sofia, the word 'Europe' evokes pre-war associations. Europe is the normality that preceded Communist totalitarianism; Europe is life before the war, the sum of everything that was part of the 'good old days'. From this viewpoint, Europe has the ambience of a bygone epoch, a faded photograph, a memory.

For the Western Europeans, on the other hand, Europe is far more future-oriented. Europe represents something that still has to be shaped and achieved. They are heading for a new Europe, a Europe with new institutions, a new financial mechanism, new rules and a new meaning. In brief, while Europe represents for the Eastern Europeans a lost model that must be rediscovered and revived, for the Western Europeans it is a project that must be realised in the coming years. The Westerners' typical emotion is hope; for the Easterners it is nostalgia. For the Westerners, the risk is utopianism; for the Easterners, it is disillusionment and an excessive obsession with the past.

But the West cannot 'integrate' Eastern Europe without integrating the Eastern European idea of Europe as well. Reuniting with the East will inevitably mean the reintegration of the European past (whether conciliatory or not); of the recent past with all its disasters, and of the older one, which we define as tradition. The new Europe cannot be healthy and capable of a valid survival without internalising its own past: the Balkans, Byzantium, and the Mediterranean Basin. However, the process of European reintegration does not seem to set any great store by this internalisation. It needs to do two things: first, it should come to terms uncompromisingly with history, including both the Nazi and the Communist toxins, and then it should responsibly evaluate the past in a way that would consolidate the carefully stratified identity of the Continent and its culture. The integration of Central and Eastern Europe could provide excellent practice for these two processes, which are essential for the future well-being of Europe.

In its efforts to fit back into Europeanness, Eastern Europe will inevitably encounter numerous obstacles. The greatest fear in Eastern Europe is that European reunification could be transformed into an ideology. Yet another ideology! Eastern Europe is far more allergic to ideologies than Western Europe. The slightest sign of demagogy, of triumphalist rhetoric, of the glorification of harmony and standardisation evokes nightmare memories and gives rise to serious concern. Everything that has the ring of wooden language, that reminds us of arrogant centralism and resembles compulsory programme gymnastics fills us with distrust, suspicion and scepticism. Are we going to replace proletarian internationalism with the imperatives of globalisation? Moscow with Brussels? 'The brotherhood of peoples' with 'Europe, our common home'? The 'Socialist camp' with the Schengen Area?

Of course, the new slogans are more promising, trustworthy and humane than the old ones. But we do not want simply to replace a bad ideology with a better one, a slogan that was forced upon us with one that we take willingly upon us. We want a change of style, a liberation – even if only temporary – from any ideology and slogan. Before we re-enter the race, we need a little time to catch our breath and regain some strength.


Far too little attention is devoted to the inevitable asymmetry between Eastern and Western Europe which has been brought about by their different historical development. A few examples come to mind in connection with the restructuring of academic research in the former Communist countries. For more than ten years, they have made efforts to revitalise an effective academic elite in Eastern academic centres. When I say 'elite', I am in no way referring to an exclusive club of privileged people, but rather people who are excellently qualified for specific areas of activity. There is an elite among farmers, among intellectuals, among workers, a political elite and so on. Under the Communist dictatorship, the representatives of these elites, if they weren't simply liquidated, were programmatically marginalised. The 'normalisation' of Eastern Europe is being held up by, among other things, the weakness of the elites, by a certain degree of 'underqualification', which is difficult to even out overnight despite considerable inherent natural potential.

In contrast, the West seems to have long ago progressed beyond this stage of identifying and encouraging elites. Even the word 'elite' is a little dusty and derogatory; overuse of the term is accompanied by the risk of political incorrectness. We are told over and over again that we should avoid the image of the ivory tower, and that elitist bodies (of the type 'Institutes for Advanced Studies') favour unworldliness and should only be funded with great caution. We can obviously accept that the ivory tower, when understood as a dividing wall between nebulous scholarly activity and the public arena, should be condemned.

On the other hand, it would be questionable if the condemnation of elitism led to the sabotaging of elites. Nevertheless it is clear that for the time being, the Eastern clock is showing a different time from the Western one. Elites already seem superfluous in the West, while the East is still panting for them.

But the asymmetry does not end here. In the West, the doctrine of 'useful research' is currently very strong. Basic research, the free exchange of ideas, purely scientific curiosity without any immediate end in sight are classified as being profligately out of tune with current social needs, everyday priorities and the interests of the taxpayer. This attitude can only create a feeling of melancholy for the researcher in the East because this is precisely the type of dialogue with which Communist party activists gagged – even choked – them: the only justification for the intellectuals' existence is as servants of the masses. They must fulfil the demands of the moment. They must dedicate themselves to the people, contribute to the increase in production and lay the foundations for a brighter future. Any other form of scientific life is bourgeois daydreaming demonstrating contempt for the working class and its immediate needs. For years, Eastern European researchers hoped that they would live to see the time when they would at last be able to devote themselves to free-flowing thought. When they would have the right to devote themselves to subjects which were not forced upon them, and to explore areas dictated purely by their own scientific curiosity and the internal problems of their subject.

The differences in mentality (which are a result of the fatal differences in historical development) can even be found in minutiae: Western sponsors prefer to fund projects rather than infrastructure. The sponsor is quite justified in wanting to avoid the mammoth infrastructures of Communist research, which are as extensive and elaborate as they are scientifically inconsistent. Against this background, the desire to fund only clearly defined projects with exact objectives and time-scales demonstrates legitimate and understandable prudence. However, this prudence will be exaggerated if one loses sight of the major differences between the state of logistical support in Western and Eastern research.

In Eastern Europe, the academic infrastructure is extremely weak and fragile. This means that projects run the risk of hovering vaguely in an undefined space, without having the necessary equipment or any of the requisites for normal working conditions. Limited in this way, the efforts of Eastern European scientists are greatly hindered by the necessity for improvisation, the lack of an institutional identity and little likelihood of stability. After all, you cannot fund the production of a cake without first investing enough in the kitchen and its equipment.

The European Commission is working intensively on building up a 'European Research Area' which will accept specialists from West and East without discrimination. For the Eastern Europeans, this programme is highly respectable and very stimulating. But isn't it also a bit utopian? Are the Community's research priorities (genome research, nanotechnology, space travel) also priorities in the candidate nations? Is the proportion between the means that are available to the

Western world and those that are available to the Eastern world fair? To the best of my knowledge, it has been decided that about 95 percent of the required funding for European research will have to come from national budgets. But the financial situation of the Eastern states is lamentable; in order to gain access to Community funds, a certain competitive level has to be reached and to do this one needs ... funds. A vicious circle which gives Eastern European scholars little chance of success. The Eastern Europeans would stand a greater chance of becoming competitive in the less-expensive field of the humanities. But, of course, the humanities are not on the list of priorities accepted by the European Research Area.

The above includes only a few of the asymmetries which make the process of rehomogenisation on which we are all working – in the West as well as in the East – extremely complicated. If the Eastern Europeans are not granted the same development opportunities, they will feel they are being treated unfairly. But if they are given the same opportunities, they are lost because to be suddenly granted equality of opportunity cannot lessen the burden of inequality that has been built up over the last fifty years.

In this situation, how realistic is it to be optimistic about European reunification? Can we simply get rid of the difficulties inherent in such an ambitious timetable? We can if we keep in mind four prerequisites for success:

- We must exhibit genuine, honest mutual sympathy. In other words we must show solidarity in our efforts to get to know one another, free of feelings of superiority or inferiority complexes.
- We must retain our sense of humour undiluted.
- We should avoid thinking of reunification as a process that will ever more radically remove differences, but rather as an ever more subtle harmonisation of those differences.
- And we should harbour no great illusions while continuing to work full of hope.

Is that all? Certainly not. I could list another 1003 prerequisites. Still, fulfilling the first four by 2050 seems a sensible objective to me...

**Andrei Pleşu**
Born in Bucharest, 1948. Principal of the New Europe College, Bucharest. Founded the cultural journal *Dilemma* in 1993. Romanian culture minister between 1989 and 1991, Romanian foreign minister from 1997 to 1999.

# The Developing Organism

*Europe is proud of its humanistic roots. They provide a solid and worthy foundation for the future European organism. But what are these roots? Heterogeneous, certainly, and over the centuries, nurtured more in strife than in peaceful consensus. We are quick to identify contributing elements; the heritage of Greece and Rome, the Judeo-Christian ethos. But what of Islam? Do we give the Islamic contribution enough credit? And looking to the future – the European organism is still in its infancy. We can identify the roots, but what do they tell us of the coming buds?*

Jacques Le Goff

# The Roots of European Identity

Identity, the way I see it, is to a large extent historical. This does not mean that I subscribe to historical or geographical determinism. History and geography always offer people choices.

The concept of Europe was born in the midst of the oldest stratum of Western high culture, Greek culture, in the context of a fundamental conflict with Asia. The mythical nymph Europa came from Phoenicia; Zeus carried her off from Asia, and in the west she gave birth to a race of people who stood up to the people of Asia. Hippocrates defined the Europeans as lovers of both freedom and battle, unlike the Asians, who were peaceful and liable to fall victim to despotic rule.

This individualisation of a continent called 'Europe' was in no way a geographical necessity. Africa or the two Americas are defined by their coastlines; Europe is merely the tip of the Asian continent, which really should be called Eurasia. The Greek geographers also discussed the problem of the eastern border of Europe, which has not been solved to this day. They suggested the Tanais, otherwise known as the Don, a suggestion taken up again by the medieval encyclopaedists. Historically, Europe did not stretch 'from the Atlantic to the Urals', as De Gaulle suggested; whether Russia is or is not part of Europe remains a problem, although Russia was very strongly drawn into European history from the 16th to the 20th century.

Greek culture provided basic values which are still intellectual and ethical instruments for Europeans today: in philosophy and science they developed the critical spirit which remains one of the essential tools of European thinking and action, and provides the Europeans with a great advantage over other systems of thought characterised by ritualism or fundamentalism, and unable to adopt methodical doubt. In ethics, humanism developed: Socrates' 'know yourself' makes the human being the central focus of the European mind. In politics there was democracy, even if it was still imperfect, excluding women and foreigners. In Rome, interest in justice led to the codification of laws which were ultimately used by the Europeans in their relations with one another. In Europe, rule of law became the defining feature of the state.

Despite these classical foundations, one might still ask if Europe did not really come into existence in the Middle Ages. The great French historian, Marc Bloch, locates the emergence of Europe between the 4th and 8th centuries as a result of the fusion and acculturation of the peoples who inhabited the Latin-speaking part of the Roman Empire (e.g. the Italo-Romans, Gallo-Romans, Hispano-Romans and Celto-Romans) with the 'barbarian' newcomers from the British Isles, northern Gaul and Germania.

What held this new Europe together was Christianity, particularly after the Christian Arians, Ostrogoths and Visigoths converted to the orthodox Roman faith. For a people in medieval Europe, this meant more or less joining international European society. Thus a Europe with a mixed population came into being and, in spite of some dramatic episodes and the attempt to dictate an 'Arian model', this ethnic mixture has remained characteristic of Europe ever since. Acculturation processes of this kind reveal what a Europe that remains open to the idea of waves of immigration will be: a Europe of cultural diversity and mixed races.

Through its institutions Christianity too left its mark on Europe, and because it imposed a monastic network on all the

Christian states, a world was created in which a unified rule, that of St Benedict, prevailed from the beginning of the 9th century. Benedictine monastic life accustomed the Europeans in subsequent centuries to ways of looking at time that still provide the basis of our present temporal divisions.

Around the year 1000, conversion to Christianity brought new people into Europe: the Scandinavians, Hungarians and Slavs; finally, from the 13th to the 15th centuries, the Prussians and Lithuanians. But even if Christianity was the element that welded Europe together, I do not believe that this role and this inheritance should necessarily be reflected in a future European constitution. Unlike Islamic countries, European states are not defined by their religion. Even medieval Europe in its Western, Roman domain failed to develop a theocratic regime, and has ever since adhered to the separation of the spiritual and secular life in strict accordance with the Gospel: 'Render unto Caesar that which is Caesar's.'

Europe today is a laicised universe, even if an important part of the laicised ethics that characterise the identity of Europe is rooted in Christianity, secularised since the 18th century. The Middle Ages also reinforced, if not created, a characteristic process that represents a serious problem and a threat to any European identity. I am speaking here of the division which, beginning with religion, grew up between Latin-Roman Christianity in the West and Greek Orthodox Christianity in the East: that is, between Eastern and Western Europe. Even if it cannot be closed, this gap must ultimately be bridged if the European Union is to be based on a truly coherent identity.

A first design for Europe therefore has two basic foundations: the first is the community of Christianity, formed by religion and culture; the second is the diversity of the various kingdoms, founded on either old multicultural traditions or new ethnic traditions introduced from outside. This anticipates the 'Europe of the Nations', since from the very beginning, Europe has demonstrated that unity can be created out of national diversity: European nationhood and European unity are closely connected. The modern concept of the sovereignty of the state first developed in the 19th century (after first being propounded by Rousseau). The sovereignty of the state need not stand in the way of the formation of a European Union. Unity and diversity are by no means irreconcilable contradictions for Europe.

Because of its internal development and its contacts with opponents and rivals, Europe gradually acquired a political and cultural face. These contacts were most beneficial to Europe. Via Spain and Sicily, technology, the sciences and philosophy were brought to Europe by the Arabs who had inherited them from the Greeks, the Indians, the Persians, the Egyptians and the Jews. Since Europe was able to assimilate and adapt them, these imports produced that extraordinary flowering of the European Middle Ages which enabled Europe to outstrip the power of the great Chinese, Indian, Muslim and Byzantine political and cultural areas, and to achieve a civilisation which was their equal.

At the same time, Europe was caught between two currents that were flowing in opposite directions. The first was dictated by self-defence and protectionism in the face of internal and external opposition, the response to the risks posed by its economic and intellectual openness. This is a movement of closure, of excluding others, of oppression and inner 'cleansing'. Thus in the Middle Ages, what the British historian Robert I. Moore calls a 'society of persecution' came into being, a society which excludes and persecutes those who are 'other': heretics, Jews, homosexuals, lepers. This is the Europe of intolerance, the Inquisition, torture, burning at the stake, incarceration, banishment and expulsion.

The second movement is expansion, giving in to the temptation to use and to misuse the newly acquired power. This movement progresses in differing ways: peacefully in the case of the expansion of trade; militarily and aggressively in the case of the Crusades. Ultimately the borders of Christianity came to agree more closely with those of Europe. A further aspect of expansion is the origin of many later conflicts: moving out eastwards in the direction of that undetermined open border. This is only occasionally warlike, and consists of missionary activity and establishing settlements. But eastward expansion is carried out by one ethnic group, the Germanic peoples, and collides with another ethnic group, the Slavs. This is the source of centuries of conflict between the Germanic and Slavonic peoples, all the more harmful for Europe because it is a conflict between Christians, between Europeans.

Dealing with the conflicts that arose in this way has remained a challenge for Europe to the present day.

Europe's identity is based on its common store of knowledge, its common culture and its art. This common knowledge had its basis in classical antiquity, but was in reality the result of a common cultural effort on the part of the Europeans, and one which led to the creation of their identity, even if one single region, one people and one political system provided the impetus for it. This European advance was given the name 'Renaissance'. The term refers in the first instance to the Carolingian Renaissance (Irish, Anglo-Saxon, Frankish, Germanic, Italian and Spanish scholars under Charlemagne and his successors). In my view, the most important Renaissance is that of the 12th century. This brought the foundation of the universities of Bologna, Paris and Oxford, which grew in importance as they spread the methods of the liberal arts and scholastic philosophy throughout Europe in the 15th century, and are still centres of, and enthusiasts for, European unification. It was a European network in which, despite the development of a certain degree of national feeling, international mobility prevailed. Finally, there was the great Renaissance that began in Italy. The emblematic figure of Erasmus, the critical European humanist of 1500, has today once again become the symbol of the 'Europe of Ideas', which might lead us to suspect that the Europe of yesterday was not so incapable of measuring up to the demands of the present day.

Romanesque and Gothic art (the latter spreading from northern France) were European movements which still continually appear in modern European art. The art historian Roland Recht remarks: 'If we look at the outstanding works of art of the 20th century carefully, we observe that they often carry on, enrich and modernise the artistic achievements of northern Europe in the period between 1140 and 1350. It is to these achievements that artists like Poelzig, Bruno Taut, Mies van der Rohe, Niemeyer, and Gaudi, but also Nervi, Gaudin, Gehry and others owe a great deal of their architectural culture.'

In the sphere of manners and literature, completely new cultural models spread throughout the whole of Europe: the ideal of courtliness and what the German sociologist Norbert Elias describes as the 'process of civilisation'. The diversity of vernacular languages that spread to fill the spaces left by the increasing retreat of Latin provides no barrier to exchange and communication in Europe.

At the beginning of the 16th century, Europe possessed the technical ability to look outwards, to discover and conquer the world. China had the same potential, but unlike Europe, failed to use it. The reason for this behavioural difference is doubtless to be found in the areas of culture and mentality, in the way the Europeans adhered less to ritual and tradition, and were socially more mobile.

Europe's cultural unity grew steadily down the centuries: the Baroque and the Enlightenment were European movements. Enlightened despotism appears in 18th-century Europe as a magic formula which seems to have been inspired by the philosophers from Lisbon to St Petersburg. Literary fashion, which quickly adopts a country or a language as its latest enthusiasm, distributes their works all over Europe. Before the French Revolution, Italy, Spain, France and England are in the forefront. In the 19th century, German literature and the Russian novel are being read all over Europe.

Political thought also had its European dimension. In 17th- and 18th-century England, the political ideas and the practice of law that made Europe commit itself to democracy were developed. *Leviathan* by Thomas Hobbes (1651), the works *On Tolerance* (1689) and *On Government* (1690) by John Locke, the *Habeas Corpus Acts* (1679) and the *Bill of Rights* (1689) were taken up by the French philosophers of the Enlightenment and in Rousseau's *Contrat Social* and are subsequently found all over Europe. The Declaration of Human and Civil Rights in the French Revolution left an even deeper mark on European identity.

But it is not just art, not just the culture of the word and of the idea that have marked European culture: agricultural tradition has also played its part. In the Middle Ages land was the basis of the economy, power and status, and this paramount importance of land, of the possessor of land and territory and of the farmer has retained its symbolic power until today. Indeed, it is the power of land and of those who own and work it that make the agricultural problems of the EU particularly awkward. The other basis of European feudalism is people's relationship to one another; above all the idea of loyalty. It remains to this very day – sometimes a hindrance, but more often a dynamic factor – one of the essential elements of the European mentality and European behaviour.

Europe was in the past, especially in the Middle Ages, first and foremost the Europe of culture, ideology, manners and moral values. The concept of Europe at that time embraced not just a geographical area, but also a collective identity that was valued and stood for community and agreement. The Europe that we see coming into being today is an economic Europe, with all its familiar difficulties, particularly in the agricultural sphere. However, we do seem to be moving into a political phase, which is a good thing. But strangely enough, the phase of cultural upturn seems to be lagging behind, even though the historically real Europe was a cultural Europe. I certainly want a cultural Europe, but above all I want a Europe of values, because values are a stabilising factor; they lead us forward while protecting what has already been achieved.

Today, European identity is faced with new challenges. First, the rise of the new nationalisms. The misfortune of the old Europe lies in the fact that it allowed oppressed nationalisms to ripen for too long, nationalisms that are anachronistic today because they were not able to develop at the same time as the others. They threaten to endanger Europe and take it backwards before the 'Europe of the Nations' is complete, despite the existence of what can be seen as a united Europe in the largest part of the Continent.

Secondly, we observe the resurgence of racism and an exclusionary mentality. Even in its most united phases, Europe was diverse: under the Roman Empire, in the Christian period or during the Industrial Revolution. Europe's *longue durée* can be seen to be a dialectic between the effort to create unity and the preservation of diversity. That is why Europe of the Nations seems to be the most suitable model for the current requirements of European unity.

This is not only a matter of inner necessity, it is also a reaction to the external challenges that Europe faces in the world today. The existence of giant players on the historical stage (gigantic because of their geographical size or their economic strength or both) forces Europe to achieve a similar greatness if it wishes to preserve and develop its existence and its identity. Against America, against Japan – tomorrow against

China – Europe must possess the necessary weight to be in an economic, demographic and political position to ensure its independence. Fortunately, it has the strength of its culture and its common heritage.

The same myths, the same images, the same ideals are the most valuable inheritance of the European. Material or intellectual images are information for the collective memory of these societies, and present us with dreams, ideas of value, role models, hopes, possibilities of escape, but also incentives that play an important role in the formation of a common European consciousness. The Europe of the imagination stands at the centre of the Europe that must be built.

The Europe of the future? Let us hope that it will be a Europe of justice and human rights, that it will be a home for tolerance which will strengthen us against the racist instincts which have unfortunately found new nourishment in the great number of immigrants, especially from the Third World.

The Europe of the future must be a Europe of close friends. The wars of the modern era have divided, ruined and destroyed Europe in a kind of infernal crescendo, from the Italian wars of the Renaissance through the Thirty Years War, the Revolutionary Wars and the Napoleonic Wars to the two great wars of the 20th century and the war in the Balkans at the end of the 1990s. A future Europe must be a peaceful Europe.

The boundaries of the Europe of the future – and its relationship with geography – must now be determined, with due regard to its history. I do not believe that we can include Turkey in a European identity. Fortunately, the conflict between the Turks and the Europeans is a thing of the distant past, and Turkey is not being excluded because of Islam or its democratic defects (which are decreasing anyway). However, geographical borders and a common historical patriotism must form the basis of the European identity, and these are not shared by Turkey.

A decision for Europe does not lie in a choice between tradition and modernity. It lies in the proper use of tradition, in returning to our heritage as an incentive, as a support for the preservation and renewal of another European tradition, that of creativity. It used to be one of Europe's demons to confuse European civilisation with civilisation in general, to wish to have a world made in its own image. If Europe wants to be a model for the modern world it must respect, and open itself, to others. Let us be aware that the world does not consist of Europeans alone. Let us put ourselves in a position to observe others and to change places with them. It is precisely because, since the time of the Greeks, Europe has continuously been open to others that it has produced greatness.

The Europe of tomorrow will be a humanist Europe, or it will be nothing. The Europe of tomorrow needs a humanism which has mastered and integrated progress in science and technology, the achievements of modernity. The difficult task facing us – which is taking place through freedom, tolerance and diversity within a human framework and to some extent in the light of history – is the creation of a new European humanism. If its history is kept in mind, Europe can build its identity on solid foundations.

**Jacques Le Goff**
Born in Toulon, France, 1924. French historian and publicist. Former president of the Ecole des Hautes Etudes en Sciences Sociales, Paris. Key representative of the French historical school 'Nouvelle Histoire'. Publications include: *The Birth of Purgatory; The Medieval Imagination.*

Ilija Trojanow

# Forgotten Roots Remembered

Anyone educated in the Eurocentric tradition will have been taught that Charles Martel saved 'our' civilisation on a windswept field near the town of Poitiers in AD 732 by defeating the forces of Islam. Fact or fiction? The problem with this account of history is that it stands reality on its head, for the dreaded 'Moors' were far closer to our modern understanding of civilisation than the barbarians on 'our' side. The famous battle of Poitiers was just another skirmish between the multi-religious and multifaceted world of Al-Andalus and a horde of Christian warriors (some of whose ancestors had only recently migrated to 'Europe' from Central Asia), tribes still struggling to settle down, to construct political entities and civic institutions. The rendition in the schoolbooks is a monumental inversion, one of those fundamental falsehoods on which the self-perception of European identity has been based. Everything good and worthy comes either from Ancient Greece or from 'our' common European heritage, goes the myth. But it ignores the substantial debt owed by Hellenic antiquity to Egyptian and West Asian predecessors, and it excludes the Mediterranean Islamic world from our parentage. The effect is debilitating, both in the 'West' and in the 'East', the former frozen in imperial arrogance, the latter fighting defensive battles of self-assertion.

In order to plough the fertile common ground, one has first to rid oneself of the essentialist idea of Europe, a peninsula passing itself off as a continent, its very name derived from a Phoenician princess, 'Europa'. Its current demarcations are not congruent with the outline of its heritage – many of the centres of what is regarded as the cradle of European civilisation were geographically not even part of Europe. The grand Hellas consisted in the initial phase of a multitude of city-states and small kingdoms, many of which were situated in Asia Minor. Although Athens and Sparta were on the European side of the Aegean, important 'polises' such as Ephesus, Miletus, Rhodos, Halikarnasos and Ilion were located along the coastline of today's Turkey. Of 1500 Greek cities, only 200 were in the Aegean; the other 1300 were scattered around the Mediterranean and Black Sea[1]. The cities of Asia Minor were not only far more affluent than those of the Greek mainland, but they were able to interact more closely with the myriad cultures and traditions of western Asia, and therefore had a greater share in the initial development of the Hellenist civilisation. Homer 'as a finished achievement was a product of Ionia' (Bertrand Russell), a region in what is now western Turkey. Thales, commonly celebrated as the father of philosophy, was a citizen of Miletus, at the time one of the leading centres of Asia Minor. Thales won fame by predicting an eclipse and thereby earned his reputation as a genius. As well he may have been, but his prediction probably had less to do with genius than with knowledge gained through the close relations between Miletus and Lydia on the one hand, and Lydia and Babylon on the other. Babylonian astronomers were already aware that eclipses follow a cycle of about nineteen years. Thales' famous Milesian school of philosophy flourished until the beginning of the 5th century BC, when Persia conquered the region and Ionia became marginalised.

The demarcation of the polity 'Europe' has always been drawn at the Christian boundaries of this subcontinent. As a result, the westernmost part of the land mass – for centuries by far its most civilised and progressive region – is generally not regarded as originally Europe: the Islamic Al-Andalus. Likewise, the equally long-standing presence of the Ottoman Empire in south-eastern Europe also fails to make it into our political ancestry. The sovereignty of Europe is simplistically defined by two exorcisms of this presence: the triumphs near the gates of Poitiers (AD 732) and in Vienna (AD 1683). European mainstream refuses to accept Islam as one of its ancestors and a fellow inhabitant of Europe, an attitude that explains the recent hesitation of the European Union to admit Turkey as a member state.

Viewing Islam as inherently regressive, most Westerners simply ignore or dismiss the fact that it originally stood for a social and scientific revolution, at a time when Christianity had completed a circle from revolution to status quo. With the edicts of Emperor Constantine, Christianity had become a state religion; with its network of land-owning monasteries and churches, it had assured itself a prime position in the agrarian economy of early medieval Europe. The councils of Nicaea, Constantinople, Ephesus and Chalcedon had cemented a canon and introduced laws establishing excommunication, which was to become a deadly weapon in the hands of the Inquisition. The gospel of love and tolerance was supplanted by the first ideology in human history to systematically deprive a minority of its rights: the Jews suffered discrimination and pogroms and many of them were forced to flee to Persia. The glory of Christianity was waning; Islam arose to take its place.

The current reduction of Islam's complex diversity to reactionary Wahabism should not obscure the fact that, for centuries, Islam was the most progressive cultural force in the Mediterranean region and West Asia. A force not necessarily Arab by birth – Greek and Persian influences abound – but Islamic by translation, incubation and diffusion. The cultural frontier between the Islamic world and the Christian world was often the border between light and darkness, between open and closed, between urban sophistication and rural gaucherie, between mobility and inertia, between a predominantly mercantile and a largely feudal economy. It is hardly surprising that the great minds of the European awakening would turn to Al-Andalus and its cultural products to broaden their horizon and to reinvent themselves. It is meanwhile widely, but also vaguely, accepted that most of the knowledge flourishing in Europe at the onset of the Renaissance was derived from the Arabic, be it due to the translations of Greek classics or to the high quality of scientific work in centres such as Baghdad, Damascus, Cordoba or Toledo, especially in the fields of medicine, physics, astronomy and mathematics.

Al-Andalus, a partly united, partly fragmented polity inside the boundaries of the Iberian peninsula, not only tolerated Christianity and Judaism, but interacted with these minority cultures, thus producing a supremely confluent and accomplished civilisation. Throughout close to eight centuries, through crests and troughs, one thing remained constant in Al-Andalus: the co-existence of Islam, Christianity and Judaism, and the intense and often fruitful dialogue between the three. The levels of tolerance were very high even by our contemporary 'democratic' standards: Rabbi Samuel the Nagid, leading spiritual figure of his community and the reviver of Hebrew as a literary language, was at the same time vizier at the court of Granada. Imagine that today, the Imam of the Friday Mosque in Marseilles were to become Prime Minister of France. Without overlooking the iconoclastic and intolerant tendencies among some of the Islamic rulers, one has to note that in Al-Andalus, the destruction of churches or synagogues and the oppression of non-believers was a rare occurrence.

The accomplishments of the Andalusian civilisation that influenced the cultures of the Europe to come were manifold. They reached from religion to technology, they included astronomy, irrigation methods as well as different aspects of architecture, from the concept of a formal garden to many elements of interior decoration. Some of these influences are self-evident (for example, the carpet), others are submerged and need to be salvaged, but taken all together, these examples prove conclusively how much Western civilisation owes to Asian and African predecessors through the intermediate services of Al-Andalus.

In the field of surveying, for example, the Eastern practice of triangulation led to techniques which went beyond the know-how of the Roman *agrimensores*. These techniques were facilitated by a small but remarkable instrument called the astrolabe, which allowed for accurate astronomical measurements to calibrate the positions of the stars. It was introduced to Christian Europe by the scholar Gerbert d'Aurillac at the end of the 10th century. Gerbert, by the way, is an excellent example of how perceptions change: lauded by his contemporaries for travelling to Cordoba for the sake of knowledge, he was derided several generations later for practising Saracen divinations and interacting with Muslim necromancers. The astrolabe became something of an intellectual craze, with just about everyone in the scientific discourse centred around the influential monastery of Cluny having something to say on its usage. It was so fashionable that Heloise (of Abelard fame) named her son Astrolabe. Such technological transfer was to continue. In the early 13th century, the mathematician Leonardo Fibonacci, who had studied accounting in North Africa, wrote the *Book of the Abacus,* a Latin treatise that popularised the Arab ciphers which soon replaced the Roman numerals.

Examples are manifold: hydraulic devices, textile techniques, pottery glazing. Moreover, there is compelling evidence in literature. William IX of Aquitaine, for example, was the first troubadour and therefore the first high poet of postclassical Europe. It is less widely known that he and his successors were deeply influenced by the poetic forms and principles of Al-Andalus. When William IX was still young, his father brought back a strange booty from his forays into the southern foothills of the Pyrenees: hundreds of *qiyan*, female singers, dancers and poets in one, entertainers of the Andalusian elite, versed in the Arabic *muwashsha* and the Jewish *zajal*. Their performances were deeply appreciated at the court of Aquitaine, where all things Andalusian were regarded as the epitome of cultural accomplishment. William (Guilhem), the young son of the Aquitaine king, grew up with this inspiring presence. The first songs he wrote studiously followed the Arabic and Jewish role models.

On another trail leading out of Al-Andalus, consider Petrus Alfonsi, a Jew who converted to Catholicism on his journey to his new home, England. In addition to becoming a physician at the court of Henry I, he wrote treatises on learned subjects as befitted an Andalusian gentleman. His books were the 'best-sellers' of his day, even though they were no more than average productions for a person of his background. He wrote only one piece of fiction, the 'Disciplina Clericalis', a garland of stories which was to become an important source of early European national literatures. Alfonsi infused into the 'European' mainstream the rich heritage of Arabic, Persian and Indian story-telling, great cycles of fables, parables and adventures from the East, such as the *Alf Laila wa Laila* (1001 Nights), the *Vetala-pancavimsati* (25 Tales of the Vampire) or the *Panchatantra*, already travelling under the assumed name and altered style of the *Dastan Kalilah wa Dimnah*. Both Boccaccio and Chaucer were directly influenced by Alfonsi; some of his stories were collected in the *Gesta Romanorum,* which would go on to inspire generations of European authors all the way to the bard of all bards.

Of course, the formative energy of European civilisation was Christianity, canonically represented as a quintessentially Western system of thought and belief. Outside the tyranny of dogma, it is hard to comprehend how a religion that was born in Palestine, developed in the Levant, disseminated in the beginning mostly into northern Africa and western Asia, could be regarded as 'European'[2]. By the time the West had gained control over the Christian enterprise, it was already a fully established ideology and system of ritual. The decisive period of crystallisation was dominated by syncretist tendencies. Far from being a heresy or a corruption of the True Law, syncretism lies at the heart of Christianity – as indeed it does of all religions. The claim of revelation presupposes a rupture with all prior traditions, in the case of Jesus, with the pagan and Jewish worlds. But in fact, Christianity as a pillar of European civilisation is an incorporation of the ideas, images and practices of the diverse cults of Adonis, Mithras, Isis and Cybele, among many others. The Virgin Mary owes her existence to the earth-goddess, a female force of fertility in many ancient religions who was worshipped as 'The Great Mother'. The Greeks in Asia Minor named her Artemis; she went on to become 'Diana of the Ephesians'. Nearly everything we subsume under soteriology, to give a further example, arises from the meeting of Kushan Buddhism and Sassanid Zoroastrianism: the figure of the Saviour as Redeemer, Warrior and Judge, the idea of the Second Coming and the End of the World, and the mythology of the afterlife. These are themes that would flow east and flower in the Buddhist myth of Maitreya, and themes that would flow west and form the auratic framework for the execution of a rebellious carpenter in Galilea.

From the beginning of civilised time, there existed a system of interrelationships that linked the littoral regions of the Mediterranean: Crete formed a symbiosis with Pharaonic Egypt, Phoenicians ploughed the sea of mercantile profitability, Hellenic cities relied on the mines of Iberia, Romans and Carthaginians had an alternate trade-and-hate relationship. So when Arabs and Berbers crossed the Straits of Gibraltar and quickly occupied the dysfunctional Visigoth fiefdoms of Hispania, it was not such a landmark as the propagandists of a natural European identity might claim. Being used to regarding reality through the prism of maps, we tend to see the blue stretch of water as a division; more often, it is a fluid bridge. Neither the great forms nor indeed the peak achievements of European culture would have been possible without this initial confluence of an underdeveloped society with a stream of cultures from elsewhere, flowing past all border posts, toll collectors, immigration officials and copyright lawyers.

We continue to regard fluidity of form, shifting identity and indeterminacy of definition as problems rather than as opportunities: the hybrid threatens the stability of the system, the viviparous fish that crawls causes headaches. The serious debates among natural scientists of the 19th century on the definition of species echoed the comicality of the great medieval debate among North European monks on whether the barnacle goose was a fish or a fowl. What are you, fish or fowl? The question is still asked of individuals and communities whose identity slips through the reticulation of nation, province, language group, ethnicity and locality. A Europe that is well poised for coming challenges needs to acknowledge the confluent presence both in its past as well as in its present.

Notes

1 The geography of fauna and flora similarly does not distinguish between Europe and Asia. The botanical demarcation separates Arabia, the Indian subcontinent and South East Asia from the rest of the continent, including the Mediterranean belt of North Africa. The zoological atlas on the other hand defines an 'African-Eurasian Province', which encompasses all of Northern Africa and all of Asia, excluding only the Indian subcontinent and South East Asia as well as the arctic stretch in the north.
2 In the early councils there were far more Asian (even Indian!) than European delegates.

**Ilija Trojanow**
Born in Sofia, 1965. Lives and works as a freelance journalist and author in Mumbai. Lived in Kenya for ten years and worked as a publisher of African literature. Publications include: *The World is Big and Salvation Lurks Everywhere* (in German).

Friedrich Cardinal Wetter

# Europe's Religious Origins and Future

When the Spanish philosopher Ortega y Gasset was asked why he had returned from exile in Argentina to Spain and thus to Europe, he readily answered that Europe '[is] the only continent that has a content'.[1] This self-confidence on the part of a European thinker might well give rise to astonishment today – indeed disapproval. But even if we do not go along with this claim to exclusivity, we are still faced with the question of what makes Europe Europe, what is the 'content' that fills its name?

From among the multiplicity of philosophical, ideological, academic, scientific, artistic and political definitions which can all be included under the weighty concept of culture, we are going to present a few observations on the religious origins and shape of Europe. They do not attempt to give a comprehensive account of the development of religious ideas or practically lived belief. Rather, they sketch a few lines which reveal the importance of the Christian religion for the formation of Europe and beyond in the past, the present, and possibly even in the future. In the process our attention will be directed particularly to the question of the responsibility borne by Christians for the process of developing the Europe in which we find ourselves.

## On the religious origin and form of Europe

Classical Greek thought and the Bible represent the basic components of Europe. Simultaneously naming both of these major determining, formative factors does not, however, overlook the fact that they express mutually connected but also partly contradictory conceptions of humanity, of the way we understand the world and of the image of God. Thus the requirement to love one's enemy as formulated in the Sermon on the Mount in New Testament Scripture expresses a demand that can hardly be comprehended in terms of classical thought. The Holy Scripture of Israel, the Old Testament, was solely a product of the religious sphere of the Orient, no matter how much the belief in one God who has chosen His people as presented there differs from polytheistic oriental religions. Thus we can say, 'The European spirit is partly an oriental spirit.'[2]

Even if the Christian foundation of Europe represents a 'synthesis between the faith of Israel and the Greek mind',[3] it is still not limited to this geographical and philosophical religious space, but reveals itself from the very beginning as a religion that breaks down boundaries throughout the world. Christianity, which through Greece and the Roman Empire became one of the decisive formative forces in Europe, gave the developing continent its unmistakable sense of itself. Europe did not see itself as intended 'to mediate itself to the world as a continent in its own name',[4] instead Europe became 'the instrument of the transmission of the event that was intended for humanity: God in Christ.'[5]

The universalistic tendency which is to be found in Christianity, and thus developed in Europe, required from the very beginning many laborious processes of reception. The Europeans, understood here as Romans, Germans and Slavs, developed over the centuries a culture and a civilisation that consisted primarily in the appropriation of the religion of Israel, the person and the works of Jesus Christ, the Roman conception of law, the classical languages, classical art and craft techniques. 'Everything that was alive in the Middle Ages could ultimately be called "Renaissance"'[6] Thus it is not surprising that, in the ages that followed, the transmission of European culture and civilisation always contained essential elements derived from the Christian religion, and that, conversely, the missionary presence of the Church in countries outside Europe also brought with it contents and methods derived from European culture and civilisation; a reciprocal process that in addition to providing concrete aid for the development of these peoples in some limited areas of civilisation, also led to not inconsiderable conflicts.

From this Judaeo-Christian and Graeco-Roman heritage there developed – not least because of the integrative power of the Church as a living community with Christ and the societal form of belief – together with the emancipation of knowledge and the bourgeoisie, what is called the modern heritage of Europe. This consists essentially in the separation of religion as a personal and communal confession from the legal order of civil society as expressed in the law. Consequently the modern European heritage continues to formulate the claims of religion, but also those of a moral ethos which has no explicit reference to religion: humane values make a humane society possible. From the store of Christian ideas a central canon of values is formed, which is lodged in the general consciousness: a canon of values that includes the recognition of freedom of conscience, unconditional respect for human rights and the ability and duty of human reason to accept responsibility.[7]

From these religious roots develop the differentiations that were once defined as 'Socratic distinction', a distinction based on wisdom and reason:[8] the distinction between the good in itself, and the good in its various individual forms, the distinction between the right as such and its various juristic formulations in the law, of democracy as majority rule in connection with Plato's 'eunomia' as the indispensable rule of good laws founded on morality.[9]

The above-mentioned theological and political philosophical considerations ensured that, from the moment when Christianity had to come to terms with the state and society, religion removed any trace of divinity from the state and its ruler, so that the ruler could no longer be seen as a God-Emperor. In this way, Christianity created the fundamental distinction between state and religion, of the secular rule of order and the power of the spiritual order, thus laying the foundations of the free constitutional state.

It was the claim of religion and theology to absolute truth that would not accept that the world and God, or the ruler and God, were identical. The limits of the state were therefore demonstrated, and mankind was promised an inviolable sanctuary which could not be abolished by the state. The idea of the separation of worldly and spiritual power – even if this was not consistently pursued down the centuries – contains the seeds of the development of pluralism, democratic decision-making processes and personal freedom. Nonetheless, this concept of the theology of the state, which determined the development of the whole medieval period, also contains an 'internal paradox'[10] as far as the social order is concerned. On the one hand, individual human beings were promised individuality and therefore freedom; on the other, they were 'subject to two universal powers simultaneously, the Church and the King'.[11]

The religious shape of modern Europe is extremely diverse and complex. Europe has not forgotten its Christian origins, and even seems to be rediscovering them as it formulates basic human rights and rules for European unification. However, the Council of Europe has not yet been able to bring itself to make explicit reference to God in its formulation of the basic European principles. God, as a word that reminds us of what lies beyond politics, is perceived as an infringement of the ideological neutrality of the state and therefore also of European unity. But this represents a false interpretation of historical facts. Pope John Paul II expresses this when he underlines: 'the recognition of an undeniable historical fact in no way means ignoring the modern demand for the legitimate ideological neutrality of the state, and thus of Europe.'[12]

In modern Europe, God is recognised as the fundamental basis of faith and life not only by Christians and Jews, but also by a large number of Islamic believers. At the same time we have to admit that Christian belief in God and the monotheism of other religions are confronted in Europe with a clearly materialistic and hedonistic tendency in ideas about the meaning of life, which reveals traits that are atheistic in practice even if they do not explicitly deny the existence and power of God. Instead of the deep mysticism of the experience of God and the human encounter with the self, we have the fascinating power of technology, which gives rise to fantasies of omnipotence. The Christian social principles of personality, subsidiarity and solidarity are often challenged by a broad consumerism that is oblivious to common humanity and the love of one's neighbour.

## The Christian contribution to Europe

Christianity is a doctrine of redemption which is concerned with the ultimate salvation of the whole human being. Even if this includes striving for justice in the political, economic and social fields, Christianity does not represent any political theory or economic doctrine. The principles of Christianity include taking all spheres of human culture seriously, that is, keeping their meaning in terms of the ultimate perfection of humanity and the world in view, but relativising all forms of cultural activity. In this respect, salvation can neither be sought nor found in the state. Thus the state is not conceived as the final revelation, as a kind of incarnation of human and divine reason. Instead, the New Testament announces that a time will come when Jesus Christ 'shall have put down all rule and all authority and power' (1. Corinthians 15, 24).

Even economic success – no matter how indispensable it is for maintaining social harmony and fit human living conditions, even a certain degree of prosperity – cannot be regarded as the final goal of human efforts. In the same way, it is impossible to deify mankind's cultural achievements, however valuable and admirable they are, since this would ultimately mean that mankind was setting itself up as its own idol. Thus substitute religions of all kinds, which could be the result of regarding money, status or sex as absolute values, should be rejected. Even the cognitive and ordering power of human reason does not in itself represent an absolute value. Reason that remains isolated within itself and is not conceived as transcendental reason falls, as it were, into the bottomless pit of the merely human and ousts God from our consciousness. Anyone, however, who ousts God from the consciousness of human reason is promoting indifference and the neutralising of values in every sphere of life.

History, particularly the history of the 20th century, makes it necessary for Christians in Europe to be particularly on their guard when the 'dark side of Europe', the 'intellectual distortion' of European thought, takes the floor.[13] The Conference of European Churches and the Council of the European Conference of Bishops admitted in the *Charta Oecumenica*, following the words of the Gospel, 'Blessed are the peacemakers, for they shall be called the children of God' (Matthew 5, 9), that Europe has occasionally betrayed its own origins in a disastrous way, and thus put its future at risk: 'Down the centuries, a Europe that in religious and cultural terms is predominantly Christian has developed. At the same time, the failures of the Christians in Europe and beyond its boundaries have caused a great deal of damage. We admit our joint responsibility for this guilt, and beg God and mankind for forgiveness.'[14]

The ideologising of politics, which found its last form in 'total war', together with the ideologising of human races which led to the destruction of countless human beings, have asked Germany and many people in Europe whether Europe may not have forfeited the moral right to act and appear on the world stage as a political and cultural role model. Even if historical guilt is recognised in this self-criticism, and it becomes clear at the same time that mankind can be led astray to evil, this admission also releases intellectual and moral forces which correspond very closely to the spirit of Christian Europe. But if this self-criticism leads to the loss of our own intellectual and religious roots, then Europe is wounded in a vital spot. Abandoning the intellectual and religious basis of individual human life, social processes and political actions leads to the world being left to its own devices. This cannot be reconciled with the way in which Christians understand the world, without at the same time calling into question the relative independence of secular cultural spheres.[15]

With the approaching expansion of Europe, we will also have to look at ways of reinforcing it. Here it might help to recall the concept of the 'Abendland' [the Christian West] which in geographical terms is somewhat narrower than Europe but whose meaning is more clearly circumscribed. This concept, occasionally used in an elitist and exclusive way, is here used to mean 'the cultural community of the Western European peoples, from which modern world culture derives'.[16] As a geographical and a Christian religious term, it needs to be complemented by the concept which Luther coined following the [German] Gospels, namely 'Morgenland' (Matthew 2,1, where the German wording of 'there came wise men from the East' has the word *Morgenland* 'Orient', land of the rising sun). This comprises the Churches of the Byzantine Empire and its Christian cultural sphere of influence, especially the eastern Slavonic peoples. Europe would not be complete if it did not breathe – in the words of Pope John Paul II – with two lungs. The Pope's words on this subject, spoken on 6 October 1989, bear witness to great love: 'Lux ex oriente. Faith, religious life, is coming anew to us in Europe from Eastern Europe.'[17]

The most important contribution made by the Christians to Europe has always been the moulding and the promulgation of the Christian concept of mankind, which represents the foundation of a way of thinking about the state and order in a Christian way. With the formation of the Europe that is now coming into being, we are presumably once more confronted with the question of redefining the meaning of liberty, equality and fraternity. Even if they were in their day – although born in the bosom of the Church – formulated in an atmosphere of misunderstanding and of hostility to the Church, the Church today once again feels called upon to make people aware of these postulates, and to rediscover their theological meaning.

The struggle for individual, social and political freedom is an indispensable element of the history of European ideas. This history of freedom is – like all such histories of human freedom – still unfinished, and is in a constant state of development. This can sometimes cause deep disquiet. But freedom that asks for what is true and morally acceptable need not frighten people. It appears, rather, as an incontrovertible sign of mankind's being made in God's image. This freedom is aware that it will come up against the absolute boundary constituted by the human being's responsibility in the face of himself, his fellow beings and God. The religiously based value of the equality of all human beings stands in stark contradiction to all experience, since the human race by nature, and throughout history, has always treated its equals in a most unequal way.

In this emphasis on the equal value of all human beings, in spite of their apparent inequality, lies one of the most important and exciting statements of Christian anthropology. This most abstract statement about human beings reveals itself as a most powerful and effective idea. As human beings and Christians, and also as members of our Church, we are well aware how often the idea of the equal value of all human beings with its corollary, equal rights before the law, have been, and still are, ignored. Brotherhood, which today we call brother-and-sisterhood, implies first of all the effort to ensure that everyone receives that to which they are entitled. Thus this brother-and-sisterhood becomes a social principle and does not remain confined to the sphere of the emotions, which can change so quickly. Today, brotherhood means in particular worldwide solidarity: 'As Christians we cannot be satisfied with a united Europe in a divided world, with a peaceful Europe in a world full of conflicts, with a rich Europe in a world that is confronted with the challenge of poverty.'[18]

With the concepts of freedom, equality and brotherhood, we devise universal dimensions without which states and communities of states cannot in the long run live in peace, especially when we look at global developments.

To formulate the vision of a new Europe means referring to the most valuable inheritance of European humanism. This inheritance can give form to the unity of the old continent and at the same time provide it, in the present and in the future, with significance in terms of culture and civilisation. It represents a total scheme of values which, in the words of Pope John Paul II:

> is the characteristic intellectual and spiritual element that has formed the European identity in the course of the centuries and are part of the real cultural assets of this continent. As I have reminded people on many occasions, these values concern the dignity of the individual; the inviolability of human life; the central role of the marriage-based family; the importance of upbringing and education; freedom of thought and speech and the freedom to profess one's own convictions and religion; the protection of the law for individuals and groups; everyone working together for the common good; work, which can be regarded as a personal and a social good; political power understood as service subject to reason and the law, and limited by the rights of individuals and nations.[19]

These words reveal the most significant inheritance of European humanism, which was, in its essence, moulded by Christianity: humanity's knowledge of what it is to be human.

### Notes

1. E. Straub (n. d.), '"Abendland" gegen One-World-Ideologie', in R. C. Meier-Walser and B. Rill (eds), *Der europäische Gedanke. Hintergrund und Finalität*, p. 124.
2. W. Sternberger (1979), 'Komponenten der geistigen Gestalt Europas', in *zur debatte* (Hg. v. d. Katholischen Akademie in Bayern), 9(3): 5.
3. J. Ratzinger (1979), 'Verpflichtendes Erbe': Speech on 29 April 1979 in Straßburg. Extracts in *zur debatte* (Hg. v. d. Katholischen Akademie in Bayern), 9(3): 1–4.
4. cf. H. Bürkle (n. d.), 'Das Christentum und die Integration Europas', in R. C. Meier-Walser and B. Rill (eds), *Der europäische Gedanke. Hintergrund und Finalität*, pp. 114–23.
5. Bürkle, ibid., p. 115.
6. J. Huizinga quoted in K. Kluxen (1986) 'Athen – Rom – Jerusalem. Auf den Spuren abendländischer Existenz' in *Wirkung des Schöpferischen. Kurt Herberts zum 80. Geburtstag* (ed. L. Bossle), Würzburg, p. 394.
7. cf. Ratzinger 1979 (see note 3).
8. H. Kuhn, quoted by Ratzinger 1979 (see note 3).
9. cf. Ratzinger 1979 (see note 3).
10. F. Seibt (2002), *Die Begründung Europas. Ein Zwischenbericht über die letzten tausend Jahre*, Frankfurt/M.; quotation from H. A. Winkler in *Die Welt* ('Die literarische Welt'), 5 October 2002, p. 9.
11. Seibt, ibid., p. 9.
12. Pope John Paul II., Address at the New Year reception for the Diplomatic Corps, 10 January 2002, quoted in *Europa-infos* (ed. OCIPE and ComECE), February 2002, No. 35, p. 2.
13. Sternberger 1979 (see note 2).
14. *Charta Oecumenica* (published by KEK/CCEE, Geneva/St. Gallen), April 2001.
15. Kluxen 1986 (see note 6), pp. 393–8.
16. A. Halder (1957), 'Abendland', in *LThK*, I, col. 17.
17. L. Accattoli (2000), *Johannes Paul II: Die Biografie,* Graz/Vienna/Cologne, p. 237.
18. Closing declaration of the European Colloquium 'Taking Responsibility for a New Epoch of European Integration'. Central Committee of German Catholics/ZdK and Semaines Sociales de France, 2 March 2002.
19. Message from Pope John Paul II to the participants in the European study conference on the theme: 'On the way to a European constitution?', in *L' Osservatore Romano* (German), **32**(36): 7 (2002).

**Friedrich Cardinal Wetter**
Born in Landau, 1928. Archbishop of Munich and Freising and Chair of the Freising Bishops' Conference since 1982. Chairman of the German Bishops' Conference Faith Commission.

David J. Goldberg

# The Diversity of Jews in Europe

A few years ago, a well-known Israeli politician wrote an article in which he predicted that by the year 2025 the American Jewish community of nearly six million would have dwindled to no more than a million adherents, European Jewry would have all but disappeared, and the vast majority of the world's fourteen million Jews would be living in the State of Israel.

At the time, there was superficial plausibility to his scenario. The Iron Curtain had come down and highly qualified immigrants from the former Soviet Union were flocking to Israel in their hundreds of thousands. The Oslo Accords had been signed with the PLO, there was a peace treaty with Egypt and Jordan, progress was being made towards self-government for the Palestinian inhabitants of Gaza and the West Bank and in the new spirit of hope and optimism, the economy was booming. Buildings were going up as exuberantly as in reunified Berlin, super highways were being constructed which one day, it was said, would link Jerusalem to Cairo and Damascus, high-tech industries were turning the coastal plain into a miniature Silicon Valley, and Shimon Peres' dream of a Middle Eastern Common Market galvanised by Israeli drive and know-how seemed closer to realisation.

But something about the triumphalist tone of this politician's article irked me. I was tempted to write to him quoting the aphorism that Mark Twain attributed to Benjamin Disraeli, 'There are three kinds of lies: lies, damned lies and statistics', and adding 'there is a fourth: demographic projections'. One thing I have learnt is that graphs never behave with remorseless exponential logic, no matter how painstakingly statisticians compile them. The rosy future painted for his country by the Israeli politician depended crucially on a satisfactory solution to the Israeli-Palestinian conflict; without it, all his demographic projections were built on quicksand.

And so it has proved. Prime Minister Rabin was assassinated by a Jewish extremist, the Oslo Accords unravelled in an atmosphere of mutual suspicion and mistrust, a hard-line Likud government has reiterated its attachment to the settlements, and a second intifada has plumbed new levels of savagery with Palestinian suicide bombings and Israeli military reprisals; as always, innocent civilians on both sides are the main victims. Where there was hope and optimism, there is now hatred and despair. Those who can, leave. There is a substantial Israeli (and Palestinian) diaspora in the United States, in Europe – in any country that offers the prospect of a more peaceful existence than that in the homeland over which two peoples are locked in deadly struggle. In Holland, for example, there are about 30,000 resident Jews and 10,000 expatriate Israelis.

European Jewry, so long dormant after the Nazi genocide, has been rediscovering its voice. Only 3.1 million Jews remained in Europe in 1945 out of a total Jewish population of 9.2 million before the Second World War. It could truly be said that European Jewry in the post-war years was a remnant of a decimated people. As such, its influence was marginal, its identity fractured. There was hardly a Jewish family from the Baltic to the Mediterranean that had not been seared in some way by the events of 1939–1945. It was no longer possible to move easily from one country or one province to another, confident in the knowledge of being able to make contact with fellow Jews in a local synagogue, and if all other languages failed, using a smattering of Yiddish as the shared tongue. Those Jews who actually *chose* to go back to live in Germany were regarded with incredulous disbelief. Traumatised and ageing, with intermarriage soaring and birth rates below the national averages in the West, and behind the Iron Curtain subject to hostility and discrimination from communist regimes that disliked *all* religion, European Jewry regularly had the last rites pronounced over it. The mere 22 miles of the English Channel had saved Anglo-Jewry from the fate of its continental European brethren, so in terms of memory and experience they were poles apart; but the same gloomy statistics applied.

Two factors have brought about a remarkable transformation. First, the collapse of communism in the 1990s loosened the restraints that had made East Europeans circumspect about admitting their Jewish identity. It was no longer shameful to have had Jewish ancestry. Especially among the young, curiosity about their roots, stifled under communism, has led many to affirm Judaism. As they have migrated westwards in search of job opportunities, they in turn have reinvigorated moribund communities. Germany has the fastest growing Jewish population in Europe with an estimated 60,000 Russian immigrants. In Russia itself, there has been a remarkable upsurge of Jewish activity, from ultra-Orthodox to cultural. New congregations have been established and old ones revived in Hungary, the Czech Republic and Slovakia.

This has led to problems about recognising Jewish status. The traditional definition of being Jewish depends upon having a Jewish mother, but with intermarriage in every European Jewish community at over 50 percent, and mainstream Orthodox Judaism steadily losing ground to more outward-looking progressive Judaism, or Jewish humanism, that ruling has become increasingly inoperable. Nevertheless, following the example of Israel, where the Orthodox rabbinate determines Jewish status, and despite the fact that both in Israel and Europe the overwhelming majority of the population is decidedly non-Orthodox, the traditional definition is still the norm. It is nominal Orthodoxy (or as it is quaintly called in Germany 'secular Orthodoxy') that is the official Jewish link with government and state agencies. The anomaly is so glaring between the fiction of Jewish communities throughout Europe observing standardised Orthodox law and the reality of its widely divergent application that it can only be a matter of time before the governments of Germany, France, Holland, Italy and elsewhere acknowledge by legislation that in the modern world there is more than one way of observing or affirming Jewishness.

Secondly, although Zionism might not have been successful in persuading most European Jews to go and settle in Israel, the perpetual controversy surrounding the Jewish state has sharpened Jewish awareness and identity. Support for Israel is the bond uniting almost all of diaspora Jewry. If God died in Auschwitz – as more than one Jewish theologian has claimed – then Israel, to an important extent, has filled the spiritual vacuum. Religious practice and observance may be waning, but ethnicity is in vogue, and almost all of modern Jewry, from left to right of the political spectrum, identifies with and shares vicariously in the triumphs and tribulations of the Jewish state. Fallout from the Middle East conflict has repercussions in Europe, especially now that there are large Muslim populations in France, Great Britain, Germany and elsewhere. It is a matter of self-respect to declare one's Jewishness and metaphorically mount the barricades in defence of a heavily criticised country, no matter how privately disturbed many Jews are by Israeli government policy.

So can we talk about a collective European Jewish identity? No more than we could ascribe that attribute to the English, French, or Germans. Reactions for and against greater European integration vary as widely among Jews as among any other sector of the populace. I would be tempted to propose that Jews, as a result of our historical experience, are inclined to be more cosmopolitan and universal in outlook than people who have been settled in a particular piece of territory for a long time. Nationalism had a relatively late flowering among Jews. It might be reasonable to infer, therefore, that most Jews would look favourably upon the notion of a unified Europe, where borders are geographical rather than military, and a common currency is valid throughout; but some of the strongest British opponents of entry into the euro are prominent Jewish businessmen. The 'Little Englander' mentality, like its Austrian, Italian or German equivalents, is not confined to a single religious or ethnic grouping.

There is an old folk saying to the effect that as the wider Christian community is, so are the Jews within it. *Wie es christelt zich, juedelt es zich*. Our European experience has invariably been as a minority grouping within larger civic structures. Minorities learn to adapt if they wish to survive; they take on the culture and *mores* of their environment, while still retaining their distinctive characteristics. We Jews have been particularly adept at this and even make self-mocking jokes about it, as in the story of the Galician immigrant who goes to a Savile Row tailor and asks him, in broken English, to make him an English gentleman's three-piece suit. The suit fits perfectly. He then asks for a bowler hat. That too fits perfectly. He completes the outfit with a rolled umbrella. The tailor murmurs discreetly that the entire ensemble looks superb, but is disconcerted to see that his customer is crying and asks why. Answers the Jew: 'I'm crying for our lost empire.'

That kind of self-deprecatory Jewish humour has been around since the Rothschilds first rose to prominence over two hundred years ago. It recognises the temptation for a *parvenu* to want to become more Catholic than the Pope. The European Jew is first and foremost a citizen of his or her country and a product of the local environment. If one is going to indulge in crude stereotyping, it should be on the basis of national, not religious, characteristics. So the Italian Jew is preoccupied with style and *la bella figura,* the English Jew is phlegmatic, the German Jew hard-working, the Irish Jew laid-back, etc. Simply cataloguing these prejudices demonstrates how inaccurate and wide of the mark such generalisations are; but doing so demonstrates that 'European Jewry' is not a discrete entity but an amorphous concept, as is the 'European Community'.

Nevertheless, certain modest propositions can be advanced about European Jewry. First, the old Talmudic adage that all Jews are responsible for one another resonates strongly with post-Holocaust generations. Should any one sector of European Jewry be threatened, the others would vigorously come to its aid, with the State of Israel and the American community offering support. Never again will we passively acquiesce, as dictated by force of circumstances between 1933 and 1945.

Secondly, European Jewry is no longer a vanishing diaspora quietly fading away. The opportunities and advantages offered by the Common Market have been beneficial to the Jews living within the European Community. Global markets and multinational corporations have led to Jewish personnel in banking, commerce and industry locating to the major European centres, where they contribute to local Jewish life. New congregations conduct their services in Hebrew, the native tongue, and English. Jewish cultural activity is lively and varied.

Thirdly, Judaism, in common with most other religious denominations throughout Europe, has witnessed a decline in organised worship. Fewer Jews attend services on a regular basis and only the tiny Orthodox minority observe the ancient tenets of the faith, from not eating 'forbidden' food to not working on the Sabbath. Whereas most Jews like to describe themselves as 'traditional' – meaning that they maintain a nostalgic memory of the customs of their forebears – in reality they lead the normal, daily lives of their fellow citizens in secular democracies. In contemporary society, religion is a matter of personal choice, and the modern Jew picks and chooses what to believe and what to practise as does the modern Catholic or Protestant.

Fourthly, European Jewry is more inclined nowadays to challenge the hegemony of America and Israel. It has grown more self-confident as its numbers have increased and its institutions have become established. The influence, wealth and pre-eminence of the two largest centres of Jewish population is acknowledged but no longer automatically deferred to. Just as Europe feels it offers a collective counterweight and alternative perspective to that of the world's sole remaining superpower, so too does European Jewry. There is little inclination to agree, for example, with American Jewry's simplistic assessment of resurgent European anti-Semitism.

The world view emanating from Washington nowadays tends to see things in stark black or white – 'either you are for us or against us'. The American Jewish community, with few exceptions, finds this scenario useful to drum up unconditional support for Israel, 'the only democracy in the Middle East, America's truest ally', etc. American Jewry still feels guilty about not having done more to help European Jews when there was a chance to do so before the Second World War. It is a significant pointer that Holocaust memorials and museums are more prevalent in America than in Europe. As compensation for its perceived lack of effort then, the American Jewish establishment now tends to denounce in strident and generalised terms every criticism of Israel as a resurgence of anti-Semitism masquerading as anti-Zionism, and to regard Europe as irredeemably tainted by the bacillus of anti-Jewish prejudice. Essentially, this is the Zionist version of Jewish history, which views Jewish experience in the Diaspora as one long weeping by the waters of Babylon until Theodor Herzl came along with his vision of a Jewish homeland. A book like Daniel Goldhagen's sensationalist *Hitler's Willing Executioners* was lapped up by American Jewry, but received a distinctly cooler reception from European Jews.

And it causes caustic comment in European Jewish circles that organisations like the Simon Wiesenthal Center in Los Angeles (which bears his name but has no connection with the Nazi hunter) or the Anti-Defamation League, are largely staffed by people born in America after the war, who depend for their funding on unearthing a regular supply of aged former Nazis or monitoring an alleged rise in anti-Semitic incidents throughout Europe since the second intifada began. I would take their dossiers more seriously if I did not know for a fact that the breaking of two windows at my synagogue by young hooligans was catalogued as 'an anti-Semitic incident', or that minor damage at another London synagogue was logged twice under two different addresses.

This is not to be complacent about such events. A few synagogues and cemeteries certainly have been damaged, usually after the Middle East has dominated the news. All sober observers can point to evidence of a rise in anti-Israel hostility, which in turn affects local Jewish communities. Unsurprisingly, it is students who bear the brunt of such criticism. Jewish societies on university campuses are subjected to intimidation and harassment that would not be tolerated if directed against other ethnic groups. Economic and academic boycotts of Israel are growing. These are real and serious concerns; but it is the height of irresponsibility to make PR capital out of these incidents by suggesting, as American and Israeli commentators have done, that Europe is in the grip of the worst bout of anti-Semitism since Hitler.

Broadly speaking, European Jews live in greater physical security and material affluence than ever before. They share similar hopes, aspirations and anxieties. But unity is not the same as uniformity. There is superficial European unity in the sense of common economic, military and legal policies, but member states retain their individuality and cultural diversity. The same is true of European Jewry – or more accurately, *Jewries*. Those who define themselves as Jewish in modern Europe cover the spectrum from Chasidic to secular, from ultra-observant to devoutly humanist, with many gradations of belief, practice and political affiliation in between. It is a varied and pluralist population, and its strength lies in its diversity.

**David J. Goldberg**
Born in London in 1940. Senior Rabbi of the Liberal Jewish Synagogue in London. Publications include: *To the Promised Land: A History of Zionist Thought.*

Yaşar Nuri Öztürk

# Islam in Europe: Confrontation or Embrace?

## A few initial facts

Proper consideration of Islam in its relationship with other cultures and civilisations, but in particular with Europe, demands first of all an unambiguous definition of what we mean by Islam. When we talk about it – even among Muslims – we think on the one hand of 'traditional Islam', which is based on the ethics and customs of the Near East, and on the other of the 'true Islam', brought to us by the Koran and proclaimed by the Prophet Mohammed. This distinction, first made by the famous scholar Ibn Taymiyya (d. 728 H./AD 1327) and continually affirmed by contemporary reform-oriented scholars, defines the 'two Islams' as follows: the former is the traditional, invented, or also false Islam; the latter is the true revealed religion, the true Islam.

Europe – or to put it more generally, the West – needs to be clear which of the two it means when it uses the term. That is the only way to escape the chaos that characterises the concept of Islam. It is also the only way that we can avoid causing great damage and paying a high price on our path to long-term brotherly coexistence, even if we apparently achieve 'positive' results in terms of short-term political calculations.

Regrettably, the West has, until today or at least until the horrific terrorist attack on September 11th, only had its short-term political calculations in view, and profited from a conceptual chaos that Muslims themselves find lamentable. Whether we will be able to speak of coexistence that is consensual, commensurate with human dignity and beneficial to the future of humanity in the relationship between the West and Islam will also depend on whether the West is prepared, when dealing with Islam, to make far clearer distinctions and to abandon policies that simply seek to profit from this conceptual confusion.

The number of Muslims in Europe has now reached the equivalent of the populations of two or three European countries. In total, fifteen million Muslims are living in Western Europe; in France alone, there are more than five million and in Germany more than three million. In order to avoid this great religious and energy potential being regarded as a problem by either the Muslims or the Europeans, the true face of Islam must be revealed. If this does not happen, traditional Islam, which uses this potential for religious purposes, will cause great problems for Europe because the character of traditional Islam does not have a positive attitude to integration, consensus and assimilation. Traditional Islam would thus radically contradict its nature, its rules and its basic assumptions.

On the other hand, the centuries of Western colonial rule and the despotic repression connected with it have intensified the resistance and hatred of the Islamic peoples. The need to 'settle scores with the West' is therefore very strong. This cannot be defused by using political slogans, or with strategies that regard stirring nations up against each other and letting them fight it out among themselves as a solution. The Islamic population which is dispersed in various different European regions and is at the moment split into rival factions would see through this game sooner or later and would eventually seek and achieve the necessary unity. It is a false conclusion to think that this unity could be permanently hindered by a cleverly implemented policy of divide and rule.

In short, the West has no option but to recognise the true face of Islam. Both for the sake of human rights and human dignity as well as for the long-term peace and well-being of Europe, the true Islam must be functionally deployed.

The strategy of creating terminologically different, regionally limited versions of Islam, for example a 'European Islam', would in the long run be deceptive and would lead to results quite different from those expected. An 'artificial Islam' of this kind would not be respected by either traditional Islam or Koranic Islam with its more modern attitudes. A 'product' like this would lead Muslims to believe that outsiders were making an effort to degenerate their religion and mould it for their own purposes and profit. This would lead to insecurity and defensive attitudes.

Let us put it still more clearly: if we speak of Islam, and mean by that the traditional, invented Islam, we will be presented with a type of 'Muslim' who is not ready to reach any compromises with the age we live in, with civilisation or with people of other beliefs. This type will always emphatically give rise to conflict, problems and chaos, because such characteristics are part of the nature of the traditional religion that is deaf to the message of the Koran. This kind of Muslim cannot live in peace with the world or with his co-religionists. If he is not even able to do so with the descendants of his own Prophet, it would be utterly wrong to assume that he can do so with other people.

This traditional Islam is very useful for Western ways of seeing things which give precedence to confrontation, for example in Huntington's concept of the 'clash of civilisations'. This is because traditional Islam, as crystallised in traditional Islamic jurisprudence, divides the world into two blocks – which once again confirms Huntington's thesis and the understanding of the world that underlies it – by means of a falsification that can in no way be reconciled with the

Koran: that is, *dar al-islam* and *dar al-harb*. By *dar al-harb* they understand all religions that lie outside traditional Islam. These are regarded as a battlefield on which the fight must be carried on. The people there are the 'others', who deserve every kind of violence, pressure and intimidation, including death, until they bow to the commands of traditional Islam. According to traditional Islam, this war against the 'others' contains the essence of their religion.

This conception of religion results from the fact that the policies of the Umayyads were declared to be a religion. The Umayyad dynasty made use of Islam to found and consolidate their Arabic rule, and in so doing, did not even shrink from killing the descendants of the Prophet. The classical law handbooks, as found in traditional Islam, are full of texts in which the commandments of this 'religion of power' are declared to be the norm.

In the Koran and the teaching of the Prophet Mohammed (i.e. in Koranic Islam) the world is not divided into *dar al-islam* and *dar al-harb*. The whole world belongs to God, and it is the right of peace-loving, just people who are prepared to share with others to benefit from the blessings of this world (cf. Koran, sura 21, v. 105). Traditional Islam, which does not accept the Koranic teaching, not only makes war on the 'others', but also fills the lives of its own adherents with conflict and violence. Traditional Islam, the false Islam, is not a religion for, but against humankind. The basic concept of traditional Islam is that 'humankind is created for religion' while in the Islam of the Koran, 'religion is created for humankind'.

## Food for thought

A few examples will be enough to demonstrate how traditional Islam steers the life of Muslims in a particular direction. This will make it clear that many of its commandments and the duties it imposes are not in accordance with the Koran.

True Islam addresses the 'human being', irrespective of skin colour, gender, origin, region, time, place, social status, dress, wealth or poverty. These human beings are pure and free from the moment of birth. They are chosen by God and loved by Him. To possess these qualities does not require the mediation of any other person; they have been given to them from the beginning of eternity. The human being has a direct relationship with God, he can celebrate his divine service and think about God in any place and in any language he knows without any mediator or guide.

Traditional Islam, in contrast, links humankind's relationship with God to a series of rules and laws. Thus it elevates the idea that divine service and thinking about God can only be celebrated in Arabic into an irrevocable commandment of their religion. The attitude of traditional Islam is that the prayers of people who do not celebrate their services in Arabic are invalid.

Traditional Islam is far from treating human rights with respect. It has no scruples about oppressing people, instead it undertakes this as a service to God. For this reason the International Declaration of Human Rights was not signed by any of the countries ruled by traditional Islam.

True Islam does not grant anyone the right to be a deputy or representative of God. Only the Prophets have the right to speak and lead in the name of God, but the age of the Prophets is over. The legitimate right to lead a group of people can only be given by the group that is to be led. The right to lead a people cannot be God-given or an accident of birth, but must be obtained from that people, and by their free choice. The Koran calls this *bay'at* (social contract). The right to lead a people obtained through *bay'at* is then exercised through the system of counsel, consultation and control known as *shura*. This system ensures that the leaders keep an eye on those who are being led, as well as vice versa. By the *shura* the people, who watch over the rulers, can remove their right to rule if they think it necessary. This is what we today call democracy.

True Islam therefore accepts laicism. We should not regard laicism as a division between religion and state which is there to defend the state from religious influence, but as a means of binding the rulers and governors to the legitimation which they have received from the people and not from God. Otherwise religion becomes an instrument of political power, because the concept of the division between religion and state stands in contradiction to the commandments of creation and the reality of the Koran and humankind. The attitude that sees the right to rule as being legitimised by God contradicts these commandments.

The Koran in no way speaks out against secularisation. It says to its own believers: 'Our Lord, grant us good in this world good in the hereafter' (sura 2, v. 201). The basic commandment is formulated as follows in the Koran: 'And seek by means of what Allah has given you the future abode, and do not neglect your portion of this world' (sura 28, v. 77). The aim of the Koran is to prevent the exclusion of the spiritual realm which is concerned with the hereafter. Its aim is not to ensure that earthly good deeds and the physical material sphere are excluded. The unifying commandment that the Koran takes as its basis is aimed at uniting the spiritual, transcendental sphere with the physical, material sphere.

In fact, in true Islam the nodal point of the question of secularisation (or laicism) is in whose name power is exercised. On this point, traditional Islam stands in complete contradiction to the religion of the Koran. In traditional Islam's understanding of power, legitimation is God-given and lasts for life. This is the monarchic system. In the Koran it is presented as an inadequate and unjust system (cf. sura 27, v. 34). Regrettably, the commandments of traditional Islam about monarchy, sheikdom and sultanate have delivered the Islamic world into the clutches of despotism for centuries. These despotic powers have excised true Islam's admonition not to behave 'like a herd of cattle' from the consciousness of the people and condemned them to backwardness. The bitterest and most repressive consequence of this backwardness can be seen in the fact that human rights are not respected in Islamic regions.

Traditional Islam, which was formed by proclaiming Near Eastern moral values and customs to be a religion, provides that those who lapse from the Islamic faith and adopt another religion should be killed, their possessions plundered and their wives enslaved. In the view of the true, Koranic Islam, anyone who changes his faith has to answer to God alone. No one else should interfere in such a matter.

Traditional Islam regards it as a religious commandment to exert pressure on all humankind, Muslims and non-Muslims, in different ways. In true Islam, however, no pressure or violence may be exerted on any person, for the Koran says quite clearly: 'There is no compulsion in religion' (sura 2, v. 256). True Islam grants human beings the freedom to go to Hell in their own way. Traditional Islam does not even grant them the freedom to enter Paradise.

In traditional Islam, animals which have been slaughtered by non-Muslims are regarded as ritually impure (*haram*) and may not be eaten. In true Islam, meat and all food which has been prepared by people who believe in God are regarded as ritually pure (*helal*) and may be eaten.

Traditional Islam does not allow Muslim women to marry Christians or Jews. In true Islam, Muslim women and men are only forbidden to marry polytheists.

Traditional Islam understands the commandment to unity to mean that all humankind should gather around it and join it, that all humankind should be united under its commandments and rules. True Islam proceeds from the idea that the will of the Creator has not created a monotone and monolithic world, and that the different forms of the evolution of life and human beings have all come into being in the same way. The commandment to unity in true Islam consists in the formula 'unity in diversity', and so it is a democratic unity. For God's commandment to unity to produce happiness and good requires this unity in diversity.

Following this principle, the character of true Islam is unifying and seeks dialogue. In Koranic Islam we find what is probably the first and most lasting call to dialogue between the religions:

> Say: O followers of the Book! come to an equitable agreement between us and you that we shall not serve any but Allah and (that) we shall not associate with any but with Him, and (that) some of us shall not take others for lords besides Allah; but if they turn their backs, then say: Bear witness that we are Muslims (sura 3, v. 64).

True Islam sees humankind as a unity, as a whole, and holds the view that the achievements that have been made since the very first day and our heritage must be treated with consideration and respect. It respects the creators of the religious, intellectual, historical and scientific heritage, and does not allow any egoism or claims to monopoly in terms of history, culture, science and spiritual life. Traditional Islam behaves in completely the opposite way. Instead of respecting humanity's common heritage, it deifies the achievements of its history and its region. It denies the existence of the 'other' creators of this common heritage, refuses them any respect and exposes them to threats and hostility.

True Islam promises all people of good will who make the effort the way to eternal life and entry into Paradise. To achieve eternal life, different peoples' regional and cultural commandments and rules are not compulsory. True Islam does not use its name 'Islam' to describe a group of people. Rather, it regards this word as a common descriptor for all the human beings who, from the beginnings of humankind down to the present day, have accepted the will of God.

True Islam sets only three conditions for achieving eternal life. First, belief in God's creation. This belief is reduced to a feeling that all human beings whose natural disposition has not been corrupted can feel in their consciences. It is very broadly defined and consists in the acceptance that a creative power exists. Any human being who senses an inner connection between his soul and creation already fulfils this first requirement. The Koran speaks of *fitrat* at this point, which is the natural disposition of humankind. According to the Koran, true belief consists on a clear conscience deriving from this *fitrat*.

The second condition is the belief in a continuation of life, i.e. that the human soul continues to exist after death. And finally a recognition that human beings should do their bit for peace, the good, the beautiful and the happiness of all. Anyone who fulfils these three conditions is ensured of eternal life; he will receive God's mercy and blessing. Traditional Islam, on the other hand, makes eternal life dependent on hundreds of conditions, most of which it has invented itself. It condemns all 'other' religions and their adherents to Hell.

Traditional Islam has developed a discipline which aims at being even more religious, even more dismissive of the adherents of other religions and behaving even more harshly. The position in true Islam is completely the opposite. True Islam desires that 'human nearness' (in the words of the Koran, neighbourliness) should dominate in human life, something that stands over and above religions, philosophies, skin colour, regions and social status. True Islam opens the door of 'neighbourliness and unity' to everyone, even to the polytheists, the group it most criticises, and commands Muslims to extend this neighbourliness and unity still further:

> And if one of the idolaters (polytheists) seek protection from you, grant him protection till he hears the word of Allah, then make him attain his place of safety; this is because they are a people who do not know' (sura 9, v. 6).
> Allah does not forbid you respecting those who have not made war against you on account of (your) religion, and have not driven you forth from your homes, that you show

them kindness and deal with them justly; surely Allah loves the doers of justice.
Allah only forbids you respecting those who made war upon you on account of (your) religion, and drove you forth from your homes and backed up (others) in your expulsion, that you make friends with them, and whoever makes friends with them, these are the unjust (sura 60, vv. 8–9).

True Islam allows war only when there is painful oppression and bloody attacks on religion and human rights. If this happens, the war should serve to protect people's livelihoods and rights (cf. sura 4, v. 75 and sura 22, vv. 39–40). Traditional Islam, on the other hand, does not shrink from waging war to conquer a country, to plunder people's goods and possessions and to change other people's beliefs by force. Even worse, it actually declares such a war to be a holy war.

True Islam therefore strives for a relationship, a closeness between God and humankind and between human beings, based on a foundation of justice, mutual sharing, peace, respect and dialogue. And it wishes this closeness to produce mutually shared values. True Islam points the way in this direction, and emphasises the fact that a happy world can be created only with the following three values: peace with the Creator, peace with nature and peace with our fellow human beings.

## What can we expect?

If by 'Islam' we mean traditional Islam, and this gains the upper hand, the attitude of the Muslims to the West will take a terrible form. It is not excessively pessimistic to think of a relationship that is painful, characterised by conflict and perhaps even bloody. One of the characteristic features of this relationship will be that violence and terror will become part of everyday life. Regrettably, the nature of the false Islam and the system of law that produced this (the French scholar Roger Garaudy describes it as a 'legal system for the desert') are of such a nature that they produce violence. The law of the desert (that is, the legal system which traditional Islam declares inviolable) does not use religion as an institution of love and peace that embraces the whole of humanity, but as a political ideology. The gift of traditional Islam to our century is the disease of a 'political Islam' which is destroying true Islam.

It would be wishful thinking to expect anything but conflict, rancour and disagreement from the inviolable legal system of traditional Islam, with its tendency to violence. But it would be even more wishful thinking for the West to place its hopes in a 'moderate Islam' invented by the West as an occasional refuge or which it uses for a certain time as a means to its short-term ends. Even if a moderate Islam grows out of the invented traditional Islam like a kind of 'test-tube Islam', and even if it then sits quietly and well-behaved in a corner for a while, sooner or later it will cause great problems to the West and Muslims alike. On this point, too, the West is fooling itself: its calculations are simply false.

The dream of a moderate Islam will end as a nightmare for the West. I believe that this dream should be replaced by 'revealed Islam', that is, true Islam, so that peace can be preserved both among Muslims and in the West. If this happens, then Muslim scholars, societies and even whole countries can benefit from the achievements and experience of the true Islam.

In this respect, Turkey represents a major opportunity. Anyone who talks about a successful union of the West and Islam and a promising mutual future will, sooner or later, come to Mustafa Kemal Atatürk, the founder of modern Turkey, and his heritage which has, unfortunately, not been properly appreciated. Both the deceived Islamic world and the West, which wishes to keep this world at arm's length from civilisation because this is apparently necessary for its policies, will suffer from serious pangs of conscience when they realise that their negative attitude to Atatürk's heritage has been unjust and wrong.

The West cannot ring in a new age of continuity and happiness if it disregards the powerful religious and structural energy of Islam, and continues to represent Islam as unattractive, excludes it, or if it stirs Muslims up against one another. The West will not be able to see any light on the horizon of a world characterised by conflict when looked at through the lens of Samuel P. Huntington. Instead the West must get to know the true Islam, interest itself in it and make friends with it. The West must also expend some energy to ensure that Muslims are united with this true Islam. It seems probable that fate is compelling the West to expend at least some of the energy that it has so long used to depict Islam as unattractive to present the truth of Islam. The West must recognise this fact. If this does not happen, then the achievements of the false Islam which the West supported for so long will cause it great difficulties. But then the West would not have the right to complain about these developments.

We believe in the following: the true Islam, the Islam of the Koran (which regards not just Moses and Jesus, not just Judaism and Christianity, as holy and values them) will not have any negative effects on the West either today or in the future. The negative things come not from the true, but from the traditional, false Islam. Do we therefore wish to get to know the true Islam, whose name and foundation is peace, or do we prefer to fight against the false Islam, which was wrenched away from its original name and its foundations to become a source of violence and hate?

What do we want? Do we want a religious ideology which provides fodder for Huntington's theory of violence and confrontation, or do we want a fraternal, friendly religion which brings the peaceful and unifying principles of Moses, Jesus and Mohammed into people's lives?

*Translator's note*
We have not used scientific phonetic transcriptions. Well-known concepts and names such as Koran, sura or Mohammed are given in their English spellings. The death date of the historical personality mentioned in the text is given first in its Islamic (H for Hegira), and then its Christian form.

The translations from the Koran are based on the electronic text provided by the University of Virginia (URL: http://etext.lib.virginia.edu/koran.html).

We use the term Umayyad to refer to the dynasty of 14 Caliphs which ruled from AD 661 to 749 and made the office of Caliph hereditary.

**Yaşar Nuri Öztürk**
Born in Bayburt, Turkey, 1945. Dean of the Faculty of Theology at the University of Istanbul. A leading contemporary theologian in Turkey. Publications include: *Islam in the Qur'an; Islam in 400 Questions; On Understanding the Qur'an.*

# Implementing Visions

*Gone are the days of post-war European complacency. A rapidly changing world is shaking up the Continent (EU and beyond) and presenting it with unwelcome challenges. The end of history may not be at hand, but the era of nation-states may well be. The enemy is at the door and the time for platitudes is over – Europe has to deliver. Will it become the cosmopolitan superstate that it pays lip service to, or will it disintegrate into bickering provincial fiefdoms? The opportunity to become a radically open society is as close as it ever has been – can Europe seize it?*

William Wallace

# Organised Europe: its Regional and Global Responsibilities

The institutional framework of Europe is no longer unresolved. 'Europe' – the European region defined in political, economic and security terms – is shaped by two interlinked international institutions: the European Union and NATO. With the acceptance of ten new members at the Copenhagen European Council in December 2002, the EU outgrew its origins as a Western European construction, built around the transformation of the Franco-German relationship and the containment of Germany within a supranational framework. NATO, similarly, has now outgrown its original design as the Cold War security alliance for Western Europe against the threat of Soviet expansion, to become a pan-European body with a close relationship with Russia and institutionalised partnerships stretching across Eurasia to the Chinese border.

Membership of these integrated organisations is not identical, but the overlap is extensive. NATO's three non-EU European member states – Norway, Iceland and Turkey – are closely associated with the EU, with Turkey now accepted as a candidate for future EU membership, and with Iceland and Norway associated with the EU not only within the European Economic Area but also within the Schengen common travel area. The EU's four non-NATO member states are all associated with NATO in the Partnership for Peace; all have contributed troops to peacekeeping operations in south-eastern Europe within the NATO framework. Eight of the ten states invited to join the EU in December 2002 had already been invited to join NATO; eight of the ten states invited to join NATO since 1997 were now joining the EU.

Yet European institutions, and the member states that constitute them, remain confused and incoherent about how far this 25-state entity needs to take responsibility for the stability and prosperity of its dependent neighbours, let alone to shoulder wider responsibilities for global order and economic strategy. European integration, institutionalised through the European Economic Community (now the EU) has been essentially inward-looking throughout its forty-five years of operation so far. Its greatest success has been the creation of a highly integrated internal market, now complemented by an integrated travel area with shared rights of residence, work and study for citizens of member states. NATO has managed European security, under American leadership and through American military predominance. The United States has also led on managing threats to global order outside Europe, in the Middle East and Asia, with its European allies providing limited support. Thirty years of cooperation among EU foreign ministries – first within the framework of European Political Cooperation, and since 1992 within the more ambitiously titled Common Foreign and Security Policy – have made little impact on these established patterns. Nor, yet, have four years of negotiations on European security and defence policy, the shape and content of which remain unclear.

The European Commission, it is true, has pursued a 'civilian' foreign policy, creating a complex network of economic association agreements: with former European colonies, with states around the southern shores of the Mediterranean, even with Canada and Latin American states. On international trade negotiations the EEC and its Commission rapidly emerged as a major player, bargaining with the US through successive GATT rounds, often to the exclusion and at the expense of the states with which it had so carefully negotiated its own association agreements. Collectively and separately, the EU and its member states provide a larger share of development assistance than the US and Japan together; though there is little effective coordination between the EU and national contributions, and much discontent within national capitals at the structural inefficiencies of the EC's distribution of aid to Third World countries.

The EU's most effective instrument of external policy, particularly since the end of the Cold War, has been the promise of future membership subject to applicants satisfying a range of political, economic and administrative conditions. 'Conditionality', with the Commission regularly reporting on progress within the applicant states towards meeting what became known as the Copenhagen Criteria, has pushed forward the transformation of the former socialist states of Central and Eastern Europe into democratic market societies. The promise of eventual entry, and the incentives of transitional technical and financial assistance, have been key elements in this successful strategy. With the completion of the current round of enlargement, however, the question of how much further the process of expansion can go must be faced. If the promise of enlargement is a necessary element in managing relations with the EU's neighbours – as negotiations with Turkey since 1997 have clearly indicated – then institutionalised Europe may gradually expand until it contains the whole of its eastern and southern peripheries. If enlargement is not to extend across Eastern Europe, around the Black Sea and the Mediterranean, then the EU now needs a coherent policy towards the many states around the edge of Europe: all of them dependent on access to the EU's internal market for their hopes of prosperity, all of them linked to the EU by flows of labour and of remittances, of investment and of tourism.

## Managing the neighbours

The strongest arguments for EU and NATO enlargement across Central and Eastern Europe after the demolition of the Berlin Wall came not from ideals of democracy or historical obligation, but from self-interest. The Iron Curtain, after all, had represented Western Europe's most secure frontier. Once the barriers had been torn down and the troops withdrawn, the EU's comfortable societies discovered that the only way to avoid importing disorder from Eastern Europe was to export security and prosperity. Transnational criminal networks, minorities seeking a better life through migration, asylum seekers from further east, sufficiently discomfited Western Europe for the public to give reluctant assent to the principle of enlargement. Nevertheless, there has remained throughout the 1990s an awkward gap between the rhetorical commitments which the EU and its member governments have made to hopeful applicants and the unwillingness of governments or established interests to adjust. Neither through the EU nor through NATO were Western governments willing to contemplate large-scale financial assistance to these countries in transition in any way comparable to the economic and military assistance they had received from the US to help them through their own painful transition in the ten years after 1945. The terms of entry offered in December 2002 to Poland, the largest of the applicant states, were much less generous than those from which current member states already benefit. Hard bargaining to defend established interests triumphed over any strategic view of long-term advantages.

Even before the success of this ambitious round of enlargement is assured, however, the EU must engage with others hopeful that they may follow. The offer of NATO membership to Romania and Bulgaria was, among other factors, intended as a signal that these still weak and insecure states will become full members of institutionalised Europe as soon as economic reconstruction and administrative reform allow; their governments hope to join the EU within the next five to six years. Croatia, now recovering from the political and economic devastation of the post-Yugoslav conflict, is confident that it will accompany them. Without the full understanding of Western European parliaments or publics, Western governments – through the Stability Pact for South Eastern Europe – have also effectively promised the remaining states of the former Yugoslavia eventual inclusion, and Albania as well. This represents a significant political and financial commitment, over perhaps fifteen or twenty years, before Serbia, Montenegro (Kosovo in one form or another), Bosnia, Macedonia and Albania, all take their places round NATO and EU tables. Then there is Turkey, already a long-standing member of NATO – with an elite determined to gain full membership of the EU and a public which has scarcely begun to understand the implications of doing so – to which EU member governments have now made a firm commitment, without persuading their publics of the rationale for admitting such a large state so far to the east.

Beyond these, institutionalised Europe is surrounded by a circle of uncertain states with which it shares boundaries that are hard to police. Relations with Russia have attracted most attention because Russia is unavoidably important – in security terms and as a key source of European energy supplies. NATO has in many ways moved furthest to accommodate Russian status and interests. The new NATO-Russia Council has granted a privileged association, which so far appears to satisfy both sides. The EU, in contrast, has so far only a range of limited initiatives towards Russia rather than any well-articulated strategy for future partnership. But Russia, at least, has been enjoying rapid economic growth, reinforced by greater political stability, in recent years. The three 'orphan' states of the Western Soviet Union, Belarus, Ukraine and Moldova, by contrast, are entangled in political and economic corruption – pools of poverty and instability along

Europe's eastern borders, threatening to spill over if conditions deteriorate further. NATO and the EU need here to coordinate responses with Russia, even though Western interests and those of Russia do not always coincide. But there appears to be little interest in Western European capitals in any further active engagement with these failing states, with all the political, financial and potentially military implications to which this might lead.

Then there is Europe's Mediterranean south, most of it colonised by European states a hundred years ago, most of it heavily dependent on European markets for exports, on European tourists and on remittances from migrant workers within the EU for foreign currency earnings. Both NATO and the EU have launched their own 'Mediterranean' strategies; neither have so far made much progress. The ambiguous presence of Israel within both, as one of the Mediterranean 'partners', inhibits the building of mutual trust. Resistance by EU Mediterranean states to opening trade barriers to North African agriculture and textiles, resistance by North African states in their turn to the EU's 'neo-colonial' efforts to impose political conditions on economic assistance, breed resentment and slow reform.

Acceptance of Turkey as a candidate for EU membership has encouraged the Moroccan government to hope to raise the long-term prospect of accession, at least as a bargaining counter in transforming its unhappy dependence on its northern neighbours. Think-tanks within Israel are discussing whether EU membership could provide an 'anchor' for Israel in any move towards a two-state settlement of their conflict with the Palestinians. Until political conditions deteriorated within Ukraine in 2002, American diplomats had encouraged its government to think of joining the EU and NATO as a strategic objective; if a different regime emerged in Belarus, there would probably be a similar call for reassurance through acceptance as a future NATO and EU member. Even in Georgia, reformers have called on their government to declare that incorporation within institutionalised Europe is their long-term goal, as providing a road map for reform and an incentive for economic assistance. The process of enlargement might thus roll slowly on, further east and further south, unless Western European governments can develop their own strategy for partnership as an alternative.

Completion of the current round of enlargement thus makes a common foreign policy towards the states of Europe's wider periphery far more urgent. Peacekeeping and policing, the 'Petersberg tasks' of European defence integration, may play a role – for example in helping to stabilise the Caucasus. But the familiar civilian instruments of EU external relations, used much more generously than in recent years, are most required: openness to trade in sensitive sectors (food, textiles, labour-intensive manufactures) with non-member states, substantial financial transfers, acceptance of migrant labour, and institutions for political dialogue.

## Stabilising the south

It is difficult for governments preoccupied with the complexities of multilateral bargaining to pay sufficient attention to those outside. Much of the discussion on European defence cooperation in European capitals, until the events of September 2001, did not allow for deployment further than the Balkans. Eighteen months later, a German-Dutch command is taking over the largely European International Stabilization Assistance Force in Kabul from the Turks (and, before them, the British), while Spanish, British, French and German frigates patrol the Arabian Sea and the Persian Gulf. Western European governments still hesitate, however, to make a sustained commitment to promoting order, reconstructing states, and economic and social development in Africa and Asia. The post-colonial pattern of association with the group of 'African, Caribbean and Pacific' states has almost exhausted its usefulness, caught in the same clash of interests over agriculture and labour-intensive manufactures that has blighted the Mediterranean dialogue. Apart from France and Britain, there has been firm resistance across Western Europe to more active intervention in resisting the rising tide of disorder in Africa south of the Sahara.

Yet comfortable Europe cannot insulate itself from disorder to its south. When countries collapse into conflict, when regimes are violently overthrown, the desperate and determined reach Berlin and Paris, London and Rome, however hard the border controls erected to deter them. When epidemics sweep across Africa, or new strains of disease emerge in disintegrating societies, they are quickly carried through European airports. When the discontented conspire against authoritarian governments their terrorist acts spill over into Europe. Rapid population growth, compounded by poverty and by political and economic failure, will continue to push young people towards the rich world to their north. European publics demand that their governments control and limit the incoming tide of migrants from the south; but have not yet accepted that this tide can only be managed by strengthening the states and the economies from which these migrants come, and by investing more heavily in the promotion of education and social development.

## Transatlantic partners or reluctant followers of American leadership?

Western European integration developed within a wider Atlantic framework. NATO allowed EU member governments to avoid the hard choices of security and defence policy, and to avoid developing an international strategy towards regions outside Europe. On East-West relations and on the Middle East, the US reserved strategic decisions for Washington, and expressed sharp displeasure at any autonomous European initiatives. Since the end of the Cold War, however, the European region has ceased to be a priority for US foreign policy, while successive administrations have called on their European allies to take up a broader share of the burden of maintaining global order and managing the global economy. Successive European governments have been unable to agree on what response to make; European discontent with American pursuit of its own interests, wrapped in the rhetoric of global order, has not been matched by either a move towards greater autonomy or an attempt to build a more balanced transatlantic partnership. The Middle East has long been a particular source of difficulties in US-European relations; divergent perceptions and interests provide ample opportunity for misunderstanding and dispute.

Further enlargement will make it even more difficult for institutionalised Europe to remain a junior partner under American leadership. EU-25 will form a potentially influential group within global institutions; numerical European dominance within NATO will sharpen the contradictions of continuing subservience to an American-led agenda. The EU is now the world's largest single market, its economic dynamism or stagnation a major factor in the global economy. It has the world's second reserve currency. Even though its member governments are falling further behind the US, their combined expenditure on defence ranks well above that of China, Russia and Japan. American officials and Congressmen rightly consider themselves entitled to demand that European governments take a more active part in political, security and economic issues beyond the borders of their own region.

In the short term, it is easier for Western European governments to pursue their individual special relationships with the US than to negotiate the delicate transition to a more balanced transatlantic partnership. In the long term, however, the current imbalances of power and influence between the two sides of the Atlantic are unlikely to be sustainable given the underlying resentments these breed on both sides. The most difficult, but also the most important, task for collective Europe after the successful completion of the coming NATO and EU enlargements will be to define a common strategy towards its most important external partners, and to develop the instruments to put that strategy into practice.

## Institutional capabilities, political imagination

The idea of a common European foreign policy has been sceptically described by one participant as designed to create 'a single voice, but silent; a single chair, but empty'. European governments have found it easier to set up new institutional mechanisms than to agree on common policies, let alone to shoulder the implications of implementing what has been agreed. More than ten years after the Treaty of European Union declared that 'a Common Foreign and Security Policy is hereby established', and more than four years after France and Britain launched their initiative to integrate European defence, the scope for common action remains limited – and the resources available are even more limited.

The European Convention in 2002–3 struggled with further institutional reform; to strengthen the role of the High Representative for CFSP and to remove the discontinuities inherent in a six-monthly Council Presidency. Institutional reform on its own, however, without the political commitment from national governments – which can only come from informed national debates that link into shared European concepts – can provide only a stronger shadow, rather than substantial common policy. What is absent, both in domestic debates about foreign policy priorities and in contributions by national political leaders to the European debate, is any sense that the larger Europe now emerging must shoulder a larger role in the world: must seek a different, more equal, partnership with the US; must pay more attention to economic needs and political crises in other continents; must devote more of its scarce resources to the economic development of its neighbours and the underdeveloped south, and more also to the equipment needed to deploy military forces for peacekeeping and peace enforcement outside its own region.

There is a risk in member states committing themselves to common policies: their governments and parliaments may assume that they thus transfer responsibility for difficult decisions from national capitals to Brussels. Smaller states may make the assumption that any particular contribution they might make is scarcely significant in global terms; larger states may feel that they stand to gain more by acting alone rather than cooperating closely with their partners. For these reasons and others, collective Europe has underperformed in shouldering its regional and global responsibilities since the end of the Cold War. Extension of its boundaries to incorporate much of former socialist Eastern Europe, to bring in a further 100 million citizens organised into ten new member states, with the EU surrounding the Baltic and NATO extending further around the Black Sea, and above all, with an unstable south and a conflict-ridden Middle East – this wider institutionalised Europe can no longer afford this underperformance. It is the task of political leadership, not only at the European level but also within larger and smaller member states, to redefine the agenda of European foreign policy to meet these wider responsibilities.

**Lord William Wallace**
Born in Leicester, England, 1941. Professor of International Relations and Political Science at the London School of Economics. Spokesman for foreign affairs for the Liberal Democrats in the British House of Lords since 2001.

Ralf Dahrendorf

# Workaday Europe, Soapbox Europe: Who Will Close the Gap?

The European Union has many problems to deal with – some of them small and some of them not so small – but one big problem hangs over it like the sword of Damocles because on it hinges the issue of whether the Union will continue to exist in the long term or whether it will, after all, lose its strength. That problem can be posed as a question: who will close the gap between the great soapbox speeches about Europe's future and the petty realities of workaday Europe?

Anyone who has ever worked in European institutions is well aware of the contradiction. This is true most of all for the members of the European Parliament. In order to get elected, they speak to the public about war and peace and about the need to create a countervailing power to other superpowers – meaning, nowadays, the one big superpower. But once they are elected, they spend most of their time harmonising guidelines for the noise made by construction machinery, for example, while all talk of global politics fades into the background.

The new candidates for accession to the EU in particular are acutely aware of this gap. The post-Communist countries currently in the process of joining the EU have long dreamt of returning to the European fold. For them, this meant finding their way into a community committed to values they have felt drawn towards for a long time. The negotiations over accession, however, brought them up against quite different experiences. The old members forced them to accept all manner of expensive regulations. It was once the negotiations were over that the haggling over money began. On this occasion, this was such a 'success' that the new – and poor – members ended up being net contributors and were only able to get themselves into a break-even situation by engaging in budgetary contortions. The embarrassment felt by leading politicians from the candidate countries – who experienced all this and then had to go and sell the EU to their voters – was palpable.

People in the old member countries of the EU have long been used to this kind of thing. While many of them may only half listen when some head of government or foreign minister unfurls a dazzling vision of Europe's future, nonetheless most of them, to a certain extent, have internalised this kind of thinking sufficiently not to respond by saying: 'Just a moment, Mr President/Minister, how does that square with the subsidising of tobacco growing from taxation?' These, meanwhile, are quite happy harping on about their visions while showing a superior disinterest in the real Europe.

But it is important to avoid making an error here: the examples of construction machinery noise and subsidies for tobacco-growing offer what is only an inadequate description of the real Europe. In certain significant ways it really has become a single market, and the value of this sort of single market is not to be underestimated. It certainly represents a huge step forward in terms of mobility compared with the situation in 1945, 1957, or even 1969. At the end of the war, when the European Economic Community was founded until the important summit took place in The Hague in December 1969, Europe was fragmented and presented an obstacle course for anyone wanting to transport people, goods, services or money from one part to another. In a series of courageous decisions and laboriously detailed initiatives, these obstacles were dismantled. First the Common Market and then the European single market came into being.

And there was more to come. In addition to the single market, a habit of working together has developed in a range of important policy areas, something that nowadays is called into question by only a few people. This occurs in certain areas of domestic policy, particularly in relation to issues of immigration and combating crime, and is also the case in issues of foreign and security policy. Outside these core areas, regular meetings between ministers and officials have become commonplace.

But the habit of working together should not be overestimated. Intergovernmental cooperation is all well and good, but it does not make a superpower. The truth is that there is no common foreign and security policy in the EU; nor, as far as one can see, will there be one. The issue of seats on the UN Security Council says it all: the allocation of a single seat for Europe with the right of veto must be ruled out. Moreover, policy on Iraq is only the latest example of how the European countries put their own national interests to the fore when things get serious. The Falklands war, France's involvement in Africa, and indeed German reunification are all examples of the same phenomenon, albeit especially visible ones.

Another fact should not be forgotten either. The EU has set an upper limit of 1.27 percent of its gross domestic product to finance its expenditure. This limit has not been reached, nor do the major member states intend that it should be reached in the foreseeable future. In the states themselves, however, governments are responsible for 40 percent or more of their GDP. It might be something of an exaggeration to say that each individual state is therefore 40 times as important as the EU, but the size of the difference should not be forgotten.

The fine words that spill so easily from some people's lips

when they are talking about the future of Europe need to be measured against facts such as these. In his draft of a European constitutional treaty, Giscard d'Estaing helped to nourish the tendency to think in fine words when he suggested a range of alternative names for the political entity of Europe: 'European Community', 'European Union', 'United States of Europe', 'United Europe'. There can be no question of applying any of these – nor should there be, unless the intention of European politicians is to mislead their electorate or, ultimately, themselves. The gap between reality and vision vis-à-vis Europe is huge, and the burning European question is: who will close it? Because if it is not closed, then someday the bubble full of visions will burst and the realities facing Europe will be harmed by its alluring sheen.

Who will close the gap? The personalisation is intended. In the following I will talk about three people, each of whom has made a thoughtful contribution to closing the gap: Walter Hallstein, Valéry Giscard d'Estaing and Jacques Delors.

The first president of the EEC, Walter Hallstein, was well aware of the gap that existed between expectations and European reality. He was not overly worried by it, however, because he had his own theory as to how the gap might be closed – indeed how it would almost necessarily be closed. In a rather delightful way he brought the concept of a 'never failing "situational logic"' into the picture, which he held to be the 'final factor of European unification'. This situational logic is 'an anonymous force', even if it only takes effect 'by means of human will'. The force 'inherent in its workings' can be summed up by the simple formula: 'Whoever says A must also say B.'

In the section of his great work *The European Community* on 'The logic of the situation', Hallstein explains what he means. The Common Market is the first step. (Hallstein knew, of course, that it was not really the first step, but that projects aimed at achieving political union and a defence community had failed before it came along.) But, he continued, where free market rules do not apply and state policies come into play instead, 'there is no other alternative than to bring these policies under one common rule of discipline'. This provides the basis for 'something as fundamentally new, something as revolutionary as a common European agricultural policy'. This in turn demands not only market rules but common prices. Creating a unit of account is but the first step in this; by the end, currency union becomes a necessity. Taxation policy, budgetary policy and economic policy then follow on. It soon becomes clear 'that the psychological chain reaction of integration does not stop at the gates of economic and social policy'. Foreign and defence policy must follow, for 'policy is a single entity'.

While this impressive conceptual scheme is fine in theory, in practice it has some serious weaknesses. One of them is that situational logic occasionally – and by no means seldom – fails. There are many in politics who say A without saying B, let alone getting around to saying E and U. The other weakness is that in the world of situational logic, democracy comes to be dispensable as it were. The referenda on treaties negotiated by governments in Maastricht or Nice do not fit with that scenario. Both weaknesses have a common central feature: the conceptual scheme has no political underpinning. It fails to take the issue of voter legitimation into account. Yet in order to do justice to its proponents' aspirations, the EU must become more political; in other words it must be more willing to take decisions and at the same time become more democratic.

There are certainly sufficient examples of what is needed. If ever there was a stage in the process of European integration that set in train a situational logic, then it was the introduction of the euro in twelve countries of the EU. Not only would the euro – so one assumed – soon become the general

European currency, but it would necessarily lead to the coordination and ultimately the integration of national economic policies. Doubts now attend both of these. Once the enlargement process is completed, only half of the EU's member states will belong to 'Euroland'. The British euro referendum is encountering resistance from parties and voters alike for good reasons that are underestimated on the Continent. And as far as a common economic policy is concerned, national traditions and interests pose considerable obstacles. Every now and again the question is raised as to whether the common currency is the keystone to the internal market or the beginning of a new phase of economic integration.

So situational logic does not work. It exists only in theory; reality follows a logic of its own. We need to find ways other than Hallstein's to close the gap.

Currently the most recent means of bringing Europe from its modest reality closer to the big vision is that of a European constitutional treaty. The method was not exactly invented by President Giscard d'Estaing, but he has made it his own and advocated it with great resolve in the course of consultation over the Convention on the Future of Europe. The basic idea of this approach – at least in the context of the argument developed here – is that the creation of sound institutional structures for political action will guarantee that Europe will find a way towards the union it desires.

We do not want to argue endlessly over concepts here, but what exactly is a constitution? The fact that even the scholars argue over this is almost a source of consolation for the rest of us. Some believe 'that the concept of a constitution, beyond the limits of traditional constitutional law, could be suitable for saying something about public organisations' (D. Schefold). Others insist on the difference between a 'treaty' and a 'constitution' (D. Grimm). Treaties can be concluded between states while constitutions exist in relation to a sovereign power. Whether the latter actually exists in the case of Europe – others speak of the *demos* – is open to doubt, however. The EU (according to Grimm) is 'an effective political association without having the quality of a state'.

The difference is important and is muddled in an unfortunate way when people speak of a 'European constitutional treaty'. What is actually at issue is indeed a treaty, even if it serves primarily to establish rules of cooperation. In any case, there still remain two key questions which need to be answered if the gap between expectation and reality in Europe is to be closed using institutional means: does the construct of Europe have identifiable and recognised *finalités politiques,* in other words political objectives (such as 'increasingly closer union')? And what is this construct about?

The answer to these questions cannot be derived from European reality. Indeed, there may be no straightforward, correct answer to them. My answer, at any rate – which is not especially popular in Brussels – is that we simply do not know with any exactitude. Certainly there are no identifiable and recognised *finalités politiques* in Europe, even if some are convinced they know what these should be. We find ourselves in a process that has an uncertain end – it might lead to the United States of Europe, but it might also lead to a re-emphasising of national political life, or indeed to a fragmentation of politics. The direction we actually pursue is a matter for concrete political decision-making – how to handle Iraq, the stability pact, asylum seekers and immigrants – and not about general rules. A constitutional text will not help with these kinds of decisions because it creates the false impression that something has already been achieved which is actually still just an intention – and the intention of a few at that, not of all. In its present state, Europe is a process, not a goal, and it is a process without a definite or defined goal. Because of this it is – as the Polish Prime Minister Miller put it recently – a topic for biology, not geology. It needs to have the conditions for its development to be acknowledged, not for existing structures to be set down in a constitution.

If this sounds too negative, it may help to mention a few formulations offered by Swiss Professor Francis Cheneval. He speaks of the 'paradox' of the EU, which is neither a federation nor a confederation and whose constitutional rules, if indeed they exist, 'are not anchored in a people and do not constitute a people'. Europe 'is an open constitutional process'. For Cheneval, this is by no means a weakness; on the contrary it is a highly original state of affairs because it 'is in keeping with the central cosmopolitan idea of a political community made up of nation-states'. This idea is a reference to Kant, who says that we should act as if cooperation in Europe is right to the extent to which it can be applied to a wider global cosmopolitan community.

The benefit of this idea is that it provides a measure which has both moral as well as constitutional qualities. Of course, this is not a description of the actual EU, which in contrast manifests some of the worst protectionist traits of nation-states. But that is another story. The question here is: whither the Union? And would a constitutional text help it on its way?

There are no clear answers to these questions. Instead of answers, we merely encounter new questions. For example, it is no longer quite so easy to give reasons for why we should actually have an increasingly close union in Europe. In the early days of the EEC, the answer followed on from the Cold War. The 'Russian doll' principle obtained: German-French friendship inside the European Community inside NATO inside the West. The key element at the time was to control German development. But now? The widespread notion that Europe must be in a position to provide a counterpart to the United States of America seems to me to be just as eccentric as the desire to establish a European social model using a constitution. In both cases there is a denial, indeed a violation, of cosmopolitan demands for freedom upheld under all circumstances by the constitution. In spite of all the soapbox speeches and the visions they contain, there are basically no plausible answers to the question of why we need to have an increasingly close Union.

A second set of observations might begin with European reality. Europe exists, so it is said, and it has an identity which must find expression in the form of a constitution. Here, too, we need to ask first whether this is really true. One aspect of European reality which we rightly celebrate and defend is democracy. How is it, then, that we tolerate the deeply undemocratic institutions of the EU? The Pope would like to see Europe's Christian roots anchored in a European constitution. But then what about the many millions of Europeans who do not identify with this tradition? And then again: is there even a European *demos*, a body politic that can support a democratic Union? At this point a question arises that is seldom aired but is nonetheless important. It is frequently said and generally acknowledged that Europe is strong on account of the diversity of its cultures. There is merit in this theory. But is Europe's diversity really compatible with the goal of ever-closer union? Have we not perhaps embarked on a process in the course of which we are destroying our great values by an exaggerated desire for unity?

These are sensitive questions, some of them difficult but all of them important. They will not be answered by a Convention nor by the text of a constitutional treaty. They must, however, be answered if we want to close the gap between vision and reality in Europe.

It is most likely the case, then, that neither the Hallstein route nor the Giscard route will be of much help to us in closing the gap between soapbox Europe and everyday Europe. Neither tackles the actual problem. But what is the way, then? Let me introduce a third name into the discussion, that of Jacques Delors.

Delors represents the last great step forward in the process of European unification. As President of the Commission, he made the goal of the single market a concrete reality and brought about the specific decisions necessary for implementing that goal. This was a thoroughly political process; indeed, Delors's strength lies in not being diverted by visions but instead getting on with mapping the way from A to B and then setting out on it.

Jacques Delors has also played his part towards promoting currency union among the first twelve European countries. This process is by no means completed. The stability pact that is a part of it has been called 'stupid' by the Commission President; it certainly is in need of improvement. And in any case it would again be wrong to rely on situational logic to anchor the currency union in economic policy. At this point a new Delors is called for who can clearly point out the necessary steps with political nous and start to take them.

The gap that has been the subject of this piece will not be closed automatically. Nor is it a matter of introducing some set of high-faluting procedural rules. It demands decisive and practical political action in the spirit of Jacques Delors. Such action can only be successful if it represents the common interests of the participating countries. For a long time to come – and possibly forever – it will take place in the constitutional twilight that Francis Cheneval described so vividly. However, one must not allow the other side, the Kantian side of Cheneval's argument, to be ignored. It is not a matter of pursuing visions. It is a matter of remembering that, whatever actions Europe takes, it takes them in anticipation of what might become globally valid rules. If Europe needs any guiding idea, then it is the 'idea of a common history in the interests of a global citizenry'.

**Lord Ralf Dahrendorf**
Born in Hamburg, 1929. Sociologist, Baron of Clare Market in the City of Westminster and member of the British House of Lords since 1993. Director of the London School of Economics from 1974 to 1984. Considered one of the most important representatives of liberal, social and political theory. Publications include: *Reflexions on the Revolution in Europe; Liberals and Others: Portraits; After 1989: Morals, Revolution and Civil Society; Society and Democracy in Germany.*

Ulrich Beck

# Cosmopolitan Europe: A Confederation of States, a Federal State or Something Altogether New?

Imagine for a moment that the European Union wanted to apply for membership of the EU – what would be the response? Its application to join the EU would have to be deferred (as has happened in the case of Turkey) or rejected outright. Why? Quite simply because the EU does not satisfy its own criteria for democracy.

This imaginary scenario goes to the very heart of the reasons why scepticism towards Europe is rife. How is it possible that for the majority of people living in very different countries, the image of the EU hovers somewhere between dutiful celebration and hostility? The EU, it will be remembered, was brought into being precisely in order to liberate Europe from the spell cast by its bellicose history. How, then, could it be that European self-critique, source of inspiration for conservative politicians such as Winston Churchill, Charles de Gaulle and Konrad Adenauer in the aftermath of the horrors of the Second World War and crimes against humanity perpetrated by the Nazi regime, has ended up in the mire of an institutionalised lack of imagination? Will the spectrum of well-meaning indifference through to open, sometimes hateful rejection be sufficient to cope with the predictable breaches and breakdowns to which the project of European transformation exposes itself as it approaches the historic moment of eastwards expansion?

To put the question even more bluntly: is there indeed a reality that deserves the title 'Europe', or is this merely an elite idealised term for an illusion that fails to stand up to critical interrogation? Could it be that the concept of Europe – a concept with the character of an appeal rather than of substance – is in fact a front for the very opposite of all that Europe stands for, namely a departure from democracy, freedom, separation of powers, transparency and political accountability? Is the experiment of a European confederation of states not condemned to failure, just like all the other empires with similar ambitions that have gone before – from the empire of Charles V, of Napoleon and the Austro-Hungarian Empire, to the British Empire, the Soviet Union or, today, the United States? Why, after all, should something that world history has otherwise consigned to the category 'failed' work for the EU?

What the critics fail to see, however, is the *reality* of Europe. Anti-Europeanism is based on a false image of Europe. It is caught up in the contradictions of its member nations' misunderstanding of themselves, a factor that continues to keep Europe captive even today. By way of contrast, I shall sketch out here four steps that introduce the concept of a cosmopolitan Europe, and I shall do this by turning the tables on the critics: nation-based realism is wrong, indeed it is a nation-based illusion that has led all our thinking, acting and researching in and about Europe down a dead end.

*First step*: The EU is not a club with an exclusively Christian membership, nor is it a transcendental community of common descent. The only human and cultural landscape that deserves the label 'European' is one that is non-anthropological, anti-ontological, radically open, that is determined by procedure – in other words is politically pragmatic. The crunch point comes with the question 'Where do you stand on Turkey?', which has become the sixty-four thousand dollar question of European politics. This is the point at which the ways part and the contrasts are ignited between the old, nation-based Europe and a new cosmopolitan Europe.

All of a sudden, a European discourse of origins is on everyone's lips. Those who would keep the Turks out discover that the roots of Europe lie in the Christian heritage, the Christian West: only those who have always been a part of this 'common occidental destiny' belong with 'us'. The others are Europe's *excluded* Others. According to this view of the world, each person has a single homeland, their own; they cannot choose it, it is innate to them and it accords with the geography of nations and the stereotypes built into them.

This kind of awful, wrong-headed and indeed dangerous territorial understanding of culture haunts even the well-meaning notion of cultural dialogue: as if Islam and the West each existed in its own exclusive space and needed to seek dialogue with the other. Where in all this is 'Londistan' – *the* capital city of Islam outside the Islamic world? Where are the Western Muslims, the Arab bourgeoisie, the Oriental Christians, the Israeli Arabs and so on and so forth? Those who would reinvent the Christian West in order to erect barriers around Europe are making Europe into a religion, indeed virtually a race, and are turning the project of European Enlightenment upside down.

This is one way in which the political theory of Carl Schmitt, with his friend-or-foe categories, insinuates its way into the debate around European identity. The idea here is that if you want to hold onto your cultural identity then you have to exclude those who are culturally different from you. And since in the political realm this view emerges not from a critical hermeneutics based on cultural research but is rather a self-fulfilling political prophesy, stereotypes of ethnic-religious belonging are borrowed from the past and cemented *politically* for the future. The term 'cosmopolitan Europe' can be understood as precisely the negation of this sort of territorial social ontology, which would seek to barricade all paths to the future.

For one thing, the term 'cosmopolitan Europe' is empirically significant, as it opens our eyes to the 'entangled modernities' (Shalini Randeria) in which we live: including, for example, the fact that the Turks some want to keep on the outside are already inside and have been for a long time! NATO, trading partnerships, transnational ways of living – Turkey arrived on the European scene a long time ago. And large parts of Turkey have become Europeanised. To those people who live in the capital cities of the Islamic world such as Istanbul, Beirut or Teheran and who belong to the middle classes, the customs and values of an Anatolian villager are no less alien than they would be to a middle-class Parisian or Berliner. And if one wanted to cling to the illusion that clear boundaries could be drawn between the European world and the Muslim world, one would have to attribute a monopoly on 'Europeanness' to the EU and completely ignore the overlapping domains of identity constituted by Europe, the Atlantic community and NATO. To allow a principle of descent based on the Christian West to be resurrected from the mass graves of Europe is to fail to recognise Europe's *inner cosmopolitanisation*. For one thing, it is to deny the reality of the roughly seventeen million people living in the EU who are unable to accept this ethnic-cultural heritage of Europeanness on account of being Muslims and/or people of colour, but who nonetheless understand and organise themselves culturally and politically as Europeans. For another, however, it is to fail to recognise Europe as a microcosm of global society. In the world of the 21st century there is no longer a closed-off space called the Christian West. In the face of growing transnational interconnections and obligations, Europe is turning into an open network with blurring boundaries, where the outside is always already inside.

There is no doubt that the current state of the EU is deserving of critique. But where should one look to find the standards for such a critique? In national self-images, in lamentations over the loss of national sovereignty? No. The concept of a cosmopolitan Europe enables a form of critique of EU reality to emerge that is not nostalgic and not national but instead is, as it were, radically European. This critique says: much about the current state of the EU is un-European. That is why Europe is paralysed. The diagnosis of the crisis is 'too little Europe' – and the therapeutic cure, 'more Europe' – understood correctly, namely cosmopolitically! And that goes both for Europe internally as well as for its relations with those outside. For example, it is utterly un-European to equate and thereby reduce Muslims to Islam. It is precisely because European values are secular values that they are not tied to any particular religion or heritage. No one would say: this person is a Catholic and comes from Bavaria and so therefore they cannot be a democrat, yet in the eyes of many nationalistic Europeans, being a Muslim is still a totalitarian determinant that excludes the possibility of 'really' being a democrat. In this sense, the national Western view is a fundamentalist view, one that paradoxically fits rather well alongside the anti-modern fundamentalism of an Osama bin Laden and serves to confirm it reciprocally in a dangerous way. 'Europeanness', by contrast, means being able to combine in one existence those things that appear logically to be mutually exclusive in the small-mindedness of ethnic thinking: it is, after all, possible to be a Muslim and a democrat, a socialist and a small businessperson, to love the Bavarian landscape and way of life *and* to belong to an anti-foreigner organisation. Radical openness is one essential characteristic of the European project and is the real secret of its success.

The political union that is Europe must be conceived as a cosmopolitan union – in opposition to the false normativity of the 'national'. Paradoxically, hatred of the West comes about not only or primarily because Muslims who want to live by the Qur'an reject human rights or democracy. The hatred that emanates from those who are deemed to be culturally different and who, on that basis, are excluded by the supposedly true Europeans, emerges from a state of affairs that constitutes precisely the opposite: namely, that in its dealings with those who are deemed to be culturally different, Europe is forgetting and denying its own values. It is an exclusionary Europe that sows the seeds of disappointment from which hatred springs.

*Second step:* Cosmopolitan Europe is executing the departure from postmodernity. Put more simply, the order of events is: nationalistic Europe, postmodernity, cosmopolitan Europe. Cosmopolitan Europe was launched after the Second World War in a politically conscious act as the *antithesis to a nationalistic Europe* and its physical and moral devastation. It was in this spirit of new beginnings that Winston Churchill, standing amidst the ruins of a destroyed continent in 1946, enthused: 'If Europe were once united … there would be no limit to the happiness, to the prosperity and glory which its three or four hundred million people would enjoy.' It is the charismatic statesmen of the Western democracies, and in particular the individuals and groups involved in active resistance, who invented Europe anew beyond the nations' cemeteries and mass graves, by consciously referring back to the European history of ideas. Cosmopolitan Europe is a project born of resistance. It is important to recognise this because two things come together in it: first, resistance is ignited through the lived experience of European values being perverted. So the point of origin is not constituted by humanism at all, but rather by anti-humanism in the sense of the bitter realisation that totalitarian regimes have always based themselves on the idea of the 'true human' precisely in order to be able to separate out, exclude, re-model or destroy those people who did not want to accommodate themselves to this ideal. But if it is no longer a question of saving some purported human substance, if what we are dealing with is a decentred quasi-subject that eludes all interrogation as to what it is, what it wants and even what is inviolable about it anymore – well then, what is there left to preserve? In the name of what can we guarantee that it won't be carried off, tortured and killed? This is precisely the point at which the origins of public protest and resistance are crucial. For it is here too that the principles of defending human dignity on the basis of felt compassion can be found. People's awareness of global norms arises, as it were, posthoc – as a side effect of the violation of these same norms – and it is this that leads them to engage in political action.

Cosmopolitan Europe is a Europe that struggles morally, politically, economically and historically for *reconciliation*. In a decisive break with the past, 1500 years of European warfare are to be brought definitively to an end. Right from the start, this reconciliation – groundless and without foundation – is not so much preached idealistically as brought into being materialistically: the limitless happiness that Churchill foresaw equates in the first instance with a limitless market. It is to be realised quite profanely as a creation of interdependencies in the political spheres of security, the economy, science and culture. The adjective 'cosmopolitan' refers to this openness, constrained by the critique of ethno-nationalism, which argues for recognition of cultural difference and diversity.

It is especially in the memory of the Holocaust that the dilemmas of an institutionalised cosmopolitanism reveal themselves. If one were to inquire about the documents and discourses where the origin of this institutionalised cosmopolitanism can be studied and documented, one would come across, among other things, the Nuremberg Trials of those responsible for the Nazi terror in Germany. This was the first international court. What is remarkable is that it was the creation of legal categories as well as of a trial procedure that went *beyond* nation-state sovereignties which make it possible to capture in legal concepts and court procedures the historical monstrosity of the systematic, state-organised extermination of Jews; these concepts and procedures in turn constitute what can and must be interpreted as a central source of the new European cosmopolitanism.

Article 6 of the *Charter of the International Military Tribunal* delineates three sorts of crime – crimes against peace, war crimes and crimes against humanity – on the basis of which Nazi criminals were sentenced. Interestingly, crimes against peace and war crimes presuppose nation-state sovereignty, that is, they obey the logic of the national view, whereas crimes against humanity, in contradistinction, suspend national sovereignty and seek to embed the cosmopolitan view in legal categories; and it is doubtless no coincidence that the judges who participated in the Nuremberg Tribunal were ultimately unable to get to grips with the historically new category of crimes against humanity. After all, what was being introduced here was not only a new law or a new principle but a new legal logic that broke with all previous nation-state logics of international law. I quote from Article 6c: '*Crimes against humanity*: namely, murder, extermination, enslavement, deportation and other inhumane acts committed against any civilian population, before or during the war; or persecutions on political, racial or religious grounds in execution of or in connection with any crime within the jurisdiction of the Tribunal, whether or not in violation of domestic law of the country were perpetrated.'

In the formulation 'before and during the war', crimes against humanity are clearly demarcated from war crimes. This creates the notion of responsibility of individual perpetrators towards the community of nations, towards humanity *outside* the national legal context. If the state becomes a criminal state, the individual who serves it must reckon with being charged and sentenced for his or her deeds before an international court of law. The phrase 'any civilian population' suspends the national principle according to which a person's obligations within a border are all-encompassing and their lack of obligations beyond that border equally all-encompassing; it replaces this with the legal principle of cosmopolitan responsibility. The cosmopolitan legal principle that breaks with nation-state law protects civilian populations not only from the violence of other, hostile states (something already contained in the term 'war crimes'), but in a much more far-reaching and provocative sense from the random acts of violence committed by sovereign states against their own citizens. Ultimately, what a cosmopolitan morality of law does is switch the priority around the other way, so that the principles of cosmopolitan law breach national law. Crimes against humanity can be neither legitimated using nation-state law nor tried and condemned on a nation-state basis. In sum, it is in this sense that the historically new category of 'crimes against humanity' suspends the principles of nation-state legislation and adjudication.

At this point, questions arise to which there are no easy answers: who are the victims of crimes against humanity – the Jews? Humanity, or in other words, everybody? And does this include the perpetrators? How can a crime against humanity be perpetrated when humanity is an empty concept with no substance or perpetuity? With the death of the human subject long since proclaimed, do we not now need to defend the rights of the dead under the banner of 'human rights'?

In this respect, cosmopolitan Europe generates a *genuinely European internal contradiction,* morally, legally and politically. If the traditions from which colonialistic, nationalistic and genocidal horror originates are European, then so are the values and legal categories against which these acts are measured and proclaimed *as* crimes against humanity and are tried under the spotlight of world publicity. The victors could have simply placed the elite responsible for Nazi terror before a firing squad – as indeed Stalin and Churchill initially demanded – or else they could have been put before their own national judges to be sentenced in accordance with national law (as happened with the Eichmann trial in Jerusalem and the Auschwitz trials in Germany). Instead, however, the European tradition of recognising the other was mobilised along with the law, based on that recognition, against ethnic perversion of the law.

Social scientific reflection on the Holocaust has brought forth a discourse of despair and with good reason. According to Horkheimer and Adorno, it is the Enlightenment itself whose dialectic generates perversion. This supposition of causality between modernity and barbarism continues to be felt in Zygmunt Bauman's great book *Modernity and the Holocaust*. But this despairing farewell to modernity does not have to be the last word on the matter. Indeed one could even say that it is blind to the fact that, and the ways in which, the creation of the EU has initiated a struggle over institutions with the aim of countering European horror with European values and methods: thus the Old World invents itself anew.

In this sense, the memory of the Holocaust becomes a beacon that warns of the ever-present modernisation of barbarism (Levy/Sznaider, *Die Globalisierung der Erinnerung: der Holocaust,* Frankfurt/Main, 2001). The negativity of modernity and its European consciousness is not a mere attitude, an ideology of the tragic. This finds expression in the historical invention of a modernity that has gone off the rails with regard to nation and state, a modernity that has mercilessly unfurled the potential for moral, political, economic and technological disaster with no consideration for its own self-destruction. The mass graves of the 20th century – of the world wars, the Holocaust, the atomic bombs of Hiroshima and Nagasaki, of Stalinist death camps and genocides – bear testimony to this. Yet an unreflected and unbroken link also exists between European pessimism, the critique of modernity and postmodernity which makes this despair a permanent feature – Jürgen Habermas is right on this point. To put it a little differently, there is a paradoxical coalition between the Europe of nations and the Europe of postmodernity, because the theoreticians of postmodernity deny the possibility and reality of combating the horror of European history with more Europe, a radicalised, cosmopolitan Europe.

Europeanisation means struggling to find institutional responses to the barbarism of European modernity and, by the same token, taking leave of postmodernity, which fails to recognise this very issue. In this sense, Cosmopolitan Europe constitutes *the European way's own institutionalised critique of itself*. This process is not complete, indeed it cannot be completed. In fact it has only just begun, with the sequence: Enlightenment, postmodernity, cosmopolitan modernity. Perhaps this radical self-critique is what distinguishes the EU from the US or from Islamic societies. Is this the secret of success that makes a self-critical Europe so attractive in the contest over definitions of the future and of modernity in our one world? A cosmopolitan Europe is a Europe that is rooted in its history, breaks with its history and gains the strength to do so out of its history; a Europe that is *self-critically* experimental. It is therefore the Europe of reflexive modernisation in which the foundations, boundaries and key ideas of nation-state politics and society are suspended and renegotiated.

*Third step:* To think of Europe in national terms is not only to fail to recognise the reality and future of Europe, it is also to (re)produce the internal blockages that have become an essential characteristic of political action in Europe. One place where this becomes apparent is in the canon of established concepts relating to politics and the state: the reality of a cosmopolitan Europe can only be realised in *negation*, that is, in a radical self-critique of common, taken-for-granted concepts relating to politics and the state.

The national gaze sees two, and only two, ways of reading European politics and integration – either as a federal state (federalism) or as a confederation of states (intergovernmentalism). Both models are empirically wrong. When conceived in normative and political terms, however, they deny the very thing that is at stake in reality and in the future: a Europe of diversity.

A national Great Europe – a federal superstate – entails the disempowerment of European nations and their consignment to the role of museum; while nation-states within a confederation of states jealously defend their nation-state sovereignty against the expansion of European power. In the national perspective, European integration *has to* be conceived ultimately as an internalisation of colonialism – either us or them. What we give up, they gain. Either there is *one single* state of Europe (federalism), in which case there are *no* national member states; or the national member states remain the masters of Europe, in which case there is *no* Europe (intergovernmentalism).

The same is true for the current debate about a constitution. Britain, for example, as is well known, has no constitution and yet speaks (now and again) with an un-European, undemocratic, cosmopolitan voice. This means that to seek to create *a single* constitution for Europe is to abolish Europe, to take the heart out of Europe, to rob it of its delightful, liberal-minded provincialities. However, to choose the option of no European constitution means, banally enough, that once again there is no Europe. Caught up in the false alternatives of the national viewpoint, then, we are faced with a choice between no Europe – and no Europe! In other words: Europe's reality emerged only in contradiction to the established range of concepts offered by political science and this is how it should be comprehended. Political science is, to a large extent, deeply entrenched in methodological nationalism and proceeds according to the motto: the uprising of European reality against its royal concepts must be crushed using all means at the disposal of empirical research. Yet this uprising of reality has a name, a concept – cosmopolitan Europe.

In a way similar to the Westphalian Peace, which brought an end to the religion-based civil wars of the 16th century through the division of state and religion, the nation-based world (civil) wars of the 20th and the fledgling 21st century can be responded to by dividing state from nation – this is the key hypothesis of the cosmopolitan confederation of European states. Just as an a-religious state allows citizens to practise a variety of religions, so too a cosmopolitan Europe ought to safeguard the coexistence of ethnic, national, religious and political identities and cultures beyond national boundaries, through the principle of constitutional tolerance. Europe teaches the following lesson: the political evolution of the world of states, of concepts of state, of theories of the state, is by no means at an end. How could it be? Modernisation means that everything is and will become history.

The other aspect of the decline of the order of nation-states is the opportunity available to European-cosmopolitan state entities to re-model themselves in the face of economic globalisation, transnational terrorism and the political consequences of climate change. Given the global problems that are gathering ominously all around and which refuse to yield to nation-state solutions, the only way in which politics can regain credibility is by undertaking the quantum leap from a national to a cosmopolitan state. This is exactly what is at stake in a cosmopolitan Europe: in an age of globalised problems that are nonetheless of concern to people in their everyday lives, there is a need to regain credibility both in the sphere of politics as well as political science, through interstate forms of cooperation and cooperative strategies at the regional level and through corresponding political theories. This is also true of Asia, America and Africa, but it is particularly true for the experiment that is the EU. The old nation-state game is no longer an option. National *realpolitik* is becoming unreal, or else it is turning into a lose–lose game. Europeanisation means taking part in a meta-power game. This power game, involving radical change to the apparently eternal rules of the national–international order, has already long begun. Those who do not join in (and Britain will soon have to make its decision on this) may well find themselves with egg on their faces (Ulrich Beck, *Macht und Gegenmacht im globalen Zeitalter,* Frankfurt/Main, 2002).

The primary principle of cosmopolitan realism is the following: *Europe will never be possible as a project of national homogeneity.* To build the common house of Europe along the lines of national–international logics is neither realistic nor desirable; in fact, it is downright counter-productive. Only a cosmopolitan Europe that is able, paradoxically, to overcome its national tradition (as its founding fathers intended) – overcome it by acknowledging it (in other words exclude the possibility of a national Great Europe, but celebrate the diversity of the national as an essential characteristic of Europe) – and yet simultaneously to acknowledge that national tradition is both European (in the sense of not national) as well as national, because it is plural-national, that is, European.

In the cosmopolitan Europe a new *realpolitik* of political action is starting to emerge: at the start of the third millennium the circular maxim of national *realpolitik* – national interests must be pursued nationally – needs to be replaced by the maxim of cosmopolitan *realpolitik*: our politics are more successfully national the more European, the more cosmopolitan they are. Only multilateral politics open up unilateral options for action. The European question, the question as to how a cosmopolitan Europe can increase its capacity to act and its power to persuade, is: how can the vicious circle of the national zero-sum game be replaced by the virtuous circle of a European plus-sum game? How can it become possible, if not to overcome national egotistical tendencies, then at least to tame them in a European way? How might *European* interests emerge as a nation's own interests? How can the exploitation of the EU by national egotistical tendencies be prevented? And what actually happens if individual states say 'no'? To put it another way: why does that so seldom happen?

Here too the concept of cosmopolitan *realpolitik* proves to be fruitful. The creation of interdependencies in every field of politics, the politics of integration that puts Europeanisation onto a permanent footing, is not a one-off form of cooperation that ultimately leaves the nation-states involved untouched – as the intergovernmental perspective implies. Instead, Europeanisation seizes and transforms the power of the state and national sovereignty at the core of its being. Nation-states turn into *trans*nation-states, and this in a dual sense: on the one hand, national and European interests become merged in such a way that national interests are Europeanised and can be pursued and maximised *as* European interests. On the other, the instrumentalisation of Europe, the pursuit of a *non*-genuine cosmopolitanism, is an option for *all* states: every member government must anticipate that the other member states could well act in exactly the same way. This leads to a situation in which the instrumentalisation of the European common good is ever-present in the form of the threat of diminishment of one's own 'national-European' interests.

Thus if all goes well, Europeanisation means that strategies of *reflexive self-limitation on the part of member states in nations' own self-interest* emerge. For pragmatic reasons the member states do not make use of their latent sovereignty, sticking instead to the European rules laid down by European institutions in order permanently to maximise their own national interests. This brings out clearly once again that cosmopolitanism does not equate with altruism or idealism, but rather with realism, or, to put it more precisely: reflexive self-interest of transnation-states.

What paralyses Europe, however, is the fact that its intellectual elites are living a nation-based lie. They lament the existence of faceless European bureaucracy and the departure from democracy and yet tacitly base their complaints on the totally unrealistic assumption that there could ever be a turning back to the nation-state idyll. Blind faith in the nation-state rules in the face of its own historicity: there is an insistent and disconcerting naivety that enables people to consider those things eternal and natural that just two or three hundred years ago were considered unnatural and absurd. This sort of intellectual protectionism, this lived illusion steeped in nostalgia predominates not only in the shabby enclaves of the popular right in Europe. It reigns – cutting right through the right–left distinction – even in the most educated cultivated circles; even the most reflexive of political theories continues to cling to this myth of the nation-state. True, the nation-state has not sunk into the grave of history. It does still exist, of that there is no doubt – as a reality of state and international law. But in Europe, with the creation of a common currency – indeed even before this, with the dissolution of Europe's internal borders, with the implementation of European law, and so on – its very essence has been transformed, 'Europeanised', 'cosmopolitanised'. More than fifty percent of all decisions that impact on our daily lives are taken not within national boundaries but rather in the EU.

Whenever things that seemed eternal and certain begin to shift, the good old truths are wheeled out and dressed up in even more militant style. So it is no wonder that there is virtually a causal relationship between the successes of Europeanisation and the rise of neo-nationalism and right-wing populism in Europe. While European nation-states are becoming integrated in processes of mutual absorption, combination and synthesis, the national imagination rules more than ever in people's heads, becoming a sentimental ghost, a rhetorical habit, in which the fearful and bewildered seek refuge and a future. But it is precisely this inability of intellectuals – as well as of the established parties on both sides of the political spectrum – to comprehend and to play the European power game as a transnational plus-sum game and to explain it as such to the broader public that lends right-wing populism in Europe unprecedented popularity.

*Fourth step:* A cosmopolitically renewed Europe can and must, as an actor on the global political stage, acquire and sharpen its profile as a rival to *global America*. The catchphrase might be: Move over, America – Europe is back!

The 'McDonaldisation' of Europe is much like the 'cappuccino-isation' of America. To put it in political terms: a *global America* that seeks to bestow its favours by military means finds itself confronted in the non-existent world parliament with the oppositional voice of Europe calling back: *Make law, not war!* (Mary Kaldor). A cosmopolitan Europe must seize this oppositional role and play it out, because as we know only too well, without opposition, dictatorship – and at a global level, global dictatorship – threatens, in this case the dictatorship of the *American way of life.* At the same time Europe must take over the role of domestic opposition in the US, since the latter has all but left the stage. To bring a touch of irony to the issue, one might say that the democratisation of the world – and of the US! – requires at least the Europeanisation of the world as well, including the US.

The brave new world of military security promised by the Bush administration plunges the real world into a danger-filled abyss because it replaces the logic of the treaty with the logic of war. While the US government prepares itself for a crusade in Baghdad, it is systematically discarding or devaluing the treaties and principles that could prohibit and destroy its deadly arsenal. Even in the ideal scenario of a quick victory, little would have been achieved as far as the spread of weapons of mass destruction is concerned unless there had been recourse to the tried-and-tested methods of international agreements and controls: without an effective United Nations there can be no internal security for the US either.

State-sponsored terrorism, along with all the dangers of chemical, biological and nuclear weapons, always opens up two possibilities in terms of combating it: the option of war and the option of the treaty, in other words, the practical reinforcement of international conventions to achieve further disarmament of weapons of mass destruction. However, since the US refuses flat out to submit to the norms of disarmament that it demands of all other states – where necessary using military violence – it destroys the treaty-based architecture of security which ultimately provides a protective shield for American citizens as well.

And once Iraq has been occupied, will the dual blessing of liberty – a free market and democracy – really unfold right away throughout the Middle East, as the Bush government seems to dream of in true neo-romantic style? Will the voracious caterpillar of militant Islam suddenly be transformed into a colourful butterfly proclaiming only tidings of peace and goodwill? This naive military glint in the dewy eyes of American idealists needs the counterbalance that Europe can provide, an oppositional European voice that says: make law, not war. A cosmopolitan Europe can and must contribute to a situation in which international relations are no longer militarised or international treaties and institutions thrown onto the rubbish heap of the Cold War. The fact is that without them, there can be no security in our radically unequal, divided one world.

By the same token, however, Europe likes to think this is not the case: without the military hegemony of the US, the romance of Europe's policy of reconciliation would soon evaporate. One reason for the superior might of the US can be traced back to internal European policy, namely the collective renunciation of military force. It is not until this failure is recognised and fixed that the EU will be capable of enacting a foreign policy that is deserving of the name. It will demand an answer to the sixty-four thousand dollar question as to the authority of common European institutions. A European foreign policy can only be formulated when capital cities recognise that handing over certain areas of authority to

Brussels does not weaken but rather strengthens them, because this cosmopolitan turn increases the global influence of all the EU states.

But America can rest assured. As long as the existence or non-existence of the EU is caught up in quarrels over milk quotas and farming subsidies – and as long as there is Britain! – American supremacy will remain unchallenged.


**Ulrich Beck**
Born in Stolp/Pomerania, 1944. Teaches sociology at the Ludwig Maximilian University in Munich and at the London School of Economics. Publications include: *Risk Society: Towards a New Modernity; The Reinvention of Politics; Democracy Without Enemies.*

# The Architects

*There are those who sit back and criticise, and those who devote their professional lives to making things happen. The latter are the architects of Europe. They have a hard and usually thankless task. Brussels – synonym for all that is cumbersome and incomprehensible in the EU – is doing its best to introduce transparency, but the task is mammoth. The ambition of Europe's constitution-in-the-making is to simplify the process. In the meantime, decisions with far-reaching consequences continue to be made while the citizens of 'Old' Europe wonder if the last decision – to add another ten countries to the EU in 2004 – was wise, or simply the last straw.*

Valéry Giscard d'Estaing

# The Calligraphy of History

The Convention on the Future of Europe is just over halfway through its task – time to report on the progress of our efforts. What have we achieved so far, and what do we still have to do?

The results achieved by the Convention have improved its standing. The European Union governments are now following our proceedings more closely and are sending 'heavyweights' such as their foreign ministers to represent them. What results does the Convention have to show for itself? First and foremost, the suggestion that the principle of subsidiarity should be made subject to political control. This will ensure that the EU does not intervene in the affairs of the member states more than is necessary for the exercise of its responsibilities – or rather, will no longer do so. We will no longer hear the complaint, 'Why is Brussels meddling in everything?' It will be sufficient for national parliaments to exercise this control.

The second result of the Convention's work is the simplification of treaties. Instead of four very complex and difficult treaties, we will have a single constitutional treaty: the European Constitution. This simplification will affect the way the EU arrives at decisions, as well as the way those decisions are implemented. Currently, there are ten different legal instruments; their number could be reduced to five. This will finally provide the answer to the question, 'Who does what in Europe?'

To combat international crime more effectively, the Convention intends to propose the inclusion in the Constitution of a precise definition of serious cross-border crime. This will enable us to work out a code of criminal law which can then be applied to this kind of crime throughout the Community. And finally the Convention is going to suggest making the EU Human Rights Charter part of the Constitution.

The Convention must also be active in other areas, for example, in the future shape of Europe's economic and social policies. Moreover, there is one area on which everyone is agreed: currency matters fall within the purview of the EU, while economic matters are still the responsibility of the member states.

The fact that all these major results have been achieved can be explained by the way the Convention works: we constantly strive to achieve a majority consensus, that is, the agreement of as many as possible, without letting ourselves be blocked by the need for unanimity. The increased importance of the Convention should nevertheless not lead to our committee becoming a kind of governmental conference, where the representatives of the various capitals negotiate outside the framework of the Convention. The Convention is a democratic space, and its negotiations will continue to take place in public. With moderation and respect for history, without any external pressure, its members must aim to produce the best possible European Constitution.

The responsibility of the last stage of the Convention will be to write the articles of the Constitution and to work out the changes to the framework of the EU necessitated by its forthcoming enlargement. Without these changes, the EU runs the risk of losing the confidence of its citizens, of getting bogged down – even of becoming diluted.

In the articles of Europe's future constitution, we must fix long-term guidelines which will protect the weak while at the same time clearing the way for the greatest possible progress. In style, the Constitution should not resemble a legal document or the kind of international treaty which attempts to anticipate any possible misinterpretation or trickery. We must produce a clear, interesting and creative text. The poetry of a constitution is in some ways the calligraphy of history. At the end of January 2003, the Praesidium will present the first articles of the Constitution. The Convention will provide detailed commentaries on the articles – and if necessary set up round-table discussions – before the Praesidium issues its final suggestions.

Parallel to our work on the text of the Constitution, we are presenting observations about the regulation of Europe's institutions. In doing this, we must investigate in detail two major questions. What institutional changes are unavoidable if we wish to be fair to all twenty-five member states in an enlarged Europe? Do we need to question the structure chosen by the EU's founding fathers – that is, the framework of Parliament, Council of Ministers and Commission – to cope adequately with the new demands that will be made of the Union?

The forthcoming EU enlargement will affect all three EU institutions. The Council of Europe had 19 members in 1975, today there are 32; within the framework of EU enlargement this will increase to 52, consisting of the president or head of government of each member state as well as their foreign ministers, with the addition of two members of the Commission. Secondly, the European Parliament: this will soon exceed its self-imposed maximum of seven hundred members and become the largest assembly in the Western world. Thirdly, there is the Commission, which originally consisted of 9 Commissioners, whereas in future there will be 25. After expansion, the Commissioners from the five largest states, who previously represented 78 percent of the population of the EU, will represent only 24 percent of EU citizens.

In the case of all three Brussels institutions, it is legitimate to ask if and how they will in future be able to provide clear and rapid decisions. For example, the Council of Europe; so far, the EU heads of state and government have democratically followed the principle of 'one man, one vote'. In the future, how will they reach decisions and what voting procedures will they adopt? At the same time, the current six-monthly change in the presidency of the Council of Ministers will mean that when there are twenty-five member states, each country will hold the presidency of the EU only once every twelve and a half years. This will impair efficiency since there will be a lack of continuity in policy terms and it will become more difficult to make decisions. Thus the idea of the rotating presidency will have to be abandoned.

The problems that will be caused by this increase in numbers have not, in my opinion, been analysed carefully enough. In the EU Commission's remit to the Convention, the problem complex was not even mentioned. Only the European Parliament has so far worked out proposals to deal with it.

The other major question concerns the internal architecture of the EU. Can we retain this or must it be altered and improved? This is a fascinating debate for insiders and of great concern to politicians in Brussels, although it does not engage the interest of the public at large. Ordinary citizens already have enough trouble finding their way about the complicated systems.

Until now, the EU has been made up of three institutions: the European Parliament, which is directly elected; the Council of Ministers, which represents the member states in determining EU policy; and the European Commission, which acts as an independent and non-political organ that defines the general welfare of Europe. The way their roles are divided can be described as follows: the Commission proposes measures which are in the general European interest, the Parliament considers and promulgates laws and the Council makes decisions.

This construction has stood the test of the last fifty years very well. Even if this structure, like all institutions created by human hand, has become a little dated, it has coped with many crises and even its opponents, who have often sat in its ranks, do not question it. In an unstable, not to say dangerous world, permanence and legitimacy are strengths which we should foster without reservation.

If you wish to better understand the debate about the institutions in Brussels, you need, in my opinion, to keep your sights firmly fixed on the actual goal of the European project. This gives rise to four questions. The first question I put to the Convention was: should the EU become a unified whole – with, perhaps, a single government – which is the dream of some and the nightmare of others? The answer was almost unanimously negative. The second question is do we wish to divide the power differently between the institutions to the extent of producing a 'community system' (Commission and Parliament) or do we wish to improve cooperation between the three institutions that already exist? Thirdly: when we talk about equal rights within the EU, do we mean equal rights for the states or for their citizens? And finally: do Europe's heads of state and government possess the political will to allow the EU to have its own legal identity, with, perhaps one day, a common diplomatic policy?

The EU is both a union of peoples and a union of states; this is what produces its ambiguously unique quality. If one departs from the concept of a confederation of states, then the rights of each state must be equal. If one departs from the concept of a confederation of peoples, however, the rights of each individual citizen must be equal. The advantage of the present structure is that it deals satisfactorily with both aspects of the question. This implies that the EU must be transformed to deal with the effects of enlargement.

Any attempt to alter this equilibrium and to concentrate power in only one of the EU's institutions risks causing a conflict in terms of the legitimacy and equal rights of its citizens and states; this would endanger its unity. Retaining the double legitimacy of the EU seems to be the most sensible way of proceeding. The future structure of the EU must, however, improve cooperation between the three institutions. The monolithic exercise of power, in spite of its obvious simplicity, does not appear to be the best solution to the question of the political leadership of the most diverse and (next to China and India) third greatest population group in the world.

It is frequently foreign policy, or rather diplomacy, that makes people consider a new distribution of power. This debate was initiated as if we could determine who will decide on a common European foreign policy in the future. Reality looks somewhat different: there is still no such thing as a common EU foreign policy. Certainly there are Community political actions, which are often very successful, as in the Balkans at present. But on the international stage there is still no common diplomatic activity. For example, since 1 January 2003, four of the fifteen members of the UN Security Council have been EU member states: France, Great Britain, Germany and Spain. A fifth member of the Council, Bulgaria, is a candidate for membership. So when the moment of decision about military activity in Iraq comes, a third of the Security Council will be EU members. If we had a common diplomatic strategy, the EU would have a key role which the world would have to recognise.

We cannot blame our present foreign policy defects on either individuals or institutions. The two people who have the major responsibilities in the EU at the moment, Javier Solana in the Council and Chris Patten in the Commission, are competent. But how great is their influence on the current attitude of the countries of the EU to the crisis in Iraq?

What is the cause of the problem? The answer is the lack of political will required to transfer diplomatic responsibility to the Community step by step, and thus to reduce the scope for national initiative. This is the decisive point. Could one imagine bringing the changes about by external pressure? That would not only be naive, but would instead drive every member state to retreat to its own national position. We can only progress if we set up an organisation that will carry out analyses for the Community as a whole, formulate positions and act as a catalyst for a common foreign policy.

Promoting the High Representative to the rank of an EU foreign minister would be one way of doing this. He should also be given the permanent presidency of the Council of EU Foreign Ministers. No force or pressure would be applied, but this could create the convergence necessary to bring about a common diplomatic presence of the EU states. The coordination between this new institution and the international activities of the Commission would have to be defined, and at the same time we should not lose sight of the nature and character of the Commission – i.e. its independence and cohesion.

I believe it would be beneficial to consider the form of the institutional structure of the EU and to concentrate on its political goals. Uncertainty about the division of powers would fade the more the double legitimacy of the Union – as a union of peoples and a union of states – were confirmed, and the Community dimension and the responsibilities of the individual states within Community actions were consolidated. When I presented the draft structure of a European constitution to the Praesidium, I allowed myself to formulate the first article: 'A union of states and peoples which decides their policies in close collaboration and exercises certain responsibilities in a federal way.'

It was a pleasant surprise to find this text almost unaltered in the Commission's draft report. I feel that it describes the essentials of the European project: an aeroplane can only fly with two wings. And this demonstrates that positive development is possible: the creation of federal functions in both executive institutions – the Council and the Commission – which will one day merge into a unity to form the government of a united Europe.

The above text was written expressly for this book. Permission has been given to *Le Monde* and the *Süddeutsche Zeitung* to publish it prior to the publication of the book.

**Valéry Giscard d'Estaing**
Born in Koblenz, 1926. President of the European Convention on the Future of Europe since 2002. President of the Council of European Municipalities and Regions and member of the Committee of the Regions since 1997. State President of France from 1974 to 1981.

Romano Prodi

# Reform and Proximity: The European Union Defines its Borders

Any private enterprise considering a move as mammoth as the expansion of the European Union (EU) would be holding its breath and hoping for success. Yet the mere prospect of a further unforeseeable enlargement would send the stock of 'Europe plc' through the roof. As things stand, we can already say that the EU is given top ratings by its neighbours. They have high expectations of us. How should we be dealing with them?

## Stock-taking

The EU has every reason to be proud of the eastward enlargement that I consider to be the pinnacle of this Commission's achievements – just look back ten years to when the EU worked out in Copenhagen the criteria for the acceptance of new members and thus opened its doors to the then just recently liberated states. However, mixed in with the joy at the end of the post-war era, there were also serious concerns: political instability, corruption, economic decline, wild west capitalism, environmental dumping, organised crime and a tidal wave of immigration were all spectres on the horizon.

In the event, we have been spared the horror scenarios. On the contrary: as an instrument of a stability policy that has been successful in all senses, opening up a reliable prospect for Eastern Europe, enlargement has been an unparalleled success story. It represents the triumph of stability in Europe, the extension of democracy and market democracy and, above, all, our common European values.

Let us not forget that the fact that the countries of Central and Eastern Europe are now being accepted into the EU simply means that we are catching up – admittedly at breathtaking speed – on a development which was historically overdue, politically desired and culturally indispensable. If postwar history had taken a different turn, the question of membership would still have arisen for Estonia, Latvia, Lithuania, Poland, Slovakia, Slovenia, the Czech Republic and Hungary – and indeed also for Romania, Bulgaria and the Balkan states, which are of course also part of Europe. But it would have happened sooner and in a less dramatic fashion.

In the post-1989 situation, there was no alternative either to expressly opening up the EU to new members or to the time frame for the process initiated in 1993. Only by opening up to the East could the EU durably stabilise the Continent, secure its own interest in an ordered political and economic reunification of the geographical entity of Europe, and accept its historic responsibility.

For the candidate countries, the certainty of accession was decisive: only with the documented, tangible prospect of membership in the EU could the governments of the candidate countries justify and sustain their double *tour de force*: managing to bring about economic transformation *and* complete preparations for accession in less than a decade is an impressive, even dazzling achievement. And it must be acknowledged that simple association with the EU would not have been sufficient motivation to drive this effort.

With the conclusion of the accession negotiations decided upon in December 2002 by the Copenhagen European Council, the successful endeavours of the candidates have been acknowledged. There is still plenty of work to do, but for eight Central and Eastern European states – as well as for the Mediterranean states of Cyprus and Malta – 2004 will usher in the era of internal European politics. Enlargement is thus the keystone of a highly successful development which has definitively put an end to the post-war era in Europe.

Let me return to my comparison of the EU with an economic enterprise: for the latter, this step would be merely one stage on the path to global expansion. This option does not exist for the EU. A Union expanding limitlessly would behave like a dying star, which would first flare up into a so-called red giant and then collapse into a black hole – not really an appealing option. So the EU cannot just keep on growing indefinitely, and not because there would be no demand for the EU resource, but because questions arise which relate to the way we are constituted internally, to our role at the regional and global level and to our identity.

The problem is that if we want to stay as we are we have to change: in the Community of six countries, it was possible to reach agreement by just a glance round the then-still small table, but in a community of twenty-five, twenty-seven – or, at some point, up to thirty-five – that is no longer possible. We can't avoid questions about the procedures, instruments and institutions which can fulfil the demands of the enlarged EU and the new situation in the world.

This is the huge, historic task of the Convention on the constitution, which will soon submit its draft constitution for a simpler, more democratic, more efficient and more politically transparent EU.

One thing is clear: in order to cover a far greater area, we cannot and must not simply stretch the essential substance that makes up the economic, political and social EU until it becomes untenably thin. If we cannot solve all the potential problems with our neighbours by accepting them into the

EU, then we must start to develop a more effective proximity policy, able to deal with problems as they arise.

## The way ahead

Thus we cannot, for example, ignore the fact that while the extension of the EU means that old borders are disappearing, new ones are also coming into existence. In accordance with the provisions of the Schengen *acquis*, we want borders to be permeable enough not to seriously affect the existing human and economic contacts. The more similar neighbours are in economic, political and social terms, the easier it is to keep the borders between them permeable. We must work on this.

In other words: we must endeavour to develop a relationship with our non-EU neighbours that allows them to participate in Europe's prosperity and stability. How can we achieve this? Ideally through market integration and having our neighbours adopt European regulations. In some areas, this is no easy task for them. It is clear that the golden opportunity that these countries are being offered through enlargement, the direct proximity with a market of almost 450 million consumers, is also a major challenge.

It is always easier to meet and overcome major challenges if the goals are clear. This is in the shared interest of both the EU and its neighbours. It is both right and proper to ask what the likely prospects are of a cooperation (and eventual EU membership) with any particular neighbour. Whether we like it or not, we will always have to ask whether a given country has any chance of joining. Ukraine is already asking this question; others will follow. Are there any patent answers? What signals do we give to countries which would like to see their future in Europe?

We want enlargement policy to succeed in terms of stability and growth, but we cannot allow our proximity policy to act only as a step on the way to an enlargement policy. If we did, the EU would bring itself to the brink of extinction. We must keep in mind that even without any more potential accession countries, the EU will continue growing: if we calculate roughly which states the EU has already granted at least the *prospect* of accession and add to this what emerges from the EU Treaty[1] and the map of Europe, we are already looking at a Union of around thirty-five member states.

I therefore consider it irresponsible to start handing out the prospect of membership to additional candidates. However, it would be equally irresponsible to refuse to give to those countries that want to orientate themselves towards the EU advice as to how to do this. I will expand on this at the end of this contribution.

First of all, however, I'd like to stress that the current promises – however long term their vision – cannot be upheld without decisive reforms of the EU to ensure its capacity to act in the future. So far, in the dual strategy of widening and deepening the EU, we have put widening first. Now the time has come to switch our priorities and put deepening first. Here are some of my thoughts on the deepening process.

Enlargement may be the answer to an internal problem we have long had, but were able to avoid until now. The EU needs to streamline its decision-making procedures, it needs an internal overhaul. Until now, some of the EU's known weaknesses have grown in a gradual and almost imperceptible fashion. With enlargement, there is no way to ignore this. Reform has become an imperative. This is not simply a matter of sheer size: we are now faced with new fields of Community activity which require new approaches. This is particularly true, for example, in the case of the common foreign and security policy, which is still in a fledgling state. Our global responsibility is growing faster than our capacity to act in accordance with that responsibility. This was recently brought home to us with painful clarity in the Balkans. If the necessary institutional measures are not taken, the EU will continue to be an economic giant but political dwarf.

So first of all we need a more efficient EU, determined by majority rule and capable of both internal and external action. It is hard for the general public to understand why the cross-border fight against crime does not work better, why the states' economic policy is not better coordinated and why the EU can't generate more clout internationally. I'll come back to that in a moment.

Secondly, we need a simpler, more streamlined EU with transparent procedures and a clear, comprehensible division of powers. The legal framework of the EU has become too opaque; people do not know how it works and what it actually does. That has to change. I am sure that the Convention will make appropriate proposals in this regard; the Commission has been and will be actively involved in drawing these up.

And thirdly, we need more democracy in the EU: the role of the European Parliament must be strengthened, both in the legislative process and in the choice of the President of the Commission. I would like the President of the Commission to be elected by a two-thirds majority of the European Parliament.

## The EU and its external relations

The EU undeniably has a certain political clout, at least on a regional level. This has a lot to do with its economic pull. As long as other countries find it attractive to trade with Europe and gain access to its markets, the EU has quite a bit of leverage in exerting political influence on the formulation of desired trade conditions. As a result of its market of almost half a billion consumers, the EU has become a standard-setting authority in such areas of legislation as environmental protection, production, social security and governance, to name but a few.

However, the political reach of this power diminishes with increasing geographical distance. In other words, direct neighbours have almost no chance to evade the pressure of EU economic and political norms. Precisely because the EU makes its cooperation with neighbours and partners dependent on the fulfilment of political criteria, it offers them effective incentives to follow the model of democracies based on the rule of law and market economies that it itself embodies.

Far distant neighbours may trade with the EU, but are scarcely touched by it on a political level. Nobody thinks that European norms for tractor seats are going to make despots on the other side of the globe quake in their boots. In other words, our regional and economic weight depends on the building-up of our international and global influence.

Europeans are often considered to be naïve in their choice of means to achieve political ends. We do, however, well understand that the European path of economic integration and political dialogue cannot do much against determined military regimes. At the same time, we can be justly proud of our record in bringing peace and stability to a Europe of huge unrest during the first half of the last century. Today, in terms of stability, we are a shining example for the rest of the Continent and indeed the world. But here again, we need to be careful: I would warn against trying to construct an American and a European way in opposition to each other. It was, after all, massive American engagement which, during and after the Second World War, made it possible for Europe to go its own way again.

What we can learn from America is decisiveness in implementing what has been acknowledged as right. To do that, we, as a Union, need the powers, the instruments and the procedures for an ordered building-up of the political will and a concentration of accountability. In all these areas there is still a great deal of work ahead of us. If the Commission's proposals are taken up in the draft constitution which is to be presented by the Convention in mid-2003, then we will come considerably closer to our goal. A Union Secretary who is also simultaneously Vice-President of the Commission would be the person 'in charge' of external affairs, the public face. He or she would ensure that the Commission's right of initiative was maintained and thus anchor the Community method in the field of external relations. This would be an important step towards a common external policy worthy of the name.

We are now setting the course for the future. As we have seen, the challenges the Community of States has to set itself have become more varied and, to a certain extent, more diffuse and more difficult to classify. The tasks facing the world community cannot be achieved without a substantial contribution by Europe.

However, we cannot become an actor on the global stage if we concentrate all of our energy in constant new rounds of enlargement, the usefulness of which will become ever harder to explain to our population. This is why we now need to concentrate on deepening rather than widening. This should not prevent or slow down the current round of enlargement. However, we should beware of creating new candidates for accession before we have put our own house in order. This is certainly not to say that any European state which shares the fundamental political principles of the EU will be denied the right to apply for membership of the EU. That right is enshrined in EU law.

In this situation, then, a situation in which the EU cannot for the time being formulate any further possibilities of accession, the proximity co-existence concept for our neighbours becomes all the more important. The EU must surround itself with a circle of friends with which it maintains particularly close relations. We must be prepared to share everything with these countries except for the existing EU institutions. How can such a circle be constructed?

Essentially, if we are talking about diminishing the differences between the EU and its neighbours in terms of quality of life and security – for only this brings sustainable stability for the EU and its neighbours – then we need a long-term programme. I am thinking in terms of a system of small steps which, on the basis of the fulfilment of certain criteria, lead to concrete, tangible advantages for the countries in question. The end goal of these small steps would be a status corresponding to membership of today's European Economic Area. For most states within the circle of friends, it would take longer before they had the full status of today's EFTA states with which we already share a common market. However, the fact that the journey may be long must not be an argument against the direction in which it is heading.

The aim of a structured, conditional expanded proximity policy might well ultimately be EU membership, but without the process having to begin with the promise of accession. The following points would characterise a proximity policy towards the ring of friends of the EU:

- The policy must be attractive. It must offer future prospects to the states concerned within a dynamic framework.
- Anyone who wants to move on more quickly should be able to do so. Anyone who needs more time to adapt to the core areas of the *acquis communautaire* should be able to take their time without dropping out of the framework.
- This policy must motivate those involved to develop closer cooperation with the EU: the closer the cooperation, the better for the EU and its neighbours in terms of security, prosperity and stability.
- There should be a kind of 'Copenhagen Criteria' for the granting of advantages linked with membership of the circle of friends. Perhaps a catalogue of criteria could help us to judge when a country can take the next step of integration into the internal market.
- The policy would have the advantage of not starting out from the promise of subsequent membership, but neither would it have to exclude the possibility of it, as long as the prerequisite criteria were fulfilled.

This economic area would be huge, including the current and future neighbours. It would stretch from the southern edge of the Mediterranean to the Arctic Circle and from Morocco via Russia to China and Japan.

We have not reached that stage yet. This area is still a dream for the future. But we can already foresee that it will bring the EU into contact with ever more regions with a high potential for conflict. Even though simple contact does not bring with it any direct political engagement, it does nonetheless make it even more important for the EU in the future to act decisively and present a common front towards the outside world.

This emphasises yet again that it is high time to replace enlargement as the main instrument of our near-abroad external policy with a new, structured proximity policy. The time has now come to implement reform and to develop our capacity to act. An efficient proximity policy is a vital element in this.

Note

1 Treaty on European Union, Article 49: 'Any European State which respects the principles set out in Article 6(1) *[these are the principles of liberty, democracy, respect for human rights and fundamental freedoms and the rule of law]* may apply to become a member of the Union.

**Romano Prodi**
Born in Scandiano, Italy, 1939. President of the European Commission since 1999. Prime Minister of Italy from 1996 to 1998. Chairman of the centre-left alliance Ulivo in 1995.

Pat Cox

# Europe's Constitution in the Making

*Il faut oser poser toutes les questions qui passent d'habitude sous silence.*

Guy Verhofstadt, 15 December 2001

During the first 50 years of its existence, Europe has been under constant construction – at any given time described as being at a turning point, as indeed it probably was in most cases. Dramas such as the 'policy of the empty chair' or the ensuing 'Luxembourg compromise' – a classic example of agreeing not to agree – were at the time serious and even dangerous for Europe's evolution. Still, it is certainly not hyperbole to state that the European Union is presently in the midst of a historical transformation. Few of us, even those of us intimately involved in the EU's daily business, can say with much firmness where we will stand ten or twenty years from now.

This high degree of uncertainty is due in part to the fifth and largest ever enlargement of the EU which will take place in 2004. After my compatriots voted 'Yes' to the Treaty of Nice on 19 October 2002, and the successful outcome of the Copenhagen Summit on 13 December 2002, there can be little doubt that the EU will have twenty-five member states by the end of 2004. The changes following the fall of the Berlin Wall have made the widening of the EU a moral and political necessity. As a result, the old debate as to whether to deepen first and widen later or vice versa has taken on a different perspective: all European institutions and member state governments feel the obligation to prepare enlargement as quickly as possible.

In the European context the dichotomy between intergovernmentalism and federalism is overly simplistic. Experience over the past ten years has amply demonstrated, however, that the Commission's exclusive 'right of initiative' and Parliament's increasing involvement in legislation via the co-decision procedure have made the EU more coherent and efficient in the areas where they apply.

## The Convention on the Future of Europe

When writing about the future of Europe, one cannot ignore the ongoing work of the Convention on the Future of Europe, which opened in the European Parliament in Brussels on 28 February 2002. According to the Laeken Declaration of December 2001, the Convention has as its objective 'to pave the way for the next Intergovernmental Conference as broadly and openly as possible'. The Convention itself is a radical (and I believe positive) break with the tradition of EU treaty-making. While final decisions will still be taken by member state governments at the Intergovernmental Conference (IGC), for the first time the preparatory stages involve a wide and open consultation process.

The European Parliament was largely responsible for the concept of a constitutional convention, which we believed was needed for two reasons: first, Parliament considered that the previous convention on drafting a Charter of Fundamental Rights was a good exercise in open dialogue among the many players; secondly, we felt that there had to be a better way to discuss and develop thinking about the future of Europe than the road to the Nice Treaty.

When we first suggested the Convention, we had little support. We were then very pleased to receive the full backing of Romano Prodi and the European Commission, and, eventually, the need for such a body began to emerge as conventional wisdom. Now, the Convention is generally accepted as an unprecedented innovation that will allow us to build the foundations for a Europe-wide common future which is truly continental.

I think the political will to make the Convention work has already been amply demonstrated during the past months; after all, the willingness to engage is the first important ingredient in any political exercise. I believe that Parliament will continue to play a dynamic and creative role, not just because we claim paternity for the Convention idea, but because we recognise that this process must be seized as a defining moment.

Since it was directly elected for the first time in 1979, Parliament has continually supported the constitutionalisation of the European order: a modern and enlightened restatement of its basic objectives; a renewed statement of shared values; a definition of rights and responsibilities; a clear definition of our institutions, their interaction and the checks and balances in our system. The pre-draft mentioned above goes a long way in this direction.

On a more practical level, Parliament has been consistent over the years in asking for the abolition of the pillar structure of the Treaty on European Union (thereby extending legal personality to the EU, or to its successor); for the integration of the Charter of Fundamental Rights into the future treaty; for the further expansion of qualified majority voting in the Council and co-decision between Council and Parliament in European legislation. All this can already be found in the Spinelli draft, the first draft constitution proposed by the European Parliament in 1984, and in many subsequent resolutions.

## Tentative results and deliberations

I shall not expand here on the Convention working groups, whose final reports have just been adopted; these documents will of course be debated and possibly modified by the Convention itself. Convention President Giscard d'Estaing presented a pre-draft of a constitutional treaty on 28 October 2002, but most decisions remain to be taken. Nevertheless, I would like to dwell briefly on some of the results that have already been achieved. The reports propose to integrate the Charter of Fundamental Rights into the future treaty, although it is not yet clear whether this will be in the main text (as in most national constitutions), or in a protocol to which reference would have to be made in the treaty. Integration is of major importance because the Charter has great symbolic value – not only for Parliament but also for many political leaders and academic experts. We have understood for some time that the EU urgently needs to win more trust and approval from its citizens, and that without this popular confidence, we will not be able to tackle the enormous challenges which will inevitably be presented by enlargement. Our citizens need to trust the EU and its institutions to share resources equitably and in the common interest, but to do this effectively, we run the risk of alienating Europeans from the new member states – and indeed, from the rest of Europe. The Charter should be seen as the solemn expression of a common political will to make European institutions – and national administrations when they implement European law – both responsible and responsive to the citizens and to provide them with a partly legal, partly political framework in which they can begin to develop an understanding of their common values, interests and responsibilities.

Parliament will continue to watch closely how the Charter will be dealt with by the Convention. To our mind, an essential element is to recognise that when the EU acts formally as law-maker, or as executive and budgetary authority, it must not only reflect best practice and be explicitly or implicitly a respecter of rights, but it must also have a duty and an obligation in law – and that is still missing currently.

As to the EU's legal personality, I feel strongly that this is far more than just a nicety for specialists: it is the basis for a more assertive stance to be adopted in global politics. The euro is just one salient example: without an effective common representation of the Eurozone in the Bretton Woods institutions, the common currency will never fulfil its potential as an instrument of Europe's external policies.

The Convention is not the sole source of ideas demanding consideration. An idea which is apparently close to Giscard d'Estaing's heart concerns the institution of a long-term President of the European Council (or European President), possibly to be appointed by the heads of state and government; another idea concerns the creation of a Congress of European Peoples. Personally, I remain to be fully convinced of the merits of the congress idea. A bicameral system could possibly make some sense, but a tricameral system on a complex and diverse continental scale could result in greater delay or obstruction. If the only job conferred on the Congress were to delay the legislative process or if, as was already proposed, such an institution were to be given a 'right of initiative' and the power of veto over certain types of legislation, I believe that would create negative rather than creative tension; and whereas I have no problem with creative tension between institutions, negative tension is not in the interest of the EU.

Although President Giscard d'Estaing has underlined that the Convention is not concerned with power struggles between member states and European institutions, or among European institutions themselves, it is still true that any constitutional exercise is an exercise in the distribution and limitation of power. It is no coincidence that, historically, new constitutions have usually followed military defeat or violent revolutions. Seen against the background of a currently peaceful Europe, the European Parliament may sometimes appear to guard its institutional prerogatives rather jealously, but the same could be said of the Council, national diplomats and parliamentarians, and heads of state or government, although the latter may often prefer to be less outspoken on matters of power relations.

It seems to me that the positions of Parliament on constitutional issues are as responsible as they can be under the circumstances. We are fully aware of the astonishing speed with which some aspects of Europe's constitutionalisation have forged ahead lately. Who would have thought a year ago that the British government would agree to the drafting of a European constitution or the integration of the Charter? Hence, we should not fall into the trap of self-defeating pessimism: the Convention has made giant leaps forward. Still, there are risks of defeat and backward moves, as is always the case when political institutions and processes are radically revisited. With this in mind, Parliament will take care to distinguish between careful evolution and self-interested resistance to change.

## Beyond 2005

The constitutional treaty to be drafted by the Convention and adopted by the subsequent IGC could at best enter into force by 2005. Thus we seem to be tackling the EU's medium-term problems. I am convinced, however, that it would be foolish to try to preclude any future institutional and political evolution; it is essential to keep the European project open-ended and to maintain flexibility.

Europe can derive its democratic vitality only from a dual legitimation: direct legitimation coming from the European citizens and the legitimacy of the member states, which in turn is based on democratic national elections. The European Parliament, as the expression of Europe-wide direct universal suffrage, is the institution specifically dedicated to representing the Union of the peoples of Europe. It is from its endorsement that the Commission derives its democratic legitimacy. This then complements the other source of legitimacy, namely the member states represented in the Council. Enhancing the intergovernmental model at the expense not only of the Commission but also, ultimately, of the Council – which, let us not forget, is also a Community institution – would undermine the democratic nature of the whole European enterprise and would be a serious step backwards. In short, we would run grave risks if we called into question the principle of an EU based on the rule of law, respect for which is guaranteed by the Court of Justice to which any European citizen has the right to appeal.

This was a description of the classic EU model which has served Europe well. But we have arrived at a stage where fairly deep-seated national characteristics are coming to the fore – characteristics which it will take several generations to change. The Convention, at best, could establish a baseline for this process. If we look at a more distant future, the European process must stress the primacy of politics and the need to accentuate and develop the democratic extent, so that we achieve the right measure of creative tension between the democratic and technocratic dimensions.

Constitutions can influence the way people conceive of themselves, but founding mothers and fathers must not lose touch with reality and those they represent. Whatever our nationality, we Europeans are very much at home in our sense of region or of local or national identity. We have a complex multiple set of identities of which Europe is only one.


## Pat Cox
Born in Dublin, 1952. President of the European Parliament since 2002. Member of the European Parliament since 1989, where he represented the Munster constituency in the Republic of Ireland.

Jean-Claude Trichet

# European Monetary Integration
Lessons for EU Candidate States

After almost ten years of working hard to harmonise their economic and legal systems with those practised by the European Union (EU), ten countries from Central, Eastern and Southern Europe have now qualified themselves to be accepted into the EU club. While their accession treaties still have to be signed by the EU and ratified by their own national governments, the integration schedule foresees that these countries will be able to gain full EU membership in May 2004.

But no matter how great the efforts of the accession countries have been, especially in adopting the legal framework of the EU – the so-called *acquis communautaire* – they will have to be redoubled if these countries also want to join the Eurozone. To do so, they will have to achieve monetary integration that will be possible only if they put into place a framework based on the following principles:

- a convergence towards the best economic practices and performances, rather than a convergence towards an average;
- a long-lasting process designed to ensure credibility;
- fiscal and monetary policies aimed at achieving macroeconomic stability.

Once put into practice, such principles will contribute to the stability of the future EU members and of the whole EU area.

## Lessons of history

To reach these clear goals as painlessly as possible, the ten EU novices would do well to heed the lessons of the recent history of European monetary integration.

*Lesson 1: The successful launch of the euro has crowned a very long process of monetary integration in Europe.*
This process has taken almost thirty years and has consisted of a number of steps. Among the most significant was the Werner Plan of 1971, which set the creation of a European Economic and Monetary Union (EMU) as a distant but clear goal. A year later came the so-called 'snake' monetary agreement that tied together the participating European currencies and led to the formation in 1979 of the European Monetary System. Ten years later, the Delors Plan mapped the road towards a fully-fledged EMU, while in 1992 the Maastricht Treaty finalised the schedule for the adoption of the single currency by 1999.

The euro was successfully launched as planned on 1 January 1999 on eleven EU countries' financial and foreign exchange markets. Greece adopted it two years later, having passed the Maastricht criteria and joined the EMU. And the final step of this monetary integration was made on 1 January 2002, when euro banknotes and coins began circulating as legal tender in all the euro area countries. This was a unique and highly symbolic event for Europe.

The international role of the euro is clearly developing, as is demonstrated by the increased circulation of euro banknotes and coins outside the euro area, the growing share of euro deposits in total deposits in EU-contiguous regions expected to join the EU and the growing use of the euro as an anchor currency. To date (early 2003), over fifty states, mainly in Europe and Africa, have adopted exchange rate arrangements that are based fully or partially on the euro to facilitate the intensive trade and financial transactions which take place between them.

Such a spectacularly successful launch of the euro has owed nothing to chance. It has taken a sound institutional and macroeconomic policy framework combined with meticulous technical preparation to ensure the successful launch of the new currency.

*Lesson 2: A sound institutional and macroeconomic policy framework and a transparent single monetary policy have been of paramount importance for the euro's success.*
The single monetary policy is formulated and implemented within *a solid institutional framework,* the so-called Eurosystem, which is the team comprising the European Central Bank (ECB) and the twelve national central banks of the euro area. The Eurosystem is built on three core principles: independence, transparency and decentralisation.

The *independence* of the ECB and national central banks is enshrined in the Maastricht Treaty. When exercising their powers and carrying out their tasks and duties, neither the central banks of the Eurosystem nor any member of their decision-making bodies shall seek or take instructions from EU institutions, from any government of its member state or from any other body. The Eurosystem considers its institutional, operational and financial independence as an essential contribution to the clarity and the credibility of the single monetary policy.

The independence of a central bank and its democratic accountability are two sides of the same coin. In this respect, *transparency and communication* by monetary authorities are crucial: elected authorities, key economic players, as well as all citizens must be kept fully informed about the conduct of the single monetary policy. At the EU level, the ECB maintains a permanent dialogue with the European Council and the European Parliament, as do national central banks with their respective national institutions. The ECB is one of the few central banks in the world to practise regular, frequent, real-time communication in the field of monetary policy. Indeed, immediately after each first monthly meeting of the ECB Governing Council, the ECB President holds a press conference.

Lastly, *decentralisation*: since the principle of subsidiarity underlies the entire European structure, monetary policy decisions are taken at the centre by the ECB Governing Council and implemented by the national central banks in close coordination.

The euro area's *single monetary policy* is geared to a sound and relevant ultimate objective, namely maintaining price stability, clearly defined as a year-on-year *increase* in the Headline Index of Consumer Prices of *below 2 percent* in the whole euro area. The euro area's monetary authorities consider price stability to be the Eurosystem's greatest contribution to promoting an environment that fosters sustainable growth and employment in the longer run. Price stability also contributes to limit unnecessary volatility of output and employment in the short run.

The relatively low yields on long-term euro-denominated bonds are testimony to investors' confidence in the new currency. The euro has actually been founded on a benchmarking principle of convergence towards the three best performances regarding interest rates and inflation, and not on convergence towards an average.

It goes without saying that for the EMU to function well, its member states, especially the major ones, must be aware of the spill-over effects that their domestic budgetary policies may have in other euro-area countries. This requires *close coordination on economic policies* by the EMU member states. The Maastricht Treaty exhorts its member states to treat national economic policies *'as a matter of common concern'*.

A coherent operational framework has been provided for a broad coordination of economic policies through close mutual surveillance (under the responsibility of the 'Eurogroup' and the Ecofin Council) and through the implementation of the 'Stability and Growth Pact' (SGP) as regards fiscal policies. The main goal of the SGP is to promote fiscal discipline with a view to reducing risk premium on long-term interest rates and enhancing the member states' ability to respond to asymmetric shocks. Moreover, 'Broad Economic Policy Guidelines', discussed each year by the heads of EMU states and governments help monitor macroeconomic and structural developments in its member states.

The successful launch of the euro resulted in EU candidate countries expressing interest in joining the EMU as early as possible. But the road that EMU member states have followed on their way from the EU to the Eurozone points to the need for future members to keep a prudent strategy towards an EMU membership in order to ensure economic growth and stability in the countries themselves.

## Defining a prudent strategy

When defining policies aimed at fostering economic growth and stability, the accession countries would again benefit from taking into account the experience of the European monetary integration.

While the accession candidates have clearly made major improvements in stabilising and strengthening their economies and institutions, and bringing them further towards convergence with the EU, they should keep in mind that the current EU member states were sometimes quite slow in implementing macroeconomic discipline or policies on trade and price liberalisation.

There is also widespread agreement that the gap between the accession countries and the euro area, in terms of average GDP per capita, albeit declining, remains quite significant. The size of this gap, together with a rather limited growth differential, suggests that the process of real convergence will be very gradual. It also means that the accession countries have to continue their efforts beyond the tentative dates of their EU accession.

As long as they do not disrupt the functioning of the single market, residual differences in income levels are compatible both with a country's EU membership as well as with its participation in the EMU. However, it is extremely important for accession countries to attain real convergence. Such convergence is essential to creating economic cohesion within the EMU and promoting integration among its member states, thereby helping to minimise the risk and the effects of asymmetric shocks.

Monetary stability, financial soundness, reasonable fiscal policy and appropriate wages and salaries restraint are indispensable pre-conditions for the EMU membership as all of them must be in place in order to preserve and foster sustainable competitiveness of the accession candidates.

Our experience shows that five requirements are of particular relevance for the accession countries on their road towards catching-up with the current EU member states and striving for EMU membership.

*1. Accession countries must achieve a sustainable nominal convergence.*
Nominal convergence is not only an objective that must be met at a given date but rather, a goal that must be achieved consistently. Strict compliance with the Maastricht criteria will be the key for joining the euro area. Indeed, as a prerequisite for adopting the euro, the EU Treaty calls for a high degree of *sustainable* convergence in price and exchange rate stability, government fiscal position, and long-term interest rate levels. The sustainability of nominal convergence itself presumes that sufficient progress has been made towards real and structural convergence, i.e. the existence of a fully-fledged market economy and economic and social infrastruc-

tures, catching-up in income and productivity levels, upgrading of the legal system, etc. Conversely, a sustainable catching-up process requires macroeconomic stability. Therefore, nominal and real convergence should be pursued in parallel; it is clear that a sustainable nominal convergence (as required by the Maastricht criteria) implies an appropriate level of structural and real convergence.

*2. Accession countries should consider membership of the new Exchange Rate Mechanism (ERM II) as a regular step in the process towards the adoption of the euro.*
Several accession countries have already expressed their intention to join the ERM II as soon as possible after EU entry. While such a move is welcome, it should be made clear that an ERM II membership does not have to follow EU accession immediately, nor does it have to be limited to only two years, which is the minimum period of required delay before a country can adopt the euro. It would be totally misleading to consider the ERM II as a mere 'waiting room' before joining the euro area. Quite the opposite is true: an ERM II membership allows countries to retain some limited exchange rate flexibility during the catching-up process and offers a meaningful, flexible and credible framework for increasing nominal and real convergence with the euro area by contributing to macroeconomic and exchange rate stability and by helping determine the appropriate level for the eventual irrevocable fixation of parities – all in the best interest of the candidate countries themselves. Entering the Eurozone is a momentous and irrevocable act. Neither the accession country concerned nor the Eurozone could afford the risks associated with a mistaken decision.

*3. Accession countries must strengthen their fiscal and external positions.*
Given the aim of attaining real convergence over time, accession countries will have to devote significant public

resources to funding public sector investment. This crucial objective may conflict with the constraint of limiting budget deficits in keeping with EU fiscal discipline. It may also put some pressure on exchange rates if accession countries were to adopt lax fiscal policies or did not tackle existing imbalances. The constraints on fiscal policies are likely to be severe in view of the current deficits, which leave little room, if any, for allocating resources to very much needed public investment. Indeed, candidate countries' weighted average public deficit amounted to 3.6 percent of the GDP in 2001 and is forecast to rise to 4.1 percent in 2002. At the same time, the average current account deficit, due in part to a high level of domestic investment, is expected to amount to 4.6 percent of the GDP in 2002 and 4.7 percent in 2003[1]. The fiscal consolidation currently planned by some accession countries is likely to require sizeable expenditure cuts. Their current fiscal structure is characterised by a growing proportion of social transfers and mandatory expenditures. Looking ahead, accession countries will have to implement fiscal consolidation very credibly in order to avoid the risks associated with the existence of high 'twin deficits', i.e. fiscal and external shortfalls.

*4. A sound and efficient banking and financial system is the key to success.*
Significant progress has been made over the past few years by the accession countries in rehabilitating their banking sector and encouraging foreign ownership. The latter has contributed to greater integration into the EU financial system. Nevertheless, adapting the legal and regulatory framework is a process entirely in the hands of the accession countries. The intermediation role of the banking sector remains fundamental for the efficient use of capital and sustained growth. Progress in corporate governance, the enhancement of the legal and supervisory frameworks that support the banking sector and an efficient fight against money laundering are es-

sential. These improvements are conducive to achieving the macroeconomic objectives of the accession countries.

*5. Central bank independence is crucial.*
Central bank independence is an integral part of the *acquis communautaire,* which is laid down not only in national legislation but above all in the Maastricht Treaty. Not only is the adoption of the *acquis communautaire* a legal prerequisite for EU accession, it also underpins the actual transformation of accession countries' economic framework, which should facilitate their integration into the EU and, later, into the euro area. In this context, it should be ensured that there is no discrepancy between the central banks' formal status in the legislation and the implementation of that legislation. It is of the utmost importance that all present and future member states comply with this key requirement.

The EU enlargement to Central, Southern and Eastern Europe involves very complex issues because of the number and diversity of countries planning to become EU members. It is a major challenge for the present EU. It has to be prepared with extreme care. The process of convergence will be gradual and needs to be enhanced through active cooperation between the current members and the accession countries.

It goes without saying that these requirements remain valid after acceptance into the euro area. The overall success of the process for accession to the EMU implies a solid and lasting convergence.

Note

1 *Accession briefing – a regular review of the accession process,* ECB, November 2002.

**Jean-Claude Trichet**
Born in Lyon, 1942. Governor of the Bank of France, member of the Governing Council of the European Central Bank (ECB). Designated successor to Wim Duisenberg, President of the European Central Bank.

Günter Verheugen

# Construction Site Europe

The Copenhagen European Summit in December 2002 changed the face of Europe by laying the foundations of European life both for the current generation and for generations to come. This truly brings within reach the fulfilment of an age-old European dream: peace, security and equal opportunity for the peoples of this continent who, united under one roof, are shaping their common future. Once the task of enlargement has been completed, Europe will enter an entirely new phase of its history. We shall have attained a unprecedented degree of European unity.

However, before turning to the future, I need to cast my gaze into the past in order to illustrate the significance of the project as a whole. Most of the candidate countries seeking to join the European Union were unfortunate enough to live for decades on the wrong side of the Iron Curtain. This was a direct result of German policies based on aggression and annihilation. At the end of the war in Poland, for example, communism was completely insignificant; this country would never have joined the Soviet bloc of its own accord. The peoples of Central and Eastern Europe have had the freedom to vote only since the radical changes of 1989. Very early on they turned resolutely towards Europe, where unification was already underway. The logic behind this was crystal clear: the emergence of another *Zwischeneuropa* was to be avoided. This invented term was previously – and occasionally still is – used to refer to the 'buffer' role attributed to the countries of Eastern Europe. The need to avoid this happening, however, was not accepted by everybody as a matter of course. I can well remember a conversation I had with the most prestigious foreign policy thinker of our times, Henry Kissinger, shortly after the Wall came down, who saw the future role of these states as forming a safety barrier between Western Europe and the then still existing Soviet Union. In one crucial point, of course, Kissinger was right: there was a clear need to explore ways to develop and safeguard lasting peace and stability for Europe out of the new situation. Subsequent events in the Balkans provided clear proof of this. Peace and stability in Europe are only guaranteed in those places where Europe unites. Wherever this perspective is absent, the classic causes of conflict in Europe remain. The military clashes in the Balkans also demonstrated that conflicts always pose a threat to Europe as a whole, no matter where in Europe they take place.

Just as it was the issue when Spain, Portugal and Greece joined the EU, so it is now: to safeguard the stability of young democracies and eliminate the old trouble spots once and for all. There is no doubt that in Central and Eastern Europe the prospect of European integration acted as a powerful accelerator in this process. I am firmly convinced that the great achievement of systemic transformation would not have been as successful without the prospect of future EU membership.

It occasionally has been – and still is – argued that eastwards enlargement is not so urgent because the essential goal has already been achieved. The new democracies and developing market economies should just wait a little longer, so the argument goes, while the EU consolidates further. Some even warn of the dangers of overstretching, that what is growing together does not belong together, either historically or culturally. They fear that what will emerge instead will be a 'pick-and-mix' Europe, far removed from the vision of its founding generation.

I have always spoken out clearly against this notion. What the doubters are forgetting, as far as the time factor is concerned, is that the motor behind reform was and still is the expectation of becoming an equal member of the EU. True, the markets are already open, the great opportunities for growth already exist, but only because EU membership has been the clear goal. European integration is both the means and the end for the states of Central and Eastern Europe. If their way into the EU had been blocked, or if they had had but a vague hope of accession, then their political and economic stability, in my view, would have soon been lost.

As far as historical and cultural ties are concerned, I do not believe that the cultural differences that exist between Finland and Greece are any less great than those that exist between Bulgaria and the Netherlands. Cultural and national differences as well as each country's own national history are not seen in Europe as divisive factors. Diversity is a key characteristic of Europe. Unlike the United States (although it does not apply absolutely), Europe has never been a melting pot nor will it become one. The ties that unite Europe are strong enough even without such melting. They are based on values and interests.

We in Europe share the common conviction that democracy, the rule of law, respect for human rights and the protection of minorities form the crucial prerequisite – indeed the essential core – of political and economic stability. As for our common interests, they too are of a political and economic nature. A united Europe will no longer sap its own energies in never-ending conflicts between neighbours and tribal wars, but will instead use its political and economic strengths to protect the opportunities available to its citizens in terms of freedom and personal advancement in the face of fast-growing globalisation of the markets and competition in the 21st century.

## The negotiation process

The negotiation process – established officially with the first six countries at the Luxembourg Summit in 1996 and with the six others in Helsinki three years later – was prolonged and not always easy. Basically, the so-called negotiations were really 'only' about the candidate countries' complete acceptance of EU law and about any transitional periods this might involve. The way this was done was to divide up the complete set of laws and regulations into thirty-one chapters for negotiation. A detailed timetable that established when which chapter should be opened with which country lent the process its crucial dynamic. This mode of proceeding enabled those states which joined the process later on to advance speedily and to catch up, provided they had done their homework diligently. It was by no means the case that the less problematic issues for negotiation were dealt with at the beginning and the difficult ones only at the end. On the contrary, chapters such as the freedom of movement of labour and capital, involving among other things the sensitive issue of land acquisition in candidate countries, were already successfully concluded in 2001 and at the start of 2002. In order to counteract certain negative effects on both sides, transition periods were agreed in some areas. Longer periods of adjustment were granted, especially in those cases – such as the environment – where immediate implementation is not possible because of the levels of investment required and the duration of the measures needed.

The chapters on financial technicalities, including agriculture, were dealt with at the end, so that eventually only a few points were left for the final round of negotiations. This meant that it was possible to achieve the scheduled precision landing when negotiations were concluded in Copenhagen. Let us not forget the additional obstacles that lay before us on this not-always-straightforward path, obstacles which at times seemed to endanger the entire process of enlargement.

I have in mind the referendum on the Nice Treaty in Ireland. With the Irish population voting in favour of it, we were able to keep to the timetable – otherwise there would have been no other choice but to postpone the entire project. However, on occasion other difficulties also developed an unexpected dynamic, which could only be countered with a great deal of diplomatic skill and a lot of work. One only has to think of the conflict between the Czech Republic and Austria over the nuclear power station at Temelin, or the implications of the tragic history of the Sudenten Germans, or again the problems facing Russia around the issue of access to the Kaliningrad enclave.

## The process is not yet over

In Copenhagen, it was possible at last to reap the harvest sown by millions of people in Central and Eastern Europe when they struggled to attain democracy and freedom, when they courageously undertook reforms and shouldered difficult burdens without hesitation – with their eyes fixed always on Europe. In this sense, the European Council of Copenhagen really did signify the end of divided Europe.

Nevertheless the work is not yet complete, either for the EU or for the candidate countries. This is true first of all for the preparations towards accession that are being undertaken in the candidate countries and which will have to be energetically and forcefully continued. The Commission will observe this process closely and take final stock six months before the planned accession date.

This is the year in which the accession treaty must be proven to be a good treaty. The European Parliament, individual national parliaments and the people in the candidate countries must agree to the contents of the treaty. By 2004 the EU could have twenty-five member states. Two countries, Bulgaria and Romania, can trust that they will be supported more intensively in their efforts to become members of the EU in 2007. Turkey has a clear opportunity to take up negotiations, once the important political criterion established in Copenhagen is fulfilled. It is the same opportunity as all the other candidate countries received and which they bravely made the most of. The Commission will present its report and recommendations on this in 2004.

## What does the future hold?

The future member states are already participating in the current great debate over a constitution for Europe and contributing their suggestions. The issues at stake in the European Convention are, in many respects, those of a constitutional nature. Creating a European basic treaty, delimiting areas of responsibility, implementing the principle of subsidiarity, anchoring the charter of fundamental rights in treaties and establishing the role of national parliaments in the European machinery of unification – all these are constitutional issues.

A constitution for the EU sounds more revolutionary than it is, because in actual fact we already have one, even if it is apocryphal and not easily accessible to everybody. The European treaties contain all the elements required for a classic constitution. However, if anyone thought that we might solve the problem of growing alienation between European institutions and their decisions on the one hand, and the citizens of Europe on the other, simply by making the treaties easier to understand, they would be wrong. We need seriously to tackle the root causes of this alienation. Analysing the problem is not an especially complicated matter. Citizens feel that 'Brussels' is having an ever-greater impact on their lives in terms of the regulations it imposes, and that they are unable either to understand, control or influence this; such feelings might well increase as the enlargement process moves forward. This is a classic description of the failure of democracy.

The entire political structure of the EU community must therefore be raised to the level of democracy that is taken for granted in its member states. In addition to improving the democratic quality of the EU, it is also necessary to strengthen the community idea at the same time. In my current office, I often see the community method being called into question – sometimes out of ignorance, but sometimes also because someone or other thinks it is more worthwhile to regulate European affairs via direct contact between centres of government. This is dangerous. The community principle is what makes the EU exceptional and gives it supranational status. While it may be tempting to rely on intergovernmental cooperation, ultimately this can only lead to an endless battle of wills. In such a scenario, either the law of the stronger applies, or else the principle of the smallest common denominator. What is certainly clear is that the intergovernmental approach can no longer work in an EU consisting of twenty-seven or more states.

The enlargement soon to take place will change the EU, probably to a greater extent than most observers today might think. First there will be increasing pressure to undertake far-reaching internal reforms. The institutional side is only one part of the problem: the reform and development of our policies will become just as important.

By 2006 at the latest, decisions will need to be made about the EU's financial prospects in the years leading up to 2013. A number of preliminary decisions have already been made in this regard. Agricultural spending will remain stable until 2013 even for the enlarged community, so that a genuine saving will be made here. This will lead to adjustments in taxation which could have a positive impact on the EU's negotiating position in the current World Trade Organization (WTO) negotiations, known as the Doha Round.

I also think it is necessary to put the structural funds to the test – both with regard to whether they can continue to be financed in the context of ongoing enlargement, and with regard to optimising regional funding in the context of the 'Lisbon strategy'.

More far-reaching and controversial, however, will be efforts to introduce reforms in other areas of policy. At the top of the list is foreign and security policy. Although it did introduce some improvements, not even the Treaty of Amsterdam was able fundamentally to change the much-lamented situation that an economic world power such as the EU does not have adequate resources to back up its foreign and security policy. Once the twenty-seven member EU is complete, when the prospect of the Balkan States' accession approaches and if Turkey's hopes of accession to the EU are to be realised, then the EU will have to resolve to take steps towards becoming a global actor – not in competition to the US and not as a military superpower, but as a strong political and diplomatic centre of power.

Geography and the new constellation of neighbouring states will force this to happen. I do not believe that a foreign and security policy coordinated between the governments of individual member states will be able to fulfil our own expectations or those of the rest of the world. Not only do we need greater commonality in general, we also need to develop more common policies in this area, one step at a time.

Great changes can also be expected to occur in the sphere of domestic and legal policy. The touchstone for this policy will be migration: how will the EU deal with issues of migration and immigration? This is a question of crucial importance for the future: the domestic political impacts it could have are hard to calculate, while conflicts of interest and contradictions in individual countries' policies are already becoming evident. Does it make sense, for example, to finance expensive development projects in less-developed countries while simultaneously taking away these same countries' prospects for development in the form of immigration regulations?

Ultimately, when we are talking of political reform, we also need to look at economic and fiscal policy, and to an extent, at social policy. While I am convinced that in the long term, the common currency will receive the political underpinning it needs in order to be a successful currency, the question is whether we can hold out long enough for this to happen. Recent experiences with the stability pact seem to me to prove, on the contrary, that here too a qualitative leap from the intergovernmental method to the community method will be necessary.

The new member countries will have their role to play in all these discussions. The concern that the new members might adopt a conservative approach to EU structures is unfounded. On the contrary, we can expect to see them contribute their tried and tested dynamics of reform to the EU.

It would also be wrong to assume that enlargement to twenty-five and a little later to twenty-seven members means that member nations will increasingly emphasise their own identities. Previous experience shows that new member countries are interested in creating a strong Community policy, strong Community institutions and also an efficient Community budget.

But more challenges are yet to come. In the final phase of the great EU enlargement towards the East, the issue as to the borders of the EU will increasingly come to the fore. Can the EU expand further and further until eventually the whole of Europe and perhaps even parts of the neighbouring regions belong to it? This is a question that requires considered debate. A few comments will suffice at this point. With the exception of the EFTA countries, each new enlargement in the future will be even more difficult than the last. This has to do both with the stage of development of potential new candidates and with rapidly advancing integration. If we wanted to create prospects for accession now for all those European states that might be interested in joining, we would soon reach the limits of our political and financial capacity for integration.

Naturally, any decisions we make cannot be set in stone; they may need to be reversed by later generations. But I consider it wise to remember that the offer of full membership in the EU cannot be the only instrument to use if we want to promote peace, stability and prosperity in our region of the world. Before we consider new talks about enlargement, it would be sensible first to undertake a careful assessment of experiences with the enlarged EU thus far.

Three candidate countries are currently seeking to find a way into the EU. Bulgaria and Romania are guaranteed a welcome from 2007 as long as they fulfil all the preconditions. The prospect of European membership for Turkey will be decided upon at the end of 2004. It has a chance and it is up to Turkey to seize it. But it must be able to depend on its prior achievements being honoured. The western Balkan countries also have prospects to join. Just how soon this can lead to accession negotiations depends on those countries' will and capacity to reform. It is absolutely impossible to allocate a time scale at present; but one day they will be members.

For the EU's other neighbours – namely Russia, the Ukraine, White Russia and the Caucasus States – there is at present only one sensible policy to pursue. We must build up privileged neighbourly relations which may well bring about the establishment of a Europe-wide trade zone; far-reaching integration is conceivable in other areas as well. Everything else must be left to the future.

Work on the construction site of Europe will not stop for some considerable time to come.

**Günter Verheugen**
Born in Bad Kreuznach, 1944. Member of the European Commission, Expansion Section, since 1999. Minister of state in the German foreign office from 1998 to 1999. Previously spokesman for the SPD party executive, SPD national party whip and member of the SPD national executive.

Noëlle Lenoir

# France and Germany: The Odd Couple or Future Motor of an Enlarged Europe?

The fall of the Berlin Wall ten years ago and the peaceful revolutions that it engendered in Central and Eastern Europe aroused great hopes throughout Europe, as much in France as everywhere else. The dissolution of the blocs, the rebirth of sovereign European states, the patching up of the splits created by the cynical dividing up of the world decided at Yalta and Potsdam: with all these events, an old world came to an abrupt end. Watching the outbursts of joy in the streets of Berlin, Prague, Warsaw, Tallinn, Vilnius and other capitals in the East prompted a tremendous wave of sympathy throughout Western Europe. But this sympathy was already mixed with a vague sense of anxiety, due to the consequences of the previous break-up of the Soviet empire. Everyone was uneasily aware that the traditional structures of Western Europe would have to adapt to the new realities so unexpectedly shaking up a European landscape that would have to be rebuilt on new foundations.

The mythical 'end of history', so hastily and so imprudently proclaimed in 1989, became an increasingly distant prospect ... And a great many questions started bubbling to the surface as to the best way to tackle Europe's new situation: how to assume the increased weight of a reunified Germany, heavily burdened with overwhelming financial costs and, since the beginning of the 1990s, demonstrating disturbing outbreaks of xenophobia? How to avoid the reappearance of murderous nationalisms in Europe? How to ensure that the aspirations of certain linguistic or geographic groups after the recognition of their rights as minorities would not degenerate into a fratricidal reawakening of nationalities? How to prevent the resurgence of ethnic conflicts with their human dramas and their influx of refugees into wretched and overpopulated camps (as in fact was tragically the case in post-war ex-Yugoslavia)? How to assure the nations of Central and Eastern Europe the political stability they need to be able to enjoy their regained freedom? What prospects of European integration might be offered to these countries of Central and Eastern Europe, so long and so unjustly deprived of democratic guarantees?

The fear of things going awry due to unforeseeable disturbances in the East quickly became clear in the West: how then to establish a system of security encompassing Eastern Europe, especially given Russian reluctance to see NATO expand its sphere of activity? How to incorporate the economies of new independent states into the liberal and regulated market of Western Europe? There were many questions, the answers to which were far from obvious.

Today, these questions have been settled in a satisfactory manner. Criticism about the ostensible slowness in the integration process of the ten countries which are to join the European Union in 2004 has thus been unfounded. No, this process has not been too slow. The fifteen years that have gone by between the fall of the Communist bloc and the joining of the ten were indispensable for the success of this unprecedented enlargement of the EU. One can understand the impatience to finally see the European family reunited; but any haste could have been dangerous. It took time for the protagonists of the reunification to overcome the numerous obstacles placed in their path: the settling of certain questions relating to European defence, the stabilisation of still fragile political regimes in the new independent states, or even the adaptation of these countries to a market economy, the very memory of which they had forgotten. Already, Poland, the Czech Republic and Hungary have become members of NATO. At the Prague Summit of November 2002, other states were allowed to join NATO, among which were former republics of the USSR, and this without any objection on the part of Moscow. In May 2004, the EU will thus be made up of twenty-five member states, among which eight will have had rediscovered democracy, human rights and the market economy in very few years, after having been deprived of them for close to half a century. Even more extraordinary: reunified Europe will shortly adopt a constitution, including a Charter of Fundamental Rights of Citizens, which will describe the organisation and powers of its democratic institutions. Even the most optimistic predictions have thus been surpassed. And quite remarkably, the changes, considerable as they are, have not provoked the anticipated crisis, which was not to be taken for granted in advance

Faced with those changes, France, together with Germany, the historic founder of the European Community, had particular reason for concern. Given Germany's anchorage in Western Europe, and France's parity with Germany within the Community, the equilibrium between the two countries seemed to be at risk. Germany – until reunification, of a demographic weight comparable to that of France – had become almost a third larger in terms of population alone. The opening, to Germany's advantage, of additional economic outlets in Central Europe suddenly made it appear a giant compared to its partners in the EU. Hence the fear of a Germany which felt stronger and more in control of its destiny, and thus freer to question its post-war alliances, to the point of renouncing its privileged ties with France. As to Germany itself, it was led to rethink its role in the EU and thus its relations with France.

Despite these fears, the Franco-German couple did not break up. Far from it. Like their predecessors – Robert Schuman and Konrad Adenauer, Charles de Gaulle and Konrad Adenauer, Georges Pompidou and Willy Brandt, Helmut Schmidt and Valéry Giscard d'Estaing – François Mitterand and Helmut Kohl knew how to form relations of trust that could weather any political storm, relations that have remained unaltered despite the upheavals of the autumn of 1989. The great European advances, always rooted in the Franco-German alliance, as for example the ECSC, continue in the same tradition. The case of the euro, created by the Maastricht Treaty in 1992 and put into circulation in 2002, is but one dazzling instance of this.

The changes that took place in Germany's domestic policy in 1998/1999 momentarily cast new doubt on the durability of the Franco-German motor. The victory of the SPD and the Greens in the 1998 federal election, followed by the relocating of the German federal government and parliament to Berlin in 1999, marked a turning point whose effects seemed uncertain. Would the 'Berlin Republic' keep the same European road map as the 'Bonn Republic'? Would Gerhard Schröder, the first federal Chancellor of the truly post-war generation, remain as convinced as were his predecessors of the virtues of the Franco-German alliance as the motor of Europe?

German participation, authorised by the *Bundestag*, in the NATO force that assured the protection of the civil population of Kosovo in 1999 seemed like an initial response to the concerns expressed in the chancelleries of Europe and across the Atlantic: Germany was agreeing to assume its share of responsibility by joining military operations. On the other hand, as far as the EU was concerned, another development had the potential to threaten Germany's privileged alliance with France. With the publication of the famous 'Blair–Schröder' document, the prospect arose that new alliances, with different rules according to the circumstances and subjects to be dealt with, would take shape in the future, in this way replacing the very idea of the Franco-German couple as the motor of European construction. The difficult negotiations at the Berlin Summit of 1999 (on the 'financial package' for 2000–2006 and on the common agricultural policy) had certainly left their mark in the minds of the German leaders, just as, moreover, the negotiations at the Nice Summit at the end of 2000 (on the distribution of votes to the Council and the allocation of seats to the European Parliament) had unquestionably tested the nerves of the French leaders. From there to announcing the programmed end of the Franco-German alliance in its European specificity, there was just a short step which the press did not hesitate to take. The newspaper headlines were full of 'disagreements between Germany and France' and 'breakdowns' of the Franco-German motor. No European initiative should be henceforth undertaken by this famous couple, for, commentators claimed, the Franco-German alliance had always rested on the principle of parity between the two partners. Now this parity had been upset by German reunification. Perhaps Germany's attitude at the time gave credit to this argument. Germany was in fact giving the impression that it no longer attached the importance it had traditionally given to the continuity of the Franco-German couple. The Franco-German meetings initiated by the Elysée Treaty of 1963 were certainly as frequent as they had ever been. But they made – so they were saying – more room for protocol than for substance. These pessimistic predictions proved to be inaccurate.

As a German proverb goes, 'Totgesagte leben länger' (Those pronounced dead live longer). The revival of the Franco-German couple in 2002 was all the more spectacular. The agreement concluded between Jacques Chirac and Gerhard Schröder on the financing of the Common Agricultural Policy (CAP) after 2006, taken up by the European Council of Heads of State and Government in Brussels in October 2002, was in fact celebrated as both the unexpected and long-awaited sign of the return to force of the Franco-German couple. Not only was this agreement the necessary blessing for the EU's enlargement process to come to a conclusion under the best of conditions, but it was followed by almost weekly announcements of Franco-German initiatives: joint propositions to the Convention on the Future of Europe (on European security and defence policies, on justice and home affairs, on economic governance and soon on the institutional architecture of the enlarged New Europe), joint positions on the methods of enlargement (supplementary aids granted to the candidate countries at the time of the European Council of Copenhagen in December 2002), and joint positions on the next stages of the Turkish candidacy, to cite just a few examples.

There is a lesson in prudence to be learned from this. Namely, that one should never trust appearances alone, and especially not appearances relayed by a media on the lookout for a story. In reality, the disappointment caused by certain tensions in Franco-German relations was in proportion to the illusion that some people cherish of a pre-established harmony between France and Germany. But the cultures and mentalities between two peoples are different. That is why, from the first attempts at Franco-German rapprochements in the last century, the emphasis was placed on the setting up of common policies, starting from different approaches to the problems. That is the lesson that Jean Monnet drew from his remarkable professional and political experience before as well as after the war.

For Monnet, France and Germany had to remain two entities of equal weight, for the secret to their harmony lay in the fact that one was unable to dominate the other. It was not just a matter of identifying their differences in approach, but also the convergences in views and interest between France and Germany, so as to identify a common path useful to Europe as a whole. This is how the European construction progressed from the beginning. And it continues to do so in this manner, in an almost 'mechanical' fashion, to use President Jacques Chirac's expression, meaning that when the Franco-German motor runs, Europe moves forward.

The recipe that allowed Monnet, Schuman and Adenauer to create the revolutionary organisation European Coal and Steel Research (ECSC), and to then start up an absolutely unprecedented process of European integration, remains valuable to this day. While they may not have shared the same vision from the start as to the best means of having Europe move forward, France and Germany do share the same European values and, above all, they share the aim of constructing a Europe of peace and stability, built on a social model going beyond a mere free market. Of course, each of the two countries may want to project its own political system, the fruit of its traditions and its history, into its own vision of institutions and European policies. It is thus the will to forge the European project together – and not a harmony pre-established upon the conception of this project – that produces, in its tension, this unparalleled dynamic of the Franco-German motor.

As astonishing as it may seem, the partners of these two countries are not jealous of their privileged ties. On the contrary, they worry when these ties seem to slacken, which clearly shows that above all, it is Europe that counts.

The Franco-German couple cannot, however, remain static. It must perpetually redefine itself according to what is at stake at the different stages of the European construction, and to the world context into which it fits. Thus the notion of the Franco-German reconciliation on which the European edifice was built after the war, today gives way to that of Europe's reunification. From the romanticism of the 'Vergangenheitsbewältigung' (coming to terms with the past) that inspired the first stages of the construction of the European edifice, now follows the realist vision of a threatening international situation with the rise of terrorism and the worsening of social and economic imbalances brought on by a badly regulated globalisation.

Globalisation itself creates new needs for regional, national and European identity. The latent conflicts brought to light by the events of September 11th oblige us to redefine the role that we, as Europeans, want to play in the world to ensure our own security, preserve our democratic values and our liberty, and intervene if possible to prevent and manage crises in the foreign arena. On the economic and social level, we must face unprecedented technological revolutions, and control their consequences, whether they be communication and information technologies, space technologies or even biotechnologies. As to international commerce, a source of growth, we must participate in its regulation on the basis of our European model and the lasting development that we intend to see taken into account on a planetary level. If there is no such regulation, notably with the World Trade Organization (WTO), the wealth of certain nations will continue to shamefully flout the poverty of other peoples. Finally, Europe must assert itself with the cultural and linguistic diversity it has inherited from a thousand-year history, a history that shapes our collective identity as Europeans.

Faced with these challenges and with the prospect of the expansion of the European family, we have two choices: we can resign ourselves to making Europe a simple space for free trade, without any communal political ambition; or we can continue in the direction of an increasingly closer political Union of the nations of Europe. But in reality, do we really have such a choice? No, for by renouncing the project of a political Union, Europe, as a community of the world, would sentence itself to death. The world is changing with an accelerated speed and it isn't waiting for Europe. To be at the centre of this world in transformation, to be able to continue to weigh up our destiny as Europeans, we must be demanding of ourselves. We must provide ourselves the means for our own autonomy. And that can only happen through the strengthening of the European construction, a construction that, far from menacing nations, makes them, on the contrary, stronger and freer.

That is why the work of the Convention on the Future of Europe is so fundamental to our future. One of the keys to any attempt at making European institutions more effective – an urgent need that the French Foreign Minister, Dominique de Villepin, recently emphasised – would be the extension of the rule of the qualified majority, instead of unanimity, at the level of decision-making processes. In a club enlarged to twenty-five, the rule of unanimity can only cause blockage. Indeed, there is a high likelihood that in the majority of cases, one of the member states – for reasons of domestic policy – would use the veto. The example of community patent law, the rationale for which nobody questions, but on which the states, even at fifteen, have not managed to agree, is convincing. If, by any chance, the states finally come to an agreement, there is good reason to fear that it would be on the basis of the lowest common denominator, and at the cost of adopting a juridical scheme so complex that it deprives the patent in question of part of its practical interest. One could multiply examples of this sort in the economic and social domains. Let's not delude ourselves: even with the common foreign and security policy (CFSP), there lies the risk of powerlessness. Which is why it is indispensable that thought be given – and by France and Germany in particular – to an implementation of decisions by the qualified majority along the lines already agreed in the treaties.

In Germany, the great contemporary Europeans Karl Lamers and Wolfgang Schäuble evoked in 1994 the first-rate idea of a 'hard core (whose juridical extension can be found in the notion taken up since the Amsterdam Treaty in 'reinforced cooperation'). German Foreign Minister Joschka Fischer also alluded to it in his 'I-am-speaking-to-you-as-a-private-citizen' talk at Berlin's Humboldt University in 2000. This does not mean that there would be an exclusively

Franco-German vanguard. The participation of other member countries was emphasised by French President Jacques Chirac before the *Bundestag* in Berlin in June 2000, when he created the notion of a 'pioneer group'. It is in that sense that one must understand the dynamism of the Franco-German relationship. What would the European security and defence policy be today without the previous creation of the Franco-German Brigade and the Eurocorps? Could we even speak of a European aerospace industry without the existence of Airbus and Eurocopter?

The relations between France and Germany today transcend standard diplomacy. This being the case, why not try to institutionalise them even further? Why not, for example, replace traditional summits with meetings of a 'Franco-German Council of Ministers' (Deutsch-französisches Kabinett), co-chaired by the French President and the German Chancellor, which would lead to concrete decisions: joint initiatives on the European or international level, cooperative programs, financial decisions related to common goals …? This would imply setting up, within each governmental administration, a permanent body to coordinate and oversee. The two bodies would hold joint meetings and would report to the two governments. In the same spirit of dialogue, it would be interesting to create a Franco-German inter-parliamentary committee, to which Franco-German cooperation projects could be submitted for evaluation and which would also be able to make proposals in the most varied domains. Ethics, for example. Joint meetings between German and French ethics committees have already been initiated to give thought to an ethical thinking which in this day and age can only be European and international if we make it lead to effective decisions. Given that a sect is already making grand announcements on the cloning of human beings, it is time to act. The European Group on Ethics (EGE), attached to the European Commission in Brussels, cannot, of course, totally replace the national ethics committees.

As to the content of the policies, much remains to be done between France and Germany to energise them. The will is there, as was demonstrated throughout the second half of 2002 by the deposition of Franco-German contributions at the Convention. One of the favoured domains for the Franco-German collaboration is that of security and defence, the topic of one of these contributions. As France has just decided through its law on military programming, we must increase the military capacity of the leading European countries. We must unite our armaments industries and launch joint programs of research and technological development. Can we be content in the present context to produce tanks, firearms and submarines of strictly national manufacture? The answer is no: an answer that led France and Germany to reach a decision clearly in favour of the creation of a European armaments bureau as well as a European planning of armaments programs. This vision of a European defence must still be shared by France and Germany's European partners, who must be convinced that we cannot make Europe political if it is denied the ability to ensure its security; and that we must be equipped with an armaments industry which has truly European outlets. There will be no European defence if the EU's member countries prefer to buy American rather than European. As to civil aviation, the example of Airbus and Eurocopter speaks for itself. It shows that by concentrating on the quality of joint productions and by surmounting national rivalries, Europe can meet international, and notably American, competition. By the same token, in the aerospace domain, it is imperative that we equip ourselves with common Franco-German research structures.

France and Germany have another common interest, that of safeguarding Europe's cultural diversity. Some people reproach the French and Germans for their insistence on wanting to preserve their languages. Let us instead be proud of our singularities and enhance them through a linguistic approach that avoids the standardisation of European culture. This is the reason that Germany and France have agreed to ask each European public service candidate to master at least two languages in addition to their mother tongue. To speak at least three languages must be understood as a challenge, and not as a handicap. Should we demonstrate ourselves less skilled than our ancestors, for whom the mastery of a half dozen languages was the most natural means of acquiring knowledge in cultivated milieus, as Stefan Zweig described so well in his admirable *The World of Yesterday*? Like yesterday, multilingualism today responds to a humanist ambition that must be claimed loudly and strongly. It is the best passport for a European youth, who asks only to travel, exchange, and cooperate.

The Franco-German couple is thus far from having reached the end of its history. In the context of an enlarged Europe, it is, on the contrary, moving into a new stage. The year 2002 illustrated perfectly the driving force of the Franco-German initiatives that have been systematically adopted by the two countries' partners. It is more than likely that these partners will continue to ask France and Germany to do the spadework on difficult problems, which they will then take on themselves. The image of the Franco-German motor has thus lost none of its actuality. For this motor to retain its driving force, it is still necessary that young people, whom General De Gaulle and Chancellor Adenauer appealed to in their joint declaration accompanying the Élysée Treaty, remain ready and willing to consolidate the Franco-German friendship. That is the mission, after all, of the education systems of both countries.

### Noëlle Lenoir
Born in Neuilly-sur-Seine, France, 1948. Since 2002, French Minister for European Affairs. Former member of the European Group on Ethics in Science and New Technologies established by the European Commission. Member of the French Constitutional Council from 1992 to 2001.

Matthias Berninger

# Europe – A Continent for Consumers

'Money rules the world.' Although by no means a new idea, it is of major importance because from the 12th century onwards this realisation was an indispensable element in the development of modern Europe according to Ferdinand Seibt in his latest work, *Die Begründung Europas – Ein Zwischenbericht über die letzten tausend Jahre* (The foundation of Europe – an interim report on the last thousand years). The 'commercial revolution' began it all, setting in motion a process which Bert Brecht described pointedly in *The Threepenny Opera*: 'If the money is there, the end is usually good.'

However, ensuring that the end would be good required yet another mental jump: the spirit of capitalism. As we know from Max Weber, this sprang from the Protestant ethos. The commercial revolution of the Middle Ages and the Calvinist revolution of the early modern period were crucial for the rapid economic development of Europe. According to David Landes, who explored the reasons why some people are rich and others are poor, there were two other contributory factors: build-up, i.e., the accumulation of knowledge and know-how; and breakthrough, i.e. reaching and passing certain threshold values. While in other regions of the world stasis was institutionalised, in Europe a 'continuum of accumulation' prevailed. Landes names the following factors as specifically European reasons for the prosperity of the European nations: the increasing autonomy of thought-based research; the creation of unity in diversity; and the invention of invention.

In *The Wealth of Nations,* Adam Smith describes 'the natural progress of prosperity'. However, Smith's classical economic liberalism produced not only the belief that the market was guided by an invisible hand – by which Smith obviously meant the hand of God – but also the theory of the sovereignty of the consumer. In essence, the sovereignty of the consumer means that consumers control the production of goods by their demand behaviour and that their requirements are thus optimally satisfied. Effective consumer rights are an important plank in the process of globalisation, one which also admittedly interacts with and intensifies the social and ecological demands made on production and trade.

The idea of consumer rights was first proclaimed in terms of general economic activity in the sphere of food safety following the graphic description of conditions in Chicago slaughterhouses at the turn of the century in Upton Sinclair's *The Jungle,* and later in a crucial speech by the then President of the United States, John F. Kennedy, on 15 March 1962: the right to safety, to be informed, to choose and to be heard. The better these requirements of safety, freedom of choice and information are fulfilled, the better the market functions. To this extent, consumer protection is an essential element of modern economic policies.

## Consumer protection in Europe

In a globalised world, consumer protection obviously cannot be confined to the national level. The BSE crisis showed how much the animal fodder industry and the meat market are part of an international network. A glance at the company reports of the multinational food giants clearly shows that one cannot develop improved consumer policies if one thinks merely within national boundaries. Therefore national consumer protection for the German government must also mean European consumer protection. In this field we can benefit from the experience of other countries. The Anglo-Saxon nations in particular have made, and are making, a positive contribution to consumer protection. Since the 1920s, for example, there have been consumer groups in the US that carry out comparative product testing. There was a delay of forty years before Stiftung Warentest (the German consumer association) was founded in 1964. The success of consumer politics in the US is also connected with the originator principle, even if we are sometimes surprised at vexatious court decisions concerning spilt coffee cups, which suggest that it is necessary to inform users that the contents of such cups are likely to be hot.

At a European level, independent consumer policies developed in parallel with the European Commission and the European Union. The initial incompetence with which the BSE crisis was dealt with later also strengthened the position of consumer policies in the EC. The administrative failures that occurred in dealing with BSE not only led to the premature resignation of the Commission, they also made its successors more sensitive to questions of consumer policy.

As early as 1975, the EC produced its first consumer policy programme which closely followed President Kennedy's 'Charter' and formulated five fundamental consumer rights: protection of health and safety; protection of economic interests; compensation for any damage suffered; education and information; and representation.

While the 1957 Treaty of Rome still did not provide the basis for an independent consumer policy at a European level, the Single European Act of 1987 included for the first time the requirement for a high level of protection in the areas of health, safety, and environmental and consumer protection in the setting up and functioning of the internal market that Europe was trying to create. With the 1992 Maastricht Treaty, consumer policy has been raised to the level of a Community policy based on a treaty that is formally independent of the objective of creating the internal market. We should not, however, overlook the fact that consumer policy was at first subordinated to the liberalisation and opening of markets. The countless PR offices that are maintained in Brussels by economic confederations and businesses sing every day for their well-paid supper a song of the potentially disastrous consequences of any sensible consumer protection measures. Since many decisions are made in Brussels, this anti-propaganda should not be underestimated; the influence of the individual interests in question is being extended further and further into areas in which democratic control and transparency are absent.

We should also encourage reform of the EU in order to provide consumers with a more powerful lobby than now exists. Consumer interests and social and ecological matters need a voice in Europe. European trade unions, non-governmental organisations (NGOs) and citizens' action groups must play as big a role as the business lobbyists do today. We must help the formation of European interest groups and strengthen their position by including them in the political dialogue. For the citizens of Europe, they are a decisive factor in the development of a European civil society.

With the European Court of Justice, a powerful ally has now joined the consumer lobbies. To take just one example: the right to change one's mind after property sales 'on the doorstep'. The relevant EU guidelines were inadequately implemented (limited) by the Kohl government at the instigation of the insurance lobby: the European Court of Justice declared this limitation to be inconsistent with EU law.

Consumer protection has been formally laid down as a prop for the internal market for many years. Admittedly, this can provide no more than the basis of a proper consumer policy, since in concrete decisions made in the EU, all too often consumer interests are given no priority at all.

Harmonisation measures aimed at the lowest common denominator ('race to the bottom'), which are looming at the moment, underline that it is sometimes necessary for nations to press ahead on their own to promote consumer protection in Europe. In the complicated web of political opinion creation, it is thanks to countries with progressive consumer protection that a broad enough spectrum is produced to enable the EC to push forward compromises in the face of those who would apply the brakes on consumer policy. The ban on using bone meal in animal fodder is a good example. The EU was in favour of restricting the ban to just a few months until Germany and other countries drew attention to the real state of affairs – above all the deficient monitoring systems in the animal feed industry. As a result, a total ban (now law) on this form of feeding is now in place.

## Democracy and transparency for the EU

Konrad Adenauer coined the sentence: 'European unity was the dream of a few, it became a hope for many and now it is a necessity for all of us.' Since that time, so many areas of our lives have been affected by what the EU does that a European constitution is a vital necessity. Overall, the EU must be reformed so that it is more transparent and therefore closer to its citizens; it is important the citizens of Europe understand who is responsible for specific decisions. Any European constitution must clearly define the interrelationships of the various institutions, including the division of powers between the European Parliament, the Council of Ministers and the EC. It should make clear what role national parliaments play in European policies and in the control of their governments.

Despite its shortcomings, we need a strong EU. Joschka Fischer made this clear in his lecture 'Quo vadis Europa? From confederation of states to federation – thoughts about the finality of European integration' (delivered at Humboldt

University on 12 May 2000). His words were rightly understood as the breaking of a taboo: by using the concept of finality, he was the first to openly address the vision of a federal Europe.

The EU cannot avoid basic reforms. Its structures are too cumbersome and opaque to be able to work effectively after enlargement. It is against this background that the Convention on the Future of the Europe has been meeting since the end of February 2002. Its representatives are charged with making the EU fit for the 21st century and of creating a workable democratic foundation for it by drafting a European constitution. Priority reforms are the transition to majority decision-making, the strengthening of the European Parliament, the election of the President of the Commission and a more exact delimitation of areas of responsibility.

## Expand and advance

The next step in European enlargement was decided in Copenhagen at the end of 2002. For my generation, this decision, thirteen years after the fall of the Wall, offers opportunities that our parents and grandparents on both sides of the Iron Curtain would hardly have believed possible.

For Germany in particular, there was a historic duty to support the entry into the EU of the Eastern European countries. However, this enlargement gives rise to anxiety in some people who are afraid of serious distortion of the labour market. However, the experience of the previous enlargement of the then European Community with the entry of Greece, Portugal and Spain shows that people do not migrate in great hordes. They stay at home because conditions there improve and linguistic barriers do not make mobility easy. Of course, some regions will be more affected by enlargement than others. We need to be particularly concerned about the rural areas in Poland because if the more than a million small farmers who live there are uprooted, we can expect population movements similar to those of the impoverished maize farmers in Mexico after they joined NAFTA, which could definitely affect the labour market in the EU. Closing the labour markets off from one another would remove the pressure on the current member states of the EU and create short-term benefits and long-term prosperity for the poorest regions of the new member states.

In view of the historical importance of enlargement, emphasised by politicians and the media, one might actually have expected the participants to demonstrate the long-sightedness and solidarity necessary to overcome the division of Europe once and for all. Instead, the Austrian daily paper, *Der Standard*, rightly compared the main negotiations at the Copenhagen Summit to a bazaar where people unscrupulously haggled over national interests. To the very end, the member states squabbled over money, quotas and national vested rights. I got a taste of this at the first meeting of EU agriculture ministers with representatives of the governments of the prospective member nations. Although there was an almost Babylonian linguistic confusion, they all spoke the same language: each of them wanted to present their wishes to Brussels like a child's Christmas list. This came as no surprise to the current EU ministers because that is, after all, the way they have run the common agricultural policy (CAP) for decades. In the foreground we have the classical subsidising of the concerns, which distorts the markets and cannot be reconciled with the forthcoming world trade discussions. There was no mention of encouragement for rural areas, support for small farmers or rewards for good ecological practice in this round. Some participants were obviously surprised that the prospective members had so quickly learned which way the wind blows. For this very reason a radical change in agricultural policy is necessary – as soon as possible. If it doesn't happen, as the experienced EU commissioner Franz Fischler knows well, change will be impossible. This will lead to accelerated rural depopulation, unfair world trade practices, ecologically damaging subsidies and false priorities in the community budget. The 'success' of the Polish government in the entry negotiations confirms this fear. It was permitted, in the final hours of the Copenhagen Summit negotiations, to distribute greater milk quotas. In the mid-term review, the Commission had proposed the exact opposite, i.e. the separation of production and support. The Poles can also distribute more money to their farmers in the first column with funds transferred by virement from the second column, which is intended for the promotion of rural areas. Here, too, the forces favouring reform recommend exactly the opposite.

Germany and France had provided the overture to all this when they tried, before the Brussels Summit in October 2002, to achieve a breakthrough in the controversy about agricultural policy after the enlargement of the EU. An agreement was reached on the basis of maintaining the EU agricultural budget at the level of 2006 but without demanding any essential changes. The *tageszeitung* carried the headline 'Reform Postponed'. I would like to suggest that the Franco-German axis is always cultivated at the expense of agricultural reform. I do not know if this happens out of respect, prudence or fear of damaging the axis, or if the structural conservatism of those who wish to preserve the status quo in terms of vested rights is acting as a normative force on what happens in reality. Perhaps this all simply demonstrates the truth of what Charles de Gaulle once said: 'A state worthy of the name has no friends, but only interests.'

France obviously has a different policy to that of Germany with regard to rural areas. The age of the Junkers in German politics is long past, but in France we can see a clear connection between political office and size of landholding. Rural areas elect their representatives to the National Assembly with up to seven times fewer votes per constituency than urban areas, so that in Paris they often joke that many a deputy has been elected not by voters but by acres. As ever, the farmers' unions have a very strong lobby in France. The political pursuit of their interests often leads to the blocking of EU reforms. The EU is currently faced with enormous reforms in terms of the functioning and finance of the EU. I feel that the Franco-German axis will bear rather more weight than we have dared to put on it so far. This famous axis will be of little use to us if we pay too much lip-service to it and thus entrench in an enlarged Europe conditions which will make decisions favouring integration impossible and encourage the flow of billions of euros in subsidies at the expense of the environment, agricultural structures, and not least fields such as education and research, which are so important for our future. The burdens that this will produce are far more dangerous for the axis than the fear of conflict in the minds of a generation of foreign office diplomats who, even in Willy Brandt's time, hindered sensible changes in agricultural policy by making them a major Franco-German bargaining counter (which still doesn't prevent the same diplomats from sniping critically at the nonsensical character of many aspects of the CAP from the sidelines). With Chancellor Schröder's announcement of the introduction of far-reaching agricultural reforms following the occurrence of the first case of BSE, we have an opportunity to put an end to this false principle in German foreign and European policy. There is no better time for this than the next few years, especially in 2003, when the CAP will be extended to the new member states and a new framework will be created for world trade.

It was possible to say of post-war Germany that it was a political dwarf and an economic giant. Yet Europe will have a permanently flourishing economy only if the national governments can work their way through to establishing a common Community foreign policy. NATO may have fulfilled this function after the war – based on the foundation myth expressed by its first General Secretary, General Hastings Lionel Ismay: 'To keep the Americans in, the Russians out, and the Germans down' – by acting as a barrier against the member states of the Warsaw Pact. Even the extension of the North Atlantic Alliance to the east will not in itself be sufficient, only an extra element in the laborious search. Laborious because for many nations it is a major step to redirect their foreign policy to follow European rather than national interests.

We need a politically unified EU in order to cope with the challenges posed by enlargement and globalisation. Mario Monti and Pascal Lamy, both European commissioners, show what influence the EU can exert when it represents a common European position. Under Monti's leadership, mergers have been hindered even if the Americans had previously encouraged them. As European representative in the forthcoming cycle of World Trade Organization (WTO) negotiations, Lamy is prepared to defy the US, as he recently demonstrated in the quarrel about US steel tariffs. But these are the only two strong men in the EU. Even Franz Fischler, who administers the EU agricultural budget with its volume of almost 50 billion euros, cannot throw his political weight fully into the balance because agricultural reform is being delayed and even held back by some individual member states. All the other EU commissioners are playing in a different league in international terms. Nevertheless, the supporters of national governments should not see this as a cause for celebration, because national governments have produced even less political volume in the international choral concert.

For the EU to proceed in a politically effective and sensible way requires it to become more efficient and democratic within the framework of the forthcoming reforms. The Kyoto protocol demonstrated how much political influence the EU can have internationally if it speaks with a single voice. We also saw this in the Johannesburg Summit at the end of August 2002. But Johannesburg was a 'summit of lost opportunities' as well. I had hoped that Johannesburg would broadcast a clear signal of mutual assurances from the north and the south. The north should obviously state that it is prepared to allow more restraint in international relations: fairer competition in world trade, the scrapping of environmentally damaging subsidies, and an increase in development aid. The EU is also very deficient in this area; while half of the world's population, some three billion people, has to live on less than two dollars a day, we subsidise every cow in the EU by $2.80. By so doing, we distort the markets in Africa. Milk powder from Europe is cheaper in southern Africa than milk from a local cow.

Only if the EU also pays heed to the principle of international justice can it expect the southern nations to commit themselves to using natural resources carefully, to ensuring the rule of law and so to dealing constructively with their human problems. Therefore it is also the EU's duty, at the forthcoming WTO agricultural negotiations, to ensure that the developing countries are given the right to protect their markets against food imports.

Even if Johannesburg was called a 'summit that merely prevented us from going backwards' or a 'summit of minor progress', it can be seen as a hopeful sign that, thanks to the unified front presented by the EU, eighteen states committed themselves to do more in terms of renewable energy than had been suggested in the programme of action. The EU member states should see this as a commitment to developing a common strategy for renewable raw materials and natural resources such as sun, wind and water.

## The future of Europe in the age of globalisation

The process of unification and the wealth of prospects it offers may be just what is needed to give us hope that we can challenge successfully the unbridled processes of uncontrolled capitalism, and also act at the same level as the last surviving world power – the US – in the foreseeable future. My American friends share this view. They too want a partnership based on equal rights, as expressed by Daniel Cohn-Bendit: 'We are partners only if we can also say no. Europe can make a major contribution to more democracy and global justice if it is in a position to say no, and if it makes its own proposals for protecting the climate, regulating financial markets, reforming the World Trade Organisation, reforming UNO, ensuring the creation of an International Court of Justice.'

Europe belongs to everyone. We are bonded by a common history and are devoting ourselves to a common peaceful future. Above all, it is young people who have come to know Europe as an entity that unites people rather than separates them. We are used to working with democratic institutions, and we have internalised democratic principles. The artist Oskar Kokoschka once said: 'Europe is not a geographical but a cultural continent.' Europe is what the Europeans make of it. It is not just Christianity, but other influences as well that have stamped our culture of democracy, the rule of law and human rights. The civil wars in the former Yugoslavia have increased our sensitivity to the co-existence of cultures; September 11th shows us dramatically what can happen if we do not accept this challenge in a world of great material and cultural differences.

These differences become particularly clear in the case of Turkey. We know that the proportion of the agricultural labour force in Turkey is 43 percent – even Poland has only 20 percent and the EU as a whole less than 5 percent. Turkey's gross national product of 3,200 euros is only about a seventh of the EU's gross national product. Infant mortality in Turkey is nine times higher than in the EU. But if we are to enter into serious membership negotiations with Turkey, we should not just look at problems and differences, nor should we, as the German Conservatives recently suggested on their banners, dig ourselves into new trenches.

We cannot ignore the enormous differences between the EU member states and Turkey. Accepting Turkey as a member of the EU and the serious negotiations that are already taking place to that end are a signal to the Muslim world – and also to the Christian West – that with courage and vision, a 'clash of civilisations' in Huntington's sense is something that can be actively worked against. A generation of young Europeans who are benefiting from the end of the division of their continent will be well advised to take up arms against new barriers and the exclusion of a Turkish nation that is prepared to undertake reforms. There can be no doubt that this will be much more effective than a third Gulf War as a focus of common EU foreign policy in the fight against terrorism. Turkey offers great opportunities to the EU, because, as a country 'between cultures' it opens up new horizons for Europe. At the same time, it contributes to an increase in our security at a time when only predictive and preventive measures offer our people long-term protection, since they can no longer be protected from the new modes of attack by military means alone.

Europe is a fascinating project which, in spite of all the difficulties and deficiencies, has a great future. I will continue to work for Europe.


**Matthias Berninger**
Born in Kassel, 1971. Parliamentary State Secretary in the German ministry for consumer protection, food and agriculture since 2001. Member of the German Bundestag (Bündnis 90/The Greens) since 1994.

Ernst-Ludwig Winnacker

# Joining Forces: Plea for a European Scientific Research Centre

Europe is a continent, a union of nations, an agglomeration of cultures. This fragmentation can be seen as a disadvantage, but also as an asset. In these days of growing scepticism about a unified Europe, a search for examples of true European collaboration would be helpful. Jean Monnet, the spiritus rector of the European Union of Coal and Steel in the 1950s, wrote in his biography of 1972 that if he were given the opportunity to do it all over again, he would start out with science and culture. Why science and culture, one might wonder? Presumably because he realised that science and culture are global enterprises in and of themselves and thus comparatively easy to organise beyond national boundaries. In fact, the internationality of science is synonymous with excellence. When Conrad Wilhelm Röntgen discovered X-rays in early December 1895, the news travelled from Würzburg to Vienna in two days, to London in three days, and to New York in two weeks. Apparently the standards of novelty and quality are readily recognised worldwide.

A research area such as the European Research Area, however, requires more than scientific excellence. In order for scientists to excel, the appropriate surroundings, instruments and structures have to be provided. Three of these instruments have gained worldwide recognition and acceptance: the universities, the academies of sciences, and the research councils – the latter being the most recent addition to this trio. The German Research Foundation (DFG) was established in 1920 as an emergency instrument to support a research system that had been heavily damaged in the First World War and had lost most of its international connections. The Japan Society for the Promotion of Science followed suit in 1932. Most councils, however, date back to the time immediately after the Second World War when the United States created the National Science Foundation, based on the conviction that science is an endless frontier and a vigorous engine for innovation without which the Second World War could never have been won. The many 50th anniversaries of research councils which we are celebrating these days attest to the wave of optimism and foresightedness that characterised the post-war years.

The one research council which, so far, has not been officially founded is a European Research Council (ERC). Due to the strength of the national research councils and the presence of the European Union, this initially appeared unnecessary and perhaps even undesirable. In fact, the EU framework programs were never designed to specifically foster research in a bottom-up process. This notwithstanding, the EU has occasionally ventured into the domain of national research councils, as in the case of the European Yeast Genome Project from the late 1980s and the early 1990s. However, this has remained the exception rather than the rule. Thus, European science and research lack a European institution, comparable to the individual national institutions, that exists side-by-side with EU-funded, i.e. government-driven, research. What is needed, therefore, is an ERC.

Being aware of this conclusion, the national research councils have recently felt a certain increasing pressure from the scientific community to offer support for joint international projects. The European Science Foundation was one instrument used to fund such networks through a set of programs to which individual councils could participate as deemed necessary by their respective communities. In addition, the EUROHORCs (Heads of European Research Councils) began to test and initiate a variety of joint funding programs, such as the chemistry program CERC3, which united at least ten research councils and was managed by their respective administrations. The program 'Money Follows Researchers', agreed upon by the DFG and their partners in Switzerland, Austria, the Netherlands, and the UK (EPSRC), for the first time permits scientists to take their grants with them when they move to another country. Most recently, the EUROHORCs have agreed, in principle, on a European Young Investigators Awards Program, to be organised as a two-tier mechanism. Potential candidates are first selected by their respective national councils and subsequently enter an international competition. Taken together, all of these activities can and must be regarded as already-existing elements of an ERC; thus, to a certain extent, this ERC already exists.

What, then, should an ERC look like? My vision of such a council is certainly not the simple merger of the national research councils into a single, giant European Council, but rather consists of a set of funding instruments that provide international and/or national added value. The image I have is that of a Greek temple with the columns representing the national research councils and the roof representing their bi- or multinational endeavours. Such a roof is needed for several reasons: in certain programs it is necessary to broaden the basis of competition from a national to a European level. Not only will it raise the profile and visibility of the respective programs, but it will also be a sure indicator to the national research councils as to their international standing.

Not all fields of science or funding instruments require such a European scope, and research councils have other means to guarantee international standards, i.e. through the use of international reviewers in order to establish scientific excellence in such fields of science. In this sense, restricted to European added value, the ERC as a tool of the national funding agencies would follow the principle of subsidiarity.

Two frequently raised questions ask whether the diversified European system could ever agree on joint thematic programs, and whether, in its developmental phase, the ERC might be overwhelmed by a Europe-wide wave of interest. Evidence would indicate that this latter should give no cause for alarm. Consider, for example, the Human Frontier Science Program (HFSP). Although this program has an annual budget of only about US$ 70 million, it nevertheless serves a worldwide community of potential applicants and ventures into thematic areas. However, instead of offering grants in classical scientific fields, it tries to define interdisciplinary subjects such as the study of complex mechanisms of living organisms. Thereby, it effectively limits the applications to those which can live up to truly interdisciplinary if not transdisciplinary standards. There is no reason to believe that an ERC could not venture into similar regions.

How can an ERC secure sufficient funding for its effort? According to a recent quote, Hans Wigzell from Sweden suggests splitting the framework budget right down the middle, with half being allocated to the ERC. Although attractive as a valuable long-term goal, I consider this impractical – if not downright harmful – since such a proposal does not explain how to fund the many necessary activities of the framework programs, activities guaranteed by legally binding decisions of the member states. Rather, I suggest as a first step establishing the ERC by using funds of the national research councils and, simultaneously, of the EU; subsequently additional funds from member states would have to be added. As far as the national funding agencies are concerned, some financial support for networking is already allotted through bilateral agreements. In addition, the EUROHORCs should consider allocating up to 0.5 percent of their funds to the European Young Investigators Award and/or to other funding schemes.

This would amount to a total of up to 50 million euro annually, enough to support such a program with a significant impact. From then on, money should come from the EU, but with no strings attached other than to follow the principles of scientific excellence and subsidiarity.

Undoubtedly, the science ministers of the member states and the European Commission will eventually recognise the necessity of a science-driven ERC and start to support it. Nonetheless, the national agencies should now take the initiative and demonstrate the feasibility of such an organisation.

An ERC cannot remain virtual; it requires a solid administrative base. The pursuit of their international activities already puts a considerable administrative burden on the national research councils, and the administrative burden on the ERC will certainly be just as complex. The organisation will require an administration which will (1) be science driven (2) have no regional or political priorities (3) have no entitlement to juste retour and (4) provide added value on a national and/or European level.

Thus, it will have to follow the following guidelines:

– minimal bureaucracy;
– use of existing structures as much as possible;
– flexibility in scale and instruments;
– full transparency of its decisions;
– central location in Brussels.

In this context, I suggest that the EUROHORCs broaden the scope of the services already provided for them by their own representations in Brussels, for example, KOWI (Koordinierungsstelle EG der Wissenschaftsorganisationen) for the DFG, MPG (*Max-Planck-Gesellschaft*), and other German agencies. These Brussels-based offices could at least provide space and other logistic support. Building on this, the EUROHORCs will not find it difficult to create a lean and effective central office from which joint efforts could be organised. The governing council of the European Science Foundation (ESF) has recently agreed to continue cooperation deliberations with COST (Cooperation in the fields of Scientific and Technical Research), an intergovernmental framework outside the EU but financed by it, which provides funding for cooperation costs of international projects including meetings and travel. If these deliberations are successful, COST could and would provide the ESF with the long-overdue and necessary representation in Brussels. The EU has decided to outsource this activity and is discussing with the ESF how to provide it with a framework. I see no major difficulties in eventually fusing the ESF/COST Brussels activities with the corresponding EUROHORCs efforts as described above.

There is currently a window of opportunity in Europe for a future-oriented structuring of science and research in Europe. In contrast to many other activities, science lags far behind in its organisation. No doubt there are already many scientific enterprises in which the European idea excels, namely CERN, EMBO, ESA, and ESO as well as certain parts of the Framework Program. In my view, the Lisbon decisions of the European heads of state, as well as the concept of a European Research Area developed by Commissioner Philip Busquin, have provided the go-ahead for additional endeavours.

**Ernst-Ludwig Winnacker**
Born in Frankfurt am Main, 1941. President of the German Research Foundation, Bonn. Vice President of the Alexander von Humboldt Foundation since 1998. Numerous publications, including several on genetic technology. Publications include: *Protein Structure and Protein Engineering.*

# The Core

*While the rest of the world (including the Europeans) ponder the nature and fate of Europe, its Union and beyond, there are some – the happy few perhaps – whose* Europaanschauung *is less tangible than those of the architects or consumers, but who provide the inner fibres, so to speak, of the European organism. Europe is: it is beautiful. It exists, it has a life of its own. It will change, and it will be something else: equally existent, equally beautiful. Europe is words, sounds, colours. It has a shape and a meaning. It belongs to the world, it is the rest of the world.*

Peter Ruzicka

# Unfinished Europe, United in Music

We have only to glance back into history to realise that music is wiser than we are. In 1809 when Napoleon's troops were besieging the city of Vienna, one of its captive inhabitants, Ludwig van Beethoven, lamented: 'What a destructive, barren life all around me, nothing but drums, cannons, human misery in all its forms.' In the same year he began to compose the stage music to Goethe's tragedy *Egmont*. The historic conflicts contained in the action, set around 1568 – the Spaniards' violent regime-wielding power over the disenfranchised Dutch – must have seemed to him like an allegory, a mirror image of the tormented present. Beethoven noted on a piece of paper on which he was drafting the *Egmont Overture*: 'The main point is that in the end the Dutch are victorious over the Spaniards.'

Of course, when he wrote the *Victory Symphony* which Goethe demanded for the conclusion of the drama, all thinking in terms of friend or foe had suddenly vanished. Beethoven chose a musical language which he owed, ironically enough, to the country of the occupiers. The electrifying tension contained in the closing bars of the piece – their activist pathos, their irresistible, combative procession, their sweeping fanfares and trumpet sounds – seem so thoroughly characteristic of this composer, for the Beethoven 'sound', and yet they are in fact a brilliant creative borrowing from the contemporary music of the French revolution.

Quite obviously, music is more knowing than mortals. It knows only victors, not the defeated, it overcomes borders and battle fronts, it defuses hostilities and conflicts which in political reality cost thousands of lives. Music seals peaceful alliances while princes and peoples carry on butchering one another in wars. A single glance suffices for us to recognise that in terms of music, Europe had already long been united when the trenches between hostile fatherlands were still being dug. A song may praise the beauty of a landscape, a dance may bear the name of a river, and yet no one can prevent either from being sung or danced throughout the world: 'It will always be: all thoughts are free!'

The Iberian peninsula experienced a period of high culture that lasted for centuries and was based on respect and dialogue between the Muslim rulers, the Christian Mozarabs and the Jewish diaspora. The 'reconquista' put a violent end to this epoch in bloody crusades and a policy of expulsion. However, the era lives on in Spanish music: in the *Cante jondo*, for example, an ancient form of Andalusian folksong which embraces Byzantine-liturgical, Moorish and Jewish influences, untouched by the hateful prayers and pogroms of the powerful. For music cannot be driven out or subjugated. But neither can it be hemmed in or held onto as the exclusive property of a nation or culture.

'When a German talks of symphonies', declared Robert Schumann in 1839, 'he is talking of Beethoven: both names are one and the same for him, they are indivisible, his pride and his joy.' Let us momentarily disregard the fact that Beethoven the composer was extremely Francophile in his orientation: when a German talks of symphonies (if at all) today, he finds himself in very good company alongside the Russians, the Americans and not least the Japanese, who sing with true fervour of 'joy' and of the 'beautiful spark of the gods'. Even music that we think of as Spanish does not necessarily have a Spaniard as its originator; often it comes from the pen of a Russian, e.g. Rimsky-Korsakov's

*Capriccio espagnol,* or a Frenchman, e.g. Emmanuel Chabrier's *España.*

While on the face of it, music in Europe has reinforced national pride, simultaneously it has secretly made a nonsense of it. The tragédie lyrique, a manifesto and self-celebration of French absolutism, was created by an Italian, Giovanni Battista Lulli, as Jean-Baptiste Lully, court composer for the sun king Louis XIV. A hundred years later it was a German, Christoph Willibald Gluck, who set in motion the reform of French musical theatre. The Swedish national opera *Gustaf Vasa* was composed by the Saxon Johann Gottlieb Naumann. And when Bedrich Smetana wrote a cycle of symphonic poems under the programmatic title of *My Fatherland* in the wake of the Czech independence movement, he took as his main orientation – without a second thought – the composition ideals of the 'New German School', thereby merely reinforcing the cultural hegemony enjoyed by the reviled German minority in Bohemia and Moravia. *Moldavia,* Smetana's most famous sound poem, flows today in triumph through the entire world, a treasured possession of all humanity that survived the age of national romanticism, as did Grieg's theatre music to *Peer Gynt* and Mussorgsky's *Pictures at an Exhibition.*

However, although it is in the nature of music to work against any overemphasis of the fatherland or glorification of one's homeland and heritage, this has by no means prevented generations of musicians – as well as architects, poets and painters – from placing their art at the service of some imaginary national culture. Albert Schweitzer identified in this attitude of mind the 'symptom of a pathology'; while in Lambarene in Africa he looked towards Europe, full of concern, and expounded his 'cultural philosophy':

> In every sphere efforts are increasingly spent on ensuring that cultural products should make the feelings, understandings and thoughts of the national folk traditions out of which

they emerged as visible as possible. This idiosyncrasy, which has been deliberately preserved and cultivated, indicates that the natural way of being has been lost. The specificity of a people's personality no longer signals its twinkling presence within intellectual life in general as something unconscious or semi-conscious. It becomes mania, artifice, fashion, a sham. What occurs is an inbreeding of ideas.

In the history of music the question of identity, particularly when limited to a region or even ethnically defined, proves to be the unmistakable symptom of a crisis: an inappropriate attempt to make time stand still or to turn back the wheel of history. That which once was taken for granted is shaken to its very foundations, is no longer comprehensible. A frightening example in our day is provided by commercialised second-hand 'folk music' which is supposed to evoke the image of an unspoilt way of life lived in harmony with nature, something long since lost. To be fair, it should be said that the popularity of such nostalgia is not without its reasons. The close-knit nature of village communities in the past, the cyclical understanding of time that rural-dwellers possessed, the settled form of existence that families accepted and never called into doubt, the ways in which change occurred slowly and almost imperceptibly – all this accounted for a traditional, rooted sensibility, a cultural stasis, which the modern city-dweller no longer knows and therefore transforms into the ideal image of a simple, unspoilt existence. The songs heard at the cradle, in the field or beneath the linden tree had been sung by their great grandmothers, and indeed the folk music of isolated settlements often preserved archaic musical forms, metres and sound patterns.

At the start of the 20th century, Hungarian composer Béla Bartók initiated a systematic investigation of folk music by 'collecting' the songs and dances of peasants while on walks through extremely remote areas and recording them using paper and pencil or, later, a phonograph. It was also Bartók who discovered – in his own country! – an ancient culture that was completely new to him, an astonishing, austere, primeval music, about whose mere existence academically trained musicians had not the slightest clue. But Bartók was not on a search for national identity: he did not limit his excursions to the Hungarian population, nor did he allow language barriers or country borders to hinder him. Instead he extended his studies, naturally enough, to Romanian, Slovakian, Ukrainian, Southern Slavonic, Bulgarian and Turkish music – indeed he even journeyed to North Africa and became immersed in Arab musical traditions. Wherever he went he became more and more convinced that it was the open exchange of ideas between peoples, the 'giving and taking', the 'crossing and recrossing', that yielded music's inexhaustible diversity. 'If there is to be any hope in the near or not-so-near future that folk music shall survive', Bartók emphasised, 'then clearly to artificially erect something like the Great Wall of China to separate one people from another is extremely detrimental to the development of folk music. To block oneself off completely from foreign influences is to invite decline; ideas from external sources, when well assimilated, provide opportunities for enrichment.'

Bartók eventually came to the conviction 'that basically all the folk music in the world derives from a small number of original forms, original types, original styles'. In an interwar climate poisoned by nationalism he provoked bitter opposition with this theory, facing forceful hostile reactions and suspicion and having to bear the indignity of being called an anti-patriot in Hungary. 'Where politics begins', noted Bartók, unimpressed by such smear campaigns, 'there art and science, law and reason end.' Peoples who had long since become allies through music were, for some time to come, to continue to be stirred up against one another in the battle plans of their rulers. Generations would pass before the unfinished work of uniting Europe politically as well as musically was completed.

European music knows no bounds; neither walls nor coastlines nor mountains have been able to isolate it – either internally or externally – and now it has not only conquered the other continents, it is even penetrating into the expanses of outer space. The Voyager probes sent out by NASA each have a gold-covered copper plate on board, an acoustic portrait of the Earth's inhabitants in word and sound. Europe is represented first and foremost by Bach and Beethoven, whose selected works may one day – who knows? – come to the ears of extraterrestrial beings (that is, of course, if they have ears and have first managed to follow NASA's instruction manual and build a record player – something that has long since become obsolete on our own planet). Selected movements from the *Brandenburg Concerto No. 2* and the *Partita in E Major* for violin solo, along with the prelude and fugue in C major from the second volume of the *Well-Tempered Clavier,* are offered as an introduction to the work of Johann Sebastian Bach for an as yet unidentified audience. A good choice, at least from an earthly point of view, for reflected in Bach's music, after all, are the heavens, the numerical harmony of the universe, the divine plan of creation, the inaudible musica mundana, which in the Western understanding is made to resound in the musica instrumentalis – 'numbers in sound'.

This ancient notion of music, which reaches back as far as Pythagoras and Cicero's visions in the *Somnium Scipionis,* found its ultimate expression in the speculative science of composition developed by Bach, the Thomist choirmaster from Leipzig. Eyes closed and deep in contemplation, Goethe listened to Bach's preludes and fugues played to him by an organist friend: 'I declared to myself: it was as if the eternal harmony was conversing within itself, as it may have done in the bosom of God, just before the creation of the world, so did I too feel moved deep within and it was as if I neither possessed nor had need of ears, still less eyes, nor any other senses.'

Per aspera ad astra. The golden record on board the Voyager probes is also carrying the first movement of Ludwig van Beethoven's *Fifth Symphony* from the depths of the Earth out to the stars. The 'through the night to the light' dramaturgy of this work not only shaped a prototype of European symphonic music, it also represents a fundamental strand of Western thought, namely, faith in progress: 'freedom, to go further, is the sole purpose in the world of art as in the great wide creation', wrote Beethoven, with unflinching confidence in the rationality of history and the hidden wisdom of the way of the world. This goal-oriented, linear logic underlies not a few Western classical compositions. But then again, European music also encompasses quite different principles of form: variation and stasis (as found in the passacaglia, for example), the cycle, circling around itself with no beginning and no end; reflections and symmetry; palimpsests: music about music; fragments, labyrinths, meandering paths...

Even if they do not (yet) enjoy a similar reception on other planets, nonetheless creative works by European composers are an ever-welcome presence in just about every country on Earth. Accompanying these works as they set out on their victory parade across the continents of the globe were also the institutions of European musical culture: the traveller of today need not forego the pleasure of symphony concerts, chamber music, piano evenings, songs or festivals whether in Cairo or Cape Town, Tokyo or Melbourne – not to mention North American orchestras. Moreover, symphonies, string quartets and piano sonatas have longed ceased to be the sole domain of Haydn's and Beethoven's successors – just as, vice versa, musicians from the Old World turn to the music emerging from India and the Far East with gratitude and curiosity.

Opera, Europeans' most characteristic and popular gift to music-loving humanity, deserves more than just a mention. Often enough – and largely justifiably – it became the target of mockery because, as can hardly be disputed, it puts the audience's sense of reality severely to the test. For example, in his novel *Vanity Fair,* William Makepeace Thackeray describes with malicious glee the celebrated prima donna of a fictitious court theatre, a singer blessed with great talent but unfortunately

> not in her first youth and beauty, and certainly too stout; when she came on in the last scene of the *Sonnambula* for instance in her night-chemise with a lamp in her hand, and had to go out of the window, and pass over the plank of the mill, it was all she could do to squeeze out of the window, and the plank used to bend and creak again under her weight – but how she poured out the finale of the opera! and with what a burst of feeling she rushed into Elvino's arms – almost fit to smother him!

Sobering experiences such as this have always brought sung drama into disrepute. On its good days, however, opera forges a virtually unbeatable alliance between music and poetry, acting and choreography, painting, sculpture and architecture. And an *Alcina*, a *Don Giovanni,* a *Tristan* is capable of transforming unrealistic scenery into a symbol of a higher truth.

Whether it be the opera house or a concert – bourgeois musical life suffers from an ugly dichotomy, a fundamental internal contradiction. Once the art of composition was no longer the sole privilege of the nobility and began to free itself from being the servant of liturgy, the composers themselves, the 'free artists', assumed the role of prince, priest and prophet. At the same time, however, as entrepreneurs for their cause they had to keep an eye on their public. They had to suffer the humiliation of having some of their most distinguished works assessed first of all as to their value as commodities and examined in terms of their saleability. Inevitably the mundane marketing of art triggered idealistic resistance. Having moved from the church into the concert hall, music itself was now canonised, 'its deepest meaning' was as 'religious culture', taught E. T. A. Hoffmann; clearly drawing on notions of the ancient musica mundane, he wrote: 'Discernment of that which is highest and holiest, of that spiritual power which ignites the spark of life in all of nature, is expressed audibly in sound, and thus are music and song the expression of the greatest fullness of being – praise of the creator!' But Hoffmann could not conceal his concern: 'Those who view music as mere tomfoolery, as a mere pastime for idle hours, as a momentary stimulation for dull ears, or as being useful for one's own ostentation, should leave it well alone.'

This stern warning went unheeded. With business in this 'pastime' flourishing, it became an unequal contest. International musical life reflects the glory and misery of the market economy, Bach and Beethoven are treated as lucrative brand names, sales success will justify almost any methods, and reservations based on taste or piety are considered to be anachronistic quirks of hopeless, sour-faced killjoys.

And yet there is no reason for us to strike up a pessimistic lament over the decline of culture. Never before in the history of music has it been easier to get access to music of all kinds; concerts, sheet music and sound carriers are available to everybody, and the hardest task facing someone studying a city's musical offerings or a record dealer's catalogues is that of making a choice. European musical culture today is unfolding within a series of paradoxes, within unholy, fertile contradictions: on the one hand there is professional specialisation in all areas of music theory and performance practice, while on the other, an alarming degree of musical illiteracy is on the advance that undermines and destabilises the multi-storey edifice of our musical life.

We do not need to go so far as to declare music a substitute for religion in order nevertheless to defend it as a purifying, limitlessly reconciling force which has consistently served to promote peace in Europe's past. Thus we would be well advised to ensure that the future of the European community is likewise grounded in music. The Greek myths tell of Orpheus, the Thracian singer who was able to move even the rocks with song and string music. Goethe took up this legend, conjuring up the ideal of an architecture, market place, streets and walls that would be built and perfected by the power of music: 'The sounds die away, but the harmony remains. The citizens of such a city walk and weave between eternal melodies; the spirit cannot sink, activity cannot slumber, the eye takes on the function, charge and duty of the ear, and the citizens feel themselves to be in an ideal state of being even on the worst of days: without reflecting, without asking as to the source, they partake of the highest moral and religious enjoyment.' Music knows better.

**Peter Ruzicka**
Born in Düsseldorf, 1948. Composer and conductor. Director of the Salzburg Festival since 2002. Artistic director for the Munich Biennial Festival. Former director of the Hamburg State Opera and the State Philharmonic Orchestra.

Adolf Muschg

# The Splintered Plinth of Europe

It's a windy, October morning in Brussels. Like a forgotten suitcase, I am standing in a grey stucco hall of the Central Station. I want to leave. But where should I go? A booking error in my lecture schedule has given me a free day: an unexpected gap between Goethe (Institute, where I talked about 'virtual libraries') and Grass (whose 75th anniversary we'll be celebrating tomorrow in Göttingen). A rush of office workers is pushing me out of the way. Helpless but free, I look up at the train schedule: no, no, I've already been to Bruges. And to Antwerp too, my favourite city, right at the start of my trip, still nursing a slight head cold: bland shops squeezing raucous diamond dealers out of the nooks of the train station vestibule, and poor Eulenspiegel's ghost, who used to snatch at me from dark street corners and oddly named houses, losing out to the ugly chic of lit-up shop windows. Tournai? Hmm, sounds good ... doesn't it have a famous cathedral? OK, off to Tournai! But the train's leaving in five minutes and relying on delays in Belgium is risky, so I rush to the ticket counter. The train takes off; I'm on it, still without a clue in which direction of the compass I am moving.

By lunchtime, I've found this town on the local map: I'm close to the French border. But I am standing on the train platform again, ready to leave. Not much to see in Tournai: a couple of prettied-up medieval alleyways running through the shadows of the grey cathedral, which, it's true, is unbelievably huge. It soars into the cloudy skies like a mighty five-master with a Romanic stern and a high Gothic bow, and you have to go inside to understand that you're looking at a ghost ship: inside, it's just one huge building site, utterly empty except for the scaffolding. A notice tells the shivering tourists that a 1999 tornado dangerously shifted the towers and affected the entire structure of the edifice. It isn't clear when the reconstruction will be finished, but we can rest assured that the building will look as good as new and be a proud asset of this little town.

Yesterday I was having a drink with a Swiss émigré in an art nouveau pub in Brussels, somewhere at the edge of a spacious construction site. A colossal, elegantly curved new building of the European Parliament rose behind the pub. This used to be an artistic quarter before it was bulldozed to make room for this towering glass cliff, complained my university friend, who added, 'Europe is swelling in this city like a cancer tumour.' Does Switzerland have any more new ideas? This is what Max Frisch asked of the Swiss when we were still students. And since my friend thought he knew the answer, he left for Brussels, the capital city of his Europe. Now that Europe has become Euroland, does it still have any new ideas or maybe the feeling is that it's enough to have a common currency and impressive but globally fungible architecture?

It took me until noon to get to Tournai, and as I was listening to the cathedral bells ring, it dawned on me where I truly wanted to go: to Europe. But the station clerk said that my ticket – round trip Brussels–Tournai – allowed no transfers, not even if I paid more. If I wanted to return to Brussels via Ghent, I would have to buy a new ticket. I didn't want to ask if this was just a Belgian attitude or the European service industry already at play. But what was I looking for in Ghent?

This became clear only when I was standing in front of it, in the side chapel of the St Bavon cathedral. I would've missed it altogether had I not seen the ticket counter. I said to myself, it must be worth seeing if they make you pay for it.

This was the Ghent Altarpiece, all twenty panels of it, painted by the van Eyck brothers in 1432 (the famous Jan and the shadowy Hubert) for the banker Joos Vyd who obviously hoped to buy himself an eternal blessing by putting up and fully outfitting a chapel. Their work of art was his payment. Standing in front of this pious masterpiece, I lost track of time. Its central panel *Adoration of the Lamb* astounded me. There it stands lightly on a red box, its white fleece soft and wavy, and looks you straight in the eye. Blood flows from a breast wound into a chalice, a few drops mar the virgin-white altar cloth between its front hooves, while its hind legs and a little plump tail are ready to move on. The fourteen angels surrounding the lamb are holding the cross and the torture rack, its symbols of suffering, and sing its praise. Meanwhile, four dense groups of human worshippers are coming out of the bushes into this paradise-like glade. A veritable Agnus Dei, as described in the Holy Scriptures, and yet – as if it were standing somewhere else, and something discordant and provocative was radiating from the wreath shimmering above its head. On the back of the altarpiece, I see the praying donor: dressed in a fiery red robe, he is giving the heavens a look that seems to me, perhaps undeservedly, a rather hypocritical expectation of a dividend.

Then a dark suspicion comes over me like a cloud as I look again at the lamb's expression: What if it is the Golden Calf staring at me? Or, maybe, the Evil Creature, hiding in a sheep's coat, is showing me its innocent visage? Luckily, as though fish scales have fallen from my eyes, and I understood the true, a scandalously true secret of the lamb: it has no secret. This is clear as day. There stands a sheep, nothing else. But nothing less than a sheep, either. Because the devout reality of this sheep has a quality of a proper sermon. You could hardly paint the most profound allegory with more piety. Now I can even see this animal through the eyes of Albrecht

Dürer, who used to stay in the inn I just passed on the way here. What was he looking for in Ghent, if not for this fully accomplished sheep? And, of course, for the forty-two identifiable plants of the Garden of Paradise: only genuine scientific interest could make the plants come alive with sap and blossom. Van Eyck's Eve could also have come from Dürer's brush, but the textiles of the painting couldn't. The magnificent mantle worn by the angel playing the organ – you'd have to wait much longer for this kind of mastery: Pieter de Hoogh, Velazquez, Degas...

Now I have arrived where I wanted to be: in Europe. Here I'm standing at the font of European vision, the entirely new perception of the autonomy of objects. Here Europe has learnt how to see things as they appear, instead of viewing them through a prism of pious prejudice and adhering to the one and only possible interpretation. There is no more distinction between small and great things. The dove of the Holy Spirit is no more or less important than any other dove: Art has made it into this pigeon just as it made Agnus Dei into this sheep.

The representation of the lamb in the devoutly Christian Europe around 1430 would have given any other artist a pretext, an excuse to paint his adoration, as it were, between quotation marks. The van Eyck brothers, on the contrary, got rid of them: they have used the adoration – for the first time ever – as a pretext for a true-to-life presentation. Such a reversal did more than put the purpose of art back on its feet (and science was also considered art back then); it also revolutionised Europe, and through Europe, the rest of the world. This was an emancipating turn for the humankind that prepared it for Copernicus and his universe. Thereafter the progress took it so far and so fast that often it was difficult to say whether the man was the driving force of the process or the driven. 'Nothing but the best', 'the sky is the limit' – this is what the Ghent-born Charles V, on whose empire the sun never set, wrote on his banner. (He was also the first ruler of the world to hide behind high monastery walls from the globalisation process.)

I believe this was how Europe began, with the human eye finally free to see things as external, independent objects, rather than as pre-packaged concepts, while risking that its own vision would be questioned. Initially, however, this was just the all-consuming desire to know everything about the world around us. The keyword of the new faith was 'objective', and this faith blew the old world to pieces and dominated them. Divide and Rule ... Yet the artist's first desire was akin to a lover's passion, as in the Ghent Altarpiece: it is the passion of art that sets the lamb free of the sufferings of sainthood. In the beginning, the emancipation of the object served as the allegory of a new freedom of the subject. The innocence that the countenance of van Eyck's sheep is expressing is but a mirror reflection of the artist's joy. For the first time ever he sees a sheep and dares to paint what he sees. 'An experiment is a medium between an object and a subject' – that's how Goethe will define this newly found love of objectivity, and he has set the emphasis right: In the Beginning, there was an object!

This is where the source of our contemporary epoch lies: in the revolutionary, yet so obvious idea that you can fully utilise an object only if you accept it as it is rather than trying to change it to fit your own preconception. And that it can satisfy your need fully only when you have understood how this object functions. This is what you must figure out – at whatever price.

Really? The new approach that brought so much progress to Europe was born out of interest for the Other, for the Outside, and the curiosity about their existence. But what became Europe's undoing was that the curious used the knowledge thus gained exclusively to benefit themselves rather than the object of their curiosity. People became more thorough and smarter when they acted in their own interest. A symmetrical relationship, a disinterested observation of an object became an attempt to control it. The closer you got to the Other or Others, the better you were able to dominate them. This meant you could economise – up to a point. You didn't want to view the whole object, least of all the whole person. All you needed was to examine their useful qualities. Which, in turn, became 'interesting' only while they were examined. Such an objective approach became a business enterprise. Europe – and its missionary offspring America – has infected the rest of the world with just such a razor-sharp way of scrutinising things. It's become a search for a calculable profit. Nature itself has provided its philosophical underpinnings. It is based on mathematics. Natural laws apply everywhere, independent of time and place. They possess an absolute authority and cannot be interpreted subjectively. They prove that a number, not a letter, holds a key to the world's secrets. You can argue endlessly about how to interpret things, but it's a calculation that produces a finite result. A word thrives on its imprecision and resists generalisation; a calculation needs and demands the latter.

Thus the means to an end slowly became the end in itself: the calculability of an object determined not only whether this object was interesting, but also whether it was an object at all. The key factor was: could it be quantified? (Getting ready for computers?)

How do you quantify Europe? (No problem if you're a statistician.) What will remain of Europe if we try to measure it with the yardstick Europe itself has invented? Just growth, nothing else but growth, a cancerous growth of glassy towers?


Brussels is the first capital city of EU-Europe; Luxembourg and Strasbourg are the two others. All three belong to the countries whose lot it was to be split up: religiously, politically and culturally. All of them have seen internal conflicts, underdeveloped identities, and weak state systems which made them an easy prey for their stronger neighbours. If you draw a line through these countries and continue it southward through the Alps and all the way through Italy, you'll see where the Continent splinters. You'll see the traces of a major historical rift that swallowed entire key episodes of the European history and disgorged them later under a different name. When the Verdun Treaty forced Emperor Lothair I in 843 to divide the Carolingian kingdom, he gave up two parts of it to his brothers Charles II and Louis the German. For himself, he left the choicest piece: a fertile ribbon of land stretching from Flanders to Sicily. A central kingdom in trouble. This trouble was pre-programmed, just like in Gottfried Keller's novel *Romeo and Julia on a Farm,* which tells a story about an abandoned piece of land between the plots owned by the farmers Manz and Marti. First, they plough it away furrow by furrow, and then each claims the rest for himself – which leads to a fight between the two clans and their eventual demise.

Not that Emperor Lothair's legacy was abandoned. As the Van Eyck brothers were painting the Ghent Altarpiece, the master of their country, Philip the Good, the Duke of Burgundy, had already become one of Europe's most glamorous rulers. But Burgundy fell apart soon after he died, and the brave role, which the Swiss confederates – as pawns of the politicians of the French and Roman Emperor's courts – played in this process, has been described in my own country's school textbooks as an act of heroism. One could also say that it was an historical misfortune. The smaller this central European kingdom became, the more it turned into a war zone of the rising greater powers. The rich remains of Lorraine made it – from Flanders to Lombardy – into Europe's classical battlefield, which couldn't be protected by any guarantee of neutrality. The Swiss confederates were the only exception: they were happy to take on not only a feared military power but also a natural fortress.

In the 20th century, this disputed stretch of land became a bloody fissure, a stretched-out death zone. This is where the Maginot and Siegfried defence lines went up that couldn't defend anything, least of all the lofty goals, the holy claims, and the well-founded intentions in whose name civilised nations were led to slaughter. What remained was a gaping black hole, which sucked in almost completely the self-confidence of the Europeans and practically drained their desire to fight again. This was a lucky consequence born of the misfortune of their own making: it left no winners, and it forced those who remained to become Europeans. The only possible consequence of their civil wars, genocides and fratricides was to create a totally new, different history. They were ready not only to think the unthinkable but also to make it work by putting their oppressed continent gradually together. They started by filling up the trenches left wide open by the Franco-German Hundred and Fifty Years' War. And the once-great powers set up their capitals of reconciliation on the old death strip and entrusted their keys to the ever-minor powers, which used to be the first victims of their wars – as if they were trying to clamp together the edges of a poorly healed fracture.

To be sure, a new, common front against the Soviet empire pushed West European states even closer together, albeit initially only with America's backing. Yet history lessons had an even stronger impact than the Cold War, as the post-1989 years have shown us. Europe's unity has become possible without having to have one common Big Enemy – now Europe is slowly figuring out how to get rid of its own Big Brother. After almost half a century, our common ground has become so firm that we can return to building the European house instead of just defending it. Now we're facing a job of absorbing a once-lost Central Europe, of reintegrating this pacified war zone with the rest of the Continent. And while Western Europeans seem to be turning into a bunch of smug, calculating super-achievers, the newcomers, kept frozen for decades within the Communist bloc, as they stretch out towards their European homeland, have unleashed such an impulse of energy that it is sure to wake up the 'old countries' and help them rediscover the uniqueness of the European alliance, as well as the obligations that such attraction creates. True, the enlargement eastwards won't come for free. Yet, whatever the price of solidarity, it will have to be adequate to pay for a once-in-a-lifetime opportunity to make Europe whole. And who of us, born in the 20th century, could even dream that Europe would move so far and so fast?

Does Europe have any new ideas? Does it need an identity at all? We've learnt at our own cost what harm ideas can cause, what nonsense the talk of identity can propagate. What Europe does need is to show cultural imagination and political tact, and muster courage to cheerfully accept its own history and then find civilised ways to deal with unavoidable conflicts. What it cannot afford to do is to forget.

The reason for that is simple: the House of Europe is standing on a splintered plinth, a fractured foundation. Europeans will benefit only if they never forget this fact. It is this memory that makes them so special – to their glory and to their shame. This is a rift that defines Europeans' true identity; they can always stumble over it and fall. This is a wound that has to remain open but must not rend any further. Cover it up, and it will poison the entire body. The trouble spots where ancient strife can flare up again need our attention and care. And I believe that countries like Belgium, whose own unity is predicated on being part of Europe, are in the right spot. Wherever people are pinning their hopes on Europe – be it in Alsace, South Tyrol, Ireland, or (hopefully soon enough) in the Balkans – they know why they are doing so. The newly refurbished nation-states, playing catch-up, will depend on the entire edifice being there to just help them cope with their own conflicts. And the ex-vassal cantons of the old confederation have campaigned convincingly for a state that would be strong enough not only to put up with their obstinate federalism but also to guarantee it.

Adolf Muschg

'Diversity in Unity' is the motto that my country likes to apply to itself. Its structure, location and history should make it a European state par excellence. Yet, for now, it has chosen not to join Europe politically. Switzerland has had the fortune – through good or bad luck? – of sticking to the principle of 'perpetual neutrality' that the Vienna Congress proclaimed in 1815. It has been so successful in this policy that it has turned the means of its existence as a state into its purpose. Moreover, it's grumbling that it is surrounded by only friendly countries. The breakdown of the old European order has only reinforced its self-confidence rather than shaken it. Why should it give a hand to rebuilding Europe? It refused to realise how a European union one day could make redundant the premises that underpin Switzerland. And now, as it watches its own brand of the best of all possible worlds crumbling, it feels left alone and lonely, and sees that it can hardly avoid applying European laws, no matter how 'independent' it tries to look. In the meantime, it's wasting a truly favourable opportunity to impress on others the many obvious structural, political and psychological associations between the way the Swiss confederation was formed and the current process of European integration. Switzerland could have had much to say, had it not cut itself off. A typical angst of an artisan who hates to see his model, his masterpiece melting down in a crucible! And the worry that others would be dealt better cards could be countered simply by getting in on the game.

Here's a joke about a mental patient who thinks he is a grain of barley and runs away every time he sees a chicken. He's been treated and pronounced fit. His doctor is doing his final check-up:

"What are you, Mr Meier?"

"I am a man."

"And what are you not?"

"I am not a grain of barley."

Five minutes after leaving the doctor's office he runs back in, screaming "A chicken! A chicken!"

"Mr Meier," sighs the doctor, "what **are** you?"

"I know, I know I'm a man," gasps the patient, "but how is the chicken supposed to know?"

**Adolf Muschg**
Born in Zollikon, Switzerland, 1934. He has published numerous novels, stories and dramatic works since 1965. Professor for German language and literature at the ETH Zürich between 1970 and 1999. First director of the Collegium Helveticum in 1997. Publications include: *Blue Man and Other Stories.*

Cees Nooteboom

# Kruisbestuiving

An Interview

*At the beginning of 1988 the French Foreign Ministry held a symposium on European identity in Paris. In preparation for this, you were invited to the Maison Descartes in Amsterdam. 'I don't really know what to make of this kind of abstraction', is what you said at the time. Can you now make something more of it?*

If anything, rather less. I had decided at that time not to bother with philosophical abstractions, but to tell a story about my Europe: not the Europe of ideas, but the Europe of my own personal experience. The only item on the programme whose meaning was completely clear to me was: 8 p.m. – Dinner at the Quai d'Orsay.

*And as such, the event in Paris fitted neatly into that time honoured European tradition of having a fantastic meal with wine followed by a lively discussion of things you don't understand as soon as you try to think about them: this is what we call philosophy. The first of those wine-drinking seekers after wisdom who realised, in the pursuit of definitions in the service of Delphic Apollo, that generalities resist definition was Socrates of Athens. With Plato, generalisations began to be viewed as the real stuff. This was the beginning of metaphysics and the Europe of ideas.*

I can't restrict the diversity of reality to the confines of general norms. I'm not a philosopher, I'm a writer – a travel writer – and so I am interested in the transient.

*Isn't travel a European invention? In other parts of the world people traditionally only travelled for definite reasons: the traveller visited relations, sought buyers for his own or other people's wares or went on a pilgrimage to holy places. But travelling as an end in itself?*

For me, travel is a movement that leads to thinking. As a nomad, I have settled within myself. I experience the world by wandering in and against time, and subsequently express in images what I have seen.

*So movement in space is also simultaneously time travel. For most people today, travel seems to be more of a flight from the constraint of the here and now, nourished by a longing for freedom and the hope of fulfilling dreams which apparently cannot be fulfilled in everyday life. Freedom and leisure ...*

... as if leisure were the holy of holies. You don't find that in Asia. When I was in Japan for the first time, a KLM manager told me how they tried to reward an employee who had sold a particularly large number of tickets by giving him a week off. He, however, didn't want this extra free time at all, but believed that if he took it, they would think he didn't like working. Of course there are people in Europe who like their work, but there aren't many of them ...

*'By the sweat of thy brow...': the Christian religion sees work as a punishment for the original sin of disobeying God by eating the fruit of the tree of the knowledge of good and evil. Holidays on Bali as a return to Paradise? Yet the masses have no idea what to do with their longed-for leisure time.*

Not just the anonymous masses. I know someone, for example, a very intelligent, well-read person, who had a relatively important job until she became seriously ill. Then her illness took her whole attention. When she recovered, she'd reached retirement age, and so did not return to work. She told me that she had very great difficulty knowing what to do with her free time. The phenomenon of boredom is interesting. It also makes me think of an extremely productive writer like Graham Greene, who complained over and over again that he was so bored.

*Anyone who doesn't know what to do with his time feels discontented. The desire for fulfilment is part of this discontent. In fact, Westerners are constantly searching. For other cultures, this almost compulsive urge towards physical and spiritual movement is somewhat alien. In Japanese Zen Buddhism, it is nothingness itself that becomes fulfilment. Every Zen Buddhist aims to achieve* satori *(enlightenment) by overcoming, even annihilating his or her differentiating awareness. Isn't this goal diametrically opposed to the European way of thinking?*

I think so. Since the time of Socrates, Europeans have been on an endless search, first in the realm of ideas, but then in the real world too. When – having now become Christians – they later set forth to teach other peoples their idea of God, they were also after money and spices. That's why they finally searched for the sea route to India. And in so doing they discovered America, which they weren't actually looking for. Then they gradually lost the idea of God and found the Enlightenment.

*…the Western form of illumination, which they weren't actually looking for either.*

This searching is still within us. But we have to keep on

searching further and further – and then it gets problematic, because we then have to find something.

*Perhaps just emptiness in the end.*

Yes. That has already been written about – by Heidegger and Sartre. But for Sartre, as you know, we have just been thrown up here; we have nothing else. And we have nothing afterwards, so we have to find fulfilment here. Of course, Sartre and Heidegger are also known to Japanese intellectuals – their ideas have supporters there as well.

*And if we ultimately find nothing?*

Then many people need a substitute; the Bayer Leverkusen football team for example. A friend of mine wanted to publish a book of illustrations taken from old postcards of football stadiums and asked me, 'Will you write something for it?' And I thought – in those days at least, not every one of the twenty-two men running around was a millionaire. Today, by contrast, we have on the one hand the game, which has been elevated to a kind of religion, and on the other materialism, pure and simple. Both are indivisibly connected. That is particularly noticeable in Spain where I live from time to time. In Holland football is quite important, but in Spain people are mad about it: on some days they even cancel the news because of football.

*Nowadays this amalgam of business and almost religious fanaticism on the part of football fans is not restricted to Europe. Think of the World Cup in Korea and Japan – or China, where the party is using the Olympic Games to legitimise its power. It was no different in Ancient Rome:* panem et circenses. *But perhaps that was a Roman – and therefore European – invention, which is now infecting other cultures. The Church might well be envious of sport, the substitute religion.*

The churches could also be envious of the immense crowds of people who queue up at the Rijksmuseum, the Louvre or wherever for a Monet exhibition. Hundreds of people wait patiently for hours to take part – let's say – in a Monet service. Are they all really so interested in Monet? And yet they crowd in to stare for half a minute each at a couple of Monets. These people are hardly connoisseurs of art – they probably don't even enjoy art – but they have some kind of desire. With music I think it's just the same.

*And how about literature?*

With literature it's somewhat different from painting or music because it mirrors people's problems for them, including their metaphysical ones. And in terms of literature the most important thing for me is poetry. I can hardly imagine how people can live without poetry. And yet there are people who say: 'We've read your novel: wonderful, and your book about Spain: fantastic! But poems?' They aren't so important to them. It is in the business world in particular that one is continually surprised to meet people with whom one can really have a sensible conversation about poetry. But they do exist, even if there are only a few of them. For example, Wallace Stevens, who led a double life his whole life long as a businessman – a very successful one (he was the vice president of an insurance company in Hartford, Connecticut) – and as a poet who interprets reality as a construct of human perception.

*If fine art and music still fulfil a religious need in people today, this probably reveals the originally sacral purpose of art. Art served the divine and was a part of and a model for the cosmic order. But this ontological meaning of art also included the element of power. Whether one thinks of the Athens Treasury at Delphi, the Shōsōin in Nara or the Palace Museum in Taipei: the possession of works of art always implied the legitimisation of authority and power.*

Yes, but it is precisely there – and that is the interesting thing about the relationship between art and the business world – that the material element is just around the corner, because money is also power. Banks, but also a lot of collectors, invest in art with the ulterior motive of increasing their capital. This brings in a dubious element, because if the Such-and-Such Bank sponsors a concert by maestro So-and-So, it makes itself greater, more beautiful and more powerful. The same is true of buying paintings. Just to give one example, a few years ago someone from Japan bought Van Gogh's *Sunflowers* for X million dollars. At the very moment when the transcendental element in art became so important, the material element slipped in as well. This is less true of literature, and not at all true of poetry.

*So is poetry particularly valuable because it escapes the clutches of power?*

I would say so. But that is why it is important for so few people. Still, this relationship between capitalism and art has always existed. There were collectors as early as the Medici. They began it and they were the first capitalists. This happened in Holland too, of course. The rich citizen had his paintings and showed off his wealth. But then there was a further development, which I find particularly interesting, in which the material and art were linked in a very special way: Dutch still-life painting. Previously they painted princes, earls, nobles, and all kinds of people who wanted to show themselves off. But then the Dutch suddenly began to paint everyday things like cheese or oysters in a deceptively realistic way. In Eastern art, for example, this never happened.

*No similar development took place in any other culture, possibly because they lacked the thing that caused it, which was the conflict between spiritual and secular power – just like the opposition between spirit and matter. It was only as a result of the collapse of the medieval cosmos because of the Copernican revolution on the one hand and the rise of the merchant and banking families in the Renaissance on the other that the function of art changed in Europe: it lost its sacral function. The ownership of works of art was an expression of worldly power. Secular subjects and still lives came into fashion. This secularisation of art went hand in hand with a profound change in the conception of art. In place of ontological meaning, purely artistic and aesthetic values came into play. Art became autonomous. As Malraux says in* Le Musée imaginaire, *in Asia museums were first introduced by the Europeans.*

Another thing that doesn't happen in the art of other cultures is the consequences of the most recent change in our view of the world because of modern physics: it was precisely at the time that Einstein was developing the theory of relativity that European painting suddenly began to make human bodies fall apart. Think, for example, of *Les Demoiselles d'Avignon*. It's the same collapse of harmony that is announced for me – I'm no musicologist – in Beethoven's last string quartets. When you look at those women, then it becomes clear how science, without the artist being scientifically minded, becomes visible in art. This also demonstrates that art plays a totally different role in Europe than it does in other cultures. Japanese art practised infinite refinement, but it basically goes on repeating itself. And if there are any new developments there now, then they tend to come from the West. Though at the same time one should not forget that Picasso was strongly influenced by African art.

*While European art, as it developed after the Renaissance, infiltrated the art of other cultures, it is also simultaneously subject to outside influences. The continents are beginning to intermingle extremely slowly, as you once put it. Another reason for Picasso's fascination with African sculptures was their expressive power, which is based not on some normative aesthet-*

*ics but on their religious function. Here we can see a coincidence of the archaic and the modern, the synchronous and the asynchronous.*

In a word: the world is round. By that I mean that with the aid of the modern media we are informed about practically everything that happens in the world, but that at the same time large sections of humanity are still, from our point of view, stuck in medieval fundamentalism. So that you can be sitting in a plane next to someone who believes that he will fly straight to Paradise if he blows himself up together with the whole aircraft. And he wants to do that because he is still in a world which the rest of us have left behind long ago and by which he feels threatened.

*At the same time the Islamic terrorist is paradoxically making use of the technological products of the very civilisation that he would like to destroy.*

Fatwa by computer – that is what I call asynchronicity in a synchronous world. But it's not always just the Muslims. In Spain it's the Basque nationalists of the ETA. So it is not always religion. Nationalism that doesn't necessarily have a religious basis is just as dangerous.

*Even more dangerous is a mixture of the two. But isn't it true that we force our seemingly more successful Western system on other cultures in the belief that it is the only sensible one?*

Yes, and yet the others are slowly coming to us. As I said before, I don't know many business people who read poetry. But I read, for example, the *Financial Times* from time to time because I'm trying to understand what's going on in the world. And I travel a lot in the Third World. For example, I was invited to New Delhi a while ago where they put me up in a very pleasant hotel. But I also wanted to go to Benares. I asked one of the hotel employees if he could reserve a room for me there, in a simple hotel with a view over the Ganges. He found a good, clean one. When he told me the price, I couldn't help remarking, 'That's interesting.' 'Why?' he asked. 'Because a night in the hotel in Benares costs exactly the same as a single glass of wine here in this hotel.' I don't want to simplify anything, but it just isn't the case that most people in the Third World want to become terrorists. They are more likely to want to earn their living in peace. But for many of them that's impossible, because we don't give them the chance: 100 million people in the world are dependent on coffee production. Coffee has never been as expensive as it is today, but it has never made less for the producers. You have to think about that as well when you talk about terrorism. Because that is the reason for the temporal difference I was just talking about, and not the other way around.

*Yet poverty is not the only – probably not even the most important – breeding ground for terrorism.*

But it is for migration. Over twenty years ago I wrote *Rituals*, which contains the following sentences, which I have to think of in this context: You don't have to worry about it. The Third World is already on its way. In Amsterdam, where the book takes place, fifty percent of the population are probably of foreign origin already. It's coming, drop by drop. When I read that in view of dramatically falling birth rates there will only be twenty million Italians in 2080, the country is going to look very different in a few decades. But it won't be empty. There will be others there, who may well be called Italians, but they will no longer be Italian Italians. The same is true of Spain, and of Germany, France, Britain etc.

*Whether they are Turks in Germany, Moroccans in Holland or Algerians in France, none of them are integrated into Europe enough...*

But that will come in the end because there's no other way. It's a question of time. People will still live separately, that is true, but demographic development alone will ensure that this changes because our women are having ever fewer children, while the women from other cultures who live among us have more children – and earlier.

*Will they become Europeans?*

Yes, they will become Europeans, it's just that Europe will look different. But it's always been like that. Think of the colonisation of the Mediterranean Basin, the Migration Period, the Franks, the Saxons, the Normans...

*Again and again Europe has experienced movements of peoples which have never occurred in other regions in the same form or to the same extent. What effects might that have on literature and art?*

You can already see it in Holland. For example, we have an Iranian writer who writes in Dutch. There are even some Moroccans whose Dutchlanguage works are being translated into French with the support of the Dutch Foundation for the Promotion of Literature. Thank God that it is like that. It brings new impulses that are not conditioned by race, religion or nationality.

*Europe has never been static. European history would have followed another course if, around a thousand years ago, Islamic and Jewish scholars like Avicenna, Averroës or Maimonides hadn't acted as channels to bring Greek philosophy – above all Aristotle – to the West. They provided the soil in which the teachings of Albertus Magnus and Thomas Aquinas, the founders of scholasticism, flourished, out of which our Western civilisation – the technological as well as the literary – grew up.*

I have been personally deeply influenced by Ezra Pound, an American who lived in Europe and worked with material and styles from, among others, Greek, Latin and medieval Provençal, wrote the *Pisan Cantos* as an American prisoner of war and translated ancient Chinese poetry into English. So we still have cross-fertilisation.

*Intermingling...*

... first it is us with the Americans, and then the Americans with us – just like the bees.

*... Hiroshige in van Gogh and then van Gogh in Japan again...*

I'll say it again: just like the bees – kruisbestuiving – the flowers with the bees, the bees with the flowers, and so on.

*Or the art of Gandhâra...*

... the very early Buddhas ...

*... which thanks to the Graeco-Roman models of their creators accidentally turned out like statues of Apollo, which can be seen right up to the Great Buddha of Kamakura.*

Or as a counter-example Blue Delft Fayence with its Chinese imagery: the world is round. That wouldn't mean anything if it were static, because then the drops could never find their way from the top to the bottom. But it is in constant motion. We have to learn to accept that, even if it is painful. Herein lies great danger, but perhaps also a huge opportunity.

*The conversation was conducted by Karl-Heinz Ludwig*

**Cees Nooteboom**
Born in The Hague, 1933. Dutch author, living in Amsterdam and Minorca. Writes travelogues, novels, stories and poems. Publications include: *All Souls Day; The Following Story; Rituals.*

László F. Földényi

# A Longing for Metaphysics: Europe and its Literature

There are those who cannot see the wood for the trees; there are others who are no longer able to find the trees in the wood. Bring them together and they can barely communicate. What they say to each other falls on deaf ears. How alarming that they have nothing in common – almost nothing, that is. What unites them is that each has lost sight of the horizon and of the great canopy of heaven above. The foliage that conceals its blueness and expansiveness is their cave. For the one, it is home, for the other, a prison. Both, though, have lost their sense of the infinite. The 'open', conjured up around two centuries ago by Hölderlin in *Bread and Wine,* remains barred to them.

And so it is also with Europe today. As far as the Corsicans are concerned, the Norwegian fjords are light years away, to the Basques, the Friesian lowlands lie beyond the bounds of their imagination; and while the Balkan would lose his way in the Scottish highlands, the Dutchman would become short of breath in the Carpathian Mountains. At this point a hand is raised – it is the 'European': he can see neither Tuscany nor Brittany, Siebenburgen or the Mazury Lakeland – he swears only by Europe. By a continent that has been seen by no one in its entirety unless from a spaceship. And yet there are those who swear just as resolutely by this part of the Earth, which cartographers alone are capable of outlining, as others do by their own home town. However suspiciously they might eye one another, both are confined, captive to their ideologies. And this captivity bars their view of the 'open': those who allow themselves to be locked in deny themselves a chance to experience the infinite or, in the language of the European tradition, to experience 'the divine'. Europe is homesick for metaphysics.

Those who nowadays would call themselves Europeans cannot avoid confronting the dangerous pitfalls of ideology, especially those who would pass themselves off as European authors. They must avoid these pitfalls while carrying the burden of a 2,500-year-old metaphysical tradition on their shoulders. For one of the greatest temptations faced by European authors today is to liberate themselves from what was, until about the second half of the 20th century, the stock-in-trade in European literature. The culture of globalisation, now spreading across the globe like a glaze over ceramics in a kiln, demands that those things which for thousands of years went by the name 'divine' or 'metaphysical' should be thrown onto the rubbish heap of history like so much old-fashioned junk and left at the mercy of forgetfulness.

What was once called European literature began to become problematic when global literature came onto the scene. One of its defining features is that it is not tied to a specific place: it can turn up in Europe just as readily as in Australia or the United States or again on the continent of Asia. It might well make an appearance in Europe as well, although it cannot, in all good conscience, be described as European literature. It lacks precisely those peculiarities that made European literature 'European'.

What are these peculiarities? To answer this, we should put the word 'European' in quotation marks in order to subject it, as Ortega y Gasset suggests, to closer inspection. The adjective 'European' became widespread at the very moment when it began to become problematic: in the 18th century. It was around this time that the concept of ideology also arose, used in 1796 by Destutt de Tracy to denote the 'science of ideas'. It was precisely then that Europe awoke to its special position in the world just as, at the same time, it was feeling ever more threatened and vulnerable. The abstract concept of Europeanness was an ideological shield: it allowed Europe to distinguish itself and set itself apart from others.

An early and revealing example of this is Jonathan Swift's magnificently bitter masterpiece, *Gulliver's Travels*. In the first edition of 1726, Gulliver uses the word 'English' to compare his experiences in far-off lands with what he observed at home – the English solve this *like so* and that *like so,* the English think *this* about *that* or *that* about *this*, the English clothe themselves *thus* and eat *thus*, etc. In later editions, the 'European' had taken the place of the despised 'English' and then became universally 'man', and 'the whole of humanity' took the place of 'so many other governments'. But the abstract figure of 'man' is, in reality, no rational, almost superhuman, perfect and enlightened world citizen, liberated from all natural instincts. On the contrary. When Gulliver sets out on his last journey, he finally encounters 'man'. And this 'man' is nothing other than a 'Yahoo'. 'Man', stripped down to an abstract concept, turns out in reality to be an animal. This is all that remains of European man: the only similarity with what was once known as 'man' resides at most in his essence.

Gulliver's case illuminates the contradictions which the term 'European' brings in its train when it becomes ideological. Swift was not the only one to notice this. Two generations later, Lichtenberg noted in *Über die Macht der Liebe* (On the Power of Love): 'We need not conclude, from what man is in Europe at this time, anything about what man could be. He is, after all, different in other parts of the world, quite different.' Even if Lichtenberg, we presume, did not have 'Yahoo' in mind, he too was nonetheless sceptical as far as the destiny of the European was concerned. Herder took a similar stance in his *Letters for the Advancement of Humanity*: 'Thus least of all can our European culture be the measure of universal human good and human values; it is no measure or a false measure. European culture is an abstract concept, a name. Where does it exist fully? With which people? In what times?'

According to this, being a 'European' is nothing other than an abstract existence, and what we call 'European culture' a kind of distillate. Sophocles was Greek, Shakespeare English, Gongora Spanish, Racine French – and at the same time each of them is so self-evidently a European that to apply the adjective 'European' to them would be tautological and pointless. And just when the term 'European literature' emerges, this very self-evidence of literature is put in question.

Soon after Herder it is Hegel who, looking at the history of Europe, declares that this continent will no longer be capable of creating the most perfect of all literary genres, the epic. Its resurrection should be expected to occur on another continent, America. Europe is exhausted, observes Hegel. A little later, on 3 October 1819, Byron notes in his diary: 'In Europe there is no freedom ... and in any event this part of the globe is so tired.'

This scepticism towards Europe also explains why all of a sudden so many wanted to give the word 'European' a new meaning. It was Novalis who brought the highest expectations to bear; in his study *Christianity or Europe* he turned to the past in order to discover there a non-existent ideal Christianity which might serve as the spiritual foundation of a likewise non-existent ideal Europe. But for him, too, Europe has lost its taken-for-grantedness. Instead, it seems like a utopia, an object of eternal longing, an abstract ultimate embodiment, measured against which the Continent, capable of being experienced and mapped, merely triggers a sense of inadequacy. For Novalis, Europe is a 'universal measure', but one which cannot be applied to the real Europe. Herder too is thinking of a similar measure when he writes of the paradox of 'European world spirit'. Europe may find itself in possession of the world spirit but the latter cannot be confined to Europe, even if it is nowhere to be encountered outside Europe. The spectre of the 'global spirit' may also be found in Goethe, when he makes European literature synonymous with world literature. 'World literature' for Goethe means above all European literature, and in this regard, little has changed since. Europe continues to consider itself identical to the world, while the world has long since ceased being confined to Europe.

Just as the word 'European' became dubious, so too did the idea of Europe itself. And here it is worth returning to the metaphor at the start of this piece: there are those who cannot see the wood for the trees, while others can no longer find the trees in the wood. At the same time, both have lost the feel for those things that liberate humans from their prisons and allow them to experience the infinite, even in circumstances deemed to be finite. The history of Europe was identical with the history of this metaphysical openness. As metaphysics had to give way more and more to the accelerated process of secularisation in the 18th century, so the idea of Europe became fragile. The fate of European literature, from then on, is inextricably bound up with the death of metaphysics. The issue of whether or not it has a future will be decided by whether literature is buried beneath this dying or whether it is able to put up a resistance.

The history of the myth of Europe – especially the version of it that appears in Ovid's *Metamorphoses* – contains an important lesson for us. The wedding of the immortal god to the mortal girl immediately draws our attention to something that has had a determining influence on the Continent's culture for more than two thousand years. In order to get to the girl with whom he was in love, Zeus took on the form of an animal – a bull. But this was not merely a mask. Zeus put aside his sceptre and trident, which struck fear throughout the entire earth, and joined a herd of cattle where he actually turned into a bull. He remained a god by leaving behind him the proof of his divinity. At the same time, however, he appeared in the guise not of an animal but of a human. Experiencing love's torments awakened in him thoroughly human feelings. When he fell in love with the daughter of King Agenor, the mortal Europa, he not only ceased to exist as a god, but he could no longer be looked upon as a human.

At least three levels of existence shaped his form, and thus something unimaginable became reality. First, Zeus stood above humans (for he retained his immortal divinity); second, his love for the girl made him human, and third, as a bull he remained subordinate to humans. Rising up from the ocean, Zeus had 'three faces'. As a human he is untouchable because he is a god, as a god he is unrecognisable because he is an animal. Neither human, nor god, nor animal. And yet he is someone (or something). He is and yet is not. The impossible takes on a form. God possesses a new kind of identity – one that is only expressed when the three levels of his existence are equally present.

History teaches us that god can be experienced by earthly beings when this new identity is revealed. And at this point Europa comes into the story, the mortal girl whose name remains immortal. She sits on the back of the bull, her cloak flaps in the wind, she looks behind her to the shore, but her hands grasp hold of the bull's horns and she urges the creatures onwards. Seen from afar, she appears to be one with the animal. Like a centaur. The mortal has become a prisoner of the immortal, and in this way she too has become divine. And it is when she arrives at the island of Crete from the coasts of Asia, where Zeus seized her (in Phoenicia) that she gains her final identity.

From this time on, the history of Europe is a history of the discovery of the human – of one, at least, that will be called *European man* and has been the main figure of the Continent's literature since the legends of Greek mythology through to the 20th century. He is to be found in Odysseus and Leopold Bloom, in Achilles and the ever-absent Godot, in Oedipus and Josef K. Unlike the literatures of other continents, European literature finds a human with three faces: a human one, a divine one and a cosmic one; and this, therefore, is ultimately where the traces of a metaphysical being can be identified. European literature can be called 'European' as long as these three faces are superimposed on one another. As soon as this face falls apart, use of the word 'European' starts to become tenuous.

The process of disintegration is an ever-present threat. Not only because of the acceleration of the process of secularisation but already before that, when it all began. The king's daughter, Europa, was the embodiment of the measure. To it she owed not only her beauty but also her wisdom: from the alliance between Europa and Zeus emerged Minos, the wise king and law-giver of Crete. At the same time, this measure was constantly under threat: Minos's wife, Pasiphaë, lost it and fell in love with a bull who, however, was not a god but only an animal. From this bull she delivered not wisdom but the Minotaur, in whom wisdom turns into its antithesis. She too is inseparable from the story of the king's daughter, Europa. The Minotaur embodies a threat to everyone: it is what man turns into when he cuts his own ties to the divine and becomes a prisoner of the underworld. The figure of the Minotaur allows us to glimpse the contours of a later human, that of the 20th century. This human is characterised by something which Nietzsche describes in *The Gay Science* as the threat of the 'onset of madness': 'this means the onset of randomness in sensibility, sight and hearing, pleasure in the lack of discipline of the head, joy in human unreason'. In other words, if Europa is a model for man as a being concerned with metaphysics and if, as such, she is the guarantor of beauty, then the Minotaur embodies a being that cuts through the metaphysical ties, he is a monster whose face – as in Picasso's drawings – has fallen into three parts. In his form we assume we are seeing man at the close of the 20th century who, like the Minotaur, is loathe to expose himself to any experience of the divine or to his own cosmic ties.

European literature begins with the birth of a human who opens himself to metaphysical questions. And parallel to his gradual disappearance, this literature too goes into decline. Towards the end of the second millennium, this process seemed to be accelerating markedly. The Hungarian poet Mihály Babits published a book in 1935 about the history of European literature; in the foreword, he quite correctly writes that while European literature may not have emerged in Europe, nonetheless European culture emerged out of this literature. Just like the king's daughter, European literature found its own independent voice when man discovered his identity at the intersection of divine, human and cosmic connections and began to shape his own history as a metaphysical being. No matter which important epoch of European literature we consider, it has always been literature's task to nurture man's metaphysical ties. This was not only so with the Greeks but also with the Romans; it is equally true of the medieval epic, Italian Renaissance poetry, troubadour poetry, Elizabethan literature, English metaphysical poetry, the dramas of the Golden Age in Spain, the French classics, classic Weimar literature, Jena and Heidelberg Romanticism, the English and French epic of the 18th and 19th centuries and the great innovators of the 20th century from Kafka to Beckett, Proust to Gombrowicz. And of course the great Russians, from Gogol to Chekhov. In their time, both Tolstoy and Dostoevsky were received as revelations in Europe;

as different as they are from one another, both were attempting to hold back the 'gentle dying' of the metaphysical tradition – doing so, indeed, with a determination that is unprecedented to this day.

This short list encompasses the history of European literature in a nutshell. This literature is not European because it was written on this continent, but rather because it is infused with the spirit of European metaphysics. It is in relation to this spirit that Leszek Kolakowski poses the following questions in his book *Metaphysical Horror*:

> Is there not in the human mind some independent cause which feeds the suspicion that the really real world is concealed beneath its *tangible surface*? Do we not carry within ourselves an instinctive suspicion which our sober, empirical mind often despises and mocks, perhaps, but which in the long history of civilization has never completely fallen asleep and which tells us that the eye of God (or the transcendental ego) sees things quite differently from us, that we are not for ever and ever excluded from becoming a part of this infallible vision.

Whichever canon we establish for European literature, the reason for posing each one of these questions was self-evident. This was especially apparent, however, from the second half of the 18th century onwards, when man's embeddedness in – or rather his having been flung into – the cosmos increasingly evaporated and European man's metaphysical connection was fundamentally shaken. The task that awaited literature, in a civilisation which proclaimed ever more exclusively the omnipotence of man, was to continue to emphasise his fragility and to interest the reader in something that tried to talk him out of civilisation. From the end of the 18th century, since Romanticism, literature has no longer merely had to 'nurture' man's metaphysical ties, but to uphold them – if necessary, by force. 'Poetry Fetter'd, Fetters the Human

Race!' so wrote William Blake in 1804, and he continued: 'Nations are Destroy'd, or Flourish, in proportion as Their Poetry Painting and Music, are Destroy'd or Flourish!' In other words, the task of literature is to defend man's existential freedom throughout Europe.

But why should something be expected of literature which the globalised world rejects ever more plainly? Why should we defend the feeling for metaphysics in an age when history desires to liberate itself ever more clearly from any metaphysical ties as it appeals to the promise of a generalised happiness that lies ahead? The answer is simple: with no measure and no morality, with no knowledge of his place in the cosmos, man wanders about aimlessly with nothing to hold onto, and instead of influencing events actively, he is at their mercy. However, being at the mercy of events is something that has significance not only for his personal life history: it also has an impact on the course of history. The 20th century gave rise not only to technological and civilisational progress on a scale previously unimagined, it also saw the greatest atrocities of all times – signs of the European spirit having gone astray.

European literature, which for more than two millennia had helped in one way or another those who turned to it for counsel, has obviously failed in the 20th century because European development has pulled out the rug from underneath the feet of even European literature. It may not be particularly surprising that literature was unable to prevent the vast crimes of the 20th century from occurring, but what is surprising is that even after all this, literature is still in the process of becoming and the literary enterprise is blossoming as never before. Quite as though nothing had happened and the century had merely been a series of technical hitches rather than the height of a centuries-long anti-metaphysics movement. In the face of the death of the metaphysical ties that had lasted for two-and-a-half millennia, one would be quite right to ask whether nowadays it is still possible to speak of European literature. Europe has never simply been just a place, it has also been the spirit of a place. With the decline of this spirit, however, the place is reduced to mere geographical coordinates. The word 'European', with regard to literature, refers less and less to something specific. Literature in Europe is in danger of becoming global, while precisely this process of becoming global appears to be so terribly attractive in the eyes of many – especially, of course, in the eyes of those who make up the rearguard of the literary business. Nowadays too, literature is subject to the logic of a consumer society. And just as most of the commodities that are sold on the market are there to satisfy not genuine but artificially awakened needs, so too, in the place reserved for literature, there arises a kind of literature that aspires to do justice to artificial expectations. It fills holes where there is no need to fill them, and rather than satisfying the human hunger for metaphysics, it provides appetisers instead. In contrast to the 2,500-year-old history of literature, this kind of literature draws our attention not to the existential liberty and fragility of man and not to death – on the contrary, it seeks to divert attention away from it.

Nietzsche writes of Wagner, Delacroix and contemporary authors in *Beyond Good and Evil* that they are 'one and all fanatics for expression', who 'at any cost' strive to have an effect. 'At any cost' was still a metaphor for him; today we can take this expression literally. And when we do this we should take further note of Nietzsche's description: 'one and all talents far beyond their genius – virtuosos through and through, with uncanny access to everything that seduces, lures, constrains, overwhelms ... hankering after the strange, the exotic, the monstrous, the crooked, the self-contradictory'. A glance at the current best-seller list of any European country or a flick of the switch to any European television channel suffices to show us how the literary heritage is being destroyed by an inflationary disposable literature. Those who would hold onto this heritage and uphold metaphysical ties are strangers to this world. Gombrowicz or Kertész, Milosz or Handke, Sebald or Nádas, Zagajewski or Nooteboom, Hrabal or Goytosolo – grains of sand in the works of the literary machine. As many names as it may amount to, they no longer amount to a legion.

Europe is at a crossroads. It offers its 'spirit' to foreign, European interests and expectations as if on a plate. Its literature has put on the mask of global literature, an indication of how wounded this spirit is whose crisis was already being lamented more than two hundred years ago, a crisis whose effects one could never have imagined. This spirit is wounded but has not been destroyed. Leszek Kolakowski writes that man can never free himself from the desire for transcendence and metaphysics, even if all of civilisation wishes to convince him otherwise. If for no other reason then at the least on account of the knowledge of his own mortality, he is condemned to yearn for metaphysics from the moment he is born. Global literature is 'horizontal', European 'vertical'. A literature that would call itself 'European' has one task only: to keep this yearning for transcendence alive.

**László F. Földényi**
Born in Debrecen, Hungary, 1952. Hungarian art critic, literary scholar and essayist. He has worked as a literary manager at various theatres and translated plays by contemporary dramatists, including Max Frisch and Heiner Müller. Publications include: *Melankólia*.

# Appendix

# The Alfred Herrhausen Society for International Dialogue

Board of Trustees:

Josef Ackermann, Frankfurt am Main, Chairman

Jean-Christophe Ammann, Frankfurt am Main
Sybille Ebert-Schifferer, Rome
Wolfgang Frühwald, Bonn
Tessen von Heydebreck, Frankfurt am Main
Wolfgang Ischinger, Washington
Jürgen Jeske, Frankfurt am Main
Josef Joffe, Hamburg
Hans Werner Kilz, Munich
Joachim-Felix Leonhard, Munich
Ingo Metzmacher, Hamburg
Eckard Minx, Berlin
Julia Neuberger, London
Wolfgang Nowak, Berlin
Christoph Schwöbel, Heidelberg

Executive Board:

Hanns Michael Hölz, Frankfurt am Main
Norbert Walter, Frankfurt am Main

Managing Director:

Maike Tippmann

Deutsche Bank is part of society and accepts its responsibility as an active corporate citizen. One expression of our societal commitment is the Alfred Herrhausen Society for International Dialogue. Set up in 1992 by Deutsche Bank, the Herrhausen Society provides a forum for examining socially relevant issues, identifying the problems and discussing their possible solutions. We owe this to the work and memory of Alfred Herrhausen.

Our search for paths into the future extends far beyond national borders; our many programmes match the global reach of Deutsche Bank's business activities.